KT-144-191

THE CONSTANT PRINCESS

Philippa Gregory is an established writer and broadcaster for radio and television. She holds a PhD in eighteenth-century literature from the University of Edinburgh. She has been widely praised for her historical novels, including *Earthly Joys*, *Virgin Earth*, *A Respectable Trade*, *The Other Boleyn Girl* (which was adapted for BBC television), *The Queen's Fool* and *The Virgin's Lover*, as well as her works of contemporary suspense. Philippa Gregory lives in the North of England with her family.

For more information, visit www.philippagregory.com and for exclusive updates on Philippa Gregory, visit www.AuthorTracker.co.uk.

By the same author

WIDEACRE

THE FAVOURED CHILD

MERIDON

THE WISE WOMAN

MRS HARTLEY AND THE GROWTH CENTRE

FALLEN SKIES

A RESPECTABLE TRADE

PERFECTLY CORRECT

THE LITTLE HOUSE

EARTHLY JOYS

VIRGIN EARTH

ZELDA'S CUT

BREAD AND CHOCOLATE

THE OTHER BOLEYN GIRL

THE QUEEN'S FOOL

THE VIRGIN'S LOVER

PHILIPPA GREGORY

THE CONSTANT PRINCESS

WITHDRAWN

LORETTO SCHOOL LIBRARY

Loretto School

12731

HarperCollins*Publishers*
77–85 Fulham Palace Road,
Hammersmith, London W6 8JB

www.harpercollins.co.uk

This paperback edition 2006
1

First published in Great Britain by
HarperCollins*Publishers* 2005

Copyright © Philippa Gregory Ltd 2005
Prelims show reconstructions of letters written by Katherine of Aragon
Lettering © Stephen Raw 2005

Philippa Gregory asserts the moral right to
be identified as the author of this work

A catalogue record for this book
is available from the British Library

ISBN-10 0 00 719031 X
ISBN-13 978 0 00 719 031 7

Printed and bound in Great Britain by
Clays Ltd, St Ives plc

All rights reserved. No part of this publication may be
reproduced, stored in a retrieval system, or transmitted,
in any form or by any means, electronic, mechanical,
photocopying, recording or otherwise, without the prior
permission of the publishers.

This novel is entirely a work of fiction.
The names, characters and incidents portrayed in it,
while based on historical events, are
the work of the author's imagination.

For Anthony

They tell me nothing but lies here and ⟨...⟩
can break my spirit. But I believe wh⟨...⟩
say nothing. I am not as simple as I ⟨...⟩

Katherine

My Lord and dear husband, I ⟨...⟩
my death draweth fast on, and ⟨...⟩
love you forceth me, with a few ⟨...⟩
of the health and safeguard of ⟨...⟩
before all worldly matters, and ⟨...⟩
your own body, for the which ⟨...⟩
and your self into many cares ⟨...⟩
yea, I do wish and devoutly ⟨...⟩

Lastly, I make this vow, that ⟨...⟩

hey think they
I choose and
m.

ommend me unto you. The hour of
case being such the tender love I
ords, to put you in remembrance
ur soul which you ought to prefer
efore the care and tenderness of
u have cast me into many miseries
. For my part I do pardon you all,
y God that He will pardon you.

nine eyes desire you above all things.
arewell.

Katherine of Aragon

Princess of Wales

Granada, 1491

There was a scream, and then the loud roar of fire enveloping silken hangings, then a mounting crescendo of shouts of panic that spread and spread from one tent to another as the flames ran too, leaping from one silk standard to another, running up guy ropes and bursting through muslin doors. Then the horses were neighing in terror and men shouting to calm them, but the terror in their own voices made it worse, until the whole plain was alight with a thousand raging blazes, and the night swirled with smoke and rang with shouts and screams.

The little girl, starting up out of her bed in her fear, cried out in Spanish for her mother and screamed: 'The Moors? Are the Moors coming for us?'

'Dear God, save us, they are firing the camp!' her nurse gasped. 'Mother of God, they will rape me, and spit you on their sickle blades.'

'Mother!' cried the child, struggling from her bed. 'Where is my mother?'

She dashed outside, her nightgown flapping at her legs, the hangings of her tent now alight and blazing up behind her in an inferno

3

of panic. All the thousand, thousand tents in the camp were ablaze, sparks pouring up into the dark night sky like fiery fountains, blowing like a swarm of fireflies to carry the disaster onwards.

'Mother!' She screamed for help.

Out of the flames came two huge, dark horses, like great, mythical beasts moving as one, jet black against the brightness of the fire. High up, higher than one could dream, the child's mother bent down to speak to her daughter who was trembling, her head no higher than the horse's shoulder. 'Stay with your nurse and be a good girl,' the woman commanded, no trace of fear in her voice. 'Your father and I have to ride out and show ourselves.'

'Let me come with you! Mother! I shall be burned. Let me come! The Moors will get me!' The little girl reached her arms up to her mother.

The firelight glinted weirdly off the mother's breastplate, off the embossed greaves of her legs, as if she were a metal woman, a woman of silver and gilt, as she leaned forwards to command. 'If the men don't see me, then they will desert,' she said sternly. 'You don't want that.'

'I don't care!' the child wailed in her panic. 'I don't care about anything but you! Lift me up!'

'The army comes first,' the woman mounted high on the black horse ruled. 'I have to ride out.'

She turned her horse's head from her panic-stricken daughter. 'I will come back for you,' she said over her shoulder. 'Wait there. I have to do this now.'

Helpless, the child watched her mother and father ride away. 'Madre!' she whimpered. 'Madre! Please!' but the woman did not turn.

'We will be burned alive!' Madilla, her servant, screamed behind her. 'Run! Run and hide!'

'You can be quiet.' The child rounded on her with sudden angry spite. 'If I, the Princess of Wales herself, can be left in a burning campsite, then you, who are nothing but a Morisco anyway, can certainly endure it.'

She watched the two horses go to and fro among the burning tents. Everywhere they went the screams were stilled and some discipline returned to the terrified camp. The men formed lines, passing buckets all the way to the irrigation channel, coming out of terror back into order. Desperately, their general ran among his men, beating them with the side of his sword into a scratch battalion from those who had been fleeing only a moment before, and arrayed them in defence formation on the plain, in case the Moors had seen the pillar of fire from their dark battlements, and sallied out to attack and catch the camp in chaos. But no Moors came that night; they stayed behind the high walls of their castle and wondered what fresh devilry the mad Christians were creating in the darkness, too fearful to come out to the inferno that the Christians had made, suspecting that it must be some infidel trap.

The five-year-old child watched her mother's determination conquer fire itself, her queenly certainty douse panic, her belief in success overcome the reality of disaster and defeat. The little girl perched on one of the treasure chests, tucked her nightgown around her bare toes, and waited for the camp to settle.

When the mother rode back to her daughter she found her dry-eyed and steady.

'Catalina, are you all right?' Isabella of Spain dismounted and turned to her youngest, most precious daughter, restraining herself from pitching to her knees and hugging the little girl. Tenderness would not raise this child as a warrior for Christ, weakness must not be encouraged in a princess.

The child was as iron-spined as her mother. 'I am all right now,' she said.

'You weren't afraid?'

'Not at all.'

The woman nodded her approbation. 'That is good,' she said. 'That is what I expect of a princess of Spain.'

'And Princess of Wales,' her daughter added.

5

This is me, this little five-year-old girl, perching on the treasure chest with a face white as marble and blue eyes wide with fear, refusing to tremble, biting my lips so I don't cry out again. This is me, conceived in a camp by parents who are rivals as well as lovers, born in a moment snatched between battles in a winter of torrential floods, raised by a strong woman in armour, on campaign for all of my childhood, destined to fight for my place in the world, to fight for my faith against another, to fight for my word against another's: born to fight for my name, for my faith and for my throne. I am Catalina, Princess of Spain, daughter of the two greatest monarchs the world has ever known: Isabella of Castile and Ferdinand of Aragon. Their names are feared from Cairo to Baghdad to Constantinople to India and beyond by all the Moors in all their many nations: Turks, Indians, Chinamen; our rivals, admirers, enemies till death. My parents' names are blessed by the Pope as the finest kings to defend the faith against the might of Islam, they are the greatest crusaders of Christendom as well as the first kings of Spain; and I am their youngest daughter, Catalina, Princess of Wales, and I will be Queen of England.

Since I was a child of three I have been betrothed in marriage to Prince Arthur, son of King Henry of England, and when I am fifteen I shall sail to his country in a beautiful ship with my standard flying at the top of the mast, and I shall be his wife and then his queen. His country is rich and fertile – filled with fountains and the sound of dripping water, ripe with warm fruits and scented with flowers; and it will be my country, I shall take care of it. All this has been arranged almost since my birth, I have always known it will be; and though I shall be sorry to leave my mother and my home, after all, I was born a princess, destined to be queen, and I know my duty.

I am a child of absolute convictions. I know that I will be Queen of England because it is God's will, and it is my mother's order. And I believe, as does everyone in my world, that God and my mother are generally of the same mind; and their will is always done.

In the morning the campsite outside Granada was a dank mess of smouldering hangings, destroyed tents, heaps of smoky forage, everything destroyed by one candle carelessly set. There could be nothing but retreat. The Spanish army had ridden out in its pride to set siege to the last great kingdom of the Moors in Spain, and had been burned to nothing. It would have to ride back again, to regroup.

'No, we don't retreat,' Isabella of Spain ruled.

The generals, called to a makeshift meeting under a singed awning, batted away the flies that were swarming around the camp, feasting off the wreckage.

'Your Majesty, we have lost for this season,' one of the generals said gently to her. 'It is not a matter of pride nor of willingness. We have no tents, we have no shelter, we have been destroyed by ill luck. We will have to go back and provision ourselves once more, set the siege again. Your husband –' he nodded to the dark, handsome man who stood slightly to one side of the group, listening '– he knows this. We all know this. We will set the siege again, they will not defeat us. But a good general knows when he has to retreat.'

Every man nodded. Common sense dictated that nothing could be done but release the Moors of Granada from their siege for this season. The battle would keep. It had been coming for seven centuries. Each year had seen generations of Christian kings increase their lands at the cost of the Moors. Every battle had pushed back the time-honoured Moorish rule of al Andalus a little further to the south. Another year would make no difference. The little girl, her back against a damp tent post that smelled of wet embers, watched her mother's serene expression. It never changed.

'Indeed it *is* a matter of pride,' she corrected him. 'We are fighting an enemy who understands pride better than any other. If we crawl away in our singed clothes, with our burned carpets rolled up under our arms, they will laugh themselves to al-Yanna, to their paradise. I cannot permit it. But more than all of this: it is God's will that we fight the Moors, it is God's will that we go forwards. It is not God's will that we go back. So we must go forwards.'

The child's father turned his head with a quizzical smile but he did not dissent. When the generals looked to him he made a small gesture with his hand. 'The queen is right,' he said. 'The queen is always right.'

'But we have no tents, we have no camp!'

He directed the question to her. 'What do you think?'

'We shall build one,' she decided.

'Your Majesty, we have laid waste to the countryside for miles all around. I daresay we could not sew so much as a kamiz for the Princess of Wales. There is no cloth. There is no canvas. There are no watercourses, no crops in the fields. We have broken the canals and ploughed up the crops. We have laid them waste; but it is we that are destroyed.'

'So we build in stone. I take it we have stone?'

The king turned a brief laugh into clearing his throat. 'We are surrounded by a plain of arid rocks, my love,' he said. 'One thing we do have is stone.'

'Then we will build, not a camp, but a city of stone.'

'It cannot be done!'

She turned to her husband. 'It will be done,' she said. 'It is God's will and mine.'

8

He nodded. 'It will be done.' He gave her a quick, private smile. 'It is my duty to see that God's will is done; and my pleasure to enforce yours.'

The army, defeated by fire, turned instead to the elements of earth and water. They toiled like slaves in the heat of the sun and the chill of the evenings. They worked the fields like peasants where they had thought they would triumphantly advance. Everyone, cavalry officers, generals, the great lords of the country, the cousins of kings, was expected to toil in the heat of the sun and lie on hard, cold ground at night. The Moors, watching from the high, impenetrable battlements of the red fort on the hill above Granada, conceded that the Christians had courage. No-one could say that they were not determined. And equally, everyone knew that they were doomed. No force could take the red fort at Granada, it had never fallen in two centuries. It was placed high on a cliff, overlooking a plain that was itself a wide, bleached bowl. It could not be surprised by a hidden attack. The cliff of red rock that towered up from the plain became imperceptibly the walls of red stone of the castle, rising high and higher; no scaling ladders could reach the top, no party could climb the sheer face.

Perhaps it could be betrayed by a traitor; but what fool could be found who would abandon the steady, serene power of the Moors, with all the known world behind them, with an undeniable faith to support them, to join the rabid madness of the Christian army whose kings owned only a few mountainous acres of Europe and who were hopelessly divided? Who would want to leave al-Yanna, the garden, which was the image of paradise itself, inside the walls of the most beautiful palace in Spain, the most beautiful palace in Europe, for the rugged anarchy of the castles and fortresses of Castile and Aragon?

Reinforcements would come for the Moors from Africa, they had kin and allies from Morocco to Senegal. Support would come for them from Baghdad, from Constantinople. Granada might look small compared with the conquests that Ferdinand and Isabella had made, but standing behind Granada was the greatest empire in the world – the empire of the Prophet, praise be his name.

But, amazingly, day after day, week after week, slowly, fighting the heat of the spring days and the coldness of the nights, the Christians did the impossible. First there was a chapel built in the round like a mosque, since the local builders could do that most quickly; then, a small house, flat-roofed inside an Arabic courtyard, for King Ferdinand, Queen Isabella and the royal family: the Infante, their precious son and heir, the three older girls, Isabel, Maria, Juana, and Catalina the baby. The queen asked for nothing more than a roof and walls, she had been at war for years, she did not expect luxury. Then there were a dozen stone hovels around them where the greatest lords reluctantly took some shelter. Then, because the queen was a hard woman, there were stables for the horses and secure stores for the gunpowder and the precious explosives for which she had pawned her own jewels to buy from Venice; then, and only then, were built barracks and kitchens, stores and halls. Then there was a little town, built in stone, where once there had been a little camp. No-one thought it could be done; but, bravo! it was done. They called it Santa Fe and Isabella had triumphed over misfortune once again. The doomed siege of Granada by the determined, foolish Christian kings would continue.

Catalina, Princess of Wales, came upon one of the great lords of the Spanish camp in whispered conference with his friends. 'What are you doing, Don Hernando?' she asked with all the precocious confidence of a five-year-old who had never been far from her mother's side, whose father could deny her very little.

'Nothing, Infanta,' Hernando Perez del Pulgar said with a smile that told her that she could ask again.

'You are.'

'It's a secret.'

'I won't tell.'

'Oh! Princess! You would tell. It is such a great secret! Too big a secret for a little girl.'

'I won't! I really won't! I truly won't!' She thought. 'I promise upon Wales.'

'On Wales! On your own country?'

'On England?'

'On England? Your inheritance?'

She nodded. 'On Wales and on England, and on Spain itself.'

'Well, then. If you make such a sacred promise I will tell you. Swear that you won't tell your mother?'

She nodded, her blue eyes wide.

'We are going to get into the Alhambra. I know a gate, a little postern gate, that is not well guarded, where we can force an entry. We are going to go in, and guess what?'

She shook her head vigorously, her auburn plait swinging beneath her veil like a puppy's plump tail.

'We are going to say our prayers in their mosque. And I am going to leave an Ave Maria stabbed to the floor with my dagger. What d'you think of that?'

She was too young to realise that they were going to a certain death. She had no idea of the sentries at every gate, of the merciless rage of the Moors. Her eyes lit up in excitement. 'You are?'

'Isn't it a wonderful plan?'

'When are you going?'

'Tonight! This very night!'

'I shan't sleep till you come back!'

11

'You must pray for me, and then go to sleep, and I will come myself, Princess, and tell you and your mother all about it in the morning.'

She swore she would never sleep and she lay awake, quite rigid in her little cot-bed, while her maid tossed and turned on the rug at the door. Slowly, her eyelids drooped until the lashes lay on the round cheeks, the little plump hands unclenched and Catalina slept.

But in the morning, he did not come, his horse was missing from its stall and his friends were absent. For the first time in her life, the little girl had some sense of the danger he had run – mortal danger, and for nothing but glory and to be featured in some song.

'Where is he?' she asked. 'Where is Hernando?'

The silence of her maid, Madilla, warned her. 'He will come?' she asked, suddenly doubtful. 'He will come back?'

Slowly, it dawns on me that perhaps he will not come back, that life is not like a ballad, where a vain hope is always triumphant and a handsome man is never cut down in his youth. But if he can fail and die, then can my father die? Can my mother die? Can I? Even I? Little Catalina, Infanta of Spain and Princess of Wales?

I kneel in the sacred circular space of my mother's newly built chapel; but I am not praying. I am puzzling over this strange world that is suddenly opening up before me. If we are in the right – and I am sure of that; if these handsome young men are in the right – and I am sure of that – if we and our cause are under the especial hand of God, then how can we ever fail?

But if I have misunderstood something, then something is very wrong, and we are all indeed mortal, perhaps we can fail. Even handsome Hernando Perez del Pulgar and his laughing friends, even my mother and father can fail. If Hernando can die, then so too can my mother and father. And if this is so, then what safety is there in the world? If Madre can die, like a common soldier, like a mule pulling a baggage cart, as I have seen men and mules die, then how can the world go on? How could there be a God?

Then it was time for her mother's audience for petitioners and friends, and suddenly he was there, in his best suit, his beard combed, his eyes dancing, and the whole story spilled out: how they had dressed in their Arab clothes so as to pass for townspeople in the darkness, how they had crept in through the postern gate, how they had dashed up to the mosque, how they had kneeled and gabbled an Ave Maria and stabbed the prayer into the floor of the mosque, and then, surprised by guards, they had fought their way, hand to hand, thrust and parry, blades flashing in the moonlight; back down the narrow street, out of the door that they had forced only moments earlier, and were away into the night before the full alarm had been sounded. Not a scratch on them, not a man lost. A triumph for them and a slap in the face for Granada.

It was a great joke to play on the Moors, it was the funniest thing in the world to take a Christian prayer into the very heart of their holy place. It was the most wonderful gesture to insult them. The queen was delighted, the king too, the princess and her sisters looked at their champion, Hernando Perez del Pulgar, as if he were a hero from the romances, a knight from the time of Arthur at Camelot. Catalina clapped her hands in delight at the story, and commanded that he tell it and re-tell it, over and over again. But in the back of her mind, pushed far away from thought, she remembered the chill she had felt when she had thought that he was not coming back.

Next, they waited for the reply from the Moors. It was certain to happen. They knew that their enemy would see the venture as the challenge that it was, there was bound to be a response. It was not long in coming.

The queen and her children were visiting Zubia, a village near to Granada, so Her Majesty could see the impregnable walls of the fort herself. They had ridden out with a light guard and the commander was white with horror when he came dashing up to them in the little village square and shouted that the gates of the red fort had opened and the Moors were thundering out, the full army, armed for attack. There was no time to get back to camp, the queen and the three princesses could never outrun Moorish horsemen on Arab stallions, there was nowhere to hide, there was nowhere even to make a stand.

In desperate haste Queen Isabella climbed to the flat roof of the nearest house, pulling the little princess by her hand up the crumbling stairs, her sisters running behind. 'I have to see! I have to see!' she exclaimed.

'Madre! You are hurting me!'

'Quiet, child. We have to see what they intend.'

'Are they coming for us?' the child whimpered, her little voice muffled by her own plump hand.

'They may be. I have to see.'

It was a raiding party, not the full force. They were led by their champion, a giant of a man, dark as mahogany, a glint of a smile beneath his helmet, riding a huge black horse as if he were Night riding to overwhelm them. His horse snarled like a dog at the watching guard, its teeth bared.

'Madre, who is that man?' the Princess of Wales whispered to her mother, staring from the vantage point of the flat roof of the house.

'That is the Moor called Yarfe, and I am afraid he has come for your friend, Hernando.'

'His horse looks so frightening, like it wants to bite.'

'He has cut off its lips to make it snarl at us. But we are not made fearful by such things. We are not frightened children.'

'Should we not run away?' asked the frightened child.

Her mother, watching the Moor parade, did not even hear her daughter's whisper.

'You won't let him hurt Hernando, will you? Madre?'

'Hernando laid the challenge. Yarfe is answering it. We will have to fight,' she said levelly. 'Yarfe is a knight, a man of honour. He cannot ignore the challenge.'

'How can he be a man of honour if he is a heretic? A Moor?'

'They are most honourable men, Catalina, though they are unbelievers. And this Yarfe is a hero to them.'

'What will you do? How shall we save ourselves? This man is as big as a giant.'

'I shall pray,' Isabella said. 'And my champion Garallosco de la Vega will answer Yarfe for Hernando.'

As calmly as if she were in her own chapel at Cordoba, Isabella kneeled on the roof of the little house and gestured that her daughters should do the same. Sulkily, Catalina's older sister, Juana, dropped to her knees, the princesses Isabel and Maria, her other two older sisters, followed suit. Catalina saw, peeping through her clasped hands as she kneeled in prayer, that Maria was shaking with fear, and that Isabel, in her widow's gown, was white with terror.

'Heavenly Father, we pray for the safety of ourselves, of our cause, and of our army.' Queen Isabella looked up at the brilliantly blue sky. 'We pray for the victory of Your champion, Garallosco de la Vega, at this time of his trial.'

'Amen,' the girls said promptly, and then followed the direction of their mother's gaze to where the ranks of the Spanish guard were drawn up, watchful and silent.

'If God is protecting him . . .' Catalina started.

'Silence,' her mother said gently. 'Let him do his work, let God do His, and let me do mine.' She closed her eyes in prayer.

Catalina turned to her eldest sister and pulled at her sleeve. 'Isabel, if God is protecting him, then how can he be in danger?'

Isabel looked down at her little sister. 'God does not make the way smooth for those He loves,' she said in a harsh whisper. 'He sends hardships to try them. Those that God loves the best are those who suffer the worst. I know that. I, who lost the only man that I will ever love. You know that. Think about Job, Catalina.'

'Then how shall we win?' the little girl demanded. 'Since God loves Madre, won't He send her the worst hardships? And so how shall we ever win?'

'Hush,' their mother said. 'Watch. Watch and pray with faith.'

Their small guard and the Moorish raiding party were drawn up opposite each other, ready for battle. Then Yarfe rode forwards on his great black charger. Something white bobbed at the ground, tied to the horse's glossy black tail. There was a gasp as the soldiers in the front rank recognised what he had. It was the Ave Maria that Hernando had left speared to the floor of the mosque. The Moor had tied it to the tail of his horse as a calculated insult, and now rode the great creature forwards and back before the Christian ranks, and smiled when he heard their roar of rage.

'Heretic,' Queen Isabella whispered. 'A man damned to hell. God strike him dead and scourge his sin.'

The queen's champion, de la Vega, turned his horse and rode towards the little house where the royal guards ringed the court-yard, the tiny olive tree, the doorway. He pulled up his horse beside the olive tree and doffed his helmet, looking up at his queen and the princesses on the roof. His dark hair was curly and sparkling with sweat from the heat, his dark eyes sparkled with anger. 'Your Grace, do I have your leave to answer his challenge?'

'Yes,' the queen said, never shrinking for a moment. 'Go with God, Garallosco de la Vega.'

'That big man will kill him,' Catalina said, pulling at her mother's long sleeve. 'Tell him he must not go. Yarfe is so much bigger. He will murder de la Vega!'

'It will be as God wills,' Isabella maintained, closing her eyes in prayer.

'Mother! Your Majesty! He is a giant. He will kill our champion.'

Her mother opened her blue eyes and looked down at her daughter

16

and saw her little face was flushed with distress and her eyes were filling with tears. 'It will be as God wills it,' she repeated firmly. 'You have to have faith that you are doing God's will. Sometimes you will not understand, sometimes you will doubt, but if you are doing God's will you cannot be wrong, you cannot go wrong. Remember it, Catalina. Whether we win this challenge or lose it, it makes no difference. We are soldiers of Christ. You are a soldier of Christ. If we live or die, it makes no difference. We will die in faith, that is all that matters. This battle is God's battle, He will send a victory, if not today, then tomorrow. And whichever man wins today, we do not doubt that God will win, and we will win in the end.'

'But de la Vega . . .' Catalina protested, her fat lower lip trembling.

'Perhaps God will take him to His own this afternoon,' her mother said steadily. 'We should pray for him.'

Juana made a face at her little sister, but when their mother knelt again the two girls clasped hands for comfort. Isabel kneeled beside them, Maria beside her. All of them squinted through their closed eyelids to the plain where the bay charger of de la Vega rode out from the line of the Spaniards, and the black horse of the Moor trotted proudly before the Saracens.

The queen kept her eyes closed until she had finished her prayer, she did not even hear the roar as the two men took up their places, lowered their visors, and clasped their lances.

Catalina leapt to her feet, leaning over the low parapet so that she could see the Spanish champion. His horse thundered towards the other, racing legs a blur, the black horse came as fast from the opposite direction. The clash when the two lances smacked into solid armour could be heard on the roof of the little house, as both men were flung from their saddles by the force of the impact, the lances smashed, their breastplates buckled. It was nothing like the ritualised jousts of the court. It was a savage impact designed to break a neck or stop a heart.

'He is down! He is dead!' Catalina cried out.

'He is stunned,' her mother corrected her. 'See, he is getting up.'

The Spanish knight staggered to his feet, unsteady as a drunkard from the heavy blow to his chest. The bigger man was up already, helmet and heavy breastplate cast aside, coming for him with a huge sickle sword at the ready, the light flashing off the razor-sharp edge. De la Vega drew his own great weapon. There was a tremendous crash as the swords smacked together and then the two men locked blades and struggled, each trying to force the other down. They circled clumsily, staggering under the weight of their armour and from their concussion; but there could be no doubt that the Moor was the stronger man. The watchers could see that de la Vega was yielding under the pressure. He tried to spring back and get free; but the weight of the Moor was bearing down on him and he stumbled and fell. At once the black knight was on top of him, forcing him downwards. De la Vega's hand closed uselessly on his long sword, he could not bring it up. The Moor raised his sword to his victim's throat, ready to give the death blow, his face a black mask of concentration, his teeth gritted. Suddenly he gave a loud cry and fell back. De la Vega rolled up, scrabbled to his feet, crawling on his hands and knees like a rising dog.

The Moor was down, plucking at his breast, his great sword dropped to one side. In de la Vega's left hand was a short stabbing dagger stained with blood, a hidden weapon used in a desperate riposte. With a superhuman effort the Moor got to his feet, turned his back on the Christian and staggered towards his own ranks. 'I am lost,' he said to the men who ran forwards to catch him. 'We have lost.'

At a hidden signal the great gates of the red fort opened and the soldiers started to pour out. Juana leapt to her feet. 'Madre, we must run!' she screamed. 'They are coming! They are coming in their thousands!'

Isabella did not rise from her knees, even when her daughter dashed across the roof and ran down the stairs. 'Juana, come back,' she ordered in a voice like a whip crack. 'Girls, you will pray.'

She rose and went to the parapet. First she looked to the marshalling of her army, saw that the officers were setting the men into formation ready for a charge as the Moorish army, terrifying in their forward rush, came pouring on. Then she glanced down to see Juana, in a frenzy of fear, peeping around the garden wall, unsure whether to run for her horse or back to her mother.

Isabella, who loved her daughter, said not another word. She returned to the other girls and kneeled with them. 'Let us pray,' she said and closed her eyes.

'She didn't even look!' Juana repeated incredulously that night when they were in their room, washing their hands and changing their dirty clothes, Juana's tear-streaked face finally clean. 'There we are, in the middle of a battle, and she closes her eyes!'

'She knew that she would do more good appealing for the intercession of God than running around crying,' Isabel said pointedly. 'And it gave the army better heart than anything else to see her, on her knees, in full sight of everyone.'

'What if she had been hit by an arrow or a spear?'

'She was not. We were not. And we won the battle. And you, Juana, behaved like a half-mad peasant. I was ashamed of you. I don't know what gets into you. Are you mad or just wicked?'

'Oh, who cares what you think, you stupid widow?'

6th January 1492

Day by day the heart went out of the Moors. The Queen's Skirmish turned out to be their last battle. Their champion was dead, their city encircled, they were starving in the land that their fathers had made fertile. Worse, the promised support from Africa had failed them, the Turks had sworn friendship but the janissaries did not come, their king had lost his nerve, his son was a hostage with the Christians, and before them were the Princes of Spain, Isabella and Ferdinand, with all the power of Christendom behind them, with a holy war declared and a Christian crusade gathering pace with the scent of success. Within a few days of the meeting of the champions, Boabdil, the King of Granada, had agreed terms of peace, and a few days after, in the ceremony planned with all the grace that was typical of the Moors of Spain, he came down on foot to the iron gates of the city with the keys to the Alhambra Palace on a silken pillow and handed them over to the King and Queen of Spain in a complete surrender.

Granada, the red fort that stood above the city to guard it, and the gorgeous palace which was hidden inside the walls – the Alhambra – were given to Ferdinand and to Isabella.

Dressed in the gorgeous silks of their defeated enemy, turbaned, slippered, glorious as caliphs, the Spanish royal family, glittering with the spoils of Spain, took Granada. That afternoon Catalina, the Princess of Wales, walked with her parents up the winding, steep path through the shade of tall trees, to the most beautiful palace in Europe, slept that night in the brilliantly tiled harem and woke to the sound of rippling water in marble fountains, and thought herself a Moorish princess born to luxury and beauty, as well as a Princess of England.

And this is my life, from this day of victory. I had been born as a child of the camp, following the army from siege to battle, seeing things that perhaps no child should see, facing adult fears every day. I had marched past the bodies of dead soldiers rotting in the spring heat because there was no time to bury them, I had ridden behind mules whipped into

staggering bloodstained corpses, pulling my father's guns through the high passes of the Sierra. I saw my mother slap a man's face for weeping with exhaustion. I heard children of my own age crying for their parents burned at the stake for heresy; but at this moment, when we dressed ourselves in embroidered silk and walked into the red fort of Granada and through the gates to the white pearl that is the Alhambra Palace, at this moment I became a princess for the first time.

I became a girl raised in the most beautiful palace in Christendom, protected by an impregnable fort, blessed by God among all others, I became a girl of immense, unshakeable confidence in the God that had brought us to victory, and in my destiny as His most favourite child and my mother's most favourite daughter.

Alhambra proved to me, once and for all, that I was uniquely favoured by God, as my mother had been favoured by God. I was his chosen child, raised in the most beautiful palace in Christendom, and destined for the highest things.

The Spanish family with their officers ahead and the royal guard behind, glorious as Sultans, entered the fort through the enormous square tower known as the Justice Gate. As the shadow of the first arch of the tower fell on Isabella's upturned face the trumpeters played a great shout of defiance, like Joshua before the walls of Jericho, as if they would frighten away the lingering devils of the infidel. At once there was an echo to the blast of sound, a shuddering sigh, from everyone gathered inside the gateway, pressed back against the golden walls, the women half-veiled in their robes, the men standing tall and proud and silent, watching, to see what the conquerors would do next. Catalina looked above the sea of heads and saw the flowing shapes of Arabic script engraved on the gleaming walls.

'What does that say?' she demanded of Madilla, her nursemaid.

Madilla squinted upwards. 'I don't know,' she said crossly. She always denied her Moorish roots. She always tried to pretend that she knew nothing of the Moors or their lives though she had been born and bred a Moor herself and only converted – according to Juana – for convenience.

'Tell us, or we'll pinch you,' Juana offered sweetly.

The young woman scowled at the two sisters. 'It says: "May God allow the justice of Islam to prevail within."'

Catalina hesitated for a moment, hearing the proud ring of certainty, a determination to match her own mother's voice.

'Well, He hasn't,' Juana said smartly. 'Allah has deserted the Alhambra and Isabella has arrived. And if you Moors knew Isabella like we do, you would know that the greatest power is coming in and the lesser power going out.'

'God save the queen,' Madilla replied quickly. 'I know Queen Isabella well enough.'

As she spoke the great doors before them, black wood studded with black nails, swung open on their black hammered hinges, and with another blast of trumpets the king and queen strode into the inner courtyard.

Like dancers rehearsed till they were step-perfect, the Spanish guard peeled off to right and left inside the town walls, checking that the place was safe, and no despairing soldiers were preparing a last ambush. The great fort of the Alcazaba, built like the prow of a ship, jutting out over the plain of Granada, was to their left, and the men poured into it, running across the parade square, ringing the walls, running up and down the towers. Finally, Isabella the queen looked up to the sky, shaded her eyes with her hand clinking with Moorish gold bracelets, and laughed aloud to see the sacred banner of St James and the silver cross of the crusade flying where the crescent had been.

Then she turned to see the domestic servants of the palace slowly approaching, their heads bowed. They were led by the Grand Vizier, his height emphasised by his flowing robes, his piercing black eyes meeting hers, scanning King Ferdinand at her side, and the royal family behind them: the prince and the four princesses. The king and the prince were dressed as richly as sultans, wearing rich, embroidered tunics over their trousers, the queen and the princesses were wearing the traditional kamiz tunics made from the finest silks, over white linen trousers, with veils falling from their heads held back by filets of gold.

'Your Royal Highnesses, it is my honour and duty to welcome you to the Alhambra Palace,' the Grand Vizier said, as if it were the most ordinary thing in the world to hand over the most beautiful palace in Christendom to armed invaders.

The queen and her husband exchanged one brief glance. 'You can take us in,' she said.

The Grand Vizier bowed and led the way. The queen glanced back at her children. 'Come along, girls,' she said and went ahead of them, through the gardens surrounding the palace, down some steps and into the discreet doorway.

'This is the main entrance?' She hesitated before the small door set in the unmarked wall.

The man bowed. 'Your Highness, it is.'

Isabella said nothing but Catalina saw her raise her eyebrows as if she did not think much of it, and then they all went inside.

But the little doorway is like a keyhole to a treasure chest of boxes, the one opening out from another. The man leads us through them like a slave opening doors to a treasury. Their very names are a poem: the Golden Chamber, the Courtyard of the Myrtles, the Hall of the Ambassadors, the Courtyard of the Lions, or the Hall of the Two Sisters. It will take us weeks to find our way from one exquisitely tiled room to another. It will take us months to stop marvelling at the pleasure of

the sound of water running down the marble gulleys in the rooms, flowing to a white marble fountain that always spills over with the cleanest, freshest water of the mountains. And I will never tire of looking through the white stucco tracery to the view of the plain beyond, the mountains, the blue sky and golden hills. Every window is like a frame for a picture, they are designed to make you stop, look and marvel. Every window frame is like white-work embroidery – the stucco is so fine, so delicate, it is like sugar-work by confectioners, not like anything real.

We move into the harem as the easiest and most convenient rooms for my three sisters and me, and the harem servants light the braziers in the cool evenings, and scatter the scented herbs as if we were the sultanas who lived secluded behind the screens for so long. We have always worn Moorish dress at home and sometimes at great state occasions so still there is the whisper of silks and the slap of slippers on marble floors, as if nothing has changed. Now, we study where the slave girls read, we walk in the gardens that were planted to delight the favourites of the sultan. We eat their fruits, we love the taste of their sherbets, we tie their flowers into garlands for our own heads, and we run down their allées where the heavy scent of roses and honeysuckle is sweet in the cool of the morning.

We bathe in the hammam, standing stock still while the servants lather us all over with a rich soap that smells of flowers. Then they pour golden ewer after golden ewer of hot water over us, splashing from head to toe, to wash us clean. We are soothed with rose oil, wrapped in fine sheets and lie, half-drunk with sensual pleasure, on the warm marble table that dominates the entire room, under the golden ceiling where the star-shaped openings admit dazzling rays of sunlight into the shadowy peace of the place. One girl manicures our toes while another works on our hands, shaping the nails and painting delicate patterns of henna. We let the old woman pluck our eyebrows, paint our eyelashes. We are served as if we are sultanas, with all the riches of Spain and all the luxury of the East, and we surrender utterly to

*the delight of the palace. It captivates us, we swoon into submission;
the so-called victors.*

*Even Isabel, grieving for the loss of her husband, starts to smile
again. Even Juana, who is usually so moody and so sulky, is at peace.
And I become the pet of the court, the favourite of the gardeners who
let me pick my own peaches from the trees, the darling of the harem
where I am taught to play and dance and sing, and the favourite of
the kitchen where they let me watch them preparing the sweet pastries
and dishes of honey and almonds of Arabia.*

*My father meets with foreign emissaries in the Hall of the
Ambassadors, he takes them to the bath house for talks, like any leisurely
sultan. My mother sits cross-legged on the throne of the Nasrids who
have ruled here for generations, her bare feet in soft leather slippers,
the drapery of her kamiz falling around her. She listens to the emissaries of the Pope himself, in a chamber that is walled with coloured
tiles and dancing with pagan light. It feels like home to her, she was
raised in the Alcazar in Seville, another Moorish palace. We walk in
their gardens, we bathe in their hammam, we step into their scented
leather slippers and we live a life that is more refined and more lux-
urious than they could dream of in Paris or London or Rome. We live
graciously. We live, as we have always aspired to do, like Moors. Our
fellow Christians herd goats in the mountains, pray at roadside cairns
to the Madonna, are terrified by superstition and lousy with disease,
live dirty and die young. We learn from Moslem scholars, we are
attended by their doctors, study the stars in the sky which they have
named, count with their numbers which start at the magical zero, eat
of their sweetest fruits and delight in the waters which run through
their aqueducts. Their architecture pleases us, at every turn of every
corner we know that we are living inside beauty. Their power now
keeps us safe; the Alcazabar is, indeed, invulnerable to attack once
more. We learn their poetry, we laugh at their games, we delight in
their gardens, in their fruits, we bathe in the waters they have made
flow. We are the victors but they have taught us how to rule. Sometimes*

I think that we are the barbarians, like those who came after the Romans or the Greeks, who could invade the palaces and capture the aqueducts, and then sit like monkeys on a throne, playing with beauty but not understanding it.

We do not change our faith, at least. Every palace servant has to give lip service to the beliefs of the One True Church. The horns of the mosque are silenced, there is to be no call to prayer in my mother's hearing. And anyone who disagrees can either leave for Africa at once, convert at once, or face the fires of the Inquisition. We do not soften under the spoils of war, we never forget that we are victors and that we won our victory by force of arms and by the will of God. We made a solemn promise to poor King Boabdil, that his people, the Moslems, should be as safe under our rule as the Christians were safe under his. We promise the convivencia – a way of living together – and they believe that we will make a Spain where anyone, Moor or Christian or Jew, can live quietly and with self-respect since all of us are 'People of the Book'. Their mistake is that they meant that truce, and they trusted that truce, and we – as it turns out – do not.

We betray our word in three months, expelling the Jews and threatening the Moslems. Everyone must convert to the True Faith and then, if there is any shadow of doubt, or any suspicion against them, their faith will be tested by the Holy Inquisition. It is the only way to make one nation: through one faith. It is the only way to make one people out of the great varied diversity which had been al Andalus. My mother builds a chapel in the council chamber and where it had once said 'Enter and ask. Do not be afraid to seek justice for here you will find it,' in the beautiful shapes of Arabic, she prays to a sterner, more intolerant God than Allah; and no-one comes for justice any more.

But nothing can change the nature of the palace. Not even the stamp of our soldiers' feet on the marble floors can shake the centuries-old sense of peace. I make Madilla teach me what the flowing inscriptions mean in every room, and my favourite is not the promises of justice, but the words written in the Courtyard of the Two Sisters which says:

'Have you ever seen such a beautiful garden?' and then answers itself: 'We have never seen a garden with greater abundance of fruit, nor sweeter, nor more perfumed.'

It is not truly a palace, not even as those we had known at Cordoba or Toledo. It is not a castle, nor a fort. It was built first and foremost as a garden with rooms of exquisite luxury so that one could live outside. It is a series of courtyards designed for flowers and people alike. It is a dream of beauty: walls, tiles, pillars melting into flowers, climbers, fruit and herbs. The Moors believe that a garden is a paradise on earth, and they have spent fortunes over the centuries to make this 'al-Yanna': the word that means garden, secret place, and paradise.

I know that I love it. Even as a little child I know that this is an exceptional place; that I will never find anywhere more lovely. And even as a child I know that I cannot stay here. It is God's will and my mother's will that I must leave al-Yanna, my secret place, my garden, my paradise. It is to be my destiny that I should find the most beautiful place in all the world when I am just six years old, and then leave it when I am fifteen; as homesick as Boabdil, as if happiness and peace for me will only ever be short-lived.

Dogmersfield Palace, Hampshire, Autumn 1501

'I say, you cannot come in! If you were the King of England himself – you could not come in.'

'I *am* the King of England,' Henry Tudor said, without a flicker of amusement. 'And she can either come out right now, or I damned well will come in and my son will follow me.'

'The Infanta has already sent word to the king that she cannot see him,' the duenna said witheringly. 'The noblemen of her court rode out to explain to him that she is in seclusion, as a lady of Spain. Do you think the King of England would come riding down the road when the Infanta has refused to receive him? What sort of a man do you think he is?'

'Exactly like this one,' he said and thrust his fist with the great gold ring towards her face. The Count de Cabra came into the hall in a rush, and at once recognised the lean forty-year-old man threatening the Infanta's duenna with a clenched fist, a few aghast servitors behind him, and gasped out: 'The king!'

At the same moment the duenna recognised the new badge of England, the combined roses of York and Lancaster, and recoiled. The count skidded to a halt and threw himself into a low bow.

'It is the king,' he hissed, his voice muffled by speaking with his head on his knees. The duenna gave a little gasp of horror and dropped into a deep curtsey.

'Get up,' the king said shortly. 'And fetch her.'

'But she is a princess of Spain, Your Grace,' the woman said, rising but with her head still bowed low. 'She is to stay in seclusion. She cannot be seen by you before her wedding day. This is the tradition. Her gentlemen went out to explain to you . . .'

'It's *your* tradition. It's not *my* tradition. And since she is my daughter-in-law in my country, under my laws, she will obey my tradition.'

'She has been brought up most carefully, most modestly, most properly . . .'

'Then she will be very shocked to find an angry man in her bedroom. Madam, I suggest that you get her up at once.'

'I will not, Your Grace. I take my orders from the Queen of Spain herself and she charged me to make sure that every respect was shown to the Infanta and that her behaviour was in every way . . .'

'Madam, you can take your working orders from me; or your marching orders from me. I don't care which. Now send the girl out or I swear on my crown I will come in and if I catch her naked in bed then she won't be the first woman I have ever seen in such a case. But she had better pray that she is the prettiest.'

The Spanish duenna went quite white at the insult.

'Choose,' the king said stonily.

'I cannot fetch the Infanta,' she said stubbornly.

'Dear God! That's it! Tell her I am coming in at once.'

She scuttled backwards like an angry crow, her face blanched with shock. Henry gave her a few moments to prepare, and then called her bluff by striding in behind her.

The room was lit only by candles and firelight. The covers of the bed were turned back as if the girl had hastily jumped up. Henry registered the intimacy of being in her bedroom, with her sheets still warm, the scent of her lingering in the enclosed space, before he looked at her. She was standing by the bed, one small white hand on the carved wooden post. She had a cloak of dark blue thrown over her shoulders and her white nightgown trimmed with priceless lace peeped through the opening at the front. Her rich auburn hair, plaited for sleep, hung down her back, but her face was completely shrouded in a hastily thrown mantilla of dark lace.

Dona Elvira darted between the girl and the king. 'This is the Infanta,' she said. 'Veiled until her wedding day.'

'Not on my money,' Henry Tudor said bitterly. 'I'll see what I've bought, thank you.'

He stepped forwards. The desperate duenna nearly threw herself to her knees. 'Her modesty . . .'

'Has she got some awful mark?' he demanded, driven to voice his deepest fear. 'Some blemish? Is she scarred by the pox and they did not tell me?'

'No! I swear.'

Silently, the girl put out her white hand and took the ornate lace hem of her veil. Her duenna gasped a protest but could do nothing to stop the princess as she raised the veil, and then flung it back. Her clear blue eyes stared into the lined, angry face of Henry Tudor without wavering. The king drank her in, and then gave a little sigh of relief at the sight of her.

She was an utter beauty: a smooth, rounded face, a straight, long nose, a full, sulky, sexy mouth. Her chin was up, he saw; her gaze challenging. This was no shrinking maiden fearing ravishment. This was a fighting princess standing on her dignity even in this most appalling moment of embarrassment.

He bowed. 'I am Henry Tudor, King of England,' he said.

She curtseyed.

He stepped forwards and saw her curb her instinct to flinch away. He took her firmly at the shoulders, and kissed one warm, smooth cheek and then the other. The perfume of her hair and the warm, female smell of her body came to him and he felt desire pulse in his groin and at his temples. Quickly he stepped back and let her go.

'You are welcome to England,' he said. He cleared his throat. 'You will forgive my impatience to see you. My son too is on his way to visit you.'

'I beg your pardon,' she said icily, speaking in perfectly phrased French. 'I was not informed until a few moments ago that Your Grace was insisting on the honour of this unexpected visit.'

Henry fell back a little from the whip of her temper. 'I have a right . . .'

She shrugged, an absolutely Spanish gesture. 'Of course. You have every right over me.'

At the ambiguous, provocative words, he was again aware of his closeness to her: of the intimacy of the small room, the tester bed hung with rich draperies, the sheets invitingly turned back, the pillow still impressed with the shape of her head. It was a scene for ravishment, not for a royal greeting. Again he felt the secret thud-thud of lust.

'I'll see you outside,' he said abruptly, as if it was her fault that he could not rid himself of the flash in his mind of what it would be like to have this ripe little beauty that he had bought. What would it be like if he had bought her for himself, rather than for his son?

'I shall be honoured,' she said coldly.

He got himself out of the room briskly enough, and nearly collided with Prince Arthur, hovering anxiously in the doorway.

'Fool,' he remarked.

Prince Arthur, pale with nerves, pushed his blond fringe back from his face, stood still and said nothing.

'I'll send that duenna home at the first moment I can,' the king said. 'And the rest of them. She can't make a little Spain in England, my son. The country won't stand for it, and I damned well won't stand for it.'

'People don't object. The country people seem to love the princess,' Arthur suggested mildly. 'Her escort says . . .'

'Because she wears a stupid hat. Because she is odd: Spanish, rare. Because she is young and –' he broke off '– pretty.'

'Is she?' he gasped. 'I mean: is she?'

'Haven't I just gone in to make sure? But no Englishman will stand for any Spanish nonsense once they get over the novelty. And neither will I. This is a marriage to cement an alliance; not to flatter her vanity. Whether they like her or not, she's marrying you. Whether you like her or not, she's marrying you. Whether she likes it or not, she's marrying you. And she'd better get out here now or *I* won't like her and that will be the only thing that can make a difference.'

I have to go out, I have won only the briefest of reprieves and I know he is waiting for me outside the door to my bedchamber and he has demonstrated, powerfully enough, that if I do not go to him, then the mountain will come to Mohammed and I will be shamed again.

I brush Dona Elvira aside as a duenna who cannot protect me now, and I go to the door of my rooms. My servants are frozen, like slaves enchanted in a fairy tale by this extraordinary behaviour from a king. My heart hammers in my ears and I know a girl's embarrassment at having to step forwards in public, but also a soldier's desire to let battle be joined, the eagerness to know the worst, to face danger rather than evade it.

Henry of England wants me to meet his son, before his travelling party, without ceremony, without dignity as if we were a scramble of peasants. So be it. He will not find a princess of Spain falling back for fear. I grit my teeth, I smile as my mother commanded me.

I nod to my herald, who is as stunned as the rest of my companions. 'Announce me,' I order him.

His face blank with shock, he throws open the door. 'The Infanta Catalina, Princess of Spain and Princess of Wales,' he bellows.

This is me. This is my moment. This is my battle cry.

I step forwards.

The Spanish Infanta – with her face naked to every man's gaze – stood in the darkened doorway and then walked into the room, only a little flame of colour in both cheeks betraying her ordeal.

At his father's side, Prince Arthur swallowed. She was far more beautiful than he had imagined, and a million times more haughty. She was dressed in a gown of dark black velvet, slashed to show an undergown of carnation silk, the neck cut square and low over her plump breasts, hung with ropes of pearls. Her auburn hair, freed from the plait, tumbled down her back in a great wave of red-gold. On her head was a black lace mantilla flung determinedly back. She swept a deep curtsey and came up with her head held high, graceful as a dancer.

'I beg your pardon for not being ready to greet you,' she said in French. 'If I had known you were coming I would have been prepared.'

'I'm surprised you didn't hear the racket,' the king said. 'I was arguing at your door for a good ten minutes.'

'I thought it was a pair of porters brawling,' she said coolly.

Arthur suppressed a gasp of horror at her impertinence; but his father was eyeing her with a smile as if a new filly was showing promising spirit.

'No. It was me; threatening your lady-in-waiting. I am sorry that I had to march in on you.'

She inclined her head. 'That was my duenna, Dona Elvira. I am sorry if she displeased you. Her English is not good. She cannot have understood what you wanted.'

'I wanted to see my daughter-in-law, and my son wanted to see his bride, and I expect an English princess to behave like an English princess, and not like some damned sequestered girl in a harem. I thought your parents had beaten the Moors. I didn't expect to find them set up as your models.'

Catalina ignored the insult with a slight turn of her head. 'I am sure that you will teach me good English manners,' she said. 'Who better to advise me?' She turned to Prince Arthur and swept him a royal curtsey. 'My lord.'

He faltered in his bow in return, amazed at the serenity that she could muster in this most embarrassing of moments. He reached into his jacket for her present, fumbled with the little purse of jewels, dropped them, picked them up again and finally thrust them towards her, feeling like a fool.

She took them and inclined her head in thanks, but did not open them. 'Have you dined, Your Grace?'

'We'll eat here,' he said bluntly. 'I ordered dinner already.'

'Then can I offer you a drink? Or somewhere to wash and change your clothes before you dine?' She examined the long, lean length of him consideringly, from the mud spattering his pale, lined face to his dusty boots. The English were a prodigiously dirty nation, not even a great house such as this one had an adequate hammam or even piped water. 'Or perhaps you don't like to wash?'

A harsh chuckle was forced from the king. 'You can order me a cup of ale and have them send fresh clothes and hot water to the best bedroom and I'll change before dinner.' He raised a hand. 'You needn't take it as a compliment to you. I always wash before dinner.'

Arthur saw her nip her lower lip with little white teeth as if to refrain from some sarcastic reply. 'Yes, Your Grace,' she said pleasantly. 'As you wish.' She summoned her lady-in-waiting to her side and gave her low-voiced orders in rapid Spanish. The woman curtseyed and led the king from the room.

The princess turned to Prince Arthur.

'*Et tu?*' she asked in Latin. 'And you?'

'I? What?' he stammered.

He felt that she was trying not to sigh with impatience.

'Would you like to wash and change your coat also?'

'I've washed,' he said. As soon as the words were out of his mouth he could have bitten off his own tongue. He sounded like a child being scolded by a nurse, he thought. 'I've washed,' indeed. What was he going to do next? Hold out his hands palms-upwards so that she could see he was a good boy?

'Then will you take a glass of wine? Or ale?'

Catalina turned to the table, where the servants were hastily laying cups and flagons.

'Wine.'

She raised a glass and a flagon and the two chinked together, and then chink-chink-chinked again. In amazement, he saw that her hands were trembling.

She poured the wine quickly and held it to him. His gaze went from her hand and the slightly rippled surface of the wine to her pale face.

She was not laughing at him, he saw. She was not at all at ease with him. His father's rudeness had brought out the pride in her, but alone with him she was just a girl, some months older than him, but still just a girl. The daughter of the two most formidable monarchs in Europe; but still just a girl with shaking hands.

'You need not be frightened,' he said very quietly. 'I am sorry about all this.'

He meant – your failed attempt to avoid this meeting, my father's brusque informality, my own inability to stop him or soften him, and, more than anything else, the misery that this business must be for you: coming far from your home among strangers and meeting your new husband, dragged from your bed under protest.

She looked down. He stared at the flawless pallor of her skin, at the fair eyelashes and pale eyebrows.

Then she looked up at him. 'It's all right,' she said. 'I have seen far worse than this, I have been in far worse places than this, and I have known worse men than your father. You need not fear for me. I am afraid of nothing.'

No-one will ever know what it cost me to smile, what it cost me to stand before your father and not tremble. I am not yet sixteen, I am far from my mother, I am in a strange country, I cannot speak the language and I know nobody here. I have no friends but the party of companions and servants that I have brought with me, and they look to me to protect them. They do not think to help me.

I know what I have to do. I have to be a Spanish princess for the English, and an English princess for the Spanish. I have to seem at ease where I am not, and assume confidence when I am afraid. You may be my husband, but I can hardly see you, I have no sense of you yet. I have no time to consider you, I am absorbed in being the princess that your father has bought, the princess that my mother has delivered, the princess that will fulfil the bargain and secure a treaty between England and Spain.

No-one will ever know that I have to pretend to ease, pretend to confidence, pretend to grace. Of course I am afraid. But I will never, never show it. And, when they call my name I will always step forwards.

The king, having washed and taken a couple of glasses of wine before he came to his dinner, was affable with the young princess, determined to overlook their introduction. Once or twice she caught him glancing at her sideways, as if to get the measure of her, and she turned to look at him, full on, one sandy eyebrow slightly raised as if to interrogate him.

'Yes?' he demanded.

'I beg your pardon,' she said equably. 'I thought Your Grace needed something. You glanced at me.'

'I was thinking you're not much like your portrait,' he said.

She flushed a little. Portraits were designed to flatter the sitter, and when the sitter was a royal princess on the marriage market, even more so.

'Better-looking,' Henry said begrudgingly, to reassure her. 'Younger, softer, prettier.'

She did not warm to the praise as he expected her to do. She merely nodded as if it were an interesting observation.

'You had a bad voyage,' Henry remarked.

'Very bad,' she said. She turned to Prince Arthur. 'We were driven back as we set out from Corunna in August and we had to wait for the storms to pass. When we finally set sail it was still terribly rough, and then we were forced into Plymouth. We couldn't get to Southampton at all. We were all quite sure we would be drowned.'

'Well, you couldn't have come overland,' Henry said flatly, thinking of the parlous state of France and the enmity of the French king. 'You'd be a priceless hostage for a king who was heartless enough to take you. Thank God you never fell into enemy hands.'

She looked at him thoughtfully. 'Pray God I never do.'

'Well, your troubles are over now,' Henry concluded. 'The next boat you are on will be the royal barge when you go down the Thames. How shall you like to become Princess of Wales?'

'I have been the Princess of Wales ever since I was three years old,' she corrected him. 'They always called me Catalina, the Infanta, Princess of Wales. I knew it was my destiny.' She looked at Arthur, who still sat silently observing the table. 'I have known we would be married all my life. It was kind of you to write to me so often. It made me feel that we were not complete strangers.'

He flushed. 'I was ordered to write to you,' he said awkwardly. 'As part of my studies. But I liked getting your replies.'

'Good God, boy, you don't exactly sparkle, do you?' asked his father critically.

Arthur flushed scarlet to his ears.

'There was no need to tell her that you were ordered to write,' his father ruled. 'Better to let her think that you were writing of your own choice.'

'I don't mind,' Catalina said quietly. 'I was ordered to reply. And, as it happens, I should like us always to speak the truth to each other.'

The king barked out a laugh. 'Not in a year's time you won't,' he predicted. 'You will be all in favour of the polite lie then. The great saviour of a marriage is mutual ignorance.'

Arthur nodded obediently, but Catalina merely smiled, as if his observations were of interest, but not necessarily true. Henry found himself piqued by the girl, and still aroused by her prettiness.

'I daresay your father does not tell your mother every thought that crosses his mind,' he said, trying to make her look at him again.

He succeeded. She gave him a long, slow, considering gaze from her blue eyes. 'Perhaps he does not,' she conceded. 'I would not know. It is not fitting that I should know. But whether he tells her or not: my mother knows everything anyway.'

He laughed. Her dignity was quite delightful in a girl whose head barely came up to his chest. 'She is a visionary, your mother? She has the gift of Sight?'

She did not laugh in reply. 'She is wise,' she said simply. 'She is the wisest monarch in Europe.'

The king thought he would be foolish to bridle at a girl's devotion to her mother, and it would be graceless to point out that her mother might have unified the kingdoms of Castile and Aragon but that she was still a long way from creating a peaceful and united Spain. The tactical skill of Isabella and Ferdinand had forged a single country from the Moorish kingdoms, they had yet to make everyone accept their peace. Catalina's own journey to London had been disrupted by rebellions of Moors and Jews who could not bear the tyranny of the Spanish kings. He changed the subject. 'Why don't you show us a dance?' he demanded, thinking that he would like to see her move. 'Or is that not allowed in Spain either?'

'Since I am an English princess I must learn your customs,' she said. 'Would an English princess get up in the middle of the night and dance for the king after he forced his way into her rooms?'

Henry laughed at her. 'If she had any sense she would.'

She threw him a small, demure smile. 'Then I will dance with my ladies,' she decided, and rose from her seat at the high table and went down to the centre of the floor. She called one by name, Henry noted, Maria de Salinas, a pretty, dark-haired girl who came quickly to stand beside Catalina. Three other young women, pretending shyness but eager to show themselves off, came forwards.

Henry looked them over. He had asked Their Majesties of Spain that their daughter's companions should all be pretty, and he was pleased to see that however blunt and ill-mannered they had found his request, they had acceded to it. The girls were all good-looking but none of them outshone the princess who stood, composed, and then raised her hands and clapped, to order the musicians to play.

He noticed at once that she moved like a sensual woman. The dance was a pavane, a slow ceremonial dance, and she moved with her hips swaying and her eyes heavy-lidded, a little smile on her face. She had been well-schooled, any princess would be taught how to dance in the courtly world where dancing, singing, music and poetry mattered more than anything else; but she danced like a woman who let the music move her, and Henry, who had some experience, believed that women who could be summoned by music were the ones who responded to the rhythms of lust.

He went from pleasure in watching her to a sense of rising irritation that this exquisite piece would be put in Arthur's cold bed. He could not see his thoughtful, scholarly boy teasing and arousing the passion in this girl on the edge of womanhood. He imagined that Arthur would fumble about and perhaps hurt her, and she would grit her teeth and do her duty as a woman and a queen must, and then, like as not, she would die in childbirth; and the whole performance of finding a bride for Arthur would have to be undergone again, with no benefit for himself but only this irritated, frustrated arousal that she seemed to inspire in him. It was good that she was desirable, since she would be an ornament to his court; but it was a nuisance that she should be so very desirable to him.

Henry looked away from her dancing and comforted himself with the thought of her dowry which would bring him lasting benefit and come directly to him, unlike this bride who seemed bound to unsettle him and must go, however mismatched, to his son. As soon as they were married her treasurer would hand over the first payment of her dowry: in solid gold. A year later he would deliver the second part in gold and in her plate and jewels. Having fought his way to the throne on a shoestring and uncertain credit, Henry trusted the power of money more than anything in life; more even than his throne, for he knew he could buy a throne with money, and far more than women, for they are cheaply bought; and far, far more than the joy of a smile from a virgin princess who stopped her dance now, swept him a curtsey and came up smiling.

'Do I please you?' she demanded, flushed and a little breathless.

'Well enough,' he said, determined that she should never know how much. 'But it's late now and you should go back to your bed. We'll ride with you a little way in the morning before we go ahead of you to London.'

She was surprised at the abruptness of his reply. Again, she glanced towards Arthur as if he might contradict his father's plans; perhaps stay with her for the remainder of the journey, since his father had bragged of their informality. But the boy said nothing. 'As you wish, Your Grace,' she said politely.

The king nodded and rose to his feet. The court billowed into deep curtseys and bows as he stalked past them, out of the room. 'Not so informal, at all,' Catalina thought as she watched the King of England stride through his court, his head high. 'He may boast of being a soldier with the manners of the camp, but he insists on obedience and on the show of deference. As indeed, he should,' added Isabella's daughter to herself.

Arthur followed behind his father with a quick 'Goodnight' to the princess as he left. In a moment all the men in their train had gone too, and the princess was alone but for her ladies.

'What an extraordinary man,' she remarked to her favourite, Maria de Salinas.

'He liked you,' the young woman said. 'He watched you very closely, he liked you.'

'And why should he not?' she asked with the instinctive arrogance of a girl born to the greatest kingdom in Europe. 'And even if he did not, it is all already agreed, and there can be no change. It has been agreed for almost all my life.'

He is not what I expected, this king who fought his way to the throne and picked up his crown from the mud of a battlefield. I expected him to be more like a champion, like a great soldier, perhaps like my father. Instead he has the look of a merchant, a man who puzzles over profit indoors, not a man who won his kingdom and his wife at the point of a sword.

I suppose I hoped for a man like Don Hernando, a hero that I could look up to, a man I would be proud to call father. But this king is lean and pale like a clerk, not a knight from the romances at all.

I expected his court to be more grand, I expected a great procession and a formal meeting with long introductions and elegant speeches, as we would have done it in the Alhambra. But he is abrupt; in my view he is rude. I shall have to become accustomed to these northern ways, this scramble to do things, this brusque ordering. I cannot expect things to be done well or even correctly. I shall have to overlook a lot until I am queen and can change things.

But, anyway, it hardly matters whether I like the king or he likes me. He has engaged in this treaty with my father and I am betrothed to his son. It hardly matters what I think of him, or what he thinks of me. It is not as if we will have to deal much together. I shall live and rule Wales and he will live and rule England, and when he dies it will be my husband on his throne and my son will be the next Prince of Wales, and I shall be queen.

As for my husband-to-be – oh! – he has made a very different first impression. He is so handsome! I did not expect him to be so hand-some! He is so fair and slight, he is like a page boy from one of the old romances. I can imagine him waking all night in a vigil, or singing up to a castle window. He has pale, almost silvery skin, he has fine golden hair, and yet he is taller than me and lean and strong like a boy on the edge of manhood.

He has a rare smile, one that comes reluctantly and then shines. And he is kind. That is a great thing in a husband. He was kind when he took the glass of wine from me, he saw that I was trembling, and he tried to reassure me.

I wonder what he thinks of me? I do so wonder what he thinks of me?

Just as the king had ruled, he and Arthur went swiftly back to Windsor the next morning and Catalina's train, with her litter carried by mules, with her trousseau in great travelling chests, her ladies-in-waiting, her Spanish household, and the guards for her dowry treasure, laboured up the muddy roads to London at a far slower pace.

She did not see the prince again until their wedding day, but when she arrived in the village of Kingston-upon-Thames her train halted in order to meet the greatest man in the kingdom, the young Edward Stafford, Duke of Buckingham, and Henry, Duke of York, the king's second son, who were appointed to accompany her to Lambeth Palace.

'I'll come out,' Catalina said hastily, emerging from her litter and walking quickly past the waiting horses, not wanting another quarrel with her strict duenna about young ladies meeting young men before their wedding day. 'Dona Elvira, say nothing. The boy is a child of ten years old. It doesn't matter. Not even my mother would think that it matters.'

'At least wear your veil!' the woman implored. 'The Duke of Buck ... Buck ... whatever his name, is here too. Wear your veil when you go before him, for your own reputation, Infanta.'

'Buckingham,' Catalina corrected her. 'The Duke of Buckingham. And call me Princess of Wales. And you know I cannot wear my veil because he will have been commanded to report to the king. You know what my mother said: that he is the king's mother's ward, restored to his family fortunes, and must be shown the greatest respect.'

The older woman shook her head, but Catalina marched out bare-faced, feeling both fearful and reckless at her own daring, and saw the duke's men drawn up in array on the road and before them, a young boy: helmet off, bright head shining in the sunshine.

Her first thought was that he was utterly unlike his brother. While Arthur was fair-haired and slight and serious-looking, with a pale complexion and warm brown eyes, this was a sunny boy who looked as if he had never had a serious thought in his head. He did not take after his lean-faced father, he had the look of a boy for whom life came easily. His hair was red-gold, his face round and still baby-plump, his smile when he first saw her was genuinely friendly and bright, and his blue eyes shone as if he was accustomed to seeing a very pleasing world.

'Sister!' he said warmly, jumped down from his horse with a clatter of armour, and swept her a low bow.

'Brother Henry,' she said, curtseying back to him to precisely the right height, considering that he was only a second son of England, and she was an Infanta of Spain.

43

'I am so pleased to see you,' he said quickly, his Latin rapid, his English accent strong. 'I was so hoping that His Majesty would let me come to meet you before I had to take you into London on your wedding day. I thought it would be so awkward to go marching down the aisle with you, and hand you over to Arthur, if we hadn't even spoken. And call me Harry. Everyone calls me Harry.'

'I too am pleased to meet you, Brother Harry,' Catalina said politely, rather taken-aback at his enthusiasm.

'Pleased! You should be dancing with joy!' he exclaimed buoyantly. 'Because Father said that I could bring you the horse which was to be one of your wedding-day presents and so we can ride together to Lambeth. Arthur said you should wait for your wedding day, but I said, why should she wait? She won't be able to ride on her wedding day. She'll be too busy getting married. But if I take it to her now we can ride at once.'

'That was kind of you.'

'Oh, I never take any notice of Arthur,' Harry said cheerfully.

Catalina had to choke down a giggle. 'You don't?'

He made a face and shook his head. 'Serious,' he said. 'You'll be amazed how serious. And scholarly, of course, but not gifted. Everyone says I am very gifted, languages mostly, but music also. We can speak French together if you wish, I am extraordinarily fluent for my age. I am considered a pretty fair musician. And of course I am a sportsman. Do you hunt?'

'No,' Catalina said, a little overwhelmed. 'At least, I only follow the hunt when we go after boar or wolves.'

'Wolves? I should so like to hunt wolves. D'you really have bears?'

'Yes, in the hills.'

'I should so like to hunt a bear. Do you hunt wolves on foot like boar?'

'No, on horseback,' she said. 'They're very fast, you have to take very fast dogs to pull them down. It's a horrid hunt.'

'I shouldn't mind that,' he said. 'I don't mind anything like that. Everyone says I am terribly brave about things like that.'

'I am sure they do,' she said, smiling.

A handsome man in his mid-twenties came forwards and bowed. 'Oh, this is Edward Stafford, the Duke of Buckingham,' Harry said quickly. 'May I present him?'

Catalina held out her hand and the man bowed again over it. His intelligent, handsome face was warm with a smile. 'You are welcome to your own country,' he said in faultless Castilian. 'I hope everything has been to your liking on your journey? Is there anything I can provide for you?'

'I have been well cared for indeed,' Catalina said, blushing with pleasure at being greeted in her own language. 'And the welcome I have had from people all along the way has been very kind.'

'Look, here's your new horse,' Harry interrupted, as the groom led a beautiful black mare forwards. 'You'll be used to good horses, of course. D'you have Barbary horses all the time?'

'My mother insists on them for the cavalry,' she said.

'Oh,' he breathed. 'Because they are so fast?'

'They can be trained as fighting horses,' she said, going forwards and holding out her hand, palm upwards, for the mare to sniff at and nibble at her fingers with a soft, gentle mouth.

'Fighting horses?' he pursued.

'The Saracens have horses which can fight as their masters do, and the Barbary horses can be trained to do it too,' she said. 'They rear up and strike down a soldier with their front hooves, and they will kick out behind, too. The Turks have horses that will pick up a sword from the ground and hand it back to the rider. My mother says that one good horse is worth ten men in battle.'

'I should so like to have a horse like that,' Harry said longingly. 'I wonder how I should ever get one?'

He paused, but she did not rise to the bait. 'If only someone would give me a horse like that, I could learn how to ride it,' he said transparently. 'Perhaps for my birthday, or perhaps next week, since it is not me getting married, and I am not getting any wedding gifts. Since I am quite left out, and quite neglected.'

'Perhaps,' said Catalina, who had once seen her own brother get his way with exactly the same wheedling.

'I should be trained to ride properly,' he said. 'Father has promised that though I am to go into the church I shall be allowed to ride at the quintain. But My Lady the King's Mother says I may not joust. And it's really unfair. I should be allowed to joust. If I had a proper horse I could joust, I am sure I would beat everyone.'

'I am sure you would,' she said.

'Well, shall we go?' he asked, seeing that she would not give him a horse for asking.

'I cannot ride, I do not have my riding clothes unpacked.'

He hesitated. 'Can't you just go in that?'

Catalina laughed. 'This is velvet and silk. I can't ride in it. And besides, I can't gallop around England looking like a mummer.'

'Oh,' he said. 'Well, shall you go in your litter then? Won't it make us very slow?'

'I am sorry for that, but I am ordered to travel in a litter,' she said. 'With the curtains drawn. I can't think that even your father would want me to charge around the country with my skirts tucked up.'

'Of course the princess cannot ride today,' the Duke of Buckingham ruled. 'As I told you. She has to go in her litter.'

Harry shrugged. 'Well, I didn't know. Nobody told me what you were going to wear. Can I go ahead then? My horses will be so much faster than the mules.'

'You can ride ahead but not out of sight,' Catalina decided. 'Since you are supposed to be escorting me you should be with me.'

'As I said,' the Duke of Buckingham observed quietly and exchanged a little smile with the princess.

'I'll wait at every crossroads,' Harry promised. 'I am escorting you, remember. And on your wedding day I shall be escorting you again. I have a white suit with gold slashing.'

'How handsome you will look,' she said, and saw him flush with pleasure.

'Oh, I don't know . . .'

'I am sure everyone will remark what a handsome boy you are,' she said, as he looked pleased.

'Everyone always cheers most loudly for me,' he confided. 'And I like to know that the people love me. Father says that the only way to keep a throne is to be beloved by the people. That was King Richard's mistake, Father says.'

'My mother says that the way to keep the throne is to do God's work.'

'Oh,' he said, clearly unimpressed. 'Well, different countries, I suppose.'

'So we shall travel together,' she said. 'I will tell my people that we are ready to move on.'

'I will tell them,' he insisted. 'It is me who escorts you. I shall give the orders and you shall rest in your litter.' He gave one quick sideways glance at her. 'When we get to Lambeth Palace you shall stay in your litter till I come for you. I shall draw back the curtains and take you in, and you should hold my hand.'

'I should like that very much,' she assured him, and saw his ready rush of colour once again.

He bustled off and the duke bowed to her with a smile. 'He is a very bright boy, very eager,' he said. 'You must forgive his enthusiasm. He has been much indulged.'

'His mother's favourite?' she asked, thinking of her own mother's adoration for her only son.

'Worse still,' the duke said with a smile. 'His mother loves him as she should; but he is the absolute apple of his grandmother's eye, and it is she who rules the court. Luckily he is a good boy, and well-mannered. He has too good a nature to be spoiled, and the king's mother tempers her treats with lessons.'

'She is an indulgent woman?' she asked.

He gave a little gulp of laughter. 'Only to her son,' he said. 'The rest of us find her – er – more majestic than motherly.'

'May we talk again at Lambeth?' Catalina asked, tempted to know more about this household that she was to join.

'At Lambeth and London, I shall be proud to serve you,' the young man said, his eyes warm with admiration. 'You must command me as you wish. I shall be your friend in England, you can call on me.'

I must have courage, I am the daughter of a brave woman and I have prepared for this all my life. When the young duke spoke so kindly to me there was no need for me to feel like weeping, that was foolish. I must keep my head up and smile. My mother said to me that if I smile no-one will know that I am homesick or afraid, I shall smile and smile however odd things seem.

And though this England seems so strange now, I will become accustomed. I will learn their ways and feel at home here. Their odd ways will become my ways, and the worst things – the things that I utterly cannot bear – those I shall change when I am queen. And anyway, it will be better for me than it was for Isabel, my sister. She was only married a few months and then she had to come home, a widow. Better for me than for Maria, who had to follow in Isabel's footsteps to Portugal, better for me than for Juana, who is sick with love for her husband Philip. It must be better for me than it was for Juan, my poor brother, who died so soon after finding happiness. And always better for me than for my mother, whose childhood was lived on a knife edge.

My story won't be like hers, of course. I have been born to less exciting times. I shall hope to make terms with my husband Arthur and with his odd, loud father, and with his sweet little braggart brother. I shall hope that his mother and his grandmother will love me or at the very least teach me how to be a Princess of Wales, a Queen of England. I shall not have to ride in desperate dashes by night from one besieged fortress to another, as my mother did. I shall not have to pawn my own jewels to pay mercenary soldiers, as she did. I shall not have to ride out in my own armour to rally my troops. I shall not be threatened by the wicked French on one side and the heretic Moors on the other, as my mother was. I shall marry Arthur and when his father dies – which must be soon, for he is so very old and so very bad-tempered – then we shall be King and Queen of England and my mother will rule in Spain as I rule in England and she will see me keep England in alliance with Spain as I have promised her, she will see me hold my country in an unbreakable treaty with hers, she will see I shall be safe forever.

London, 14th November 1501

On the morning of her wedding day Catalina was called early; but she had been awake for hours, stirring as soon as the cold, wintry sun had started to light the pale sky. They had prepared a great bath – her ladies told her that the English were amazed that she was going to wash before her wedding day and that most of them thought that she was risking her life. Catalina, brought up in the Alhambra where the bath houses were the most beautiful suite of rooms in the palace, centres of gossip, laughter and scented water, was equally amazed to hear that the English thought it perfectly adequate to bathe only occasionally, and that the poor people would bathe only once a year.

She had already realised that the scent of musk and ambergris which had wafted in with the king and Prince Arthur had underlying notes of sweat and horse, and that she would live for the rest of her life among people who did not change their underwear from

49

one year to the next. She had seen it as another thing that she must learn to endure, as an angel from heaven endures the privations of earth. She had come from al Yanna – the garden, the paradise – to the ordinary world. She had come from the Alhambra Palace to England, she had anticipated some disagreeable changes.

'I suppose it is always so cold that it does not matter,' she said uncertainly to Dona Elvira.

'It matters to us,' the duenna said. 'And you shall bathe like an Infanta of Spain though all the cooks in the kitchen have had to stop what they are doing to boil up water.'

Dona Elvira had commanded a great tureen from the flesh kitchen which was usually deployed to scald beast carcases, had it scoured by three scullions, lined it with linen sheets and filled it to the brim with hot water scattered with rose petals and scented with oil of roses brought from Spain. She lovingly supervised the washing of Catalina's long white limbs, the manicuring of her toes, the filing of her fingernails, the brushing of her teeth and finally the three-rinse washing of her hair. Time after time the incredulous English maids toiled to the door to receive another ewer of hot water from exhausted page boys, and tipped it in the tub to keep the temperature of the bath hot.

'If only we had a proper bath house,' Dona Elvira mourned. 'With steam and a tepidarium and a proper clean marble floor! Hot water on tap and somewhere for you to sit and be properly scrubbed.'

'Don't fuss,' Catalina said dreamily as they helped her from the bath and patted her all over with scented towels. One maid took her hair, squeezed out the water and rubbed it gently with red silk soaked in oil to give it shine and colour.

'Your mother would be so proud of you,' Dona Elvira said as they led the Infanta towards her wardrobe and started to dress her in layer after layer of shifts and gowns. 'Pull that lace tighter, girl, so that the skirt lies flat. This is her day, as well as yours, Catalina. She said that you would marry him whatever it cost her.'

Yes, but she did not pay the greatest price. I know they bought me this wedding with a king's ransom for my dowry, and I know that they endured long and hard negotiations, and I survived the worst voyage anyone has ever taken, but there was another price paid that we never speak of – wasn't there? And the thought of that price is in my mind today, as it has been on the journey, as it was on the voyage, as it has been ever since I first heard of it.

There was a man of only twenty-four years old, Edward Plantagenet, the Duke of Warwick and a son of the kings of England, with – truth be told – a better claim to the throne of England than that of my father-in-law. He was a prince, nephew to the king, and of blood royal. He committed no crime, he did nothing wrong, but he was arrested for my sake, taken to the Tower for my benefit, and finally killed, beheaded on the block, for my gain, so that my parents could be satisfied that there were no pretenders to the throne that they had bought for me.

My father himself told King Henry himself that he would not send me to England while the Duke of Warwick was alive, and so I am like Death himself, carrying the scythe. When they ordered the ship for me to come to England: Warwick was a dead man.

They say he was a simpleton. He did not really understand that he was under arrest, he thought that he was housed in the Tower as a way of giving him honour. He knew he was the last of the Plantagenet princes, and he knew that the Tower has always been royal lodgings as well as a prison. When they put a pretender, a cunning man who had tried to pass himself off as a royal prince, into the room next door to poor Warwick, he thought it was for company. When the other man invited him to escape, he thought it was a clever thing to do, and like the innocent he was, he whispered of their plans where his guards could hear. That gave them the excuse they needed for a charge of treason.

They trapped him very easily, they beheaded him with little protest from anyone.

The country wants peace and the security of an unchallenged king. The country will wink at a dead claimant or two. I am expected to wink at it also. Especially as it is done for my benefit. It was done at my father's request, for me. To make my way smooth.

When they told me that he was dead, I said nothing, for I am an Infanta of Spain. Before anything else, I am my mother's daughter. I do not weep like a girl and tell all the world my every thought. But when I was alone in the gardens of the Alhambra in the evening with the sun going down and leaving the world cool and sweet, I walked beside a long canal of still water, hidden by the trees, and I thought that I would never walk in the shade of trees again and enjoy the flicker of hot sunshine through cool green leaves without thinking that Edward, Duke of Warwick, will see the sun no more, so that I might live my life in wealth and luxury. I prayed then that I might be forgiven for the death of an innocent man.

My mother and father have fought down the length of Castile and Aragon, have ridden the breadth of Spain to make justice run in every village, in the smallest of hamlets – so that no Spaniard can lose his life on the whim of another. Even the greatest lords cannot murder a peasant; they have to be ruled by the law. But when it came to England and to me, they forgot this. They forgot that we live in a palace where the walls are engraved with the promise: 'Enter and ask. Do not be afraid to seek justice for here you will find it.' They just wrote to King Henry and said that they would not send me until Warwick was dead, and in a moment, at their expressed wish, Warwick was killed.

And sometimes, when I do not remember to be Infanta of Spain nor Princess of Wales but just the Catalina who walked behind her mother through the great gate into the Alhambra Palace, and knew that her mother was the greatest power the world had ever known; sometimes I wonder childishly, if my mother has not made a great mistake? If she has not driven God's will too far? Farther even than

God would want? For this wedding is launched in blood, and sails in a sea of innocent blood. How can such a wedding ever be the start of a good marriage? Must it not – as night follows sunset – be tragic and bloody too? How can any happiness ever come to Prince Arthur and to me that has been bought at such a terrible price? And if we could be happy would it not be an utterly sinfully-selfish joy?

Prince Harry, the ten-year-old Duke of York, was so proud of his white taffeta suit that he scarcely glanced at Catalina until they were at the west doors of St Paul's Cathedral and then he turned and stared, trying to see her face through the exquisite lace of the white mantilla. Ahead of them stretched a raised pathway, lined with red cloth, studded with golden nails, running at head height from the great doorway of the church where the citizens of London crowded to get a better view, up the long aisle to the altar where Prince Arthur stood, pale with nerves, six hundred slow ceremonial paces away.

Catalina smiled at the young boy at her side, and he beamed with delight. Her hand was steady on his proffered arm. He paused for a moment more, until everyone in the enormous church realised that the bride and prince were at the doorway, waiting to make their entrance, a hush fell, everyone craned to see the bride, and then, at the precise, most theatrical moment, he led her forwards.

Catalina felt the congregation murmur around her feet as she went past them, high on the stage that King Henry had ordered to be built so that everyone should see the flower of Spain meet the rosebush of England. The prince turned as she came towards him, but was blinded for a moment by irritation at the sight of his brother, leading the princess as if he himself were the bridegroom, glancing around as he walked, acknowledging the doffing of caps and the whispering of curtseys with his smug little smile, as if it were him that everyone had come to see.

Then they were both at Arthur's side and Harry had to step back, however reluctantly, as the princess and prince faced the archbishop together and kneeled together on the specially embroidered white taffeta cushions.

'Never has a couple been more married,' King Henry thought sourly, standing in the royal pew with his wife and his mother. 'Her parents trusted me no further than they would a snake, and my view of her father has always been that of a half-Moor huckster. Nine times they have been betrothed. This will be a marriage that nothing can break. Her father cannot wriggle from it, whatever second thoughts he has. He will protect me against France now; this is his daughter's inheritance. The very thought of our alliance will frighten the French into peace with me, and we must have peace.'

He glanced at his wife at his side. Her eyes were filled with tears, watching her son and his bride as the archbishop raised their clasped hands and wrapped them in his holy stole. Her face, beautiful with emotion, did not stir him. Who ever knew what she was thinking behind that lovely mask? Of her own marriage, the union of York and Lancaster which put her as a wife on the throne that she could have claimed in her own right? Or was she thinking of the man she would have preferred as a husband? The king scowled. He was never sure of his wife, Elizabeth. In general, he preferred not to consider her.

Beyond her, his flint-faced mother, Margaret Beaufort, watched the young couple with a glimmer of a smile. This was England's triumph, this was her son's triumph, but far more than that, this was *her* triumph – to have dragged this base-born bastard family back from disaster, to challenge the power of York, to defeat a reigning king, to capture the very throne of England against all the odds. This was her making. It was her plan to bring her son back from France at the right moment to claim his throne. They were her alliances who gave him the soldiers for the battle. It was her battle plan which left the usurper Richard to despair on the field at

Bosworth, and it was her victory that she celebrated every day of her life. And this was the marriage that was the culmination of that long struggle. This bride would give her a grandson, a Spanish–Tudor king for England, and a son after him, and after him: and so lay down a dynasty of Tudors that would be never-ending.

Catalina repeated the words of the marriage vow, felt the weight of a cold ring on her finger, turned her face to her new husband and felt his cool kiss, in a daze. When she walked back down that absurd walkway and saw the smiling faces stretching from her feet to the walls of the cathedral she started to realise that it was done. And when they went from the cool dark of the cathedral to the bright wintry sunlight outside and heard the roar of the crowd for Arthur and his bride, the Prince and Princess of Wales, she realised that she had done her duty finally and completely. She had been promised to Arthur from childhood, and now, at last, they were married. She had been named the Princess of Wales since she was three years old and now, at last, she had taken her name, and taken her place in the world. She looked up and smiled and the crowd, delighted with the free wine, with the prettiness of the young girl, with the promise of safety from civil war that could only come with a settled royal succession, roared their approval.

They were husband and wife; but they did not speak more than a few words to each other for the rest of the long day. There was a formal banquet, and though they were seated side by side, there were healths to be drunk and speeches to be attended to, and musicians playing. After the long dinner of many courses there was an entertainment with poetry and singers and a tableau. No-one had ever seen so much money flung at a single occasion. It was a greater celebration than the king's own wedding, greater even than his own coronation. It was a redefinition of the English kingly state, and it told the world that this marriage of the Tudor rose to the Spanish princess was one of the greatest events of the new age. Two new dynasties were proclaiming themselves by this union: Ferdinand and Isabella of the new country that they were forging from al Andalus, and the Tudors who were making England their own.

The musicians played a dance from Spain and Queen Elizabeth, at a nod from her mother-in-law, leaned over and said quietly to Catalina, 'It would be a great pleasure for us all if you would dance.'

Catalina, quite composed, rose from her chair and went to the centre of the great hall as her ladies gathered around her, formed a circle and held hands. They danced the pavane, the same dance that Henry had seen at Dogmersfield, and he watched his daughter-in-law through narrowed eyes. Undoubtedly, she was the most beddable young woman in the room. A pity that a cold fish like Arthur would be certain to fail to teach her the pleasures that could be had between sheets. If he let them both go to Ludlow Castle she would either die of boredom or slip into complete frigidity. On the other hand, if he kept her at his side she would delight his eyes, he could watch her dance, he could watch her brighten the court. He sighed. He thought he did not dare.

'She is delightful,' the queen remarked.

'Let's hope so,' he said sourly.

'My lord?'

He smiled at her look of surprised inquiry. 'No, nothing. You are right, delightful indeed. And she looks healthy, doesn't she? As far as you can tell?'

'I am sure she is, and her mother assured me that she is most regular in her habits.'

He nodded. 'That woman would say anything.'

'But surely not; nothing that would mislead us? Not on a matter of such importance?' she suggested.

He nodded and let it go. The sweetness of his wife's nature and her faith in others was not something he could change. Since she had no influence on policy, her opinions did not matter. 'And Arthur?' he said. 'He seems to be growing and strong? I would to God he had the spirits of his brother.'

They both looked at young Harry who was standing, watching the dancers, his face flushed with excitement, his eyes bright.

'Oh, Harry,' his mother said indulgently. 'But there has never been a prince more handsome and more full of fun than Harry.'

The Spanish dance ended and the king clapped his hands. 'Now Harry and his sister,' he commanded. He did not want to force Arthur to dance in front of his new bride. The boy danced like a clerk, all gangling legs and concentration. But Harry was raring to go and was on the floor with his sister Princess Margaret in a moment. The musicians knew the young royals' taste in music and struck up a lively galliard. Harry tossed his jacket to one side and threw himself into the dance, stripped down to his shirtsleeves like a peasant.

There was a gasp from the Spanish grandees at the young prince's shocking behaviour, but the English court smiled with his parents at his energy and enthusiasm. When the two had romped their way through the final turns and gallop, everyone applauded, laughing. Everyone but Prince Arthur, who was staring into the middle distance, determined not to watch his brother dance. He came to with a start only when his mother put her hand on his arm.

'Please God he's daydreaming of his wedding night,' his father remarked to Lady Margaret his mother. 'Though I doubt it.'

She gave a sharp laugh. 'I can't say I think much of the bride,' she said critically.

'You don't?' he asked. 'You saw the treaty yourself.'

'I like the price but the goods are not to my taste,' she said with her usual sharp wit. 'She is a slight, pretty thing, isn't she?'

'Would you rather a strapping milkmaid?'

'I'd like a girl with the hips to give us sons,' she said bluntly. 'A nursery-full of sons.'

'She looks well enough to me,' he ruled. He knew that he would never be able to say how well she looked to him. Even to himself he should never even think it.

Catalina was put into her wedding bed by her ladies, Maria de Salinas kissed her goodnight, and Dona Elvira gave her a mother's blessing; but Arthur had to undergo a further round of backslapping ribaldry, before his friends and companions escorted him to her door. They put him into bed beside the princess, who lay still and silent as the strange men laughed and bade them goodnight, and then the archbishop came to sprinkle the sheets with holy water and pray over the young couple. It could not have been a more public bedding unless they had opened the doors for the citizens of London to see the young people side by side, awkward as bolsters, in their marital bed. It seemed like hours to both of them until the doors were finally closed on the smiling, curious faces and the two of them were quite alone, seated upright against the pillows, frozen like a pair of shy dolls.

There was silence.

'Would you like a glass of ale?' Arthur suggested in a voice thin with nerves.

'I don't like ale very much,' Catalina said.

'This is different. They call it wedding ale, it's sweetened with mead and spices. It's for courage.'

'Do we need courage?'

He was emboldened by her smile and got out of bed to fetch her a cup. 'I should think we do,' he said. 'You are a stranger in a new land, and I have never known any girls but my sisters. We both have much to learn.'

She took the cup of hot ale from him and sipped the heady drink. 'Oh, that *is* nice.'

Arthur gulped down a cup and took another. Then he came back to the bed. Raising the cover and getting in beside her seemed an imposition; the idea of pulling up her night shift and mounting her was utterly beyond him.

'I shall blow out the candle,' he announced.

The sudden dark engulfed them, only the embers of the fire glowed red.

'Are you very tired?' he asked, longing for her to say that she was too tired to do her duty.

'Not at all,' she said politely, her disembodied voice coming out of the darkness. 'Are you?'

'No.'

'Do you want to sleep now?' he asked.

'I know what we have to do,' she said abruptly. 'All my sisters have been married. I know all about it.'

'I know as well,' he said, stung.

'I didn't mean that you don't know, I meant that you need not be afraid to start. I know what we have to do.'

'I am not afraid, it is just that I . . .'

To his absolute horror he felt her hand pull his nightshirt upwards, and touch the bare skin of his belly.

'I did not want to frighten you,' he said, his voice unsteady, desire rising up even though he was sick with fear that he would be incompetent.

'I am not afraid,' said Isabella's daughter. 'I have never been afraid of anything.'

In the silence and the darkness he felt her take hold of him and grasp firmly. At her touch he felt his desire well up so sharply that he was afraid he would come in her hand. With a low groan he rolled over on top of her and found she had stripped herself naked to the waist, her nightgown pulled up. He fumbled clumsily and felt her flinch as he pushed against her. The whole process seemed quite impossible, there was no way of knowing what a man was supposed

59

to do, nothing to help or guide him, no knowing the mysterious geography of her body, and then she gave a little cry of pain, stifled with her hand, and he knew he had done it. The relief was so great that he came at once, a half-painful, half-pleasurable rush which told him that, whatever his father thought of him, whatever his brother Harry thought of him, the job was done and he was a man and a husband; and the princess was his wife and no longer a virgin untouched.

Catalina waited till he was asleep and then she got up and washed herself in her privy chamber. She was bleeding but she knew it would stop soon, the pain was no worse than she had expected, Isabel her sister had said it was not as bad as falling from a horse, and she had been right. Margot, her sister-in-law, had said that it was paradise; but Catalina could not imagine how such deep embarrassment and discomfort could add up to bliss – and concluded that Margot was exaggerating, as she often did.

Catalina came back to the bedroom. But she did not go back to the bed. Instead she sat on the floor by the fire, hugging her knees and watching the embers.

'Not a bad day,' I say to myself, and I smile; it is my mother's phrase. I want to hear her voice so much that I am saying her words to myself. Often, when I was little more than a baby, and she had spent a long day in the saddle, inspecting the forward scouting parties, riding back to chivvy up the slower train, she would come into her tent, kick off her riding boots, drop down to the rich Moorish rugs and cushions by the fire in the brass brazier and say: 'Not a bad day.'

'Is there ever a bad day?' I once asked her.

'Not when you are doing God's work,' she replied seriously. 'There are days when it is easy and days when it is hard. But if you are on God's work then there are never bad days.'

I don't for a moment doubt that bedding Arthur, even my brazen touching him and drawing him into me, is God's work. It is God's work that there should be an unbreakable alliance between Spain and England. Only with England as a reliable ally can Spain challenge the spread of France. Only with English wealth, and especially English ships, can we Spanish take the war against wickedness to the very heart of the Moorish empires in Africa and Turkey. The Italian princes are a muddle of rival ambitions, the French are a danger to every neighbour, it has to be England who joins the crusade with Spain to maintain the defence of Christendom against the terrifying might of the Moors; whether they be black Moors from Africa, the bogeymen of my childhood, or light-skinned Moors from the dreadful Ottoman Empire. And once they are defeated, then the crusaders must go on, to India, to the East, as far as they have to go to challenge and defeat the wickedness that is the religion of the Moors. My great fear is that the Saracen kingdoms stretch forever, to the end of the world and even Cristóbal Colón does not know where that is.

'What if there is no end to them?' I once asked my mother, as we leaned over the sun-warmed walls of the fort and watched the despatch of a new group of Moors leaving the city of Granada, their baggage loaded on mules, the women weeping, the men with their heads bowed low, the flag of St James now flying over the red fort where the crescent had rippled for seven centuries, the bells ringing for Mass where once horns had blown for heretic prayers. 'What if now we have defeated these, they just go back to Africa and in another year, they come again?'

'That is why you have to be brave, my Princess of Wales,' my mother had answered. 'That is why you have to be ready to fight them whenever they come, wherever they come. This is war till the end of the world, till the end of time when God finally ends it. It will take many shapes. It will never cease. They will come again and again, and you will have to be ready in Wales as we will be ready in Spain. I bore you to be a fighting princess as I am a Queen Militant. Your father and I placed you in England as Maria is placed in Portugal, as Juana is

placed with the Hapsburgs in the Netherlands. You are there to defend the lands of your husbands, and to hold them in alliance with us. It is your task to make England ready and keep it safe. Make sure that you never fail your country, as your sisters must never fail theirs, as I have never failed mine.'

Catalina was awakened in the early hours of the morning by Arthur gently pushing between her legs. Resentfully, she let him do as he wanted, knowing that this was the way to get a son and make the alliance secure. Some princesses, like her mother, had to fight their way in open warfare to secure their kingdom. Most princesses, like her, had to endure painful ordeals in private. It did not take long, and then he fell asleep. Catalina lay as still as a frozen stone in order not to wake him again.

He did not stir until daybreak, when his grooms of the bedchamber rapped brightly on the door. He rose up with a slightly embarrassed 'Good morning' to her; and went out. They greeted him with cheers and marched him in triumph to his own rooms. Catalina heard him say, vulgarly, boastfully, 'Gentlemen, this night I have been in Spain,' and heard the yell of laughter that applauded his joke. Her ladies came in with her gown and heard the men's laughter. Dona Elvira raised her thin eyebrows to heaven at the manners of these English.

'I don't know what your mother would say,' Dona Elvira remarked.

'She would say that words count less than God's will, and God's will has been done,' Catalina said firmly.

It was not like this for my mother. She fell in love with my father on sight and she married him with great joy. When I grew older I began to understand that they felt a real desire for each other – it was not

just a powerful partnership of a great king and queen. My father might take other women as his lovers; but he needed his wife, he could not be happy without her. And my mother could not even see another man. She was blind to anybody but my father. Alone, of all the courts in Europe, the court of Spain had no tradition of love-play, of flirtation, of adoration of the queen in the practice of courtly love. It would have been a waste of time. My mother simply did not notice other men and when they sighed for her and said her eyes were as blue as the skies she simply laughed and said, 'What nonsense,' and that was an end to it.

When my parents had to be apart they wrote every day, he would not move one step without telling her of it, and asking for her advice. When he was in danger she hardly slept.

He could not have got through the Sierra Nevada if she had not been sending him men and digging teams to level the road for him. No-one else could have driven a road through there. He would have trusted no-one else to support him, to hold the kingdom together as he pushed forwards. She could have conquered the mountains for no-one else, he was the only one that could have attracted her support. What looked like a remarkable unity of two calculating players was deceptive – it was their passion which they played out on the political stage. She was a great queen because that was how she could evoke his desire. He was a great general in order to match her. It was their love, their lust, which drove them; almost as much as God.

We are a passionate family. When Isabel, my sister, now with God, came back from Portugal a widow she swore that she had loved her husband so much that she would never take another. She had been with him for only six months but she said that without him, life had no meaning. Juana, my second sister, is so in love with her husband Philip that she cannot bear to let him out of her sight, when she learns that he is interested in another woman she swears that she will poison her rival, she is quite mad with love for him. And my brother . . . my darling brother Juan . . . simply died of love. He and his beautiful wife

Margot were so passionate, so besotted with each other, that his health failed, he was dead within six months of their wedding. Is there anything more tragic than a young man dying six months into his marriage? I come from passionate stock – but what about me? Shall I ever fall in love?

Not with this clumsy boy, for a certainty. My early liking for him has quite melted away. He is too shy to speak to me, he mumbles and pretends he cannot think of the words. He forced me to command in the bedroom, and I am ashamed that I had to be the one to make the first move. He makes me into a woman without shame, a woman of the marketplace when I want to be wooed like a lady in a romance. But if I had not invited him – what could he have done? I feel a fool now, and I blame him for my embarrassment. 'In Spain,' indeed! He would have got no closer than the Indies if I had not showed him how to do it. Stupid puppy.

When I first saw him I thought he was as beautiful as a knight from the romances, like a troubadour, like a poet. I thought I could be like a lady in a tower and he could sing beneath my window and persuade me to love him. But although he has the looks of a poet he doesn't have the wit. I can never get more than two words out of him, and I begin to feel that I demean myself in trying to please him.

Of course, I will never forget that it is my duty to endure this youth, this Arthur. My hope is always for a child, and my destiny is to keep England safe against the Moors. I shall do that; whatever else happens, I shall be Queen of England and protect my two countries: the Spain of my birth and the England of my marriage.

London, Winter 1501

Arthur and Catalina, standing stiffly side by side on the royal barge, but not exchanging so much as one word, led a great fleet of gaily painted barges downriver to Baynard's Castle, which would be their London home for the next weeks. It was a huge, rectangular palace of a house overlooking the river, with gardens running down to the water's edge. The Mayor of London, the councillors, and all the court followed the royal barge; and musicians played as the heirs to the throne took up residence in the heart of the City.

Catalina noticed that the Scots envoys were much in attendance, negotiating the marriage of her new sister-in-law, Princess Margaret. King Henry was using his children as pawns in his game for power, as every king must do. Arthur had made the vital link with Spain, Margaret, though only twelve years old, would make Scotland into a friend, rather than the enemy that it had been for generations. Princess Mary also would be married, when her time came, either to the greatest enemy that the country faced, or the greatest friend that they hoped to keep. Catalina was glad that she had known from childhood that she should be the next Queen of England. There had been no changes of policy and no shifting alliances. She had been

Queen of England-to-be almost from birth. It made the separation from her home and from her family so much easier.

She noticed that Arthur was very restrained in his greeting when he met the Scots lords at dinner at the Palace of Westminster.

'The Scots are our most dangerous enemies,' Edward Stafford, the Duke of Buckingham, told Catalina in whispered Castilian, as they stood at the back of the hall, waiting for the company to take their seats. 'The king and the prince hope that this marriage will make them our friend forever, will bind the Scots to us. But it is hard for any of us to forget how they have constantly harried us. We have all been brought up to know that we have a most constant and malignant enemy to the north.'

'Surely they are only a poor little kingdom,' she queried. 'What harm can they do us?'

'They always ally with France,' he told her. 'Every time we have a war with France they make an alliance and pour over our northern borders. And, they may be small and poor but they are the doorway for the terrible danger of France to invade us from the north. I think Your Grace knows from your own childhood that even a small country on your frontier can be a danger.'

'Well, the Moors had only a small country at the end,' she observed. 'My father always said that the Moors were like a disease. They might be a small irritation but they were always there.'

'The Scots are our plague,' he agreed. 'Once every three years or so, they invade and make a little war, and we lose an acre of land or win it back again. And every summer they harry the border countries and steal what they cannot grow or make themselves. No northern farmer has ever been safe from them. The king is determined to have peace.'

'Will they be kind to the Princess Margaret?'

'In their own rough way.' He smiled. 'Not as you have been welcomed, Infanta.'

Catalina beamed in return. She knew that she was warmly

welcomed in England. Londoners had taken the Spanish princess to their hearts, they liked the gaudy glamour of her train, the oddness of her dress, and they liked the way the princess always had a smile for a waiting crowd. Catalina had learned from her mother that the people are a greater power than an army of mercenaries and she never turned her head away from a cheer. She always waved, she always smiled, and if they raised a great bellow of applause she would even bob them a pretty little curtsey.

She glanced over to where the Princess Margaret, a vain, precocious girl, was smoothing down her dress and pushing back her headdress before going into the hall.

'Soon you will be married and going away, as I have done,' Catalina remarked pleasantly in French. 'I do hope it brings you happiness.'

The younger girl looked at her boldly. 'Not as you have done, for you have come to the finest kingdom in Europe, whereas I have to go far away into exile,' she said.

'England may be fine to you; but it is still strange to me,' Catalina said, trying not to flare up at the rudeness of the girl. 'And if you had seen my home in Spain you would be surprised at how fine our palace is there.'

'There is nowhere better than England,' Margaret said with the serene conviction of one of the spoiled Tudor children. 'But it will be good to be queen. While you are still only a princess, I shall be queen. I shall be the equal of my mother.' She thought for a moment. 'Indeed, I shall be the equal of your mother.'

The colour rushed into Catalina's face. 'You would never be the equal of my mother,' she snapped. 'You are a fool to even say it.'

Margaret gasped.

'Now, now, Your Royal Highnesses,' the duke interrupted quickly. 'Your father is ready to take his place. Will you please to follow him into the hall?'

Margaret turned and flounced away from Catalina.

'She is very young,' the duke said soothingly. 'And although she would never admit to it, she is afraid to leave her mother and her father and go so far away.'

'She has a lot to learn,' Catalina said through gritted teeth. 'She should learn the manners of a queen if she is going to be one.' She turned to find Arthur at her side, ready to conduct her into the hall behind his parents.

The royal family took their seats. The king and his two sons sat at the high table under the canopy of state, facing out over the hall, to their right sat the queen and the princesses. My Lady, the King's Mother, Margaret Beaufort, was seated beside the king, between him and his wife.

'Margaret and Catalina were having cross words as they came in,' she observed to him with grim satisfaction. 'I thought that the Infanta would irritate our Princess Margaret. She cannot bear to have too much attention shown to another, and everyone makes such a fuss over Catalina.'

'Margaret will soon be gone,' Henry said shortly. 'Then she can have her own court, and her own honeymoon.'

'Catalina has become the very centre of the court,' his mother complained. 'The palace is crowded out with people coming to watch her dine. Everyone wants to see her.'

'She's a novelty only, a seven-day wonder. And anyway, I want people to see her.'

'She has charm of a sort,' the older woman noted. The groom of the ewer presented a golden bowl filled with scented water and Lady Margaret dipped her fingertips and then wiped them on the napkin.

'I think her very pleasing,' Henry said as he dried his own hands. 'She went through the wedding without one wrong step, and the people like her.'

His mother made a small, dismissive gesture. 'She is sick with her own vanity, she has not been brought up as I would bring up a child of mine. Her will has not been broken to obedience. She thinks that she is something special.'

Henry glanced across at the princess. She had bent her head to listen to something being said by the youngest Tudor princess, Princess Mary; and he saw her smile and reply. 'D'you know? *I* think she is something special,' he said.

The celebrations continued for days and days, and then the court moved on to the new-built, glamorous palace of Richmond, set in a great and beautiful park. To Catalina, in a swirl of strange faces and introductions, it felt as if one wonderful joust and fete merged into another, with herself at the very centre of it all, a queen as celebrated as any sultana with a country devoted to her amusement. But after a week the party was concluded with the king coming to the princess and telling her that it was time for her Spanish companions to go home.

Catalina had always known that the little court which had accompanied her through storms and near-shipwreck to present her to her new husband would leave her once the wedding was done and the first half of the dowry paid; but it was a gloomy couple of days while they packed their bags and said goodbye to the princess. She would be left with her small domestic household, her ladies, her chamberlain, her treasurer, and her immediate servants, but the rest of her entourage must leave. Even knowing as she did that this was the way of the world, that the wedding party always left after the wedding, did not make her feel any less bereft. She sent them with messages to everyone in Spain and with a letter for her mother.

From her daughter, Catalina, Princess of Wales, to Her Royal Highness of Castile and Aragon, and most dearest Madre,
   Oh, Madre!
   As these ladies and gentlemen will tell you, the prince and I have a

good house near the river. It is called Baynard's Castle although it is not a castle but a palace and newly built. There are no bath houses, for either ladies or men. I know what you are thinking. You cannot imagine it.

Dona Elvira has had the blacksmith make a great cauldron which they heat up on the fire in the kitchen and six serving men heave it to my room for my bath. Also, there are no pleasure gardens with flowers, no streams, no fountains, it is quite extraordinary. It all looks as if it is not yet built. At best, they have a tiny court which they call a knot garden where you can walk round and round until you are dizzy. The food is not good and the wine very sour. They eat nothing but preserved fruit and I believe they have never heard of vegetables.

You must not think that I am complaining, I wanted you to know that even with these small difficulties I am content to be the princess. Prince Arthur is kind and considerate to me when we meet, which is generally at dinner. He has given me a very beautiful mare of Barbary stock mixed with English, and I ride her every day. The gentlemen of the court joust (but not the princes); my champion is often the Duke of Buckingham who is very kind to me, he advises me as to the court and tells me how to go on. We all often dine in the English style, men and women together. The women have their own rooms but men visitors and male servants come and go out of them as if they were public, there is no seclusion for women at all. The only place I can be sure to be alone is if I lock myself in the necessary house – otherwise there are people everywhere.

Queen Elizabeth, though very quiet, is very kind to me when we meet and I like being in her company. My Lady the King's Mother is very cold; but I think she is like that with everyone except the king and the princes. She dotes on her son and grandsons. She rules the court as if she were queen herself. She is very devout and very serious. I am sure she is very admirable in every way.

You will want to know if I am with child. There are no signs yet. You will want to know that I read my Bible or holy books for two hours every day, as you ordered, and that I go to Mass three times a day and I take communion every Sunday also. Father Alessandro Geraldini is well, and

70

as great a spiritual guide and advisor in England as he was in Spain, and I trust to him and to God to keep me strong in the faith to do God's work in England as you do in Spain. Dona Elvira keeps my ladies in good order and I obey her as I would you. Maria de Salinas is my best friend, here as at home, though nothing here is like Spain, and I cannot bear her to talk of home at all.

I will be the princess that you want me to be. I shall not fail you or God. I will be queen and I will defend England against the Moors.

Please write to me soon and tell me how you are. You seemed so sad and low when I left, I hope that you are better now. I am sure that the darkness that you saw in your mother will pass over you, and not rest on your life as it did on hers. Surely, God would not inflict sadness on you, who has always been His favourite? I pray for you and for Father every day. I hear your voice in my head, advising me all the time. Please write soon to your daughter who loves you so much,

Catalina

PS Although I am glad to be married, and to be called to do my duty for Spain and God, I miss you very much. I know you are a queen before a mother but I would be so glad to have one letter from you. C

The court bade a cheerful farewell to the Spanish but Catalina found it hard to smile and wave. After they had gone she went down to the river to see the last of the barges shrink and then disappear in the distance and King Henry found her there, a lonely figure, on the pier looking downstream, as if she wished she were going too.

He was too skilled with women to ask her what was wrong. He knew very well what was wrong: loneliness, and homesickness natural enough in a young woman of nearly sixteen years old. He had been an exile from England for almost all his own life, he knew very well the rise and fall of yearning that comes with an unexpected scent, the change of seasons, a farewell. To invite an explanation would only trigger a flood of tears and achieve nothing. Instead, he tucked her cold little hand under his arm and said that she must see his library which he had newly assembled at the palace and she could borrow books to read at any time. He threw an order over his shoulder to one of his pages as he led the princess to the library and walked her round the beautiful shelves, showing her not only the classical authors and the histories that were his own interest, but also the stories of romance and heroism which he thought more likely to divert her.

She did not complain, he noticed with pleasure, and she had rubbed her eyes dry as soon as she had seen him coming towards her. She had been raised in a hard school. Isabella of Spain had been a soldier's wife and a soldier herself, she did not raise any of her girls to be self-indulgent. He thought there was not a young woman in England who could match this girl for grit. But there were shadows under the princess's blue eyes and though she took the proffered volumes with a word of thanks she still did not smile.

'And do you like maps?' he asked her.

She nodded. 'Of course,' she said. 'In my father's library we have maps of the whole world, and Cristóbal Colón made him a map to show him the Americas.'

'Does your father have a large library?' he asked, jealous of his reputation as a scholar.

Her polite hesitation before she replied told him everything, told him that his library here, of which he had been so proud, was nothing to the learning of the Moors of Spain. 'Of course my father has inherited many books, they are not all his own collection,' Catalina said tactfully. 'Many of them are Moorish authors, from Moorish scholars. You know that the Arabs translated the Greek authors before they were ever made into French or Italian, or English. The Arabs had all the sciences and all the mathematics when they were forgotten in Christendom. He has all the Moorish translations of Aristotle and Sophocles and everyone.'

He could feel his longing for the new learning like a hunger. 'He has many books?'

'Thousands of volumes,' she said. 'Hebrew and Arabic, Latin, and all the Christian languages too. But he doesn't read them all, he has Arab scholars to study them.'

'And the maps?' he asked.

'He is advised mostly by Arab navigators and map-makers,' she said. 'They travel so far overland, they understand how to chart their way by the stars. The sea voyages are just the same to them as a journey through the desert. They say that a watery waste is the same as a plain of sand, they use the stars and the moon to measure their journey in both.'

'And does your father think that much profit will come from his discoveries?' the king asked curiously. 'We have all heard of these great voyages of Cristóbal Colón and the treasures he has brought back.'

He admired how her eyelashes swept down to hide the gleam. 'Oh, I could not say.' Cleverly, she avoided the question. 'Certainly, my mother thinks that there are many souls to save for Jesus.'

Henry opened the great folder with his collection of maps and spread them before her. Beautifully illuminated sea monsters frolicked in the corners. He traced for her the coastline of England, the borders of the Holy Roman Empire, the handful of regions of France, the new widening borders of her own country of Spain and the papal lands in Italy. 'You see why your father and I have to be friends,' he said to her. 'We both face the power of France on our doorstep. We cannot even trade with each other unless we can keep France out of the narrow seas.'

'If Juana's son inherits the Hapsburg lands then he will have two kingdoms,' she indicated. 'Spain and also the Netherlands.'

'And your son will have all of England, an alliance with Scotland, and all our lands in France,' he said, making a sweep with his spread palm. 'They will be a powerful pair of cousins.'

She smiled at the thought of it, and Henry saw the ambition in her. 'You would like to have a son who would rule half of Christendom?'

'What woman would not?' she said. 'And my son and Juana's son could surely defeat the Moors, could drive them back and back beyond the Mediterranean Sea?'

'Or perhaps you might find a way to live in peace,' he suggested. 'Just because one man calls Him Allah, and another calls him God is no reason for believers to be enemies, surely?'

At once Catalina shook her head. 'It will have to be a war forever, I think. My mother says that it is the great battle between Good and Evil which will go on until the end of time.'

'Then you will be in danger forever,' he started, when there was a tap on the great wooden door of the library. It was the page that Henry had sent running, bringing a flustered goldsmith who had been waiting for days to show his work to the king and was rather surprised to be summoned in a moment.

'Now,' Henry said to his daughter-in-law, 'I have a treat for you.'

She looked up at him. 'Good God,' he thought. 'It would be a man of stone who did not want this little flower in his bed. I swear that I could make her smile, and at any rate, I would enjoy trying.'

'Have you?'

Henry gestured to the man who flapped out a cloth of maroon velvet from his pocket, and then spilled the contents of his knapsack on to the scarlet background. A tumble of jewels, diamonds, emeralds, rubies, pearls, chains, lockets, earrings and brooches was swiftly spread before Catalina's widening gaze.

'You shall have your pick,' Henry said, his voice warm and intimate. 'It is my private gift to you, to bring the smile back to your pretty face.'

She hardly heard him, she was at the table in a moment, the goldsmith holding up one rich item after another. Henry watched her indulgently. So she might be a princess with a pure blood line of

Castilian aristocrats, while he was the grandson of a working man; but she was a girl as easily bought as any other. And he had the means to please her.

'Silver?' he asked.

She turned a bright face to him. 'Not silver,' she said decisively.

Henry remembered that this was a girl who had seen the treasure of the Incas cast at her feet.

'Gold then?'

'I do prefer gold.'

'Pearls?'

She made a little moue with her mouth.

'My God, she has a kissable mouth,' he thought. 'Not pearls?' he asked aloud.

'They are not my greatest favourite,' she confided. She smiled up at him. 'What is your favourite stone?'

'Why, she is flirting with me,' he said to himself, stunned at the thought. 'She is playing me like she would an indulgent uncle. She is reeling me in like a fish.'

'Emeralds?'

She smiled again.

'No. This,' she said simply.

She had picked out, in a moment, the most expensive thing in the jeweller's pack, a collar of deepest blue sapphires with a matching pair of earrings. Charmingly, she held the collar against her smooth cheeks so that he could look from the jewels to her eyes. She took a step closer towards him so that he could smell the scent on her hair, orange-blossom water from the gardens of the Alhambra. She smelled as if she were an exotic flower herself. 'Do they match my eyes?' she asked him. 'Are my eyes as blue as sapphires?'

He took a little breath, surprised at the violence of his response. 'They are. You shall have them,' he said, almost choking on his desire for her. 'You shall have this and anything else you like. You shall name your . . . your . . . wish.'

The look she threw up at him was of pure delight. 'And my ladies too?'

'Call your ladies, they shall have their pick.'

She laughed with pleasure and ran to the door. He let her go. He did not trust himself to stay in the room without chaperones. Hastily, he took himself out into the hall and met his mother, returning from hearing Mass.

He kneeled and she put her fingers on his head in her blessing. 'My son.'

'My lady mother.'

He rose to his feet. She quickly took in the flush of his face and his suppressed energy. 'Has something troubled you?'

'No!'

She sighed. 'Is it the queen? Is it Elizabeth?' she asked wearily. 'Is she complaining about the Scots' marriage for Margaret again?'

'No,' he said. 'I have not seen her today.'

'She will have to accustom herself,' she said. 'A princess cannot choose whom she marries and when she leaves home. Elizabeth would know that if she had been properly brought up. But she was not.'

He gave his crooked smile. 'That is hardly her fault.'

His mother's disdain was apparent. 'No good would ever have come from her mother,' she said shortly. 'Bad breeding, the Woodvilles.'

Henry shrugged and said nothing. He never defended his wife to his mother – her malice was so constant and so impenetrable that it was a waste of time to try to change her mind. He never defended his mother to his wife; he never had to. Queen Elizabeth never commented on her difficult mother-in-law or her demanding husband. She took him, his mother, his autocratic rule, as if they were natural hazards, as unpleasant and as inevitable as bad weather.

'You should not let her disturb you,' his mother said.

'She has never disturbed me,' he said, thinking of the princess who did.

I am certain now that the king likes me, above all his daughters, and I am so glad of it. I am used to being the favourite daughter, the baby of the family. I like it when I am the favourite of the king, I like to feel special.

When he saw that I was sad at my court going back to Spain and leaving me in England he spent the afternoon with me, showing me his library, talking about his maps, and finally, giving me an exquisite collar of sapphires. He let me pick out exactly what I wanted from the goldsmith's pack, and he said that the sapphires were the colour of my eyes.

I did not like him very well at first, but I am becoming accustomed to his abrupt speech and his quick ways. He is a man whose word is law in this court and in this land and he owes thanks to no-one for anything, except perhaps his Lady Mother. He has no close friends, no intimates but her and the soldiers who fought with him, who are now the great men of his court. He is not tender to his wife nor warm to his daughters, but I like it that he attends to me. Perhaps I will come to love him as a daughter. Already I am glad when he singles me out. In a court such as this, which revolves around his approval, it makes me feel like a princess indeed when he praises me, or spends time with me.

If it were not for him then I think I would be even more lonely than I am. The prince my husband treats me as if I were a table or a chair. He never speaks to me, he never smiles at me, he never starts a conversation, it is all he can do to find a reply. I think I was a fool when I thought he looked like a troubadour. He looks like a milksop and that is the truth. He never raises his voice above a whisper, he never says anything of any interest. He may well speak French and Latin and half a dozen languages, but since he has nothing to say – what good are they? We live as strangers and if he did not come to my bedchamber at night, once a week as if on duty, I would not know I was married at all.

I show the sapphires to his sister, the Princess Margaret, and she is eaten up with jealousy. I shall have to confess to the sin of vanity and of pride. It is not right for me to flaunt them before her; but if she had ever been kind to me by word or deed then I would not have showed her. I want her to know that her father values me, even if she and her grandmother and her brother do not. But now all I have done is upset her and put myself in the wrong, and I will have to confess and make a penance.

Worst of all, I did not behave with the dignity that a princess of Spain should always show. If she were not such a fishwife's apprentice then I could have been better. This court dances around the king as if nothing matters more in the world than his favour, and I should know better than to join in. At the very least I should not be measuring myself against a girl four years younger than me and only a princess of England, even if she calls herself Queen of Scotland at every opportunity.

The young Prince and Princess of Wales finished their visit to Richmond and started to make their own royal household in Baynard's Castle. Catalina had her rooms at the back of the house, overlooking the gardens and the river, with her household, her Spanish ladies, her Spanish chaplain, and duenna, and Arthur's rooms overlooked the City, with his household, his chaplain, and his tutor. They met formally only once a day for dinner, when the two households sat at opposite sides of the hall and stared at each other with mutual suspicion, more like enemies in the middle of a forced truce than members of a united home.

The castle was run according to the commands of Lady Margaret, the king's mother. The feast days and fast days, the entertainments and the daily timetable were all commanded by her. Even the nights when Arthur was to visit his wife in her bedchamber had been appointed by her. She did not want the young people becoming exhausted, nor did she want them neglecting their duties. So once a week the prince's household and friends solemnly escorted him to the princess's rooms and left him there overnight. For both young people the experience was an ordeal of embarrassment. Arthur became no more skilled, Catalina endured his silent determination as politely as she could. But then, one day in early December, Catalina's monthly course started and she told Dona Elvira. The duenna at once told the prince's groom of the bedchamber that the prince could not come to the Infanta's bed for a week; the Infanta was indisposed. Within half an hour, everyone from the king at Whitehall to the spit boy at Baynard's Castle knew that the Princess of Wales was having her course and so no child had yet been conceived; and everyone from the king to the spit boy wondered, since the girl was lusty and strong and since she was bleeding – obviously fertile – if Arthur was capable of doing his side of their duty.

In the middle of December, when the court was preparing for the great twelve-day feast of Christmas, Arthur was summoned by his father and ordered to prepare to leave for his castle at Ludlow.

'I suppose you'll want to take your wife with you,' the king said, smiling at his son in an effort to seem unconcerned.

'As you wish, sir,' Arthur replied carefully.

'What would you wish?'

After enduring a week's ban from Catalina's bed, with everyone remarking among themselves that no child had been made – but to be sure, it was early days yet, and it might be nobody's fault – Arthur felt embarrassed and discouraged. He had not gone back to her bedroom and she had sent no message to invite him. He could not expect an invitation – he knew that was ridiculous – a princess of Spain could hardly send for the prince of England; but she had not smiled or encouraged him in any way at all. He had received no message to tell him to resume his visits, and he had no idea how long these mysteries usually took. There was no-one that he could ask, and he did not know what he should do.

'She does not seem very merry,' Arthur observed.

'She's homesick,' his father said briskly. 'It's up to you to divert her. Take her to Ludlow with you. Buy her things. She's a girl like any other. Praise her beauty. Tell her jokes. Flirt with her.'

Arthur looked quite blank. 'In Latin?'

His father barked his harsh laugh. 'Lad. You can do it in Welsh if your eyes are smiling and your cock is hard. She'll know what you mean. I swear it. She's a girl who knows well enough what a man means.'

There was no answering brightness from his son. 'Yes, sir.'

'If you don't want her with you, you're not obliged to take her this year, you know. You were supposed to marry and then spend the first year apart.'

'That was when I was fourteen.'

'Only a year ago.'

'Yes, but . . .'

'So you do want her with you?'

His son flushed. The father regarded the boy with sympathy. 'You want her, but you are afraid she will make a fool of you?' he suggested.

The blond head drooped, nodded.

'And you think if you and she are far from court and from me, then she will be able to torment you.'

Another small nod. 'And all her ladies. And her duenna.'

'And time will hang heavy on your hands.'

The boy looked up, his face a picture of misery.

'And she will be bored and sulky and she will make your little court at Ludlow a miserable prison for both of you.'

'If she dislikes me . . .' he started, his voice very low.

Henry rested a heavy hand on his boy's shoulder. 'Oh, my son.

It doesn't matter what she thinks of you,' he said. 'Perhaps your mother was not my choice, perhaps I was not hers. When a throne is involved the heart comes in second place if it ever matters at all. She knows what she has to do; and that is all that counts.'

'Oh, she knows all about it!' the boy burst out resentfully. 'She has no . . .'

His father waited. 'No . . . what?'

'No shame at all.'

Henry caught his breath. 'She is shameless? She is passionate?' He tried to keep the desire from his voice, a sudden lascivious picture of his daughter-in-law, naked and shameless, in his mind.

'No! She goes at it like a man harnessing a horse,' Arthur said miserably. 'A task to be done.'

Henry choked down a laugh. 'But at least she does it,' he said. 'You don't have to beg her, or persuade her. She knows what she has to do?'

Arthur turned from him to the window and looked out of the arrow slit to the cold river Thames below. 'I don't think she likes me. She only likes her Spanish friends, and Mary, and perhaps Henry. I see her laughing with them and dancing with them as if she were very merry in their company. She chatters away with her own people, she is courteous to everyone who passes by. She has a smile for everyone. I hardly ever see her, and I don't want to see her, either.'

Henry dropped his hand on his son's shoulder. 'My boy, she doesn't know what she thinks of you,' he assured him. 'She's too busy in her own little world of dresses and jewels and those damned gossipy Spanish women. The sooner you and she are alone together, the sooner you two will come to terms. You can take her with you to Ludlow and you can get acquainted.'

The boy nodded, but he did not look convinced. 'If it is your wish, sire,' he said formally.

'Shall I ask her if she wants to go?'

The colour flooded into the young man's cheeks. 'What if she says no?' he asked anxiously.

His father laughed. 'She won't,' he promised. 'You'll see.'

Henry was right. Catalina was too much of a princess to say either yes or no to a king. When he asked her if she would like to go to Ludlow with the prince she said that she would do whatever the king wished.

'Is Lady Margaret Pole still at the castle?' she asked, her voice a little nervous.

He scowled at her. Lady Margaret was now safely married to Sir Richard Pole, one of the solid Tudor warhorses, and warden of Ludlow Castle. But Lady Margaret had been born Margaret Plantagenet, beloved daughter of the Duke of Clarence, cousin to King Edward and sister to Edward of Warwick whose claim to the throne had been so much greater than Henry's own.

'What of it?'

'Nothing,' she said hastily.

'You have no cause to avoid her,' he said gruffly. 'What was done, was done in my name, by my order. You don't bear any blame for it.'

She flushed as if they were talking of something shameful. 'I know.'

'I can't have anyone challenging my right to the throne,' he said abruptly. 'There are too many of them, Yorks and Beauforts, and Lancasters too, and endless others who fancy their chances as pretenders. You don't know this country. We're all married and intermarried like so many coneys in a warren.' He paused to see if she would laugh, but she was frowning, following his rapid French. 'I can't have anyone claiming by their pretended right what I have won by conquest,' he said. 'And I won't have anyone else claiming by conquest either.'

'I thought you were the true king,' Catalina said hesitantly.

'I am now,' said Henry Tudor bluntly. 'And that's all that matters.'

'You were anointed.'

'I am now,' repeated with a grim smile.

'But you are of the royal line?'

'I have royal blood in my veins,' he said, his voice hard. 'No need to measure how much or how little. I picked up my crown off the battlefield, literally, it was at my feet in the mud. So I knew; everyone knew – everyone saw God give me the victory because I was his chosen king. The archbishop anointed me because he knew that too. I am as much king as any in Christendom, and more than most because I did not just inherit as a baby, the fruit of another man's struggle – God gave me my kingdom when I was a man. It is my just desert.'

'But you had to claim it . . .'

'I claimed my own,' he said finally. 'I won my own. God gave my own to me. That's an end to it.'

She bowed her head to the energy in his words. 'I know, sire.'

Her submissiveness, and the pride that was hidden behind it, fascinated him. He thought that there had never been a young woman whose smooth face could hide her thoughts like this one.

'D'you want to stay here with me?' Henry asked softly, knowing that he should not ask her such a thing, praying, as soon as the words were out of his mouth, that she would say 'no' and silence his secret desire for her.

'Why, I wish whatever Your Majesty wishes,' she said coolly.

'I suppose you want to be with Arthur?' he asked, daring her to deny it.

'As you wish, sire,' she said steadily.

'Tell me! Would you like to go to Ludlow with Arthur, or would you rather stay here with me?'

She smiled faintly, and would not be drawn. 'You are the king,' she said quietly. 'I must do whatever you command.'

Henry knew he should not keep her at court beside him but he could not resist playing with the idea. He consulted her Spanish advisors, and found them hopelessly divided and squabbling among themselves. The Spanish ambassador, who had worked so hard to deliver the intractable marriage contract, insisted that the princess should go with her new husband, and that she should be seen to be a married woman in every way. Her confessor, who alone of all of them seemed to have a tenderness for the little princess, urged that the young couple should be allowed to stay together. Her duenna, the formidable and difficult Dona Elvira, preferred not to leave London. She had heard that Wales was a hundred miles away, a mountainous and rocky land. If Catalina stayed in Baynard's Castle and the household was rid of Arthur, then they would make a little Spanish enclave in the heart of the City, and the duenna's power would be unchallenged, she would rule the princess and the little Spanish court.

The queen volunteered her opinion that Catalina would find Ludlow too cold and lonely in mid-December and suggested that perhaps the young couple could stay together in London until spring.

'You just hope to keep Arthur with you, but he has to go,' Henry said brusquely to her. 'He has to learn the business of kingship and there is no better way to learn to rule England than to rule the Principality.'

'He's still young, and he is shy with her.'

'He has to learn to be a husband too.'

'They will have to learn to deal together.'

'Better that they learn in private then.'

In the end, it was the king's mother who gave the decisive advice. 'Send her,' she said to her son. 'We need a child off her. She won't make one on her own in London. Send her with Arthur to Ludlow.' She laughed shortly. 'God knows, they'll have nothing else to do there.'

'Elizabeth is afraid that she will be sad and lonely,' the king remarked. 'And Arthur is afraid that they will not deal well together.'

'Who cares?' his mother asked. 'What difference does that make? They are married and they have to live together and make an heir.'

He shot her a swift smile. 'She is only just sixteen,' he said, 'and the baby of her family, still missing her mother. You don't make any allowances for her youth, do you?'

'I was married at twelve years old, and gave birth to you in the same year,' she returned. 'No-one made any allowances for me. And yet I survived.'

'I doubt you were happy.'

'I was not. I doubt that she is. But that, surely, is the last thing that matters?'

Dona Elvira told me that I must refuse to go to Ludlow. Father Geraldini said that it was my duty to go with my husband. Dr de Puebla said that for certain my mother would want me to live with my husband, to do everything to show that the marriage is complete in word and deed. Arthur, the hopeless beanpole, said nothing, and his father seems to want me to decide; but he is a king and I don't trust him.

All I really want to do is to go home to Spain. Whether we are in London or whether we live in Ludlow it will be cold, and it will rain all the time, the very air feels wet, I cannot get anything good to eat, and I cannot understand a word anybody says.

I know I am Princess of Wales and I will be Queen of England. That is true, and it will be true. But, this day, I cannot feel very glad about it.

'We are to go to my castle at Ludlow,' Arthur remarked awkwardly to Catalina. They were seated side by side at dinner, the hall below them, the gallery above and the wide doors crowded with people who had come from the City for the free entertainment of watching the court dine. Most people were observing the Prince of Wales and his young bride.

She bowed her head but did not look at him. 'Is it your father's command?' she asked.

'Yes.'

'Then I shall be happy to go,' she said.

'We will be alone, but for the warden of the castle and his wife,' Arthur went on. He wanted to say that he hoped she would not mind, that he hoped she would not be bored, or sad or – worst of all – angry with him.

She looked at him without a smile. 'And so?'

'I hope you will be content,' he stumbled.

'Whatever your father wishes,' she said steadily, as if to remind him that they were merely prince and princess and had no rights and no power at all.

He cleared his throat. 'I shall come to your room tonight,' he asserted.

She gave him a look from eyes as blue and hard as the sapphires around her neck. 'Whatever you wish,' she said in the same neutral tone.

He came when she was in bed and Dona Elvira admitted him to the room, her face like a stone, disapproval in every gesture. Catalina sat up in bed and watched as his groom of the bedchamber took his gown from his shoulders and went quietly out, closing the door behind him.

'Wine?' Arthur asked. He was afraid his voice quavered slightly.

'No, thank you,' she said.

Awkwardly the young man came to the bed, turned back the sheets, got in beside her. She turned to look at him, and he knew he was blushing beneath her inquiring gaze. He blew out the candle so she could not see his discomfort. A little torchlight from the guard outside flickered through the slats of the shutters, and then was gone as the guard moved on. Arthur felt the bed move as she lay back and pulled her nightdress out of the way. He felt as if he were a thing to her, an object of no importance, something she had to endure in order to be Queen of England.

He threw back the covers and jumped from the bed. 'I'm not staying here. I'm going to my room,' he said tersely.

'What?'

'I shan't stay here. I'm not wanted . . .'

'Not wanted? I never said you were not . . .'

'It is obvious. The way you look . . .'

'It's pitch black! How d'you know how I look? And anyway, you look as if someone forced you here!'

'I? It isn't me who sent a message that half the court heard, that I was not to come to your bed.'

He heard her gasp. 'I did not say you were not to come. I had to tell them to tell you . . .' She broke off in embarrassment. 'It was my time . . . you had to know . . .'

'Your duenna told my steward that I was not to come to your bed. How do you think that made me feel? How d'you think that looked to everyone?'

'How else was I to tell you?' she demanded.

'Tell me yourself!' he raged. 'Don't tell everyone else in the world.'

'How could I? How could I say such a thing? I should be so embarrassed!'

'Instead it is me who is made to look a fool!'

Catalina slipped out of bed and steadied herself, holding the tall carved bedpost. 'My lord, I apologise if I have offended you, I don't know how such things are done here . . . In future I will do as you wish . . .'

He said nothing.

She waited.

'I'm going,' he said and went to hammer on the door for his groom to come to him.

'Don't!' The cry was forced out of her.

'What?' He turned.

'Everyone will know,' she said desperately. 'Know that there is something wrong between us. Everyone will know that you have just come to me. If you leave at once, everyone will think . . .'

'I won't stay here!' he shouted.

Her pride rushed up. 'You will shame us both!' she cried out. 'What do you want people to think? That I disgust you, or that you are impotent?'

'Why not? If both are true?' He hammered on the door even louder.

She gasped in horror and fell back against the bedpost.

'Your Grace?' came a shout from the outer chamber and the door opened to reveal the groom of the bedchamber and a couple of pages, and behind them Dona Elvira and a lady-in-waiting.

Catalina stalked over to the window and turned her back to the room. Uncertainly, Arthur hesitated, glancing back at her for help, for some indication that he could stay after all.

'For shame!' Dona Elvira exclaimed, pushing past Arthur and running to throw a gown around Catalina's shoulders. Once the woman was standing with her arm around Catalina, glaring at him, Arthur could not return to his bride; he stepped over the threshold and went to his own rooms.

I cannot bear him. I cannot bear this country. I cannot live here for the rest of my life. That he should say that I disgust him! That he should dare to speak to me so! Has he run mad like one of their filthy dogs that pant everywhere? Has he forgotten who I am? Has he forgotten himself?

I am so furious with him I should like to take a scimitar and slice his stupid head off. If he thought for a moment he would have known that everyone in the palace, everyone in London, probably everyone in this gross country, will laugh at us. They will say I am ugly and that I cannot please him.

I am crying with temper, it's not grief. I tuck my head into the pillow of my bed, so that no-one can hear me and tell everyone else that the princess cried herself to sleep because her husband would not bed her. I am choking on tears and temper, I am so angry with him.

After a little while I stop, I wipe my face, I sit up. I am a princess by birth and by marriage, I should not give way. I shall have some dignity even if he has none. He is a young man, a young English man at that – how should he know how to behave? I think of my home in the moonlight, of how the walls and the tracery gleam white and the yellow stone is bleached to cream. That is a palace, where people know how to behave with grace and dignity. I wish with all my heart that I was still there.

I remember that I used to watch a big yellow moon reflected in the water of the sultana's garden. Like a fool, I used to dream of being married.

Oxford, Christmas 1501

They set off a few days before Christmas. Resolutely, they spoke to each other in public with utter courtesy, and ignored each other completely when no-one was watching. The queen had asked that they might at least stay for the twelve-day feast but My Lady the King's Mother had ruled that they should take their Christmas at Oxford, it would give the country a chance to see the prince and the new Princess of Wales, and what the king's mother said was law.

Catalina travelled by litter, jolted mercilessly over the frozen roads, her mules foundering in the fords, chilled to the bone however many rugs and furs they packed around her. The king's mother had ruled that she should not ride for fear of a fall. The unspoken hope was that Catalina was carrying a child. Catalina herself said nothing to confirm or deny the hope. Arthur was silence itself.

They had separate rooms on the road to Oxford, and separate rooms at Magdalene College when they arrived. The choristers were ready, the kitchens were ready, the extraordinarily rich hospitality of Oxford was ready to make merry; but the Prince and Princess of Wales were as cold and as dull as the weather.

They dined together, seated at the great table facing down the hall, and as many of the citizens of Oxford who could get into the gallery took their seats and watched the princess put small morsels of food in her mouth, and turn her shoulder to her husband, while he looked around the hall for companions and conversation, as if he were dining alone.

They brought in dancers and tumblers, mummers and players. The princess smiled very pleasantly but never laughed, gave small purses of Spanish coins to all the entertainers, thanked them for their attendance; but never once turned to her husband to ask him if he was enjoying the evening. The prince walked around the room, affable and pleasant to the great men of the city. He spoke in English, all the time, and his Spanish-speaking bride had to wait for someone to talk to her in French or Latin, if they would. Instead, they clustered around the prince and chatted and joked and laughed, almost as if they were laughing at her, and did not want her to understand the jest. The princess sat alone, stiffly on her hard, carved wooden chair, her head held high and a small, defiant smile on her lips.

At last it was midnight and the long evening could end. Catalina rose from her seat and watched the court sink into bows and curtseys. She dropped a low Spanish curtsey to her husband, her duenna behind her with a face like flint. 'I bid you goodnight, Your Grace,' said the princess in Latin, her voice clear, her accent perfect.

'I shall come to your room,' he said. There was a little murmur of approval; the court wanted a lusty prince.

The colour rose in her cheeks at the very public announcement. There was nothing she could say. She could not refuse him; but the way she rose and left the room did not promise him a warm welcome when they were alone. Her ladies dipped their curtseys and followed her in a little offended flurry, swishing off like a many-coloured veil trailing behind her. The court smiled behind their hands at the high spirits of the bride.

Arthur came to her half an hour later, fired up by drink and resentment. He found her still dressed, waiting by the fire, her duenna at her side, her room ablaze with candles, her ladies still talking and playing cards as if it were the middle of the afternoon. Clearly, she was not a young woman on her way to bed.

'Sire, good evening,' she said and rose and curtseyed as he entered.

Arthur had to check his backwards step, in retreat at the first encounter. He was ready for bed, in his nightgown with only a robe thrown over his shoulders. He was acutely aware of his bare feet and vulnerable toes. Catalina blazed in her evening finery. The ladies all turned and looked at him, their faces unfriendly. He was acutely conscious of his nightgown and his bare legs and a chuckle of barely suppressed laughter from one of his men behind him.

'I expected you to be in bed,' he said.

'Of course, I can go to bed,' she returned with glacial courtesy. 'I was about to go to bed. It is very late. But when you announced so publicly that you would visit me in my rooms I thought you must be planning to bring all the court with you. I thought you were telling everyone to come to my rooms. Why else announce it at the top of your voice so that everybody could hear?'

'I did not announce it at the top of my voice!'

She raised an eyebrow in wordless contradiction.

'I shall stay the night,' he said stubbornly. He marched to her bedroom door. 'These ladies can go to their beds, it is late.' He nodded to his men. 'Leave us.' He went into her room and closed the door behind him.

She followed him and closed the door behind her, shutting out the bright, scandalised faces of the ladies. Her back to the door, she watched him throw off his robe and nightgown so he was naked, and climb into her bed. He plumped up the pillows and leaned back, his arms crossed against his narrow bare chest, like a man awaiting an entertainment.

It was her turn to be discomforted. 'Your Grace . . .'

'You had better get undressed,' he taunted her. 'As you say, it's very late.'

She turned one way, and then the other. 'I shall send for Dona Elvira.'

'Do. And send for whoever else undresses you. Don't mind me, please.'

Catalina bit her lip. He could see her uncertainty. She could not bear to be stripped naked in front of him. She turned and went out of the bedchamber.

There was a rattle of irritable Spanish from the room next door. Arthur grinned, he guessed that she was clearing the room of her ladies and undressing out there. When she came back, he saw that he was right. She was wearing a white gown trimmed with exquisite lace and her hair was in a long plait down her back. She looked more like a little girl than the haughty princess she had been only moments before, and he felt his desire rise up with some other feeling: a tenderness.

She glanced at him, her face unfriendly. 'I will have to say my prayers,' she said. She went to the prie-dieu and kneeled before it. He watched her bow her head over her clasped hands and start to whisper. For the first time his irritation left him, and he thought how hard it must be for her. Surely, his unease and fear must be nothing to hers: alone in a strange land, at the beck and call of a boy a few months younger than her, with no real friends and no family, far away from everything and everyone she knew.

The bed was warm. The wine he had drunk to give him courage now made him feel sleepy. He leaned back on the pillow. Her prayers were taking a long time but it was good for a man to have a spiritual wife. He closed his eyes on the thought. When she came to bed he thought he would take her with confidence but with gentleness. It was Christmas, he should be kind to her. She was probably lonely and afraid. He should be generous. He thought warmly of how loving he would be to her, and how grateful she would be. Perhaps they would learn to give each other pleasure, perhaps he would make her happy. His breathing deepened, he gave a tiny little snuffly snore. He slept.

Catalina looked around from her prayers and smiled in pure triumph. Then, absolutely silently, she crept into bed beside him and, carefully arranging herself so that not even the hem of her nightgown could touch him, she composed herself for sleep.

You thought to embarrass me before my women, before all the court. You thought you could shame me and triumph over me. But I am a princess of Spain and I have known things and seen things that you, in this safe little country, in this smug little haven, would never dream of. I am the Infanta, I am the daughter of the two most powerful monarchs in the whole of Christendom who alone have defeated the greatest threat ever to march against it. For seven hundred years the Moors have occupied Spain, an empire mightier than that of the Romans, and who drove them out? My mother! My father! So you needn't think I am afraid of you – you rose-petal prince, or whatever they call you. I shall never stoop to do anything that a princess of Spain should not do. I shall never be petty or spiteful. But if you challenge me, I shall defeat you.

Arthur did not speak to her in the morning, his boy's high pride was utterly cut to the quick. She had shamed him at his father's court by denying him her rooms, and now she had shamed him in private. He felt that she had trapped him, made a fool of him, and was even now laughing at him. He rose up and went out in sullen silence. He went to Mass and did not meet her eyes, he went hunting and was gone all day. He did not speak to her at night. They watched a play, seated side by side, and not one word was exchanged all evening. A whole week they stayed at Oxford and they did not say more than a dozen words to each other every day. He swore a private bitter oath to himself that he would never, ever speak to her again. He would get a child on her, if he could, he would humiliate her in every way that he could, but he would never say one direct word to her, and he would never, never, never sleep again in her bed.

When the morning came for them to move on to Ludlow the sky was grey with clouds, fat-bellied with snow. Catalina came out of the doorway of the college and recoiled as the icy, damp air hit her in the face. Arthur ignored her.

She stepped out into the yard where the train was all drawn up and waiting for her. She hesitated before the litter. It struck him that she was like a prisoner, hesitating before a cart. She could not choose.

'Will it not be very cold?' she asked.

He turned a hard face to her. 'You will have to get used to the cold, you're not in Spain now.'

'So I see.'

She drew back the curtains of the litter. Inside there were rugs for her to wrap around herself and cushions for her to rest on, but it did not look very cosy.

'It gets far worse than this,' he said cheerfully. 'Far colder, it rains or sleets or snows, and it gets darker. In February we have only a couple of hours of daylight at best, and then there are the freezing fogs which turn day into night so it is forever grey.'

She turned and looked up at him. 'Could we not set out another day?'

'You agreed to come,' he taunted her. 'I would have been happy to leave you at Greenwich.'

'I did as I was told.'

'So here we are. Travelling on as we have been ordered to do.'

'At least you can move about and keep warm,' she said plaintively. 'Can I not ride?'

'My Lady the King's Mother said you could not.'

She made a little face but she did not argue.

'It's your choice. Shall I leave you here?' he asked briskly, as if he had little time for these uncertainties.

'No,' she said. 'Of course not,' and climbed into the litter and pulled the rugs over her feet and up around her shoulders.

Arthur led the way out of Oxford, bowing and smiling at the people who had turned out to cheer him. Catalina drew the curtains of her litter against the cold wind and the curious stares, and would not show her face.

They stopped for dinner at a great house on the way and Arthur went in to dine without even waiting to help her from the litter. The lady of the house, flustered, went out to the litter and found Catalina stumbling out, white-faced and with red eyes.

'Princess, are you all right?' the woman asked her.

'I am cold,' Catalina said miserably. 'I am freezing cold. I think I have never been so cold.'

She hardly ate any dinner, they could not make her take any wine. She looked ready to drop with exhaustion; but as soon as they had eaten Arthur wanted to push on, they had twenty more miles to go before the early dusk of winter.

'Can't you refuse?' Maria de Salinas asked her in a quick whisper.

'No,' the princess said. She rose from her seat without another word. But when they opened the great wooden door to go out into the courtyard, small flakes of snow swirled in around them.

'We cannot travel in this, it will soon be dark and we shall lose the road!' Catalina exclaimed.

'I shall not lose the road,' Arthur said, and strode out to his horse. 'You shall follow me.'

The lady of the house sent a servant flying for a heated stone to put in the litter at Catalina's feet. The princess climbed in, hunched the rugs around her shoulders, and tucked her hands in deep.

'I am sure that he is impatient to get you to Ludlow to show you his castle,' the woman said, trying to put the best aspect on a miserable situation.

'He is impatient to show me nothing but neglect,' Catalina snapped; but she took care to say it in Spanish.

They left the warmth and lights of the great house and heard the doors bang behind them as they turned the horses' heads to the west, and to the white sun which was sinking low on the horizon. It was two hours past noon but the sky was so filled with snow clouds that there was an eerie grey glow over the rolling landscape. The road snaked ahead of them, brown tracks against brown fields, both of them bleaching to whiteness under the haze of swirling snow. Arthur rode ahead, singing merrily, Catalina's litter laboured along behind. At every step the mules threw the litter to one side and then the other, she had to keep a hand on the edge to hold herself in place, and her fingers became chilled and then cramped, blue from cold. The curtains kept out the worst of the snowflakes but not the insistent, penetrating draughts. If she drew back a corner to look out at the country she saw a whirl of whiteness as the snowflakes danced and circled the road, the sky seeming greyer every moment.

The sun set white in a white sky and the world grew more shadowy. Snow and clouds closed down around the little cavalcade which wound its way across a white land under a grey sky.

Arthur's horse cantered ahead, the prince riding easily in the saddle, one gloved hand on the reins, the other on his whip. He had stout woollen undergarments under his thick leather jerkin and soft, warm leather boots. Catalina watched him ride forwards. She was too cold and too miserable even to resent him. More than anything else she wished he would ride back to tell her that the journey was nearly over, that they were there.

An hour passed, the mules walked down the road, their heads bowed low against the wind that whirled flakes around their ears and into the litter. The snow was getting thicker now, filling the air and drifting into the ruts of the lane. Catalina had hunched up under the covers, lying like a child, the rapidly cooling stone at her belly, her knees drawn up, her cold hands tucked in, her face ducked down, buried in the furs and rugs. Her feet were freezing cold, there was a gap in the rugs at her back and now and then she shivered at a fresh draught of icy air.

All around, outside the litter, she could hear men chattering and laughing about the cold, swearing that they would eat well when the train got into Burford. Their voices seemed to come from far away; Catalina drifted into a sleep from coldness and exhaustion.

Groggily, she woke when the litter bumped down to the ground and the curtains were swept back. A wave of icy air washed over her and she ducked her head down and cried out in discomfort.

'Infanta?' Dona Elvira asked. The duenna had been riding her mule, the exercise had kept her warm. 'Infanta? Thank God, at last we are here.'

Catalina would not lift her head.

'Infanta, they are waiting to greet you.'

Still Catalina would not look up.

'What's this?' It was Arthur's voice, he had seen the litter put down and the duenna bending over it. He saw that the heap of rugs made no movement. For a moment, with a pang of dismay, he thought that the princess might have been taken ill. Maria de Salinas gave him a reproachful look. 'What's the matter?'

'It is nothing.' Dona Elvira straightened up and stood between the prince and his young wife, shielding Catalina as he jumped from his horse and came towards her. 'The princess has been asleep, she is composing herself.'

'I'll see her,' he said. He put the woman aside with one confident hand and kneeled down beside the litter.

'Catalina?' he asked quietly.

'I am frozen with cold,' said a little thread of voice. She lifted her head and he saw that she was as white as the snow itself and her lips were blue. 'I am so c . . . cold that I shall die and then you will be happy. You can b . . . bury me in this horrible country and m . . . marry some fat, stupid Englishwoman. And I shall never see . . .' She broke off into sobs.

'Catalina?' He was utterly bemused.

'I shall never see my m . . . mother again. But she will know that you killed me with your miserable country and your cruelty.'

'I have not been cruel!' he rejoined at once, quite blind to the gathering crowd of courtiers around them. 'By God, Catalina, it was not me!'

'You have been cruel.' She lifted her face from the rugs. 'You have been cruel because –'

It was her sad, white, tearstained face that spoke to him far more than her words could ever have done. She looked like one of his sisters when their grandmother scolded them. She did not look like an infuriating, insulting princess of Spain, she looked like a girl who had been bullied into tears – and he realised that it was he who had bullied her, he had made her cry, and he had left her in the cold litter for all the afternoon while he had ridden on ahead and delighted in the thought of her discomfort.

He reached into the rugs and pulled out her icy hand. Her fingers were numb with cold. He knew he had done wrong. He took her blue fingertips to his mouth and kissed them, then he held them against his lips and blew his warm breath against them. 'God forgive me,' he said. 'I forgot I was a husband. I didn't know I had to be a husband. I didn't realise that I could make you cry. I won't ever do so again.'

She blinked, her blue eyes swimming in unshed tears. 'What?'

'I was wrong. I was angry but quite wrong. Let me take you inside and we will get warm and I shall tell you how sorry I am and I will never be unkind to you again.'

At once she struggled with her rugs and Arthur pulled them off her legs. She was so cramped and so chilled that she stumbled when she tried to stand. Ignoring the muffled protests of her duenna, he swept her up into his arms and carried her like a bride across the threshold of the hall.

Gently he put her down before the roaring fire, gently he put back her hood, untied her cloak, chafed her hands. He waved away the servants who would have come to take her cloak, offered her wine. He made a little circle of peace and silence around them, and he watched the colour come back to her pale cheeks.

'I am sorry,' he said, heartfelt. 'I was very, very angry with you but I should not have taken you so far in such bad weather and I should never have let you get cold. It was wrong of me.'

'I forgive you,' she whispered, a little smile lighting her face.

'I didn't know that I had to take care of you. I didn't think. I have been like a child, an unkind child. But I know now, Catalina. I will never be unkind to you again.'

She nodded. 'Oh, please. And you too must forgive me. I have been unkind to you.'

'Have you?'

'At Oxford,' she whispered, very low.

He nodded. 'And what do you say to me?'

She stole a quick upwards glance at him. He was not making a play of offence. He was a boy still, with a boy's fierce sense of fairness. He needed a proper apology.

'I am very, very sorry,' she said, speaking nothing but the truth. 'It was not a good thing to do, and I was sorry in the morning, but I could not tell you.'

'Shall we go to bed now?' he whispered to her, his mouth very close to her ear.

'Can we?'

'If I say that you are ill?'

She nodded, and said nothing more.

'The princess is unwell from the cold,' Arthur announced generally. 'Dona Elvira will take her to her room, and I shall dine there, alone with her, later.'

'But the people have come to see Your Grace . . .' his host pleaded. 'They have an entertainment for you, and some disputes they would like you to hear . . .'

'I shall see them all in the hall now, and we shall stay tomorrow also. But the princess must go to her rooms at once.'

'Of course.'

There was a flurry around the princess as her ladies, led by Dona Elvira, escorted her to her room. Catalina glanced back at Arthur. 'Please come to my room for dinner,' she said clearly enough for everyone to hear. 'I want to see you, Your Grace.'

It was everything to him: to hear her publicly avow her desire for him. He bowed at the compliment and then he went to the great hall and called for a cup of ale and dealt very graciously with the half-dozen men who had mustered to see him, and then he excused himself and went to her room.

Catalina was waiting for him, alone by the fireside. She had dismissed her women, her servants, there was no-one to wait on them, they were quite alone. He almost recoiled at the sight of the empty room; the Tudor princes and princesses were never left alone. But she had banished the servants who should wait at the table, she had sent away the ladies who should dine with them. She had even dismissed her duenna. There was no-one to see what she had done to her apartments, nor how she had set the dinner table.

She had swathed the plain wooden furniture in scarves of light cloth in vivid colours, she had even draped scarves from the tapestries to hide the cold walls, so the room was like a beautifully trimmed tent.

She had ordered them to saw the legs of the table down to stumps, so the table sat as low as a footstool, a most ridiculous piece of furniture. She had set big cushions at either end, as if they should recline like savages to eat. The dinner was set out on the table at knee level, drawn up to the warmth of the burning logs like some barbaric feast, there were candles everywhere and a rich smell like incense, as heady as a church on a feast day.

Arthur was about to complain at the wild extravagance of sawing up the furniture; but then he paused. This was, perhaps, not just some girlish folly; she was trying to show him something.

She was wearing a most extraordinary costume. On her head was a twist of the finest silk, turned and knotted like a coronet with a tail hanging down behind which she had tucked nonchalantly in one side of the headdress as if she would pull it over her face like a veil. Instead of a decent gown she wore a simple shift of the finest, lightest silk, smoky blue in colour, so fine that he could almost see through it, to glimpse the paleness of her skin underneath. He could feel his heartbeat thud when he realised she was naked beneath this wisp of silk. Beneath the chemise she was wearing a pair of hose – like men's hose – but nothing like men's hose, for they were billowy leggings which fell from her slim hips where they were tied with a drawstring of gold thread, to her feet where they were tied again, leaving her feet half bare in dainty crimson slippers worked with a gold thread. He looked her up and down, from barbaric turban to Turkish slippers, and found himself bereft of speech.

'You don't like my clothes,' Catalina said flatly, and he was too inexperienced to recognise the depth of embarrassment that she was ready to feel.

'I've never seen anything like them before,' he stammered. 'Are they Arab clothes? Show me!'

She turned on the spot, watching him over her shoulder and then coming back to face him again. 'We all wear them in Spain,' she said. 'My mother too. They are more comfortable than gowns, and cleaner. Everything can be washed, not like velvets and damask.'

He nodded, he noticed now a light rosewater scent which came from the silk.

'And they are cool in the heat of the day,' she added.

'They are . . . beautiful.' He nearly said 'barbaric' and was so glad that he had not, when her eyes lit up.

'Do you think so?'

'Yes.'

At once she raised her arms and twirled again to show him the flutter of the hose and the lightness of the chemise.

'You wear them to sleep in?'

She laughed. 'We wear them nearly all the time. My mother always wears them under her armour, they are far more comfortable than anything else, and she could not wear gowns under chain mail.'

'No . . .'

'When we are receiving Christian ambassadors, or for great state occasions, or when the court is at feast, we wear gowns and robes, especially at Christmas when it is cold. But in our own rooms, and always in the summer, and always when we are on campaign, we wear Morisco dress. It is easy to make, and easy to wash, and easy to carry, and best to wear.'

'You cannot wear it here,' Arthur said. 'I am so sorry. But My Lady the King's Mother would object if she knew you even had them with you.'

She nodded. 'I know that. My mother was against me even bringing them. But I wanted something to remind me of my home and I thought I might keep them in my cupboard and tell nobody. Then tonight, I thought I might show you. Show you myself, and how I used to be.'

Catalina stepped to one side and gestured to him that he should come to the table. He felt too big, too clumsy, and on an instinct, he stooped and shucked off his riding boots and stepped on to the rich rugs barefoot. She gave a little nod of approval and beckoned him to sit. He dropped to one of the gold-embroidered cushions.

Serenely, she sat opposite him and passed him a bowl of scented water, with a white napkin. He dipped his fingers and wiped them.

She smiled and offered him a gold plate laid with food. It was a dish of his childhood, roasted chicken legs, devilled kidneys, with white manchet bread: a proper English dinner. But she had made them serve only tiny portions on each individual plate, dainty bones artfully arranged. She had sliced apples served alongside the meat, and added some precious spiced meats next to sliced sugared plums. She had done everything she could to serve him a Spanish meal, with all the delicacy and luxury of the Moorish taste.

Arthur was shaken from his prejudice. 'This is . . . beautiful,' he said, seeking a word to describe it. 'This is . . . like a picture. You are like . . .' He could not think of anything that he had ever seen that was like her. Then an image came to him. 'You are like a painting I once saw on a plate,' he said. 'A treasure of my mother's from Persia. You are like that. Strange, and most lovely.'

She glowed at his praise. 'I want you to understand,' she said, speaking carefully in Latin. 'I want you to understand what I am. Cuiusmodi sum.'

'What you are?'

'I am your wife,' she assured him. 'I am the Princess of Wales, I will be Queen of England. I will be an Englishwoman. That is my destiny. But also, as well as this, I am the Infanta of Spain, of al Andalus.'

'I know.'

'You know; but you don't know. You don't know about Spain, you don't know about me. I want to explain myself to you. I want you to know about Spain. I am a princess of Spain. I am my father's favourite. When we dine alone, we eat like this. When we are on campaign, we live in tents and sit before the braziers like this, and we were on campaign for every year of my life until I was seven.'

'But you are a Christian court,' he protested. 'You are a power in Christendom. You have chairs, proper chairs, you must eat your dinner off a proper table.'

'Only at banquets of state,' she said. 'When we are in our private rooms we live like this, like Moors. Oh, we say grace; we thank the

One God at the breaking of the bread. But we do not live as you live here in England. We have beautiful gardens filled with fountains and running water. We have rooms in our palaces inlaid with precious stones and inscribed with gold letters telling beautiful truths in poetry. We have bath houses with hot water to wash in and thick steam to fill the scented room, we have ice houses packed in winter with snow from the sierras so our fruit and our drinks are chilled in summer.'

The words were as seductive as the images. 'You make yourself sound so strange,' he said reluctantly. 'Like a fairy tale.'

'I am only just realising now how strange we are to each other,' Catalina said. 'I thought that your country would be like mine but it is quite different. I am coming to think that we are more like Persians than like Germans. We are more Arabic than Visigoth. Perhaps you thought that I would be a princess like your sisters, but I am quite, quite different.'

He nodded. 'I shall have to learn your ways,' he proposed tentatively. 'As you will have to learn mine.'

'I shall be Queen of England, I shall have to become English. But I want you to know what I was, when I was a girl.'

Arthur nodded. 'Were you very cold today?' he asked. He could feel a strange new feeling, like a weight in his belly. He realised it was discomfort, at the thought of her being unhappy.

She met his look without concealment. 'Yes,' she said. 'I was very cold. And then I thought that I had been unkind to you and I was very unhappy. And then I thought that I was far away from my home and from the heat and the sunshine and my mother and I was very homesick. It was a horrible day, today. I had a horrible day, today.'

He reached his hand out to her. 'Can I comfort you?'

Her fingertips met his. 'You did,' she said. 'When you brought me in to the fire and told me you were sorry. You do comfort me. I will learn to trust that you always will.'

He drew her to him; the cushions were soft and easy, he laid her beside him and he gently tugged at the silk that was wrapped around her head. It slipped off at once and the rich red tresses tumbled down. He touched them with his lips, then her sweet slightly trembling mouth, her eyes with the sandy eyelashes, her light eyebrows, the blue veins at her temples, the lobes of her ears. Then he felt his desire rise and he kissed the hollow at the base of her throat, her thin collarbones, the warm, seductive flesh from neck to shoulder, the hollow of her elbow, the warmth of her palm, the erotically deep-scented armpit, and then he drew her shift over her head and she was naked, in his arms, and she was his wife, and a loving wife, at last, indeed.

I love him. I did not think it possible, but I love him. I have fallen in love with him. I look at myself in the mirror, in wonderment, as if I am changed, as everything else is changed. I am a young woman in love with my husband. I am in love with the Prince of Wales. I, Catalina of Spain, am in love. I wanted this love, I thought it was impossible, and I have it. I am in love with my husband and we shall be King and Queen of England. Who can doubt now that I am chosen by God for His especial favour? He brought me from the dangers of war to safety and peace in the Alhambra Palace and now He has given me England and the love of the young man who will be its king.

In a sudden rush of emotion I put my hands together and pray: 'Oh God, let me love him forever, do not take us from each other as Juan was taken from Margot, in their first months of joy. Let us grow old together, let us love each other for ever.'

Ludlow Castle, January 1502

The winter sun was low and red over the rounded hills as they rattled through the great gate that pierced the stone wall around Ludlow.

Arthur, who had been riding beside the litter, shouted to Catalina over the noise of the hooves on the cobbles. 'This is Ludlow, at last!'

Ahead of them the men-at-arms shouted: 'Make way for Arthur! Prince of Wales!' and the doors banged open and people tumbled out of their houses to see the procession go by.

Catalina saw a town as pretty as a tapestry. The timbered second storeys of the crowded buildings overhung cobbled streets with prosperous little shops and working yards tucked cosily underneath them on the ground floor. The shopkeepers' wives jumped up from their stools set outside the shops to wave to her and Catalina smiled, and waved back. From the upper storeys the glovers' girls and shoemakers' apprentices, the goldsmiths' boys and the spinsters leaned out and called her name. Catalina laughed, and caught her breath as one young lad looked ready to overbalance but was hauled back in by his cheering mates.

They passed a great bull ring with a dark-timbered inn, as the church bells of the half-dozen religious houses, college, chapels and hospital of Ludlow started to peal their bells to welcome the prince and his bride home.

Catalina leaned forwards to see her castle, and noted the unassailable march of the outer bailey. The gate was flung open, they went in, and found the greatest men of the town, the mayor, the church elders, the leaders of the wealthy trades guilds, assembled to greet them.

Arthur pulled up his horse and listened politely to a long speech in Welsh and then in English.

'When do we eat?' Catalina whispered to him in Latin and saw his mouth quiver as he held back a smile.

'When do we go to bed?' she breathed, and had the satisfaction of seeing his hand tremble on the rein with desire. She gave a little giggle and ducked back into the litter until finally the interminable speeches of welcome were finished and the royal party could ride on through the great gate of the castle to the inner bailey.

It was a neat castle, as sound as any border castle in Spain. The curtain wall marched around the inner bailey high and strong, made in a curious rosy-coloured stone that made the powerful walls more warm and domestic.

Catalina's eye, sharpened by her training, looked from the thick walls to the well in the outer bailey, the well in the inner bailey, took in how one defensible area led to another, thought that a siege could be held off for years. But it was small, it was like a toy castle, something her father would build to protect a river crossing or a vulnerable road. Something a very minor lord of Spain would be proud to have as his home.

'Is this it?' she asked blankly, thinking of the city that was housed inside the walls of her home, of the gardens and the terraces, of the hill and the views, of the teeming life of the town centre, all inside defended walls. Of the long hike for the guards: if they went all around the battlements they would be gone for more than an hour. At Ludlow a sentry would complete the circle in minutes. 'Is this it?'

At once he was aghast. 'Did you expect more? What were you expecting?'

She would have caressed his anxious face, if there had not been hundreds of people watching. She made herself keep her hands still. 'Oh, I was foolish. I was thinking of Richmond.' Nothing in the world would have made her say that she was thinking of the Alhambra.

He smiled, reassured. 'Oh, my love. Richmond is new-built, my father's great pride and joy. London is one of the greatest cities of Christendom, and the palace matches its size. But Ludlow is only a town, a great town in the Marches, for sure, but a town. But it is wealthy, you will see, and the hunting is good and the people are welcoming. You will be happy here.'

'I am sure of it,' said Catalina, smiling at him, putting aside the thought of a palace built for beauty, only for beauty, where the builders had thought firstly where the light would fall and what reflections it would make in still pools of marble.

She looked around her and saw, in the centre of the inner bailey, a curious circular building like a squat tower.

'What's that?' she asked, struggling out of the litter as Arthur held her hand.

He glanced over his shoulder. 'It's our round chapel,' he said negligently.

'A round chapel?'

'Yes, like in Jerusalem.'

At once she recognised with delight the traditional shape of the mosque – designed and built in the round so that no worshipper was better placed than any others, because Allah is praised by the poor man as well as the rich. 'It's lovely.'

Arthur glanced at her in surprise. To him it was only a round tower built with the pretty plum-coloured local stone, but he saw that it glowed in the afternoon light, and radiated a sense of peace.

'Yes,' he said, hardly noticing it. 'Now this,' he indicated the great building facing them, with a handsome flight of steps up to the open door, 'this is the great hall. To the left are the council chambers of Wales and, above them, my rooms. To the right are the guest bedrooms and chambers for the warden of the castle and his lady: Sir Richard and Lady Margaret Pole. Your rooms are above, on the top floor.'

He saw her swift reaction. 'She is here now?'

'She is away from the castle at the moment.'

She nodded. 'There are buildings behind the great hall?'

'No. It is set into the outer wall. This is all of it.'

Catalina schooled herself to keep her face smiling and pleasant.

'We have more guest rooms in the outer bailey,' he said defensively. 'And we have a lodge house, as well. It is a busy place, merry. You will like it.'

'I am sure I will,' she smiled. 'And which are my rooms?'

He pointed to the highest windows. 'See up there? On the right-hand side, matching mine, but on the opposite side of the hall.'

She looked a little daunted. 'But how will you get to my rooms?' she asked quietly.

He took her hand and led her, smiling to his right and to his left, towards the grand stone stairs to the double doors of the great hall. There was a ripple of applause and their companions fell in behind them. 'As My Lady the King's Mother commanded me, four times a month I shall come to your room in a formal procession through the great hall,' he said. He led her up the steps.

'Oh.' She was dashed.

He smiled down at her. 'And all the other nights I shall come to you along the battlements,' he whispered. 'There is a private door that goes from your rooms to the battlements that run all around the castle. My rooms go on to them too. You can walk from your rooms to mine whenever you wish and nobody will know whether we are together or not. They will not even know whose room we are in.'

He loved how her face lit up. 'We can be together, whenever we want?'

'We will be happy here.'

Yes I will, I will be happy here. I will not mourn like a Persian for the beautiful courts of his home and declare that there is nowhere else fit for life. I will not say that these mountains are a desert without oases like a Berber longing for his birthright. I will accustom myself to Ludlow, and I will learn to live here, on the border, and later in England. My mother is not just a queen, she is a soldier, and she raised me to know my duty and to do it. It is my duty to learn to be happy here and to live here without complaining.

I may never wear armour as she did, I may never fight for my country, as she did; but there are many ways to serve a kingdom, and to be a merry, honest, constant queen is one of them. If God does not call me to arms, He may call me to serve as a lawgiver, as a bringer of justice. Whether I defend my people by fighting for them against an enemy or by fighting for their freedom in the law, I shall be their queen, heart and soul, Queen of England.

It was night time, past midnight. Catalina glowed in the firelight. They were in bed, sleepy, but too desirous of each other for sleep.

'Tell me a story.'

'I have told you dozens of stories.'

'Tell me another. Tell me the one about Boabdil giving up the Alhambra Palace with the golden keys on a silk cushion and going away crying.'

'You know that one. I told it to you last night.'

'Then tell me the story about Yarfa and his horse that gnashed its teeth at Christians.'

'You are a child. And his name was Yarfe.'

'But you saw him killed?'

'I was there; but I didn't see him actually die.'

'How could you not watch it?'

'Well, partly because I was praying as my mother ordered me to, and because I was a girl and not a bloodthirsty, monstrous boy.'

Arthur tossed an embroidered cushion at her head. She caught it and threw it back at him.

'Well, tell me about your mother pawning her jewels to pay for the crusade.'

She laughed again and shook her head, making her auburn hair swing this way and that. 'I shall tell you about my home,' she offered.

'All right.' He gathered the purple blanket around them both and waited.

'When you come through the first door to the Alhambra it looks like a little room. Your father would not stoop to enter a palace like that.'

'It's not grand?'

'It's the size of a little merchant's hall in the town here. It is a good hall for a small house in Ludlow, nothing more.'

'And then?'

'And then you go into the courtyard and from there into the golden chamber.'

'A little better?'

'It is filled with colour, but still it is not much bigger. The walls are bright with coloured tiles and gold leaf and there is a high balcony, but it is still only a little space.'

'And then, where shall we go today?'

'Today we shall turn right and go into the Court of the Myrtles.'

He closed his eyes, trying to remember her descriptions. 'A courtyard in the shape of a rectangle, surrounded by high buildings of gold.'

'With a huge, dark wooden doorway framed with beautiful tiles at the far end.'

'And a lake, a lake of a simple rectangle shape, and on either side of the water, a hedge of sweet-scented myrtle trees.'

'Not a hedge like you have,' she demurred, thinking of the ragged edges of the Welsh fields in their struggle of thorn and weed.

'Like what, then?' he asked, opening his eyes.

'A hedge like a wall,' she said. 'Cut straight and square, like a block of green marble, like a living green sweet-scented statue. And the gateway at the end is reflected back in the water, and the arch around it, and the building that it is set in. So that the whole thing is mirrored in ripples at your feet. And the walls are pierced with light screens of stucco, as airy as paper, like white on white embroidery. And the birds . . .'

'The birds?' he asked, surprised, for she had not told him of them before.

She paused while she thought of the word. '*Apodes?*' she said in Latin.

'*Apodes?* Swifts?'

She nodded. 'They flow like a turbulent river of birds just above your head, round and round the narrow courtyard, screaming as they go, as fast as a cavalry charge, they go like the wind, round and round, as long as the sun shines on the water they go round, all day. And at night –'

'At night?'

She made a little gesture with her hands, like an enchantress. 'At night they disappear, you never see them settle or nest. They just disappear – they set with the sun, but at dawn they are there again, like a river, like a flood.' She paused. 'It is hard to describe,' she said in a small voice. 'But I see it all the time.'

'You miss it,' he said flatly. 'However happy I may make you, you will always miss it.'

She made a little gesture. 'Of course. It is to be expected. But I never forget who I am. Who I was born to be.'

Arthur waited.

She smiled at him, her face was warmed by her smile, her blue eyes shining. 'The Princess of Wales,' she said. 'From my childhood I knew it. They always called me the Princess of Wales. And so Queen of England, as destined by God. Catalina, Infanta of Spain, Princess of Wales.'

He smiled in reply and drew her closer to him, they lay back together, her head on his shoulder, her dark red hair a veil across his chest.

'I knew I would marry you almost from the moment I was born,' he said reflectively. 'I can't remember a time when I was not betrothed to you. I can't remember a time when I was not writing letters to you and taking them to my tutor for correction.'

'Lucky that I please you, now I am here.'

He put his finger under her chin and turned her face up towards him for a kiss. 'Even luckier, that I please you,' he said.

'I would have been a good wife anyway,' she insisted. 'Even without this . . .'

He pulled her hand down beneath the silky sheets to touch him where he was growing big again.

'Without this, you mean?' he teased.

'Without this . . . joy,' she said and closed her eyes and lay back, waiting for his touch.

Their servants woke them at dawn and Arthur was ceremonially escorted from her bed. They saw each other again at Mass but they were seated at opposite sides of the round chapel, each with their own household, and could not speak.

The Mass should be the most important moment of my day, and it should bring me comfort – I know that. But I always feel lonely during Mass. I do pray to God and thank Him for His especial care of me, but just being in this chapel – shaped like a tiny mosque – reminds me so much of my mother. The smell of incense is as evocative of her as if it were her perfume, I cannot believe that I am not kneeling beside her as I have done four times a day for almost every day of my life. When I say 'Hail Mary, full of grace' it is my mother's round, smiling, determined face that I see. And when I pray for courage to do my duty in this strange land with these dour, undemonstrative people, it is my mother's strength that I need.

I should give thanks for Arthur but I dare not even think of him when I am on my knees to God. I cannot think of him without the sin of desire. The very image of him in my mind is a deep secret, a pagan pleasure. I am certain that this is not the holy joy of matrimony. Such intense pleasure must be a sin. Such dark, deep desire and satisfaction cannot be the pure conception of a little prince that is the whole point and purpose of this marriage. We were put to bed by an archbishop but our passionate coupling is as animal as a pair of sun-warmed snakes twisted all around in their pleasure. I keep my joy in Arthur a secret from everyone, even from God.

I could not confide in anyone, even if I wanted to. We are expressly forbidden from being together as we wish. His grandmother, My Lady the King's Mother, has ordered this, as she orders everything, even every-thing here in the Welsh Marches. She has said that he should come to my room once a week every week, except for the time of my courses, he should arrive before ten of the clock and leave by six. We obey her of course, everybody obeys her. Once a week, as she has commanded, he comes through the great hall, like a young man reluctantly obedient, and in the morning he leaves me in silence and goes quietly away as a young man who has done his duty, not one that has been awake all night in breathless delight. He never boasts of pleasure, when they come to fetch him from my chamber he says nothing, nobody knows the joy we take in each other's passion. No-one will ever know that we are together every night. We meet on the battlements which run from his rooms to mine at the very top of the castle, grey-blue sky arching above us, and we consort like lovers in secret, concealed by the night, we go to my room, or to his, and we make a private world together, filled with hidden joy.

Even in this crowded small castle filled with busybodies and the king's mother's spies, nobody knows that we are together, and nobody knows how much we are in love.

After Mass the royal pair went to break their fast in their separate rooms, though they would rather have been together. Ludlow Castle was a small reproduction of the formality of the king's court. The king's mother had commanded that after breakfast Arthur must work with his tutor at his books or at sports as the weather allowed; and Catalina must work with her tutor, sew, or read, or walk in the garden.

'A garden!' Catalina whispered under her breath in the little patch of green with the sodden turf bench on one side of a thin border, set in the corner of the castle walls. 'I wonder if she has ever seen a real garden?'

In the afternoon they might ride out together to hunt in the woods around the castle. It was a rich countryside, the river fast-flowing through a wide valley with old thick woodlands on the sides of the hills. Catalina thought she would grow to love the pasture lands around the River Teme and, on the horizon, the way the darkness of the hills gave way to the sky. But in the mid-winter weather it was a landscape of grey and white, only the frost or the snow bringing brightness to the blackness of the cold woods. The weather was often too bad for the princess to go out at all. She hated the damp fog or when it drizzled with icy sleet. Arthur often rode alone.

'Even if I stayed behind I would not be allowed to be with you,' he said mournfully. 'My grandmother would have set me something else to do.'

'So go!' she said, smiling, though it seemed a long, long time until dinner and she had nothing to do but to wait for the hunt to come home.

They went out into the town once a week, to go to St Laurence's Church for Mass, or to visit the little chapel by the castle wall, to attend a dinner organised by one of the great guilds, or to see a cockfight, a bull baiting, or players. Catalina was impressed by the neat prettiness of the town; the place had escaped the violence of the wars between York and Lancaster that had finally been ended by Henry Tudor.

'Peace is everything to a kingdom,' she observed to Arthur.

'The only thing that can threaten us now is the Scots,' he said.

'The Yorkist line are my forebears, the Lancasters too, so the rivalry ends with me. All we have to do is keep the north safe.'

'And your father thinks he has done that with Princess Margaret's marriage?'

'Pray God he is right, but they are a faithless lot. When I am king I shall keep the border strong. You shall advise me, we'll go out together and make sure the border castles are repaired.'

'I shall like that,' she said.

'Of course, you spent your childhood with an army fighting for border lands, you would know better than I what to look for.'

She smiled. 'I am glad it is a skill of mine that you can use. My father always complained that my mother was making Amazons, not princesses.'

They dined together at dusk, and thankfully, dusk came very early on those cold winter nights. At last they could be close, seated side by side at the high table looking down the hall of the castle, the great hearth heaped with logs on the side wall. Arthur always put Catalina on his left, closest to the fire, and she wore a cloak lined with fur, and had layer upon layer of linen shifts under her ornate gown. Even so, she was still cold when she came down the icy stairs from her warm rooms to the smoky hall. Her Spanish ladies, Maria de Salinas, her duenna Dona Elvira and a few others, were seated at one table, the English ladies who were supposed to be her companions at another and her retinue of Spanish servants were seated at another. The great lords of Arthur's council, his chamberlain, Sir Richard Pole, warden of the castle, Bishop William Smith of Lincoln, his physician, Dr Bereworth, his treasurer Sir Henry Vernon, the steward of his household, Sir Richard Croft, his groom of the privy chamber, Sir William Thomas of Carmarthen, and all the leading men of the Principality, were seated in the body of the hall. At the back and in the gallery every nosy parker, every busybody in Wales could pile in to see the Spanish princess take her dinner, and speculate if she pleased the young prince or no.

There was no way to tell. Most of them thought that he had failed to bed her. For see! The Infanta sat like a stiff little doll and rarely leaned towards her young husband. The Prince of Wales spoke to her as if by rote, every ten minutes. They were little patterns of good behaviour, and they scarcely even looked at each other. The gossips said that he went to her rooms, as ordered, but only once a week and never of his own choice. Perhaps the young couple did not please each other. They were young, perhaps too young for marriage.

No-one could tell that Catalina's hands were gripped tight in her lap to stop herself from touching her husband, nor that every half-hour or so he glanced at her, apparently indifferent, and whispered so low that only she could hear: 'I want you right now.'

After dinner there would be dancing and perhaps mummers or a storyteller, a Welsh bard or strolling players to watch. Sometimes the poets would come in from the high hills and tell old, strange tales in their own tongue that Arthur could follow only with diffi-culty, but which he would try to translate for Catalina.

'When the long yellow summer comes and victory comes
  to us,
And the spreading of the sails of Brittany,
And when the heat comes and when the fever is kindled
There are portents that victory will be given to us.'

'What is that about?' she asked him.

'The long yellow summer is when my father decided to invade from Brittany. His road took him to Bosworth and victory.'

She nodded.

'It was hot, that year, and the troops came with the Sweat, a new disease, which now curses England as it does Europe with the heat of every summer.'

She nodded again. A new poet came forwards, played a chord on his harp and sang.

'And this?'

'It's about a red dragon that flies over the Principality,' he said. 'It kills the boar.'

'What does it mean?' Catalina asked.

'The dragon is the Tudors: us,' he said. 'You'll have seen the red dragon on our standard. The boar is the usurper, Richard. It's a compliment to my father, based on an old tale. All their songs are ancient songs. They probably sang them in the ark.' He grinned. 'Songs of Noah.'

'Do they give you Tudors credit for surviving the flood? Was Noah a Tudor?'

'Probably. My grandmother would take credit for the Garden of Eden itself,' he returned. 'This is the Welsh border, we come from Owen ap Tudor, from Glendower, we are happy to take the credit for everything.'

As Arthur predicted, when the fire burned low they would sing the old Welsh songs of magical doings in dark woods that no man could know. And they would tell of battles and glorious victories won by skill and courage. In their strange tongue they would tell stories of Arthur and Camelot, and Merlin the prince, and Guinevere: the queen who betrayed her husband for a guilty love.

'I should die if you took a lover,' he whispered to her as a page shielded them from the hall and poured wine.

'I can never even see anyone else when you are here,' she assured him. 'All I see is you.'

Every evening there was music or some entertainment for the Ludlow court. The king's mother had ruled that the prince should keep a merry house – it was a reward for the loyalty of Wales that had put her son Henry Tudor on an uncertain throne. Her grandson must pay the men who had come out of the hills to fight for the Tudors and remind them that he was a Welsh prince, and he would go on counting on their support to rule the English, whom no-one could count on at all. The Welsh must join with England and together, the two of them could keep out the Scots, and manage the Irish.

When the musicians played the slow formal dances of Spain, Catalina would dance with one of her ladies, conscious of Arthur's gaze on her, keeping her face prim, like a little mummer's mask of respectability; though she longed to twirl around and swing her hips like a woman in the seraglio, like a Moorish slave girl dancing for a sultan. But My Lady the King's Mother's spies watched everything, even in Ludlow, and would be quick to report any indiscreet behaviour by the young princess. Sometimes, Catalina would slide a glance at her husband and see his eyes on her, his look that of a man in love. She would snap her fingers as if part of the dance, but in fact to warn him that he was staring at her in a way that his grandmother would not like; and he would turn aside and speak to someone, tearing his gaze away from her.

Even after the music was over and the entertainers gone away, the young couple could not be alone. There were always men who sought council with Arthur, who wanted favours or land or influence, and they would approach him and talk low-voiced, in English, which Catalina did not yet fully understand, or in Welsh, which she thought no-one could ever understand. The rule of law barely ran in the border lands, each landowner was like a war-lord in his own domain. Deeper in the mountains there were people who still thought that Richard was on the throne, who knew nothing of the changed world, who spoke no English, who obeyed no laws at all.

Arthur argued, and praised, and suggested that feuds should be forgiven, that trespasses should be made good, that the proud Welsh chieftains should work together to make their land as prosperous as their neighbour England, instead of wasting their time in envy. The valleys and coastal lands were dominated by a dozen petty lords, and in the high hills the men ran in clans like wild tribes. Slowly, Arthur was determined to make the law run throughout the land.

'Every man has to know that the law is greater than his lord,'

Catalina said. 'That is what the Moors did in Spain, and my mother and father followed them. The Moors did not trouble themselves to change people's religions nor their language, they just brought peace and prosperity and imposed the rule of law.'

'Half of my lords would think that was heresy,' he teased her. 'And your mother and father are now imposing their religion, they have driven out the Jews already, the Moors will be next.'

She frowned. 'I know,' she said. 'And there is much suffering. But their intention was to allow people to practise their own religion. When they won Granada that was their promise.'

'D'you not think that to make one country, the people must always be of one faith?' he asked.

'Heretics can live like that,' she said decidedly. 'In al Andalus the Moors and Christians and Jews lived in peace and friendship along-side one another. But if you are a Christian king, it is your duty to bring your subjects to God.'

Catalina would watch Arthur as he talked with one man and then another, and then, at a sign from Dona Elvira, she would curtsey to her husband and withdraw from the hall. She would read her evening prayers, change into her robe for the night, sit with her ladies, go to her bedroom and wait, and wait and wait.

'You can go, I shall sleep alone tonight,' she said to Dona Elvira.

'Again?' The duenna frowned. 'You have not had a bed companion since we came to the castle. What if you wake in the night and need some service?'

'I sleep better with no-one else in the room,' Catalina would say. 'You can leave me now.'

The duenna and the ladies would bid her goodnight and leave, the maids would come and unlace her bodice, unpin her headdress, untie her shoes and pull off her stockings. They would hold out her warmed linen nightgown and she would ask for her cape and say she would sit by the fire for a few moments, and then send them away.

In the silence, as the castle settled for the night, she would wait for him. Then, at last she would hear the quiet sound of his footfall at the outer door of her room, where it opened on to the battlements that ran between his tower and hers. She would fly to the door and unbolt it, he would be pink-cheeked from the cold, his cape thrown over his own nightshirt as he tumbled in, the cold wind blowing in with him as she threw herself into his arms.

'Tell me a story.'

'Which story tonight?'

'Tell me about your family.'

'Shall I tell you about my mother when she was a girl?'

'Oh yes. Was she a princess of Castile like you?'

Catalina shook her head. 'No, not at all. She was not protected or safe. She lived in the court of her brother, her father was dead, and her brother did not love her as he should. He knew that she was his only true heir. He favoured his daughter; but everyone knew that she was a bastard, palmed off on him by his queen. She was even nicknamed by the name of the queen's lover. They called her La Beltraneja after her father. Can you think of anything more shameful?'

Arthur obediently shook his head. 'Nothing.'

'My mother was all but a prisoner at her brother's court; the queen hated her, of course, the courtiers were unfriendly and her brother was plotting to disinherit her. Even their own mother could not make him see reason.'

'Why not?' he asked, and then caught her hand when he saw the shadow cross her face. 'Ah, love, I am sorry. What is the matter?'

'Her mother was sick,' she said. 'Sick with sadness. I don't understand quite why, or why it was so very bad. But she could hardly speak or move. She could only cry.'

'So your mother had no protector?'

'No, and then the king her brother ordered that she should be betrothed to Don Pedro Giron.' She sat up a little and clasped her hands around her knees. 'They said he had sold his soul to the devil, a most wicked man. My mother swore that she would offer her soul to God and God would save her, a virgin, from such a fate. She said that surely no merciful God would take a girl like her, a princess, who had survived long years in one of the worst courts of Europe, and then throw her at the end into the arms of a man who wanted her ruin, who desired her only because she was young and untouched, who wanted to despoil her?'

Arthur hid a grin at the romantic rhythm of the story. 'You do this awfully well,' he said. 'I hope it ends happily.'

Catalina raised her hand like a troubadour calling for silence. 'Her greatest friend and lady-in-waiting Beatriz had taken up a knife and sworn that she would kill Don Pedro before he laid hands on Isabella; but my mother kneeled before her prie-dieu for three days and three nights and prayed without ceasing to be spared this rape.

'He was on his journey towards her, he would arrive the very next day. He ate well and drank well, telling his companions that tomorrow he would be in the bed of the highest-born virgin of Castile.

'But that very night he died.' Catalina's voice dropped to an awed whisper. 'Died before he had finished his wine from dinner. Dropped dead as surely as if God had reached down from the heavens and pinched the life out of him as a good gardener pinches out a greenfly.'

'Poison?' asked Arthur, who knew something of the ways of determined monarchs, and who thought Isabella of Castile quite capable of murder.

'God's will,' Catalina answered seriously. 'Don Pedro found, as everyone else has found, that God's will and my mother's desires always run together. And if you knew God and my mother as I know them, you would know that their will is always done.'

He raised his glass and drank a toast to her. 'Now that is a good story,' he said. 'I wish you could tell it in the hall.'

'And it is all true,' she reminded him. 'I know it is. My mother told me it herself.'

'So she fought for her throne too,' he said thoughtfully.

'First for her throne, and then to make the kingdom of Spain.'

He smiled. 'For all that they tell us that we are of royal blood, we both come from a line of fighters. We have our thrones by conquest.'

She raised her eyebrows. 'I come from royal blood,' she said. 'My mother has her throne by right.'

'Oh yes. But if your mother had not fought for her place in the world she would have been Dona whatever his name was –'

'Giron.'

'Giron. And you would have been born a nobody.'

Catalina shook her head. The idea was quite impossible for her to grasp. 'I should have been the daughter of the sister of the king whatever happened. I should always have had royal blood in my veins.'

'You would have been a nobody,' he said bluntly. 'A nobody with royal blood. And so would I if my father had not fought for his throne. We are both from families who claim their own.'

'Yes,' she conceded reluctantly.

'We are both the children of parents who claim what rightfully belongs to others.' He went further.

Her head came up at once. 'They do not! At least my mother did not. She was the rightful heir.'

Arthur disagreed. 'Her brother made his daughter his heir, he recognised her. Your mother had the throne by conquest. Just as my father won his.'

Her colour rose. 'She did not,' she insisted. 'She is the rightful heir to the throne. All she did was defend her right from a pretender.'

'Don't you see?' he said. 'We are all pretenders until we win. When we win, we can rewrite the history and rewrite the family trees, and execute our rivals, or imprison them, until we can argue that there was always only one true heir: ourselves. But before then, we are one of many claimants. And not even always the best claimant with the strongest claim.'

She frowned. 'What are you saying?' she demanded. 'Are you saying that I am not the true princess? That you are not the true heir to England?'

He took her hand. 'No, no. Don't be angry with me,' he soothed her. 'I am saying that we have and we hold what we claim. I am saying that we make our own inheritance. We claim what we want, we say that we are Prince of Wales, Queen of England. That we decide the name and the title we go by. Just like everyone else does.'

'You are wrong,' she said. 'I was born Infanta of Spain and I will die Queen of England. It is not a matter of choice, it is my destiny.'

He took her hand and kissed it. He saw there was no point pursuing his belief that a man or a woman could make their own destiny with their own conviction. He might have his doubts; but with her the task was already done. She had complete conviction, her destiny was made. He had no doubt that she would indeed defend it to death. Her title, her pride, her sense of self were all one. 'Katherine, Queen of England,' he said, kissing her fingers, and saw her smile return.

I love him so deeply, I did not know that I could ever love anyone like this. I can feel myself growing in patience and wisdom, just through my love for him. I step back from irritability and impatience, I even bear my homesickness without complaint. I can feel myself becoming a better woman, a better wife, as I seek to please him and make him

proud of me. I want him always to be glad that he married me. I want us always to be as happy as we are today. There are no words to describe him . . . there are no words.

A messenger came from the king's court bringing the newlyweds some gifts: a pair of deer from the Windsor forest, a parcel of books for Catalina, letters from Elizabeth the queen, and orders from My Lady the King's Mother who had heard, though no-one could imagine how, that the prince's hunt had broken down some hedges, and who commanded Arthur to make sure that they were restored and the landowner compensated.

He brought the letter to Catalina's room when he came at night. 'How can she know everything?' he demanded.

'The man will have written to her,' she said ruefully.

'Why not come direct to me?'

'Because he knows her? Is he her liege man?'

'Could be,' he said. 'She has a network of alliances like spider threads across the country.'

'You should go to see him,' Catalina decided. 'We could both go. We could take him a present, some meat or something, and pay what we owe.'

Arthur shook his head at the power of his grandmother. 'Oh yes, we can do that. But how can she know everything?'

'It's how you rule,' she said. 'Isn't it? You make sure that you know everything and that anyone with a trouble comes to you. Then they take the habit of obedience and you take the habit of command.'

He chuckled. 'I can see I have married another Margaret Beaufort,' he said. 'God help me with another one in the family.'

Catalina smiled. 'You should be warned,' she admitted. 'I am the daughter of a strong woman. Even my father does as he is bid by her.'

He put down the letter and gathered her to him. 'I have longed for you all day,' he said into the warm crook of her neck.

She opened the front of his nightshirt so she could lay her cheek against his sweet-smelling skin. 'Oh, my love.'

With one accord they moved to the bed. 'Oh, my love.'

'Tell me a story.'

'What shall I tell you tonight?'

'Tell me about how your father and mother were married. Was it arranged for them, as it was for us?'

'Oh no,' she exclaimed. 'Not at all. She was quite alone in the world, and though God had saved her from Don Pedro she was still not safe. She knew that her brother would marry her to anyone who would guarantee to keep her from inheriting his throne.

'They were dark years for her, she said that when she appealed to her mother it was like talking to the dead. My grandmother was lost in a world of her own sorrow, she could do nothing to help her own daughter.

'My mother's cousin, her only hope, was the heir to the neighbouring kingdom: Ferdinand of Aragon. He came to her in disguise. Without any servants, without any soldiers, he rode through the night and came to the castle where she was struggling to survive. He had himself brought in, and threw off his hat and cape so she saw him, and knew him at once.'

Arthur was rapt. 'Really?'

Catalina smiled. 'Isn't it like a romance? She told me that she loved him at once, fell in love on sight like a princess in a poem. He proposed marriage to her then and there, and she accepted him then and there. He fell in love with her that night, at first sight, which is something that no princess can expect. My mother, my father, were blessed by God. He moved them to love and their hearts followed their interests.'

'God looks after the kings of Spain,' Arthur remarked, half-joking.

She nodded. 'Your father was right to seek our friendship. We are making our kingdom from al Andalus, the lands of the Moorish princes. We have Castile and Aragon, now we have Granada and we will have more. My father's heart is set on Navarre, and he will not stop there. I know he is determined to have Naples. I don't think he will be satisfied until all the south and western regions of France are ours. You will see. He has not made the borders he wants for Spain yet.'

'They married in secret?' he asked, still amazed at this royal couple who had taken their lives into their own hands and made their own destiny.

She looked slightly sheepish. 'He told her he had a dispensation, but it was not properly signed. I am afraid that he tricked her.'

He frowned. 'Your wonderful father lied to his saintly wife?'

She gave a little rueful smile. 'Indeed, he will do anything to get his own way. You quickly learn it when you have dealings with him. He always thinks ahead, two, perhaps three, steps ahead. He knew my mother was devout and would not marry without the dispensation and *ole!* – there is a dispensation in her hand.'

'But they put it right later?'

'Yes, and though his father and her brother were angry, it was the right thing to do.'

'How could it be the right thing to do? To defy your family? To disobey your own father? That's a sin. It breaks a commandment. It is a cardinal sin. No Pope could bless such a marriage.'

'It was God's will,' she said confidently. 'None of them knew that it was God's will. But my mother knew. She always knows what God wills.'

'How can she be so sure? How could she be so sure then, when she was only a girl?'

She chuckled. 'God and my mother have always thought alike.'

He laughed and tweaked the lock of her hair. 'She certainly did the right thing in sending you to me.'

'She did,' Catalina said. 'And we shall do the right thing by the country.'

'Yes,' he said. 'I have such plans for us when we come to the throne.'

'What shall we do?'

Arthur hesitated. 'You will think me a child, my head filled with stories from books.'

'No I shan't. Tell me!'

'I should like to make a council, like the first Arthur did. Not like my father's council, which is just filled with his friends who fought for him, but a proper council of all the kingdom. A council of knights, one for each county. Not chosen by me because I like their company, but chosen by their own county – as the best of men to represent them. And I should like them to come to the table and each of them should know what is happening in their own county, they should report. And so if a crop is going to fail and there is going to be hunger we should know in time and send food.'

Catalina sat up, interested. 'They would be our advisors. Our eyes and ears.'

'Yes. And I should like each of them to be responsible for building defences, especially the ones in the north and on the coasts.'

'And for mustering troops once a year, so we are always ready for attack,' she added. 'They will come, you know.'

'The Moors?'

She nodded. 'They are defeated in Spain for now, but they are as strong as ever in Africa, in the Holy Lands, in Turkey and the lands beyond. When they need more land they will move again into Christendom. Once a year in the spring, the Ottoman sultan goes to war, like other men plough the fields. They will come against us. We cannot know when they will come, but we can be very certain that they will do so.'

'I want defences all along the south coast against France, and against the Moors,' Arthur said. 'A string of castles, and beacons behind them, so that when we come under attack in – say – Kent, we can know about it in London, and everyone can be warned.'

'You will need to build ships,' she said. 'My mother commissioned fighting ships from the dockyard in Venice.'

'We have our own dockyards,' he said. 'We can build our own ships.'

'How shall we raise the money for all these castles and ships?' Isabella's daughter asked the practical question.

'Partly from taxing the people,' he said. 'Partly from taxing the merchants and the people who use the ports. It is for their safety, they should pay. I know people hate the taxes but that is because they don't see what is done with the money.'

'We will need honest tax collectors,' Catalina said. 'My father says that if you can collect the taxes that are due and not lose half of them along the way it is better than a regiment of cavalry.'

'Yes, but how d'you find men that you can trust?' Arthur thought aloud. 'At the moment, any man who wants to make a fortune gets himself a post of collecting taxes. They should work for us, not for themselves. They should be paid a wage and not collect on their own account.'

'That has never been achieved by anyone but the Moors,' she said. 'The Moors in al Andalus set up schools and even universities for the sons of poor men, so that they had clerks that they could trust. And their great offices of court are always done by the young scholars, sometimes the young sons of their king.'

'Shall I take a hundred wives to get a thousand clerks for the throne?' he teased her.

'Not another single one.'

'But we have to find good men,' he said thoughtfully. 'You need loyal servants to the crown, those who owe their salary to the crown and their obedience to the crown. Otherwise they work for themselves and they take bribes and all their families become over-mighty.'

'The church could teach them,' Catalina suggested. 'Just as the imam teaches the boys for the Moors. If every parish church was as learned as a mosque with a school attached to it, if every priest knew he had to teach reading and writing, then we could found new colleges at the universities, so that boys could go on and learn more.'

'Is it possible?' he asked. 'Not just a dream?'

She nodded. 'It could be real. To make a country is the most real thing anyone can do. We will make a kingdom that we can be proud of, just as my mother and father did in Spain. We can decide how it is to be, and we can make it happen.'

'Camelot,' he said simply.

'Camelot,' she repeated.

Ludlow Castle, Spring 1502

It snowed for a sennight in February, and then came a thaw and the snow turned to slush and now it is raining again. I cannot walk in the garden, nor go out on a horse, nor even ride out into the town by mule. I have never seen such rain in my life before. It is not like our rain that falls on the hot earth and yields a rich, warm smell as the dust is laid and the plants drink up the water. But this is cold rain on cold earth, and there is no perfume and only standing pools of water with dark ice on it like a cold skin.

I miss my home with an ache of longing in these cold dark days. When I tell Arthur about Spain and the Alhambra it makes me yearn that he should see it for himself, and meet my mother and father. I want them to see him, and know our happiness. I keep wondering if his father would not allow him out of England . . . but I know I am dreaming. No king would ever let his precious son and heir out of his lands.

Then I start to wonder if I might go home for a short visit on my own. I cannot bear to be without Arthur for even a night, but then I think that unless I go to Spain alone I will never see my mother again, and the thought of that, never feeling the touch of her hand on my hair or seeing her smile at me – I don't know how I would bear to never see her again.

I am glad and proud to be Princess of Wales and the Queen of England-to-be, but I did not think, I did not realise – I know, how silly this is of me – but I did not quite understand that it would mean that I would live here forever, that I would never come home again. Somehow, although I knew I would be married to the Prince of Wales and one day be Queen of England, I did not fully understand that this would be my home now and forever; and that I may never see my mother or my father or my home again.

I expected at least that we would write, I thought I would hear from her often. But it is as she was with Isabel, with Maria, with Juana; she sends instructions through the ambassador, I have my orders as a princess of Spain. But as a mother to her daughter, I hear from her only rarely.

I don't know how to bear it. I never thought such a thing could happen. My sister Isabel came home to us after she was widowed, though she married again and had to leave again. And Juana writes to me that she will go home on a visit with her husband. It isn't fair that she should go and I not be allowed to. I am only just sixteen. I am not ready to live without my mother's advice. I am not old enough to live without a mother. I look for her every day to tell me what I should do – and she is not there.

My husband's mother, Queen Elizabeth, is a cipher in her own household. She cannot be a mother to me, she cannot command her own time, how should she advise me? It is the king's mother, Lady Margaret, who rules everything; and she is a most well-thought-of, hard-hearted woman. She cannot be a mother to me, she couldn't be a mother to anyone. She worships her son because thanks to him she is the mother of the king; but she does not love him, she has no tenderness. She does not even love Arthur and if a woman could not love him she must be utterly without a heart. Actually, I am quite sure that she dislikes me, though I don't know why she should.

And anyway, I am sure my mother must miss me as I miss her?
Surely, very soon, she will write to the king and ask him if I can come
home for a visit? Before it gets much colder here? And it is terribly cold
and wet already. I am sure I cannot stay here all the long winter. I am
sure I will be ill. I am sure she must want me to come home . . .

Catalina, seated at the table before the window, trying to catch the
failing light of a grey February afternoon, took up her letter, asking
her mother if she could come for a visit to Spain, and tore it gently
in half and then in half again and fed the pieces into the fire in her
room. It was not the first letter she had written to her mother asking
to come home, but – like the others – it would never be sent. She
would not betray her mother's training by turning tail and running
from grey skies and cold rain and people whose language no-one
could ever understand and whose joys and sorrows were a mystery.

She was not to know that even if she had sent the letter to the
Spanish ambassador in London, then that wily diplomat would have
opened it, read it, and torn it up himself, and then reported the
whole to the King of England. Rodrigo Gonsalvi de Puebla knew,
though Catalina did not yet understand, that her marriage had
forged an alliance between the emerging power of Spain and the
emerging power of England against the emerging power of France.
No homesick princess wanting her mother would be allowed to
unbalance that.

'Tell me a story.'

'I am like Scheherazade, you want a thousand stories from me.'

'Oh yes!' he said. 'I will have a thousand and one stories. How
many have you told me already?'

'I have told you a story every night since we were together, that first night, at Burford,' she said.

'Forty-nine days,' he said.

'Only forty-nine stories. If I was Scheherazade I would have nine hundred and fifty-two to go.'

He smiled at her. 'Do you know, Catalina, I have been happier in these forty-nine days than ever in my life before?'

She took his hand and put it to her lips.

'And the nights!'

Her eyes darkened with desire. 'Yes, the nights,' she said quietly.

'I long for every nine hundred and fifty-two more,' he said. 'And then I will have another thousand after that.'

'And a thousand after that?'

'And a thousand after that forever and ever until we are both dead.'

She smiled. 'Pray God we have long years together,' she said tenderly.

'So what will you tell me tonight?'

She thought. 'I shall tell you of a Moor's poem.'

Arthur settled back against the pillows as she leaned forwards and fixed her blue gaze on the curtains of the bed, as if she could see beyond them, to somewhere else.

'He was born in the deserts of Arabia,' she explained. 'So when he came to Spain he missed everything about his home. He wrote this poem.

> "*A palm tree stands in the middle of Rusafa,*
> *Born in the west, far from the land of palms.*
> *I said to it: How like me you are, far away and in exile*
> *In long separation from your family and friends.*
> *You have sprung from soil in which you are a stranger*
> *And I, like you, am far from home.*"'

He was silent, taking in the simplicity of the poem. 'It is not like our poetry,' he said.

'No,' she replied quietly. 'They are a people who have a great love of words, they love to say a true thing simply.'

He opened his arms to her and she slid alongside him so that they were lying, thigh to thigh, side to side. He touched her face, her cheek was wet.

'Oh my love! Tears?'

She said nothing.

'I know that you miss your home,' he said softly, taking her hand in his and kissing the fingertips. 'But you will become accustomed to your life here, to your thousand, thousand days here.'

'I am happy with you,' Catalina said quickly. 'It is just . . .' Her voice trailed away. 'My mother,' she said, her voice very small. 'I miss her. And I worry about her. Because . . . I am the youngest, you see. And she kept me with her as long as she could.'

'She knew you would have to leave.'

'She's been much . . . tried. She lost her son, my brother, Juan, and he was our only heir. It is so terrible to lose a prince, you cannot imagine how terrible it is to lose a prince. It is not just the loss of him, but the loss of everything that might have been. His life has gone, but his reign and his future have gone too. His wife will no longer be queen, everything that he hoped for will not happen. And then the next heir, little Miguel, died at only two years old. He was all we had left of my sister Isabel, his mother, and then it pleased God to take him from us too. Poor Maria died far away from us in Portugal, she went away to be married and we never saw her again. It was natural that my mother kept me with her for comfort. I was her last child to leave home. And now I don't know how she will manage without me.'

Arthur put his arm around her shoulders and drew her close. 'God will comfort her.'

'She will be so lonely,' she said in a little voice.

'Surely she, of all women in the world, feels God's comfort?'

'I don't think she always does,' Catalina said. 'Her own mother was tormented by sadness, you know. Many of the women of our family can get quite sick with sorrow. I know that my mother fears sinking into sadness just like her mother: a woman who saw things so darkly that she would rather have been blind. I know she fears that she will never be happy again. I know that she liked to have me with her so that I could make her happy. She said that I was a child born for joy, that she could tell that I would always be happy.'

'Does your father not comfort her?'

'Yes,' she said uncertainly. 'But he is often away from her. And anyway, I should like to be with her. But you must know how I feel. Didn't you miss your mother when you were first sent away? And your father and your sisters and your brother?'

'I miss my sisters; but not my brother,' he said so decidedly that she had to laugh.

'Why not? I thought he was such fun.'

'He is a braggart,' Arthur said irritably. 'He is always pushing himself forwards. Look at our wedding, he had to be at the centre of the stage all the time, look at our wedding feast when he had to dance so that all eyes were on him. Pulling Margaret up to dance and making a performance of himself.'

'Oh no! It was just that your father told him to dance, and he was merry. He's just a boy.'

'He wants to be a man. He tries to be a man, he makes a fool of all of us when he tries. And nobody ever checks him! Did you not see how he looked at you?'

'I saw nothing at all,' she said truthfully. 'It was all a blur for me.'

'He fancies himself in love with you, and dreamed that he was walking you up the aisle on his own account.'

She laughed. 'Oh! How silly!'

'He's always been like that,' he said resentfully. 'And because he is the favourite of everyone he is allowed to say and do exactly as he wants. I have to learn the law, and languages, and I have to live here and prepare myself for the crown; but Harry stays at Greenwich or Whitehall at the centre of court as if he were an ambassador; not an heir who should be trained. He has to have a horse when I have a horse – though I had been kept on a steady palfrey for years. He has a falcon when I have my first falcon – nobody makes him train a kestrel and then a goshawk for year after year, then he has to have my tutor and tries to outstrip me, tries to outshine me whenever he can, and always takes the eye.'

Catalina saw he was genuinely irritated. 'But he is only a second son,' she observed.

'He is everyone's favourite,' Arthur said glumly. 'He has everything for the asking and everything comes easily to him.'

'He is not the Prince of Wales,' she pointed out. 'He may be liked; but he is not important. He only stays at court because he is not important enough to be sent here. He does not have his own Principality. Your father will have plans for him. He will probably be married and sent away. A second son is no more important than a daughter.'

'He is to go into the church,' he said. 'He is to be a priest. Who would marry him? So he will be in England forever. I daresay I shall have to endure him as my archbishop, if he does not manage to make himself Pope.'

Catalina laughed at the thought of the flushed-faced blond, bright boy as Pope. 'How grand we shall all be when we are grown up,' she said. 'You and me, King and Queen of England, and Harry, archbishop; perhaps even a cardinal.'

'Harry won't ever grow up,' he insisted. 'He will always be a selfish boy. And because my grandmother – and my father – have always given him whatever he wanted, just for the asking, he will be a greedy, difficult boy.'

'Perhaps he will change,' she said. 'When my oldest sister, poor Isabel, went away to Portugal the first time, you would have thought her the vainest, most worldly girl you could imagine. But when her husband died and she came home she cared for nothing but to go into a convent. Her heart was quite broken.'

'Nobody will break Harry's heart,' his older brother asserted. 'He hasn't got one.'

'You'd have thought the same of Isabel,' Catalina argued. 'But she fell in love with her husband on her wedding day and she said she would never love again. She had to marry for the second time, of course. But she married unwillingly.'

'And did you?' he asked, his mood suddenly changing.

'Did I what? Marry unwillingly?'

'No! Fall in love with your husband on your wedding day?'

'Certainly not on my wedding day,' she said. 'Talk about a boastful boy! Harry is nothing to you! I heard you tell them all the next morning that having a wife was very good sport.'

Arthur had the grace to look abashed. 'I may have said something in jest.'

'That you had been in Spain all night?'

'Oh, Catalina. Forgive me. I knew nothing. You are right, I was a boy. But I am a man now, your husband. And you did fall in love with your husband. So don't deny it.'

'Not for days and days,' she said dampeningly. 'It was not love at first sight at all.'

'I know when it was, so you can't tease me. It was the evening at Burford when you had been crying and I kissed you for the first time properly, and I wiped your tears away with my sleeves. And then that night I came to you, and the house was so quiet that it was as if we were the only people alive in the whole world.'

She snuggled closer into his arms. 'And I told you my first story,' she said. 'But do you remember what it was?'

'It was the story of the fire at Santa Fe,' he said. 'When the luck was against the Spanish for once.'

She nodded. 'Normally, it was us who brought fire and the sword. My father has a reputation of being merciless.'

'Your father was merciless? Though it was land he was claiming for his own? How did he hope to bring the people to his will?'

'By fear,' she said simply. 'And anyway, it was not his will. It was God's will, and sometimes God is merciless. This was not an ordinary war, it was a crusade. Crusades are cruel.'

He nodded.

'They had a song about my father's advance. The Moors had a song.'

She threw back her head and in a haunting, low voice, translating the words into French, she sang to him:

> 'Riders gallop through the Elvira gate, up to the Alhambra,
> Fearful tidings they bring the king,
> Ferdinand himself leads an army, flower of Spain,
> Along the banks of the Jenil; with him comes
> Isabel, Queen with the heart of a man.'

Arthur was delighted. 'Sing it again!'

She laughed and sang again.

'And they really called her that: "Queen with the heart of a man"?'

'Father says that when she was in camp it was better than two battalions for strengthening our troops and frightening the Moors. In all the battles they fought, she was never defeated. The army never lost a battle when she was there.'

'To be a king like that! To have them write songs about you.'

'I know,' Catalina said. 'To have a legend for a mother! It's not surprising I miss her. In those days she was never afraid of anything. When the fire would have destroyed us, she was not afraid then. Not of the flames in the night and not of defeat. Even when my father and all the advisors agreed that we would have to pull back to Toledo and re-arm, come again next year, my mother said no.'

'Does she argue with him in public?' Arthur asked, fascinated at the thought of a wife who was not a subject.

'She does not exactly argue,' she said thoughtfully. 'She would never contradict him or disrespect him. But he knows very well when she doesn't agree with him. And mostly, they do it her way.'

He shook his head.

'I know what you're thinking, a wife should obey. She would say so herself. But the difficulty is that she's always right,' said her daughter. 'All the times I can think of, whenever it has been a great question as to whether the army should go on, or whether something can be done. It's as if God advises her, it really is; she knows best what should be done. Even Father knows that she knows best.'

'She must be an extraordinary woman.'

'She is queen,' Catalina said simply. 'Queen in her own right. Not a mere queen by marriage, not a commoner raised to be queen. She was born a princess of Spain like me. Born to be a queen. Saved by God from the most terrible dangers to be Queen of Spain. What else should she do but command her kingdom?'

That night I dream I am a bird, an apus, a swift, flying high and fearless over the kingdom of new Castile, south from Toledo, over Cordoba, south to the kingdom of Granada; the ground below me laid out like a tawny carpet, woven from the gold-fleeced sheep of the Berbers, the brass earth pierced by bronze cliffs, the hills so high that not even olive trees can cling to their steep slopes. On I fly, my little bird-heart thudding until I see the rosy walls of the Alcazar, the great fort which encloses the palace of the Alhambra, and flying low and fast, I skim the brutal squareness of the watchtower where the flag of the sickle moon once waved, to plunge down towards the Court of Myrtles to fly round and around in the warm air, enclosed by dainty buildings of stucco and tile, looking down on the mirror of water, and seeing at last the one I am looking for: my mother, Isabella of Spain,

walking in the warm evening air, and thinking of her daughter in faraway England.

Ludlow Castle, March 1502

'I want to ask you to meet a lady who is a good friend of mine and is ready to be a friend of yours,' Arthur said, choosing his words with care.

Catalina's ladies-in-waiting, bored on a cold afternoon with no entertainment, craned forwards to listen while trying to appear engaged in their needlework.

At once she blanched as white as the linen she was embroidering. 'My lord?' she asked anxiously. He had said nothing of this in the early hours of the morning when they had woken and made love. She had not expected to see him until dinner. His arrival in her rooms signalled that something had happened. She was wary, waiting to know what was going on.

'A lady? Who is she?'

'You may have heard of her from others, but I beg you to remember that she is eager to be your friend, and she has always been a good friend to me.'

Catalina's head flew up, she took a breath. For a moment, for a dreadful moment, she thought that he was introducing a former mistress into her court, begging a place among ladies-in-waiting for some woman who had been his lover, so that they might continue their affair.

If this is what he is doing, I know what part I must play. I have seen my mother haunted by the pretty girls that my father, God forgive him,

cannot resist. Again and again we would see him pay attention to some new face at court. Each time my mother behaved as if she had noticed nothing, dowered the girl handsomely, married her off to an eligible courtier, and encouraged him to take his new bride far, far away. It was such a common occurrence that it became a joke: that if a girl wanted to marry well with the queen's blessing, and travel to some remote province, all she had to do was to catch the eye of the king, and in no time she would find herself riding away from the Alhambra on a fine new horse with a set of new clothes.

I know that a sensible woman looks the other way and tries to bear her hurt and humiliation when her husband chooses to take another woman to his bed. What she must not do, what she absolutely must never do, is behave like my sister Juana, who shames herself and all of us by giving way to screaming fits, hysterical tears, and threats of revenge.

'It does no good,' my mother once told me when one of the ambassadors relayed to us some awful scene at Philip's court in the Netherlands: Juana threatening to cut off the woman's hair, attacking her with a pair of scissors, and then swearing she would stab herself.

'It only makes it worse to complain. If a husband goes astray you will have to take him back into your life and into your bed, whatever he has done; there is no escape from marriage. If you are queen and he is king you have to deal together. If he forgets his duty to you, that is no reason to forget yours to him. However painful, you are always his queen and he is always your husband.'

'Whatever he does?' I asked her. 'However he behaves? He is free though you are bound?'

She shrugged. 'Whatever he does cannot break the marriage bond. You are married in the sight of God: he is always your husband, you are always queen. Those whom God has joined together, no man can put asunder. Whatever pain your husband brings you, he is still your husband. He may be a bad husband; but he is still your husband.'

'What if he wants another?' I asked, sharp in my young girl's curiosity.

'If he wants another he can have her or she can refuse him, that is *between them. That is for her and her conscience,' my mother had said steadily. 'What must not change is you. Whatever he says, whatever she wants: you are still his wife and his queen.'*

Catalina summoned this bleak counsel and faced her young husband. 'I am always glad to meet a friend of yours, my lord,' she said levelly, hoping that her voice did not quaver at all. 'But, as you know, I have only a small household. Your father was very clear that I am not allowed any more companions than I have at present. As you know, he does not pay me any allowance. I have no money to pay another lady for her service. In short, I cannot add any lady, even a special friend of yours, to my court.'

Arthur flinched at the reminder of his father's mean haggling over her train. 'Oh no, you mistake me. It is not a friend who wants a place. She would not be one of your ladies-in-waiting,' he said hastily. 'It is Lady Margaret Pole, who is waiting to meet you. She has come home here at last.'

Holy Mary, Mother of God, pray for us. This is worse than if it was his mistress. I knew I would have to face her one day. This is her home, but she was away when we got here and I thought she had deliberately snubbed me by being away and staying away. I thought she was avoiding me out of hatred, as I would avoid her from shame. Lady Margaret Pole is sister to that poor boy, the Duke of Warwick, beheaded to make the succession safe for me, and for my line. I have been dreading the moment when I would have to meet her. I have been praying to the saints that she would stay away, hating me, blaming me, but keeping her distance.

Arthur saw her quick gesture of rejection, but he had known of no way to prepare her for this. 'Please,' he said hurriedly. 'She has been away caring for her children or she would have been here with her husband to welcome you to the castle when we first arrived. I told you she would return. She wants to greet you now. We all have to live together here. Sir Richard is a trusted friend of my father, the lord of my council and the warden of this castle. We will all have to live together.'

Catalina put out a shaking hand to him and at once he came closer, ignoring the fascinated attention of her ladies.

'I cannot meet her,' she whispered. 'Truly, I can't. I know that her brother was put to death for my sake. I know my parents insisted on it, before they would send me to England. I know he was innocent, innocent as a flower, kept in the Tower by your father so that men should not gather round him and claim the throne in his name. He could have lived there in safety all his life but for my parents demanding his death. She must hate me.'

'She doesn't hate you,' he said truthfully. 'Believe me, Catalina, I would not expose you to anyone's unkindness. She does not hate you, she doesn't hate me, she doesn't even hate my father who ordered the execution. She knows that these things happen. She is a princess, she knows as well as you do that it is not choice but policy that governs us. It was not your choice, nor mine. She knows that your father and mother had to be sure that there were no rival princes to claim the throne, that my father would clear my way, whatever it cost him. She is resigned.'

'Resigned?' she gasped incredulously. 'How can a woman be resigned to the murder of her brother, the heir of the family? How can she greet me with friendship when he died for my convenience? When we lost my brother our world ended, our hopes died with him. Our future was buried with him. My mother, who is a living saint, still cannot bear it. She has not been happy since the day of his death. It is unbearable to her. If he had been executed for some stranger I swear she would have taken a life in return. How could Lady Margaret lose her brother and bear it? How can she bear me?'

'She has resignation,' he said simply. 'She is a most spiritual woman and if she looked for reward, she has one in that she is married to Sir Richard Pole, a man most trusted by my father, and she lives here in the highest regard and she is my friend and I hope will be yours.'

He took her hand and felt it tremble. 'Come, Catalina. This isn't like you. Be brave, my love. She won't blame you.'

'She must blame me,' she said in an anguished whisper. 'My parents insisted that there should be no doubt over your inheritance. I know they did. Your own father promised that there would be no rival princes. They knew what he meant to do. They did not tell him to leave an innocent man with his life. They let him do it. They wanted him to do it. Edward Plantagenet's blood is on my head. Our marriage is under the curse of his death.'

Arthur recoiled, he had never before seen her so distressed. 'My God, Catalina, you cannot call us accursed.'

She nodded miserably.

'You have never spoken of this.'

'I could not bear to say it.'

'But you have thought it?'

'From the moment they told me that he was put to death for my sake.'

'My love, you cannot really think that we are accursed?'

'In this one thing.'

He tried to laugh off her intensity. 'No. You must know we are blessed.' He drew closer and said very quietly, so that no-one else could hear, 'Every morning when you wake in my arms, do you feel accursed then?'

'No,' she said unwillingly. 'No, I don't.'

'Every night when I come to your rooms, do you feel the shadow of sin upon you?'

'No,' she conceded.

'We are not cursed,' he said firmly. 'We are blessed with God's favour. Catalina, my love, trust me. She has forgiven my father, she certainly would never blame you. I swear to you, she is a woman with a heart as big as a cathedral. She wants to meet you. Come with me and let me present her to you.'

'Alone then,' she said, still fearing some terrible scene.

'Alone. She is in the castle warden's rooms now. If you come at once, we can leave them all here, and go quietly by ourselves and see her.'

She rose from her seat and put her hand on the crook of his arm. 'I am walking alone with the princess,' Arthur said to her ladies. 'You can all stay here.'

They looked surprised to be excluded, and some of them were openly disappointed. Catalina went past them without looking up.

Once out of the door he preceded her down the tight spiral staircase, one hand on the central stone post, one on the wall. Catalina followed him, lingering at every deep-set arrowslit window, looking down into the valley where the Teme had burst its banks and was like a silver lake over the water meadows. It was cold, even for March in the Borders, and Catalina shivered as if a stranger was walking on her grave.

'My love,' he said, looking back up the narrow stairs towards her. 'Courage. Your mother would have courage.'

'She ordered this thing,' she said crossly. 'She thought it was for my benefit. But a man died for her ambition, and now I have to face his sister.'

'She did it for you,' he reminded her. 'And nobody blames you.' They came to the floor below the princess's suite of rooms and without hesitation, Arthur tapped on the thick wooden door of the warden's apartments and went in.

The square room overlooking the valley was the match of Catalina's presence chamber upstairs, panelled with wood and hung with bright tapestries. There was a lady waiting for them, seated by the fireside, and when the door opened she rose. She was dressed in a pale grey gown with a grey hood on her hair. She was about thirty years of age; she looked at Catalina with friendly interest, and then she sank into a deep, respectful curtsey.

Disobeying the nip of his bride's fingers, Arthur withdrew his arm and stepped back as far as the doorway. Catalina looked back at him reproachfully and then bobbed a small curtsey to the older woman. They rose up together.

'I am so pleased to meet you,' Lady Pole said sweetly. 'And I am sorry not to have been here to greet you. But one of my children was ill and I went to make sure that he was well nursed.'

'Your husband has been very kind,' Catalina managed to say.

'I hope so, for I left him a long list of commandments; I so wanted your rooms to be warm and comfortable. You must tell me if there is anything you would like. I don't know Spain, so I didn't know what things would give you pleasure.'

'No! It is all . . . absolutely.'

The older woman looked at the princess. 'Then I hope you will be very happy here with us,' she said.

'I hope to . . .' Catalina breathed. 'But I . . . I . . .'

'Yes?'

'I was very sorry to hear of the death of your brother.' Catalina dived in. Her face, which had been white with discomfort, now flushed scarlet. She could feel her ears burning, and to her horror she heard her voice tremble. 'Indeed, I was very sorry. Very . . .'

'It was a great loss to me, and to mine,' the woman said steadily. 'But it is the way of the world.'

'I am afraid that my coming . . .'

'I never thought that it was any choice or any fault of yours, Princess. When our dear Prince Arthur was to be married his father was bound to make sure that his inheritance was secured. I know that my brother would never have threatened the peace of the

Tudors, but they were not to know that. And he was ill-advised by a mischievous young man, drawn into some foolish plot . . .' She broke off as her voice shook; but rapidly she recovered herself. 'Forgive me. It still grieves me. He was an innocent, my brother. His silly plotting was proof of his innocence, not of his guilt. There is no doubt in my mind that he is in God's keeping now, with all innocents.'

She smiled at the princess. 'In this world, we women often find that we have no power over what men do. I am sure you would have wished my brother no harm, and indeed, I am sure that he would not have stood against you or against our dearest prince here – but it is the way of the world that harsh measures are sometimes taken. My father made some bad choices in his life, and God knows he paid for them in full. His son, though innocent, went the way of his father. A turn of the coin and it could all have been different. I think a woman has to learn to live with the turn of the coin even when it falls against her.'

Catalina was listening intently. 'I know my mother and father wanted to be sure that the Tudor line was without challenge,' she breathed. 'I know that they told the king.' She felt as if she had to make sure that this woman knew the depth of her guilt.

'As I might have done if I had been them,' Lady Margaret said simply. 'Princess, I do not blame you, nor your mother or father. I do not blame our great king. Were I any one of them, I might have behaved just as they have done, and explained myself only to God. All I have to do, since I am not one of these great people but merely the humble wife to a fine man, is to take care how I behave, and how I will explain myself to God.'

'I felt that I came to this country with his death on my conscience,' Catalina admitted in a sudden rush.

The older woman shook her head. 'His death is not on your conscience,' she said firmly. 'And it is wrong to blame yourself for another's doing. Indeed, I would think your confessor would tell you: it is a form of pride. Let that be the sin that you confess, you need not take the blame for the sins of others.'

Catalina looked up for the first time and met the steady eyes of Lady Pole, and saw her smile. Cautiously she smiled back, and the older woman stretched out her hand, as a man would offer to shake on a bargain. 'You see,' she said pleasantly. 'I was a Princess Royal myself once. I was the last Plantagenet princess, raised by King Richard in his nursery with his son. Of all the women in the world, I should know that there is more to life than a woman can ever control. There is the will of your husband, and of your parents, and of your king, and of your God. Nobody could blame a princess for the doings of a king. How could one ever challenge it? Or make any difference? Our way has to be obedience.'

Catalina, her hand in the warm, firm grasp, felt wonderfully reassured. 'I am afraid I am not always very obedient,' she confessed.

The older woman laughed. 'Oh yes, for one would be a fool not to think for oneself,' she allowed. 'True obedience can only happen when you secretly think you know better, and you choose to bow your head. Anything short of that is just agreement, and any ninny-in-waiting can agree. Don't you think?'

And Catalina, giggling with an English woman for the first time, laughed aloud and said: 'I never wanted to be a ninny-in-waiting.'

'Neither did I,' gleamed Margaret Pole, who had been a Plantagenet, a Princess Royal and was now a mere wife buried in the fastness of the Tudor Borders. 'I always know that I am myself, in my heart, whatever title I am given.'

I am so surprised to find that the woman whose presence I have dreaded is making the castle at Ludlow feel like a home for me. Lady Margaret Pole is a companion and friend to comfort me for the loss of my mother and sisters. I realise now that I have always lived in a

world dominated by women: the queen my mother, my sisters, our ladies- and maids-in-waiting, and all the women servants of the seraglio. In the Alhambra we lived almost withdrawn from men, in rooms built for the pleasure and comfort of women. We lived almost in seclusion, in the privacy of the cool rooms, and ran through the courtyards and leaned on the balconies secure in the knowledge that half the palace was exclusively in the ownership of us women.

We would attend the court with my father, we were not hidden from sight; but the natural desire of women for privacy was served and emphasised by the design of the Alhambra where the prettiest rooms and the best gardens were reserved for us.

It is strange to come to England and find the world dominated by men. Of course I have my rooms and my ladies, but any man can come and ask for admittance at any time. Sir Richard Pole or any other of Arthur's gentlemen can come to my rooms without notice and think that they are paying me a compliment. The English seem to think it right and normal that men and women should mix. I have not yet seen a house with rooms that are exclusive to women, and no woman goes veiled as we sometimes did in Spain, not even when travelling, not even among strangers.

Even the royal family is open to all. Men, even strangers, can stroll through the royal palaces as long as they are smart enough for the guards to admit them. They can wait around in the queen's presence chamber and see her any time she walks by, staring at her as if they were family. The great hall, the chapel, the queen's public rooms are open to anyone who can find a good hat and a cape and pass as gentry. The English treat women as if they are boys or servants, they can go anywhere, they can be looked at by anyone. For a while I thought this was a great freedom, and for a while I revelled in it; then I realised the English women may show their faces but they are not bold like men, they are not free like boys; they still have to remain silent and obey.

Now with Lady Margaret Pole returned to the warden's rooms it feels as if this castle has come under the rule of women. The evenings in the hall are less hearty, even the food at dinner has changed. The troubadours sing of love and less of battles, there is more French spoken and less Welsh.

My rooms are above, and hers are on the floor below, and we go up and down stairs all day to see each other. When Arthur and Sir Richard are out hunting, the castle's mistress is still at home and the place does not feel empty any more. Somehow, she makes it a lady's castle, just by being here. When Arthur is away, the life of the castle is not silent, waiting for his return. It is a warm, happy place, busy in its own day's work.

I have missed having an older woman to be my friend. Maria de Salinas is a girl as young and silly as I am, she is a companion, not a mentor. Dona Elvira was nominated by my mother the queen to stand in a mother's place for me; but she is not a woman I can warm to, though I have tried to love her. She is strict with me, jealous of her influence over me, ambitious to run the whole court. She and her husband, who commands my household, want to dominate my life. Since that first evening at Dogmersfield when she contradicted the king himself, I have doubted her judgement. Even now she continually cautions me against becoming too close with Arthur, as if it were wrong to love a husband, as if I could resist him! She wants to make a little Spain in England, she wants me to still be the Infanta. But I am certain that my way ahead in England is to become English.

Dona Elvira will not learn English. She affects not to be able to understand French when it is spoken with an English accent. The Welsh she treats with absolute contempt as barbarians on the very edge of civilisation, which is not very comfortable when we are visiting the townspeople of Ludlow. To be honest, sometimes she behaves more grandly than any woman I have ever known, she is prouder than my mother herself. She is certainly grander than me. I have to admire her, but I cannot truly love her.

But Margaret Pole was educated as the niece of a king and is as

fluent in Latin as me. We speak French easily together, she is teaching
me English, and when we come across a word we don't know in any
of our shared languages, we compose great mimes that set us wailing
with giggles. I made her cry with laughing when I tried to demon-
strate indigestion, and the guards came running, thinking we were
under attack when she used all the ladies of the court and their maid-
servants to demonstrate to me the correct protocol for an English hunt
in the field.

With Margaret, Catalina thought she could raise the question of her
future, and her father-in-law of whom she was frankly nervous.

'He was displeased before we came away,' she said. 'It is the question of the dowry.'

'Oh, yes?' Margaret replied. The two women were seated in a
window, waiting for the men to come back from hunting. It was
bitterly cold and damp outside, neither of them had wanted to go
out. Margaret thought it better to volunteer nothing about the vexed
question of Catalina's dowry; she had already heard from her husband
that the Spanish king had perfected the art of double dealing. He
had agreed a substantial dowry for the Infanta, but then sent her to
England with only half the money. The rest, he suggested, could be
made up with the plate and treasure that she brought as her household goods. Outraged, King Henry had demanded the full amount.
Sweetly Ferdinand of Spain replied that the Infanta's household had
been supplied with the very best, Henry could take his pick.

It was a bad way to start a marriage that was, in any case, founded
only on greed and ambition, and a shared fear of France. Catalina
was caught between the determination of two cold-hearted men.
Margaret guessed that one of the reasons that Catalina had been
sent to Ludlow Castle with her husband was to force her to use her
own household goods and so diminish their value. If King Henry

had kept her at court in Windsor or Greenwich or Westminster, she would have eaten off his plates and her father could have argued that the Spanish plate was as good as new, and must be taken as the dowry. But now, every night they ate from Catalina's gold plates and every scrape of a careless knife knocked a little off the value. When it was time to pay the second half of the dowry, the King of Spain would find he would have to pay cash. King Ferdinand might be a hard man and a cunning negotiator but he had met his match in Henry Tudor of England.

'He said that I should be a daughter to him,' Catalina started carefully. 'But I cannot obey him as a daughter should, if I am to obey my own father. My father tells me not to use my plate and to give it to the king. But he won't accept it. And since the dowry is unpaid the king sends me away with no provision, he doesn't even pay my allowance.'

'Does the Spanish ambassador not advise you?'

Catalina made a little face. 'He is the king's own man,' she said. 'No help to me. I don't like him. He is a Jew, but converted. An adaptable man. A Spaniard, but he has lived here for years. He is become a man for the Tudors, not for Aragon. I shall tell my father that he is poorly served by Dr de Puebla, but in the meantime, I have no good advice, and in my household Dona Elvira and my treasurer never stop quarrelling. She says that my goods and my treasure must be loaned to the goldsmiths to raise money, he says he will not let them out of his sight until they are paid to the king.'

'And have you not asked the prince what you should do?'

Catalina hesitated. 'It is a matter between his father and my father,' she said cautiously. 'I didn't want to let it disturb us. He has paid for all my travelling expenses here. He is going to have to pay for my ladies' wages at midsummer, and soon I will need new gowns. I don't want to ask him for money. I don't want him to think me greedy.'

'You love him, don't you?' Margaret asked, smiling, and watched the younger woman's face light up.

'Oh yes,' the girl breathed. 'I do love him so.'

The older woman smiled. 'You are blessed,' she said gently. 'To be a princess and to find love with the husband you are ordered to marry. You are blessed, Catalina.'

'I know. I do think it is a sign of God's especial favour to me.'

The older woman paused at the grandness of the claim, but did not correct her. The confidence of youth would wear away soon enough without any need for warnings. 'And do you have any signs?'

Catalina looked puzzled.

'Of a child coming? You do know what to look for?'

The young woman blushed. 'I do know. My mother told me. There are no signs yet.'

'It's early days,' Lady Margaret said comfortingly. 'But if you had a child on the way I think there would be no difficulty with a dowry. I think nothing would be too good for you if you were carrying the next Tudor prince.'

'I ought to be paid my allowance whether I have a child or not,' Catalina observed. 'I am Princess of Wales, I should have an allowance to keep my state.'

'Yes,' said Margaret drily. 'But who is going to tell the king that?'

'Tell me a story.'

They were bathed in the dappled gold of candlelight and fire-light. It was midnight and the castle was silent but for their low voices, all the lights were out but for the blaze of Catalina's chambers where the two young lovers were resisting sleep.

'What shall I tell you about?'

'Tell me a story about the Moors.'

She thought for a moment, throwing a shawl around her bare shoulders against the cold. Arthur was sprawled across the bed but when she moved he gathered her to him so her head rested on his naked chest. He ran his hand through her rich red hair and gathered it into his fist.

'I will tell you a story about one of the sultanas,' she said. 'It is not a story. It is true. She was in the harem; you know that the women live apart from the men in their own rooms?'

He nodded, watching the candlelight flicker on her neck, on the hollow at her collarbone.

'She looked out of the window and the tidal river beneath her window was at low ebb. The poor children of the town were playing in the water. They were on the slipway for the boats and they had spread mud all around and they were slipping and sliding, skating in the mud. She laughed while she watched them and she said to her ladies how she wished that she could play like that.'

'But she couldn't go out?'

'No, she could never go out. Her ladies told the eunuchs who guarded the harem and they told the Grand Vizier and he told the sultan, and when she left the window and went to her presence chamber, guess what?'

He shook his head, smiling. 'What?'

'Her presence chamber was a great marble hall. The floor was made of rose-veined marble. The sultan had ordered them to bring great flasks of perfumed oils and pour them on the floor. All the perfumiers in the town had been ordered to bring oil of roses to the palace. They had brought rose petals and sweet-smelling herbs and they had made a thick paste of oil of roses and rose petals and herbs and spread it, one foot thick, all across the floor of her presence chamber. The sultana and her ladies stripped to their chemises and slid and played in the mud, threw rose water and petals and all the afternoon played like the mudlarks.'

He was entranced. 'How glorious.'

She smiled up at him. 'Now it is your turn. You tell me a story.'

'I have no stories like that. It is all fighting and winning.'

'Those are the stories you like best when I tell them,' she pointed out.

'I do. And now your father is going to war again.'

'He is?'

'Did you not know?'

Catalina shook her head. 'The Spanish ambassador sometimes sends me a note with the news, but he has told me nothing. Is it a crusade?'

'You are a bloodthirsty soldier of Christ. I should think the infidels shake in their sandals. No, it is not a crusade. It is a far less heroic cause. Your father, rather surprisingly to us, has made an alliance with King Louis of France. Apparently they plan to invade Italy together and share the spoils.'

'King Louis?' she asked in surprise. 'Never! I had thought they would be enemies until death.'

'Well, it seems that the French king does not care who he allies with. First the Turks and now your father.'

'Well, better that King Louis makes alliance with my father than with the Turks,' she said stoutly. 'Anything is better than they are invited in.'

'But why would your father join with our enemy?'

'He has always wanted Naples,' she confided to him. 'Naples and Navarre. One way or another he will have them. King Louis may think he has an ally but there will be a high price to pay. I know him. He plays a long game but he usually gets his own way. Who sent you the news?'

'My father. I think he is vexed not to be in their counsel. He fears the French worse only than the Scots. It is a disappointment for us that your father would ally with them on anything.'

'On the contrary, your father should be pleased that my father is keeping the French busy in the south. My father is doing him a service.'

He laughed at her. 'You are a great help.'

'Will your father not join with them?'

Arthur shook his head. 'Perhaps, but his one great desire is to

156

keep England at peace. War is a terrible thing for a country. You are a soldier's daughter and you should know. My father says it is a terrible thing to see a country at war.'

'Your father only fought one big battle,' she said. 'Sometimes you have to fight. Sometimes you have to beat your enemy.'

'I wouldn't fight to gain land,' he said. 'But I would fight to defend our borders. And I think we will have to fight against the Scots unless my sister can change their very nature.'

'And is your father prepared for war?'

'He has the Howard family to keep the north for him,' he said. 'And he has the trust of every northern landlord. He has reinforced the castles and he keeps the Great North Road open so that he can get his soldiers up there if needs be.'

Catalina looked thoughtful. 'If he has to fight he would do better to invade them,' she said. 'Then he can choose the time and the place to fight and not be forced into defence.'

'Is that the better way?'

She nodded. 'My father would say so. It is everything to have your army moving forwards and confident. You have the wealth of the country ahead of you, for your supplies; you have the movement forwards: soldiers like to feel that they are making progress. There is nothing worse than being forced to turn and fight.'

'You are a tactician,' he said. 'I wish to God I had your childhood and knew the things you know.'

'You do have,' she said sweetly. 'For everything I know is yours, and everything I am is yours. And if you and our country ever need me to fight for you then I will be there.'

It has become colder and colder and the long week of rain has turned into showers of hail and now snow. Even so it is not bright, cold wintry weather but a low, damp mist with swirling cloud and flurries of slush

which clings in clumps to trees and turrets and sits in the river like old sherbet.

When Arthur comes to my room he slips along the battlements like a skater and this morning, as he went back to his room, we were certain we would be discovered because he slid on fresh ice and fell and cursed so loud that the sentry on the next tower put his head out and shouted 'Who goes there?' and I had to call back that it was only me, feeding the winter birds. So Arthur whistled at me and told me it was the call of a robin and we both laughed so much that we could barely stand. I am certain that the sentry knew anyway, but it was so cold he did not come out.

Now today Arthur has gone out riding with his council, who want to look at a site for a new corn mill while the river is in spate and partly blocked by snow and ice, and Lady Margaret and I are staying at home and playing cards.

It is cold and grey, it is wet all the time, even the walls of the castle weep with icy moisture, but I am happy. I love him, I would live with him anywhere, and spring will come and then summer. I know we will be happy then too.

The tap on the door came late at night. She threw it open.

'Ah love, my love! Where have you been?'

He stepped into the room and kissed her. She could taste the wine on his breath. 'They would not leave,' he said. 'I have been trying to get away to be with you for three hours at the very least.'

He picked her up off her feet and carried her to the bed. 'But Arthur, don't you want . . . ?'

'I want you.'

'Tell me a story.'

'Are you not sleepy now?'

'No. I want you to sing me the song about the Moors losing the battle of Malaga.'

Catalina laughed. 'It was the battle of Alhama. I shall sing you some of the verses; but it goes on and on.'

'Sing me all of them.'

'We would need all night,' she protested.

'We have all night, thank God,' he said, joy in his voice. 'We have all night and we have every night for the rest of our lives, thank God for it.'

'It is a forbidden song,' she said. 'Forbidden by my mother herself.'

'So how did you learn it?' Arthur demanded, instantly diverted.

'Servants,' she said carelessly. 'I had a nursemaid who was a Morisco and she would forget who I was, and who she was, and sing to me.'

'What's a Morisco? And why was the song banned?' he asked curiously.

'A Morisco means "little Moor" in Spanish,' she explained. 'It's what we call the Moors who live in Spain. They are not really Moors like those in Africa. So we call them little Moors, or Moros. As I left, they were starting to call themselves Mudajjan – one allowed to remain.'

'One allowed to remain?' he asked. 'In their own land?'

'It's not their land,' she said instantly. 'It's ours. Spanish land.'

'They had it for seven hundred years,' he pointed out. 'When you Spanish were doing nothing but herding goats in the mountains, they were building roads and castles and universities. You told me so yourself.'

'Well, it's ours now,' she said flatly.

He clapped his hands like a sultan. 'Sing the song, Scheherazade. And sing it in French, you barbarian, so I can understand it.'

Catalina put her hands together like a woman about to pray and bowed low to him.

'Now that is good,' Arthur said, revelling in her. 'Did you learn that in the harem?'

She smiled at him and tipped up her head and sang.

'An old man cries to the king: Why comes this sudden calling?
  – Alas! Alhama!
Alas my friends, Christians have won Alhama – Alas! Alhama!
A white-bearded imam answers: This has thou merited, oh King!
  – Alas! Alhama!
In an evil hour thou slewest the Abencerrages, flower of Granada
  – Alas! Alhama!
Not Granada, not kingdom, not thy life shall long remain – Alas!
  Alhama!'

She fell silent. 'And it was true,' she said. 'Poor Boabdil came out of the Alhambra Palace, out of the red fort that they said would never fall, with the keys on a silk cushion, bowed low and gave them to my mother and my father and rode away. They say that at the mountain pass he looked back at his kingdom, his beautiful kingdom, and wept, and his mother told him to weep like a woman for what he could not hold as a man.'

Arthur let out a boyish crack of laughter. 'She said what?'

Catalina looked up, her face grave. 'It was very tragic.'

'It is just the sort of thing my grandmother would say,' he said delightedly. 'Thank God my father won his crown. My grandmother would be just as sweet in defeat as Boabdil's mother. Good God: "weep like a woman for what you cannot hold as a man." What a thing to say to a man as he walks away in defeat!'

Catalina laughed too. 'I never thought of it like that,' she said. 'It isn't very comforting.'

'Imagine going into exile with your mother, and she so angry with you!'

'Imagine losing the Alhambra, never going back there!'

He pulled her to him and kissed her face. 'No regrets!' he commanded.

At once she smiled for him. 'Then divert me,' she ordered. 'Tell me about your mother and father.'

He thought for a moment. 'My father was born an heir to the Tudors, but there were dozens in line for the throne before him,' he said. 'His father wanted him called Owen, Owen Tudor, a good Welsh name, but his father died before his birth, in the war. My grandmother was only a child of twelve when he was born, but she had her way and called him Henry – a royal name. You can see what she was thinking even then, even though she was little more than a child herself, and her husband was dead.

'My father's fortunes soared up and down with every battle of the civil war. One time he was a son of the ruling family, the next they were on the run. His uncle Jasper Tudor – you remember him – kept faith with my father and with the Tudor cause, but there was a final battle and our cause was lost, and our king executed. Edward came to the throne and my father was the last of the line. He was in such danger that Uncle Jasper broke out of the castle where they were being held and fled with him out of the country to Brittany.'

'To safety?'

'Of a sort. He told me once that he woke every morning expecting to be handed over to Edward. And once, King Edward said that he should come home and there would be a kind welcome and a wedding arranged for him. My father pretended to be ill on the road and escaped. He would have come home to his death.'

Catalina blinked. 'So he was a pretender too, in his time.'

He grinned at her. 'As I said. That is why he fears them so much. He knows what a pretender can do if the luck is with him. If they had caught him they would have brought him home to his death in the Tower. Just like he did to Warwick. My father would have been put to death the moment King Edward had him. But he pretended to be ill and got away, over the border into France.'

'They didn't hand him back?'

Arthur laughed. 'They supported him. He was the greatest challenge to the peace of England, of course they encouraged him. It suited the French to support him then: when he was not king but pretender.'

She nodded, she was a child of a prince praised by Machiavelli himself. Any daughter of Ferdinand was born to double-dealing. 'And then?'

'Edward died young, in his prime, with only a young son to inherit. His brother Richard first held the throne in trust and then claimed it for himself and put his own nephews, Edward's sons, the little princes, in the Tower of London.'

She nodded, this was a history she had been taught in Spain, and the greater story – of deadly rivalry for a throne – was a common theme for both young people.

'They went into the Tower and never came out again,' Arthur said bleakly. 'God bless their souls, poor boys, no-one knows what happened to them. The people turned against Richard, and summoned my father from France.'

'Yes?'

'My grandmother organised the great lords one after another, she was an arch-plotter. She and the Duke of Buckingham put their heads together and had the nobles of the kingdom in readiness. That's why my father honours her so highly: he owes her his throne. And he waited until he could get a message to my mother to tell her that he would marry her if he won the throne.'

'Because he loved her?' Catalina asked hopefully. 'She is so beautiful.'

'Not he. He hadn't even seen her. He had been in exile for most of his life, remember. It was a marriage cobbled together because his mother knew that if she could get those two married then everyone would see that the heir of York had married the heir of Lancaster and the war could be over. And her mother saw it as her only way out to safety. The two mothers brokered the deal together like a pair of crones over a cauldron. They're both women you wouldn't want to cross.'

'He didn't love her?' She was disappointed.

Arthur smiled. 'No. It's not a romance. And she didn't love him. But they knew what they had to do. When my father marched in and beat Richard and picked the crown of England out of the bodies and the wreckage of the battlefield, he knew that he would marry the princess, take the throne, and found a new line.'

'But wasn't she next heir to the throne anyway?' she asked, puzzled. 'Since it was her father who had been King Edward? And her uncle who had died in the battle, and her brothers were dead?'

He nodded. 'She was the oldest princess.'

'So why didn't she claim the throne for herself?'

'Aha, you are a rebel!' he said. He took a handful of her hair and pulled her face towards him. He kissed her mouth, tasting of wine and sweetmeats. 'A Yorkist rebel, which is worse.'

'I just thought she should have claimed the throne for herself.'

'Not in this country,' Arthur ruled. 'We don't have reigning queens in this England. Girls don't inherit. They cannot take the throne.'

'But if a king had only a daughter?'

He shrugged. 'Then it would be a tragedy for the country. You have to give me a boy, my love. Nothing else will do.'

'But if we only had a girl?'

'She would marry a prince and make him King Consort of England, and he would rule alongside her. England has to have a king. Like your mother did. She reigns alongside her husband.'

'In Aragon she does, but in Castile he rules alongside her. Castile is her country and Aragon his.'

'We'd never stand for it in England,' Arthur said.

She drew away from him in indignation. She was only half-pretending. 'I tell you this, if we have only one child and she is a girl then she will rule as queen and she will be a queen as good as any man can be king.'

'Well, she will be a novelty,' he said. 'We don't believe a woman can defend the country as a king needs to do.'

'A woman can fight,' she said instantly. 'You should see my mother in armour. Even I could defend the country. I have seen warfare, which is more than you have done. I could be as good a king as any man.'

He smiled at her, shaking his head. 'Not if the country was invaded. You couldn't command an army.'

'I could command an army. Why not?'

'No English army would be commanded by a woman. They wouldn't take orders from a woman.'

'They would take orders from their commander,' she flashed out. 'And if they don't then they are no good as soldiers and they have to be trained.'

He laughed. 'No Englishman would obey a woman,' he said. He saw by her stubborn face that she was not convinced.

'All that matters is that you win the battle,' she said. 'All that matters is that the country is defended. It doesn't matter who leads the army as long as they follow.'

'Well, at any rate, my mother had no thought of claiming the throne for herself. She would not have dreamed of it. She married my father and became Queen of England through marriage. And because she was the York Princess and he was the Lancaster heir my grandmother's plan succeeded. My father may have won the throne by conquest and acclaim; but we will have it by inheritance.'

Catalina nodded. 'My mother said there was nothing wrong with a man who is new-come to the throne. What matters is not the winning but the keeping of it.'

'We shall keep it,' he said with certainty. 'We shall make a great country here, you and me. We shall build roads and markets, churches and schools. We shall put a ring of forts around the coast-line and build ships.'

'We shall create courts of justice as my mother and father have done in Spain,' she said, settling back into the pleasure of planning a future on which they could agree. 'So that no man can be cruelly treated by another. So that every man knows that he can go to the court and have his case heard.'

He raised his glass to her. 'We should start writing this down,' he said. 'And we should start planning how it is to be done.'

'It will be years before we come to our thrones.'

'You never know. I don't wish it – God knows, I honour my father and my mother and I would want nothing before God's own time. But you never know. I am Prince of Wales, you are Princess. But we will be King and Queen of England. We should know who we will have at our court, we should know what advisors we will choose, we should know how we are going to make this country truly great. If it is a dream, then we can talk of it together at nighttime, as we do. But if it is a plan, we should write it in the daytime, take advice on it, think how we might do the things we want.'

Her face lit up. 'When we have finished our lessons for the day, perhaps we could do it then. Perhaps your tutor would help us, and my confessor.'

'And my advisors,' he said. 'And we could start here. In Wales. I can do what I want, within reason. We could make a college here, and build some schools. We could even commission a ship to be built here. There are shipwrights in Wales, we could build the first of our defensive ships.'

She clapped her hands like the girl she was. 'We could start our reign!' she said.

'Hail Queen Katherine! Queen of England!' Arthur said playfully, but at the ring of the words he stopped and looked at her more seriously. 'You know, you will hear them say that, my love. Vivat! Vivat Catalina Regina, Queen Katherine, Queen of England.'

It is like an adventure, wondering what sort of country we can make, what sort of king and queen we will be. It is natural we should think of Camelot. It was my favourite book in my mother's library and I found Arthur's own well-thumbed copy in his father's library.

I know that Camelot is a story, an ideal, as unreal as the love of a troubadour, or a fairy-tale castle or legends about thieves and treasure and genies. But there is something about the idea of ruling a kingdom with justice, with the consent of the people, which is more than a fairy tale.

Arthur and I will inherit great power, his father has seen to that. I think we will inherit a strong throne and a great treasure. We will inherit with the goodwill of the people; the king is not loved but he is respected, and nobody wants a return to endless battles. These English have a horror of civil war. If we come to the throne with this power, this wealth, and this goodwill, there is no doubt in my mind that we can make a great country here.

And it shall be a great country in alliance with Spain. My parents' heir is Juana's son, Charles. He will be Holy Roman Emperor and King of Spain. He will be my nephew and we will have the friendship of kinsmen. What a powerful alliance this will be: the great Holy Roman Empire and England. Nobody will be able to stand against us, we might divide France, we might divide most of Europe. Then we will stand, the empire and England against the Moors, then we will win and the whole of the East, Persia, the Ottomans, the Indies, even China will be laid open to us.

The routine of the castle changed. In the days which were starting to become warmer and brighter the young Prince and Princess of

Wales set up their office in her rooms, dragged a big table over to the window for the afternoon light, and pinned up maps of the Principality on the linenfold panelling.

'You look as if you are planning a campaign,' Lady Margaret Pole said pleasantly.

'The princess should be resting,' Dona Elvira remarked resentfully to no-one in particular.

'Are you unwell?' Lady Margaret asked quickly.

Catalina smiled and shook her head, she was becoming accustomed to the obsessive interest in her health. Until she could say that she was carrying England's heir she would have no peace from people asking her how she did.

'I don't need to rest,' she said. 'And tomorrow, if you will take me, I should like to go out and see the fields.'

'The fields?' asked Lady Margaret, rather taken aback. 'In March? They won't plough for another week or so, there is almost nothing to see.'

'I have to learn,' Catalina said. 'Where I live, it is so dry in summer that we have to build little ditches in every field, to the foot of every tree, to channel water to the plants to make sure that they can drink and live. When we first rode through this country and I saw the ditches in your fields, I was so ignorant I thought they were bringing water in.' She laughed aloud at the memory. 'And then the prince told me they were drains to take the water away. I could not believe it! So we had better ride out and you must tell me everything.'

'A queen does not need to know about fields,' Dona Elvira said in muted disapproval from the corner. 'Why should she know what the farmers grow?'

'Of course a queen needs to know,' Catalina replied, irritated. 'She should know everything about her country. How else can she rule?'

'I am sure you will be a very fine Queen of England,' Lady Margaret said, making the peace.

Catalina glowed. 'I shall be the best Queen of England that I can be,' she said. 'I shall care for the poor and assist the church, and if we are ever at war I shall ride out and fight for England just as my mother did for Spain.'

Planning for the future with Arthur, I forget my homesickness for Spain. Every day we think of some improvement we could make, of some law that should be changed. We read together, books of philosophy and politics, we talk about whether people can be trusted with their freedom, of whether a king should be a good tyrant or should step back from power. We talk about my home: of my parents' belief that you make a country by one church, one language, and one law. Or whether it could be possible to do as the Moors did: to make a country with one law but with many faiths and many languages, and assume that people are wise enough to choose the best.

We argue, we talk. Sometimes we break up in laughter, sometimes we disagree. Arthur is my lover always, my husband, undeniably. And now he is becoming my friend.

Catalina was in the little garden of Ludlow Castle, which was set along the east wall, in earnest conversation with one of the castle gardeners. In neat beds around her were the herbs that the cooks used, and some herbs and flowers with medicinal properties grown by Lady Margaret. Arthur, seeing Catalina as he walked back from confession in the round chapel, glanced up to the great hall to check that no-one would prevent him, and slipped off to be with her. As he drew up she was gesturing, trying to describe something. Arthur smiled.

'Princess,' he said formally in greeting.

She swept him a low curtsey, but her eyes were warm with pleasure at the sight of him. 'Sire.'

The gardener had dropped to his knees in the mud at the arrival of the prince. 'You can get up,' Arthur said pleasantly. 'I don't think you will find many pretty flowers at this time of year, Princess.'

'I was trying to talk to him about growing salad vegetables,' she said. 'But he speaks Welsh and English and I have tried Latin and French and we don't understand each other at all.'

'I think I am with him. I don't understand either. What is salad?'

She thought for a moment. '*Acetaria.*'

'*Acetaria?*' he queried.

'Yes, salad.'

'What is it, exactly?'

'It is vegetables that grow in the ground and you eat them without cooking them,' she explained. 'I was asking if he could plant some for me.'

'You eat them raw? Without boiling?'

'Yes, why not?'

'Because you will be dreadfully ill, eating uncooked food in this country.'

'Like fruit, like apples. You eat them raw.'

He was unconvinced. 'More often cooked, or preserved or dried. And anyway, that is a fruit and not leaves. But what sorts of vegetables do you want?'

'*Lactuca,*' she said.

'*Lactuca?*' he repeated. 'I have never heard of it.'

She sighed. 'I know. You none of you seem to know anything of vegetables. *Lactuca* is like . . .' She searched her mind for the truly terrible vegetable that she had been forced to eat, boiled into a pulp at one dinner at Greenwich. 'Samphire,' she said. 'The closest thing you have to *lactuca* is probably samphire. But you eat *lactuca* without cooking and it is crisp and sweet.'

'Vegetables? Crisp?'

'Yes,' she said patiently.

'And you eat this in Spain?'

She nearly laughed at his appalled expression. 'Yes. You would like it.'

'And can we grow it here?'

'I think he is telling me: no. He has never heard of such a thing. He has no seeds. He does not know where we would find such seeds. He does not think it would grow here.' She looked up at the blue sky with the scudding rain clouds. 'Perhaps he is right,' she said, a little weariness in her voice. 'I am sure that it needs much sunshine.'

Arthur turned to the gardener. 'Ever heard of a plant called *lactuca*?'

'No, Your Grace,' the man said, his head bowed. 'I'm sorry, Your Grace. Perhaps it is a Spanish plant. It sounds very barbaric. Is Her Royal Highness saying they eat grass there? Like sheep?'

Arthur's lip quivered. 'No, it is a herb, I think. I will ask her.'

He turned to Catalina and took her hand and tucked it in the crook of his arm. 'You know sometimes in summer, it is very sunny and very hot here. Truly. You would find the midday sun was too hot. You would have to sit in the shade.'

She looked disbelievingly from the cold mud to the thickening clouds.

'Not now, I know; but in summer. I have leaned against this wall and found it warm to the touch. You know, we grow strawberries and raspberries and peaches. All the fruit that you grow in Spain.'

'Oranges?'

'Well, perhaps not oranges,' he conceded.

'Lemons? Olives?'

He bridled. 'Yes, indeed.'

She looked suspiciously at him. 'Dates?'

'In Cornwall,' he asserted, straight-faced. 'Of course it is warmer in Cornwall.'

'Sugar cane? Rice? Pineapples?'

He tried to say yes, but he could not repress the giggles and she crowed with laughter, and fell on him.

When they were steady again he glanced around the inner bailey and said, 'Come on, nobody will miss us for a while,' and led her down the steps to the little sally-port and let them out of the hidden door.

A small path led them to the hillside which fell away steeply from the castle down to the river. A few lambs scampered off as they approached, a lad wandering after them. Arthur slid his arm around her waist and she let herself fall into pace with him.

'We do grow peaches,' he assured her. 'Not the other things, of course. But I am sure we can grow your *lactuca*, whatever it is. All we need is a gardener who can bring the seeds and who has already grown the things you want. Why don't you write to the gardener at the Alhambra and ask him to send you someone?'

'Could I send for a gardener?' she asked incredulously.

'My love, you are going to be Queen of England. You can send for a regiment of gardeners.'

'Really?'

Arthur laughed at the delight dawning on her face. 'At once. Did you not realise it?'

'No! But where should he garden? There is no room against the castle wall, and if we are to grow fruit as well as vegetables . . .'

'You are Princess of Wales! You can plant your garden wherever you please. You shall have all of Kent if you want it, my darling.'

'Kent?'

'We grow apples and hops there, I think we might have a try at *lactuca*.'

Catalina laughed with him. 'I didn't think. I didn't dream of sending for a gardener. If only I had brought one in the first place. I have all these useless ladies-in-waiting and I need a gardener.'

'You could swap him for Dona Elvira.'

She gurgled with laughter.

'Ah God, we are blessed,' he said simply. 'In each other and in our lives. You shall have anything you want, always. I swear it. Do you want to write to your mother? She can send you a couple of good men and I will get some land turned over at once.'

'I will write to Juana,' she decided. 'In the Netherlands. She is in the north of Christendom like me. She must know what will grow in this weather. I shall write to her and see what she has done.'

'And we shall eat *lactuca*!' he said, kissing her fingers. 'All day. We shall eat nothing but *lactuca*, like sheep grazing grass, whatever it is.'

'Tell me a story.'

'No, you tell me something.'

'If you will tell me about the fall of Granada, again.'

'I will tell you. But you have to explain something to me.'

Arthur stretched out and pulled her so that she was lying across the bed, her head on his shoulder. She could feel the rise and fall of his smooth chest as he breathed and hear the gentle thud of his heartbeat, constant as love.

'I shall explain everything.' She could hear the smile in his voice. 'I am extraordinarily wise today. You should have heard me after dinner tonight dispensing justice.'

'You are very fair,' she conceded. 'I do love it when you give a judgement.'

'I am a Solomon,' he said. 'They will call me Arthur the Good.'

'Arthur the Wise,' she suggested.

'Arthur the Magnificent.'

Catalina giggled. 'But I want you to explain to me something that I heard about your mother.'

'Oh yes?'

'One of the English ladies-in-waiting told me that she had been betrothed to the tyrant Richard. I thought I must have misunderstood her. We were speaking French and I thought I must have had it wrong.'

'Oh, that story,' he said with a little turn of the head.

'Is it not true? I hope I have not offended you?'

'No, not at all. It's a tale often told.'

'It cannot be true?'

'Who knows? Only my mother and Richard the tyrant can know what took place. And one of them is dead and the other is silent as the grave.'

'Will you tell me?' she asked tentatively. 'Or should we not speak of it at all?'

He shrugged. 'There are two stories. The well-known one, and its shadow. The story that everyone knows is that my mother fled into sanctuary with her mother and sisters, they were hiding in a church all together. They knew if they left they would be arrested by Richard the Usurper and would disappear into the Tower like her young brothers. No-one knew if the princes were alive or dead, but nobody had seen them, everyone feared they were dead. My mother wrote to my father – well, she was ordered to by her mother – she told him that if he would come to England, a Tudor from the Lancaster line, then she, a York princess, would marry him, and the old feud between the two families would be over forever. She told him to come and save her, and know her love. He received the letter, he raised an army, he came to find the princess, he married her and brought peace to England.'

'That is what you told me before. It is a very good story.'

Arthur nodded.

'And the story you don't tell?'

Despite himself he giggled. 'It's rather scandalous. They say that she was not in sanctuary at all. They say that she left the sanctuary and her mother and sisters. She went to court. King Richard's wife was dead and he was looking for another. She accepted the proposal of King Richard. She would have married her uncle, the tyrant, the man who murdered her brothers.'

Catalina's hand stole over her mouth to cover her gasp of shock, her eyes were wide. 'No!'

'So they say.'

'The queen, your mother?'

'Herself,' he said. 'Actually, they say worse. That she and Richard were betrothed as his wife lay dying. That is why there is always such enmity between her and my grandmother. My grandmother does not trust her; but she will never say why.'

'How could she?' she demanded.

'How could she not?' he returned. 'If you look at it from her point of view, she was a princess of York, her father was dead, her mother was the enemy of the king trapped in sanctuary, as much in prison as if she was in the Tower. If she wanted to live, she would have to find some way into the favour of the king. If she wanted to be acknowledged as a princess at all, she would have to have his recognition. If she wanted to be Queen of England she would have to marry him.'

'But surely, she could have . . .' she began and then she fell silent.

'No.' He shook his head. 'You see? She was a princess, she had very little choice. If she wanted to live she would have to obey the king. If she wanted to be queen she would have to marry him.'

'She could have raised an army on her own account.'

'Not in England,' he reminded her. 'She would have to marry the King of England to be its queen. It was her only way.'

Catalina was silent for a moment. 'Thank God that for me to be queen I had to marry you, that my destiny brought me so easily here.'

He smiled. 'Thank God we are happy with our destiny. For we would have married, and you would have been Queen of England, whether you had liked me or not. Wouldn't you?'

'Yes,' she said. 'There is never a choice for a princess.'

He nodded.

'But your grandmother, My Lady the King's Mother, must have planned your mother's wedding to your father. Why does she not forgive her? She was part of the plan.'

'Those two powerful women, my father's mother and my mother's mother, brokered the deal between them like a pair of washerwomen selling stolen linen.'

She gave a little squeak of shock.

Arthur chuckled, he found that he dearly loved surprising her. 'Dreadful, isn't it?' he replied calmly. 'My mother's mother was probably the most hated woman in England at one time.'

'And where is she now?'

He shrugged. 'She was at court for a while, but My Lady the King's Mother disliked her so much she got rid of her. She was famously beautiful, you know, and a schemer. My grandmother accused her of plotting against my father and he chose to believe her.'

'She is never dead? They never executed her!'

'No. He put her into a convent and she never comes to court.'

She was aghast. 'Your grandmother had the queen's own mother confined in a convent?'

He nodded, his face grave. 'Truly. You be warned by this, beloved. My grandmother welcomes no-one to court that might distract from her own power. Make sure you never cross her.'

Catalina shook her head. 'I never would. I am absolutely terrified of her.'

'So am I!' he laughed. 'But I know her, and I warn you. She will stop at nothing to maintain the power of her son, and of her family. Nothing will distract her from this. She loves no-one but him. Not me, not her husbands, no-one but him.'

'Not you?'

He shook his head. 'She does not even love him, as you would understand it. He is the boy that she decided was born to be king. She sent him away when he was little more than a baby for his safety. She saw him survive his boyhood. Then she ordered him into the face of terrible danger to claim the throne. She could only love a king.'

She nodded. 'He is her pretender.'

'Exactly. She claimed the throne for him. She made him king. He is king.'

He saw her grave face. 'Now, enough of this. You have to sing me your song.'

'Which one?'

'Is there another one about the fall of Granada?'

'Dozens, I should think.'

'Sing me one,' he commanded. He piled a couple of extra cushions behind his head, and she knelt up before him, tossed back her mane of red hair and began to sing in a low sweet voice:

'There was crying in Granada when the sun was going down
Some calling on the Trinity, some calling on Mahoun,
Here passed away the Koran and therein the Cross was borne,
And here was heard the Christian bell and there the Moorish
horn.
Te Deum Laudamus! *Was up the Alcala sung:*
Down from the Alhambra minarets were all the crescents flung,
The arms thereon of Aragon, they with Castile display
One king comes in in triumph, one weeping goes away.'

He was silent for long minutes. She stretched out again beside him on her back, looking, without seeing, the embroidered tester of the bed over their heads.

'It's always like that, isn't it?' he remarked. 'The rise of one is the fall of another. I shall be king but only at my father's death. And at my death, my son will reign.'

'Shall we call him Arthur?' she asked. 'Or Henry for your father?'

'Arthur is a good name,' he said. 'A good name for a new royal family in Britain. Arthur for Camelot, and Arthur for me. We don't want another Henry; my brother is enough for anyone. Let's call him Arthur, and his older sister will be called Mary.'

'Mary? I wanted to call her Isabella, for my mother.'

'You can call the next girl Isabella. But I want our first-born to be called Mary.'

'Arthur must be first.'

He shook his head. 'First we will have Mary so that we learn how to do it all with a girl.'

'How to do it all?'

He gestured. 'The christening, the confinement, the birthing, the whole fuss and worry, the wet nurse, the rockers, the nursemaids. My grandmother has written a great book to rule how it shall be done. It is dreadfully complicated. But if we have our Mary first then our nursery is all ready, and in your next confinement we shall put our son and heir into the cradle.'

She rose up and turned on him in mock indignation. 'You would practise being a father on my daughter!' she exclaimed.

'You wouldn't want to start with my son,' he protested. 'This will be the rose of the rose of England. That's what they call me, remember: "the rose of England". I think you should deal with my little rosebud, my little blossom, with great respect.'

'She is to be Isabella then,' Catalina stipulated. 'If she comes first, she shall be Isabella.'

'Mary, for the queen of heaven.'

'Isabella for the Queen of Spain.'

'Mary, to give thanks for you coming to me. The sweetest gift that heaven could have given me.'

Catalina melted into his arms. 'Isabella,' she said as he kissed her.

'Mary,' he whispered into her ear. 'And let us make her now.'

It is morning. I lie awake, it is dawn and I can hear the birds slowly starting to sing. The sun is coming up and through the lattice window I can see a glimpse of blue sky. Perhaps it will be a warm day, perhaps the summer is coming at last.

Beside me, Arthur is breathing quietly and steadily. I can feel my heart swell with love for him, I put my hand on the fair curls of his head and wonder if any woman has ever loved a man as I love him.

I stir and put my other hand on the warm roundness of my belly. Can it be possible that last night we made a child? Is there already, safe in my belly, a baby who will be called Mary, Princess Mary, who will be the rose of the rose of England?

I hear the footsteps of the maid moving about in my presence chamber, bringing wood for the fire, raking up the embers. Still Arthur does not stir. I put a gentle hand on his shoulder. 'Wake up, sleepyhead,' I say, my voice warm with love. 'The servants are outside, you must go.'

He is damp with sweat, the skin of his shoulder is cold and clammy. 'My love?' I ask. 'Are you well?'

He opens his eyes and smiles at me. 'Don't tell me it's morning already. I am so weary I could sleep for another day.'

'It is.'

'Oh, why didn't you wake me earlier? I love you so much in the morning and now I can't have you till tonight.'

I put my face against his chest. 'Don't. I slept late too. We keep late hours. And you will have to go now.'

Arthur holds me close, as if he cannot bear to let me go; but I can hear the groom of the chamber open the outside door to bring hot water. I draw myself away from him. It is like tearing off a layer of my own skin. I cannot bear to move away from him.

Suddenly, I am struck by the warmth of his body, the tangled heat of the sheets around us. 'You are so hot!'

'It is desire,' he says, smiling. 'I shall have to go to Mass to cool down.'

He gets out of bed and throws his gown around his shoulders. He gives a little stagger.

'Beloved, are you all right?' I ask.

'A little dizzy, nothing more,' he says. 'Blind with desire, and it is

all your fault. See you in chapel. Pray for me, sweetheart.'

I get up from bed, and unbolt the battlements door to let him out. He sways a little as he goes up the stone steps, then I see him straighten his shoulders to breathe in the fresh air. I close the door behind him, and then go back to my bed. I glance round the room, nobody could know that he has been here. In a moment, Dona Elvira taps on my door and comes in with the maid-in-waiting and behind them a couple of maids with the jug of hot water, and my dress for the day.

'You slept late, you must be overtired,' Dona Elvira says disapprovingly; but I am so peaceful and so happy that I cannot even be troubled to reply.

In the chapel they could do no more than exchange hidden smiles. After Mass, Arthur went riding and Catalina went to break her fast. After breakfast was her time to study with her chaplain and Catalina sat at the table in the window with him, their books before them, and studied the letters of St Paul.

Margaret Pole came in as Catalina was closing her book. 'The prince begs your attendance in his rooms,' she said.

Catalina rose to her feet. 'Has something happened?'

'I think he is unwell. He has sent away everyone but the grooms of the body and his servers.'

Catalina left at once, followed by Dona Elvira and Lady Margaret. The prince's rooms were crowded by the usual hangers-on of the little court: men seeking favour or attention, petitioners asking for justice, the curious come to stare, and the host of lesser servants and functionaries. Catalina went through them all to the double doors of Arthur's private chamber, and went in.

He was seated in a chair by the fire, his face very pale. Dona Elvira and Lady Margaret waited at the door as Catalina went quickly towards him.

'Are you ill, my love?' she asked quickly.

He managed a smile but she saw it was an effort. 'I have taken some kind of chill, I think,' he said. 'Come no closer, I don't want to pass it to you.'

'Are you hot?' she asked fearfully, thinking of the Sweat which came on like a fever and left a corpse.

'No, I feel cold.'

'Well, it is not surprising in this country where it either snows or rains all the time.'

He managed another smile.

Catalina looked around and saw Lady Margaret. 'Lady Margaret, we must call the prince's physician.'

'I sent my servants to find him already,' she said, coming forwards.

'I don't want a fuss made,' Arthur said irritably. 'I just wanted to tell you, Princess, that I cannot come to dinner.'

Her eyes went to his. 'How shall we be alone?' was the unspoken question.

'May I dine in your rooms?' she asked. 'Can we dine alone, privately, since you are ill?'

'Yes, let's,' he ruled.

'See the doctor first,' Lady Margaret advised. 'If Your Grace permits. He can advise what you should eat, and if it is safe for the princess to be with you.'

'He has no disease,' Catalina insisted. 'He says he just feels tired. It is just the cold air here, or the damp. It was cold yesterday and he was riding half the day.'

There was a tap on the door and a voice called out. 'Dr Bereworth is here, Your Grace.'

Arthur raised his hand in permission, Dona Elvira opened the door and the man came into the room.

'The prince feels cold and tired.' Catalina went to him at once, speaking rapidly in French. 'Is he ill? I don't think he's ill. What do you think?'

The doctor bowed low to her and to the prince. He bowed to Lady Margaret and Dona Elvira.

'I am sorry, I don't understand,' he said uncomfortably in English to Lady Margaret. 'What is the princess saying?'

Catalina clapped her hands together in frustration. 'The prince . . .' she began in English.

Margaret Pole came to her side. 'His Grace is unwell,' she said.

'May I speak with him alone?' he asked.

Arthur nodded. He tried to rise from the chair but he almost staggered. The doctor was at once at his side, supporting him, and led him into his bedchamber.

'He cannot be ill.' Catalina turned to Dona Elvira and spoke to her in Spanish. 'He was well last night. Just this morning he felt hot. But he said he was only tired. But now he can hardly stand. He cannot be ill.'

'Who knows what illness a man might take in this rain and fog?' the duenna replied dourly. 'It's a wonder that you are not sick yourself. It is a wonder that any of us can bear it.'

'He is not sick,' Catalina said. 'He is just overtired. He rode for a long time yesterday. And it was cold, there was a very cold wind. I noticed it myself.'

'A wind like this can kill a man,' Dona Elvira said gloomily. 'It blows so cold and so damp.'

'Stop it!' Catalina said, clapping her hands to her ears. 'I won't hear another word. He is just tired, overtired. And perhaps he has taken a chill. There is no need to speak of killing winds and damp.'

Lady Margaret stepped forwards and gently took Catalina's hands. 'Be patient, Princess,' she counselled. 'Dr Bereworth is a very good doctor, and he has known the prince from childhood. The prince is a strong young man and his health is good. It is probably nothing to worry about at all. If Dr Bereworth is concerned we will send for the king's own physician from London. We will soon have him well again.'

Catalina nodded, and turned to sit by the window and look out. The sky had clouded over, the sun was quite gone. It was raining again, the raindrops chasing down the small panes of glass. Catalina watched them. She tried to keep her mind from the death of her brother who had loved his wife so much, who had been looking forward to the birth of their son. Juan had died within days of taking sick, and no-one had ever known what was wrong with him.

'I shan't think of him, not of poor Juan,' Catalina whispered to herself. 'The cases are not alike at all. Juan was always slight, little; but Arthur is strong.'

The physician seemed to take a long time and when he came out of the bedchamber, Arthur was not with him. Catalina who had risen from her seat as soon as the door opened, peeped around him to see Arthur lying on the bed, half-undressed, half-asleep.

'I think his grooms of the body should prepare him for bed,' the doctor said. 'He is very weary. He would be better for rest. If they take care, they can get him into bed without waking him.'

'Is he ill?' Catalina demanded speaking slowly in Latin. '*Aegrotat?* Is he very ill?'

The doctor spread his hands. 'He has a fever,' he said cautiously in slow French. 'I can give him a draught to bring down his fever.'

'Do you know what it is?' Lady Margaret asked, her voice very low. 'It's not the Sweat, is it?'

'Please God it is not. And there are no other cases in the town, as far as I know. But he should be kept quiet and allowed to rest. I shall go and make up this draught and I will come back.'

The low-voiced English was incomprehensible to Catalina. 'What does he say? What did he say?' she demanded of Lady Margaret.

'Nothing more than you heard,' the older woman assured her. 'He has a fever and needs rest. Let me get his men to undress him and put him properly to bed. If he is better tonight, you can dine with him. I know he would like that.'

'Where is he going?' Catalina cried out as the doctor bowed and went to the door. 'He must stay and watch the prince!'

'He is going to make a draught to bring down his fever. He will be back at once. The prince will have the best of care, Your Grace. We love him as you do. We will not neglect him.'

'I know you would not . . . it is only . . . Will the doctor be long?'

'He will be as quick as he can. And see, the prince is asleep. Sleep will be his best medicine. He can rest and grow strong and dine with you tonight.'

'You think he will be better tonight?'

'If it is just a little fever and fatigue then he will be better in a few days,' Lady Margaret said firmly.

'I will watch over his sleep,' Catalina said.

Lady Margaret opened the door and beckoned to the prince's chief gentlemen. She gave them their orders and then she drew the princess through the crowd to her own rooms. 'Come, Your Grace,' she said. 'Come for a walk in the inner bailey with me and then I shall go back to his rooms and see that everything is comfortable for him.'

'I shall go back now,' Catalina insisted. 'I shall watch over his sleep.'

Margaret glanced at Dona Elvira. 'You should stay away from his rooms in case he does have a fever,' she said speaking slowly and clearly in French, so that the duenna could understand her. 'Your health is most important, Princess. I would not forgive myself if anything happened to either of you.'

Dona Elvira stepped forwards and narrowed her lips. Lady Margaret knew she could be relied on to keep the princess from danger.

'But you said he only had a slight fever. I can go to him?'

'Let us wait to see what the doctor has to say.' Lady Margaret lowered her voice. 'If you should be with child, dear Princess, we would not want you to take his fever.'

'But I will dine with him.'

'If he is well enough.'

'But he will want to see me!'

'Depend upon it,' Lady Margaret smiled. 'When his fever has broken and he is better this evening and sitting up and eating his dinner he will want to see you. You have to be patient.'

Catalina nodded. 'If I go now, do you swear that you will stay with him all the time?'

'I will go back now, if you will walk outside and then go to your room and read or study or sew.'

'I'll go!' said Catalina, instantly obedient. 'I'll go to my rooms if you will stay with him.'

'At once,' Lady Margaret promised.

This small garden is like a prison yard, I walk round and round in the herb garden, and the rain drizzles over everything like tears. My rooms are no better, my privy chamber is like a cell, I cannot bear to have anyone with me, and yet I cannot bear to be alone. I have made the ladies sit in the presence chamber, their unending chatter makes me want to scream with irritation. But when I am alone in my room I long for company. I want someone to hold my hand and tell me that everything will be all right.

I go down the narrow stone stairs and across the cobbles to the round chapel. A cross and a stone altar is set in the rounded wall, a light burning before it. It is a place of perfect peace; but I can find no peace. I fold my cold hands inside my sleeves and hug myself and I walk around the circular wall, it is thirty-six steps to the door and then I walk the circle again, like a donkey on a treadmill. I am praying; but I have no faith that I am heard.

'I am Catalina, Princess of Spain and of Wales,' I remind myself. 'I am Catalina, beloved of God, especially favoured by God. Nothing can

go wrong for me. Nothing as bad as this could ever go wrong for me. It is God's will that I should marry Arthur and unite the kingdoms of Spain and England. God will not let anything happen to Arthur nor to me. I know that He favours my mother and me above all others. This fear must be sent to try me. But I will not be afraid because I know that nothing will ever go wrong for me.'

Catalina waited in her rooms, sending her women every hour to ask how her husband did. The first few hours they said he was still sleeping, the doctor had made his draught and was standing by his bed, waiting for him to wake. Then, at three in the afternoon, they said that he had wakened but was very hot and feverish. He had taken the draught and they were waiting to see his fever cool. At four he was worse, not better, and the doctor was making up a different prescription.

He would take no dinner, he would just drink some cool ale and the doctor's cures for fever.

'Go and ask him if he will see me?' Catalina ordered one of her English women. 'Make sure you speak to Lady Margaret. She promised me that I should dine with him. Remind her.'

The woman went and came back with a grave face. 'Princess, they are all very anxious,' she said. 'They have sent for a physician from London. Dr Bereworth, who has been watching over him, does not know why the fever does not cool down. Lady Margaret is there and Sir Richard Pole, Sir William Thomas, Sir Henry Vernon, Sir Richard Croft, they are all waiting outside his chamber and you cannot be admitted to see him. They say he is wandering in his mind.'

'I must go to the chapel. I must pray,' Catalina said instantly.

She threw a veil over her head and went back to the round chapel. To her dismay, Prince Arthur's confessor was at the altar, his head bowed low in supplication, some of the greatest men of the town and castle were seated around the wall, their heads bowed. Catalina slipped into the room, and fell to her knees. She rested her chin on her hands and scrutinised the hunched shoulders of the priest for any sign that his prayers were being heard. There was no way of telling. She closed her eyes.

Dearest God, spare Arthur, spare my darling husband, Arthur. He is only a boy, I am only a girl, we have had no time together, no time at all. You know what a kingdom we will make if he is spared. You know what plans we have for this country, what a holy castle we will make from this land, how we shall hammer the Moors, how we shall defend this kingdom from the Scots. Dear God, in your mercy spare Arthur and let him come back to me. We want to have our children: Mary, who is to be the rose of the rose, and our son Arthur who will be the third Holy Roman Catholic Tudor king for England. Let us do as we have promised. Oh dear Lord, be merciful and spare him. Dear Lady, intercede for us, and spare him. Sweet Jesus, spare him. It is I, Catalina, who asks this, and I ask in the name of my mother, Queen Isabella, who has worked all her life in your service, who is the most Christian queen, who has served on your crusades. She is beloved of You, I am beloved of You. Do not, I beg You, disappoint me.

It grew dark as Catalina prayed but she did not notice. It was late when Dona Elvira touched her gently on the shoulder and said, 'Infanta, you should have some dinner and go to bed.'

Catalina turned a white face to her duenna. 'What word?' she asked.

'They say he is worse.'

Sweet Jesus, spare him, sweet Jesus, spare me, sweet Jesus, spare England. Say that Arthur is no worse.

In the morning they said that he had passed a good night, but the gossip among the servers of the body was that he was sinking. The fever had reached such a height that he was wandering in his mind, sometimes he thought he was in his nursery with his sisters and his brother, sometimes he thought he was at his wedding, dressed in brilliant white satin, and sometimes, most oddly, he thought he was in a fantastic palace. He spoke of a courtyard of myrtles, a rectangle of water like a mirror reflecting a building of gold, and a circular sweep of flocks of swifts who went round and round all the sunny day long.

'I shall see him,' Catalina announced to Lady Margaret at noon.

'Princess, it may be the Sweat,' her ladyship said bluntly. 'I cannot allow you to go close to him. I cannot allow you to take any infection. I should be failing in my duty if I let you go too close to him.'

'Your duty is to me!' Catalina snapped.

The woman, a princess herself, never wavered. 'My duty is to England,' she said. 'And if you are carrying a Tudor heir then my duty is to that child, as well as to you. Do not quarrel with me please, Princess. I cannot allow you to go closer than the foot of his bed.'

'Let me go there, then,' Catalina said, like a little girl. 'Please just let me see him.'

Lady Margaret bowed her head and led the way to the royal chambers. The crowds in the presence chamber had swollen in numbers as the word had gone around the town that their prince was fighting for his life; but they were silent, silent as a crowd in mourning. They were waiting and praying for the rose of England. A few men saw Catalina, her face veiled in her lace mantilla, and called out a blessing on her, then one man stepped forwards and dropped to his knee. 'God bless you, Princess of Wales,' he said. 'And may the prince rise from his bed and be merry with you again.'

'Amen,' Catalina said through cold lips, and went on.

The double doors to the inner chamber were thrown open and Catalina went in. A makeshift apothecary's room had been set up in the prince's privy chamber, a trestle table with large glass jars of ingredients, a pestle and mortar, a chopping board, and half a dozen men in the gaberdine gowns of physicians were gathered together. Catalina paused, looking for Dr Bereworth.

'Doctor?'

He came towards her at once, and dropped to his knee. His face was grave. 'Princess.'

'What news of my husband?' she said, speaking slowly and clearly for him in French.

'I am sorry, he is no better.'

'But he is not worse,' she suggested. 'He is getting better.'

He shook his head. '*Il est très malade,*' he said simply.

Catalina heard the words but it was as if she had forgotten the language. She could not translate them. She turned to Lady Margaret. 'He says that he is better?' she asked.

Lady Margaret shook her head. 'He says that he is worse,' she said honestly.

'But they will have something to give him?' She turned to the doctor. '*Vous avez un médicament?*'

He gestured at the table behind him, at the apothecary.

'Oh, if only we had a Moorish doctor!' Catalina cried out. 'They have the greatest skill, there is no-one like them. They had the best universities for medicines before . . . If only I had brought a doctor with me! Arab medicine is the finest in the world!'

'We are doing everything we can,' the doctor said stiffly.

Catalina tried to smile. 'I am sure,' she said. 'I just so wish . . . Well! Can I see him?'

A quick glance between Lady Margaret and the doctor showed that this had been a matter of some anxious discussion.

'I will see if he is awake,' he said, and went through the door.

Catalina waited. She could not believe that only yesterday morning Arthur had slipped from her bed complaining that she had not woken him early enough to make love. Now, he was so ill that she could not even touch his hand.

The doctor opened the door. 'You can come to the threshold, Princess,' he said. 'But for the sake of your own health, and for the health of any child you could be carrying, you should come no closer.'

Catalina stepped up quickly to the door. Lady Margaret pressed a pomander stuffed with cloves and herbs in her hand. Catalina held it to her nose. The acrid smell made her eyes water as she peered into the darkened room.

Arthur was sprawled on the bed, his nightgown pulled down for modesty, his face flushed with fever. His blond hair was dark with sweat, his face gaunt. He looked much older than his fifteen years. His eyes were sunk deep into his face, the skin beneath his eyes stained brown.

'Your wife is here,' the doctor said quietly to him.

Arthur's eyes fluttered open and she saw them narrow as he tried to focus on the bright doorway and Catalina, standing before him, her face white with shock.

'My love,' he said. '*Amo te.*'

'*Amo te,*' she whispered. 'They say I cannot come closer.'

'Don't come closer,' he said, his voice a thread. 'I love you.'

'I love you too!' She could hear that her voice was strained with tears. 'You will be well?'

He shook his head, too weary to speak.

'Arthur?' she said, demandingly. 'You will get better?'

He rested his head back on his hot pillow, gathering his strength. 'I will try, beloved. I will try so hard. For you. For us.'

'Is there anything you want?' she asked. 'Anything I can get for you?' She glanced around. There was nothing that she could do for him. There was nothing that would help. If she had brought a Moorish doctor with her, if her parents had not destroyed the learning of the Arab universities, if the church had allowed the study of medicine, and not called knowledge heresy . . .

'All I want is to live with you,' he said, his voice a thin thread.

She gave a little sob. 'And I you.'

'The prince should rest now, and you should not linger here.' The doctor stepped forwards.

'Please, let me stay!' she cried in a whisper. 'Please allow me. I beg you. Please let me be with him.'

Lady Margaret put a hand around her waist and drew her back. 'You shall come again, if you leave now,' she promised. 'The prince needs to rest.'

'I shall come back,' Catalina called to him, and saw the little gesture of his hand which told her that he had heard her. 'I shall not fail you.'

Catalina went to the chapel to pray for him, but she could not pray. All she could do was think of him, his white face on the white pillows. All she could do was feel the throb of desire for him. They had been married only one hundred and forty days, they had been passionate lovers for only ninety-four nights. They had promised that they would have a lifetime together, she could not believe that she was on her knees now, praying for his life.

This cannot be happening, he was well only yesterday. This is some terrible dream and in a moment I will wake up and he will kiss me and call me foolish. Nobody can take sick so quickly, nobody can go from strength and beauty to being so desperately ill in such a short time. In a moment I will wake up. This cannot be happening. I cannot pray, but it does not matter that I cannot pray because it is not really happening. A dream prayer would mean nothing. A dream illness means nothing. I am not a superstitious heathen to fear dreams. I shall wake up in a moment and we will laugh at my fears.

At dinner time she rose up, dipped her finger in the holy water, crossed herself, and with the water still wet on her forehead went back to his chambers, with Dona Elvira following, close behind.

The crowds in the halls outside the rooms and in the presence chamber were thicker than ever, women as well as men, silent with inarticulate grief. They made way for the princess without a word but a quiet murmur of blessings. Catalina went through them, looking neither to left nor right, through the presence chamber, past the apothecary bench, to the very door of his bedchamber.

The guard stepped to one side. Catalina tapped lightly on the door and pushed it open.

They were bending over him on the bed. Catalina heard him cough, a thick cough as though his throat was bubbling with water.

'*Madre de Dios,*' she said softly. 'Holy Mother of God, keep Arthur safe.'

The doctor turned at her whisper. His face was pale. 'Keep back!' he said urgently. 'It is the Sweat.'

At that most feared word Dona Elvira stepped back and laid hold of Catalina's gown as if she would drag her from danger.

'Loose me!' Catalina snapped and tugged her gown from the duenna's hands. 'I will come no closer, but I have to speak with him,' she said steadily.

The doctor heard the resolution in her voice. 'Princess, he is too weak.'

'Leave us,' she said.

'Princess.'

'I have to speak to him. This is the business of the kingdom.'

One glance at her determined face told him that she would not be denied. He went past her with his head low, his assistants following behind him. Catalina made a little gesture with her hand and Dona Elvira retreated. Catalina stepped over the threshold and pushed the door shut on them.

She saw Arthur stir in protest.

'I won't come any closer,' she assured him. 'I swear it. But I have to be with you. I cannot bear . . .' She broke off.

His face when he turned it to her was shiny with sweat, his hair as wet as when he came in from hunting in the rain. His young round face was strained as the disease leached the life out of him.

'*Amo te*,' he said through lips that were cracked and dark with fever.

'*Amo te*,' she replied.

'I am dying,' he said bleakly.

Catalina did not interrupt nor deny him. He saw her straighten a little, as if she had staggered beneath a mortal blow.

He took a rasping breath. 'But you must still be Queen of England.'

'What?'

He took a shaky breath. 'Love – obey me. You have sworn to obey me.'

'I will do anything.'

'Marry Harry. Be queen. Have our children.'

'What?' She was dizzy with shock. She could hardly make out what he was saying.

'England needs a great queen,' he said. 'Especially with him. He's not fit to rule. You must teach him. Build my forts. Build my navy. Defend against the Scots. Have my daughter Mary. Have my son Arthur. Let me live through you.'

'My love –'

'Let me do it,' he whispered longingly. 'Let me keep England safe through you. Let me live through you.'

'I am your wife,' she said fiercely. 'Not his.'

He nodded. 'Tell them you are not.'

She staggered at that, and felt for the door to support her.

'Tell them I could not do it.' A hint of a smile came to his drained face. 'Tell them I was unmanned. Then marry Harry.'

'You hate Harry!' she burst out. 'You cannot want me to marry him. He is a child! And I love you.'

'He will be king,' he said desperately. 'So you will be queen. Marry him. Please. Beloved. For me.'

The door behind her opened a crack and Lady Margaret said quietly, 'You must not exhaust him, Princess.'

'I have to go,' Catalina said desperately to the still figure in the bed.

'Promise me . . .'

'I will come back. You will get better.'

'Please.'

Lady Margaret opened the door wider and took Catalina's hand. 'For his own good,' she said quietly. 'You have to leave him.'

Catalina turned away from the room, she looked back over her shoulder. Arthur lifted a hand a few inches from the rich coverlet. 'Promise,' he said. 'Please. For my sake. Promise. Promise me now, beloved.'

'I promise,' burst out of her.

His hand fell, she heard him give a little sigh of relief.

They were the last words they said to each other.

Ludlow Castle, 2nd April 1502

At six o'clock, Vespers, Arthur's confessor, Dr Eldenham, adminis-tered extreme unction and Arthur died soon after. Catalina knelt on the threshold as the priest anointed her husband with the oil and bowed her head for the blessing. She did not rise from her knees until they told her that her boy-husband was dead and she was a widow of sixteen years old.

Lady Margaret on one side and Dona Elvira on the other half-carried and half-dragged Catalina to her bedchamber. Catalina slipped between the cold sheets of her bed and knew that however long she waited there, she would not hear Arthur's quiet footstep on the battlements outside her room, and his tap on the door. She would never again open her door and step into his arms. She would never again be snatched up and carried to her bed, having wanted all day to be in his arms.

'I cannot believe it,' she said brokenly.

'Drink this,' Lady Margaret said. 'The physician left it for you. It is a sleeping draught. I will wake you at noon.'

'I cannot believe it.'

'Princess, drink.'

Catalina drank it down, ignoring the bitter taste. More than anything else she wanted to be asleep and never wake again.

That night I dreamed I was on the top of the great gateway of the red fort that guards and encircles the Alhambra palace. Above my head

the standards of Castile and Aragon were flapping like the sails on Cristóbal Colón's ships. Shading my eyes from the autumn sun, looking out over the great plain of Granada, I saw the simple, familiar beauty of the land, the tawny soil intersected by a thousand little ditches carrying water from one field to another. Below me was the white-walled town of Granada, even now, ten years on from our conquest, still, unmistakably a Moorish town: the houses all arranged around shady courtyards, a fountain splashing seductively in the centre, the gardens rich with the perfume of late flowering roses, and the boughs of the trees heavy with fruit.

Someone was calling for me: 'Where is the Infanta?'

And in my dream I answered: 'I am Katherine, Queen of England. That is my name now.'

They buried Arthur, Prince of Wales, on St George's Day, this first prince of all England, after a nightmare journey from Ludlow to Worcester when the rain lashed down so hard that they could barely make way. The lanes were awash, the water meadows knee-high in flood water and the Teme had burst its banks and they could not get through the fords. They had to use bullock carts for the funeral procession, horses could not have made their way through the mire on the lanes, and all the plumage and black cloth was sodden by the time they finally straggled into Worcester.

Hundreds turned out to see the miserable cortege go through the streets to the cathedral. Hundreds wept for the loss of the rose of England. After they lowered his coffin into the vault beneath the choir, the servants of his household broke their staves of office and threw them into the grave with their lost master. It was over for them. Everything they had hoped for, in the service of such a young and promising prince was finished. It was over for Arthur. It felt as if everything was over and could never be set right again.

No, no, no.

For the first month of mourning Catalina stayed in her rooms. Lady Margaret and Dona Elvira gave out that she was ill, but not in danger. In truth they feared for her reason. She did not rave or cry, she did not rail against fate or weep for her mother's comfort, she lay in utter silence, her face turned towards the wall. Her family tendency to despair tempted her like a sin. She knew she must not give way to weeping and madness, for if she once let go she would never be able to stop. For the long month of seclusion Catalina gritted her teeth and it took all her willpower and all her strength to stop herself from screaming out in grief.

When they woke her in the morning she said she was tired. They did not know that she hardly dared to move for fear that she would moan aloud. After they had dressed her, she would sit on her chair like a stone. As soon as they allowed it, she would go back to bed, lie on her back, and look up at the brightly coloured tester that she had seen with eyes half-closed by love, and know that Arthur would never pull her into the crook of his arm again.

They summoned the physician, Dr Bereworth, but when she saw him her mouth trembled and her eyes filled with tears. She turned her head away from him and she went swiftly into her bedchamber and closed the door on them all. She could not bear to see him, the doctor who had let Arthur die, the friends who had watched it happen. She could not bear to speak to him. She felt a murderous rage at the sight of the doctor who had failed to save the boy. She wished him dead, and not Arthur.

'I am afraid her mind is affected,' Lady Margaret said to the doctor as they heard the latch click on the privy chamber door. 'She does not speak, she does not even weep for him.'

'Will she eat?'

'If food is put before her and if she is reminded to eat.'

'Get someone, someone familiar – her confessor perhaps – to read to her. Encouraging words.'

'She will see no-one.'

'Might she be with child?' he whispered. It was the only question that now mattered.

'I don't know,' she replied. 'She has said nothing.'

'She is mourning him,' he said. 'She is mourning like a young woman, for the young husband she has lost. We should let her be. Let her grieve. She will have to rise up soon enough. Is she to go back to court?'

'The king commands it,' Lady Margaret said. 'The queen is sending her own litter.'

'Well, when it comes she will have to change her ways then,' he said comfortably. 'She is only young. She will recover. The young have strong hearts. And it will help her to leave here, where she has such sad memories. If you need any advice please call me. But I will not force myself into her presence, poor child.'

No, no, no.

But Catalina did not look like a poor child, Lady Margaret thought. She looked like a statue, like a stone princess carved from grief. Dona Elvira had dressed her in her new dark clothes of mourning, and persuaded her to sit in the window where she could see the green trees and the hedges creamy with may blossom, the sun on the fields, and hear the singing of the birds. The summer had come as Arthur had promised her that it would, it was warm as he had sworn it would be; but she was not walking by the river with him, greeting the swifts as they flew in from Spain. She was not planting salad vegetables in the gardens of the castle and persuading him to try them. The summer was here, the sun was here, Catalina was here, but Arthur was cold in the dark vault of Worcester Cathedral.

Catalina sat still, her hands folded on the black silk of her gown, her eyes looking out of the window, but seeing nothing, her mouth folded tight over her gritted teeth as if she were biting back a storm of words.

'Princess,' Lady Margaret started tentatively.

Slowly, the head under the heavy black hood turned towards her. 'Yes, Lady Margaret?' Her voice was hoarse.

'I would speak with you.'

Catalina inclined her head.

Dona Elvira stepped back and went quietly out of the room.

'I have to ask you about your journey to London. The royal litter has arrived and you will have to leave here.'

There was no flicker of animation in Catalina's deep blue eyes. She nodded again, as if they were discussing the transport of a parcel.

'I don't know if you are strong enough to travel.'

'Can I not stay here?' Catalina asked.

'I understand the king has sent for you. I am sorry for it. They write that you may stay here until you are well enough to travel.'

'Why, what is to become of me?' Catalina asked, as if it was a matter of absolute indifference. 'When I get to London?'

'I don't know.' The former princess did not pretend for one moment that a girl of a royal family could choose her future. 'I am sorry. I do not know what is planned. My husband has been told nothing except to prepare for your journey to London.'

'What do you think might happen? When my sister's husband

died, they sent her back to us from Portugal. She came home to Spain again.'

'I would expect that they will send you home,' Lady Margaret said.

Catalina turned her head away once more. She looked out of the window but her eyes saw nothing. Lady Margaret waited, she wondered if the princess would say anything more.

'Does a Princess of Wales have a house in London as well as here?' she asked. 'Shall I go back to Baynard's Castle?'

'You are not the Princess of Wales,' Lady Margaret started. She was going to explain but the look that Catalina turned on her was so darkly angry that she hesitated. 'I beg your pardon,' she said. 'I thought perhaps you did not understand . . .'

'Understand what?' Catalina's white face was slowly flushing pink with temper.

'Princess?'

'Princess of what?' Catalina snapped.

Lady Margaret dropped into a curtsey, and stayed low.

'Princess of what?' Catalina shouted loudly, and the door opened behind them and Dona Elvira came quickly into the room and then checked as she saw Catalina on her feet, her cheeks burning with temper, and Lady Margaret on her knees. She went out again without a word.

'Princess of Spain,' Lady Margaret said very quietly.

There was intense silence.

'I am the Princess of Wales,' Catalina said slowly. 'I have been the Princess of Wales all my life.'

Lady Margaret rose up and faced her. 'Now you are the Dowager Princess.'

Catalina clapped a hand over her mouth to hold back a cry of pain.

'I am sorry, Princess.'

Catalina shook her head, beyond words, her fist at her mouth muffling her whimpers of pain. Lady Margaret's face was grim. 'They will call you Dowager Princess.'

'I will never answer to it.'

'It is a title of respect. It is only the English word for widow.'

Catalina gritted her teeth and turned away from her friend to look out of the window. 'You can get up,' she said through her teeth. 'There is no need for you to kneel to me.'

The older woman rose to her feet and hesitated. 'The queen writes to me. They want to know of your health. Not only if you feel well, and strong enough to travel; they really need to know if you might be with child.'

Catalina clenched her hands together, turned away her face so that Lady Margaret should not see her cold rage.

'If you are with child and that child is a boy then he will be the Prince of Wales, and then King of England, and you would be My Lady the King's Mother,' Lady Margaret reminded her quietly.

'And if I am not with child?'

'Then you are the Dowager Princess, and Prince Harry is Prince of Wales.'

'And when the king dies?'

'Then Prince Harry becomes king.'

'And I?'

Lady Margaret shrugged in silence. 'Next to nothing', said the gesture. Aloud she said, 'You are the Infanta still.' Lady Margaret tried to smile. 'As you will always be.'

'And the next Queen of England?'

'Will be the wife of Prince Harry.'

The anger went out of Catalina, she walked to the fireplace, took hold of the high mantelpiece and steadied herself with it. The little fire burning in the grate threw out no heat that she could feel through the thick black skirt of her mourning gown. She stared at the flames as if she would understand what had happened to her.

'I am become again what I was, when I was a child of three,' she said slowly. 'The Infanta of Spain, not the Princess of Wales. A baby. Of no importance.'

Lady Margaret, whose own royal blood had been carefully diluted by a lowly marriage so that she could pose no threat to the Tudor throne of England, nodded. 'Princess, you take the position of your husband. It is always thus for all women. If you have no husband and no son, then you have no position. You have only what you were born to.'

'If I go home to Spain as a widow, and they marry me to an archduke, I will be Archduchess Catalina, and not a princess at all. Not Princess of Wales, and never Queen of England.'

Lady Margaret nodded. 'Like me,' she said.

Catalina turned her head. 'You?'

'I was a Plantagenet princess, King Edward's niece, sister to Edward of Warwick, the heir to King Richard's throne. If King Henry had lost the battle at Bosworth Field it would have been King Richard on the throne now, my brother as his heir and Prince of Wales, and I should be Princess Margaret, as I was born to be.'

'Instead you are Lady Margaret, wife to the warden of a little castle, not even his own, on the edge of England.'

The older woman nodded her assent to the bleak description of her status.

'Why did you not refuse?' Catalina asked rudely.

Lady Margaret glanced behind her to see that the door to the presence chamber was shut and none of Catalina's women could hear.

'How could I refuse?' she asked simply. 'My brother was in the Tower of London, simply for being born a prince. If I had refused to marry Sir Richard, I should have joined him. My brother put his dear head down on the block for nothing more than bearing his name. As a girl, I had the chance to change my name. So I did.'

'You had the chance to be Queen of England!' Catalina protested.

Lady Margaret turned away from the younger woman's energy.

'It is as God wills,' she said simply. 'My chance, such as it was, has gone. Your chance has gone too. You will have to find a way to live the rest of your life without regrets, Infanta.'

Catalina said nothing, but the face that she showed to her friend was closed and cold. 'I will find a way to fulfil my destiny,' she said. 'Ar —' She broke off, she could not name him, even to her friend. 'I once had a conversation about claiming one's own,' she said. 'I understand it now. I shall have to be a pretender to myself. I shall insist on what is mine. I know what is my duty and what I have to do. I shall do as God wills, whatever the difficulties for me.'

The older woman nodded. 'Perhaps God wills that you accept your fate. Perhaps it is God's will that you be resigned,' she suggested.

'He does not,' Catalina said firmly.

I will tell no-one what I promised. I will tell no-one that in my heart I am still Princess of Wales, I will always be Princess of Wales until I see the wedding of my son and see my daughter-in-law crowned. I will tell no-one that I understand now what Arthur told me: that even a princess born may have to claim her title.

I have told no-one whether or not I am with child. But I know, well enough. I had my course in April, there is no baby. There is no Princess Mary, there is no Prince Arthur. My love, my only love, is dead and there is nothing left of him for me, not even his unborn child.

I will say nothing, though people constantly pry and want to know. I have to consider what I am to do, and how I am to claim the throne that Arthur wanted for me. I have to think how to keep my promise to him, how to tell the lie that he wanted me to tell. How I can make it convincing, how I can fool the king himself, and his sharp-witted, hard-eyed mother.

But I have made a promise, I do not retract my word. He begged me for a promise and he dictated the lie I must tell, and I said 'yes'. I will not fail him. It is the last thing he asked of me, and I will do it. I will do it for him, and I will do it for our love.

Oh my love, if you knew how much I long to see you.

Catalina travelled to London with the black-trimmed curtains of the litter closed against the beauty of the countryside, as it came into full bloom. She did not see the people doff their caps or curtsey as the procession wound through the little English villages. She did not hear the men and women call 'God bless you, Princess!' as the litter jolted slowly down the village streets. She did not know that every young woman in the land crossed herself and prayed that she should not have the bad luck of the pretty Spanish princess who had come so far for love and then lost her man after only five months.

She was dully aware of the lush green of the countryside, of the fertile swelling of the crops in the fields and the fat cattle in the water-meadows. When their way wound through the thick forests, she noticed the coolness of the green shade, and the thick interleaving of the canopy of boughs over the road. Herds of deer vanished into the dappled shade and she could hear the calling of a cuckoo and the rattle of a woodpecker. It was a beautiful land, a wealthy land, a great inheritance for a young couple. She thought of Arthur's desire to protect this land of his against the Scots, against the Moors. Of his will to reign here better and more justly than it had ever been done before.

She did not speak to her hosts on the road who attributed her silence to grief, and pitied her for it. She did not speak to her ladies, not even to Maria who was at her side in silent sympathy, nor to Dona Elvira who, at this crisis in Spanish affairs, was everywhere; her husband organising the houses on the road, she herself ordering the princess's food, her bedding, her companions, her diet. Catalina said nothing and let them do as they wished with her.

Some of her hosts thought her sunk so deep in grief that she was beyond speech, and prayed that she should recover her wits again, and go back to Spain and make a new marriage that would bring her a new husband to replace the old. What they did not know was that Catalina was holding her grief for her husband in some hidden place deep inside her. Deliberately, she delayed her mourning until she had the safety to indulge in it. While she jolted along in the litter she was not weeping for him, she was racking her brains how to fulfil his dream. She was wondering how to obey him, as he had demanded. She was thinking how she should fulfil her deathbed promise to the only young man she had ever loved.

I shall have to be clever. I shall have to be more cunning than King Henry Tudor, more determined than his mother. Faced with those two, I don't know that I can get away with it. But I have to get away with it. I have given my promise, I will tell my lie. England shall be ruled as Arthur wanted. The rose will live again, I shall make the England that he wanted.

I wish I could have brought Lady Margaret with me to advise me, I miss her friendship, I miss her hard-won wisdom. I wish I could see her steady gaze and hear her counsel to be resigned, to bow to my destiny, to give myself to God's will. I would not follow her advice – but I wish I could hear it.

Summer 1502

Croydon, May 1502

The princess and her party arrived at Croydon Palace and Dona Elvira led Catalina to her private rooms. For once, the girl did not go to her bedchamber and close the door behind her, she stood in the sumptuous presence chamber, looking around her. 'A chamber fit for a princess,' she said.

'But it is not your own,' Dona Elvira said, anxious for her charge's status. 'It has not been given to you. It is just for your use.'

The young woman nodded. 'It is fitting,' she said.

'The Spanish ambassador is in attendance,' Dona Elvira told her. 'Shall I tell him that you will not see him?'

'I will see him,' Catalina said quietly. 'Tell him to come in.'

'You don't have to . . .'

'He may have word from my mother,' she said. 'I should like her advice.'

The duenna bowed and went to find the ambassador. He was deep in conversation in the gallery outside the presence chamber with Father Alessandro Geraldini, the princess's chaplain. Dona

Elvira regarded them both with dislike. The chaplain was a tall, handsome man, his dark good looks in stark contrast to those of his companion. The ambassador, Dr de Puebla, was tiny beside him, leaning against a chair to support his misshaped spine, his damaged leg tucked behind the other, his bright little face alight with excitement.

'She could be with child?' the ambassador confirmed in a whisper. 'You are certain?'

'Pray God it is so. She is certainly in hopes of it,' the confessor confirmed.

'Dr de Puebla!' the duenna snapped, disliking the confidential air between the two men. 'I shall take you to the princess now.'

De Puebla turned and smiled at the irritable woman. 'Certainly, Dona Elvira,' he said equably. 'At once.'

Dr de Puebla limped into the room, his richly trimmed black hat already in his hand, his small face wreathed in an unconvincing smile. He bowed low with a flourish, and came up to inspect the princess.

At once he was struck by how much she had changed in such a short time. She had come to England a girl, with a girl's optimism. He had thought her a spoilt child, one who had been protected from the harshness of the real world. In the fairy-tale palace of the Alhambra this had been the petted youngest daughter of the most powerful monarchs in Christendom. Her journey to England had been the first real discomfort she had been forced to endure, and she had complained about it bitterly, as if he could help the weather. On her wedding day, standing beside Arthur and hearing the cheers for him, had been the first time she had taken second place to anyone but her heroic parents.

But before him now was a girl who had been hammered by unhappiness into a fine maturity. This Catalina was thinner, and paler, but with a new spiritual beauty, honed by hardship. He drew his breath. This Catalina was a young woman with a queenly presence. She had become through grief not only Arthur's widow, but her mother's daughter. This was a princess from the line that had defeated the most powerful enemy of Christendom. This was the very bone of the bone and blood of the blood of Isabella of Castile. She was cool, she was hard. He hoped very much that she was not going to be difficult.

De Puebla gave her a smile that he meant to be reassuring and saw her scrutinise him with no answering warmth in her face. She gave him her hand and then she sat in a straight-backed wooden chair before the fire. 'You may sit,' she said graciously, gesturing him to a lower chair, further away.

He bowed again, and sat.

'Do you have any messages for me?'

'Of sympathy, from the king and Queen Elizabeth and from My Lady the King's Mother, and from myself of course. They will invite you to court when you have recovered from your journey and are out of mourning.'

'How long am I to be in mourning?' Catalina inquired.

'My Lady the King's Mother has said that you should be in seclusion for a month after the burial. But since you were not at court during that time, she has ruled that you will stay here until she commands you to return to London. She is concerned for your health . . .'

He paused, hoping that she would volunteer whether or not she was with child, but she let the silence stretch.

He thought he would ask her directly. 'Infanta . . .'

'You should call me princess,' she interrupted. 'I am the Princess of Wales.'

He hesitated, thrown off course. 'Dowager Princess,' he corrected her quietly.

Catalina nodded. 'Of course. It is understood. Do you have any letters from Spain?'

He bowed and gave her the letter he was carrying in the hidden pocket in his sleeve. She did not snatch it from him like a child and open it, then and there. She nodded her head in thanks and held it.

'Do you not want to open it now? Do you not want to reply?'

'When I have written my reply, I will send for you,' she said simply, asserting her power over him. 'I shall send for you when I want you.'

'Certainly, Your Grace.' He smoothed the velvet nap of his black breeches to hide his irritation but inwardly he thought it an impertinence that the Infanta, now a widow, should command where before the Princess of Wales had politely requested. He thought he perhaps did not like this new, finer Catalina, after all.

'And have you heard from Their Majesties in Spain?' she asked. 'Have they advised you as to their wishes?'

'Yes,' he said, wondering how much he should tell her. 'Of course, Queen Isabella is anxious that you are not unwell. She asked me to inquire after your health and to report to her.'

A secretive shadow crossed Catalina's face. 'I shall write to the queen my mother and tell her my news,' she said.

'She was anxious to know . . .' he began, probing for the answer to the greatest question: was there an heir? Was the princess with child?

'I shall confide in no-one but my mother.'

'We cannot proceed to the settlement of your jointure and your arrangements until we know,' he said bluntly. 'It makes a difference to everything.'

She did not flare up as he had thought she would do. She inclined her head, she had herself under tight control. 'I shall write to my mother,' she repeated, as if his advice did not much matter.

He saw he would get nothing more from her. But at least the chaplain had told him she could be with child, and he should know. The king would be glad to know that there was at least a possibility of an heir. At any rate she had not denied it. There might be capital to make from her silence. 'Then I will leave you to read your letter.' He bowed.

She made a casual gesture of dismissal and turned to look at the flames of the little summertime fire. He bowed again and, since she was not looking at him, scrutinised her figure. She had no bloom of early pregnancy but some women took it badly in the first months. Her pallor could be caused by morning sickness. It was impossible for a man to tell. He would have to rely on the confessor's opinion, and pass it on with a caution.

I open my mother's letter with hands that are trembling so much that I can hardly break the seals. The first thing I see is the shortness of the letter, only one page.

'Oh, Madre,' I breathe. 'No more?'

Perhaps she was in haste; but I am bitterly hurt to see that she has written so briefly! If she knew how much I want to hear her voice she would have written at twice the length. As God is my witness I don't think I can do this without her; I am only sixteen and a half, I need my mother.

I read the short letter through once, and then, almost incredulously, I read it through again.

It is not a letter from a loving mother to her daughter. It is not a letter from a woman to her favourite child, and that child on the very edge of despair. Coldly, powerfully, she has written a letter from a queen to a princess. She writes of nothing but business. We could be a pair of merchants concluding a sale.

She says that I am to stay in whatever house is provided for me until I have had my next course and I know that I am not with child. If that is the case I am to command Dr de Puebla to demand my jointure as Dowager Princess of Wales and as soon as I have the full money and <u>not before</u> (underlined so there can be no mistake), I am to take ship for Spain.

If, on the other hand, God is gracious, and I am with child, then I am to assure Dr de Puebla that the money for my dowry will be paid in cash and at once, he is to secure me my allowance as Dowager Princess of Wales, and I am to rest and hope for a boy.

I am to write to her at once and tell her if I think I am with child. I am to write to her as soon as I am certain, one way or the other, and I am to confide also in Dr de Puebla and to maintain myself under the chaperonage of Dona Elvira.

I fold the letter carefully, matching the edges one to another as if tidiness matters very much. I think that if she knew of the despair that laps at the edges of my mind like a river of darkness she would have written to me more kindly. If she knew how very alone I am, how grieved I am, how much I miss him, she would not write to me of settlements and jointures and titles. If she knew how much I loved him and how I cannot bear to live without him she would write and tell me that she loves me, that I am to go home to her at once, without delay.

I tuck the letter into the pocket at my waist, and I stand up, as if reporting for duty. I am not a child any more. I will not cry for my mother. I see that I am not in the especial care of God since he could let Arthur die. I see that I am not in the especial love of my mother, since she can leave me alone, in a strange land.

She is not only a mother, she is Queen of Spain, and she has to ensure that she has a grandson, or failing a grandson, a watertight treaty. I am not just a young woman who has lost the man she loves. I am a Princess of Spain and I have to produce a grandson, or failing that a watertight treaty. And in addition, I am now bound by a promise. I have promised that I will be Princess of Wales again, and Queen of England. I have promised this to the young man to whom I promised everything. I will perform it for him, whatever anyone else wants.

The Spanish ambassador did not report at once to Their Majesties of Spain. Instead, playing his usual double game, he took the chaplain's opinion first to the King of England.

'Her confessor says that she is with child,' he remarked.

For the first time in days King Henry felt his heart lighten. 'Good God, if that were so, it would change everything.'

'Please God it is so. I should be glad of it,' de Puebla agreed. 'But I cannot guarantee it. She shows no sign of it.'

'Could be early days,' Henry agreed. 'And God knows, and I know, a child in the cradle is not a prince on the throne. It's a long road to the crown. But it would be a great comfort to me if she was with child – and to the queen,' he added as an afterthought.

'So she must stay here in England until we know for sure,' the ambassador concluded. 'And if she is not with child we shall settle our accounts, you and I, and she shall go home. Her mother asks for her to be sent home at once.'

'We'll wait and see,' Henry said, conceding nothing. 'Her mother will have to wait like the rest of us. And if she is anxious to have her daughter home she had better pay the rest of the dowry.'

'You would not delay the return of the princess to her mother over a matter of money,' the ambassador suggested.

'The sooner everything is settled the better,' the king said smoothly. 'If she is with child then she is our daughter and the mother of our heir; nothing would be too good for her. If she is not, then she can go home to her mother as soon as her dowry is paid.'

I know that there is no Mary growing in my womb, there is no Arthur; but I shall say nothing until I know what to do. I dare say nothing until I am sure what I should do. My mother and father will be planning for the good of Spain, King Henry will be planning for the good

of England. Alone, I will have to find a way to fulfil my promise. Nobody will help me. Nobody can even know what I am doing. Only Arthur in heaven will understand what I am doing and I feel far, far away from him. It is so painful, a pain I could not imagine. I have never needed him more than now, now that he is dead, and only he can advise me how to fulfil my promise to him.

Catalina had spent less than a month of seclusion at Croydon Palace when the king's chamberlain came to tell her that Durham House in the Strand had been prepared for her and she could go there at her convenience.

'Is this where a Princess of Wales would stay?' Catalina demanded urgently of de Puebla, who had been immediately summoned to her privy chamber. 'Is Durham House where a princess would be housed? Why am I not to live in Baynard's Castle again?'

'Durham House is perfectly adequate,' he stammered, taken aback by her fervour. 'And your household is not diminished at all. The king has not asked you to dismiss anyone. You are to have an adequate court. And he will pay you an allowance.'

'My jointure as the prince's widow?'

He avoided her gaze. 'An allowance at this stage. He has not been paid your dowry from your parents, remember, so he will not pay your jointure. But he will give you a good sum, one that will allow you to keep your state.'

'I should have my jointure.'

He shook his head. 'He will not pay it until he has the full dowry. But it is a good allowance, you will keep a good state.'

He saw that she was immensely relieved. 'Princess, there is no question but that the king is respectful of your position,' he said carefully. 'You need have no fears of that. Of course, if he could be assured as to your health . . .'

Again the shuttered look closed down Catalina's face. 'I don't know what you mean,' she said shortly. 'I am well. You can tell him that I am well. Nothing more.'

I am buying time, letting them think that I am with child. It is such agony, knowing that my time of the month has come and gone, that I am ready for Arthur's seed, but he is cold and gone and he will never come to my bed again, and we will never make his daughter Mary and his son Arthur.

I cannot bear to tell them the truth: I am barren, without a baby to raise for him. And while I say nothing they have to wait too. They will not send me home to Spain while they hope that I might still be My Lady the Mother of the Prince of Wales. They have to wait.

And while they wait I can plan what I shall say, and what I shall do. I have to be wise as my mother would be, and cunning as the fox, my father. I have to be determined like her, and secretive like him. I have to think how and when I shall start to tell this lie, Prince Arthur's great lie. If I can tell it so that it convinces everyone, if I can place myself so that I fulfil my destiny, then Arthur, beloved Arthur, can do as he wished. He can rule England through me, I can marry his brother and become queen. Arthur can live through the child I conceive with his brother, we can make the England we swore that we would make, despite misfortune, despite his brother's folly, despite my own despair.

I shall not give myself to heartbreak, I shall give myself to England. I shall keep my promise. I shall be constant to my husband and to my destiny. And I shall plan and plot and consider how I shall conquer this misfortune and be what I was born to be. How I shall be the pretender who becomes the queen.

The little court moved to Durham House in late June and the remainder of Catalina's court straggled in from Ludlow Castle, speaking of a town in silence and a castle in mourning. Catalina did not seem particularly pleased at the change of scene, though Durham House was a pretty palace with lovely gardens running down to the river, with its own stairs and a pier for boats. The ambassador came to visit and found her in the gallery at the front of the house, which overlooked the front courtyard below and Ivy Lane beyond.

She let him stand before her.

'Her Grace, the queen your mother, is sending an emissary to escort you home as soon as your widow's jointure is paid. Since you have not told us that you are with child she is preparing for your journey.'

De Puebla saw her press her lips together as if to curb a hasty reply. 'How much does the king have to pay me, as his son's widow?'

'He has to pay you a third of the revenues of Wales, Cornwall and Chester,' he said. 'And your parents are now asking, in addition, that King Henry return all of your dowry.'

Catalina looked aghast. 'He never will,' she said flatly. 'No emissary will be able to convince him. King Henry will never pay such sums to me. He didn't even pay my allowance when his son was alive. Why should he repay the dowry and pay a jointure when he has nothing to gain from it?'

The ambassador shrugged his shoulders. 'It is in the contract.'

'So too was my allowance, and you failed to make him pay that,' she said sharply.

'You should have handed over your plate as soon as you arrived.'

'And eat off what?' she blazed out.

Insolently, he stood before her. He knew, as she did not yet understand, that she had no power. Every day that she failed to announce she was with child her importance diminished. He was certain that she was barren. He thought her a fool now; she had bought herself a little time by her discretion – but for what? Her disapproval of him mattered very little; she would soon be gone. She might rage but nothing would change.

'Why did you ever agree to such a contract? You must have known he would not honour it.'

He shrugged. The conversation was meaningless. 'How should we think there would ever be such a tragic occurrence? Who could have imagined that the prince would die, just as he entered into adult life? It is so very sad.'

'Yes, yes,' said Catalina. She had promised herself she would never cry for Arthur in front of anyone. The tears must stay back. 'But now, thanks to this contract, the king is deep in debt to me. He has to return the dowry that he has been paid, he cannot have my plate, and he owes me this jointure. Ambassador, you must know that he will never pay this much. And clearly he will never give me the rents of – where? – Wales and, and Cornwall? – forever.'

'Only until you remarry,' he observed. 'He has to pay your jointure until you remarry. And we must assume that you will remarry soon. Their Majesties will want you to return home in order to arrange a new marriage for you. I imagine that the emissary is coming to fetch you home just for that. They probably have a marriage contract drawn up for you already. Perhaps you are already betrothed.'

For one moment de Puebla saw the shock in her face then she turned abruptly from him to stare out of the window on the courtyard before the palace and the open gates to the busy streets outside.

He watched the tightly stretched shoulders and the tense turn of her neck, surprised that his shot at her second marriage had hit her so hard. Why should she be so shocked at the mention of marriage? Surely she must know that she would go home only to be married again?

215

Catalina let the silence grow as she watched the street beyond the Durham House gate. It was so unlike her home. There were no dark men in beautiful gowns, there were no veiled women. There were no street sellers with rich piles of spices, no flower sellers staggering under small mountains of blooms. There were no herbalists, physicians, or astronomers, plying their trade as if knowledge could be freely available to anyone. There was no silent movement to the mosque for prayer five times a day, there was no constant splash of fountains. Instead there was the bustle of one of the greatest cities in the world, the relentless, unstoppable buzz of prosperity and commerce, and the ringing of the bells of hundreds of churches. This was a city bursting with confidence, rich on its own trade, exuberantly wealthy.

'This is my home now,' she said. Resolutely she put aside the pictures in her mind of a warmer city, of a smaller community, of an easier, more exotic world. 'The king should not think that I will go home and remarry as if none of this has happened. My parents should not think that they can change my destiny. I was brought up to be Princess of Wales and Queen of England. I shall not be cast off like a bad debt.'

The ambassador, from a race who had known disappointment, so much older and wiser than the girl who stood at the window, smiled at her unseeing back. 'Of course it shall be as you wish,' he lied easily. 'I shall write to your father and mother and say that you prefer to wait here, in England, while your future is decided.'

Catalina rounded on him. 'No, I shall decide my future.'

He had to bite the inside of his cheeks to hide his smile. 'Of course you will, Infanta.'

'Dowager Princess.'

'Dowager Princess.'

She took a breath; but when it came, her voice was quite steady. 'You may tell my father and mother, and you shall tell the king, that I am not with child.'

'Indeed,' he breathed. 'Thank you for informing us. That makes everything much clearer.'

'How so?'

'The king will release you. You can go home. He would have no claim on you, no interest in you. There can be no reason for you to stay. I shall have to make arrangements but your jointure can follow you. You can leave at once.'

'No,' she said flatly.

De Puebla was surprised. 'Dowager Princess, you can be released from this failure. You can go home. You are free to go.'

'You mean the English think they have no use for me?'

He gave the smallest of shrugs, as if to ask: what was she good for, since she was neither maid nor mother?

'What else can you do here? Your time here is over.'

She was not yet ready to show him her full plan. 'I shall write to my mother,' was all she would reply. 'But you are not to make arrangements for me to leave. It may be that I shall stay in England for a little while longer. If I am to be remarried, I could be remarried in England.'

'To whom?' he demanded.

She looked away from him. 'How should I know? My parents and the king should decide.'

I have to find a way to put my marriage to Harry into the mind of the king. Now that he knows I am not with child surely it will occur to him that the resolution for all our difficulties is to marry me to Harry?

If I trusted Dr de Puebla more, I should ask him to hint to the king that I could be betrothed to Harry. But I do not trust him. He muddled my first marriage contract, I don't want him muddling this one.

If I could get a letter to my mother without de Puebla seeing it then I could tell her of my plan, of Arthur's plan.

But I cannot. I am alone in this. I do feel so fearfully alone.

'They are going to name Prince Harry as the new Prince of Wales,' Dona Elvira said quietly to the princess as she was brushing her hair in the last week of June. 'He is to be Prince Harry, Prince of Wales.'

She expected the girl to break down at this last severing of her links with the past but Catalina did nothing but look around the room. 'Leave us,' she said shortly to the maids who were laying out her nightgown and turning down the bed.

They went out quietly and closed the door behind them. Catalina tossed back her hair and met Dona Elvira's eyes in the mirror. She handed her the hairbrush again and nodded for her to continue.

'I want you to write to my parents and tell them that my marriage with Prince Arthur was not consummated,' she said, smoothly. 'I am a virgin as I was when I left Spain.'

Dona Elvira was stunned, the hairbrush suspended in mid-air, her mouth open. 'You were bedded in the sight of the whole court,' she said.

'He was impotent,' Catalina said, her face as hard as a diamond.

'You were together once a week.'

'With no effect,' she said, unwavering. 'It was a great sadness to him, and to me.'

'Infanta, you never said anything. Why did you not tell me?'

Catalina's eyes were veiled. 'What should I say? We were newly wed. He was very young. I thought it would come right in time.'

Dona Elvira did not even pretend to believe her. 'Princess, there is no need for you to say this. Just because you have been a wife need not damage your future. Being a widow is no obstacle to a

218

good marriage. They will find someone for you. They will find a good match for you, you do not have to pretend . . .'

'I don't want "someone"; Catalina said fiercely. 'You should know that as well as me. I was born to be Princess of Wales and Queen of England. It was Arthur's greatest wish that I should be Queen of England.' She pulled herself back from thinking of him, or saying more. She bit her lip; she should not have tried to say his name. She forced down the tears and took a breath. 'I am a virgin untouched, now, as I was in Spain. You shall tell them that.'

'But we need say nothing, we can go back to Spain, anyway,' the older woman pointed out.

'They will marry me to some lord, perhaps an archduke,' Catalina said. 'I don't want to be sent away again. Do you want to run my household in some little Spanish castle? Or Austria? Or worse? You will have to come with me, remember. Do you want to end up in the Netherlands, or Germany?'

Dona Elvira's eyes darted away, she was thinking furiously. 'No-one would believe us if we say you are a virgin.'

'They would. You have to tell them. No-one would dare to ask me. You can tell them. It has to be you to tell them. They will believe you because you are close to me, as close as a mother.'

'I have said nothing so far.'

'And that was right. But you will speak now. Dona Elvira, if you don't seem to know, or if you say one thing and I say another, then everyone will know that you are not in my confidence, that you have not cared for me as you should. They will think you are negligent of my interests, that you have lost my favour. I should think that my mother would recall you in disgrace if she thought that I was a virgin and you did not even know. You would never serve in a royal court again if they thought you had neglected me.'

'Everyone saw that he was in love with you.'

'No they didn't. Everyone saw that we were together, as a prince and princess. Everyone saw that he came to my bedroom only as he had been ordered. No more. No-one can say what went on behind the bedroom door. No-one but me. And I say that he was impotent. Who are you to deny that? Do you dare to call me a liar?'

The older woman bowed her head to gain time. 'If you say so,' she said carefully. 'Whatever you say, Infanta.'

'Princess.'

'Princess,' the woman repeated.

'And I do say it. It is my way ahead. Actually, it is your way ahead too. We can say this one, simple thing and stay in England; or we can return to Spain in mourning and become next to nobody.'

'Of course, I can tell them what you wish. If you wish to say your husband was impotent and you are still a maid then I can say that. But how will this make you queen?'

'Since the marriage was not consummated, there can be no objection to me marrying Prince Arthur's brother Harry,' Catalina said in a hard, determined voice.

Dona Elvira gasped with shock at this next stage.

Catalina pressed on. 'When this new emissary comes from Spain you may inform him that it is God's will and my desire that I be Princess of Wales again, as I always have been. He shall speak to the king. He shall negotiate, not my widow's jointure, but my next wedding.'

Dona Elvira gaped. 'You cannot make your own marriage!'

'I can,' Catalina said fiercely. 'I will, and you will help me.'

'You cannot think that they will let you marry Prince Harry?'

'Why should they not? The marriage with his brother was not consummated. I am a virgin. The dowry to the king is half-paid. He can keep the half he already has and we can give him the rest of it. He need not pay my jointure. The contract has been signed and sealed, they need only change the names, and here I am in England already. It is the best solution for everyone. Without it I become nothing; you certainly are nobody. Your ambition, your husband's ambition, will all come to nothing. But if we can win this then you will be the mistress of a royal household, and I will be as I should be: Princess of Wales and Queen of England.'

'They will not let us!' Dona Elvira gasped, appalled at her charge's ambition.

'They will let us,' Catalina said fiercely. 'We have to fight for it. We have to be what we should be; nothing less.'

Princess in Waiting

Winter 1503

King Henry and his queen, driven by the loss of their son, were expecting another child, and Catalina, hoping for their favour, was sewing an exquisite layette of baby clothes before a small fire in the smallest room of Durham Palace in the early days of February 1503. Her ladies, hemming seams according to their abilities, were seated at a distance; Dona Elvira could speak privately.

'This should be your baby's layette,' the duenna said resentfully under her breath. 'A widow for a year, and no progress made. What is going to become of you?'

Catalina looked up from her delicate black-thread work. 'Peace, Dona Elvira,' she said quietly. 'It will be as God and my parents and the king decide.'

'Seventeen, now,' Dona Elvira said, stubbornly pursuing her theme, her head down. 'How long are we to stay in this Godforsaken country, neither a bride nor a wife? Neither at court nor elsewhere? With bills mounting up and the jointure still not paid?'

'Dona Elvira, if you knew how much your words grieve me, I don't think you would say them,' Catalina said clearly. 'Just because you mutter them into your sewing like a cursing Egyptian doesn't mean I don't hear them. If I knew what was to happen, I would tell you myself at once. You will not learn any more by whispering your fears.'

The woman looked up and met Catalina's clear gaze.

'I think of you,' she said bluntly. 'Even if no-one else does. Even if that fool ambassador and that idiot the emissary does not. If the king does not order your marriage to the prince then what is to become of you? If he will not let you go, if your parents do not insist on your return, then what is going to happen? Is he just going to keep you forever? Are you a princess or a prisoner? It is nearly a year. Are you a hostage for the alliance with Spain? How long can you wait? You are seventeen, how long can you wait?'

'I am waiting,' Catalina said calmly. 'Patiently. Until it is resolved.'

The duenna said nothing more, Catalina did not have the energy to argue. She knew that during this year of mourning for Arthur, she had been steadily pushed more and more to the margins of court life. Her claim to be a virgin had not produced a new betrothal as she had thought it would; it had made her yet more irrelevant. She was only summoned to court on the great occasions, and then she was dependent on the kindness of Queen Elizabeth.

The king's mother, Lady Margaret, had no interest in the impoverished Spanish princess. She had not proved readily fertile, she now said she had never even been bedded, she was widowed and brought no more money into the royal treasury. She was of no use to the house of Tudor except as a bargaining counter in the continuing struggle with Spain. She might as well stay at her house in the Strand, as be summoned to court. Besides, My Lady the King's Mother did not like the way that the new Prince of Wales looked at his widowed sister-in-law.

Whenever Prince Harry met her, he fixed his eyes on her with puppy-like devotion. My Lady the King's Mother had privately decided that she would keep them apart. She thought that the girl smiled on the young prince too warmly, she thought she encouraged his boyish adoration to serve her own foreign vanity. My Lady the King's Mother was resentful of anyone's influence on the only surviving son and heir. Also, she mistrusted Catalina. Why would the young widow encourage a brother-in-law who was nearly six years her junior? What did she hope to gain from his friendship? Surely she knew that he was kept as close as a child: bedded in his father's rooms, chaperoned night and day, constantly supervised? What did the Spanish widow hope to achieve by sending him books, teaching him Spanish, laughing at his accent and watching him ride at the quintain, as if he were in training as her knight errant?

Nothing would come of it. Nothing could come of it. But My Lady the King's Mother would allow no-one to be intimate with Harry but herself, and she ruled that Catalina's visits to court were to be rare and brief.

The king himself was kind enough to Catalina when he saw her, but she felt him eye her as if she were some sort of treasure that he had purloined. She always felt with him as if she were some sort of trophy – not a young woman of seventeen years old, wholly dependent on his honour, his daughter by marriage.

If she could have brought herself to speak of Arthur to her mother-in-law or to the king then perhaps they would have sought her out to share their grief. But she could not use his name to curry favour with them. Even a year since his death, she could not think of him without a tightness in her chest which was so great that she thought it could stop her breathing for very grief. She still could not say his name out loud. She certainly could not play on her grief to help her at court.

'But what will happen?' Dona Elvira continued.

Catalina turned her head away. 'I don't know,' she said shortly.

'Perhaps if the queen has another son with this baby, the king will send us back to Spain,' the duenna pursued.

Catalina nodded. 'Perhaps.'

The duenna knew her well enough to recognise Catalina's silent determination. 'Your trouble is, that you still don't want to go,' she whispered. 'The king may keep you as a hostage against the dowry money, your parents may let you stay; but if you insisted you could get home. You still think you can make them marry you to Harry; but if that was going to happen you would be betrothed by now. You have to give up. We have been here a year now and you make no progress. You will trap us all here while you are defeated.'

Catalina's sandy eyelashes swept down to veil her eyes. 'Oh no,' she said. 'I don't think that.'

There was a sharp rap at the door. 'Urgent message for the Dowager Princess of Wales!' the voice called out.

Catalina dropped her sewing and rose to her feet. Her ladies sprang up too. It was so unusual for anything to happen in the quiet court of Durham House that they were thrown into a flutter.

'Well, let him in!' Catalina exclaimed.

Maria de Salinas flung open the door and one of the royal grooms of the chamber came in and kneeled before the princess. 'Grave news,' he said shortly. 'A son, a prince, has been born of the queen and has died. Her Grace the Queen has died too. God pray for His Grace in his kingly grief.'

'What?' demanded Dona Elvira, trying to take in the astounding rush of events.

'God save her soul,' Catalina replied correctly. 'God save the King.'

'Heavenly Father, take Your daughter Elizabeth into Your keeping. You must love her, she was a woman of great gentleness and grace.'

I sit back on my heels and abandon the prayer. I think the queen's life, ended so tragically, was one of sorrow. If Arthur's version of the scandal were true, then she had been prepared to marry King Richard, however despicable a tyrant. She had wanted to marry him and be his queen. Her mother and My Lady the King's Mother and the victory of

Bosworth had forced her to take King Henry. She had been born to be Queen of England, and she had married the man who could give her the throne.

I thought that if I had been able to tell her of my promise then she would have known the pain that seeps through me like ice every time I think of Arthur, and know that I promised him I would marry Harry. I thought that she might have understood if you are born to be Queen of England you have to be Queen of England, whoever is king. Whoever your husband will have to be.

Without her quiet presence at court I feel that I am more at risk, further from my goal. She was kind to me, she was a loving woman. I was waiting out my year of mourning and trusting that she would help me into marriage with Harry, because he would be a refuge for me, and because I would be a good wife to him. I was trusting that she knew one could marry a man for whom one feels nothing but indifference and still be a good wife.

But now the court will be ruled by My Lady the King's Mother and she is a formidable woman, no friend to anyone but her own cause, no affection for anyone but her son Henry, and his son, Prince Harry.

She will help no-one but she will serve the interests of her own family first. She will consider me as only one candidate among many for his hand in marriage. God forgive her, she might even look to a French bride for him and then I will have failed not only Arthur but my own mother and father too, who need me to maintain the alliance between England and Spain and the enmity between England and France.

This year has been hard for me, I had expected a year of mourning and then a new betrothal; I have been growing more and more anxious since no-one seems to be planning such a thing. And now I am afraid that it will get worse. What if King Henry decides to surrender the second part of the dowry and sends me home? What if they betroth Harry, that foolish boy, to someone else? What if they just forget me? Hold me as a hostage to the good behaviour of Spain but neglect me?

Leave me at Durham House, a shadow princess over a shadow court, while the real world goes on elsewhere?

I hate this time of year in England, the way the winter lingers on and on in cold mists and grey skies. In the Alhambra the water in the canals will be released from frost and starting to flow again, icy cold, rushing deep with melt-water from the snows of the sierra. The earth will be starting to warm in the gardens, the men will be planting flowers and young saplings, the sun will be warm in the mornings and the thick hangings will be taken down from the windows so the warm breezes can blow through the palace again.

The birds of summer will come back to the high hills and the olive trees will shimmer their leaves of green and grey. Everywhere the farmers will be turning over the red soil, and there will be the scent of life and growth.

I long to be home; but I will not leave my post. I am not a soldier who forgets his duty, I am a sentry who wakes all night. I will not fail my love. I said 'I promise', and I do not forget it. I will be constant to him. The garden that is immortal life, al-Yanna, will wait for me, the rose will wait for me in al-Yanna, Arthur will wait for me there. I will be Queen of England as I was born to be, as I promised him I would be. The rose will bloom in England as well as in heaven.

There was a great state funeral for Queen Elizabeth, and Catalina was in mourning black again. Through the dark lace of her mantilla she watched the orders of precedence, the arrangements for the service, she saw how everything was commanded by the great book of the king's mother. Even her own place was laid down, behind the princesses, but before all the other ladies of the court.

Lady Margaret, the king's mother, had written down all the procedures to be followed at the Tudor court, from birth chambers to lying in state, so that her son and the generations which she prayed would come after him would be prepared for every occasion, so that each occasion would match another, and so that every occasion, however distant in the future, would be commanded by her.

Now her first great funeral, for her unloved daughter-in-law, went off with the order and grace of a well-planned masque at court, and as the great manager of everything she stepped up visibly, unquestionably, to her place as the greatest lady at court.

2nd April 1503

It was a year to the day that Arthur had died and Catalina spent the day alone in the chapel of Durham House. Father Geraldini held a memorial Mass for the young prince at dawn and Catalina stayed in the little church, without breaking her fast, without taking so much as a cup of small ale, all the day.

Some of the time she knelt before the altar, her lips moving in silent prayer, struggling with the loss of him with a grief which was as sharp and as raw as the day that she had stood on the threshold of his room and learned that they could not save him, that he would die, that she would have to live without him.

For some of the long hours, she prowled around the empty chapel, pausing to look at the devotional pictures on the walls or the exquisite carving of the pew ends and the rood screen. Her horror was that she was forgetting him. There were mornings when she woke and tried to see his face, and found that she could see nothing beneath her closed eyelids, or worse, all she could see was some rough sketch of him, a poor likeness: the simulacrum and no longer the real thing. Those mornings she would sit up quickly, clench her knees up to her belly, and hold herself tight so that she did not give way to her agonising sense of loss.

Then, later in the day she would be talking to her ladies, or sewing, or walking by the river, and someone would say something, or she would see the sun on the water and suddenly he would be there before her, as vivid as if he were alive, lighting up the afternoon. She would stand quite still for a moment, silently drinking him in, and then she would go on with the conversation, or continue her walk, knowing that she would never forget him. Her eyes had the print of him on their lids, her body had the touch of him on her skin, she was his, heart and soul, till death: not – as it turned out – till his death; but till her death. Only when the two of them were gone from this life would their marriage in this life be over.

But on this, the anniversary of his death, Catalina had promised herself that she should be alone, she would allow herself the indulgence of mourning, of railing at God for taking him.

'You know, I shall never understand Your purpose,' I say to the statue of the crucified Christ, hanging by His bloodstained palms over the altar. 'Can you not give me a sign? Can you not show me what I should do?'

I wait but He says nothing. I have to wonder if the God who spoke so clearly to my mother is sleeping, or gone away. Why should He direct her, and yet remain silent for me? Why should I, raised as a fervently Christian child, a passionately Roman Catholic child, have no sense of being heard when I pray from my deepest grief? Why should God desert me, when I need Him so much?

I return to the embroidered kneeler before the altar but I do not kneel on it in a position of prayer, I turn it around and sit on it, as if I were at home, a cushion pulled up to a warm brazier, ready to talk, ready to listen. But no-one speaks to me now. Not even my God.

'I know it is Your will that I should be queen,' I say thoughtfully, as if He might answer, as if He might suddenly reply in a tone as reasonable as my own. 'I know that it is my mother's wish too. I know

that my darling –' I cut short the end of the sentence. Even now, a year on, I cannot take the risk of saying Arthur's name, even in an empty chapel, even to God. I still fear an outpouring of tears, the slide into hysteria and madness. Behind my control is a passion for Arthur like a deep mill pond held behind a sluice gate. I dare not let one drop of it out. There would be a flood of sorrow, a torrent.

'I know that he wished I should be queen. On his deathbed, he asked for a promise. In Your sight, I gave him that promise. In Your name I gave it. I meant it. I am sworn to be queen. But how am I to do it? If it is Your will, as well as his, as I believe, if it is Your will as well as my mother's, as I believe, then, God: hear this. I have run out of stratagems. It has to be You. You have to show me the way to do it.'

I have been demanding this of God with more and more urgency for a year now; while the endless negotiations about the repayment of the dowry and the payment of the jointure drag on and on. Without one clear word from my mother I have come to think that she is playing the same game as me. Without doubt, I know that my father will have some long tactical play in mind. If only they would tell me what I should do! In their discreet silence I have to guess that they are leaving me here as bait for the king. They are leaving me here until the king sees, as I see, as Arthur saw, that the best resolution of this difficulty would be for me to marry Prince Harry.

The trouble is, that as every month goes by, Harry grows in stature and status at the court: he becomes a more attractive prospect. The French king will make a proposal for him, the hundred princelings of Europe with their pretty daughters will make offers, even the Holy Roman Emperor has an unmarried daughter Margaret, who might suit. We have to bring this to a decision now, this very month of April, as my first year of widowhood ends. Now that I am free from my year of waiting. But the balance of power has changed. King Henry is in no hurry, his heir is young – a boy of only eleven. But I am seventeen years old. It is time I was married. It is time I was Princess of Wales once more.

Their Majesties of Spain are demanding the moon: full restitution of their investment, and the return of their daughter, the full widow's jointure to be paid for an indefinite period. The great cost of this is designed to prompt the King of England to find another way. My parents' patience with negotiation allows England to keep both me and the money. They show that they expect the return of neither me nor the money. They are hoping that the King of England will see that he need return neither the dowry nor me.

But they underestimate him. King Henry does not need them to hint him to it. He will have seen perfectly well for himself. Since he is not progressing, he must be resisting both demands. And why should he not? He is in possession. He has half the dowry, and he has me.

And he is no fool. The calmness of the new emissary, Don Gutierre Gomez de Fuensalida, and the slowness of the negotiations has alerted this most acute king to the fact that my mother and father are content to leave me in his hands, in England. It does not take a Machiavelli to conclude that my parents hope for another English marriage – just as when Isabel was widowed they sent her back to Portugal to marry her brother-in-law. These things happen. But only if everyone is in agreement. In England, where the king is new-come to his throne and filled with ambition, it may take more skill than we can deploy to bring it about.

My mother writes to me to say she has a plan but it will take some time to come to fruition. In the meantime she tells me to be patient and never to do anything to offend the king or his mother.

'I am Princess of Wales,' I reply to her. 'I was born to be Princess of Wales and Queen of England. You raised me in these titles. Surely, I should not deny my own upbringing? Surely, I can be Princess of Wales and Queen of England, even now?'

'Be patient,' she writes back to me, in a travel-stained note which *takes weeks to get to me and which has been opened; anyone can have read it. 'I agree that your destiny is to be Queen of England. It is your destiny, God's will, and my wish. Be patient.'*

'How long must I be patient?' I ask God, on my knees to Him in His chapel on the anniversary of Arthur's death. 'If it is Your will, why do You not do it at once? If it is not Your will, why did You not destroy me with Arthur? If You are listening to me now – why do I feel so terribly alone?'

Late in the evening a rare visitor was announced in the quiet presence chamber of Durham House. 'Lady Margaret Pole,' said the guard at the door. Catalina dropped her Bible and turned her pale face to see her friend hesitating shyly in the doorway.

'Lady Margaret!'

'Dowager Princess!' She curtseyed low and Catalina went swiftly across the room to her, raised her up and fell into her arms.

'Don't cry,' Lady Margaret said quietly into her ear. 'Don't cry or I swear I shall weep.'

'I won't, I won't, I promise I won't.' Catalina turned to her ladies. 'Leave us,' she said.

They went reluctantly, a visitor was a novelty in the quiet house, and besides there were no fires burning in any of the other chambers. Lady Margaret looked around the shabby room.

'What is this?'

Catalina shrugged and tried to smile. 'I am a poor manager, I am afraid. And Dona Elvira is no help. And in truth, I have only the money the king gives me and that is not much.'

'I was afraid of this,' the older woman said. Catalina drew her to the fire and sat her down on her own chair.

'I thought you were still at Ludlow?'

'We were. We have been. Since neither the king nor the prince comes to Wales all the business has fallen on my husband. You would think me a princess again to see my little court there.'

Catalina again tried to smile. 'Are you grand?'

'Very. And mostly Welsh-speaking. Mostly singing.'

'I can imagine.'

'We came for the queen's funeral, God bless her, and then I wanted to stay for a little longer and my husband said that I might come and see you. I have been thinking of you all day, today.'

'I have been in the chapel,' Catalina said inconsequently. 'It doesn't seem like a year.'

'It doesn't, does it?' Lady Margaret agreed, though privately she thought that the girl had aged far more than one year. Grief had refined her girlish prettiness, she had the clear, decided looks of a woman who had seen her hopes destroyed. 'Are you well?'

Catalina made a little face. 'I am well enough. And you? And the children?'

Lady Margaret smiled. 'Praise God, yes. But do you know what plans the king has for you? Are you to . . .' She hesitated. 'Are you to go back to Spain? Or stay here?'

Catalina drew a little closer. 'They are talking, about the dowry, about my return. But nothing gets done. Nothing is decided. The king is holding me and holding my dowry, and my parents are letting him do it.'

Lady Margaret looked concerned. 'I had heard that they might consider betrothing you to Prince Harry,' she said. 'I did not know.'

'It is the obvious choice. But it does not seem obvious to the king,' Catalina said wryly. 'What do you think? Is he a man to miss an obvious solution, d'you think?'

'No,' said Lady Margaret, whose life had been jeopardised by the king's awareness of the obvious fact of her family's claim on his throne.

'Then I must assume that he has thought of this choice and is waiting to see if it is the best he can make,' Catalina said. She gave a little sigh. 'God knows, it is weary work, waiting.'

'Now your mourning is over, no doubt he will make arrangements,' her friend said hopefully.

'No doubt,' Catalina replied.

After weeks spent alone, mourning for his wife, the king returned to the court at Whitehall Palace, and Catalina was invited to dine with the royal family and seated with the Princess Mary and the ladies of the court. The young Harry, Prince of Wales, was placed securely between his father and grandmother. Not for this Prince of Wales the cold journey to Ludlow Castle and the rigorous training of a prince in waiting. Lady Margaret had ruled that this prince, their only surviving heir, should be brought up under her own eye, in ease and comfort. He was not to be sent away, he was to be watched all the time. He was not even allowed to take part in dangerous sports, jousting or fighting, though he was quite wild to take part, and a boy who loved activity and excitement. His grandmother had ruled that he was too precious to risk.

He smiled at Catalina and she shot him a look that she hoped was discreetly warm. But there was no opportunity to exchange so much as one word. She was firmly anchored further down the table and she could hardly see him thanks to My Lady the King's Mother, who plied him with the best of all foods from her own plate, and interposed her broad shoulder between him and the ladies.

Catalina thought that it was as Arthur had said, that the boy was spoiled by this attention. His grandmother leaned back for a moment to speak to one of the ushers and Catalina saw Harry's gaze flick towards her. She gave him a smile and then cast down her eyes. When she glanced up, he was still looking at her and then he blushed red to be caught. 'A child.' She shot a sideways little smile even as she silently criticised him. 'A child of eleven. All boasting and boyishness. And why should this plump, spoilt boy be spared when Arthur . . .' At once she stopped the thought. To compare Arthur with his brother was to wish the little boy dead, and she would not do that. To think of Arthur in public was to risk breaking down and she would never do that.

'A woman could rule a boy like that,' she thought. 'A woman could be a very great queen if she married such a boy. For the first ten years he would know nothing, and by then, perhaps he might be in such a habit of obedience that he would let his wife continue to rule. Or he might be, as Arthur told me, a lazy boy. A young man wasted. He might be so lazy that he could be diverted by games and hunting and sports and amusements, so that the business of the kingdom could be done by his wife.'

Catalina never forgot that Arthur had told her that the boy fancied himself in love with her. 'If they give him everything that he wants, perhaps he might be the one who chooses his bride,' she thought. 'They are in the habit of indulging him. Perhaps he could beg to marry me and they would feel obliged to say "yes".'

She saw him blush even redder, even his ears turned pink. She held his gaze for a long moment, she took in a little breath and parted her lips as if to whisper a word to him. She saw his blue eyes focus on her mouth and darken with desire, and then, calculating the effect, she looked down. 'Stupid boy,' she thought.

The king rose from the table and all the men and women on the crowded benches of the hall rose too, and bowed their heads.

'Give you thanks for coming to greet me,' King Henry said. 'Comrades in war and friends in peace. But now forgive me, as I wish to be alone.'

He nodded to Harry, he offered his mother his hand, and the royal family went through the little doorway at the back of the great hall to their privy chamber.

'You should have stayed longer,' the king's mother remarked as they settled into chairs by the fire and the groom of the ewery brought them wine. 'It looks bad, to leave so promptly. I had told the Master of Horse you would stay, and there would be singing.'

'I was weary,' Henry said shortly. He looked over to where Catalina and the Princess Mary were sitting together. The younger girl was red-eyed, the loss of her mother had hit her hard. Catalina was – as usual – cool as a stream. He thought she had great power of self-containment. Even this loss of her only real friend at court, her last friend in England, did not seem to distress her.

'She can go back to Durham House tomorrow,' his mother remarked, following the direction of his gaze. 'It does no good for her to come to court. She has not earned her place here with an heir, and she has not paid for her place here with her dowry.'

'She is constant,' he said. 'She is constant in her attendance on you, and on me.'

'Constant like the plague,' his mother returned.

'You are hard on her.'

'It is a hard world,' she said simply. 'I am nothing but just. Why don't we send her home?'

'Do you not admire her at all?'

She was surprised by the question. 'What is there to admire in her?'

'Her courage, her dignity. She has beauty, of course, but she also has charm. She is educated, she is graceful. I think, in other circumstances, she could have been merry. And she has borne herself, under this disappointment, like a queen.'

'She is of no use to us,' she said. 'She was our Princess of Wales; but our boy is dead. She is of no use to us now, however charming she may seem to be.'

Catalina looked up and saw them watching her. She gave a small, controlled smile and inclined her head. Henry rose, went to a window bay on his own, and crooked his finger for her. She did not jump to come to him, as any of the women of court would have jumped. She looked at him, she raised an eyebrow as if she were considering whether or not to obey, and then she gracefully rose to her feet and strolled towards him.

'Good God, she is desirable,' he thought to himself. 'No more than seventeen. Utterly in my power, and yet still she walks across the room as if she were Queen of England crowned.'

'You will miss the queen, I daresay,' he said abruptly in French as she came up to him.

'I shall,' she replied clearly. 'I grieve for you in the loss of your wife. I am sure my mother and father would want me to give you their commiserations.'

He nodded, never taking his eyes from her face. 'We share a grief now,' he observed. 'You have lost your partner in life and I have lost mine.'

He saw her gaze sharpen. 'Indeed,' she said steadily. 'We do.'

He wondered if she was trying to unravel his meaning. If that quick mind was working behind that clear lovely face there was no sign of it. 'You must teach me the secret of your resignation,' he said.

'Oh, I don't think I resign myself.'

Henry was intrigued. 'You don't?'

'No. I think I trust in God that He knows what is right for all of us, and His will shall be done.'

'Even when His ways are hidden, and we sinners have to stumble about in the dark?'

'I know my destiny,' Catalina said calmly. 'He has been gracious to reveal it to me.'

'Then you're one of the very few,' he said, thinking to make her laugh at herself.

'I know,' she said without a glimmer of a smile. He realised that she was utterly serious in her belief that God had revealed her future to her. 'I am blessed.'

'And what is this great destiny that God has for you?' he said sarcastically. He hoped so much that she would say that she should be Queen of England, and then he could ask her, or draw close to her, or let her see what was in his mind.

'To do God's will, of course, and bring His kingdom to earth,' she said cleverly, and evaded him once more.

I speak very confidently of God's will, and I remind the king that I was raised to be Princess of Wales, but in truth God is silent to me. Since the day of Arthur's death I can have no genuine conviction that I am blessed. How can I call myself blessed when I have lost the one thing that made my life complete? How can I be blessed when I do not think I will ever be happy again? But we live in a world of believers – I have to say that I am under the especial protection of God, I have to give the illusion of being sure of my destiny. I am the daughter of Isabella of Spain. My inheritance is certainty.

But in truth, of course, I am increasingly alone. I feel increasingly alone. There is nothing between me and despair but my promise to Arthur, and the thin thread, like gold wire in a carpet, of my own determination.

May 1503

King Henry did not approach Catalina for one month for the sake of decency, but when he was out of his black jacket he made a formal visit to her at Durham House. Her household had been warned that he would come, and were dressed in their best. He saw the signs of wear and tear in the curtains and rugs and hangings and smiled to himself. If she had the good sense that he thought she had, she would be glad to see a resolution to this awkward position. He congratulated himself on not making it easier for her in this last year. She should know by now that she was utterly in his power and her parents could do nothing to free her.

His herald threw open the double doors to her presence chamber and shouted: 'His Grace, King Henry of England . . .'

Henry waved aside the other titles and went in to his daughter-in-law.

She was wearing a dark-coloured gown with blue slashings on the sleeve, a richly embroidered stomacher and a dark blue hood. It brought out the amber in her hair and the blue in her eyes and he smiled in instinctive pleasure at the sight of her as she sank into a deep formal curtsey and rose up.

'Your Grace,' she said pleasantly. 'This is an honour indeed.'

He had to force himself not to stare at the creamy line of her neck, at the smooth, unlined face that looked back up at him. He had lived all his life with a beautiful woman of his own age; now here was a girl young enough to be his daughter, with the rich-scented bloom of youth still on her, and breasts full and firm. She was ready for marriage, indeed, she was over-ready for marriage. This was a girl who should be bedded. He checked himself at once, and thought he was part lecher, part lover to look on his dead son's child-bride with such desire.

'Can I offer you some refreshment?' she asked. There was a smile in the back of her eyes.

He thought if she had been an older, a more sophisticated woman he would have assumed she was playing him, as knowingly as a skilled angler can land a salmon.

'Thank you. I will take a glass of wine.'

And so she caught him. 'I am afraid I have nothing fit to offer you,' she said smoothly. 'I have nothing left in my cellars at all, and I cannot afford to buy good wine.'

Henry did not show by so much as a flicker that he knew she had trapped him into hearing of her financial difficulties. 'I am sorry for that, I will have some barrels sent over,' he said. 'Your house-keeping must be very remiss.'

'It is very thin,' she said simply. 'Will you take a cup of ale? We brew our own ale very cheaply.'

'Thank you,' he said, biting his lip to hide a smile. He had not dreamed that she had so much self-confidence. The year of widowhood had brought out her courage, he thought. Alone in a foreign land she had not collapsed as other girls might have collapsed, she had gathered her power and become stronger.

'Is My Lady the King's Mother in good health and the Princess Mary well?' she asked, as confidently as if she were entertaining him in the gold room of the Alhambra.

'Yes, thank God,' he said. 'And you?'

She smiled and bowed her head. 'And no need to ask for your health,' she remarked. 'You never look any different.'

'Do I not?'

'Not since the very first time we met,' she said. 'When I had just landed in England and was coming to London and you rode to meet me.' It cost Catalina a good deal not to think of Arthur as he was on that evening, mortified by his father's rudeness, trying to talk to her in an undertone, stealing sideways looks at her.

Determinedly she put her young lover from her mind and smiled at his father and said: 'I was so surprised by your coming, and so startled by you.'

He laughed. He saw that she had conjured the picture of when he first saw her, a virgin by her bed, in a white gown with a blue cape with her hair in a plait down her back, and how he thought then that he had come upon her like a ravisher, he had forced his way into her bedchamber, he could have forced himself on to her.

He turned and took a chair to cover his thoughts, gesturing that she should sit down too. Her duenna, the same sour-faced Spanish mule, he noticed irritably, stood at the back of the room with two other ladies.

Catalina sat perfectly composed, her white fingers interlaced in her lap, her back straight, her entire manner that of a young woman confident of her power to attract. Henry said nothing and looked at her for a moment. Surely she must know what she was doing to him when she reminded him of their first meeting? And yet surely the daughter of Isabella of Spain and the widow of his own son could not be wilfully tempting him to lust?

A servant came in with two cups of small ale. The king was served first and then Catalina took a cup. She took a tiny sip and set it down.

'D'you still not like ale?' He was startled at the intimacy in his own voice. Surely to God he could ask his daughter-in-law what she liked to drink?

'I drink it only when I am very thirsty,' she replied. 'But I don't like the taste it leaves in my mouth.' She put her hand to her mouth and touched her lower lip. Fascinated, he watched her fingertip brush the tip of her tongue. She made a little face. 'I think it will never be a favourite of mine,' she said.

'What did you drink in Spain?' He found he could hardly speak. He was still watching her soft mouth, shiny where her tongue had licked her lips.

'We could drink the water,' she said. 'In the Alhambra the Moors had piped clean water all the way from the mountains into the palace. We drank mountain spring water from the fountains, it was still cold. And juices from fruits of course, we had wonderful fruits in summer, and ices, and sherbets and wines as well.'

'If you come on progress with me this summer we can go to places where you can drink the water,' he said. He thought he was sounding like a stupid boy, promising her a drink of water as a treat. Stubbornly, he persisted. 'If you come with me we can go hunting, we can go to Hampshire, beyond, to the New Forest. You remember the country around there? Near where we first met?'

'I should like that so much,' she said. 'If I am still here, of course.'

'Still here?' He was startled, he had almost forgotten that she was his hostage, she was supposed to go home by summer. 'I doubt your father and I will have agreed terms by then.'

'Why, how can it take so long?' she asked, her blue eyes wide with assumed surprise. 'Surely we can come to some agreement?' She hesitated. 'Between friends? Surely if we cannot agree about the moneys owed, there is some other way? Some other agreement that can be made? Since we have made an agreement before?'

It was so close to what he had been thinking that he rose to his feet, discomfited. At once she rose too. The top of her pretty blue hood only came to his shoulder, he thought he would have to bend his head to kiss her, and if she were under him in bed he would have to take care not to hurt her. He felt his face flush hot at the thought of it. 'Come here,' he said thickly and led her to the window embrasure where her ladies could not overhear them.

'I have been thinking what sort of arrangement we might come to,' he said. 'The easiest thing would be for you to stay here. I should certainly like you to stay here.'

Catalina did not look up at him. If she had done so then, he would have been sure of her. But she kept her eyes down, her face downcast. 'Oh, certainly, if my parents agree,' she said, so softly that he could hardly hear.

He felt himself trapped. He felt he could not go forwards while she held her head so delicately to one side and showed him only the curve of her cheek and her eyelashes, and yet he could hardly go back when she had asked him outright if there was not another way to resolve the conflict between him and her parents.

'You will think me very old,' he burst out.

Her blue eyes flashed up at him and were veiled again. 'Not at all,' she said levelly.

'I am old enough to be your father,' he said, hoping she would disagree.

Instead she looked up at him. 'I never think of you like that,' she said.

Henry was silent. He felt utterly baffled by this slim young woman who seemed at one moment so deliciously encouraging and yet at another moment, quite opaque. 'What would you like to do?' he demanded of her.

At last she raised her head and smiled up at him, her lips curving up but no warmth in her eyes. 'Whatever you command,' she said. 'I should like most of all to obey you, Your Grace.'

What does he mean? What is he doing? I thought he was offering me Harry and I was about to say 'yes' when he said that I must think him very old, as old as my father. And of course he is, indeed, he looks far older than my father, that is why I never think of him like a father, a grandfather perhaps, or an old priest. My father is handsome; a terrible womaniser; a brave soldier; a hero on the battlefield. This king has fought one half-hearted battle and put down a dozen unheroic uprisings of poor men too sickened with his rule to endure it any more. So he is not like my father and I spoke only the truth when I said that I never see him like that.

But then he looked at me as if I had said something of great interest, and then he asked me what I wanted. I could not say to his face that I wanted him to overlook my marriage to his oldest son, and marry me anew to his youngest. So I said that I wanted to obey him. There can be nothing wrong with that. But somehow it was not what he wanted. And it did not get me to where I wanted.

I have no idea what he wants. Nor how to turn it to my own advantage.

Henry went back to Whitehall Palace, his face burning and his heart pounding, hammered between frustration and calculation. If he could persuade Catalina's parents to allow the wedding, he could claim the rest of her substantial dowry, be free of their claims for her jointure, reinforce the alliance with Spain at the very moment that he was looking to secure new alliances with Scotland and France, and perhaps, with such a young wife, get another son and heir on her. One daughter on the throne of Scotland, one daughter on the throne of France should lock both nations into peace for a lifetime. The Princess of Spain on the throne of England should keep the most Christian kings of Spain in alliance. He would have bolted the great powers of Christendom into peaceful alliance with England not just for a generation, but for generations to come. They would have heirs in common; they would be safe. England would be safe. Better yet, England's sons might inherit the kingdoms of France, of Scotland, of Spain. England might conceive its way into peace and greatness.

It made absolute sense to secure Catalina; he tried to focus on the political advantage and not think of the line of her neck nor the curve of her waist. He tried to steady his mind by thinking of the small fortune that would be saved by not having to provide her with a jointure nor with her keep, by not having to send a ship, several ships probably, to escort her home. But all he could think was that she had touched her soft mouth with her finger and told him that she did not like the lingering taste of ale. At the thought of the tip of her tongue against her lips he groaned aloud and the groom holding the horse for him to dismount looked up and said: 'Sire?'

'Bile,' the king said sourly.

It did feel like too rich a fare that was sickening him, he decided as he strode to his private apartments, courtiers eddying out of his way with sycophantic smiles. He felt that he must remember that she was little more than a child, she was his own daughter-in-law. If he listened to the good sense that had carried him so far, he should simply promise to pay her jointure, send her back to her parents, and then delay the payment till they had her married to some other kingly fool elsewhere, and he could get away with paying nothing.

But at the mere thought of her married to another man he had to stop and put his hand out to the oak panelling for support.

'Your Grace?' someone asked him. 'Are you ill?'

'Bile,' the king repeated. 'Something I have eaten.'

His chief groom of the body came to him. 'Shall I send for your physician, Your Grace?'

'No,' the king said. 'But send a couple of barrels of the best wine to the Dowager Princess. She has nothing in her cellar, and when I have to visit her I should like to drink wine and not ale.'

'Yes, Your Grace,' the man said, bowed, and went away. Henry straightened up and went to his rooms. They were crowded with people as usual: petitioners, courtiers, favour-seekers, fortune-hunters, some friends, some gentry, some noblemen attending on him for love or calculation. Henry regarded them all sourly. When he had been Henry Tudor on the run in Brittany he had not been blessed with so many friends.

'Where is my mother?' he asked one of them.

'In her rooms, Your Grace,' the man replied.

'I shall visit her,' he said. 'Let her know.'

He gave her a few moments to ready herself, and then he went to her chambers. On her daughter-in-law's death she had moved into the apartment traditionally given to the queen. She had ordered new tapestries and new furniture and now the place was more grandly furnished than any queen had ever had before.

'I'll announce myself,' the king said to the guard at her door, and stepped in without ceremony.

Lady Margaret was seated at a table in the window, the household accounts spread before her, inspecting the costs of the royal court as if it were a well-run farm. There was very little waste and no extravagance allowed in the court run by Lady Margaret, and royal servants who had thought that some of the payments which passed through their hands might leave a little gold on the side were soon disappointed.

Henry nodded his approval at the sight of his mother's supervision of the royal business. He had never rid himself of his own anxiety that the ostentatious wealth of the throne of England might prove to be hollow show. He had financed a campaign for the throne on debt and favours; he never wanted to be cap in hand again.

She looked up as he came in. 'My son.'

He kneeled for her blessing as he always did when he first greeted her every day, and felt her fingers gently touch the top of his head.

'You look troubled,' she remarked.

'I am,' he said. 'I went to see the Dowager Princess.'

'Yes?' A faint expression of disdain crossed her face. 'What are they asking for now?'

'We –' He broke off and then started again. 'We have to decide what is to become of her. She spoke of going home to Spain.'

'When they pay us what they owe,' she said at once. 'They know they have to pay the rest of her dowry before she can leave.'

'Yes, she knows that.'

There was a brief silence.

'She asked if there could not be another agreement,' he said. 'Some resolution.'

'Ah, I've been waiting for this,' Lady Margaret said exultantly. 'I knew they would be after this. I am only surprised they have waited so long. I suppose they thought they should wait until she was out of mourning.'

'After what?'

'They will want her to stay,' she said.

Henry could feel himself beginning to smile and deliberately he set his face still. 'You think so?'

'I have been waiting for them to show their hand. I knew that they were waiting for us to make the first move. Ha! That we have made them declare first!'

He raised his eyebrows, longing for her to spell out his desire. 'For what?'

'A proposal from us, of course,' she said. 'They knew that we would never let such a chance go. She was the right match then, and she is the right match now. We had a good bargain with her then, and it is still good. Especially if they pay in full. And now she is more profitable than ever.'

His colour flushed as he beamed at her. 'You think so?'

'Of course. She is here, half her dowry already paid, the rest we have only to collect, we have already rid ourselves of her escort, the alliance is already working to our benefit – we would never have the respect of the French if they did not fear her parents, the Scots fear us too – she is still the best match in Christendom for us.'

His sense of relief was overwhelming. If his mother did not oppose the plan then he felt he could push on with it. She had been his best and safest advisor for so long that he could not have gone against her will.

'And the difference in age?'

She shrugged. 'It is what? Five, nearly six years? That is nothing for a prince.'

He recoiled as if she had slapped him in the face. 'Six years?' he repeated.

'And Harry is tall for his age and strong. They will not look mismatched,' she said.

'No,' he said flatly. 'No. Not Harry. I did not mean Harry. I was not speaking of Harry!'

The anger in his voice alerted her. 'What?'

'No. No. Not Harry. Damn it! Not Harry!'

'What? Whatever can you mean?'

'It is obvious! Surely it is obvious!'

Her gaze flashed across his face, reading him rapidly, as only she could. 'Not Harry?'

'I thought you were speaking of me.'

'Of you?' She quickly reconsidered the conversation. 'Of you for the Infanta?' she asked incredulously.

He felt himself flush again. 'Yes.'

'Arthur's widow? Your own daughter-in-law?'

'Yes! Why not?'

Lady Margaret stared at him in alarm. She did not even have to list the obstacles.

'He was too young. It was not consummated,' he said, repeating the words that the Spanish ambassador had learned from Dona Elvira, which had been spread throughout Christendom.

She looked sceptical.

'She says so herself. Her duenna says so. The Spanish say so. Everybody says so.'

'And you believe them?' she asked coldly.

'He was impotent.'

'Well . . .' It was typical of her that she said nothing while she considered it. She looked at him, noting the colour in his cheeks and the trouble in his face. 'They are probably lying. We saw them wedded and bedded and there was no suggestion then that it had not been done.'

'That is their business. If they all tell the same lie and stick to it, then it is the same as the truth.'

'Only if we accept it.'

'We do,' he ruled.

She raised her eyebrows. 'It is your desire?'

'It is not a question of desire. I need a wife,' Henry said coolly, as though it could be anyone. 'And she is conveniently here, as you say.'

'She would be suitable by birth,' his mother conceded, 'but for her relationship to you. She is your daughter-in-law even if it was not consummated. And she is very young.'

'She is seventeen,' he said. 'A good age for a woman. And a widow. She is ready for a second marriage.'

'She is either a virgin or she is not,' Lady Margaret observed waspishly. 'We had better agree.'

'She is seventeen,' he corrected himself. 'A good age for marriage. She is ready for a full marriage.'

'The people won't like it,' she observed. 'They will remember her wedding to Arthur, we made such a show of it. They took to her. They took to the two of them. The pomegranate and the rose. She caught their fancy in her lace mantilla.'

'Well, he is dead,' he said harshly. 'And she will have to marry someone.'

'People will think it odd.'

He shrugged. 'They will be glad enough if she gives me a son.'

'Oh yes, if she can do that. But she was barren with Arthur.'

'As we have agreed, Arthur was impotent. The marriage was not consummated.'

She pursed her lips but said nothing.

'And it gains us the dowry and removes the cost of the jointure,' he pointed out.

She nodded. She loved the thought of the fortune that Catalina would bring.

'And she is here already.'

'A most constant presence,' she said sourly.

'A constant princess,' he smiled.

'Do you really think her parents would agree? Their Majesties of Spain?'

'It solves their dilemma as well as ours. And it maintains the alliance.' He found he was smiling, and tried to make his face stern, as normal. 'She herself would think it was her destiny. She believes herself born to be Queen of England.'

'Well then, she is a fool,' his mother remarked smartly.

'She was raised to be queen since she was a child.'

'But she will be a barren queen. No son of hers will be any good. He could never be king. If she has one at all, he will come after Harry,' she reminded him. 'He will even come after Harry's sons. It's a far poorer alliance for her than marriage to a Prince of Wales. The Spanish won't like it.'

'Oh, Harry is still a child. His sons are a long way ahead. Years.'

'Even so. It would weigh on her parents. They will prefer Prince Harry for her. That way, she is queen and her son is king after her. Why would they agree to anything less?'

Henry hesitated. There was nothing he could say to fault her logic, except that he did not wish to follow it.

'Oh. I see. You want her,' she said flatly when the silence extended so long that she realised there was something he could not let himself say. 'It is a matter of your desire.'

He took the plunge. 'Yes,' he confirmed.

Lady Margaret looked at him with calculation in her gaze. He had been taken from her as little more than a baby for safekeeping. Since then she had always seen him as a prospect, as a potential heir to the throne, as her passport to grandeur. She had hardly known him as a baby, never loved him as a child. She had planned his future as a man, she had defended his rights as a king, she had mapped his campaign as a threat to the House of York – but she had never known tenderness for him. She could not learn to feel indulgent towards him this late in her life; she was hardly ever indulgent to anyone, not even to herself.

'That's very shocking,' she said coolly. 'I thought we were talking of a marriage of advantage. She stands as a daughter to you. This desire is a carnal sin.'

'It is not and she is not,' he said. 'There is nothing wrong in honourable love. She is not my daughter. She is his widow. And it was not consummated.'

'You will need a dispensation, it is a sin.'

'He never even had her!' he exclaimed.

'The whole court put them to bed,' she pointed out levelly.

'He was too young. He was impotent. And he was dead, poor lad, within months.'

She nodded. 'So she says now.'

'But you do not advise me against it,' he said.

'It is a sin,' she repeated. 'But if you can get dispensation and her parents agree to it, then –' She pulled a sour face. 'Well, better her than many others, I suppose,' she said begrudgingly. 'And she can live at court under my care. I can watch over her and command her more easily than I could an older girl, and we know that she behaves herself well. She is obedient. She will learn her duties under me. And the people love her.'

'I shall speak to the Spanish ambassador today.'

She thought she had never seen such a bright gladness in his face. 'I suppose I can teach her.' She gestured to the books before her. 'She will have much to learn.'

'I shall tell the ambassador to propose it to Their Majesties of Spain and I shall talk to her tomorrow.'

'You will go again so soon?' she asked curiously.

Henry nodded. He would not tell her that even to wait till tomorrow seemed too long. If he had been free to do so, he would have gone back straight away and asked her to marry him that very night, as if he were a humble squire and she a maid, and not King of England and Princess of Spain; father and daughter-in-law.

Henry saw that Dr de Puebla the Spanish ambassador was invited to Whitehall in time for dinner, given a seat at one of the top tables, and plied with the best wine. Some venison, hanged to perfection and cooked in a brandywine sauce, came to the king's table, he helped himself to a small portion and sent the dish to the Spanish ambassador. De Puebla, who had not experienced such favours since first negotiating the Infanta's marriage contract, loaded his plate with a heavy spoon and dipped the best manchet bread into the gravy, glad to eat well at court, wondering quietly behind his avid smile what it might mean.

The king's mother nodded towards him, and de Puebla rose up

from his seat to bow to her. 'Most gracious,' he remarked to himself as he sat down once more. 'Extremely. Exceptionally.'

He was no fool, he knew that something would be required for all these public favours. But given the horror of the past year – when the hopes of Spain had been buried beneath the nave in Worcester Cathedral – at least these were straws in a good wind. Clearly, King Henry had a use for him again as something other than a whipping boy for the failure of the Spanish sovereigns to pay their debts.

De Puebla had tried to defend Their Majesties of Spain to an increasingly irritable English king. He had tried to explain to them in long, detailed letters that it was fruitless asking for Catalina's widow's jointure if they would not pay the remainder of the dowry. He tried to explain to Catalina that he could not make the English king pay a more generous allowance for the upkeep of her household, nor could he persuade the Spanish king to give his daughter financial support. Both kings were utterly stubborn, both quite determined to force the other into a weak position. Neither seemed to care that in the meantime Catalina, only seventeen, was forced to keep house with an extravagant entourage in a foreign land on next to no money. Neither king would take the first step and undertake to be responsible for her keep, fearing that this would commit him to keeping her and her household forever.

De Puebla smiled up at the king, seated on his throne under the canopy of state. He genuinely liked King Henry, he admired the courage with which he had seized and held the throne, he liked the man's direct good sense. And more than that, de Puebla liked living in England, he was accustomed to his good house in London, to the importance conferred on him by representing the newest and most powerful ruling house in Europe. He liked the fact that his Jewish background and recent conversion were utterly ignored in England, since everyone at this court had come from nowhere and changed their name or their affiliation at least once. England suited de Puebla, and he would do his best to remain. If it meant serving the King of

England better than the King of Spain, he thought it was a small compromise to make.

Henry rose from the throne and gave the signal that the servers could clear the plates. They swept the board and cleared the trestle tables, and Henry strolled among the diners, pausing for a word here and there, still very much the commander among his men. All the favourites at the Tudor court were the gamblers who had put their swords behind their words and marched into England with Henry. They knew their value to him, and he knew his to them. It was still a victors' camp rather than a softened civilian court.

At length Henry completed his circuit and came to de Puebla's table. 'Ambassador,' he greeted him.

De Puebla bowed low. 'I thank you for your gift of the dish of venison,' he said. 'It was delicious.'

The king nodded. 'I would have a word with you.'

'Of course.'

'Privately.'

The two men strolled to a quieter corner of the hall while the musicians in the gallery struck a note and began to play.

'I have a proposal to resolve the issue of the Dowager Princess,' Henry said as drily as possible.

'Indeed?'

'You may find my suggestion unusual, but I think it has much to recommend it.'

'At last,' de Puebla thought to himself. 'He is going to propose Harry. I thought he was going to let her sink a lot lower before he did that. I thought he would bring her down so that he could charge us double for a second try at Wales. But, so be it. God is merciful.'

'Ah yes?' de Puebla said aloud.

'I suggest that we forget the issue of the dowry,' Henry started. 'Her goods will be absorbed into my household. I shall pay her an appropriate allowance, as I did for the late Queen Elizabeth – God bless her. I shall marry the Infanta myself.'

De Puebla was almost too shocked to speak. 'You?'

'I. Is there any reason why not?'

The ambassador gulped, drew a breath, managed to say, 'No, no, at least . . . I suppose there could be an objection on the grounds of affinity.'

'I shall apply for a dispensation. I take it that you are certain that the marriage was not consummated?'

'Certain,' de Puebla gasped.

'You assured me of that on her word?'

'The duenna said . . .'

'Then it is nothing,' the king ruled. 'They were little more than promised to one another. Hardly man and wife.'

'I will have to put this to Their Majesties of Spain,' de Puebla said, desperately trying to assemble some order to his whirling thoughts, striving to keep his deep shock from his face. 'Does the Privy Council agree?' he asked, playing for time. 'The Archbishop of Canterbury?'

'It is a matter between ourselves at the moment,' Henry said grandly. 'It is early days for me as a widower. I want to be able to reassure Their Majesties that their daughter will be cared for. It has been a difficult year for her.'

'If she could have gone home . . .'

'Now there will be no need for her to go home. Her home is England. This is her country,' Henry said flatly. 'She shall be queen here, as she was brought up to be.'

De Puebla could hardly speak for shock at the suggestion that this old man, who had just buried his wife, should marry his dead son's bride. 'Of course. So, shall I tell Their Majesties that you are quite determined on this course? There is no other arrangement that we should consider?' De Puebla racked his brains as to how he could bring in the name of Prince Harry, who was surely Catalina's most appropriate future husband. Finally, he plunged in. 'Your son, for instance?'

'My son is too young to be considered for marriage as yet,' Henry disposed of the suggestion with speed. 'He is eleven and a strong, forward boy but his grandmother insists that we plan nothing for him for another four years. And by then, the Princess Dowager would be twenty-one.'

'Still young,' gasped de Puebla. 'Still a young woman, and near him in age.'

'I don't think Their Majesties would want their daughter to stay in England for another four years without husband or household of her own,' Henry said with unconcealed threat. 'They could hardly want her to wait for Harry's majority. What would she do in those years? Where would she live? Are they proposing to buy her a palace and set up a household for her? Are they prepared to give her an income? A court, appropriate to her position? For four years?'

'If she could return to Spain to wait?' de Puebla hazarded.

'She can leave at once, if she will pay the full amount of her dowry, and find her own fortune elsewhere. Do you really think she can get a better offer than Queen of England? Take her away if you do!'

It was the sticking point that they had reached over and over again in the past year. De Puebla knew he was beaten. 'I will write to Their Majesties tonight,' he said.

I dreamed I was a swift, flying over the golden hills of the Sierra Nevada. But this time, I was flying north, the hot afternoon sun was on my left, ahead of me was a gathering of cool cloud. Then suddenly, the cloud took shape, it was Ludlow Castle, and my little bird heart fluttered at the sight of it and at the thought of the night that would come when he would take me in his arms and press down on me, and I would melt with desire for him.

Then I saw it was not Ludlow but the great grey walls were those of Windsor Castle, and the curve of the river was the great grey glass of the river Thames, and all the traffic plying up and down and the great ships at anchor were the wealth and the bustle of the English. I knew I was far from my home, and yet I was at home. This would be my home, I would build a little nest against the grey stone of the towers here, just as I would have done in Spain. And here they would call me a swift; a bird which flies so fast that no-one has ever seen it land, a bird that flies so high that they think it never touches the ground. I shall not be Catalina, the Infanta of Spain. I shall be Katherine of Aragon, Queen of England, just as Arthur named me: Katherine, Queen of England.

'The king is here again,' Dona Elvira said, looking out of the window. 'He has ridden here with just two men. Not even a standard bearer or guards.' She sniffed. The widespread English informality was bad enough but this king had the manners of a stable boy.

Catalina flew to the window and peered out. 'What can he want?' she wondered. 'Tell them to decant some of his wine.'

Dona Elvira went out of the room in a hurry. In the next moment Henry strolled in, unannounced. 'I thought I would call on you,' he said.

Catalina sank into a deep curtsey. 'Your Grace does me much honour,' she said. 'And at least now I can offer you a glass of good wine.'

Henry smiled and waited. The two of them stood while Dona Elvira returned to the room with a Spanish maid-in-waiting carrying a tray of Morisco brassware with two Venetian glasses of red wine. Henry noted the fineness of the workmanship and assumed correctly that it was part of the dowry that the Spanish had withheld.

'Your health,' he said, holding up his glass to the princess.

To his surprise she did not simply raise her glass in return, she raised her eyes and gave him a long, thoughtful look. He felt himself tingle, like a boy, as his eyes met hers. 'Princess?' he said quietly.

'Your Grace?'

They both of them glanced towards Dona Elvira, who was standing uncomfortably close, quietly regarding the floorboards beneath her worn shoes.

'You can leave us,' the king said.

The woman looked at the princess for her orders, and made no move to leave.

'I shall talk in private with my daughter-in-law,' King Henry said firmly. 'You may go.'

Dona Elvira curtseyed and left, and the rest of the ladies swept out after her.

Catalina smiled at the king. 'As you command,' she said.

He felt his pulse speed at her smile. 'Indeed, I do need to speak to you privately. I have a proposal to put to you. I have spoken to the Spanish ambassador and he has written to your parents.'

'At last. This is it. At last,' Catalina thought. 'He has come to propose Harry for me. Thank God, who has brought me to this day. Arthur, beloved, this day you will see that I shall be faithful to my promise to you.'

'I need to marry again,' Henry said. 'I am still young –' He thought he would not say his age of forty-six. 'It may be that I can have another child or two.'

Catalina nodded politely; but she was barely listening. She was waiting for him to ask her to marry Prince Harry.

'I have been thinking of all the princesses in Europe who would be suitable partners for me,' he said.

Still the princess before him said nothing.

'I can find no-one I would choose.'

She widened her eyes to indicate her attention.

Henry ploughed on. 'My choice has fallen on you,' he said bluntly, 'for these reasons. You are here in London already, you have become accustomed to living here. You were brought up to be Queen of England, and you will be queen as my wife. The difficulties with the dowry can be put aside. You will have the same allowance that I paid to Queen Elizabeth. My mother agrees with this.'

At last his words penetrated her mind. She was so shocked that she could barely speak. She just stared at him. 'Me?'

'There is a slight objection on the grounds of affinity but I shall ask the Pope to grant a dispensation,' he went on. 'I understand that your marriage to Prince Arthur was never consummated. In that case, there is no real objection.'

'It was not consummated.' Catalina repeated the words by rote, as if she no longer understood them. The great lie had been part of a plot to take her to the altar with Prince Harry, not with his father. She could not now retract it. Her mind was so dizzy that she could only cling to it. 'It was not consummated.'

'Then there should be no difficulty,' the king said. 'I take it that you do not object?'

He found that he could hardly breathe, waiting for her answer. Any thought that she had been leading him on, tempting him to this moment, had vanished when he looked into her bleached, shocked face.

He took her hand. 'Don't look so afraid,' he said, his voice low with tenderness. 'I won't hurt you. This is to resolve all your problems. I will be a good husband to you. I will care for you.' Desperately, he racked his brains for something that might please her. 'I will buy you pretty things,' he said. 'Like those sapphires that you liked so much. You shall have a cupboard full of pretty things, Catalina.'

She knew she had to reply. 'I am so surprised,' she said.

'Surely you must have known that I desired you?'

I stopped my cry of denial. I wanted to say that of course I had not known. But it was not true. I had known, as any young woman would have known, from the way he had looked at me, from the way that I

had responded to him. From the very first moment that I met him there was this undercurrent between us. I ignored it. I pretended it was something easier than it was, I deployed it. I have been most at fault.

In my vanity, I thought that I was encouraging an old man to think of me kindly, that I could engage him, delight him, even flirt with him, first as a fond father-in-law and then to prevail upon him to marry me to Harry. I had meant to delight him as a daughter, I had wanted him to admire me, to pet me. I wanted him to dote on me.

This is a sin, a sin. This is a sin of vanity and a sin of pride. I have deployed his lust and covetousness. I have led him to sin through my folly. No wonder God has turned His face from me and my mother never writes to me. I am most wrong.

Dear God, I am a fool, and a childish, vain fool at that. I have not lured the king into a trap of my own satisfaction, but merely baited his trap for me. My vanity and pride in myself made me think that I could tempt him to do whatever I want. Instead, I have tempted him only to his own desires, and now he will do what he wants. And what he wants is me. And it is my own stupid fault.

'You must have known.' Henry smiled down at her confidently. 'You must have known when I came to see you yesterday, and when I sent you the good wine?'

Catalina gave a little nod. She had known something – fool that she was – she had known something was happening; and praised her own diplomatic skills for being so clever as to lead the King of England by the nose. She had thought herself a woman of the world and thought her ambassador an idiot for not achieving this outcome from a king who was so easily manipulated. She had thought she had the King of England dancing to her bidding, when in fact he had his own tune in mind.

'I desired you from the moment I first saw you,' he told her, his voice very low.

She looked up. 'You did?'

'Truly. When I came into your bedchamber at Dogmersfield.'

She remembered an old man, travel-stained and lean, the father of the man she would marry. She remembered the sweaty male scent as he forced his way into her bedroom and she remembered standing before him and thinking: what a clown, what a rough soldier to push in where he is not wanted. And then Arthur arrived, his blond hair tousled, and with the brightness of his shy smile.

'Oh yes,' she said. From somewhere deep inside her own resolution, she found a smile. 'I remember. I danced for you.'

Henry drew her a little closer and slid his arm around her waist. Catalina forced herself not to pull away. 'I watched you,' he said. 'I longed for you.'

'But you were married,' Catalina said primly.

'And now I am widowed and so are you,' he said. He felt the stiffness of her body through the hard boning of the stomacher and let her go. He would have to court her slowly, he thought. She might have flirted with him, but now she was startled by the turn that things had taken. She had come from an absurdly sheltered upbringing and her innocent months with Arthur had hardly opened her eyes at all. He would have to take matters slowly with her. He would have to wait until she had permission from Spain, he would leave the ambassador to tell her of the wealth she might command, he would have to let her women urge the benefits of the match upon her. She was a young woman, by nature and experience she was bound to be a fool. He would have to give her time.

'I will leave you now,' he said. 'I will come again tomorrow.'

She nodded, and walked with him to the door of her privy chamber. There she hesitated. 'You mean it?' she asked him, her blue eyes suddenly anxious. 'You mean this as a proposal of marriage, not as a feint in a negotiation? You truly want to marry me? I will be queen?'

He nodded. 'I mean it.' The depth of her ambition began to dawn on him and he smiled as he slowly saw the way to her. 'Do you want to be queen so very much?'

Catalina nodded. 'I was brought up to it,' she said. 'I want nothing more.' She hesitated, for a moment she almost thought to tell him that it had been the last thought of his son, but then her passion for Arthur was too great for her to share him with anyone, even his father. And besides, Arthur had planned that she should marry Harry.

The king was smiling. 'So you don't have desire, but you do have ambition,' he observed a little coldly.

'It is nothing more than my due,' she said flatly. 'I was born to be a queen.'

He took her hand and bent over it. He kissed her fingers; and he stopped himself from licking them. 'Take it slowly,' he warned himself. 'This is a girl and possibly a virgin; certainly not a whore.' He straightened up. 'I shall make you Katherine of Aragon, Queen of England,' he promised her, and saw her blue eyes darken with desire at the title. 'We can marry as soon as we have the dispensation from the Pope.'

Think! Think! I urgently command myself. You were not raised by a fool to be a fool, you were raised by a queen to be a queen. If this is a feint you ought to be able to see it. If it is a true offer you ought to be able to turn it to your advantage.

It is not a true fulfilment of the promise I made to my beloved but it is close. He wanted me to be Queen of England and to have the children that he would have given me. So what if they will be his half-brother and half-sister rather than his niece and nephew? That makes no difference.

I shrink from the thought of marrying this old man, old enough to be my father. The skin at his neck is fine and loose, like that of a turtle. I cannot imagine being in bed with him. His breath is sour, an old man's breath; and he is thin, and he will feel bony at the hips and shoulders. But I shrink from the thought of being in bed with that child Harry. His face is as smooth and as rounded as a little girl's. In truth, I cannot bear the thought of being anyone's wife but Arthur's; and that part of my life has gone.

Think! Think! This might be the very right thing to do.

Oh God, beloved, I wish you were here to tell me. I wish I could just visit you in the garden for you to tell me what I should do. I am only seventeen, I cannot outwit a man old enough to be my father, a king with a nose for pretenders.

Think!

I will have no help from anyone. I have to think alone.

Dona Elvira waited until the princess's bedtime and until all the maids-in-waiting, the ladies and the grooms of the bedchamber had withdrawn. She closed the door on them all and then turned to the princess, who was seated in her bed, her hair in a neat plait, her pillows plumped behind her.

'What did the king want?' she demanded without ceremony.

'He proposed marriage to me,' Catalina said bluntly in reply. 'For himself.'

For a moment the duenna was too stunned to speak then she crossed herself, as a woman seeing something unclean. 'God save us,' was all she said. Then: 'God forgive him for even thinking it.'

'God forgive you,' Catalina replied smartly. 'I am considering it.'

'He is your father-in-law, and old enough to be your father.'

'His age doesn't matter,' Catalina said truly. 'If I go back to Spain they won't seek a young husband for me but an advantageous one.'

'But he is the father of your husband.'

Catalina nipped her lips together. 'My late husband,' she said bleakly. 'And the marriage was not consummated.'

Dona Elvira swallowed the lie; but her eyes flicked away, just once.

'As you remember,' Catalina said smoothly.

'Even so! It is against nature!'

'It is not against nature,' Catalina asserted. 'There was no consummation of the betrothal, there was no child. So there can be no sin against nature. And anyway, we can get a dispensation.'

Dona Elvira hesitated. 'You can?'

'He says so.'

'Princess, you cannot want this?'

The princess's little face was bleak. 'He will not betroth me to Prince Harry,' she said. 'He says the boy is too young. I cannot wait four years until he is grown. So what can I do but marry the king? I was born to be Queen of England and mother of the next King of England. I have to fulfil my destiny, it is my God-given destiny. I thought I would have to force myself to take Prince Harry. Now it seems I shall have to force myself to take the king. Perhaps this is God testing me. But my will is strong. I will be Queen of England, and the mother of the king. I shall make this country a fortress against the Moors, as I promised my mother, I shall make it a country of justice and fairness defended against the Scots, as I promised Arthur.'

'I don't know what your mother will think,' the duenna said. 'I should not have left you alone with him, if I had known.'

Catalina nodded. 'Don't leave us alone again.' She paused. 'Unless I nod to you,' she said. 'I may nod for you to leave, and then you must go.'

The duenna was shocked. 'He should not even see you before your wedding day. I shall tell the ambassador that he must tell the king that he cannot visit you at all now.'

Catalina shook her head. 'We are not in Spain now,' she said fiercely. 'D'you still not see it? We cannot leave this to the ambassador, not even my mother can say what shall happen. I shall have to make this happen. I alone have brought it so far, and I alone will make it happen.'

I hoped to dream of you, but I dreamed of nothing. I feel as if you have gone far, far away. I have no letter from my mother so I don't know what she will make of the king's wish. I pray, but I hear nothing from God. I speak very bravely of my destiny and God's will but they feel now quite intertwined. If God does not make me Queen of England then I do not know how I can believe in Him. If I am not Queen of England then I do not know what I am.

Catalina waited for the king to visit her as he had promised. He did not come the next day but Catalina was sure he would come the day after. When three days had elapsed she walked on her own by the river, chafing her hands in the shelter of her cloak. She had been so sure that he would come again that she had prepared herself to keep him interested, but under her control. She planned to lead him on, to keep him dancing at arm's length. When he did not come she realised that she was anxious to see him. Not for desire – she thought she would never feel desire again – but because he was her only way to the throne of England. When he did not come, she was mortally afraid that he had had second thoughts, and he would not come at all.

'Why is he not coming?' I demand of the little waves on the river, washing against the bank as a boatman rows by. 'Why would he come so passionate and earnest one day, and then not come at all?'

I am so fearful of his mother, she has never liked me and if she turns her face from me, I don't know that he will go ahead. But then I remember that he said that his mother had given her permission. Then I am afraid that the Spanish ambassador might have said something against the match – but I cannot believe that de Puebla would ever say anything to inconvenience the king, even if he failed to serve me.

'*Then why is he not coming?*' *I ask myself.* '*If he was courting in the English way, all rush and informality, then surely he would come every day?*'

Another day went past, and then another. Finally, Catalina gave way to her anxiety and sent the king a message at his court, hoping that he was well.

Dona Elvira said nothing, but her stiff back as she supervised the brushing and powdering of Catalina's gown that night spoke volumes.

'I know what you are thinking,' Catalina said, as the duenna waved the maid of the wardrobe from the room and turned to brush Catalina's hair. 'But I cannot risk losing this chance.'

'I am thinking nothing,' the older woman said coldly. 'These are English ways. As you tell me, we cannot now abide by decent Spanish ways. And so, I am not qualified to speak. Clearly, my advice is not taken. I am an empty vessel.'

Catalina was too worried to soothe the older woman. 'It doesn't matter what you are,' she said distractedly. 'Perhaps he will come tomorrow.'

Henry, seeing her ambition as the key to her, had given the girl a few days to consider her position. He thought she might compare the life she led at Durham House, in seclusion with her little Spanish court, her furniture becoming more shabby and no new gowns, with the life she might lead as a young queen at the head of one of the richest courts in Europe. He thought she had the sense to think that through on her own. When he received a note from her, inquiring as to his health, he knew that he had been right; and the next day he rode down the Strand to visit her.

Her porter who kept the gate said that the princess was in the garden, walking with her ladies by the river. Henry went through the back door of the palace to the terrace, and down the steps through the garden. He saw her by the river, walking alone, ahead of her ladies, her head slightly bowed in thought, and he felt an old, familiar sensation in his belly at the sight of a woman he desired. It made him feel young again, that deep pang of lust, and he smiled at himself for feeling a young man's passion, for knowing again a young man's folly.

His page, running ahead, announced him and he saw her head jerk up at his name and she looked across the lawn and saw him. He smiled, he was waiting for that moment of recognition between a woman and a man who loves her – the moment when their eyes meet and they both know that intense moment of joy, that moment when the eyes say: 'Ah, it is you,' and that is everything.

Instead, like a dull blow, he saw at once that there was no leap of her heart at the sight of him. He was smiling shyly, his face lit up with anticipation; but she, in the first moment of surprise, was nothing more than startled. Unprepared, she did not feign emotion, she did not look like a woman in love. She looked up, she saw him – and he could tell at once that she did not love him. There was no shock of delight. Instead, chillingly, he saw a swift expression of calculation cross her face. She was a girl in an unguarded moment, wondering if she could have her own way. It was the look of a huckster, pricing a fool ready for fleecing. Henry, the father of two selfish girls, recognised it in a moment, and knew that whatever the princess might say, however sweetly she might say it, this would be a marriage of convenience to her, whatever it was to him. And more than that, he knew that she had made up her mind to accept him.

He walked across the close-scythed grass towards her and took her hand. 'Good day, Princess.'

Catalina curtseyed. 'Your Grace.'

She turned her head to her ladies. 'You can go inside.' To Dona Elvira she said, 'See that there are refreshments for His Grace when we come in.' Then she turned back to him. 'Will you walk, sire?'

'You will make a very elegant queen,' he said with a smile. 'You command very smoothly.'

He saw her hesitate in her stride and the tension leave her slim young body as she exhaled. 'Ah, you mean it then,' she breathed. 'You mean to marry me.'

'I do,' he said. 'You will be a most beautiful Queen of England.'

She glowed at the thought of it. 'I still have many English ways to learn.'

'My mother will teach you,' he said easily. 'You will live at court in her rooms and under her supervision.'

Catalina checked a little in her stride. 'Surely I will have my own rooms, the queen's rooms?'

'My mother is occupying the queen's rooms,' he said. 'She moved in after the death of the late queen, God bless her. And you will join her there. She thinks that you are too young as yet to have your own rooms and a separate court. You can live in my mother's rooms with her ladies and she can teach you how things are done.'

He could see that she was troubled, but trying hard not to show it.

'I should think I know how things are done in a royal palace,' Catalina said, trying to smile.

'An English palace,' he said firmly. 'Fortunately my mother has run all my palaces and castles and managed my fortune since I came to the throne. She shall teach you how it is done.'

Catalina closed her lips on her disagreement. 'When do you think we will hear from the Pope?' she asked.

'I have sent an emissary to Rome to inquire,' Henry said. 'We shall have to apply jointly, your parents and myself. But it should be resolved very quickly. If we are all agreed, there can be no real objection.'

'Yes,' she said.

'And we are completely agreed on marriage?' he confirmed.

'Yes,' she said again.

He took her hand and tucked it into his arm. Catalina walked a little closer and let her head brush against his shoulder. She was not wearing a headdress, only the hood of her cape covered her hair, and the movement pushed it back. He could smell the essence of roses on her hair, he could feel the warmth of her head against his shoulder. He had to stop himself from taking her in his arms. He paused and she stood close to him; he could feel the warmth of her, down the whole length of his body.

'Catalina,' he said, his voice very low and thick.

She stole a glance and saw desire in his face, and she did not step away. If anything, she came a little closer. 'Yes, Your Grace?' she whispered.

Her eyes were downcast but slowly, in the silence, she looked up at him. When her face was upturned to his, he could not resist the unstated invitation, he bent and kissed her on the lips.

There was no shrinking, she took his kiss, her mouth yielded under his, he could taste her, his arms came around her, he pressed her towards him, he could feel his desire for her rising in him so strongly that he had to let her go, that minute, or disgrace himself.

He released her and stood shaking with desire so strong that he could not believe its power as it washed through him. Catalina pulled her hood forwards as if she would be veiled from him, as if she were a girl from a harem with a veil hiding her mouth, only dark, promising eyes showing above the mask. That gesture, so foreign, so secretive, made him long to push back her hood and kiss her again. He reached for her.

'We might be seen,' she said coolly, and stepped back from him. 'We can be seen from the house, and anyone can go by on the river.'

Henry let her go. He could say nothing, for he knew his voice would tremble. Silently, he offered her his arm once more, and silently she took it. They fell into pace with each other, he tempering his longer stride to her steps. They walked in silence for a few moments.

'Our children will be your heirs?' she confirmed, her voice cool and steady, following a train of thought very far from his own whirl of sensations.

He cleared his throat. 'Yes, yes, of course.'

'That is the English tradition?'

'Yes.'

'They will come before your other children?'

'Our son will inherit before the Princesses Margaret and Mary,' he said. 'But our daughters would come after them.'

She frowned a little. 'How so? Why would they not come before?'

'It is first on sex, and then on age,' he said. 'The first-born boy inherits, then other boys, then girls according to age. Please God there is always a prince to inherit. England has no tradition of ruling queens.'

'A ruling queen can command as well as a king,' said the daughter of Isabella of Castile.

'Not in England,' said Henry Tudor.

She left it at that. 'But our oldest son would be king when you died,' she pursued.

'Please God I have some years left,' he said wryly.

She was seventeen, she had no sensitivity about age. 'Of course. But when you die, if we had a son, he would inherit?'

'No. The king after me will be Prince Harry, the Prince of Wales.'

She frowned. 'I thought you could nominate an heir? Can you not make it our son?'

He shook his head. 'Harry is Prince of Wales. He will be king after me.'

'I thought he was to go into the church?'

'Not now.'

'But if we have a son? Can you not make Harry king of your French dominions, or Ireland, and make our son King of England?'

Henry laughed shortly. 'No. For that would be to destroy my kingdom, which I have had some trouble to win and to keep together. Harry will have it all by right.' He saw she was disturbed. 'Catalina, you will be Queen of England, one of the finest kingdoms of Europe, the place your mother and father chose for you. Your sons and daughters will be princes and princesses of England. What more could you want?'

'I want my son to be king,' she answered him frankly.

He shrugged. 'It cannot be.'

She turned away slightly, only his grip on her hand kept her close.

He tried to laugh it off. 'Catalina, we are not even married yet. You might not even have a son. We need not spoil our betrothal for a child not yet conceived.'

'Then what would be the point of marriage?' she asked, direct in her self-absorption.

He could have said 'desire'. 'Destiny, so that you shall be queen.'

She would not let it go. 'I had thought to be Queen of England and see my son on the throne,' she repeated. 'I had thought to be a power in the court, like your mother is. I had thought that there are castles to build and a navy to plan and schools and colleges to found. I want to defend against the Scots on our northern borders and against the Moors on our coasts. I want to be a ruling queen in England, these are things I have planned and hoped for. I was named as the next Queen of England almost in my cradle, I have thought about the kingdom I would reign, I have made plans. There are many things that I want to do.'

He could not help himself, he laughed aloud at the thought of this girl, this child, presuming to make plans for the ruling of his kingdom. 'You will find that I am before you,' he said bluntly. 'This kingdom shall be run as the king commands. This kingdom is run as I command. I did not fight my way to the crown to hand it over to a girl young enough to be my daughter. Your task will be to fill the royal nurseries and your world will start and stop there.'

'But your mother . . .'

'You will find my mother guards her domains as I guard mine,' he said, still chuckling at the thought of this child planning her future at his court. 'She will command you as a daughter and you will obey. Make no mistake about it, Catalina. You will come into my court and obey me, you will live in my mother's rooms and obey her. You will be Queen of England and have the crown on your head. But you will be my wife, and I will have an obedient wife as I have always done.'

He stopped, he did not want to frighten her, but his desire for her was not greater than his determination to hold this kingdom that he had fought so hard to win. 'I am not a child like Arthur,' he said to her quietly, thinking that his son, a gentle boy, might have made all sorts of soft promises to a determined young wife. 'You will not rule beside me. You will be a child-bride to me. I shall love you and make you happy. I swear you will be glad that you married me. I shall be kind to you. I shall be generous to you. I shall give you anything you want. But I shall not make you a ruler. Even at my death you will not rule my country.'

That night I dreamed that I was a queen in a court with a sceptre in one hand and wand in the other and a crown on my head. I raised the sceptre and found it changed in my hand, it was a branch of a

tree, the stem of a flower, it was valueless. My other hand was no longer filled with the heavy orb of the sceptre, but with rose petals. I could smell their scent. I put my hand up to touch the crown on my head and I felt a little circlet of flowers. The throne room melted away and I was in the sultana's garden at the Alhambra, my sisters plaiting circlets of daisies for each other's heads.

'Where is the Queen of England?' someone called from the terrace below the garden.

I rose from the lawn of camomile flowers and smelled the bitter-sweet perfume of the herb as I tried to run past the fountain to the archway at the end of the garden. 'I am here!' I tried to call, but I made no noise above the splashing of the water in the marble bowl.

'Where is the Queen of England?' I heard them call again.

'I am here!' I called out silently.

'Where is Queen Katherine of England?'

'Here! Here! Here!'

The ambassador, summoned at daybreak to come at once to Durham House, did not trouble himself to get there until nine o'clock. He found Catalina waiting for him in her privy chamber with only Dona Elvira in attendance.

'I sent for you hours ago,' the princess said crossly.

'I was undertaking business for your father and could not come earlier,' he said smoothly, ignoring the sulky look on her face. 'Is there something wrong?'

'I spoke with the king yesterday and he repeated his proposal of marriage,' Catalina said, a little pride in her voice.

'Indeed.'

'But he told me that I would live at court in the rooms of his mother.'

'Oh.' The ambassador nodded.

'And he said that my sons would inherit only after Prince Harry.'
The ambassador nodded again.

'Can we not persuade him to overlook Prince Harry? Can we not draw up a marriage contract to set him aside in favour of my son?'

The ambassador shook his head. 'It's not possible.'

'Surely, a man can choose his heir?'

'No. Not in the case of a king come so new to his throne. Not an English king. And even if he could, he would not.'

She leapt from her chair and paced to the window. 'My son will be the grandson of the kings of Spain!' she exclaimed. 'Royal for centuries. Prince Harry is nothing more than the son of Elizabeth of York and a successful pretender.'

De Puebla gave a little hiss of horror at her bluntness and glanced towards the door. 'You would do better never to call him that. He is the King of England.'

She nodded, accepting the reprimand. 'But he has not my breeding,' she pursued. 'Prince Harry would not be the king that my boy would be.'

'That is not the question,' the ambassador observed. 'The question is of time and practice. The king's oldest son is always the Prince of Wales. He always inherits the throne. This king, of all the kings in the world, is not going to make a pretender of his own legitimate heir. He has been dogged with pretenders. He is not going to make another.'

As always, Catalina flinched at the thought of the last pretender, Edward of Warwick, beheaded to make way for her.

'Besides,' the ambassador continued, 'any king would rather have a sturdy eleven-year-old son as his heir than a new-born in the cradle. These are dangerous times. A man wants to leave a man to inherit, not a child.'

'If my son is not to be king, then what is the point of me marrying a king?' Catalina demanded.

'You would be queen,' the ambassador pointed out.

'What sort of a queen would I be with My Lady the King's Mother ruling everything? The king would not let me have my way in the kingdom, and she would not let me have my way in the court.'

'You are very young,' he started, trying to soothe her.

'I am old enough to know my own mind,' Catalina stated. 'And I want to be queen in truth as well as in name. But he will never let me be that, will he?'

'No,' de Puebla admitted. 'You will never command while he is alive.'

'And when he is dead?' she demanded, without shrinking.

'Then you would be the Dowager Queen,' de Puebla offered.

'And my parents might marry me once more to someone else, and I might leave England anyway!' she finished, quite exasperated.

'It is possible,' he conceded.

'And Harry's wife would be Princess of Wales, and Harry's wife would be the new queen. She would go before me, she would rule in my place, and all my sacrifice would be for nothing. And her sons would be Kings of England.'

'That is true.'

Catalina threw herself into her chair. 'Then I have to be Prince Harry's wife,' she said. 'I have to be.'

De Puebla was quite horrified. 'I understood you had agreed with the king to marry him! He gave me to believe that you were agreed.'

'I had agreed to be queen,' she said, white-faced with determination. 'Not some cat's-paw. D'you know what he called me? He said I would be his child-bride, and I would live in his mother's rooms, as if I were one of her ladies-in-waiting!'

'The former queen . . .'

'The former queen was a saint to put up with a mother-in-law like that one. She stepped back all her life. I can't do it. It is not what I want, it is not what my mother wants, and it is not what God wants.'

'But if you have agreed . . .'

'When has any agreement been honoured in this country?' Catalina demanded fiercely. 'We will break this agreement and make another. We will break this promise and make another. I shall not marry the king, I shall marry another.'

'Who?' he asked numbly.

'Prince Harry, the Prince of Wales,' she said. 'So that when King Henry dies I shall be queen in deed as well as name.'

There was a short silence.

'So you say,' said de Puebla slowly. 'Perhaps. But who is going to tell the king?'

God, if You are there, tell me that I am doing the right thing. If You are there, then help me. If it is Thy will that I am Queen of England, then I will need help to achieve it. It has all gone wrong now, and if this has been sent to try me, then see! I am on my knees and shaking with anxiety. If I am indeed blessed by You, destined by You, chosen by You, and favoured by You, then why do I feel so hopelessly alone?

Ambassador Dr de Puebla found himself in the uncomfortable position of having to bring bad news to one of the most powerful and irascible kings in Christendom. He had firm letters of refusal from Their Majesties of Spain in his hand, he had Catalina's determination to be Princess of Wales, and he had his own shrinking courage, screwed up to the tightest point for this embarrassing meeting.

The king had chosen to see him in the stable yard of Whitehall Palace, he was there looking at a consignment of new Barbary horses, brought in to improve English stock. De Puebla thought of making a graceful reference to foreign blood refreshing native strains, breeding best done between young animals; but he saw Henry's dark face and realised that there would be no easy way out of this dilemma.

'Your Grace,' he said, bowing low.

'De Puebla,' the king said shortly.

'I have a reply from Their Majesties of Spain to your most flattering proposal; but perhaps I should see you at a more opportune time?'

'Here is well enough. I can imagine from your tiptoeing in what they say.'

'The truth is . . .' de Puebla prepared to lie. 'They want their daughter home, and they cannot contemplate her marriage to you. The queen is particularly vehement in her refusal.'

'Because?' the king inquired.

'Because she wants to see her daughter, her youngest, sweetest daughter, matched to a prince of her own age. It is a woman's whim —' The diplomat made a little diffident gesture. 'Only a woman's whim. But we have to recognise a mother's wishes, don't we? Your Grace?'

'Not necessarily,' the king said unhelpfully. 'But what does the Dowager Princess say? I thought that she and I had an understanding. She can tell her mother of her preference.' The king's eyes were on the Arab stallion, walking proud-headed around the yard, his ears flickering backwards and forwards, his tail held high, his neck arched like a bow. 'I imagine she can speak for herself.'

'She says that she will obey you, as ever, Your Grace,' de Puebla said tactfully.

'And?'

'But she has to obey her mother.' He fell back at the sudden hard glance that the king threw at him. 'She is a good daughter, Your Grace. She is an obedient daughter to her mother.'

'I have proposed marriage to her and she has indicated that she would accept.'

'She would never refuse a king such as you. How could she? But if her parents do not consent, they will not apply for dispensation. Without dispensation from the Pope, there can be no marriage.'

'I understand that her marriage was not consummated. We barely need a dispensation. It is a courtesy, a formality.'

'We all know that it was not consummated,' de Puebla hastily confirmed. 'The princess is a maid still, fit for marriage. But all the same the Pope would have to grant a dispensation. If Their Majesties of Spain do not apply for such a dispensation, then what can anyone do?'

The king turned a dark, hard gaze on the Spanish ambassador. 'I don't know, now. I thought I knew what we would do. But now I am misled. You tell me. What can anyone do?'

The ambassador drew on the enduring courage of his race, his secret Jewishness which he held to his heart in the worst moments of his life. He knew that he and his people would always, somehow, survive.

'Nothing can be done,' he said. He attempted a sympathetic smile and felt that he was smirking. He rearranged his face into the gravest expression. 'If the Queen of Spain will not apply for dispensation there is nothing that can be done. And she is inveterate.'

'I am not one of Spain's neighbours to be overrun in a spring campaign,' the king said shortly. 'I am no Granada. I am no Navarre. I do not fear her displeasure.'

'Which is why they long for your alliance,' de Puebla said smoothly.

'An alliance how?' the king asked coldly. 'I thought they were refusing me?'

'Perhaps we could avoid all this difficulty by celebrating another marriage,' the diplomat said carefully, watching Henry's dark face. 'A new marriage. To create the alliance we all want.'

'To whom?'

At the banked-down anger in the king's face the ambassador lost his words.

'Sire . . . I . . .'

'Who do they want for her now? Now that my son, the rose, is dead and buried? Now she is a poor widow with only half her dowry paid, living on my charity?'

'The prince,' de Puebla plunged in. 'She was brought to the kingdom to be Princess of Wales. She was brought here to be wife to the prince, and later – much later, please God – to be queen. Perhaps that is her destiny, Your Grace. She thinks so, certainly.'

'She thinks!' the king exclaimed. 'She thinks like that filly thinks! Nothing beyond the next minute.'

'She is young,' the ambassador said. 'But she will learn. And the prince is young, they will learn together.'

'And we old men have to stand back, do we? She has told you of no preference, no particular liking for me? Though she gave me clearly to understand that she would marry me? She shows no regret at this turn around? She is not tempted to defy her parents and keep her freely given word to me?'

The ambassador heard the bitterness in the old man's voice. 'She is allowed no choice,' he reminded the king. 'She has to do as she is bidden by her parents. I think, for herself, there was an attraction, perhaps even a powerful attraction. But she knows she has to go where she is bid.'

'I thought to marry her! I would have made her queen! She would have been Queen of England.' He almost choked on the title, all his life he had thought it the greatest honour that a woman could think of, just as his title was the greatest in his own imagination.

The ambassador paused for a moment to let the king recover.

'You know, there are other, equally beautiful young ladies in her family,' he suggested carefully. 'The young Queen of Naples is a widow now. As King Ferdinand's niece, she would bring a good dowry, and she has the family likeness.' He hesitated. 'She is said to be very lovely, and –' He paused. 'Amorous.'

'She gave me to understand that she loved me. Am I now to think her a pretender?'

The ambassador felt a cold sweat which seeped from every pore of his body at that dreadful word. 'No pretender,' he said, his smile quite ghastly. 'A loving daughter-in-law, an affectionate girl . . .'

There was an icy silence.

'You know how pretenders fare in this country,' the king said stiffly.

'Yes! But . . .'

'She will regret it, if she plays with me.'

'No play! No pretence! Nothing!'

The king let the ambassador stand, slightly shaking with anxiety.

'I thought to finish this whole difficulty with the dowry and the jointure,' Henry remarked, at length.

'And so it can be. Once the princess is betrothed to the prince, then Spain will pay the second half of the dowry and the widow's jointure is no more,' de Puebla assured him. He noticed he was talking too rapidly, took a breath, and went slower. 'All difficulties are finished. Their Majesties of Spain would be glad to apply for dispensation for their daughter to marry Prince Harry. It would be a good match for her and she will do as she is ordered. It leaves you free to look around for your wife, Your Grace, and it frees the revenues of Cornwall and Wales and Chester to your own disposal once more.'

King Henry shrugged his shoulders and turned from the schooling ring and the horse. 'So it is over?' he asked coldly. 'She does not desire me, as I thought she did. I mistook her attention to me. She meant to be nothing but filial?' He laughed harshly at the thought of her kiss by the river. 'I must forget my desire for her?'

'She has to obey her parents as a Princess of Spain,' de Puebla reminded him. 'On her own account, I know there was a preference. She told me so herself.' He thought that Catalina's double-dealing could be covered by this. 'She is disappointed, to tell you the truth.

But her mother is adamant. I cannot deny the Queen of Castile. She is utterly determined to have her daughter returned to Spain, or married to Prince Harry. She will brook no other suggestion.'

'So be it,' said the king, his voice like ice. 'I had a foolish dream, a desire. It can finish here.'

He turned and walked away from the stable yard, his pleasure in his horses soured.

'I hope that there is no ill feeling?' the ambassador asked, hobbling briskly behind him.

'None at all,' the king threw over his shoulder. 'None in the world.'

'And the betrothal with Prince Harry? May I assure Their Catholic Majesties that it will go ahead?'

'Oh, at once. I shall make it my first and foremost office.'

'I do hope there is no offence?' de Puebla called to the king's retreating back.

The king turned on his heel and faced the Spanish ambassador, his clenched fists on his hips, his shoulders square. 'She has tried to play me like a fool,' he said through thin lips. 'I don't thank her for it. Her parents have tried to lead me by the nose. I think they will find that they have a dragon, not one of their baited bulls. I won't forget this. You Spaniards, you will not forget it either. And she will regret the day she tried to lead me on as if I were a lovesick boy, as I regret it now.'

'It is agreed,' de Puebla said flatly to Catalina. He was standing before her – 'Like an errand boy!' he thought indignantly – as she was ripping the velvet panels out of a gown to re-model the dress.

'I am to marry Prince Harry,' she said in a tone as dull as his own. 'Has he signed anything?'

'He has agreed. He has to wait for a dispensation. But he has agreed.'

She looked up at him. 'Was he very angry?'

'I think he was even angrier than he showed me. And what he showed me was bad.'

'What will he do?' she asked.

He scrutinised her pale face. She was white but she was not fearful. Her blue eyes were veiled as her father's were veiled when he was planning something. She did not look like a damsel in distress, she looked like a woman trying to outwit a most dangerous protagonist. She was not endearing, as a woman in tears would have been endearing, he thought. She was formidable; but not pleasing.

'I don't know what he will do,' he said. 'His nature is vengeful. But we must give him no advantage. We have to pay your dowry at once. We have to complete our side of the contract to force him to complete his.'

'The plate has lost its value,' she said flatly. 'It is damaged by use. And I have sold some.'

He gasped. 'You have sold it? It is the king's own!'

She shrugged. 'I have to eat, Dr de Puebla. We cannot all go uninvited to court and thrust our way in to the common table. I am not living well, but I do have to live. And I have nothing to live on but my goods.'

'You should have preserved them intact!'

She shrugged 'I should never have been reduced to this. I have had to pawn my own plate to live. Whoever is to blame, it is not me.'

'Your father will have to pay the dowry and pay you an allowance,' he said grimly. 'We must give them no excuse to withdraw. If your dowry is not paid he will not marry you to the prince. Infanta, I must warn you, he will revel in your discomfort. He will prolong it.'

Catalina nodded. 'He is my enemy too then.'

'I fear it.'

'It will happen, you know,' she said inconsequentially.

'What?'

'I will marry Harry. I will be queen.'

'Infanta, it is my dearest wish.'

'Princess,' she replied.

Whitehall, June 1503

'You are to be betrothed to Catalina of Aragon,' the king told his son, thinking of the son who had gone before.

The blond boy flushed as pink as a girl. 'Yes, sire.'

He had been coached perfectly by his grandmother. He was prepared for everything but real life.

'Don't think the marriage will happen,' the king warned him.

The boy's eyes flashed up in surprise and were then cast down again. 'No?'

'No. They have robbed us and cheated us at every turn, they have rolled us over like a bawd in a tavern. They have cozened us and promised one thing after another like a cock-teaser in drink. They say –' He broke off, his son's wide-eyed gaze reminding him that he had spoken as a man to a man, and this was a boy. Also, his resentment should not show, however fiercely it burned.

'They have taken advantage of our friendship,' he summed up. 'And now we will take advantage of their weakness.'

'Surely we are all friends?'

Henry grimaced, thinking of that scoundrel Ferdinand, and of his daughter, the cool beauty who had turned him down. 'Oh, yes,' he said. 'Loyal friends.'

'So I am to be betrothed and later, when I am fifteen, we will be married?'

The boy had understood nothing. So be it. 'Say sixteen.'

'Arthur was fifteen.'

Henry bit down the reply that much good it had done Arthur. Besides, it did not matter since it would never happen. 'Oh, yes,' he said again. 'Fifteen, then.'

The boy knew that something was wrong. His smooth forehead was furrowed. 'We do mean this, don't we, Father? I would not mislead such a princess. It is a most solemn oath I will make?'

'Oh, yes,' the king said again.

The night before my betrothal to Prince Harry, I have a dream so lovely that I do not want to wake. I am in the garden of the Alhambra, walking with my hand in Arthur's, laughing up at him, and showing him the beauty around us: the great sandstone wall which encircles the fort, the city of Granada below us and the mountains capped with silvery snow on the horizon.

'I have won,' I say to him. 'I have done everything you wanted, everything that we planned. I will be princess as you made me. I will be queen as you wanted me to be. My mother's wishes are fulfilled, my own destiny will be complete, your desire and God's will. Are you happy now, my love?'

He smiles down at me, his eyes warm, his face tender, a smile he has only for me. 'I shall watch over you,' he whispers. 'All the time. Here in al-Yanna.'

I hesitate at the odd sound of the word on his lips, and then I realise that he has used the Moorish word: 'al-Yanna', which means both heaven, a cemetery, and a garden. For the Moors, heaven is a garden, an eternal garden.

'I shall come to you one day,' I whisper, even as his grasp on my hand becomes lighter, and then fades, though I try to hold him. 'I shall be with you again, my love. I shall meet you here in the garden.'

'I know,' he says, and now his face is melting away like mist in the morning, like a mirage in the hot air of the sierra. 'I know we will be together again, Catalina, my Katherine, my love.'

25th June 1503

It was a bright, hot June day. Catalina was dressed in a new gown of blue with a blue hood, the eleven-year-old boy opposite her was radiant with excitement, dressed in cloth of gold.

They were before the Bishop of Salisbury with a small court present: the king, his mother, the Princess Mary, and a few other witnesses. Catalina put her cold hand in the prince's warm palm and felt the plumpness of childhood beneath her fingers.

Catalina looked beyond the flushed boy to his father's grave face. The king had aged in the months since the death of his wife, and the lines in his face were more deeply grooved, his eyes shadowed. Men at the court said he was sick, some illness which was thinning his blood and wearing him out. Others said that he was sour with disappointment: at the loss of his heir, at the loss of his wife, at the frustration of his plans. Some said he had been crossed in love, outwitted by a woman. Only that could have unmanned him so bitterly.

Catalina smiled shyly at him, but there was no echoing warmth from the man who would be her father-in-law for the second time, but had wanted her for his own. For a moment, her confidence dimmed. She had allowed herself to hope that the king had surrendered to her determination, to her mother's ruling, to God's will. Now, seeing his cold look, she had a moment of fear that perhaps this ceremony – even something as serious and sacred as a betrothal – might perhaps be nothing more than a revenge by this most cunning of kings.

Chilled, she turned away from him to listen to the bishop recite the words of the marriage service and she repeated her part, making sure not to think of when she had said the words before, only a year and a half ago, when her hand had been cool in the grasp of the most handsome young man she had ever seen, when her bridegroom had given her a shy sideways smile, when she had stared at him through the veil of her mantilla and been aware of the thousands of silently watching faces beyond.

The young prince, who had been dazzled then by the beauty of his sister-in-law the bride, was now the bridegroom. His beam was the boisterous joy of a young boy in the presence of a beautiful older girl. She had been the bride of his older brother, she was the young woman he had been proud to escort on her wedding day. He had begged her for a present of a Barbary horse for his tenth birthday. He had looked at her at her wedding feast and that night prayed that he too might have a Spanish bride just like her.

When she had left the court with Arthur he had dreamed of her, he had written poems and love-songs, secretly dedicating them to her. He had heard of Arthur's death with a bright, fierce joy that now she was free.

Now, not even two years on, she was before him, her hair brushed out bronze and golden over her shoulders signifying her virgin state, her blue lace mantilla veiling her face. Her hand was in his, her blue eyes were on him, her smile was only for him.

Harry's braggart boyish heart swelled so full in his chest that he could scarcely reply to his part of the service. Arthur was gone, and he was Prince of Wales; Arthur was gone, and he was his father's favourite, the rosebush of England. Arthur was gone, and Arthur's bride was his wife. He stood straight and proud and repeated his oaths in his clear treble voice. Arthur was gone, and there was only one Prince of Wales and one Princess: Prince Harry and Princess Katherine.

Princess Again

1504

I may think that I have won; but still I have not won. I should have won; but I have not won. Harry reaches twelve, and they declare him Prince of Wales but they do not come for me, declare our betrothal or invest me as princess. I send for the ambassador. He does not come in the morning, he does not even come that day. He comes the day after, as if my affairs have no urgency, and he does not apologise for his delay. I ask him why I have not been invested as Princess of Wales alongside Harry and he does not know. He suggests that they are waiting for the payment of my dowry and without it, nothing can go ahead. But he knows, and I know, and King Henry knows, that I no longer have all my plate to give to them, and if my father will not send his share, there is nothing I can do.

My mother the queen must know that I am desolate; but I hear from her only rarely. It is as if I am one of her explorers, a solitary Cristóbal Colón with no companions and no maps. She has sent me out into the world and if I tumble off the edge or am lost at sea, there is nothing that anyone can do.

She has nothing to say to me. I fear that she is ashamed of me, as I wait at court like a supplicant for the prince to honour his promise.

In November I am so filled with foreboding that she is ill or sad that I write to her and beg her to reply to me, to send me at least one word. That, as it happens, was the very day that she died and so she never had my letter and I never had my one word. She leaves me in death as she left me in life: to silence and a sense of her absence.

I knew that I would miss her when I left home. But it was a comfort to me to know that the sun still shone in the gardens of the Alhambra, and she was still there beside the green-trimmed pool. I did not know that the loss of her would make my situation in England so much worse. My father, having long refused to pay the second half of my dowry as part of his game with the King of England, now finds his play has become a bitter truth – he cannot pay. He has spent his life and his fortune in ceaseless crusade against the Moors and there is no money left for anyone. The rich revenues of Castile are now paid to Juana, my mother's heir; and my father has nothing in the treasury of Aragon for my marriage. My father is now no more than one of the many kings of Spain. Juana is the great heiress of Castile and, if the gossips are to be believed, Juana has run as mad as a rabid dog, tormented by love and by her husband into insanity. Anyone looking at me now no longer sees a princess of a united Spain, one of the great brides of Christendom; but a widowed pauper with bad blood. Our family fortunes are cascading down like a house of cards without my mother's steady hand and watchful eye. There is nothing left for my father but despair; and that is all the dowry he can give me.

I am only nineteen. Is my life over?

1509

And then, I waited. Incredibly, I waited for a total of six years. Six years when I went from a bride of seventeen to a woman of twenty-three. I knew then that King Henry's rage against me was bitter, and effective, and long-lasting. No princess in the world had ever been made to wait so long, or treated so harshly, or left in such despair. I am not exaggerating this, as a troubadour might do to make a better story – as I might have told you, beloved, in the dark hours of the night. No, it was not like a story, it was not even like a life. It was like a prison sentence, it was like being a hostage with no chance of redemption, it was loneliness, and the slow realisation that I had failed.

I failed my mother and failed to bring to her the alliance with England that I had been born and bred to do. I was ashamed of my failure. Without the dowry payment from Spain I could not force the English to honour the betrothal. With the king's enmity I could force them to do nothing. Harry was a child of thirteen, I hardly ever saw him. I could not appeal to him to make his promise good. I was powerless, neglected by the court and falling into shameful poverty.

Then Harry was fourteen years of age and our betrothal was still not made marriage, and that marriage not celebrated. I waited a year, *he reached fifteen years, and nobody came for me. So Harry reached his sixteenth and then his seventeenth birthday, and still nobody came for me. Those years turned. I grew older. I waited. I was constant. It was all I could be.*

I turned the panels on my gowns and sold my jewels for food. I had to sell my precious plate, one gold piece at a time. I knew it was the property of the king as I sent for the goldsmiths. I knew that each time I pawned a piece I put my wedding back another day. But I had to eat, my household had to eat. I could pay them no wages, I could hardly ask them to beg for me as well as go hungry on their own account.

I was friendless. I discovered that Dona Elvira was plotting against my father in favour of Juana and her husband Philip and I dismissed her, in a rage, and sent her away. I did not care if she spoke against me, if she named me as a liar. I did not care even if she declared that Arthur and I had been lovers. I had caught her in treason against my father; did she truly think I would ally with my sister against the King of Aragon? I was so angry that I did not care what her enmity cost me.

Also, since I am not a fool, I calculated rightly that no-one would believe her word against mine. She fled to Philip and Juana in the Netherlands, and I never heard from her again, and I never complained of my loss.

I lost my ambassador, Dr de Puebla. I had often complained to my father of his divided loyalties, of his disrespect, of his concessions to the English court. But when he was recalled to Spain I found that he had known more than I had realised, he had used his friendship with the king to my advantage, he had understood his way around this most difficult court. He had been a better friend than I had known, and I was the poorer without him. I lost a friend and an ally, through my own arrogance; and I was sorry for his absence. His replacement: the emissary who had come to take me home, Don Gutierre Gomez de Fuensalida, was a pompous fool who thought the English were honoured by his presence. They sneered at his face and laughed behind his back and I was a ragged princess with an ambassador entranced by his own self-importance.

I lost my dear father in Christ, the confessor I trusted, appointed by my mother to guide me, and I had to find another for myself. I lost the ladies of my little court, who would not live in hardship and poverty, and I could not pay anyone else to serve me. Maria de Salinas stood by me, through all these long years of endurance, for love; but the other ladies wanted to leave. Then, finally, I lost my house, my lovely house on the Strand, which had been my home, a little safe place in this most foreign land.

The king promised me rooms at court and I thought that he had at last forgiven me. I thought he was offering me to come to court, to live in the rooms of a princess and to see Harry. But when I moved my house-hold there I found that I was given the worst rooms, allocated the poorest service, unable to see the prince, except on the most formal of state occasions. One dreadful day, the court left on progress without telling us and we had to dash after them, finding our way down the unmarked country lanes, as unwanted and as irrelevant as a wagon filled with old goods. When we caught up, no-one had noticed that we were missing and I had to take the only rooms left: over the stables, like a servant.

The king stopped paying my allowance, his mother did not press my case. I had no money of my own at all. I lived despised on the fringe of the court, with Spaniards who served me only because they could not leave. They were trapped like me, watching the years slide by, getting older and more resentful till I felt like the sleeping princess of the fairy tale and thought that I would never wake.

I lost my vanity – my proud sense that I could be cleverer than that old fox who was my father-in-law, and that sharp vixen his mother. I learned that he had betrothed me to his son Prince Harry, not because he loved and forgave me, but because it was the cleverest and cruellest way to punish me. If he could not have me, then he could make sure that no-one had me. It was a bitter day when I realised that.

And then, Philip died and my sister Juana was a widow like me, and King Henry came up with a plan to marry her, my poor sister – driven from her wits by the loss of her husband – and put her over me, on the throne of England, where everyone would see that she was crazed, where everyone could see the bad blood which I share, where everyone would know that he had made her queen and thrown me down to nothing. It was a wicked plan, certain to shame and distress both me and Juana. He would have done it if he could, and he made me his pander as well – he forced me to recommend him to my father. Under my father's orders I spoke to the king of Juana's beauty; under the king's orders I urged my father to accept his suit, all the time knowing that I was betraying my very soul. I lost my ability to refuse King Henry my persecutor, my father-in-law, my would-be seducer. I was afraid to say 'no' to him. I was very much reduced, that day.

I lost my vanity in my allure, I lost my confidence in my intelligence and skills; but I never lost my will to live. I was not like my mother, I was not like Juana, I did not turn my face to the wall and long for my pain to be over. I did not slide into the wailing grief of madness nor into the gentle darkness of sloth. I gritted my teeth, I am the constant princess, I don't stop when everyone else stops. I carried on. I waited. Even when I could do nothing else, I could still wait. So I waited.

These were not the years of my defeat; these were the years when I grew up, and it was a bitter maturing. I grew from a girl of sixteen ready for love to a half-orphaned, lonely widow of twenty-three. These were the years when I drew on the happiness of my childhood in the Alhambra and my love for my husband to sustain me, and swore that whatever the obstacles before me, I should be Queen of England. These were the years when, though my mother was dead, she lived again through me. I found her determination inside me, I found her courage inside me, I found Arthur's love and optimism inside me. These were the years when although I had nothing left: no husband, no mother, no friends, no fortune and no prospects; I swore that however disregarded, however poor, however unlikely a prospect, I would still be Queen of England.

News, always slow to reach the bedraggled Spaniards on the fringe of the royal court, filtered through that Harry's sister the Princess Mary was to be married, gloriously, to Prince Charles, son of King Philip and Queen Juana, grandson to both the Emperor Maximilian and King Ferdinand. Amazingly, at this of all moments, King Ferdinand at last found the money for Catalina's dowry, and packed it off to London.

'My God, we are freed. There can be a double wedding. I can marry him,' Catalina said, heartfelt, to the Spanish emissary, Don Gutierre Gomez de Fuensalida.

He was pale with worry, his yellow teeth nipping at his lips. 'Oh, Infanta, I hardly know how to tell you. Even with this alliance, even with the dowry money – dear God, I fear it comes too late. I fear it will not help us at all.'

'How can it be? Princess Mary's betrothal only deepens the alliance with my family.'

'What if . . .' He started and broke off. He could hardly speak of the danger that he foresaw. 'Princess, all the English know that the dowry money is coming, but they do not speak of your marriage. Oh, Princess, what if they plan an alliance that does not include Spain? What if they plan an alliance between the emperor and King Henry? What if the alliance is for them to go to war against Spain?'

She turned her head. 'It cannot be.'

'What if it is?'

'Against the boy's own grandfather?' she demanded.

'It would only be one grandfather, the emperor, against another, your father.'

'They would not,' she said determinedly.

'They could.'

'King Henry would not be so dishonest.'

'Princess, you know that he would.'

She hesitated. 'What is it?' she suddenly demanded, sharp with irritation. 'There is something else. Something you are not telling me. What is it?'

He paused, a lie in his mouth; then he told her the truth. 'I am afraid, I am very afraid, that they will betroth Prince Harry to Princess Eleanor, the sister of Charles.'

'They cannot, he is betrothed to me.'

'They may plan it as part of a great treaty. Your sister Juana to marry the king, your nephew Charles for Princess Mary, and your niece Eleanor for Prince Harry.'

'But what about me? Now that my dowry money is on its way at last?'

He was silent. It was painfully apparent that Catalina was excluded by these alliances, and no provision made for her.

'A true prince has to honour his promise,' she said passionately. 'We were betrothed by a bishop before witnesses, it is a solemn oath.'

The ambassador shrugged, hesitated. He could hardly make himself tell her the worst news of all. 'Your Grace, Princess, be brave. I am afraid he may withdraw his oath.'

'He cannot.'

Fuensalida went further. 'Indeed, I am afraid it is already withdrawn. He may have withdrawn it years ago.'

'What?' she asked sharply. 'How?'

'A rumour, I cannot be sure of it. But I am afraid . . .' He broke off.

'Afraid of what?'

'I am afraid that the prince may be already released from his betrothal to you.' He hesitated at the sudden darkening of her face. 'It will not have been his choice,' he said quickly. 'His father is determined against us.'

'How could he? How can such a thing be done?'

'He could have sworn an oath that he was too young, that he was under duress. He may have declared that he did not want to marry you. Indeed, I think that is what he has done.'

'He was not under duress!' Catalina exclaimed. 'He was utterly delighted. He has been in love with me for years, I am sure he still is. He did want to marry me!'

'An oath sworn before a bishop that he was not acting of his own free will would be enough to secure his release from his promise.'

'So all these years that I have been betrothed to him, and acted on that premise, all these years that I have waited and waited and endured . . .' She could not finish. 'Are you telling me that for all these years, when I believed that we had them tied down, contracted, bound, he has been free?'

The ambassador nodded; her face was so stark and shocked that he could hardly find his voice.

'This is . . . a betrayal,' she said. 'A most terrible betrayal.' She choked on the words. 'This is the worst betrayal of all.'

He nodded again.

There was a long, painful silence. 'I am lost,' she said simply. 'Now I know it. I have been lost for years and I did not know. I have been fighting a battle with no army, with no support. Actually – with no cause. You tell me that I have been defending a cause that was gone long ago. I was fighting for my betrothal but I was not betrothed. I have been all alone, all this long time. And now I know it.'

Still she did not weep, though her blue eyes were horrified.

'I made a promise,' she said, her voice harsh. 'I made a solemn and binding promise.'

'Your betrothal?'

She made a little gesture with her hand. 'Not that. I swore a promise. A deathbed promise. Now you tell me it has all been for nothing.'

'Princess, you have stayed at your post, as your mother would have wanted you to do.'

'I have been made a fool!' burst out of her, from the depth of her shock. 'I have been fighting for the fulfilment of a vow, not knowing that the vow was long broken.'

He could say nothing, her pain was too raw for any soothing words.

After a few moments, she raised her head. 'Does everyone know but me?' she asked bleakly.

He shook his head. 'I am sure it was kept most secret.'

'My Lady the King's Mother,' she predicted bitterly. 'She will have known. It will have been her decision. And the king, the prince himself, and if he knew, then the Princess Mary will know – he would have told her. And his closest companions . . .' She raised her head. 'The king's mother's ladies, the princess's ladies. The bishop that he swore to, a witness or two. Half the court, I suppose.' She paused. 'I thought that at least some of them were my friends,' she said.

The ambassador shrugged. 'In a court there are no friends, only courtiers.'

'My father will defend me from this . . . cruelty!' she burst out. 'They should have thought of that before they treated me so! There will be no treaties for England with Spain when he hears about this. He will take revenge for this abuse of me.'

He could say nothing, and in the still silent face that he turned to her she saw the worst truth.

'No,' she said simply. 'Not him. Not him as well. Not my father. He did not know. He loves me. He would never injure me. He would never abandon me here.'

Still he could not tell her. He saw her take a deep breath.

'Oh. Oh. I see. I see from your silence. Of course. He knows, of course he knows, doesn't he? My father? The dowry money is just another trick. He knows of the proposal to marry Prince Harry to Princess Eleanor. He has been leading the king on to think that he can marry Juana. He ordered me to encourage the king to marry Juana. He will have agreed to this new proposal for Prince Harry. And so he knows that the prince has broken his oath to me? And is free to marry?'

'Princess, he has told me nothing. I think he must know. But perhaps he plans . . .'

Her gesture stopped him. 'He has given up on me. I see. I have failed him and he has cast me aside. I am indeed alone.'

'So shall I try to get us home now?' Fuensalida asked quietly. Truly, he thought, it had become the very pinnacle of his ambitions. If he could get this doomed princess home to her unhappy father and her increasingly deranged sister, the new Queen of Castile, he would have done the best he could in a desperate situation. Nobody would marry Catalina of Spain now she was the daughter of a divided kingdom. Everyone could see that the madness in her blood was coming out in her sister. Not even Henry of England could pretend that Juana was fit to marry when she was on a crazed progress across Spain with her dead husband's coffin. Ferdinand's tricky diplomacy had rebounded on him and now everyone in Europe was his enemy, with two of the most powerful men in Europe allied to make war against him. Ferdinand was lost, and going down. The best that this unlucky princess could expect was a scratch marriage to some Spanish grandee and retirement to the countryside, with a chance to escape the war that must come. The worst was to remain trapped and in poverty in England, a forgotten hostage that no-one would ransom. A prisoner who would be soon forgotten, even by her gaolers.

'What shall I do?' Finally she accepted danger. He saw her take it in. Finally, she understood that she had lost. He saw her, a queen in every inch, learn the depth of her defeat. 'I must know what I should do. Or I shall be hostage, in an enemy country, with no-one to speak for me.'

He did not say that he had thought her just that, ever since he had arrived.

'We shall leave,' he said decisively. 'If war comes they will keep you as a hostage and they will seize your dowry. God forbid that now the money is finally coming, it should be used to make war against Spain.'

'I cannot leave,' she said flatly. 'If I go, I will never get back here.'

'It is over!' he cried in sudden passion. 'You see it yourself, at last. We have lost. We are defeated. It is over for you and England. You have held on and faced humiliation and poverty, you have faced it like a princess, like a queen, like a saint. Your mother herself could not have shown more courage. But we are defeated, Infanta. You have lost. We have to get home as best we can. We have to run, before they catch us.'

'Catch us?'

'They could imprison us both as enemy spies and hold us to ransom,' he told her. 'They could impound whatever remains of your dowry goods and impound the rest when it arrives. God knows, they can make up a charge, and execute you, if they want to enough.'

'They dare not touch me! I am a princess of royal blood,' she flared up. 'Whatever else they can take from me, they can never take that! I am Infanta of Spain even if I am nothing else! Even if I am never Queen of England, at least I will always be Infanta of Spain.'

'Princes of royal blood have gone into the Tower of London before and not come out again,' the ambassador said bleakly. 'Princes of the royal blood of England have had those gates shut behind them and never seen daylight again. He could call you a pretender. You know what happens in England to pretenders. We have to go.'

Catalina curtseyed to My Lady the King's Mother and received not even a nod of the head in return. She stiffened. The two retinues had met on their way to Mass; behind the old lady was her granddaughter the Princess Mary and half a dozen ladies. All of them showed frosty faces to the young woman who was supposed to be betrothed to the Prince of Wales but who had been neglected for so long.

'My lady.' Catalina stood in her path, waiting for an acknow-ledgement.

The king's mother looked at the young woman with open dislike.

'I hear that there are difficulties over the betrothal of the Princess Mary,' she said.

Catalina looked towards the Princess Mary and the girl, hidden behind her grandmother, made an ugly grimace at her and broke off with a sudden snort of laughter.

'I did not know,' Catalina said.

'You may not know, but your father undoubtedly knows,' the old woman said irritably. 'In one of your constant letters to him you might tell him that he does his cause and your cause no good by trying to disturb our plans for our family.'

'I am very sure he does not . . .' Catalina started.

'I am very sure that he does; and you had better warn him not to stand in our way,' the old woman interrupted her sharply, and swept on.

'My own betrothal . . .' Catalina tried.

'Your betrothal?' The king's mother repeated the words as if she had never heard them before. 'Your betrothal?' Suddenly, she laughed, throwing her head back, her mouth wide. Behind her, the princess laughed too, and then all the ladies were laughing out loud at the thought of the pauper princess speaking of her betrothal to the most eligible prince in Christendom.

'My father is sending my dowry!' Catalina cried out.

'Too late! You are far too late!' the king's mother wailed, clutching at the arm of her friend.

Catalina, confronted by a dozen laughing faces, reduced to helpless hysteria at the thought of this patched princess offering her bits of plate and gold, ducked her head down, pushed through them, and went away.

That night the ambassador of Spain and an Italian merchant of some wealth and great discretion stood side by side on a shadowy quayside at a quiet corner of the London docks, and watched the quiet loading of Spanish goods on to a ship bound for Bruges.

'She has not authorised this?' the merchant whispered, his dark face lit by flickering torchlight. 'We are all but stealing her dowry! What will happen if the English suddenly say that the marriage is to go ahead and we have emptied her treasure room? What if they see that the dowry has come from Spain at last, but it never reached her treasure room? They will call us thieves. We will be thieves!'

'They will never say it is to go ahead,' the ambassador said simply. 'They will impound her goods and imprison her the moment that they declare war on Spain, and they could do that any day now. I dare not let King Ferdinand's money fall into the hands of the English. They are our enemies, not our allies.'

'What will she do? We have emptied her treasury. There is nothing in her strong-room but empty boxes. We have left her a pauper.'

The ambassador shrugged. 'She is ruined anyway. If she stays here when England is at war with Spain then she is an enemy hostage and they will imprison her. If she runs away with me she will have no kind welcome back at home. Her mother is dead and her family is ruined and she is ruined too. I would not be surprised if she did not throw herself into the Thames and drown. Her life is over. I cannot see what will become of her. I can save her money, if you will ship it out for me. But I cannot save her.'

I know I have to leave England; Arthur would not want me to stay to face danger. I have a terror of the Tower and the block that would be fitting only if I were a traitor, and not a princess who has never done anything wrong but tell one great lie, and that for the best. It would be the jest of all time if I had to put my head down on Warwick's block and die, a Spanish pretender to the throne where he died a Plantagenet.

That must not happen. I see that my writ does not run. I am not

such a fool as to think I can command any more. I do not even pray
any more. I do not even ask for my destiny. But I can run away. And
I think the time to run away is now.

'You have done what?' Catalina demanded of her ambassador. The
inventory in her hand trembled.

'I took it upon my own authority to move your father's treasure
from the country. I could not risk . . .'

'*My* dowry.' She raised her voice.

'Your Grace, we both know it will not be needed for a wedding.
He will never marry you. They would take your dowry and he would
still not marry you.'

'It was my side of the bargain!' she shouted. 'I keep faith! Even
if no-one else does! I have not eaten, I have given up my own house
so as not to pawn that treasure. I make a promise and I keep to it,
whatever the cost!'

'The king would have used it to pay for soldiers to fight against
your father. He would have fought against Spain with your father's
own gold!' Fuensalida exclaimed miserably. 'I could not let it happen.'

'So you robbed me!'

He stumbled over the words. 'I took your treasure into safe-
keeping in the hopes that . . .'

'Go!' she said abruptly.

'Princess?'

'You have betrayed me, just as Dona Elvira betrayed me, just as
everyone always betrays me,' she said bitterly. 'You may leave me. I
shall not send for you again. Ever. Be very sure that I shall never
speak to you again. But I shall tell my father what you have done.
I shall write to him at once and tell him that you have stolen my
dowry monies, that you are a thief. You will never be received at the
court in Spain.'

He bowed, trembling with emotion, and then he turned to leave, too proud to defend himself.

'You are nothing more than a traitor!' Catalina cried as he reached the door. 'And if I were a queen with the power of the queen I would have you hanged for treason.'

He stiffened. He turned, he bowed again, his voice when he spoke was ice. 'Infanta, please do not make a fool of yourself by insulting me. You are badly mistaken. It was your own father who commanded me to return your dowry. I was obeying his direct order. Your own father wanted your treasury stripped of every valuable. It is he who decided to make you a pauper. He wanted the dowry money returned because he has given up all hope of your marriage. He wanted the money kept safe and smuggled safely out of England.

'But I must tell you,' he added with weighty malice, 'he did not order me to make sure that *you* were safe. He gave no orders to smuggle you safely out of England. He thought of the treasure but not of you. His orders were to secure the safety of the goods. He did not even mention you by name. I think he must have given you up for lost.'

As soon as the words were out he wished he had not said them. The stricken look on her face was worse than anything he had ever seen before. 'He told you to send back the gold but to leave me behind? With nothing?'

'I am sure . . .'

Blindly, she turned her back to him and walked to the window so that he could not see the blank horror on her face. 'Go,' she repeated. 'Just go.'

I am the sleeping princess in the story, a snow princess left in a cold land and forgetting the feel of the sun. This winter has been a long one, even for England. Even now, in April, the grass is so frosty in the

morning that when I wake and see the ice on my bedroom windows the light filtering through is so white that I think it has snowed overnight. The water in the cup by my bed is frozen by midnight, and we cannot now afford to keep the fire in through the night. When I walk outside on the icy grass, it crunches thickly under my feet and I can feel its chill through the thin soles of my boots. This summer, I know, will have all the mild sweetness of an English summer; but I long for the burning heat of Spain. I want to have my despair baked out of me once more. I feel as if I have been cold for seven years, and if nothing comes to warm me soon I shall simply die of it, just melt away under the rain, just blow away like the mist off the river. If the king is indeed dying, as the court rumour says, and Prince Harry comes to the throne and marries Eleanor, then I shall ask my father for permission to take the veil and retire to a convent. It could not be worse than here. It could not be poorer, colder or more lonely. Clearly my father has forgotten his love for me and given me up, just as if I had died with Arthur. Indeed, now, I acknowledge that every day I wish that I had died with Arthur.

I have sworn never to despair – the women of my family dissolve into despair like molasses into water. But this ice in my heart does not feel like despair. It feels as if my rock-hard determination to be queen has turned me to stone. I don't feel as if I am giving way to my feelings like Juana; I feel as if I have mislaid my feelings. I am a block, an icicle, a princess of constant snow.

I try to pray to God but I cannot hear Him. I fear He has forgotten me as everyone else has done. I have lost all sense of His presence, I have lost my fear of His will, and I have lost my joy in His blessing. I can feel nothing for Him. I no longer think I am His special child, chosen to be blessed. I no longer console myself that I am His special child, chosen to be tested. I think He has turned His face from me. I don't know why, but if my earthly father can forget me, and forget that I was his favourite child, as he has done, then I suppose my Heavenly Father can forget me too.

In all the world I find that I care for only two things now: I can still feel my love for Arthur, like a warm, still-beating heart in a little bird that has fallen from a frozen sky, chilled and cold. And I still long for Spain, for the Alhambra Palace, for al-Yanna; the garden, the secret place, paradise.

I endure my life only because I cannot escape it. Each year I hope that my fortunes will change; each year when Harry's birthday comes around and the betrothal is not made marriage, I know that another year of my fertile life has come and gone. Each midsummer day, when the dowry payment falls due and there is no draft from my father, I feel shame: like a sickness in my belly. And twelve times a year, for seven years, that is eighty-four times, my courses have come and gone. Each time I bleed I think, there is another chance to make a prince for England wasted. I have learned to grieve for the stain on my linen as if it is a child lost. Eighty-four chances for me to have a son, in the very flush of my youth; eighty-four chances lost. I am learning to miscarry. I am learning the sorrow of miscarriage.

Each day, when I go to pray I look up at the crucified Christ and say: 'Your will be done'. That is each day for seven years, that is two thousand, five hundred and fifty-six times. This is the arithmetic of my pain. I say: 'Your will be done'; but what I mean is: 'make Your will on these wicked English councillors and this spiteful, unforgiving English king, and his old witch of a mother. Give me my rights. Make me queen. I must be queen, I must have a son, or I will become a princess of snow'.

21st April 1509

'The king is dead,' Fuensalida the ambassador wrote briefly to Catalina, knowing that she would not receive him in person, knowing that she would never forgive him for stealing her dowry and naming her as a pretender, for telling her that her father had abandoned her. 'I know you will not see me but I have to do my duty and warn you that on his deathbed the king told his son that he was free to marry whoever he chooses. If you wish me to commission a ship to take you home to Spain, I have personal funds to do so. Myself, I cannot see that you will gain anything by staying in this country but insult, ignominy, and perhaps danger.'

'Dead,' Catalina said.

'What?' one of her ladies asked.

Catalina scrunched the letter into her hand. She never trusted anyone with anything now. 'Nothing,' she said. 'I am going for a walk.'

Maria de Salinas stood up and put Catalina's patched cloak about her shoulders. It was the same cloak that she had worn wrapped around in the winter cold when she and Arthur had left London for Ludlow, seven years earlier.

'Shall we come with you?' she offered, without enthusiasm, glancing at the grey sky beyond the windows.

'No.'

I pound alongside the river, the gravelled walk pricking the soles of my feet through the thin leather, as if I am trying to run away from hope itself. I wonder if there is any chance that my luck might change, might be changing now. The king who wanted me, and then hated me for refusing him, is dead. They said he was sick; but God knows, he never weakened. I thought he would reign forever. But now he is dead. Now he has gone. It will be the prince who decides.

I dare not touch hope. After all these years of fasting, I feel as if hope would make me drunk if I had so much of a drop of it on my lips. But I do hope for just a little taste of optimism, just a little flavour which is not my usual diet of grim despair.

Because I know the boy, Harry. I swear I know him. I have watched him as a falconer wakes with a tired bird. Watched him, and judged him, and checked my judgement against his behaviour again and again. I have read him as if I were studying my catechism. I know his strengths and his weaknesses, and I think I have faint, very faint, reason for hope.

Harry is vain, it is the sin of a young boy and I do not blame him for it, but he has it in abundance. On the one hand this might make him marry me, for he will want to be seen to be doing the right thing – honouring his promise, even rescuing me. At the thought of being saved by Harry, I have to stop in my stride and pinch my nails into the palms of my hands in the shelter of my cloak. This humiliation too I can learn to bear. Harry may want to rescue me and I shall have to be grateful. Arthur would have died of shame at the thought of his little braggart brother rescuing me; but Arthur died before this hour, my mother died before this hour; I shall have to bear it alone.

But equally, his vanity could work against me. If they emphasise the wealth of Princess Eleanor, the influence of her Hapsburg family, the glory of the connection to the Holy Roman Emperor – he may be seduced. His grandmother will speak against me and her word has been his law. She will advise him to marry Princess Eleanor and he will be attracted – like any young fool – to the idea of an unknown beauty.

But even if he wants to marry her, it still leaves him with the difficulty of what to do with me. He would look bad if he sent me home, surely he cannot have the gall to marry another woman with me still in attendance at court? I know that Harry would do anything rather than look foolish. If I can find a way to stay here until they have to consider his marriage, then I will be in a strong position indeed.

I walk more slowly, looking around me at the cold river, the passing boatmen huddled in their winter coats against the cold. 'God bless you, Princess!' calls out one man, recognising me. I raise my hand in reply. The people of this odd, fractious country have loved me from the moment they scrambled to see me in the little port of Plymouth. That will count in my favour too with a prince new-come to his throne and desperate for affection.

Harry is not mean with money. He is not old enough yet to know the value of it, and he has always been given anything he might want. He will not bicker over the dowry and the jointure. I am sure of that. He will be disposed to make a lordly gesture. I shall have to make sure that Fuensalida and my father do not offer to ship me home to make way for the new bride. Fuensalida despaired long ago of our cause. But now I do not. I shall have to resist his panic, and my own fears. I must stay here to be in the field. I cannot draw back now.

Harry was attracted to me once, I know that. Arthur told me of it first, said that the little boy liked leading me into my wedding, had been dreaming that he was the bridegroom and I was the bride. I have nurtured his liking, every time I see him I pay him particular attention. When his sister laughs at him and disregards him, I glance his way, ask him to sing for me, watch him dance with admiration. On the rare occasions that I have caught a moment with him in private I ask him to read to me and we discuss our thoughts on great writers. I make sure that he knows that I find him illuminating. He is a clever boy, it is no hardship to talk with him.

My difficulty always has been that everyone else admires him so greatly that my modest warmth can hardly weigh with him. Since his grandmother My Lady the King's Mother declares that he is the handsomest prince in Christendom, the most learned, the most promising, what can I say to compare? How can one compliment a boy who is already flattered into extreme vanity, who already believes that he is the greatest prince the world has known?

These are my advantages. Against them I could list the fact that he has been destined for me for six years and he perhaps sees me as his father's choice and a dull choice at that. That he has sworn before a bishop that I was not his choice in marriage and that he does not want to marry me. He might think to hold to that oath, he might think to proclaim he never wanted me, and deny the oath of our betrothal. At the thought of Harry announcing to the world that I was forced on him and now he is glad to be free of me, I pause again. This too I can endure.

These years have not been kind to me. He has never seen me laughing with joy, he has never seen me smiling and easy. He has never seen me dressed other than poorly, and anxious about my appearance. They have never called me forwards to dance before him, or to sing for him. I always have a poor horse when the court is hunting and sometimes I cannot keep up. I always look weary and I am always anxious. He is young and frivolous and he loves luxury and fineness of dress. He might have a picture of me in his mind as a poor woman, a drag upon his family, a pale widow, a ghost at the feast. He is a self-indulgent boy, he might decide to excuse himself from his duty. He is vain and light-hearted and might think nothing of sending me away.

But I have to stay. If I leave, he will forget me in a moment, I am certain of that, at least. I have to stay.

Fuensalida, summoned to the king's council, went in with his head held high, trying to seem unbowed, certain that they had sent for him to tell him to leave and take the unwanted Infanta with him. His high Spanish pride, which had so much offended them so very often in the past, took him through the door and to the Privy Council table. The new king's ministers were seated around the table, there was a place left empty for him in the plumb centre. He felt like a boy, summoned before his tutors for a scolding.

'Perhaps I should start by explaining the condition of the Princess of Wales,' he said diffidently. 'The dowry payment is safely stored, out of the country, and can be paid in . . .'

'The dowry does not matter,' one of the councillors said.

'The dowry?' Fuensalida was stunned into silence. 'But the princess's plate?'

'The king is minded to be generous to his betrothed.'

There was a stunned silence from the ambassador. 'His betrothed?'

'Of the greatest importance now is the power of the King of France and the danger of his ambitions in Europe. It has been thus since Agincourt. The king is most anxious to restore the glory of England. And now we have a king as great as that Henry, ready to make England great again. English safety depends on a three-way alliance between Spain and England, and the emperor. The young king believes that his wedding with the Infanta will secure the support of the King of Aragon to this great cause. This is, presumably, the case?'

'Certainly,' said Fuensalida, his head reeling. 'But the plate . . .'

'The plate does not matter,' one of the councillors repeated.

'I thought that her goods . . .'

'They do not matter.'

'I shall have to tell her of this . . . change . . . in her fortunes.'

The Privy Council rose to their feet. 'Pray do.'

'I shall return when I have . . . er . . . seen her.' Pointless, Fuensalida thought, to tell them that she had been so angry with him for what she saw as his betrayal that he could not be sure that she would see him. Pointless to reveal that the last time he had seen her he had told her that she was lost and her cause was lost and everyone had known it for years.

He staggered as much as walked from the room, and almost collided with the young prince. The youth, still not yet eighteen, was radiant. 'Ambassador!'

Fuensalida threw himself back and dropped to his knee. 'Your Grace! I must . . . condole with you on the death of . . .'

'Yes, yes.' He waved aside the sympathy. He could not make himself look grave. He was wreathed in smiles, taller than ever. 'You will wish to tell the princess that I propose that our marriage takes place as soon as possible.'

Fuensalida found he was stammering with a dry mouth. 'Of course, sire.'

'I shall send a message to her for you,' the young man said generously. He giggled. 'I know that you are out of favour. I know that she has refused to see you, but I am sure that she will see you for my sake.'

'I thank you,' the ambassador said. The prince waved him away. Fuensalida rose from his bow and went towards the Princess's chambers. He realised that it would be hard for the Spanish to recover from the largesse of this new English king. His generosity, his ostentatious generosity, was crushing.

Catalina kept her ambassador waiting, but she admitted him within the hour. He had to admire the self-control that set her to watch the clock when the man who knew her destiny was waiting outside to tell her.

'Emissary,' she said levelly.

He bowed. The hem of her gown was ragged. He saw the neat, small threads where it had been stitched up, and then worn ragged again. He had a sense of great relief that whatever happened to her after this unexpected marriage, she would never again have to wear an old gown.

'Dowager Princess, I have been to the Privy Council. Our troubles are over. He wants to marry you.'

Fuensalida had thought she might cry with joy, or pitch into his arms, or fall to her knees and thank God. She did none of these things. Slowly, she inclined her head. The tarnished gold leaf on the hood caught the light. 'I am glad to hear it,' was all she said.

'They say that there is no issue about the plate.' He could not keep the jubilation from his voice.

She nodded again.

'The dowry will have to be paid. I shall get them to send the money back from Bruges. It has been in safe-keeping, Your Grace. I have kept it safe for you.' His voice quavered, he could not help it.

Again she nodded.

He dropped to one knee. 'Princess, rejoice! You will be Queen of England.'

Her blue eyes when she turned them to him were hard, like the sapphires she had sold long ago. 'Emissary, I was always going to be Queen of England.'

I have done it. Good God, I have done it. After seven endless years of waiting, after hardship and humiliation, I have done it. I go into my bedchamber and kneel before my prie-dieu and close my eyes. But I speak to Arthur, not to the risen Lord.

'I have done it,' I tell him. 'Harry will marry me, I have done as you wished me to do.'

For a moment I can see his smile, I can see him as I did so often, when I glanced sideways at him during dinner and caught him smiling down the hall to someone. Before me again is the brightness of his face, the darkness of his eyes, the clear line of his profile. And more than anything else, the scent of him, the very perfume of my desire.

Even on my knees before a crucifix I give a little sigh of longing. 'Arthur, beloved. My only love. I shall marry your brother but I am always yours.' For a moment, I remember, as bright as the first taste of early cherries, the scent of his skin in the morning. I raise my face and it is as if I can feel his chest against my cheek as he bears down on me, thrusts towards me. 'Arthur,' I whisper. I am now, I will always be, forever his.

Catalina had to face one ordeal. As she went into dinner in a hastily tailored new gown, with a collar of gold at her neck and pearls in her ears, and was conducted to a new table at the very front of the hall, she curtseyed to her husband-to-be and saw his bright smile at her, and then she turned to her grandmother-in-law and met the basilisk gaze of Lady Margaret Beaufort.

'You are fortunate,' the old lady said afterwards, as the musicians started to play and the tables were taken away.

'I am?' Catalina replied, deliberately dense.

'You married one great prince of England and lost him; now it seems you will marry another.'

'This can come as no surprise,' Catalina observed in flawless French, 'since I have been betrothed to him for six years. Surely, my lady, you never doubted that this day would come? You never thought that such an honourable prince would break his holy word?'

The old woman hid her discomfiture well. 'I never doubted our intentions,' she returned. 'We keep our word. But when you with-held your dowry and your father reneged on his payments, I wondered as to your intentions. I wondered about the honour of Spain.'

'Then you were kind to say nothing to disturb the king,' Catalina said smoothly. 'For he trusted me, I know. And I never doubted your desire to have me as your granddaughter. And see! Now I will be your granddaughter, I will be Queen of England, the dowry is paid, and everything is as it should be.'

She left the old lady with nothing to say – and there were few that could do that. 'Well, at any rate, we will have to hope that you are fertile,' was all she sourly mustered.

'Why not? My mother had half a dozen children,' Catalina said sweetly. 'Let us hope my husband and I are blessed with the fertility of Spain. My emblem is the pomegranate – a Spanish fruit, filled with life.'

My Lady the King's Grandmother swept away, leaving Catalina alone. Catalina curtseyed to her departing back and rose up, her head high. It did not matter what Lady Margaret might think or say, all that mattered was what she could do. Catalina did not think she could prevent the wedding, and that was all that mattered.

Greenwich Palace, 11th June 1509

I was dreading the wedding, the moment when I would have to say the words of the marriage vows that I had said to Arthur. But in the end the service was so unlike that glorious day in St Paul's Cathedral that I could go through it with Harry before me, and Arthur locked away in the very back of my mind. I was doing this for Arthur, the very thing he had commanded, the very thing that he had insisted on – and I could not risk thinking of him.

There was no great congregation in a cathedral, there were no watching ambassadors, or fountains flowing with wine. We were married within the walls of Greenwich Palace in the church of the Friars Observant, with only three witnesses and half a dozen people present.

There was no rich feasting or music or dancing, there was no drunkenness at court or rowdiness. There was no public bedding. I had been afraid of that – the ritual of putting to bed and then the public showing of the sheets in the morning; but the prince – the king, I now have to say – is as shy as me, and we dine quietly before the court and withdraw together. They drink our healths and let us go. His grandmother is there, her face like a mask, her eyes cold. I show her every courtesy, it doesn't matter to me what she thinks now. She can do nothing. There is no suggestion that I shall be living in her chambers under her supervision. On the contrary she has moved out of her rooms for me. I am married to Harry. I am Queen of England and she is nothing more than the grandmother of a king.

My ladies undress me in silence, this is their triumph too, this is their escape from poverty as well as mine. Nobody wants to remember the night at Oxford, the night at Burford, the nights at Ludlow. Their fortunes as much as mine depend on the success of this great deception. If I asked them, they would deny Arthur's very existence.

Besides, it was all so long ago. Seven long years. Who but I can remember that far back? Who but I ever knew the delight of waiting for Arthur, the firelight on the rich-coloured curtains of the bed, the glow of candlelight on our entwined limbs? The sleepy whispers in the early hours of the morning: 'Tell me a story!'

They leave me in one of my dozen exquisite new nightgowns and withdraw in silence. I wait for Harry, as long ago I used to wait for Arthur. The only difference is the utter absence of joy.

The men-at-arms and the gentlemen of the bedchamber brought the young king to the queen's door, tapped on it and admitted him to her rooms. She was in her gown, seated by the fireside, a richly embroidered shawl thrown over her shoulders. The room was warm, welcoming. She rose as he came in and swept him a curtsey.

Harry lifted her up with a touch on her elbow. She saw at once that he was flushed with embarrassment, she felt his hand tremble.

'Will you take a cup of wedding ale?' she invited him, she made sure that she did not think of Arthur bringing her a cup and saying it was for courage.

'I will,' he said. His voice, still so young, was unsteady in its register. She turned away to pour the ale so he should not see her smile.

They lifted their cups to each other. 'I hope you did not find today too quiet for your taste,' he said uncertainly. 'I thought with my father newly dead we should not have too merry a wedding. I did not want to distress My Lady, his mother.'

She nodded but said nothing.

'I hope you are not disappointed,' he pressed on. 'Your first wedding was so very grand.'

Catalina smiled. 'I hardly remember it, it was so long ago.'

He looked pleased at her reply, she noted. 'It was, wasn't it? We were all little more than children.'

'Yes,' she said. 'Far too young to marry.'

He shifted in his seat. She knew that the courtiers who had taken Hapsburg gold would have spoken against her. The enemies of Spain would have spoken against her. His own grandmother had advised against this wedding. This transparent young man was still anxious about his decision, however bold he might try to appear.

'Not that young; you were fifteen,' he reminded her. 'A young woman.'

'And Arthur was the same age,' she said, daring to name him. 'But he was never strong, I think. He could not be a husband to me.'

Harry was silent and she was afraid she had gone too far. But then she saw the glimpse of hope in his face.

'It is indeed true then, that the marriage was never consummated?' he asked, colouring up in embarrassment. 'I am sorry . . . I wondered . . . I know they said . . . but I did wonder . . .'

'Never,' she said calmly. 'He tried once or twice but you will remember that he was not strong. He may have even bragged that he had done it, but, poor Arthur, it meant nothing.'

'I shall do this for you,' I say fiercely, in my mind, to my beloved. 'You wanted this lie. I shall do it thoroughly. If it is going to be done, it must be done thoroughly. It has to be done with courage, conviction; and it must never be undone.'

Aloud, Catalina said: 'We married in the November, you remember. December we spent most of the time travelling to Ludlow and were apart on the journey. He was not well after Christmas, and then he died in April. I was very sad for him.'

'He was never your lover?' Harry asked, desperate to be certain.

'How could he be?' She gave a pretty, deprecatory shrug that made the gown slip off one creamy shoulder a little. She saw his eyes drawn to the exposed skin, she saw him swallow. 'He was not strong. Your own mother thought that he should have gone back to Ludlow alone, for the first year. I wish we had done that. It would have made no difference to me, and he might have been spared. He was like a stranger to me for all our marriage. We lived like children in a royal nursery. We were hardly even companions.'

He sighed as if he were free of a burden, the face he turned to her was bright. 'You know, I could not help but be afraid,' he said. 'My grandmother said . . .'

'Oh! Old women always gossip in the corners,' she said, smiling. She ignored his widened eyes at her casual disrespect. 'Thank God we are young and need pay no attention.'

'So, it was just gossip,' he said, quickly adopting her dismissive tone. 'Just old women's gossip.'

'We won't listen to her,' she said, daring him to go on. 'You are king and I am queen and we shall make up our own minds. We hardly need her advice. Why – it is her advice that has kept us apart when we could have been together.'

It had not struck him before. 'Indeed,' he said, his face hardening. 'We have both been deprived. And all the time she hinted that you were Arthur's wife, wedded and bedded, and I should look elsewhere.'

'I am a virgin, as I was when I came to England,' she asserted boldly. 'You could ask my old duenna or any of my women. They all knew it. My mother knew it. I am a virgin untouched.'

He gave a little sigh as if released from some worry. 'You are kind to tell me,' he said. 'It is better to have these things in the light, so we know, so we both know. So that no-one is uncertain. It would be terrible to sin.'

'We are young,' she said. 'We can speak of such things between ourselves. We can be honest and straightforward together. We need not fear rumours and slanders. We need have no fear of sin.'

'It will be my first time too,' he admitted shyly. 'I hope you don't think the less of me?'

'Of course not,' she said sweetly. 'When were you ever allowed to go out? Your grandmother and your father had you mewed up as close as a precious falcon. I am glad that we shall be together, that it will be the first time, for both of us, together.'

Harry rose to his feet and held out his hand. 'So, we shall have to learn together,' he said. 'We shall have to be kind to each other. I don't want to hurt you, Catalina. You must tell me if anything hurts you.'

Easily she moved into his arms, and felt his whole body stiffen at her touch. Gracefully, she stepped back, as if modestly shrinking but kept one hand on his shoulder to encourage him to press forwards until the bed was behind her. Then she let herself lean back until she was on the pillows, smiling up at him, and she could see his blue eyes darken with desire.

'I have wanted you since I first saw you,' he said breathlessly. He stroked her hair, her neck, her naked shoulder, with a hurried touch, wanting all of her, at once.

She smiled. 'And I, you.'

'Really?'

She nodded.

'I dreamed that it was me that married you that day.' He was flushed, breathless.

Slowly, she untied the ribbons at the throat of her nightgown, letting the silky linen fall apart so that he could see her throat, her round, firm breasts, her waist, the dark shadow between her legs.

Harry gave a little groan of desire at the sight of her. 'It might as well have been,' she whispered. 'I have had no other. And we are married now, at last.'

'Ah God, we are,' he said longingly. 'We are married now, at last.'

He dropped his face into the warmth of her neck, she could feel his breath coming fast and urgent in her hair, his body was pushing against hers, Catalina felt herself respond. She remembered Arthur's touch and gently bit the tip of her tongue to remind herself never, never to say Arthur's name out loud. She let Harry push against her, force himself against her and then he was inside her. She gave a little rehearsed cry of pain but she knew at once, in a heart-thud of dread, that it was not enough. She had not cried out enough, her body had not resisted him enough. She had been too warm, too welcoming. It had been too easy. He did not know much, this callow boy; but he knew that it was not difficult enough.

He checked, even in the midst of his desire. He knew that something was not as it should be. He looked down at her. 'You *are* a virgin,' he said uncertainly. 'I hope that I do not hurt too much.'

But he knew that she was not. Deep down, he knew that she was no virgin. He did not know much, this over-protected boy, but he knew this. Somewhere in his mind, he knew that she was lying.

She looked up at him. 'I was a virgin until this moment,' she said, managing the smallest of smiles. 'But your potency has overcome me. You are so strong. You overwhelmed me.'

His face was still troubled, but his desire could not wait. He started to move again, he could not resist the pleasure. 'You have mastered me,' she encouraged him. 'You are my husband, you have taken your own.' She saw him forget his doubt in his rising desire. 'You have done what Arthur could not do,' she whispered.

They were the very words to trigger his desire. The young man gave a groan of pleasure and fell down on to her, his seed pumping into her, the deed undeniably done.

He doesn't question me again. He wants so much to believe me that he does not ask the question, fearing that he might get an answer he doesn't like. He is cowardly in this. He is accustomed to hearing the answers he wants to hear and he would rather an agreeable lie than an unpalatable truth.

Partly, it is his desire to have me, and he wants me as I was when he first saw me: a virgin in bridal white. Partly it is to disprove everyone who warned him against the trap that I had set for him. But more than anything else: he hated and envied my beloved Arthur and he wants me just because I was Arthur's bride, and – God forgive him for a spiteful, envious, second son – he wants me to tell him that he can do something that Arthur could not do, that he can have something that Arthur could not have. Even though my beloved husband is cold under the nave of Worcester Cathedral, the child that wears his crown still wants to triumph over him. The greatest lie is not in telling Harry that I am a virgin. The greatest lie is in telling him that he is a better man, more of a man than his brother. And I did that too.

In the dawn, while he is still sleeping, I take my pen-knife and cut the sole of my foot, where he will not notice a scar, and drip blood on the sheet where we had lain, enough to pass muster for an inspection by My Lady the King's Grandmother, or any other bad-tempered, suspicious enemy who might still seek to discomfort me. There is to be no showing of the sheets for a king and his bride; but I know that everyone will ask, and it is best that my ladies can say that they have all seen the smear of blood, and that I am complaining of the pain.

In the morning, I do everything that a bride should do. I say I am tired, and I rest for the morning. I smile with my eyes looking downwards as if I have discovered some sweet secret. I walk a little stiffly and I refuse to ride out to hunt for a week. I do everything to indicate

that I am a young woman who has lost her virginity. I convince
everyone. And besides, no-one wants to believe anything other.

The cut on my foot is sore for a long, long time. It catches me every
time I step into my new shoes, the ones with the great diamond buckles.
It is like a reminder to me of the lie I promised Arthur that I would
tell. Of the great lie that I will live, for the rest of my life. I don't mind
the sharp little nip of pain when I slide my right foot into my shoe. It
is nothing to the pain that is hidden deep inside me when I smile at
the unworthy boy who is king and call him, in my new admiring voice:
'husband'.

Harry woke in the night and his quiet stillness woke Catalina.

'My lord?' she asked.

'Go to sleep,' he said. 'It's not yet dawn.'

She slipped from the bed and lit a taper in the red embers of the
fire, then lit a candle. She let him see her, nightgown half-open, her
smooth flanks only half-hidden by the fall of the gown. 'Would you
like some ale? Or some wine?'

'A glass of wine,' he said. 'You have one too.'

She put the candle in the silver holder and came back to the bed
beside him with the wine glasses in her hand. She could not read
his face, but suppressed her pang of irritation that, whatever it was,
she had to be woken, she had to inquire what was troubling him,
she had to demonstrate her concern. With Arthur she had known
in a second what he wanted, what he was thinking. But anything
could distract Harry, a song, a dream, a note thrown from the crowd.
Anything could trouble him. He had been raised to be accustomed
to sharing his thoughts, accustomed to guidance. He needed an
entourage of friends and admirers, tutors, mentors, parents. He liked
constant conversation. Catalina had to be everyone to him.

'I have been thinking about war,' he said.

'Oh.'

'King Louis thinks he can avoid us, but we will force war on him. They tell me he wants peace, but I will not have it. I am the King of England, the victors of Agincourt. He will find me a force to be reckoned with.'

She nodded. Her father had been clear that Harry should be encouraged in his warlike ambitions against the King of France. He had written to her in the warmest of terms as his dearest daughter, and advised her that any war between England and France should be launched, not on the north coast – where the English usually invaded – but on the borders between France and Spain. He suggested that the English should reconquer the region of Aquitaine which would be glad to be free of France and would rise up to meet its liberators. Spain would be in strong support. It would be an easy and glorious campaign.

'In the morning I am going to order a new suit of armour,' Harry said. 'Not a suit for jousting, I want heavy armour, for the battle-field.'

She was about to say that he could hardly go to war when there was so much to do in the country. The moment that an English army left for France, the Scots, even with an English bride on their throne, were certain to take advantage and invade the north. The whole tax system was riddled with greed and injustice and must be reformed, there were new plans for schools, for a king's council, for forts and a navy of ships to defend the coast. These were Arthur's plans for England, they should come before Harry's desire for a war.

'I shall make my grandmother regent when I go to war,' Harry said. 'She knows what has to be done.'

Catalina hesitated, marshalling her thoughts. 'Yes indeed,' she said. 'But the poor lady is so old now. She has done so much already. Perhaps it might be too much of a burden for her?'

He smiled. 'Not her! She has always run everything. She keeps the royal accounts, she knows what is to be done. I don't think anything would be too much for her as long as it kept us Tudors in power.'

'Yes,' Catalina said, gently touching on his resentment. 'And see how well she ruled you! She never let you out of her sight for a moment. Why, I don't think she would let you go out even now if she could prevent you. When you were a boy, she never let you joust, she never let you gamble, she never let you have any friends. She dedicated herself to your safety and your wellbeing. She could not have kept you closer if you had been a princess.' She laughed. 'I think she thought you were a princess and not a lusty boy. Surely it is time that she had a rest? And you had some freedom?'

His swift, sulky look told her that she would win this.

'Besides,' she smiled, 'if you give her any power in the country she will be certain to tell the council that you will have to come home, that war is too dangerous for you.'

'She could hardly stop me going to war,' he bristled. 'I am the king.'

Catalina raised her eyebrows. 'Whatever you wish, my love. But I imagine she will stop your funds, if the war starts to go badly. If she and the Privy Council doubt your conduct of the war they need do nothing but sit on their hands and not raise taxes for your army. You could find yourself betrayed at home – betrayed by her love, I mean – while you are attacked abroad. You might find that the old people stop you doing what you want. Like they always try to do.'

He was aghast. 'She would never work against me.'

'Never on purpose,' Catalina agreed with him. 'She would always think she was serving your interest. It is just that . . .'

'What?'

'She will always think that she knows your business best. To her, you will always be a little boy.'

She saw him flush with annoyance.

'To her you will always be a second son, the one who came after Arthur. Not the true heir. Not fitted for the throne. Old people cannot change their minds, cannot see that everything is different now. But really, how can she ever trust your judgement, when she has spent her life ruling you? To her, you will always be the youngest prince, the baby.'

'I shall not be limited by an old woman,' he swore.

'Your time is now,' Catalina agreed.

'D'you know what I shall do?' he demanded. 'I shall make you regent when I go to war! You shall rule the country for me while I am gone. You shall command our forces at home. I would trust no-one else. We shall rule together. And you will support me as I require. D'you think you could do that?'

She smiled at him. 'I know I can. I won't fail,' she said. 'I was born to rule England. I shall keep the country safe while you are away.'

'That's what I need,' Harry said. 'And your mother was a great commander, wasn't she? She supported her husband. I always heard that he led the troops but she raised the money and raised the army?'

'Yes,' she said, a little surprised at his interest. 'Yes, she was always there. Behind the lines, planning his campaigns, and making sure he had the forces he needed, raising funds and raising troops, and sometimes she was in the very forefront of the battles. She had her own armour, she would ride out with the army.'

'Tell me about her,' he said, settling himself down in the pillows. 'Tell me about Spain. About what it was like when you were a little girl in the palaces of Spain. What was it like? In – what is it called – the Alhambra?'

It was too close to what had been before. It was as if a shadow had stretched over her heart. 'Oh, I hardly remember it at all,' she said, smiling at his eager face. 'There's nothing to tell.'

'Go on. Tell me a story about it.'

'No. I can't tell you anything. D'you know, I have been an English princess for so long, I could not tell you anything about it at all.'

In the morning Harry was filled with energy, excited at the thought of ordering his suit of armour, wanting a reason to declare war at once. He woke her with kisses and was on her, like an eager boy, while she was waking. She held him close, welcomed his quick, selfish pleasure, and smiled when he was up and out of bed in a moment, hammering at the door and shouting for his guards to take him to his rooms.

'I want to ride before Mass today,' he said. 'It is such a wonderful day. Will you come with me?'

'I'll see you at Mass,' Catalina promised him. 'And then you can breakfast with me, if you wish.'

'We'll take breakfast in the hall,' he ruled. 'And then we must go hunting. It is too good weather not to take the dogs out. You will come, won't you?'

'I'll come,' she promised him, smiling at his exuberance. 'And shall we have a picnic?'

'You are the best of wives!' he exclaimed. 'A picnic would be wonderful. Will you tell them to get some musicians and we can dance? And bring ladies, bring all your ladies, and we shall all dance.'

She caught him before he went out of the door. 'Harry, may I send for Lady Margaret Pole? You like her, don't you? Can I have her as a lady-in-waiting?'

He stepped back into the room, caught her into his arms and kissed her heartily. 'You shall have whoever you want to serve you. Anyone you want, always. Send for her at once, I know she is the finest of women. And appoint Lady Elizabeth Boleyn too. She is returning to court after her confinement. She has had another girl.'

'What will she call her?' Catalina asked, diverted.

'Mary, I think. Or Anne. I can't remember. Now, about our dance . . .'

She beamed at him. 'I shall get a troupe of musicians and dancers and if I can order soft-voice zephyrs I will do that too.' She laughed at the happiness in his face. She could hear the tramp of his guard coming to the door. 'See you at Mass!'

I married him for Arthur, for my mother, for God, for our cause, and for myself. But in a very little while I have come to love him. It is impossible not to love such a sweet-hearted, energetic, good-natured boy as Harry, in these first years of his reign. He has never known anything but admiration and kindness, he expects nothing less. He wakes happy every morning, filled with the confident expectation of a happy day. And, since he is king, and surrounded by courtiers and flatterers, he always has a happy day. When work troubles him or people come to him with disagreeable complaints he looks around for someone to take the bother of it away from him. In the first few weeks it was his grandmother who commanded; slowly, I make sure that it is to me that he hands the burdens of ruling the kingdom.

The Privy Councillors learn to come to me to ascertain what the king would think. It is easier for them to present a letter or a suggestion, if he has been prepared by me. The courtiers soon know that anything that encourages him to go away from me, anything that takes the country away from the alliance with Spain will displease me, and Harry does not like it when I frown. Men seeking advantage, advocates seeking help, petitioners seeking justice, all learn that the quickest way to a fair, prompt decision is to call first at the queen's rooms and then wait for my introduction.

I never have to ask anyone to handle him with tact. Everyone knows that a request should come to him as it were fresh, for the first time. Everyone knows that the self-love of a young man is very new and very bright and should not be tarnished. Everyone takes a warning from the case of his grandmother who is finding herself put gently and implacably to one side, because she openly advises him, because she takes decisions without him, because once – foolishly – she scolded him. Harry is a king so careless that he will hand over the keys of his kingdom to anyone he trusts. The trick for me is to make sure that he trusts only me.

I make sure that I never blame him for not being Arthur. I taught myself – in the seven years of widowhood – that God's will was done when He took Arthur from me, and there is no point in blaming those who survive when the best prince is dead. Arthur died with my promise in his ears and I think myself very lucky indeed that marriage to his brother is not a vow that I have to endure; but one I can enjoy.

I like being queen. I like having pretty things and rich jewels and a lap dog, and assembling ladies-in-waiting whose company is a pleasure. I like paying Maria de Salinas the long debt of her wages and watching her order a dozen gowns and fall in love. I like writing to Lady Margaret Pole and summoning her to my court, falling into her arms and crying for joy to see her again, and having her promise that she will be with me. I like knowing that her discretion is absolute; she never says one word about Arthur. But I like it that she knows what this marriage has cost me, and why I have done it. I like her watching me make Arthur's England even though it is Harry on the throne.

The first month of marriage is nothing for Harry but a round of parties, feasts, hunts, outings, pleasure trips, boating trips, plays, and tournaments. Harry is like a boy who has been locked up in a school room for too long and is suddenly given a summer holiday. The world is so filled with amusement for him that the least experience gives him great pleasure. He loves to hunt – and he had never been allowed fast horses before. He loves to joust and his father and grandmother had never even allowed him in the lists. He loves the company of men of the world who carefully adapt their conversation and their amusements to divert him. He loves the company of women but – thank God – his childlike devotion to me holds him firm. He likes to talk to pretty women, play cards with them, watch them dance and reward them with great prizes for petty feats – but always he glances towards me to see that I approve. Always he stays at my side, looking down at me from his greater height with a gaze of such devotion that I can't help but be loving towards him for what he brings me; and in a very little while, I can't help but love him for himself.

He has surrounded himself with a court of young men and women who are such a contrast to his father's court that they demonstrate by their very being that everything has changed. His father's court was filled with old men, men who had been through hard times together, some of them battle-hardened; all of them had lost and regained their lands at least once. Harry's court is filled with men who have never known hardship, never been tested.

I have made a point of saying nothing to criticise either him or the group of wild young men that gather around him. They call themselves the 'Minions' and they encourage each other in mad bets and jests all the day and – according to gossip – half the night too. Harry was kept so quiet and so close for all his childhood that I think it natural he should long to run wild now, and that he should love the young men who boast of drinking bouts and fights, and chases and attacks, and girls who they seduce, and fathers who pursue them with cudgels. His best friend is William Compton, the two go about with their arms around each other's shoulders as if ready to dance or braced for a fight for half the day. There is no harm in William, he is as great a fool as the rest of the court, he loves Harry as a comrade, and he has a mock-adoration of me that makes us all laugh. Half of the Minions pretend to be in love with me and I let them dedicate verses and sing songs to me and I make sure that Harry always knows that his songs and poems are the best.

The older members of the court disapprove and have made stern criticisms of the king's boisterous lads; but I say nothing. When the councillors come to me with complaints I say that the king is a young man and youth will have its way. There is no great harm in any one of the comrades; when they are not drinking, they are sweet young men. One or two, like the Duke of Buckingham who greeted me long ago, or the young Thomas Howard, are fine young men who would be an ornament to any court. My mother would have liked them. But when the lads are deep in their cups they are noisy and rowdy and excitable as young men always are and when they are sober they talk

331

*nonsense. I look at them with my mother's eyes and I know that they
are the boys who will become the officers in our army. When we go to
war their energy and their courage are just what we will need. The
noisiest, most disruptive young men in peacetime are exactly the leaders
I will need in time of war.*

Lady Margaret, the king's grandmother, having buried a husband or
two, a daughter-in-law, a grandson and finally her own precious
prince, was a little weary of fighting for her place in the world and
Catalina was careful not to provoke her old enemy into open warfare.
Thanks to Catalina's discretion, the rivalry between the two women
was not played overtly – anyone hoping to see Lady Margaret abuse
her granddaughter-in-law as she had insulted her son's wife was
disappointed. Catalina slid away from conflict.

When Lady Margaret tried to claim precedence by arriving at the
dining-hall door a few footsteps before Catalina, a Princess of the
Blood, an Infanta of Spain and now Queen of England, Catalina
stepped back at once and gave way to her with such an air of
generosity that everyone remarked on the pretty behaviour of the
new queen. Catalina had a way of ushering the older woman before
her that absolutely denied all rules of precedence and instead
somehow emphasised Lady Margaret's ungainly gallop to beat her
granddaughter-in-law to the high table. They also saw Catalina
pointedly step back, and everyone remarked on the grace and
generosity of the younger woman.

The death of Lady Margaret's son, King Henry, had hit the old
lady hard. It was not so much that she had lost a beloved child; it
was more that she had lost a cause. In his absence she could hardly
summon the energy to force the Privy Councillors to report to her
before going to the king's rooms. Harry's joyful excusing of his
father's debts and freeing of his father's prisoners she took as an

insult to his father's memory, and to her own rule. The sudden leap of the court into youth and freedom and playfulness made her feel old and bad-tempered. She, who had once been the commander of the court and the maker of the rules, was left to one side. Her opinion no longer mattered. The great book by which all court events must be governed had been written by her; but suddenly, they were celebrating events that were not in her book, they invented pastimes and activities, and she was not consulted.

She blamed Catalina for all the changes she most disliked, and Catalina smiled very sweetly and continued to encourage the young king to hunt and to dance and to stay up late at night. The old lady grumbled to her ladies that the queen was a giddy, vain thing and would lead the prince to disaster. Insultingly, she even remarked that it was no wonder Arthur had died, if this was the way that the Spanish girl thought a royal household should be run.

Lady Margaret Pole remonstrated with her old acquaintance as tactfully as she could. 'My lady, the queen has a merry court but she never does anything against the dignity of the throne. Indeed, without her, the court would be far wilder. It is the king who insists on one pleasure after another. It is the queen who gives this court its manners. The young men adore her and nobody drinks or misbehaves before her.'

'It is the queen who I blame,' the old woman said crossly. 'Princess Eleanor would never have behaved like this. Princess Eleanor would have been housed in my rooms, and the place would have run by my rules.'

Tactfully, Catalina heard nothing; not even when people came to her and repeated the slanders. Catalina simply ignored her grandmother-in-law and the constant stream of her criticism. She could have done nothing that would irritate her more.

It was the late hours that the court now kept that were the old lady's greatest complaint. Increasingly, she had to wait and wait for dinner to be served. She would complain that it was so late at night that the servants would not be finished before dawn, and then she would retire before the court had even finished their dinner.

'You keep late hours,' she told Harry. 'It is foolish. You need your sleep. You are only a boy; you should not be roistering all night. I cannot keep hours like this, and it is a waste of candles.'

'Yes; but my lady grandmother, you are nearly seventy years old,' he said patiently. 'Of course you should have your rest. You shall retire whenever you wish. Catalina and I are only young. It is natural for us to want to stay up late. We like amusement.'

'She should be resting. She has to conceive an heir,' Lady Margaret said irritably. 'She's not going to do that bobbing about in a dance with a bunch of feather-heads. Masquing, every night. Whoever heard of such a thing? And who is to pay for all this?'

'We've been married less than a month!' he exclaimed, a little irritated. 'These are our wedding celebrations. I think we can enjoy good pastimes, and keep a merry court. I like to dance.'

'You act as if there was no end to money,' she snapped. 'How much has this dinner cost you? And last night's? The strewing herbs alone must cost a fortune. And the musicians? This is a country that has to hoard its wealth, it cannot afford a spendthrift king. It is not the English way to have a popinjay on the throne, a court of mummers.'

Harry flushed, he was about to make a sharp retort.

'The king is no spendthrift,' Catalina intervened quickly. 'This is just part of the wedding festivities. Your son, the late king, always thought that there should be a merry court. He thought that people should know that the court was wealthy and gay. King Harry is only following in the footsteps of his wise father.'

'His father was not a young fool under the thumb of his foreign wife!' the old lady said spitefully.

Catalina's eyes widened slightly and she put her hand on Harry's sleeve to keep him silent. 'I am his partner and his help-meet, as God has bidden me,' she said gently. 'As I am sure you would want me to be.'

The old lady grunted. 'I hear you claim to be more than that,' she began.

The two young people waited. Catalina could feel Harry shift restlessly under the gentle pressure of her hand.

'I hear that your father is to recall his ambassador. Am I right?' She glared at them both. 'Presumably he does not need an ambassador now. The King of England's own wife is in the pay and train of Spain. The King of England's own wife is to be the Spanish ambassador. How can that be?'

'My lady grandmother . . .' Harry burst out; but Catalina was sweetly calm.

'I am a princess of Spain, of course I would represent the country of my birth to my country by marriage. I am proud to be able to do such a thing. Of course I will tell my father that his beloved son, my husband, is well, that our kingdom is prosperous. Of course I will tell my husband that my loving father wants to support him in war and peace.'

'When we go to war . . .' Harry began.

'War?' the old lady demanded, her face darkening. 'Why should we go to war? We have no quarrel with France. It is only her father who wants war with France, no-one else. Tell me that not even you will be such a fool as to take us into war to fight for the Spanish! What are you now? Their errand boy? Their vassal?'

'The King of France is a danger to us all!' Harry stormed. 'And the glory of England has always been . . .'

'I am sure My Lady the King's Grandmother did not mean to disagree with you, sire,' Catalina said sweetly. 'These are changing times. We cannot expect older people always to understand when things change so quickly.'

'I'm not quite in my dotage yet!' the old woman flared. 'And I know danger when I see it. And I know divided loyalties when I see them. And I know a Spanish spy . . .'

'You are a most treasured advisor,' Catalina assured her. 'And my lord the king and I are always glad of your advice. Aren't we, Harry?'

He was still angry. 'Agincourt was . . .'

'I'm tired,' the old woman said. 'And you twist and twist things about. I'm going to my room.'

Catalina swept her a deep, respectful curtsey, Harry ducked his head with scant politeness. When Catalina came up the old woman had gone.

'How can she say such things?' Harry demanded. 'How can you bear to listen to her when she says such things? She makes me want to roar like a baited bear! She understands nothing, and she insults you! And you just stand and listen!'

Catalina laughed, took his cross face in her hands and kissed him on the lips. 'Oh, Harry, who cares what she thinks as long as she can do nothing? Nobody cares what she says now.'

'I am going to war with France whatever she thinks,' he promised.

'Of course you are, as soon as the time is right.'

I hide my triumph over her, but I know the taste of it, and it is sweet. I think to myself that one day the other tormentors of my widowhood, the princesses, Harry's sisters, will know my power too. But I can wait.

Lady Margaret may be old but she cannot even gather the senior people of court about her. They have known her forever, the bonds of kinship, wardship, rivalry and feud run through them all like veins through dirty marble. She was never well-liked: not as a woman, not as the mother of a king. She was from one of the great families of the country but when she leapt up so high after Bosworth she flaunted her important-ance. She has a great reputation for learning and for holiness but she is not beloved. She always insisted on her position as the king's mother and a gulf has grown between her and the other people of the court.

Drifting away from her, they are becoming friends of mine: Lady Margaret Pole of course, the Duke of Buckingham and his sisters, Elizabeth and Anne, Thomas Howard, his sons, Sir Thomas and Lady Elizabeth Boleyn, dearest William Warham, the Archbishop of Canterbury, George Talbot, Sir Henry Vernon that I knew from Wales. They all know that although Harry neglects the business of the realm, I do not.

I consult them for their advice, I share with them the hopes that Arthur and I had. Together with the men of the Privy Council I am bringing the kingdom into one powerful, peaceful country. We are starting to consider how to make the law run from one coast to another, through the wastes, the mountains and forests alike. We are starting to work on the defences of the coast. We are making a survey of the ships that could be commanded into a fighting navy, we are creating muster rolls for an army. I have taken the reins of the kingdom into my hands and found that I know how it is done.

Statecraft is my family business. I sat at my mother's feet in the throne room of the Alhambra Palace. I listened to my father in the beautiful golden Hall of the Ambassadors. I learned the art and the craft of kingship as I had learned about beauty, music, and the art of building, all in the same place, all in the same lessons. I learned a taste for rich tiling, for bright sunlight falling on a delicate tracery of stucco, and for power, all at the same time. Becoming a Queen Regnant is like coming home. I am happy as Queen of England. I am where I was born and raised to be.

The king's grandmother lay in her ornate bed, rich curtains drawn close so that she was lulled by shadows. At the foot of the bed an uncomplaining lady-in-waiting held up the monstrance for her to see the body of Christ in its white purity through the diamond-cut piece of glass. The dying woman fixed her eyes on it, occasionally looking to the ivory crucifix on the wall beside the bed, ignoring the soft murmur of prayers around her.

Catalina kneeled at the foot of the bed, her head bowed, a coral rosary in her hands, praying silently. My Lady Margaret, confident of a hard-won place in heaven, was sliding away from her place on earth.

Outside, in her presence chamber, Harry waited for them to tell him that his grandmother was dead. The last link to his subordinate, junior childhood would be broken with her death. The years in which he had been the second son – trying a little harder for attention, smiling a little brighter, working at being clever – would all be gone. From now on, everyone he would meet would know him only as the most senior member of his family, the greatest of his line. There would be no articulate, critical old Tudor lady to watch over this gullible prince, to cut him down with one quiet word in the very moment of his springing up. When she was dead he could be a man, on his own terms. There would be no-one left who knew him as a boy. Although he was waiting, outwardly pious, for news of her death, inside he was longing to hear that she was gone, that he was at last truly independent, at last a man and a king. He had no idea that he still desperately needed her counsel.

'He must not go to war,' the king's grandmother said hoarsely from the bed.

The lady-in-waiting gave a little gasp at the sudden clarity of her mistress's speech. Catalina rose to her feet. 'What did you say, my lady?'

'He must not go to war,' she repeated. 'Our way is to keep out of the endless wars of Europe, to keep behind the seas, to keep safe and far away from all those princeling squabbles. Our way is keep the kingdom at peace.'

'No,' Catalina said steadily. 'Our way is to take the crusade into the heart of Christendom and beyond. Our way is to make England a leader in establishing the church throughout Europe, throughout the Holy Land, to Africa, to the Turks, to the Saracens, to the edge of the world.'

'The Scots . . .'

'I shall defeat the Scots,' Catalina said firmly. 'I am well aware of the danger.'

'I did not let him marry you for you to lead us to war.' The dark eyes flared with fading resentment.

'You did not let him marry me at all. You opposed it from the first moment,' Catalina said bluntly. 'And I married him precisely so that he should mount a great crusade.' She ignored the little whimper from the lady-in-waiting, who believed that a dying woman should not be contradicted.

'You will promise me that you will not let him go to war,' the old lady breathed. 'My dying promise, my deathbed promise. I lay it on you from my deathbed, as a sacred duty.'

'No.' Catalina shook her head. 'Not me. Not another. I made one deathbed promise and it has cost me dearly. I will not make another. Least of all to you. You have lived your life and made your world as you wished. Now it is my turn. I shall see my son as King of England and perhaps King of Spain. I shall see my husband lead a glorious crusade against the Moors and the Turks. I shall see my country, England, take its place in the world, where it should be. I shall see England at the heart of Europe, a leader of Europe. And I shall be the one that defends it and keeps it safe. I shall be the one that is Queen of England, as you never were.'

'No . . .' the old woman breathed.

'Yes,' Catalina swore, without compromise. 'I am Queen of England now and I will be till my death.'

The old woman raised herself up, struggled for breath. 'You pray for me.' She laid the order on the younger woman almost as if it were a curse. 'I have done my duty to England, to the Tudor line. You see that my name is remembered as if I were a queen.'

Catalina hesitated. If this woman had not served herself, her son and her country, the Tudors would not be on the throne. 'I will pray for you,' she conceded grudgingly. 'And as long as there is a chantry in England, as long as the Holy Roman Catholic Church is in England, your name will be remembered.'

'Forever,' the old woman said, happy in her belief that some things could never change.

'Forever,' Catalina agreed.

Then, less than an hour later, she was dead; and I became queen, ruling queen, undeniably in command, without a rival, even before my coronation. No-one knows what to do in the court, there is no-one who can give a coherent order. Harry has never ordered a royal funeral, how should he know where to begin, how to judge the extent of the honour that should be given to his grandmother? How many mourners? How long the time of mourning? Where should she be buried? How should the whole ceremonial be done?

I summon my oldest friend in England, the Duke of Buckingham, who greeted me on my arrival all those years ago and is now Lord High Steward, and I ask for Lady Margaret Pole to come to me. My ladies bring me the great volume of ceremonial, The Royal Book, written by the king's dead grandmother herself, and I set about organising my first public English event.

I am lucky; tucked inside the cover of the book I find three pages of handwritten instructions. The vain old lady had laid out the order of the procession that she wanted for her funeral. Lady Margaret and I gasp at the numbers of bishops she would like to serve, the pall-bearers, the mutes, the mourners, the decorations on the streets, the duration of the mourning. I show them to the Duke of Buckingham, her one-time ward, who says nothing but in discreet silence just smiles and shakes his head. Hiding my unworthy sense of triumph I take a

quill, dip it in black ink, cut almost everything by a half, and then
start to give orders.

It was a quiet ceremony of smooth dignity, and everyone knew that
it had been commanded and ordered by the Spanish bride. Those
who had not known before realised now that the girl who had been
waiting for seven years to come to the throne of England had not
wasted her time. She knew the temperament of the English people,
she knew how to put on a show for them. She knew the tenor of
the court: what they regarded as stylish, what they saw as mean. And
she knew, as a princess born, how to rule. In those days before her
coronation, Catalina established herself as the undeniable queen,
and those who had ignored her in her years of poverty now discovered in themselves tremendous affection and respect for the princess.

She accepted their admiration, just as she had accepted their
neglect: with calm politeness. She knew that by ordering the funeral
of the king's grandmother she established herself as the first woman
of the new court, and the arbiter of all decisions of court life. She
had, in one brilliant performance, established herself as the foremost leader of England. And she was certain that after this triumph
no-one would ever be able to supplant her.

We decide not to cancel our coronation, though My Lady the King's
Grandmother's funeral preceded it. The arrangements are all in place,
we judge that we should do nothing to mar the joy of the City or of the
people who have come from all over England to see the boy Harry take
his father's crown. They say that some have travelled all the way from
Plymouth, who saw me come ashore, a frightened seasick girl, all those
years ago. We are not going to tell them that the great celebration of

Harry's coming to the throne, of my coronation, is cancelled because a cross old lady has died at an ill-judged time. We agree that the people are expecting a great celebration and we should not deny them.

In truth, it is Harry who cannot bear a disappointment. He had promised himself a great moment of glory and he would not miss it for the world. Certainly not for the death of a very old lady who spent the last years of her life preventing him from having his own way in anything.

I agree with him. I judge that the king's grandmother seized her power and enjoyed her time, and now it is time for us. I judge that it is the mood of the country and the mood of the court to celebrate the triumph of Harry's coming to the throne with me at his side. Indeed, for some of them, who have long taken an interest in me, there is the greatest delight that I shall have the crown at last. I decide – and there is no-one but me to decide – that we will go ahead. And so we do.

I know that Harry's grief for his grandmother is only superficial; his mourning is mostly show. I saw him when I came from her privy chamber, and he knew, since I had left her bedside, that she must be dead. I saw his shoulders stretch out and lift, as if he were suddenly free from the burden of her care, as if her skinny, loving, age-spotted hand had been a dead weight on his neck. I saw his quick smile – his delight that he was alive and young and lusty, and that she was gone. Then I saw the careful composing of his face into conventional sadness and I stepped forwards, with my face grave also, and told him that she was dead, in a low sad voice, and he answered me in the same tone.

I am glad to know that he can play the hypocrite. The court room in the Alhambra Palace has many doors; my father told me that a king should be able to go out of one and come in through another and nobody know his mind. I know that to rule is to keep your own counsel. Harry is a boy now, but one day he will be a man and he will have to make up his own mind and judge well. I will remember that he can say one thing and think another.

But I have learned something else about him too. When I saw that *he did not weep one real tear for his grandmother I knew that this king, our golden Harry, has a cold heart that no-one can trust. She had been as a mother to him; she had dominated his childhood. She had cared for him, watched over him, and taught him herself. She supervised his every waking moment and shielded him from every unpleasant sight, she kept him from tutors who would have taught him of the world, and allowed him to walk only in the gardens of her making. She spent hours on her knees in prayer for him and insisted that he be taught the rule and the power of the church. But when she stood in his way, when she denied him his pleasures, he saw her as his enemy; and he cannot forgive anyone who refuses him something he wants. I know from this that this boy, this charming boy, will grow to be a man whose selfishness will be a danger to himself, and to those around him. One day we may all wish that his grandmother had taught him better.*

24th June 1509

They carried Catalina from the Tower to Westminster as an English princess. She travelled in a litter made of cloth of gold, carried high by four white palfreys so everyone could see her. She wore a gown of white satin and a coronet set with pearls, her hair brushed out over her shoulders. Harry was crowned first and then Catalina bowed her head and took the holy oil of kingship on her head and breasts, stretched out her hand for the sceptre and the ivory wand, knew that, at last, she was a queen, as her mother had been: an anointed queen, a greater being than mere mortals, a step closer to the angels, appointed by God to rule His country, and under His especial protection. She knew that finally she had fulfilled the destiny that she had been born for, she had taken her place, as she had promised that she would.

She took a throne just a little lower than King Henry's, and the crowd that cheered for the handsome young king coming to his throne also cheered for her, the Spanish princess, who had been constant against the odds and was crowned Queen Katherine of England at last.

I have waited for this day for so long that when it comes it is like a dream, like the dreams I have had of my greatest desires. I go through the coronation ceremony: my place in the procession, my seat on the throne, the cool lightness of the ivory rod in my hand, my other hand tightly gripping the heavy sceptre, the deep, heady scent of the holy oil on my forehead and breasts, as if it is another dream of longing for Arthur.

But this time it is real.

When we come out of the Abbey and I hear the crowd cheer for him, for me, I turn to look at my husband beside me. I am shocked then, a sudden shock like waking suddenly from a dream – that he is not Arthur. He is not my love. I had expected to be crowned beside Arthur and for us to take our thrones together. But instead of the handsome, thoughtful face of my husband, it is Harry's round, flushed beam. Instead of my husband's shy, coltish grace, it is Harry's exuberant swagger at my side.

I realise at that moment, that Arthur really is dead, really gone from me. I am fulfilling my part of our promise, marrying the King of England, even though it is Harry. Please God, Arthur is fulfilling his part: to watch over me from al-Yanna, and to wait for me there. One day, when my work is done and I can go to my love, I will live with him forever.

'Are you happy?' the boy asks me, shouting to make himself heard above the pealing of the bells and the cheering of the crowds. 'Are you happy, Catalina? Are you glad that I married you? Are you glad to be Queen of England, that I have given you this crown?'

'I am very happy,' I promise him. 'And you must call me Katherine now.'

'Katherine?' he asks. 'Not Catalina any more?'

'I am Queen of England,' I say, thinking of Arthur saying these very words. 'I am Queen Katherine of England.'

'Oh, I say!' he exclaims, delighted at the idea of changing his name, as I have changed mine. 'That's good. We shall be King Henry, and Queen Katherine. They shall call me Henry too.'

This is the king but he is not Arthur, he is Harry who wants to be called Henry, like a man. I am the queen, and I shall not be Catalina. I shall be Katherine – English through and through, and not the girl who was once so very much in love with the Prince of Wales.

Katherine, Queen of England

Summer 1509

The court, drunk with joy, with delight in its own youth, with freedom, took the summer for pleasure. The progress from one beautiful, welcoming house to another lasted for two long months when Henry and Katherine hunted, dined in the greenwood, danced until midnight, and spent money like water. The great lumbering carts of the royal household went along the dusty lanes of England so that the next house might shine with gold and be bright with tapestries, so that the royal bed – which they shared every night – would be rich with the best linen and the glossiest furs.

No business of any worth was transacted by Henry at all. He wrote once to his father-in-law to tell him how happy he was, but the rest of the work for the king followed him in boxes from one beautiful parkland castle or mansion to another, and these were opened and read only by Katherine, Queen of England, who ordered the clerks to write her orders to the Privy Council, and sent them out herself over the king's signature.

Not until mid-September did the court return to Richmond and Henry at once declared that the party should go on. Why should they ever cease in pleasure? The weather was fair, they could have hunting and boating, archery and tennis contests, parties and masquings. The nobles and gentry flocked to Richmond to join the unending party: the families whose power and name were older than the Tudors, and the new ones, whose wealth and name was bobbing upwards on the rise of the Tudor tide, floated by Tudor wealth. The victors of Bosworth who had staked their lives on the Tudor courage in great danger found themselves alongside newcomers who made their fortunes on nothing more than Tudor amusements.

Henry welcomed everyone with uncritical delight; anyone who was witty and well-read, charming or a good sportsman could have a place at court. Katherine smiled on them all, never rested, never refused a challenge or an invitation, and set herself the task of keeping her teenage husband entertained all the day long. Slowly, but surely, she drew the management of the entertainments, then of the household, then of the king's business, then of the kingdom, into her hands.

Queen Katherine had the accounts for the royal court spread out before her, a clerk to one side, a comptroller of the household with his great book to another, the men who served as exchequers of the household standing behind her. She was checking the books of the great departments of the court: the kitchen, the cellar, the wardrobe, the servery, the payments for services, the stables, the musicians. Each department of the palace had to compile their monthly expenditure and send it to the Queen's Exchequer – just as they had sent it to My Lady the King's Mother, for her to approve their business, and if they overspent by very much, they could expect a visit from one of the exchequers for the Privy Purse to ask them pointedly if they could explain why costs had so suddenly risen?

Every court in Europe was engaged in the struggle to control the cost of running the sprawling feudal households with the newly fashionable wealth and display. All the kings wanted a great entourage, like a mediaeval lord; but now they wanted culture, wealth, architecture and rich display as well. England was managed better than any court in Europe. Queen Katherine had learned her housekeeping skills the hard way: when she had tried to run Durham House as a royal palace should be run, but with no income. She knew to a penny what was the price of a gallon loaf, she knew the difference between salted fish and fresh, she knew the price of cheap wine imported from Spain and expensive wine brought in from France. Even more rigorous than My Lady the King's Mother, Queen Katherine's scrutiny of the household books made the cooks argue with suppliers at the kitchen doors, and get the very best price for the extravagantly consuming court.

Once a week Queen Katherine surveyed the expenditure of the different departments of the court, and every day at dawn, while King Henry was out hunting, she read the letters that came for him, and drafted his replies.

It was steady, unrelenting work, to keep the court running as a well-ordered centre for the country, and to keep the king's business under tight control. Queen Katherine, determined to understand her new country, did not begrudge the hours she spent reading letters, taking advice from Privy Councillors, inviting objections, taking opinions. She had seen her own mother dominate a country by persuasion. Isabella of Spain had brokered her country out of a collection of rival kingships and lordships by offering them a trouble-free, cheap, central administration, a nationwide system of justice, an end to corruption and banditry and an infallible defence system. Her daughter saw at once that these advantages could be transferred to England.

But she was also following in the steps of her Tudor father-in-law, and the more she worked on his papers and read his letters, the more she admired the steadiness of his judgement. Oddly, she wished now, that she had known him as a ruler, as she would have bene-fited from his advice. From his records she could see how he balanced the desire of the English lords to be independent, on their own lands, with his own need to bind them to the crown. Cunningly, he allowed the northern lords greater freedom and greater wealth and status than anyone, since they were his bulwark against the Scots. Katherine had maps of the northern lands pinned around the council chamber and saw how the border with Scotland was nothing more than a handful of disputed territories in difficult country. Such a border could never be made safe from a threatening neighbour. She thought that the Scots were England's Moors: the land could not be shared with them. They would have to be utterly defeated.

She shared her father-in-law's fears of overmighty English lords at court, she learned his jealousy of their wealth and power; and when Henry thought to give one man a handsome pension in an exuberant moment, it was Katherine who pointed out that he was a wealthy man already, there was no need to make his position any stronger. Henry wanted to be a king famed for his generosity, beloved for the sudden shower of his gifts. Katherine knew that power followed wealth and that kings new-come to their throne must hoard both wealth and power.

'Did your father never warn you about the Howards?' she asked as they stood together watching an archery contest. Henry, stripped down to his shirtsleeves, his bow in his hand, had the second-highest score and was waiting for his turn to go again.

'No,' he replied. 'Should he have done so?'

'Oh no,' she said swiftly. 'I did not mean to suggest that they would play you false in any way, they are love and loyalty personi-fied, Thomas Howard has been a great friend to your family, keeping the north safe for you, and Edward is my knight, my dearest knight of all. It is just that their wealth has increased so much, and their family alliances are so strong. I just wondered what your father thought of them.'

'I wouldn't know,' Henry said easily. 'I wouldn't have asked him. He wouldn't have told me anyway.'

'Not even when he knew you were to be the next king?'

He shook his head. 'He thought I wouldn't be king for years yet,' he said. 'He had not finished making me study my books. He had not yet let me out into the world.'

She shook her head. 'When we have a son we will make sure he is prepared for his kingdom from an early age.'

At once, his hand stole around her waist. 'Do you think it will be soon?' he asked.

'Please God,' she said sweetly, withholding her secret hope. 'Do you know, I have been thinking of a name for him?'

'Have you, sweetheart? Shall you call him Ferdinand for your father?'

'If you would like it, I thought we might call him Arthur,' she said carefully.

'For my brother?' His face darkened at once.

'No, Arthur for England,' she said swiftly. 'When I look at you sometimes I think you are like King Arthur of the round table, and this is Camelot. We are making a court here as beautiful and as magical as Camelot ever was.'

'Do you think that, little dreamer?'

'I think you could be the greatest king England has ever known since Arthur of Camelot,' she said.

'Arthur it is, then,' he said, soothed as always by praise. 'Arthur Henry.'

'Yes.'

They called to him from the butts that it was his turn, and that he had a high score to beat, and he went with a kiss blown to her. Katherine made sure that she was watching as he drew his bow, and when he glanced over, as he always did, he could see that her attention was wholly on him. The muscles in his lean back rippled as he drew back the arrow, he was like a statue, beautifully poised, and

353

then slowly, like a dancer, he released the string and the arrow flew
– faster than sight – true to the very centre of the target.

'A hit!'

'A winning hit!'

'Victory to the king!'

The prize was a golden arrow and Henry came bright-faced to
his wife to kneel at her feet so that she could bend down and kiss
him on both cheeks, and then, lovingly, on the mouth.

'I won for you,' he said. 'You, alone. You bring me luck. I never
miss when you are watching me. You shall keep the winning arrow.'

'It is a Cupid's arrow,' she responded. 'I shall keep it to remind
me of the one in my heart.'

'She loves me.' He rose to his feet and turned to his court, and there
was a ripple of applause and laughter. He shouted triumphantly:
'She loves me!'

'Who could help but love you?' Lady Elizabeth Boleyn, one of the
ladies-in-waiting, called out boldly. Henry glanced at her and then
looked down from his great height to his petite wife.

'Who could help but love her?' he asked, smiling at her.

That night I kneel before my prie-dieu and clasp my hands over my
belly. It is the second month that I have not bled, I am almost certain
that I am with child.

'Arthur,' I whisper, my eyes closed. I can almost see him, as he was:
naked in candlelight in our bedroom at Ludlow. 'Arthur, my love. He
says that I can call this boy Arthur Henry. So I will have fulfilled our
hope – that I should give you a son called Arthur. And though I know
you didn't like your brother, I will show him the respect that I owe to
him; he is a good boy and I pray that he will grow to a good man. I
shall call my boy Arthur Henry for you both.'

I feel no guilt for my growing affection for this boy Henry though he can never take the place of his brother, Arthur. It is right that I should love my husband and Henry is an endearing boy. The knowledge that I have of him, from watching him for long years as closely as if he were an enemy, has brought me to a deep awareness of the sort of boy he is. He is selfish as a child, but he has a child's generosity and easy tenderness. He is vain, he is ambitious, to tell truth, he is as conceited as a player in a troupe, but he is quick to laughter and quick to tears, quick to compassion, quick to alleviate hardship. He will make a good man if he has good guides, if he can be taught to rein in his desires and learn service to his country and to God. He has been spoiled by those who should have guided him; but it is not too late to make a good man from him. It is my task and my duty to keep him from selfishness. Like any young man, he is a tyrant in the making. A good mother would have disciplined him, perhaps a loving wife can curb him. If I can love him, and hold him to love me, I can make a great king of him. And England needs a great king.

Perhaps this is one of the services I can do for England: guide him, gently and steadily, away from his spoiled childhood and towards a manhood which is responsible. His father and his grandmother kept him as a boy; perhaps it is my task to help him grow to be a man.

'Arthur, my dearest Arthur,' I say quietly as I rise and go towards the bed, and this time I am speaking to them both: to the husband that I loved first, and to the child that is slowly, quietly growing inside me.

Autumn 1509

At nighttime in October, after Katherine had refused to dance after midnight for the previous three weeks, and had insisted, instead, on watching Henry dance with her ladies, she told him that she was with child, and made him swear to keep it secret.

'I want to tell everyone!' he exclaimed. He had come to her room in his nightgown and they were seated either side of the warm fire, on their way to bed.

'You can write to my father next month,' she specified. 'But I don't want everyone to know yet. They will all guess soon enough.'

'You must rest,' he said instantly. 'And should you have special things to eat? Do you have a desire for anything special to eat? I can send someone for it at once, they can wake the cooks. Tell me, love, what would you like?'

'Nothing! Nothing!' she said, laughing. 'See, we have biscuits and wine. What more do I ever eat this late at night?'

'Oh usually, yes! But now everything is different.'

'I shall ask the physicians in the morning,' she said. 'But I need nothing now. Truly, my love.'

'I want to get you something,' he said. 'I want to look after you.'

'You do look after me,' she reassured him. 'And I am perfectly well fed, and I feel very well.'

'Not sick? That is a sign of a boy, I am sure.'

'I have been feeling a little sick in the mornings,' she said, and watched his beam of happiness. 'I feel certain that it is a boy. I hope this is our Arthur Henry.'

'Oh! You were thinking of him when you spoke to me at the archery contest.'

'Yes, I was. But I was not sure then, and I did not want to tell you too early.'

'And when do you think he will be born?'

'In early summer, I think.'

'It cannot take so long!' he exclaimed.

'My love, I think it does take that long.'

'I shall write to your father in the morning,' he said. 'I shall tell him to expect great news in the summer. Perhaps we shall be home after a great campaign against the French then. Perhaps I shall bring you a victory and you shall give me a son.'

Henry has sent his own physician, the most skilled man in London, to see me. The man stands at one side of the room while I sit on a chair at the other. He cannot examine me, of course – the body of the queen cannot be touched by anyone but the king. He cannot ask me if I am regular in my courses or in my bowels; they too are sacred. He is so paralysed with embarrassment at being called to see me that he keeps his eyes on the floor and asks me short questions in a quiet, clipped voice. He speaks English, and I have to strain to hear and understand him.

He asks me if I eat well, and if I have any sickness. I answer that I eat well enough but that I am sick of the smell and sight of cooked meats. I miss the fruit and vegetables that were part of my daily diet in Spain, I am craving baklava sweetmeats made from honey, or a tagine made with vegetables and rice. He says that it does not matter since there is no benefit to eating vegetables or fruit for humans, and indeed, he would have advised me against eating any raw stuff for the duration of my pregnancy.

He asks me if I know when I conceived. I say that I cannot say for certain, but that I know the date of my last course. He smiles as a learned man to a fool and tells me that this is little guide as to when a baby might be due. I have seen Moorish doctors calculate the date of a baby's birth with a special abacus. He says he has never heard of such things and such heathen devices would be unnatural and not wanted at the treatment of a Christian child.

He suggests that I rest. He asks me to send for him whenever I feel unwell and he will come to apply leeches. He says he is a great believer in bleeding women frequently to prevent them becoming overheated. Then he bows and leaves.

I look blankly at Maria de Salinas, standing in the corner of the room for this mockery of a consultation. 'This is the best doctor in England?' I ask her. 'This is the best that they have?'

She shakes her head in bewilderment.

'I wonder if we can get someone from Spain,' I think aloud.

'Your mother and father have all but cleared Spain of the learned men,' she says, and in that moment I feel almost ashamed of them.

'Their learning was heretical,' I say defensively.

She shrugs. 'Well, the Inquisition arrested most of them. The rest have fled.'

'Where did they go?' I ask.

'Wherever people go. The Jews went to Portugal and then to Italy, to Turkey, I think throughout Europe. I suppose the Moors went to Africa and the East.'

'Can we not find someone from Turkey?' I suggest. 'Not a heathen, of course. But someone who has learned from a Moorish physician? There must be some Christian doctors who have knowledge. Some who know more than this one?'

'I will ask the ambassador,' she says

'He must be Christian,' I stipulate. I know that I will need a better doctor than this shy ignoramus, but I do not want to go against the authority of my mother and the Holy Church. If they say that such knowledge is sin, then, surely, I should embrace ignorance. It is my duty. I am no scholar and it is better if I am guided by the ruling of the Holy Church. But can God really want us to deny knowledge? And what if this ignorance costs me England's son and heir?

Katherine did not reduce her work, commanding the clerks to the king, hearing petitioners who needed royal justice, discussing with the Privy Council the news from the kingdom. But she wrote to Spain to suggest that her father might like to send an ambassador to represent Spanish interests, especially since Henry was determined on a war against France in alliance with Spain as soon as the season for war started in the spring, and there would be much correspondence between the two countries.

'He is most determined to do your bidding,' Catalina wrote to her father, carefully translating every word into the complex code that they used. 'He is conscious that he has not been to war and is anxious that all goes well for an English–Spanish army. I am very concerned, indeed, that he is not exposed to danger. He has no heir, and even if he did, this is a hard country for princes in their minority. When he goes to war with you, I shall trust him into your safe-keeping. He should certainly feel that he is experiencing war to the full, he should certainly learn how to campaign from you. But I shall trust you to keep him from any real danger. Do not misunderstand me on this,' she wrote sternly. 'He must feel that he is at the heart of war, he must learn how battles are won; but he must not ever be in any real danger. And,' she added, 'he must never know that we have protected him.'

King Ferdinand, in full possession of Castile and Aragon once more, ruling as regent for Juana who was now said to be far beyond taking her throne, lost in a dark world of grief and madness, wrote smoothly back to his youngest daughter that she was not to worry about the safety of her husband in war, he would make sure that Henry was exposed to nothing but excitement. 'And do not let your wifely fears distract him from his duty,' he reminded her. 'In all her years with me your mother never shirked from danger. You must be the queen she would want you to be. This is a war that has to be fought for the safety and profit of us all, and the young king must play his part alongside this old king and the old emperor. This is an alliance of two old warhorses and one young colt; and he will want to be part of it.' He left a space in the letter as if for thought and then added a postscript. 'Of course, we will both make sure it is mostly play for him. Of course he will not know.'

Ferdinand was right. Henry was desperate to be part of an alliance that would defeat France. The Privy Council, the thoughtful advisors of his father's careful reign, were appalled to find that the young man was utterly set on the idea that kingship meant warfare, and he could imagine no better way to demonstrate that he had inherited the throne. The eager, boastful young men that formed the young court, desperate for a chance to show their own courage, were egging Henry on to war. The French had been hated for so long that it seemed incredible that a peace had ever been made and that it had lasted. It seemed unnatural to be at peace with the French – the normal state of warfare should be resumed as soon as victory was a certainty. And victory, with a new young king, and a new young court, must be a certainty now.

Nothing that Katherine might quietly remark could completely calm the fever for war, and Henry was so bellicose with the French ambassador at their first meeting that the astounded representative reported to his master that the new young king was out of his mind with choler, denying that he had ever written a peaceable letter to the King of France, which the Privy Council had sent in his absence. Fortunately, their next meeting went better. Katherine made sure that she was there.

'Greet him pleasantly,' she prompted Henry as she saw the man advance.

'I will not feign kindness where I mean war.'

'You have to be cunning,' she said softly. 'You have to be skilled in saying one thing and thinking another.'

'I will never pretend. I will never deny my righteous pride.'

'No, you should not pretend, exactly. But let him in his folly misunderstand you. There is more than one way to win a war, and it is winning that matters, not threatening. If he thinks you are his friend, we will catch them unprepared. Why would we give them warning of attack?'

He was troubled, he looked at her, frowning. 'I am not a liar.'

'No, for you told him last time that the vain ambitions of his king would be corrected by you. The French cannot be allowed to capture Venice. We have an ancient alliance with Venice . . .'

'Do we?'

'Oh, yes,' Katherine said firmly. 'England has an ancient alliance with Venice, and besides, it is the very first wall of Christianity against the Turks. By threatening Venice the French are on the brink of letting the heathens into Italy. They should be ashamed of themselves. But last time you met, you warned the French ambassador. You could not have been more clear. Now is the time for you to greet him with a smile. You do not need to spell out your campaign. We will keep our own counsel. We will not share it with such as him.'

'I have told him once, I need not tell him again. I do not repeat myself,' Henry said, warming to the thought.

'We don't brag of our strength,' she said. 'We know what we can do, and we know what we will do. They can find out for themselves in our own good time.'

'Indeed,' said Henry, and stepped down from the little dais to greet the French ambassador quite pleasantly, and was rewarded to see the man fumble in his bow and stutter in his address.

'I had him quite baffled,' he said to Katherine gleefully.

'You were masterly,' she assured him.

If he was a dullard I would have to bite back my impatience and curb my temper more often than I do. But he is not unintelligent. He is bright and clever, perhaps even as quick-witted as Arthur. But where Arthur had been trained to think, had been educated as a king from birth, they let this second son slide by on his charm and his ready tongue. They found him pleasing and encouraged him to be nothing more than agreeable. He has a good brain and he can read, debate and think well – but only if the topic catches his interest, and then only for a while. They taught him to study, but only to demonstrate his own cleverness. He is lazy, he is terribly lazy – he would always rather that someone does the detailed work for him, and this is a great fault in a king, it throws him into the power of his clerks. A king who will not work will always be in the hands of his advisors. It is a recipe for overmighty councillors.

When we start to discuss the terms of the contract between Spain and England he asks me to write it out for him, he does not like to do this himself, he likes to dictate and have a clerk write it out fair. And he will never bother to learn the code. It means that every letter between him and the emperor, every letter between him and my father, is either written by me, or translated by me. I am at the very centre of the emerging plans for war, whether I want to be or no. I cannot help but be the decision-maker at the very heart of this alliance, and Henry puts himself to one side.

Of course I am not reluctant to do my duty. No true child of my mother's would ever have turned away from effort, especially one that led to war with the enemies of Spain. We were all raised to know that kingship is a vocation, not a treat. To be a king means to rule; and ruling is always demanding work. No true child of my father's could have resisted being at the very heart of planning and plotting, and preparing for war. There is no-one at the English court better able than I to take our country into war.

I am no fool. I guessed from the start that my father planned to use our English troops against the French, and while we engage them at the time and place of his choosing, I wager that he will invade the kingdom of Navarre. I must have heard him a dozen times telling my mother that if he could have Navarre he would have rounded the north border of Aragon and besides, Navarre is a rich region, growing grapes and wheat. My father has wanted it from the moment he came to the throne of Aragon. I know that if he has a chance at Navarre he will win it, and if he can make the English do the work for him he would think that even better.

But I am not fighting this war to oblige my father, though I let him think that. He will not use me as his instrument, I will use him for mine. I want this war for England, and for God. The Pope himself has ruled that the French should not overrun Venice, the Pope himself is putting his own holy army into the field against the French. No true son or daughter of the church needs any greater cause than this: to know that the Holy Father is calling for support.

And for me there is another reason, even more powerful than that. I never forget my mother's warning that the Moors will come against Christendom again, I never forget her telling me that I must be ready in England as she was always ready in Spain. If the French defeat the armies of the Pope and seize Venice, who can doubt but that the Moors will see it as their chance to snatch Venice in their turn from the French? And once the Moors get a toe-hold in the heart of Christendom once more, it will be my mother's war to be fought all over again. They will come at us from the East, they will come at us from Venice, and Christian Europe will lie at their mercy. My father himself told me that Venice with its great trade, its arsenal, its powerful dockyards, must never be taken by the Moors, we must never let them win a city where they could build fighting galleys in a week, arm them in days, man them in a morning. If they have the Venetian dockyards and shipwrights then we have lost the seas. I know that it is my given duty, given to me by my mother and by God: to send English men to serve the Pope, and to defend Venice from any invader. It is easy to persuade Henry to think the same.

But I don't forget Scotland. I never forget Arthur's fear of Scotland. The Privy Council has spies along the border, and Thomas Howard, the old Earl of Surrey, was placed there, quite deliberately I think, by the old king. King Henry my father-in-law gave Thomas Howard great lands in the north so that he, of all people, would keep the border safe. The old king was no fool. He did not let others do his business and trust to their abilities. He tied them into his success. If the Scots invade England they will come through Howard lands, and Thomas Howard is as anxious as I that this will never happen. He has assured me that the Scots will not come against us this summer, in any numbers worse than their usual brigand raids. All the intelligence we can gather from English merchants in Scotland, from travellers primed to keep their eyes open, confirms the earl's view. We are safe for this summer at least. I can take this moment and send the English army to war against the French. Henry can march out in safety and learn to be a soldier.

Katherine watched the dancing at the Christmas festivities, applauded her husband when he twirled other ladies around the room, laughed at the mummers, and signed off the court's bills for enormous amounts of wine, ale, beef, and the rarest and finest of everything. She gave Henry a beautiful inlaid saddle for his Christmas gift, and some shirts that she had sewn and embroidered herself with the beautiful blackwork of Spain.

'I want all my shirts to be sewn by you,' he said, putting the fine linen against his cheek. 'I want to never wear anything that another woman has touched. Only your hands shall make my shirts.'

Katherine smiled and pulled his shoulder down to her height. He bent down like a grown boy, and she kissed his forehead. 'Always,' she promised him. 'I shall always sew your shirts for you.'

'And now, my gift to you,' he said. He pushed a large leather box towards her. Katherine opened it. There was a great set of magnificent jewels: a diadem, a necklace, two bracelets and matching rings.

'Oh, Henry!'

'Do you like them?'

'I love them,' she said.

'Will you wear them tonight?'

'I shall wear them tonight and at the Twelfth Night feast,' she promised.

The young queen shone in her happiness, this first Christmas of her reign. The full skirts of her gown could not conceal the curve of her belly; everywhere she went the young king would order a chair to be brought for her, she must not stand for a moment, she must never be wearied. He composed for her special songs that his musicians played, special dances and special masques were made up in her honour. The court, delighted with the young queen's fertility, with the health and strength of the young king, with itself, made merry late into the night and Katherine sat on her throne, her feet slightly spread to accommodate the curve of her belly, and smiled in her joy.

Westminster Palace, January 1510

I wake in the night to pain, and a strange sensation. I dreamed that a tide was rising in the river Thames and that a fleet of black-sailed ships were coming upriver. I think that it must be the Moors, coming for me, and then I think it is a Spanish fleet – an armada, but strangely, disturbingly, my enemy, and the enemy of England. In my distress I toss and turn in bed and I wake with a sense of dread and find that it is worse than any dream, my sheets are wet with blood, and there is a real pain in my belly.

I call out in terror, and my cry wakes Maria de Salinas, who is sleeping with me.

'What is it?' she asks, then she sees my face and calls out sharply to the maid at the foot of the bed and sends her running for my ladies and for the midwives, but somewhere in the back of my mind I know already that there is nothing that they can do. I clamber into my chair in my bloodstained nightdress and feel the pain twist and turn in my belly.

By the time they arrive, struggling from their beds, all stupid with sleep, I am on my knees on the floor like a sick dog, praying for the pain to pass and to leave me whole. I know that there is no point in praying for the safety of my child. I know that my child is lost. I can feel the tearing sensation in my belly as he slowly comes away.

After a long, bitter day, when Henry comes to the door again and again, and I send him away, calling out to him in a bright voice of reassurance, biting the palm of my hand so that I do not cry out, the baby is born, dead. The midwife shows her to me, a little girl, a white, limp little thing: poor baby, my poor baby. My only comfort is that it is not the boy I had promised Arthur I would bear for him. It is a girl, a dead girl, and then I twist my face in grief when I remember that he wanted a girl first, and she was to be called Mary.

I cannot speak for grief, I cannot face Henry and tell him myself. I cannot bear the thought of anyone telling the court, I cannot bring myself to write to my father and tell him that I have failed England, I have failed Henry, I have failed Spain, and worst of all – and this I could never tell anyone – I have failed Arthur.

I stay in my room, I close the door on all the anxious faces, on the *midwives wanting me to drink strawberry-leaf tisanes, on the ladies wanting to tell me about their still births, and their mothers' still births and their happy endings, I shut them away from me and I kneel at the foot of my bed, and press my hot face against the covers. I whisper through my sobs, muffled so that no-one but him can hear me. 'I am sorry, so sorry, my love. I am so sorry not to have had your son. I don't know why, I don't know why our gentle God should send me this great sorrow. I am so sorry, my love. If I ever have another chance I will do my best, the very best that I can, to have our son, to keep him safe till birth and beyond. I will, I swear I will. I tried this time, God knows, I would have given anything to have your son and named him Arthur for you, my love.' I steady myself as I can feel the words tumbling out too quickly, I can feel myself losing control, I feel the sobs starting to choke me.*

'Wait for me,' I say quietly. 'Wait for me still. Wait for me by the quiet waters in the garden where the white and the red rose petals fall. Wait for me and when I have given birth to your son Arthur and your daughter Mary, and done my duty here, I will come to you. Wait for me in the garden and I will never fail you. I will come to you, love. My love.'

The king's physician went to the king directly from the queen's apartments. 'Your Grace, I have good news for you.'

Henry turned a face to him that was as sour as a child's whose joy has been stolen. 'You have?'

'I have indeed.'

'The queen is better? In less pain? She will be well?'

'Even better than well,' the physician said. 'Although she lost one child, she has kept another. She was carrying twins, Your Grace. She has lost one child but her belly is still large and she is still with child.'

For a moment the young man could not understand the words. 'She still has a child?'

The physician smiled. 'Yes, Your Grace.'

It was like a stay of execution. Henry felt his heart turn over with hope. 'How can it be?'

The physician was confident. 'By various ways I can tell. Her belly is still firm, the bleeding has stopped. I am certain she is still with child.'

Henry crossed himself. 'God is with us,' he said positively. 'This is the sign of His favour.' He paused. 'Can I see her?'

'Yes, she is as happy at this news as you.'

Henry bounded up the stairs to Katherine's rooms. Her presence chamber was empty of anyone but the least informed sight-seers, the court and half the City knew that she had taken to her bed and would not be seen. Henry brushed through the crowd who whispered hushed blessings for him and the queen, strode through her privy chamber, where her women were sewing, and tapped on her bedroom door.

Maria de Salinas opened it and stepped back for the king. The queen was out of her bed, seated in the window seat, her book of prayers held up to the light.

'My love!' he exclaimed. 'Here is Dr Fielding come to me with the best of news.'

Her face was radiant. 'I told him to tell you privately.'

'He did. No-one else knows. My love, I am so glad!'

Her eyes were wet with tears. 'It is like a redemption,' she said. 'I feel as if a cross has been lifted from my shoulders.'

'I shall go to Walsingham the moment our baby is born and thank Our Lady for her favour,' he promised. 'I shall endow the shrine with a fortune, if it is a boy.'

'Please God that He grants it,' she murmured.

'Why should He not?' Henry demanded. 'When it is our desire, and right for England, and we ask it as holy children of the church?'

'Amen,' she said quickly. 'If it is God's will.'

He flicked his hand. 'Of course it must be His will,' he said. 'Now you must take care and rest.'

Katherine smiled at him. 'As you see.'

'Well, you must. And anything you want, you shall have.'

'I shall tell the cooks if I want anything.'

'And the midwives shall attend you night and morning to make sure that you are well.'

'Yes,' she agreed. 'And if God is willing, we shall have a son.'

It was Maria de Salinas, my true friend who had come with me from Spain, and stayed with me through our good months and our hard years, who found the Moor. He was attending on a wealthy merchant, travelling from Genoa to Paris, they had called in at London to value some gold and Maria heard of him from a woman who had given a hundred pounds to Our Lady of Walsingham, hoping to have a son.

'They say he can make barren women give birth,' she whispers to me, watching that none of my other ladies have come close enough to overhear.

I cross myself as if to avoid temptation. 'Then he must use black arts.'

'Princess, he is supposed to be a great physician. Trained by masters who were at the university of Toledo.'

'I will not see him.'

'Because you think he must use black arts?'

'Because he is my enemy and my mother's enemy. She knew that the Moors' knowledge was unlawfully gained, drawn from the devil, not from the revealed truth of God. She drove the Moors from Spain and their magical arts with them.'

'Your Grace, he may be the only doctor in England who knows anything about women.'

'I will not see him.'

Maria took my refusal and let a few weeks go by and then I woke in the night with a deep pain in my belly, and slowly, felt the blood coming. She was quick and ready to call the maids with the towels and with a ewer to wash, and when I was back in bed again and we realised that it was no more than my monthly courses returned, she came quietly and stood beside the head of the bed. Lady Margaret Pole was silent at the doorway.

'Your Grace, please see this doctor.'

'He is a Moor.'

'Yes, but I think he is the only man in this country who will know what is happening. How can you have your courses if you are with child? You may be losing this second baby. You have to see a doctor that we can trust.'

'Maria, he is my enemy. He is my mother's enemy. She spent her life driving his people from Spain.'

'We lost their wisdom with them,' Maria says quietly. 'You have not lived in Spain for nearly a decade, Your Grace, you do not know what it is like there now. My brother writes to me that people fall sick and there are no hospitals that can cure them. The nuns and the monks do their best; but they have no knowledge. If you have a stone it has to be cut out of you by a horse doctor, if you have a broken arm or leg then the blacksmith has to set it. The barbers are surgeons, the tooth drawers work in the market place and break people's jaws. The midwives go from burying a man sick with sores to a childbirth and lose as many babies as they deliver. The skills of the Moorish physicians, with their knowledge of the body, their herbs to soothe pain, their instruments for surgery, and their insistence on washing – it is all lost.'

'If it was sinful knowledge it is better lost,' I say stubbornly.

'Why would God be on the side of ignorance and dirt and disease?' she asks fiercely. 'Forgive me, Your Grace, but this makes no sense. And

you are forgetting what your mother wanted. She always said that the universities should be restored, to teach Christian knowledge. But by then she had killed or banished all the teachers who knew anything.'

'The queen will not want to be advised by a heretic,' Lady Margaret said firmly. 'No English lady would consult a Moor.'

Maria turns to me. 'Please, Your Grace.'

I am in such pain that I cannot bear an argument. 'Both of you can leave me now,' I say. 'Just let me sleep.'

Lady Margaret goes out of the door but Maria pauses to close the shutters so that I am in shadow. 'Oh, let him come then,' I say. 'But not while I am like this. He can come next week.'

She brings him by the hidden stairway which runs from the cellars through a servants' passage to the queen's private rooms at Richmond Palace. I am wearily dressing for dinner, and I let him come into my rooms while I am still unlaced, in my shift with a cape thrown on top. I grimace at the thought of what my mother would say at a man coming into my privy chamber. But I know, in my heart, that I have to see a doctor who can tell me how to get a son for England. And I know, if I am honest, that something is wrong with the baby they say I am carrying.

I know him for an unbeliever the moment I see him. He is black as ebony, his eyes as dark as jet, his mouth wide and sensual, his face both merry and compassionate, all at the same time. The back of his hands are black, dark as his face, long-fingered, his nails rosy pink, the palms brown, the creases ingrained with his colour. If I were a palmist I could trace the lifeline on his African palm like cart tracks of brown dust in a field of terracotta. I know him at once for a Moor and a Nubian; and I want to order him away from my rooms. But I know, at the same time, that he may be the only doctor in this country who has the knowledge I need.

This man's people, infidels, sinners who have set their black faces against God, have medicine that we do not. For some reason, God and his angels have not revealed to us the knowledge that these people have sought and found. These people have read in Greek everything that the Greek physicians thought. Then they have explored for themselves, with forbidden instruments, studying the human body as if it were an animal, without fear or respect. They create wild theories with forbidden thoughts and then they test them, without superstition. They are prepared to think anything, to consider anything; nothing is taboo. These people are educated where we are fools, where I am a fool. I might look down on him as coming from a race of savages, I might look down on him as an infidel doomed to hell; but I need to know what he knows.

If he will tell me.

'I am Catalina, Infanta of Spain and Queen Katherine of England,' I say bluntly, that he may know that he is dealing with a queen and the daughter of a queen who had defeated his people.

He inclines his head, as proud as a baron. 'I am Yusuf, son of Ismail,' he says.

'You are a slave?'

'I was born to a slave, but I am a free man.'

'My mother would not allow slavery,' I tell him. 'She said it was not allowed by our religion, our Christian religion.'

'Nevertheless, she sent my people into slavery,' he remarks. 'Perhaps she should have considered that high principles and good intentions end at the border.'

'Since your people won't accept the salvation of God then it doesn't matter what happens to your earthly bodies.'

His face lights up with amusement, and he gives a delightful, irrepressible chuckle. 'It matters to us, I think,' he says. 'My nation allows slavery, but we don't justify it like that. And most importantly, you cannot inherit slavery with us. When you are born, whatever the condition of your mother, you are born free. That is the law, and I think it a very good one.'

'Well, it makes no difference what you think,' I say rudely. 'Since you are wrong.'

Again he laughs aloud, in true merriment, as if I have said something very funny. 'How good it must be, always to know that you are right,' he says. 'Perhaps you will always be certain of your rightness. But I would suggest to you, Catalina of Spain and Katherine of England, that sometimes it is better to know the questions than the answers.'

I pause at that. 'But I want you only for answers,' I say. 'Do you know medicine? Whether a woman can conceive a son? If she is with child?'

'Sometimes it can be known,' he says. 'Sometimes it is in the hands of Allah, praise His holy name, and sometimes we do not yet understand enough to be sure.'

I cross myself against the name of Allah, quick as an old woman spitting on a shadow. He smiles at my gesture, not in the least disturbed. 'What is it that you want to know?' he asks, his voice filled with kindness. 'What is it that you want to know so much that you have to send for an infidel to advise you? Poor queen, you must be very alone if you need help from your enemy.'

My eyes are filling with too-quick tears at the sympathy in his voice and I brush my hand against my face.

'I have lost a baby,' I say shortly. 'A daughter. My physician says that she was one of twins, and that there is another child still inside me, that there will be another birth.'

'So why send for me?'

'I want to know for sure,' I say. 'If there is another child I will have to go into confinement, the whole world will watch me. I want to know that the baby is alive inside me now, that it is a boy, that he will be born.'

'Why should you doubt your own physician's opinion?'

I turn from his inquiring, honest gaze. 'I don't know,' I say evasively.

'Infanta, I think you do know.'

'How can I know?'

'With a woman's sense.'

'I have it not.'

He smiles at my stubbornness. 'Well, then, woman without any feelings, what do you think with your clever mind, since you have decided to deny what your body tells you?'

'How can I know what I should think?' I ask. 'My mother is dead. My greatest friend in England . . .' I break off before I can say the name of Arthur. 'I have no-one to confide in. One midwife says one thing, one says another. The physician is sure . . . but he wants to be sure. The king rewards him only for good news. How can I know the truth?'

'I should think you do know, despite yourself,' he insists gently. 'Your body will tell you. I suppose your courses have not returned?'

'No, I have bled,' I admit unwillingly. 'Last week.'

'With pain?'

'Yes.'

'Your breasts are tender?'

'They were.'

'Are they fuller than usual?'

'No.'

'You can feel the child? He moves inside you?'

'I can't feel anything since I lost the girl.'

'You are in pain now?'

'Not any more. I feel . . .'

'Yes?'

'Nothing. I feel nothing.'

He says nothing, he sits quietly, he breathes so softly it is like sitting with a quietly sleeping black cat. He looks at Maria. 'May I touch her?'

'No,' she says. 'She is the queen. Nobody can touch her.'

He shrugs his shoulders. 'She is a woman like any other. She wants a child like any woman. Why should I not touch her belly as I would touch any woman?'

'She is the queen,' she repeats. 'She cannot be touched. She has an anointed body.'

374

He smiles as if the holy truth is amusing. 'Well, I hope someone has touched her, or there cannot be a child at all,' he remarks.

'Her husband. An anointed king,' Maria says shortly. 'And take care of how you speak. These are sacred matters.'

'If I may not examine her, then I shall have to say only what I think from looking at her. If she cannot bear examination then she will have to make do with guesswork.' He turns to me. 'If you were an ordinary woman and not a queen, I would take your hands in mine now.'

'Why?'

'Because it is a hard word I have to tell you.'

Slowly, I stretch out my hands with the priceless rings on my fingers. He takes them gently, his dark hands as soft as the touch of a child. His dark eyes look into mine without fear, his face is tender, moved. 'If you are bleeding then it is most likely that your womb is empty,' he says. 'There is no child there. If your breasts are not full then they are not filling with milk, your body is not preparing to feed a child. If you do not feel a child move inside you in the sixth month, then either the child is dead, or there is no child there. If you feel nothing then that is most probably because there is nothing to feel.'

'My belly is still swollen.' I draw back my cloak and show him the curve of my belly under my shift. 'It is hard, I am not fat, I look as I did before I lost the first baby.'

'It could be an infection,' he says consideringly. 'Or – pray Allah that it is not – it could be a growth, a swelling. Or it could be a miscarriage which you have not yet expelled.'

I draw my hands back. 'You are ill-wishing me!'

'Never,' he says. 'To me, here and now, you are not Catalina, Infanta of Spain, but simply a woman who has asked for my help. I am sorry for you.'

'Some help!' Maria de Salinas interrupts crossly. 'Some help you have been!'

'Anyway, I don't believe it,' I say. 'Yours is one opinion, Dr Fielding has another. Why should I believe you, rather than a good Christian?'

He looks at me for a long time, his face tender. 'I wish I could tell you a better opinion,' he says. 'But I imagine there are many who will tell you agreeable lies. I believe in telling the truth. I will pray for you.'

'I don't want your heathen prayers,' I say roughly. 'You can go, and take your bad opinion and your heresies with you.'

'Go with God, Infanta,' he says with dignity, as if I have not insulted him. He bows. 'And since you don't want my prayers to my God (praise be to His holy name), I shall hope instead that when you are in your time of trouble that your doctor is right, and your own God is with you.'

I let him leave, as silent as a dark cat down the hidden staircase, and I say nothing. I hear his sandals clicking down the stone steps, just like the hushed footsteps of the servants at my home. I hear the whisper of his long gown, so unlike the stiff brush of English cloth. I feel the air gradually lose the scent of him, the warm spicy scent of my home.

And when he is gone, quite gone, and the downstairs door is shut and I hear Maria de Salinas turn the key in the lock, then I find that I want to weep – not just because he has told me such bad news, but because one of the few people in the world who has ever told me the truth has gone.

Katherine did not tell her young husband of the visit of the Moorish doctor, nor of the bad opinion that he had so honestly given her. She did not mention his visit to anyone, not even Lady Margaret Pole. She drew on her sense of destiny, on her pride, and on her faith that she was still especially favoured by God, and she continued with the pregnancy, not even allowing herself to doubt.

She had good reason. The English physician, Dr Fielding, remained confident, the midwives did not contradict him, the court behaved as if Katherine would be brought to bed of a child in March or April, and so she went through the spring weather, the greening gardens, the bursting trees, with a serene smile and her hand clasped gently against her rounded belly.

Henry was excited by the imminent birth of his child; he was planning a great tournament to be held at Greenwich once the baby was born. The loss of the girl had taught him no caution, he bragged all round the court that a healthy baby would soon come. He was forewarned only not to predict a boy. He told everyone that he did not mind if this first child was a prince or princess – he would love

377

this baby for being the first-born, for coming to himself and the queen in the first flush of their happiness.

Katherine stifled her doubts, and never even said to Maria de Salinas that she had not felt her baby kick, that she felt a little colder, a little more distant from everything every day. She spent longer and longer on her knees in her chapel; but God did not speak to her, and even the voice of her mother seemed to have grown silent. She found that she missed Arthur – not with the passionate longing of a young widow, but because he had been her dearest friend in England, and the only one she could have trusted now with her doubts.

In February she attended the great Shrove Tuesday feast and shone before the court and laughed. They saw the broad curve of her belly, they saw her confidence as they celebrated the start of Lent. They moved to Greenwich, certain that the baby would be born just after Easter.

We are going to Greenwich for the birth of my child, the rooms are prepared for me as laid down in My Lady the King's Mother's Royal Book – hung with tapestries with pleasing and encouraging scenes, carpeted with rugs and strewn with fresh herbs. I hesitate at the doorway, behind me my friends raise their glasses of spiced wine. This is where I shall do my greatest work for England, this is my moment of destiny. This is what I was born and bred to do. I take a deep breath and go inside. The door closes behind me. I will not see my friends, the Duke of Buckingham, my dear knight Edward Howard, my confessor, the Spanish ambassador, until my baby is born.

My women come in with me. Lady Elizabeth Boleyn places a sweet-smelling pomander on my bedside table, Lady Elizabeth and Lady Anne, sisters to the Duke of Buckingham, straighten a tapestry, one at each corner, laughing over whether it leans to one side or the other.

Maria de Salinas is smiling, standing by the great bed that is new-hung with dark curtains. Lady Margaret Pole is arranging the cradle for the baby at the foot of the bed. She looks up and smiles at me as I come in and I remember that she is a mother, she will know what is to be done.

'I shall want you to take charge of the royal nurseries,' I suddenly blurt out to her, my affection for her and my sense of needing the advice and comfort of an older woman is too much for me.

There is a little ripple of amusement among my women. They know that I am normally very formal, such an appointment should come through the head of my household after consultation with dozens of people.

Lady Margaret smiles at me. 'I knew you would,' *she says, speaking in reply as intimate as myself.* 'I have been counting on it.'

'Without royal invitation?' *Lady Elizabeth Boleyn teases.* 'For shame, Lady Margaret! Thrusting yourself forwards!'

That makes us all laugh at the thought of Lady Margaret, that most dignified of women, as someone craving patronage.

'I know you will care for him as if he were your own son,' *I whisper to her.*

She takes my hand and helps me to the bed. I am heavy and ungainly, I have this constant pain in my belly that I try to hide.

'God willing,' *she says quietly.*

Henry comes in to bid me farewell. His face is flushed with emotion and his mouth is working, he looks more like a boy than a king. I take his hands and I kiss him tenderly on the mouth. 'My love,' *I say.* 'Pray for me, I am sure everything will go well for us.'

'I shall go to Our Lady of Walsingham to give thanks,' *he tells me again.* 'I have written to the nunnery there and promised them great rewards if they will intercede with Our Lady for you. They are praying for you now, my love. They assure me that they are praying all the time.'

'God is good,' *I say. I think briefly of the Moorish doctor who told* me that I was not with child and I push his pagan folly from my mind. 'This is my destiny and it is my mother's wish and God's will,' I say.

'I so wish your mother could be here,' Henry says clumsily. I do not let him see me flinch.

'Of course,' I say quietly. 'And I am sure she is watching me from al-Yan –' I cut off the words before I can say them. 'From paradise,' I say smoothly. 'From heaven.'

'Can I get you anything?' he asks. 'Before I leave, can I fetch you anything?'

I do not laugh at the thought of Henry – who never knows where anything is – running errands for me at this late stage. 'I have everything I need,' I assure him. 'And my women will care for me.'

He straightens up, very kingly, and he looks around at them. 'Serve your mistress well,' he says firmly. To Lady Margaret he says, 'Please send for me at once if there is any news, at any time, day or night.' Then he kisses me farewell very tenderly, and when he goes out they close the door behind him and I am alone with my ladies, in the seclusion of my confinement.

I am glad to be confined. The shady, peaceful bedroom will be my haven, I can rest for a while in the familiar company of women. I can stop play-acting the part of a fertile and confident queen, and be myself. I put aside all doubts. I will not think and I will not worry. I will wait patiently until my baby comes, and then I will bring him into the world without fear, without screaming. I am determined to be confident that this child, who has survived the loss of his twin, will be a strong baby. And I, who have survived the loss of my first child, will be a brave mother. Perhaps it might be true that we have surmounted grief and loss together: this baby and I.

I wait. All through March I wait, and I ask them to pin back the tapestry that covers the window so I can smell the scent of spring on the air and hear the seagulls as they call over the high tides on the river.

Nothing seems to be happening; not for my baby nor for me. The midwives ask me if I feel any pain, and I do not. Nothing more than the dull ache I have had for a long time. They ask if the baby has quickened, if I feel him kick me, but, to tell truth, I do not understand what they mean. They glance at one another and say over-loudly, over-emphatically, that it is a very good sign, a quiet baby is a strong baby; he must be resting.

The unease that I have felt right from the start of this second pregnancy, I put right away from me. I will not think of the warning from the Moorish doctor, nor of the compassion in his face. I am determined not to seek out fear, not to run towards disaster. But April comes and I can hear the patter of rain on the window, and then feel the heat of the sunshine, and still nothing happens.

My gowns that strained so tight across my belly through the winter feel looser in April, and then looser yet. I send out all the women but Maria, and I unlace my gown and show her my belly and ask if she thinks I am losing my girth.

'I don't know,' she says; but I can tell by her aghast face that my belly is smaller, that it is obvious that there is no baby in there, ready to be born.

In another week it is obvious to everyone that my belly is going down, I am growing slim again. The midwives try to tell me that sometimes a woman's belly diminishes just before her baby is born, as her baby drops down to be born, or some such arcane knowledge. I look at them coldly, and I wish I could send for a decent physician who would tell me the truth.

'My belly is smaller and my course has come this very day,' I say to them flatly. 'I am bleeding. As you know, I have bled every month since I lost the girl. How can I be with child?'

They flutter their hands, and cannot say. They don't know. They tell me that these are questions for my husband's respected physician. It was he who had said that I was still with child in the first place, not them. They had never said that I was with child, they had merely been called in to assist with a delivery. It was not them who had said that I was carrying a baby.

'But what did you think, when he said there was a twin?' I demand. 'Did you not agree when he said that I had lost a child and yet kept one?'

They shake their heads. They did not know.

'You must have thought something,' I say impatiently. 'You saw me lose my baby. You saw my belly stay big. What could cause that if not another child?'

'God's will,' says one of them helplessly.

'Amen,' I say, and it costs me a good deal to say it.

'I want to see that physician again,' Katherine said quietly to Maria de Salinas.

'Your Grace, it may be that he is not in London. He travels in the household of a French count. It may be that he has gone.'

'Find out if he is still in London, or when they expect him to return,' the queen said. 'Don't tell anyone that it is I who have asked for him.'

Maria de Salinas looked at her mistress with sympathy. 'You want him to advise you how to have a son?' she asked in a low voice.

'There is not a university in England that studies medicine,' Katherine said bitterly. 'There is not one that teaches languages. There is not one that teaches astronomy, or mathematics, geometry, geography, cosmography, or even the study of animals, or plants. The universities of England are about as much use as a monastery full of monks colouring-in the margins of sacred texts.'

Maria de Salinas gave a little gasp of shock at Katherine's bluntness. 'The church says . . .'

'The church does not need decent physicians. The church does not need to know how sons are conceived,' Katherine snapped. 'The church can continue with the revelations of the saints. It needs nothing more than scripture. The church is composed of men who are not troubled by the illnesses and difficulties of women. But for those of us on our pilgrimage today, those of us in the world, especially those of us who are women: we need a little more.'

'But you said that you did not want pagan knowledge. You said to the doctor himself. Your said your mother was right to close the universities of the infidel.'

'My mother had half a dozen children,' Katherine replied crossly. 'But I tell you, if she could have found a doctor to save my brother she would have had him even if he had been trained in hell itself. She was wrong to turn her back on the learning of the Moors. She was mistaken. I have never thought that she was perfect, but I think the less of her now. She made a great mistake when she drove away their wise scholars along with their heretics.'

'The church itself said that their scholarship is heresy,' Maria observed. 'How could you have one without the other?'

'I am sure that you know nothing about it,' said Isabella's daughter, driven into a corner. 'It is not a fit subject for you to discuss and besides, I have told you what I want you to do.'

The Moor, Yusuf, is away from London but the people at his lodging house say that he has reserved his rooms to return within the week. I shall have to be patient. I shall wait in my confinement and try to be patient.

They know him well, Maria's servant tells her. His comings and goings are something of an event in their street. Africans are so rare in England as to be a spectacle – and he is a handsome man and generous with small coins for little services. They told Maria's servant that he insisted on having fresh water for washing in his room and he washes every day, several times a day, and that – wonder of wonders – he bathes three or four times a week, using soap and towels, and throwing water all over the floor to the great inconvenience of the housemaids, and to great danger of his health.

I cannot help but laugh at the thought of the tall, fastidious Moor

folding himself up into a washing tub, desperate for a steam, a tepid
soak, a massage, a cold shower, and then a long, thoughtful rest while
smoking a hookah and sipping a strong, sweet peppermint tea. It
reminds me of my horror when I first came to England and discovered
that they bathe only infrequently, and wash only the tips of their fingers
before eating. I think that he has done better than me – he has carried
his love of his home with him, he has re-made his home wherever he
goes. But in my determination to be Queen Katherine of England I
have given up being Catalina of Spain.

They brought the Moor to Katherine under cover of darkness, to
the chamber where she was confined. She sent the women from the
room at the appointed hour and told them that she wanted to be
alone. She sat in her chair by the window, where the tapestries were
drawn back for air, and the first thing he saw, as she rose when he
came in, was her slim candlelit profile against the darkness of the
window. She saw his little grimace of sympathy.

'No child.'

'No,' she said shortly. 'I shall come out of my confinement
tomorrow.'

'You are in pain?'

'Nothing.'

'Well, I am glad of that. You are bleeding?'

'I had my normal course last week.'

He nodded. 'Then you may have had a disease which has passed,'
he said. 'You may be fit to conceive a child. There is no need to despair.'

'I do not despair,' she said flatly. 'I never despair. That is why I
have sent for you.'

'You will want to conceive a child as soon as possible,' he guessed.

'Yes.'

He thought for a moment. 'Well, Infanta, since you have had one child, even if you did not bear it to full term, we know that you and your husband are fertile. That is good.'

'Yes,' she said, surprised by the thought. She had been so distressed by the miscarriage she had not thought that her fertility had been proven. 'But why do you speak of my husband's fertility?'

The Moor smiled. 'It takes both a man and a woman to conceive a child.'

'Here in England they think that it is only the woman.'

'Yes. But in this, as in so many other things, they are wrong. There are two parts to every baby: the man's breath of life and the woman's gift of the flesh.'

'They say that if a baby is lost, then the woman is at fault, perhaps she has committed a great sin.'

He frowned. 'It is possible,' he conceded. 'But not very likely. Otherwise how would murderesses ever give birth? Why would inno-cent animals miscarry their young? I think we will learn in time that there are humours and infections which cause miscarriage. I do not blame the woman, it makes no sense to me.'

'They say that if a woman is barren it is because the marriage is not blessed by God.'

'He is your God,' he remarked reasonably. 'Would he persecute an unhappy woman in order to make a point?'

Katherine did not reply. 'They will blame me if I do not have a live child,' she observed very quietly.

'I know,' he said. 'But the truth of the matter is: having had one child and lost it, there is every reason to think that you might have another. And there should be no reason why you should not conceive again.'

'I must bear the next child to full term.'

'If I could examine you, I might know more.'

She shook her head. 'It is not possible.'

His glance at her was merry. 'Oh, you savages,' he said softly.

She gave a little gasp of amused shock. 'You forget yourself!'

'Then send me away.'

That stopped her. 'You can stay,' she said. 'But of course, you cannot examine me.'

'Then let us consider what might help you conceive and carry a child,' he said. 'Your body needs to be strong. Do you ride horses?'

'Yes.'

'Ride astride before you conceive and then take a litter thereafter. Walk every day, swim if you can. You will conceive a child about two weeks after the end of your course. Rest at those times, and make sure that you lie with your husband at those times. Try to eat moderately at every meal and drink as little of their accursed small ale as you can.'

Katherine smiled at the reflection of her own prejudices. 'Do you know Spain?'

'I was born there. My parents fled from Malaga when your mother brought in the Inquisition and they realised that they would be tormented to death.'

'I am sorry,' she said awkwardly.

'We will go back, it is written,' he said with nonchalant confidence.

'I should warn you that you will not.'

'I know that we will. I have seen the prophecy myself.'

At once they fell silent again.

'Shall I tell you what I advise? Or shall I just leave now?' he asked, as if he did not much mind which it was to be.

'Tell me,' she said. 'And then I can pay you, and you can go. We were born to be enemies. I should not have summoned you.'

'We are both Spanish, we both love our country. We both serve our God. Perhaps we were born to be friends.'

She had to stop herself giving him her hand. 'Perhaps,' she said gruffly, turning her head away. 'But I was brought up to hate your people and hate your faith.'

'I was brought up to hate no-one,' he said gently. 'Perhaps that is what I should be teaching you before anything else.'

'Just teach me how to have a son,' she repeated.

'Very well. Drink water that has been boiled, eat as much fruit and fresh vegetables as you can get. Do you have salad vegetables here?'

For a moment I am back in the garden at Ludlow with his bright eyes on me.

'Acetaria?'

'Yes, salad.'

'What is it, exactly?'

He saw the queen's face glow.

'What are you thinking of?'

'Of my first husband. He told me that I could send for gardeners to grow salad vegetables, but I never did.'

'I have seeds,' the Moor said surprisingly. 'I can give you some seeds and you can grow the vegetables you will need.'

'You have?'

'Yes.'

'You would give me . . . you would sell them to me?'

'Yes. I would give them to you.'

For a moment she was silenced by his generosity. 'You are very kind,' she said.

He smiled. 'We are both Spanish and a long way from our homes. Doesn't that matter more than the fact that I am black and you are white? That I worship my God facing Mecca and you worship yours facing west?'

'I am a child of the true religion and you are an infidel,' she said, but with less conviction than she had ever felt before.

'We are both people of faith,' he said quietly. 'Our enemies should be the people who have no faith, neither in their God, nor in others, nor in themselves. The people who should face our crusade should be those who bring cruelty into the world for no reason but their own power. There is enough sin and wickedness to fight, without taking up arms against people who believe in a forgiving God and who try to lead a good life.'

Katherine found that she could not reply. On the one hand was her mother's teaching, on the other was the simple goodness that radiated from this man. 'I don't know,' she said finally, and it was as if the very words set her free. 'I don't know. I would have to take the question to God. I would have to pray for guidance. I don't pretend to know.'

'Now, that is the very beginning of wisdom,' he said gently. 'I am sure of that, at least. Knowing that you do not know is to ask humbly, instead of tell arrogantly. That is the beginning of wisdom. Now, more importantly, I will go home and write you a list of things that you must not eat, and I will send you some medicine to strengthen your humours. Don't let them cup you, don't let them put leeches on you, and don't let them persuade you to take any poisons or potions. You are a young woman with a young husband. A baby will come.'

It was like a blessing. 'You are sure?' she said.

'I am sure,' he replied. 'And very soon.'

Greenwich Palace, May 1510

I send for Henry, he should hear it first from me. He comes unwillingly. He has been filled with a terror of women's secrets and women's doings and he does not like to come into a room which has been prepared for a confinement. Also, there is something else: a lack of warmth, I see it in his face, turned away from me. The way he does not meet my eyes. But I cannot challenge him about coolness towards me when I first have to tell him such hard news. Lady Margaret leaves us alone, closing the door behind her. I know she will ensure no-one outside eavesdrops. They will all know soon enough.

'Husband, I am sorry, I have sad news for us,' I say.

The face he turns to me is sulky. 'I knew it could not be good when Lady Margaret came for me.'

There is no point in my feeling a flash of irritation. I shall have to manage us both. 'I am not with child,' I say, plunging in. 'The doctor must have made a mistake. There was only one child and I lost it. This confinement has been a mistake. I shall return to court tomorrow.'

'How can he have mistaken such a thing?'

I give a little shrug of the shoulders. I want to say: because he is a pompous fool and your man, and you surround yourself with people who only ever tell you the good news and are afraid to tell you bad. But instead I say neutrally: 'He must have been mistaken.'

'I shall look a fool!' he bursts out. 'You have been away for nearly three months and nothing to show for it.'

I say nothing for a moment. Pointless to wish that I were married to a man who might think beyond his appearance. Pointless to wish that I were married to a man whose first thought might be of me.

'No-one will think anything at all,' I say firmly. 'If anything, they will say that it is I who am a fool to not know whether I am with child, or no. But at least we had a baby and that means we can have another.'

'It does?' he asks, immediately hopeful. 'But why should we lose her? Is God displeased with us? Have we committed some sin? Is it a sign of God's displeasure?'

I nip my lower lip to stop the Moor's question: is God so vindictive that He would kill an innocent child to punish the parents for a sin so venial that they do not even know that they have committed it?

'My conscience is clear,' I say firmly.

'Mine too,' he says quickly, too quickly.

But my conscience is not clear. That night I go on my knees to the image of the crucified lord and for once I truly pray, I do not dream of Arthur, or consult my memory of my mother. I close my eyes and I pray.

'Lord, it was a deathbed promise,' I say slowly. 'He demanded it of me. It was for the good of England. It was to guide the kingdom and the new king in the paths of the church. It was to protect England from the Moor and from sin. I know that it has brought me wealth, and the throne, but I did not do it for gain. If it is sin, Lord, then show me now. If I should not be his wife, then tell me now. Because I believe that I did the right thing, and that I am doing the right thing. And I believe that You would not take my son from me in order to punish me for this. I believe that You are a merciful God. And I believe that I did the right thing for Arthur, for Henry, for England and for me.'

I sit back on my heels and wait for a long time, for an hour, perhaps more, in case my God, the God of my mother, chooses to speak to me in His anger.

He does not.

So I will go on assuming that I am in the right. Arthur was right to call on my promise, I was right to tell the lie, my mother was right to call it God's will that I should be Queen of England, and that whatever happens – nothing will change that.

Lady Margaret Pole comes to sit with me this evening, my last evening in confinement, and she takes the stool on the opposite side of the fire, close enough so that we cannot easily be overheard. 'I have something to tell you,' she says.

I look at her face, she is so calm that I know at once something bad has happened.

'Tell me,' I say instantly.

She makes a little moue of distaste. 'I am sorry to bring you the tittle-tattle of the court.'

'Very well. Tell me.'

'It is the Duke of Buckingham's sister.'

'Elizabeth?' I ask, thinking of the pretty young woman who had come to me the moment she knew I would be queen and asked if she could be my lady-in-waiting.

'No, Anne.'

I nod, this is Elizabeth's younger sister, a dark-eyed girl with a roguish twinkle and a love of male company. She is popular at court among the young men but – at least as long as I am present – she behaves with all the demure grace of a young matron of the highest family in the land, in service to the queen.

'What of her?'

'She has been seeing William Compton, without telling anyone. They have had assignations. Her brother is very upset. He has told her husband, and he is furious at her risking her reputation and his good name in a flirtation with the king's friend.'

I think for a moment. William Compton is one of Henry's wilder companions, the two of them are inseparable.

'William will only have been amusing himself,' I say. 'He is a heart-breaker.'

'It turns out that she has gone missing from a masque, once during dinner and once all day when the court was hunting.'

I nod. This is much more serious. 'There is no suggestion that they are lovers?'

She shrugs. 'Certainly her brother, Edward Stafford, is furious. He has complained to Compton and there has been a quarrel. The King has defended Compton.'

I press my lips together to prevent myself snapping out a criticism in my irritation. The Duke of Buckingham is one of the oldest friends of the Tudor family, with massive lands and many retainers. He greeted me with Prince Harry all those years ago, he is now honoured by the king, the greatest man in the land. He has been a good friend to me since then. Even when I was in disgrace I always had a smile and a kind word from him. Every summer he sent me a gift of game, and there were some weeks when that was the only meat we saw. Henry cannot quarrel with him as if he were a tradesman and Henry a surly farmer. This is the king and the greatest man of the state of England. The old king Henry could not even have won his throne without Buckingham's support. A disagreement between them is not a private matter, it is a national disaster. If Henry had any sense he would not have involved himself in this petty courtiers' quarrel. Lady Margaret nods at me, I need say nothing, she understands my disapproval.

'Can I not leave the court for a moment without my ladies climbing out of their bedroom windows to run after young men?'

She leans forwards and pats my hand. 'It seems not. It is a foolish young court, Your Grace, and they need you to keep them steady. The king has spoken very high words to the duke and the duke is much offended. William Compton says he will say nothing of the matter to anyone, so everyone thinks the worst. Anne has been all but imprisoned by her husband, Sir George, we none of us have seen her today. I am afraid that when you come out of your confinement he will not allow her to wait on you, and then your honour is involved.' She pauses. 'I thought you should know now rather than be surprised by it all tomorrow morning. Though it goes against the grain to be a tale-bearer of such folly.'

'It is ridiculous,' I say. 'I shall deal with it tomorrow, when I come out of confinement. But really, what are they all thinking of? This is *like a schoolyard! William should be ashamed of himself and I am surprised that Anne should so far forget herself as to chase after him. And what does her husband think he is? Some knight at Camelot to imprison her in a tower?'*

Queen Katherine came out of her confinement, without announcement, and returned to her usual rooms at Greenwich Palace. There could be no churching ceremony to mark her return to normal life, since there had been no birth. There could be no christening since there was no child. She came out of the shadowy room without comment, as if she had suffered some secret, shameful illness, and everyone pretended that she had been gone for hours rather than nearly three months.

Her ladies-in-waiting, who had become accustomed to an idle pace of life with the queen in her confinement, assembled at some speed in the queen's chambers, and the housemaids hurried in with fresh strewing herbs and new candles.

Katherine caught several furtive glances among the ladies and assumed that they too had guilty consciences over misbehaviour in her absence; but then she realised that there was a whispered buzz of conversation that ceased whenever she raised her head. Clearly, something had happened that was more serious than Anne's disgrace; and, equally clearly, no-one was telling her.

She beckoned one of her ladies, Lady Madge, to come to her side.

'Is Lady Elizabeth not joining us this morning?' she asked, as she could see no sign of the older Stafford sister.

The girl flushed scarlet to her ears. 'I don't know,' she stammered. 'I don't think so.'

'Where is she?' Katherine asked.

The girl looked desperately round for help but all the other ladies in the room were suddenly taking an intense interest in their sewing, in their embroidery, or in their books. Elizabeth Boleyn dealt a hand of cards with as much attention as if she had a fortune staked on it.

'I don't know where she is,' the girl confessed.

'In the ladies' room?' Katherine suggested. 'In the Duke of Buckingham's rooms?'

'I think she has gone,' the girl said baldly. At once someone gasped, and then there was silence.

'Gone?' Katherine looked around. 'Will someone tell me what is happening?' she asked, her tone reasonable enough. 'Where has Lady Elizabeth gone? And how can she have gone without my permission?'

The girl took a step back. At that moment, Lady Margaret Pole came into the room.

'Lady Margaret,' Katherine said pleasantly. 'Here is Madge telling me that Lady Elizabeth has left court without my permission and without bidding me farewell. What is happening?'

Katherine felt her amused smile freeze on her face when her old friend shook her head slightly, and Madge, relieved, dropped back to her seat. 'What is it?' Katherine asked more quietly.

Without seeming to move, all the ladies craned forwards to hear how Lady Margaret would explain the latest development.

'I believe the king and the Duke of Buckingham have had hard words,' Lady Margaret said smoothly. 'The duke has left court and taken both his sisters with him.'

'But they are my ladies-in-waiting. In service to me. They cannot leave without my permission.'

'It is very wrong of them, indeed,' Margaret said. Something in the way she folded her hands in her lap and looked so steadily and calmly warned Katherine not to probe.

'So what have you been doing in my absence?' Katherine turned to the ladies, trying to lighten the mood of the room.

At once they all looked sheepish. 'Have you learned any new songs? Have you danced in any masques?' Katherine asked.

'I know a new song,' one of the girls volunteered. 'Shall I sing it?'

Katherine nodded, at once one of the other women picked up a lute. It was as if everyone was quick to divert her. Katherine smiled and beat the time with her hand on the arm of her chair. She knew, as a woman who had been born and raised in a court of conspirators, that something was very wrong indeed.

There was the sound of company approaching and Katherine's guards threw open the door to the king and his court. The ladies stood up, shook out their skirts, bit their lips to make them pink, and sparkled in anticipation. Someone laughed gaily at nothing. Henry strode in, still in his riding clothes, his friends around him, William Compton's arm in his.

Katherine was again alert to some difference in her husband. He did not come in, take her in his arms, and kiss her cheeks. He did not stride into the very centre of the room and bow to her either. He came in, twinned with his best friend, the two almost hiding behind each other, like boys caught out in a petty crime: part-shame-faced, part-braggart. At Katherine's sharp look Compton awkwardly disengaged himself, Henry greeted his wife without enthusiasm, his eyes downcast, he took her hand and then kissed her cheek, not her mouth.

'Are you well now?' he asked.

'Yes,' she said calmly. 'I am quite well now. And how are you, sire?'

'Oh,' he said carelessly. 'I am well. We had such a chase this morning. I wish you had been with us. We were half way to Sussex, I do believe.'

'I shall come out tomorrow,' Katherine promised him.

'Will you be well enough?'

'I am quite well,' she repeated.

He looked relieved. 'I thought you would be ill for months,' he blurted out.

Smiling, she shook her head, wondering who had told him that.

'Let's break our fast,' he said. 'I am starving.'

He took her hand and led her to the great hall. The court fell in informally behind them. Katherine could hear the over-excited buzz of whispers. She leaned her head towards Henry so that no-one could catch her words. 'I hear there have been some quarrels in court.'

'Oh! You have heard of our little storm already, have you?' he said. He was far too loud, he was far too jovial. He was acting the part of a man with nothing to trouble his conscience. He threw a laugh over his shoulder and looked for someone to join in his forced amusement. Half a dozen men and women smiled, anxious to share his good humour. 'It is something and nothing. I have had a quarrel with your great friend, the Duke of Buckingham. He has left the court in a temper!' He laughed again, even more heartily, glancing at her sideways to see if she was smiling, trying to judge if she already knew all about it.

'Indeed?' Katherine said coolly.

'He was insulting,' Henry said, gathering his sense of offence. 'He can stay away until he is ready to apologise. He is such a pompous man, you know. Always thinks he knows everything. And his sour sister Elizabeth can go too.'

'She is a good lady-in-waiting and a kind companion to me,' Katherine observed. 'I expected her to greet me this day. I have no quarrel with her, nor with her sister Anne. I take it you have no quarrel with them either?'

'Nonetheless I am most displeased with their brother,' Henry said. 'They can all go.'

Katherine paused, took a breath. 'She and her sister are in my household,' she observed. 'I have the right to choose and dismiss my own ladies.'

She saw the quick flush of his childish temper. 'You will oblige me by sending them away from your household! Whatever your rights! I don't expect to hear talk of rights between us!'

The court behind them fell silent at once. Everyone wanted to hear the first royal quarrel.

Katherine released his hand and went around the high table to take her place. It gave her a moment to remind herself to be calm. When he came to his seat beside hers she took a breath and smiled at him. 'As you wish,' she said evenly. 'I have no great preference in the matter. But how am I to run a well-ordered court if I send away young women of good family who have done nothing wrong?'

'You were not here, so you have no idea what she did or didn't do!' Henry sought for another complaint and found one. He waved the court to sit and dropped into his own chair. 'You locked yourself away for months. What am I supposed to do without you? How are things supposed to be run if you just go away and leave everything?'

Katherine nodded, keeping her face absolutely serene. She was very well aware that the attention of the entire court was focused on her like a burning glass on fine paper. 'I hardly left for my own amusement,' she observed.

'It has been most awkward for me,' he said, taking her words at face value. 'Most awkward. It is all very well for you, taking to your bed for weeks at a time, but how is the court to run without a queen? Your ladies were without discipline, nobody knew how things were to go on, I couldn't see you, I had to sleep alone . . .' He broke off.

Katherine realised, belatedly, that his bluster was hiding a genuine sense of hurt. In his selfishness, he had transformed her long endurance of pain and fear into his own difficulty. He had managed to see her fruitless confinement as her wilfully deserting him, leaving him alone to rule over a lopsided court; in his eyes, she had let him down.

'I think at the very least you should do as I ask,' he said pettishly. 'I have had trouble enough these last months. All this reflects very badly on me, I have been made to look a fool. And no help from you at all.'

'Very well,' Katherine said peaceably. 'I shall send Elizabeth away and her sister Anne too, since you ask it of me. Of course.'

Henry found his smile, as if the sun was coming out from behind clouds. 'Yes. And now you are back we can get everything back to normal.'

Not a word for me, not one word of comfort, not one thought of under-standing. I could have died trying to bring his child into the world, without his child I have to face sorrow, grief and a haunting fear of sin. But he does not think of me at all.

I find a smile to reply to his. I knew when I married him that he was a selfish boy and I knew he would grow into a selfish man. I have set myself the task of guiding him and helping him to be a better man, the best man that he can be. There are bound to be times when I think he has failed to be the man he should be. And when those times come, as now, I must see it as my failure to guide him. I must forgive him.

Without my forgiveness, without me extending my patience further than I thought possible, our marriage will be a poorer one. He is always ready to resent a woman who cares for him – he learned that from his grandmother. And I, God forgive me, am too quick to think of the husband that I lost, and not of the husband that I won. He is not the man that Arthur was, and he will never be the king that Arthur would have been. But he is my husband and my king and I should respect him.

Indeed: I will respect him, whether he deserves it or not.

The court was subdued over breakfast, few of them could drag their eyes from the high table where, under the gold canopy of state, seated on their thrones, the king and queen exchanged conversation and seemed to be quite reconciled.

'But does she know?' one courtier whispered to one of Katherine's ladies.

'Who would tell her?' she replied. 'If Maria de Salinas and Lady Margaret have not told her already then she doesn't know. I would put my earrings on it.'

'Done,' he said. 'Ten shillings that she finds out.'

'By when?'

'Tomorrow,' he said.

I had another piece of the jigsaw when I came to look at the accounts for the weeks while I had been in confinement. In the first days that I had been away from court there had been no extraordinary expenses. But then the bill for amusements began to grow. There were bills from singers and actors to rehearse their celebration for the expected baby, bills from the organist, the choristers, from drapers for the material for pennants and standards, extra maids for polishing the gold christening bowl. Then there were payments for costumes of Lincoln green for disguising, singers to perform under the window of Lady Anne, a clerk to copy out the words of the king's new song, rehearsals for a new May Day masque with a dance, and costumes for three ladies with Lady Anne to play the part of Unattainable Beauty.

I rose from the table where I had been turning over the papers and went to the window to look down at the garden. They had set up a wrestling ring and the young men of the court were stripped to their shirtsleeves. Henry and Charles Brandon were gripped in each other's arms like blacksmiths at a fair. As I watched, Henry tripped his friend and threw him to the ground and then dropped his weight on him to hold him down. Princess Mary applauded, the court cheered.

I turned from the window. I began to wonder if Lady Anne had proved to be unattainable indeed. I wondered how merry they had been

on May Day morning when I had woken on my own, in sadness, to
silence, with no-one singing beneath my window. And why should the
court pay for singers, hired by Compton, to seduce his newest mistress?

The king summoned the queen to his rooms in the afternoon. Some messages had come from the Pope and he wanted her advice. Katherine sat beside him, listened to the report of the messenger and stretched up to whisper in her husband's ear.

He nodded. 'The queen reminds me of our well-known alliance with Venice,' he said pompously. 'And indeed, she has no need to remind me. I am not likely to forget it. You can depend on our determination to protect Venice and indeed all Italy against the ambitions of the French king.'

The ambassadors nodded respectfully. 'I shall send you a letter about this,' Henry said grandly. They bowed and withdrew.

'Will you write to them?' he asked Katherine.

She nodded. 'Of course,' she said. 'I thought that you handled that quite rightly.'

He smiled at her approval. 'It is so much better when you are here,' he said. 'Nothing goes on right when you are away.'

'Well, I am back now,' she said, putting a hand on his shoulder. She could feel the power of the muscle under her hand. Henry was a man now, with the strength of a man. 'Dearest, I am so sorry about your quarrel with the Duke of Buckingham.'

Under her hand she felt his shoulder hunch, he shrugged away her touch. 'It is nothing,' he said. 'He shall beg my pardon and it will be forgotten.'

'But perhaps he could just come back to court,' she said. 'Without his sisters if you don't want to see them . . .'

Inexplicably he barked out a laugh. 'Oh, bring them all back by all means,' he said. 'If that is your true wish, if you think it will bring you happiness. You should never have gone into confinement, there was no child, anyone could have seen that there would be no child.'

She was so taken aback that she could hardly speak. 'This is about my confinement?'

'It would hardly have happened without. But everyone could see there would be no child. It was wasted time.'

'Your own doctor . . .'

'What did he know? He only knows what you tell him.'

'He assured me . . .'

'Doctors know nothing!' he suddenly burst out. 'They are always guided by the woman; everyone knows that. And a woman can say anything. Is there a baby, isn't there a baby? Is she a virgin, isn't she a virgin? Only the woman knows and the rest of us are fooled.'

Katherine felt her mind racing, trying to trace what had offended him, what she could say. 'I trusted your doctor,' she said. 'He was very certain. He assured me I was with child and so I went into confinement. Another time I will know better. I am truly sorry, my love. It has been a very great grief to me.'

'It just makes me look such a fool!' he said plaintively. 'It's no wonder that I . . .'

'That you? What?'

'Nothing,' said Henry, sulkily.

'It is such a lovely afternoon, let us go for a walk,' I say pleasantly to my ladies. 'Lady Margaret will accompany me.'

We go outside, my cape is brought and put over my shoulders and my gloves. The path down to the river is wet and slippery and Lady Margaret takes my arm and we go down the steps together. The primroses are thick as churned butter in the hedgerows and the sun is out. There are white swans on the river but when the barges and wherries go by the birds drift out of the way as if by magic. I breathe deeply, it is so good to be out of that small room and to feel the sun on my face again that I hardly want to open the subject of Lady Anne.

'You must know what took place?' I say to her shortly.

'I know some gossip,' she says levelly. 'Nothing for certain.'

'What has angered the king so much?' I ask. 'He is upset about my confinement, he is angry with me. What is troubling him? Surely not the Stafford girl's flirtation with Compton?'

Lady Margaret's face is grave. 'The king is very attached to William Compton,' she said. 'He would not have him insulted.'

'It sounds as if all the insult is the other way,' I say. 'It is Lady Anne and her husband who are dishonoured. I would have thought the king would have been angry with William. Lady Anne is not a girl to tumble behind a wall. There is her family to consider and her husband's family. Surely the king should have told Compton to behave himself?'

Lady Margaret shrugs. 'I don't know,' she says. 'None of the girls will even talk to me. They are as silent as if it were a grave matter.'

'But why, if it was nothing more than a foolish affair? Youth calls to youth in springtime?'

She shakes her head. 'Truly, I don't know. You would think so. But if it is a flirtation, why would the duke be so very offended? Why quarrel with the king? Why would the girls not be laughing at Anne for getting caught?'

'And another thing . . .' I say.

She waits.

'Why should the king pay for Compton's courtship? The fee for the singers is in the court accounts.'

She frowned. 'Why would he encourage it? The king must have known that the duke would be greatly offended.'

'And Compton remains in high favour?'

'They are inseparable.'

I speak the thought that is sitting cold in my heart. 'So do you think that Compton is the shield and the love affair is between the king, my husband, and Lady Anne?'

Lady Margaret's grave face tells me that my guess is her own fear.
'I don't know,' she says, honest as ever. 'As I say, the girls tell me nothing,
and I have not asked anyone that question.'

'Because you think you will not like the answer?'

She nods. Slowly, I turn, and we walk back along the river in silence.

Katherine and Henry led the company into dinner in the grand hall and sat side by side under the gold canopy of state as they always did. There was a band of special singers that had come to England from the French court and they sang without instruments, very true to the note with a dozen different parts. It was complicated and beautiful and Henry was entranced by the music. When the singers paused, he applauded and asked them to repeat the song. They smiled at his enthusiasm, and sang again. He asked for it once more, and then sang the tenor line back to them: note perfect.

It was their turn to applaud him and they invited him to sing with them the part that he had learned so rapidly. Katherine, on her throne, leaned forwards and smiled as her handsome young husband sang in his clear young voice, and the ladies of the court clapped in appreciation.

When the musicians struck up and the court danced, Katherine came down from the raised platform of the high table and danced with Henry, her face bright with happiness and her smile warm. Henry, encouraged by her, danced like an Italian, with fast, dainty footwork and high leaps. Katherine clapped her hands in delight and called for another dance as if she had never had a moment's worry in her life. One of her ladies leaned towards the courtier who had taken the bet that Katherine would find out. 'I think I shall keep my earrings,' she said. 'He has fooled her. He has played her for a fool, and now he is fair game to any one of us. She has lost her hold on him.'

I wait till we are alone, and then I wait until he beds me with his eager joy, and then I slip from the bed and bring him a cup of small ale.

'So tell me the truth, Henry,' I say to him simply. 'What is the truth of the quarrel between you and the Duke of Buckingham, and what were your dealings with his sister?'

His swift sideways glance tells me more than any words. He is about to lie to me. I hear the words he says: a story about a disguising and all of them in masks and the ladies dancing with them and Compton and Anne dancing together, and I know that he is lying.

It is an experience more painful than I thought I could have with him. We have been married for nearly a year, a year next month, and always he has looked at me directly, with all his youth and honesty in his gaze. I have never heard anything but truth in his voice: boastfulness, certainly, the arrogance of a young man, but never this uncertain deceitful quaver. He is lying to me, and I would almost rather have a bare-faced confession of infidelity than to see him look at me, blue-eyed and sweet as a boy, with a parcel of lies in his mouth.

I stop him, I truly cannot bear to hear it. 'Enough,' I say. 'I know enough at least to realise that this is not true. She was your lover, wasn't she? And Compton was your friend and shield?'

His face is aghast. 'Katherine . . .'

'Just tell me the truth.'

His mouth is trembling. He cannot bear to admit what he has done. 'I didn't mean to . . .'

'I know that you did not,' I say. 'I am sure you were sorely tempted.'

'You were away for so long . . .'

'I know.'

A dreadful silence falls. I had thought that he would lie to me and I would track him down and then confront him with his lies and with his adultery and I would be a warrior queen in my righteous anger. But this is sadness and a taste of defeat. If Henry cannot remain faithful when I am in confinement with our child, our dearly needed child, then how shall he be faithful till death? How shall he obey his vow to forsake all others when he can be distracted so easily? What am I to do, what can any woman do, when her husband is such a fool as to desire a woman for a moment, rather than the woman he is pledged to for eternity?

'Dear husband, this is very wrong,' I say sadly.

'It was because I had such doubts. I thought for a moment that we were not married,' he confesses.

'You forgot we were married?' I ask incredulously.

'No!' His head comes up, his blue eyes are filled with unshed tears. His face shines with contrition. 'I thought that since our marriage was not valid, I need not abide by it.'

I am quite amazed by him. 'Our marriage? Why would it not be valid?'

He shakes his head. He is too ashamed to speak. I press him. 'Why not?'

He kneels beside my bed and hides his face in the sheets. 'I liked her and I desired her and she said some things which made me feel . . .'

'Feel what?'

'Made me think . . .'

'Think what?'

'What if you were not a virgin when I married you?'

At once I am alert, like a villain near the scene of a crime, like a murderer when the corpse bleeds at the sight of him. 'What do you mean?'

'She was a virgin . . .'

'Anne?'

'Yes. Sir George is impotent. Everyone knows that.'

'Do they?'

'Yes. So she was a virgin. And she was not . . .' He rubs his face against the sheet of our bed. 'She was not like you. She . . .' He stumbles for words. 'She cried out in pain. She bled, I was afraid when I saw how much blood, really a lot . . .' He breaks off again. 'She could not go on, the first time. I had to stop. She cried, I held her. She was a virgin. That is what it is like to lie with a virgin, the first time. I was her first love. I could tell. Her first love.'

There is a long, cold silence.

'She fooled you,' I say cruelly, throwing away her reputation, and his tenderness for her, with one sweep, making her a whore and him a fool, for the greater good.

He looks up, shocked. 'She did?'

'She was not that badly hurt, she was pretending.' I shake my head at the sinfulness of young women. 'It is an old trick. She will have had a bladder of blood in her hand and broke it to give you a show of blood. She will have cried out. I expect she whimpered and said she could not bear the pain from the very beginning.'

Henry is amazed. 'She did.'

'She thought to make you feel sorry for her.'

'But I was!'

'Of course. She thought to make you feel that you had taken her virginity, her maidenhead, and that you owe her your protection.'

'That is what she said!'

'She tried to entrap you,' I say. 'She was not a virgin, she was acting the part of one. I was a virgin when I came to your bed and the first night that we were lovers was very simple and sweet. Do you remember?'

'Yes,' he says.

'There was no crying and wailing like players on a stage. It was quiet and loving. Take that as your benchmark,' I say. 'I was a true virgin. You and I were each other's first love. We had no need for play-acting and exaggeration. Hold to that truth of our love, Henry. You have been fooled by a counterfeit.'

'She said . . .' he begins.

'She said what?' I am not afraid. I am filled with utter determination

406

that Anne Stafford will not put asunder what God and my mother have joined together.

'She said that you must have been Arthur's lover.' He stumbles before the white fierceness of my face. 'That you had lain with him, and that . . .'

'Not true.'

'I didn't know.'

'It is not true.'

'Oh, yes.'

'My marriage with Arthur was not consummated. I came to you a virgin. You were my first love. Does anyone dare say different to me?'

'No,' he says rapidly. 'No. No-one shall say different to you.'

'Nor to you.'

'Nor to me.'

'Would anyone dare to say to my face that I am not your first love, a virgin untouched, your true wedded wife, and Queen of England?'

'No,' he says again.

'Not even you.'

'No.'

'It is to dishonour me,' I say furiously. 'And where will scandal stop? Shall they suggest that you have no claim to the throne because your mother was no virgin on her wedding day?'

He is stunned with shock. 'My mother? What of my mother?'

'They say that she lay with her uncle, Richard the usurper,' I say flatly. 'Think of that! And they say that she lay with your father before they were married, before they were even betrothed. They say that she was far from a virgin on her wedding day when she wore her hair loose and went in white. They say she was dishonoured twice over, little more than a harlot for the throne. Do we allow people to say such things of a queen? Are you to be disinherited by such gossip? Am I? Is our son?'

Henry is gasping with shock. He loved his mother and he had never thought of her as a sexual being before. 'She would never have . . . she was a most . . . how can . . .'

'You see? This is what happens if we allow people to gossip about their betters.' I lay down the law which will protect me. 'If you allow someone to dishonour me, there is no stopping the scandal. It insults me, but it threatens you. Who knows where scandal will stop once it takes hold? Scandal against the queen rocks the throne itself. Be warned, Henry.'

'She said it!' he exclaims. 'Anne said that it was no sin for me to lie with her because I was not truly married!'

'She lied to you,' I say. 'She pretended to her virgin state and she traduced me.'

His face flushes red with anger. It is a relief to him to turn to rage. 'What a whore!' he exclaims crudely. 'What a whore to trick me into thinking . . . what a jade's trick!'

'You cannot trust young women,' I say quietly. 'Now that you are King of England you will have to be on your guard, my love. They will run after you and they will try to charm you and seduce you, but you have to be faithful to me. I was your virgin bride, I was your first love. I am your wife. Do not forsake me.'

He takes me into his arms. 'Forgive me,' he whispers brokenly.

'We will never ever speak of this again,' I say solemnly. 'I will not have it, and I will not allow anyone to dishonour either me or your mother.'

'No,' he says fervently. 'Before God. We will never speak of this nor allow any other to speak of it again.'

Next morning Henry and Katherine rose up together and went quietly to Mass in the king's chapel. Katherine met with her confessor and kneeled to confess her sins. She did not take very long, Henry observed, she must have no great sins to confess. It made him feel even worse to see her go to her priest for a brief confession and come away with her face so serene. He knew that she was a woman of holy purity, just like his mother. Penitently, his face in his hands, he thought that not only had Katherine never been unfaithful to her given word, she had probably never even told a lie in her life.

I go out with the court to hunt dressed in a red velvet gown, determined to show that I am well, that I am returned to the court, that everything will be as it was before. We have a long, hard run after a fine stag who takes a looping route around the great park and the hounds bring him down in the stream and Henry himself goes into the water, laughing, to cut his throat. The stream blooms red around him and stains his clothes, and his hands. I laugh with the court but the sight of the blood makes me feel sick to my very belly.

We ride home slowly, I keep my face locked in a smile to hide my weariness and the pain in my thighs, in my belly, in my back. Lady Margaret brings her horse beside mine, and glances at me. 'You had better rest this afternoon.'

'I cannot,' I say shortly.

She does not need to ask why. She has been a princess, she knows that a queen has to be on show, whatever her own feelings. 'I have the story, if you want to trouble yourself to hear such a thing.'

'You are a good friend,' I say. 'Tell me briefly. I think I know the worst that it can be already.'

'After we had gone in for your confinement the king and the young men started to go into the City in the evenings.'

'With guards?'

'No, alone and disguised.'

I stifle a sigh. 'Did no-one try to stop him?'

'The Earl of Surrey, God bless him. But his own sons were of the party and it was light-hearted fun, and you know that the king will not be denied his pastimes.'

I nod.

'One evening they came into court in their disguises and pretended to be London merchants. The ladies danced with them, it was all very amusing. I was not there that evening, I was with you in confinement; someone told me about it the next day. I took no notice. But apparently one of the merchants singled out Lady Anne and danced with her all night.'

'Henry,' I say, and I can hear the bitterness in my own whisper.

'Yes, but everyone thought it was William Compton. They are about the same height, and they were all wearing false beards and hats. You know how they do.'

'Yes,' I say. 'I know how they do.'

'Apparently they made an assignation and when the duke thought that his sister was sitting with you in the evenings she was slipping away and meeting the king. When she went missing all night, it was too much for her sister. Elizabeth went to her brother and warned him of what Anne was doing. They told her husband and all of them confronted Anne and demanded to know who she was seeing, and she said it was Compton. But when she was missing, and they thought she was with her lover, they met Compton. So then they knew, it was not Compton, it was the king.'

I shake my head.

'I am sorry, my dear,' Lady Margaret says to me gently. 'He is a young man. I am sure it is no more than vanity and thoughtlessness.'

I nod and say nothing. I check my horse, who is tossing his head against my hands, which are too heavy on the reins. I am thinking of Anne crying out in pain as her hymen was broken.

'And is her husband, Sir George, unmanned?' *I ask.* 'Was she a virgin until now?'

'So they say,' Lady Margaret replies drily. 'Who knows what goes on in a bedroom?'

'I think we know what goes on in the king's bedroom,' *I say bitterly.* 'They have hardly been discreet.'

'It is the way of the world,' she says quietly. 'When you are confined it is only natural that he will take a lover.'

I nod again. This is nothing but the truth. What is surprising to me is that I should feel such hurt.

'The duke must have been much aggrieved,' I say, thinking of the dignity of the man, and how it was he who put the Tudors on the throne in the first place.

'Yes,' she says. She hesitates. Something about her voice warns me that there is something she is not sure if she should say.

'What is it, Margaret?' I ask. 'I know you well enough to know that there is something more.'

'It is something that Elizabeth said to one of the girls before she left,' she says.

'Oh?'

'Elizabeth says that her sister did not think it was a light love affair that would last while you were in confinement and then be forgotten.'

'What else could it be?'

'She thought that her sister had ambitions.'

'Ambitions for what?'

'She thought that she might take the king's fancy and hold him.'

'For a season,' I say disparagingly.

'No, for longer,' she says. 'He spoke of love. He is a romantic young man. He spoke of being hers till death.' She sees the look on my face and breaks off. 'Forgive me, I should have said none of this.'

I think of Anne Stafford crying out in pain and telling him that she was a virgin, a true virgin, in too much pain to go on. That he was her first love, her only love. I know how much he would like that.

I check my horse again, he frets against the bit. 'What do you mean, she was ambitious?'

'I think she thought that given her family position, and the liking that was between her and the king, that she could become the great mistress of the English court.'

I blink. 'And what about me?'

'I think she thought that, in time, he might turn from you to her. I think she hoped to supplant you in his love.'

I nod. 'And if I died bearing his child, I suppose she thought she would have her empty marriage annulled and marry him?'

'That would be the very cusp of her ambition,' Lady Margaret says. 'And stranger things have happened. Elizabeth Woodville got to the throne of England on looks alone.'

'Anne Stafford was my lady-in-waiting,' I say. 'I chose her for the honour over many others. What about her duty to me? What about her friendship with me? Did she never think of me? If she had served me in Spain we would have lived night and day together . . .' I break off, there is no way to explain the safety and affection of the harem to a woman who has always lived her life alert to the gaze of men.

Lady Margaret shakes her head. 'Women are always rivals,' she says simply. 'But until now everyone has thought that the king only had eyes for you. Now everyone knows different. There is not a pretty girl in the land who does not now think that the crown is for taking.'

'It is still my crown,' I point out.

'But girls will hope for it,' she says. 'It is the way of the world.'

'They will have to wait for my death,' I say bleakly. 'That could be a long wait even for the most ambitious girl.'

Lady Margaret nods. I indicate behind me and she looks back. The ladies-in-waiting are scattered among the huntsmen and courtiers, riding and laughing and flirting. Henry has Princess Mary on one side of him and one of her ladies-in-waiting on another. She is a new girl to court, young and pretty. A virgin, without doubt, another pretty virgin.

'And which of these will be next?' I ask bitterly. 'When I next go in for my confinement and cannot watch them like a fierce hawk? Will it be a Percy girl? Or a Seymour? Or a Howard? Or a Neville? Which girl will step up to the king next and try to charm her way into his bed and into my place?'

'Some of your ladies love you dearly,' she says.

412

'And some of them will use their position at my side to get close to the king,' I say. 'Now they have seen it done they will be waiting for their chance. They will know that the easiest route to the king is to come into my rooms, to pretend to be my friend, to offer me service. First she will pretend friendship and loyalty to me and all the time she will watch for her chance. I can know that one will do it, but I cannot know which one she is.'

Lady Margaret leans forward, and strokes her horse's neck, her face grave. 'Yes,' she agrees.

'And one of them, one of the many, will be clever enough to turn the king's head,' I say bitterly. 'He is young and vain and easily misled. Sooner or later, one of them will turn him against me and want my place.'

Lady Margaret straightens up and looks directly at me, her grey eyes as honest as ever. 'This may all be true; but I think you can do nothing to prevent it.'

'I know,' I say grimly.

'I have good news for you,' Katherine said to Henry. They had thrown open the windows of her bedroom to let in the cooler night air. It was a warm night in late May and for once, Henry had chosen to come to bed early.

'Tell me some good news,' he said. 'My horse went lame today, and I cannot ride him tomorrow. I would welcome some good news.'

'I think I am with child.'

He bounced up in the bed. 'You are?'

'I think so,' she said, smiling.

'Praise God! You are?'

'I am certain of it.'

'God be praised. I shall go to Walsingham the minute you give birth to our son. I shall go on my knees to Walsingham! I shall crawl

413

along the road! I shall wear a suit of pure white. I shall give Our Lady pearls.'

'Our Lady has been gracious to us indeed.'

'And how potent they will all know that I am now! Out of confinement in the first week of May and pregnant by the end of the month. That will show them! That will prove that I am a husband indeed.'

'Indeed it will,' she said levelly.

'It is not too early to be sure?'

'I have missed my course, and I am sick in the morning. They tell me it is a certain sign.'

'And you are certain?' He had no tact to phrase his anxiety in gentle words. 'You are certain this time? You know that there can be no mistake?'

She nodded. 'I am certain. I have all the signs.'

'God be praised. I knew it would come. I knew that a marriage made in heaven would be blessed.'

Katherine nodded. Smiling.

'We shall go slowly on our progress, you shall not hunt. We shall go by boat for some of the way, barges.'

'I think I will not travel at all, if you will allow it,' she said. 'I want to stay quietly in one place this summer, I don't even want to ride in a litter.'

'Well, I shall go on progress with the court and then come home to you,' he said. 'And what a celebration we shall have when our baby is born. When will it be?'

'After Christmas,' Katherine said. 'In the New Year.'

Winter 1510

I should have been a soothsayer, I have proved to be so accurate with my prediction, even without a Moorish abacus. We are holding the Christmas feast at Richmond and the court is joyful in my happiness. The baby is big in my belly, and he kicks so hard that Henry can put his hand on me and feel the little heel thud out against his hand. There is no doubt that he is alive and strong, and his vitality brings joy to the whole court. When I sit in council, I sometimes wince at the strange sensation of him moving inside me, the pressure of his body against my own, and some of the old councillors laugh – having seen their own wives in the same state – for joy that there is to be an heir for England and Spain at last.

I pray for a boy but I do not expect one. A child for England, a child for Arthur, is all I want. If it is the daughter that he had wanted, then I will call her Mary as he asked.

Henry's desire for a son, and his love for me, has made him more thoughtful at last. He takes care of me in ways that he has never done before. I think he is growing up, the selfish boy is becoming a good man at last, and the fear that has haunted me since his affair with the Stafford girl is receding. Perhaps he will take lovers as kings always do, but perhaps he will resist falling in love with them and making the wild promises that a man can make but a king must not. Perhaps he will acquire the good sense that so many men seem to learn: to enjoy a new woman but remain constant, in their hearts, to their wife. Certainly, if he continues to be this sweet-natured, he will make a good father. I think of him teaching our son to ride, to hunt, to joust. No boy could have a better father for sports and pastimes than a son of Henry's. Not even Arthur would have made a more playful father. Our boy's education, his skill in court life, his upbringing as a Christian, his training as a ruler, these are the things that I will teach him. He will learn my mother's courage and my father's skills, and from me – I think I can teach him constancy, determination. These are my gifts now.

I believe that between Henry and me, we will raise a prince who will make his mark in Europe, who will keep England safe from the Moors, from the French, from the Scots, from all our enemies.

I will have to go into confinement again but I leave it as late as I dare. Henry swears to me that there will be no other while I am confined, that he is mine, all mine. I leave it till the evening of the Christmas feast and then I take my spiced wine with the members of my court and bid them merry Christmas as they bid me God speed, and I go once more into the quietness of my bedroom.

In truth, I don't mind missing the dancing and the heavy drinking. I am tired, this baby is a weight to carry. I rise and then rest with the winter sun, rarely waking much before nine of the morning, and ready to sleep at five in the afternoon. I spend much time praying for a safe delivery, and for the health of the child that moves so strongly inside me.

Henry comes to see me, privately, most days. The Royal Book is clear that the queen should be in absolute isolation before the birth of her child; but the Royal Book was written by Henry's grandmother and I suggest that we can please ourselves. I don't see why she should command me from beyond the grave when she was such an unhelpful mentor in life. Besides, to put it as bluntly as an Aragonese: I don't trust Henry on his own in court. On New Year's Eve he dines with me before going to the hall for the great feast, and brings me a gift of rubies, with stones as big as Cristóbal Colón's haul. I put them around my neck and see his eyes darken with desire for me as they gleam on the plump whiteness of my breasts.

'Not long now,' I say, smiling; I know exactly what he is thinking.

'I shall go to Walsingham as soon as our child is born, and when I come back you will be churched,' he says.

'And then, I suppose you will want to make another baby,' I say with mock weariness.

'I will,' he says, his face bright with laughter.

He kisses me goodnight, wishes me joy of the new year and then goes out of the hidden door in my chamber to his own rooms, and from there to the feast. I tell them to bring the boiled water that I still drink in obedience to the Moor's advice, and then I sit before the fire sewing the tiniest little gown for my baby, while Maria de Salinas reads in Spanish to me.

Suddenly, it is as if my whole belly has turned over, as if I am falling from a great height. The pain is so thorough, so unlike anything I have ever known before, that the sewing drops from my hands and I grip the arms of my chair and let out a gasp before I can say a word. I know at once that the baby is coming. I had been afraid that I would not know what was happening, that it would be a pain like that when I lost my poor girl. But this is like the great force of a deep river, this feels like something powerful and wonderful starting to flow. I am filled with joy and a holy terror. I know that the baby is coming and that he is strong, and that I am young, and that everything will be all right.

As soon as I tell the ladies, the chamber bursts into uproar. My Lady the King's Mother might have ruled that the whole thing shall be done soberly and quietly with the cradle made ready and two beds made up for the mother, one to give birth in and one to rest in; but in real life, the ladies run around like hens in a poultry yard, squawking in alarm. The midwives are summoned from the hall, they have gone off to make merry, gambling that they would not be needed on New Year's Eve. One of them is quite tipsy and Maria de Salinas throws her out of the room

417

before she falls over and breaks something. The physician cannot be found at all, and pages are sent running all over the palace looking for him.

The only ones who are settled and determined are Lady Margaret Pole, Maria de Salinas, and I. Maria, because she is naturally disposed to calm, Lady Margaret, because she has been confident from the start of this confinement, and I, because I can feel that nothing will stop this baby coming, and I might as well grab hold of the rope in one hand, my relic of the Virgin Mother in the other, fix my eyes on the little altar in the corner of the room and pray to St Margaret of Antioch to give me a swift and easy delivery and a healthy baby.

Unbelievably, it is little more than six hours – though one of those hours lingers on for at least a day – and then there is a rush and a slither, and the midwife mutters 'God be praised!' quietly and then there is a loud, irritable cry, almost a shout, and I realise that this is a new voice in the room, that of my baby.

'A boy, God be praised, a boy,' the midwife says and Maria looks up at me and sees me radiant with joy.

'Really?' I demand. 'Let me see him!'

They cut the cord and pass him up to me, still naked, still bloody, his little mouth opened wide to shout, his eyes squeezed tight in anger, Henry's son.

'My son,' I whisper.

'England's son,' the midwife says. 'God be praised.'

I put my face down to his warm little head, still sticky, I sniff him like a cat sniffs her kittens. 'This is our boy,' I whisper to Arthur, who is so close at that moment that it is almost as if he is at my side, looking over my shoulder at this tiny miracle, who turns his head and nuzzles at my breast, little mouth gaping. 'Oh, Arthur, my love, this is the boy I promised I would bear for you and for England. This is our son for England, and he will be king.'

418

Spring 1511

1st January 1511

The whole of England went mad when they learned on New Year's Day that a boy had been born. Everyone called him Prince Henry at once, there was no other name possible. In the streets they roasted oxen and drank themselves into a stupor. In the country they rang the church bells and broke into the church ales to toast the health of the Tudor heir, the boy who would keep England at peace, who would keep England allied with Spain, who would protect England from her enemies and who would defeat the Scots once and for all.

Henry came in to see his son, disobeying the rules of confinement, tiptoeing carefully, as if his footstep might shake the room. He peered into the cradle, afraid almost to breathe near the sleeping boy.

'He is so small,' he said. 'How can he be so small?'

'The midwife says he is big and strong,' Katherine corrected him, instantly on the defence of her baby.

'I am sure. It is just that his hands are so . . . and look, he has fingernails! Real fingernails!'

'He has toenails too,' she said. The two of them stood side by side and looked down in amazement at the perfection that they had made together. 'He has little plump feet and the tiniest toes you can imagine.'

'Show me,' he said.

Gently, she pulled off the little silk shoes that the baby wore. 'There,' she said, her voice filled with tenderness. 'Now I must put this back on so that he does not get cold.'

Henry bent over the crib, and tenderly took the tiny foot in his big hand. 'My son,' he said wonderingly. 'God be praised, I have a son.'

I lie on my bed as the old king's mother commanded in the Royal Book, and I receive honoured guests. I have to hide a smile when I think of my mother giving birth to me on campaign, in a tent, like any soldier's doxy. But this is the English way and I am an English queen and this baby will be King of England.

I've never known such simple joy. When I doze I wake with my heart filled with delight, before I even know why. Then I remember. I have a son for England, for Arthur and for Henry; and I smile and turn my head, and whoever is watching over me answers the question before I have asked it: 'Yes, your son is well, Your Grace.'

Henry is excessively busy with the care of our son. He comes in and out to see me twenty times a day with questions and with news of the arrangements he has made. He has appointed a household of no less than forty people for this tiny baby, and already chosen his rooms in the Palace of Westminster for his council chamber when he is a young man. I smile, and say nothing. Henry is planning the greatest christening that has ever been seen in England, nothing is too good for this Henry who will be Henry the Ninth. Sometimes when I am sitting on my bed, supposed to be writing letters, I draw his monogram. Henry IX: my son, the King of England.

His sponsors are carefully chosen: the daughter of the emperor, Margaret of Austria, and King Louis the Twelfth of France. So he is working already, this little Tudor, to cloud the French suspicion against us, to maintain our alliance with the Hapsburg family. When they bring him to me and I put my finger in the palm of his tiny hand, his fingers curl around, as if to grip on. As if he would hold my hand. As if he might love me in return. I lie quietly, watching him sleep, my finger against his little palm, the other hand cupped over his tender little head where I can feel a steady pulse throbbing.

His godparents are Archbishop Warham, my dear and true friend Thomas Howard, Earl of Surrey, and the Earl and Countess of Devon. My dearest Lady Margaret is to run his nursery at Richmond. It is the newest and cleanest of all the palaces near London, and wherever we are, whether at Whitehall or Greenwich or Westminster, it will be easy for me to visit him.

I can hardly bear to let him go away, but it is better for him to be in the country than in the City. And I shall see him every week at the very least, Henry has promised me that I shall see him every week.

Henry went to the shrine of Our Lady at Walsingham, as he had promised, and Katherine asked him to tell the nuns who kept the shrine that she would come herself when she was next with child. When the next baby was in the queen's womb she would give thanks for the safe birth of the first; and pray for the safe delivery of a second. She asked the king to tell the nuns that she would come to them every time she was with child, and that she hoped to visit them many times.

She gave him a heavy purse of gold. 'Will you give them this, from me, and ask them for their prayers?'

He took it. 'They pray for the Queen of England as their duty,' he said.

'I want to remind them.'

Henry returned to court for the greatest tournament that England had ever seen, and Katherine was up and out of her bed to organise it for him. He had commissioned new armour before he went away and she had commanded her favourite, Edward Howard, the talented younger son of the Howard house, to make sure that it would fit precisely to the slim young king's measurements, and that the workmanship was perfect. She had banners made, and tapestries hung, masques prepared with glorious themes, gold everywhere: cloth of gold banners and curtains, and swathes of cloth, gold plates and gold cups, gold tips to the ornamental lances, gold-embossed shields, even gold on the king's saddlery.

'This will be the greatest tournament that England has ever seen,' Edward Howard said to her. 'English chivalry and Spanish elegance. It will be a thing of beauty.'

'It is the greatest celebration that we have ever had,' she said, smiling. 'For the greatest reason.'

I know I have made an outstanding showcase for Henry but when he rides into the tiltyard I catch my breath. It is the fashion that the knights who have come to joust choose a motto; sometimes they even compose a poem or play a part in a tableau before they ride. Henry has kept his motto a secret, and not told me what it is going to be. He has commissioned his own banner and the women have hidden from me, with much laughter, while they embroider his words on the banner of Tudor green silk. I truly have no idea what it will say until he bows before me in the royal box, the banner unfurls and his herald shouts out his title for the joust: 'Sir Loyal Heart'.

I rise to my feet and clasp my hands before my face to hide my trembling mouth. My eyes fill with tears, I cannot help it. He has called himself 'Sir Loyal Heart' – he has declared to the world the restoration of his devotion and love for me. My women step back so that I can see the canopy that he has commanded them to hang all around the royal box. He has had it pinned all over with little gold badges of H and K entwined. Everywhere I look, at every corner of the jousting green, on every banner, on every post there are Ks and Hs together. He has used this great joust, the finest and richest that England has ever seen, to tell the world that he loves me, that he is mine, that his heart is mine and that it is a loyal heart.

I look around at my ladies-in-waiting and I am utterly triumphant. If I could speak freely I would say to them: 'There! Take this as your warning. He is not the man that you have thought him. He is not a man to turn from his true-married wife. He is not a man that you can seduce, however clever your tricks, however insidious your whispers against me. He has given his heart to me, and he has a loyal heart.' I run my eyes over them, the prettiest girls from the greatest families of England, and I know that every one of them secretly thinks that she could have my place. If she were to be lucky, if the king were to be seduced, if I were to die, she could have my throne.

But his banner tells them 'Not so.' His banner tells them, the gold Ks and Hs tell them, the herald's cry tells them that he is all mine, forever. The will of my mother, my word to Arthur, the destiny given by God to England has brought me finally to this: a son and heir in England's cradle, the King of England publicly declaring his passion for me, and my initial twined with his in gold everywhere I look.

I touch my hand to my lips and hold it out to him. His visor is up, his blue eyes are blazing with passion for me. His love for me warms me like the hot sun of my childhood. I am a woman blessed by God, especially favoured by Him, indeed. I survived widowhood and my despair at the loss of Arthur. The courtship of the old king did not seduce me, his enmity did not defeat me, the hatred of his mother did not destroy me. The love of Henry delights me but does not redeem me. With God's especial favour, I have saved myself. I myself have come from the darkness of poverty into the glamour of the light. I myself have fought that terrible slide into blank despair. I myself have made myself into a woman who can face death and face life and endure them both.

I remember once when I was a little girl, my mother was praying before a battle and then she rose up from her knees, kissed the little ivory cross, put it back on its stand and gestured for her lady-in-waiting to bring her breastplate and buckle it on.

I ran forwards and begged her not to go, and I asked her why she must ride, if God gives us His blessing? If we are blessed by God, why do we have to fight as well? Will He not just drive away the Moors for us?

'I am blessed because I am chosen to do His work.' She kneeled down and put her arm around me. 'You might say, why not leave it to God and he will send a thunderstorm over the wicked Moors?'

I nodded.

'I am the thunderstorm,' she said, smiling. 'I am God's thunderstorm to drive them away. He has not chosen a thunderstorm today, He has chosen me. And neither I nor the dark clouds can refuse our duty.'

I smile at Henry as he drops his visor and turns his horse from the royal box. I understand now what my mother meant by being God's thunderstorm. God has called me to be his sunshine in England. It is my God-given duty to bring happiness and prosperity and security to England. I do this by leading the king in the right choices, by securing the succession, and by protecting the safety of the borders. I am England's queen chosen by God and I smile on Henry as his big glossy black horse trots slowly to the end of the lists, and I smile on the people of London who call out my name and shout 'God bless Queen Katherine!' and I smile to myself because I am doing as my mother wished, as God decreed, and Arthur is waiting for me in al-Yanna, the garden.

22nd February 1511

Ten days later, when she was at the height of her happiness, they brought to Queen Katherine the worst news of her life.

It is worse even than the death of my husband, Arthur. I had not thought there could be anything worse than that; but so it proves. It is worse than my years of widowhood and waiting. It is worse than hearing from Spain that my mother was dead, that she died on the day I wrote to her, begging her to send me a word. Worse than the worst days I have ever had.

My baby is dead. More than this, I cannot say, I cannot even hear. I think Henry is here, some of the time; and Maria de Salinas. I think Margaret Pole is here, and I see the stricken face of Thomas Howard at Henry's shoulder; William Compton desperately gripping Henry's shoulder; but the faces all swim before my eyes and I can be sure of nothing.

I go into my room and I order them to close the shutters and bolt the doors. But it is too late. They have already brought me the worst news of my life; closing the door will not keep it out. I cannot bear the light. I cannot bear the sound of ordinary life going on. I hear a page boy laugh in the garden near my window and I cannot understand how there can be any joy or gladness left in the world, now that my baby has gone.

And now the courage I have held on to, for all my life, turns out to be a thread, a spider-web, a nothing. My bright confidence that I am walking in the way of God and that He will protect me is nothing more than an illusion, a child's fairy story. In the shadows of my room I plunge deep into the darkness that my mother knew when she lost her son, that Juana could not escape when she lost her husband, that was the curse of my grandmother, that runs through the women of my family like a dark vein. I am no different after all. I am not a woman who can survive love and loss, as I had thought. It has only been that, so far, I have never lost someone who was worth more than life itself to me. When Arthur died my heart was broken. But now that my baby is dead, I want nothing but that my heart should cease to beat.

I cannot think of any reason why I should live and that innocent, sinless babe be taken from me. I can see no reason for it. I cannot understand a God who can take him from me. I cannot understand a world that can be so cruel. In the moment that they told me, 'Your Grace, be brave, we have bad news of the prince,' I lost my faith in God. I lost my desire to live. I lost even my ambition to rule England and keep my country safe.

He had blue eyes and the smallest, most perfect hands. He had finger-nails like little shells. His little feet . . . his little feet . . .

Lady Margaret Pole, who had been in charge of the dead child's nursery, came into the room without knocking, without invitation, and knelt before Queen Katherine, who sat on her chair by the fire, among her ladies, seeing nothing and hearing nothing.

'I have come to beg your pardon though I did nothing wrong,' she said steadily.

Katherine raised her head from her hand. 'What?'

'Your baby died in my care. I have come to beg your pardon. I was not remiss, I swear it. But he is dead. Princess, I am sorry.'

'You are always here,' Katherine said with quiet dislike. 'In my darkest moments, you are always at my side, like bad luck.'

The older woman flinched. 'Indeed, but it is not my wish.'

'And don't call me "Princess".'

'I forgot.'

For the first time in weeks Katherine sat up and looked into the face of another person, saw her eyes, saw the new lines around her mouth, realised that the loss of her baby was not her grief alone. 'Oh God, Margaret,' she said, and pitched forwards.

Margaret Pole caught her and held her. 'Oh God, Katherine,' she said into the queen's hair.

'How could we lose him?'

'God's will. God's will. We have to believe it. We have to bow beneath it.'

'But why?'

'Princess, no-one knows why one is taken and another spared. D'you remember?'

She felt from the shudder that the woman remembered the loss of her husband in this, the loss of her son.

'I never forget. Every day. But why?'

'It is God's will,' Lady Margaret repeated.

'I don't think I can bear it.' Katherine breathed so softly that none of her ladies could hear. She raised her tearstained face from her friend's shoulder. 'To lose Arthur felt like torture, but to lose my baby is like death itself. I don't think I can bear it, Margaret.'

The older woman's smile was infinitely patient. 'Oh, Katherine. You will learn to bear it. There is nothing that anyone can do but bear it. You can rage or you can weep but in the end, you will learn to bear it.'

Slowly Katherine sat back on her chair; Margaret remained, with easy grace, kneeling on the floor at her feet, handclasped with her friend.

'You will have to teach me courage all over again,' Katherine whispered.

The older woman shook her head. 'You only have to learn it once,' she said. 'You know, you learned at Ludlow; you are not a woman

427

to be destroyed by sorrow. You will grieve but you will live, you will come out into the world again. You will love. You will conceive another child, this child will live, you will learn again to be happy.'

'I cannot see it,' Katherine said desolately.

'It will come.'

The battle that Katherine had waited for, for so long, came while she was still overshadowed with grief for her baby. But nothing could penetrate her sadness.

'Great news, the best news in the world!' wrote her father. Wearily, Katherine translated from the code and then from Spanish to English. 'I am to lead a crusade against the Moors in Africa. Their existence is a danger to Christendom, their raids terrify the whole of the Mediterranean and endanger shipping from Greece to the Atlantic. Send me the best of your knights – you who claim to be the new Camelot. Send me your most courageous leaders at the head of your most powerful men and I shall take them to Africa and we will destroy the infidel kingdoms as holy Christian kings.'

Wearily, Katherine took the translated letter to Henry. He was coming off the tennis court, a napkin twisted around his neck, his face flushed. He beamed when he saw her, then at once his look of joy was wiped from his face by a grimace of guilt, like a boy caught out in a forbidden pleasure. At that fleeting expression, at that brief, betraying moment, she knew he had forgotten that their son was dead. He was playing tennis with his friends, he had won, he saw the wife he still loved, he was happy. Joy came as easily to the men of his family as sorrow to the women of hers. She felt a wave of hatred wash over her, so powerful that she could almost taste it in her mouth. He could forget, even for a moment, that their little boy had died. She thought that she would never forget; never.

'I have a letter from my father,' she said, trying to put some interest into her harsh voice.

'Oh?' He was all concern. He came towards her and took her arm. She gritted her teeth so that she did not scream: 'Don't touch me!'

'Did he tell you to have courage? Did he write comforting words?'

The clumsiness of the young man was unbearable. She summoned her most tolerant smile. 'No. It is not a personal letter. You know he rarely writes to me in that way. It is a letter about a crusade. He invites our noblemen and lords to raise regiments and go with him against the Moors.'

'Does he? Oh, does he? What a chance!'

'Not for you,' she said, quelling any idea that Henry might have that he could go to war when they had no son. 'It is just a little expedition. But my father would welcome English men, and I think they should go.'

'I should think he would.' Henry turned and shouted for his friends, who were hanging back like guilty schoolboys caught having fun. They could not bear to see Katherine since she had become so pale and quiet. They liked her when she was the queen of the joust and Henry was Sir Loyal Heart. She made them uncomfortable when she came to dinner like a ghost, ate nothing, and left early.

'Hey! Anyone want to go to war against the Moors?'

A chorus of excited yells answered his holloa. Katherine thought that they were like nothing so much as a litter of excited puppies, Lord Thomas Darcy and Edward Howard at their head.

'I will go!'

'And I will go!'

'Show them how Englishmen fight!' Henry urged them. 'I, myself, will pay the costs of the expedition.'

'I will write to my father that you have eager volunteers,' Katherine said quietly. 'I will go and write to him now.' She turned away and walked quickly towards the doorway to the little stair that led to her rooms. She did not think she could bear to be with them for another moment. These were the men who would have taught her son to ride. These were the men who would have been his statesmen, his Privy Council. They would have sponsored him at his first communion, they would have stood proxy for him at his betrothal, they would have been godfathers to his sons. And here they were, laughing, clamouring for war, competing with each other for Henry's shouted approval, as if her son had not been born, had not died. As if the world were the same as it had ever been; when Katherine knew that it was utterly changed.

He had blue eyes. And the tiniest, most perfect feet.

In the event, the glorious crusade never happened. The English knights arrived at Cadiz but the crusade never set sail for the Holy Land, never faced a sharp scimitar wielded by a black-hearted infidel. Katherine translated letters between Henry and her father in which her father explained that he had not yet raised his troops, that he was not yet ready to leave, and then, one day, she came to Henry with a letter in her hand and her face shocked out of its usual weariness.

'Father writes me the most terrible news.'

'What is happening?' Henry demanded, bewildered. 'See, here, I have just received a letter from an English merchant in Italy, I cannot make any sense of it. He writes that the French and the Pope are at war.' Henry held out his letter to her. 'How can this be? I don't understand it at all.'

'It is true. This is from my father. He says the Pope has declared that the French armies must get out of Italy,' Katherine explained. 'And the Holy Father has put his own papal troops into the field against the French. King Louis has declared that the Pope shall no longer be Pope.'

'How dare he?' Henry demanded, shocked to his core.

'Father says we must forget the crusade and go at once to the aid of the Pope. He will try to broker an alliance between us and the Holy Roman Emperor. We must form an alliance against France. King Louis cannot be allowed to take Rome. He must not advance into Italy.'

'He must be mad to think that I would allow it!' Henry exclaimed. 'Would I let the French take Rome? Would I allow a French puppet Pope? Has he forgotten what an English army can do? Does he want another Agincourt?'

'Shall I tell my father we will unite with him against France?' Katherine asked. 'I could write at once.'

He caught her hand and kissed it. For once she did not pull away and he drew her a little closer and put his arm around her waist. 'I'll come with you while you write and we can sign the letter from us both – your father should know that his Spanish daughter and his English son are absolutely as one in his support. Thank God that our troops are in Cadiz already,' Henry exclaimed as his good fortune struck him.

Katherine hesitated, a thought forming slowly in her mind. 'It is . . . fortuitous.'

'Lucky,' Henry said buoyantly. 'We are blessed by God.'

'My father will want some benefit for Spain from this.' Katherine introduced the suspicion carefully as they went to her rooms, Henry shortening his stride to match hers. 'He never makes a move without planning far ahead.'

'Of course, but you will guard our interests as you always do,' he said confidently. 'I trust you, my love, as I trust him. Is he not my only father now?'

Summer 1511

Slowly, as the days grow warmer, and the sun is more like a Spanish sun, I grow warm too and become more like the Spanish girl I once was. I cannot reconcile myself to the death of my son, I think I will never reconcile myself to his loss; but I can see that there is no-one to blame for his death. There was no neglect or negligence, he died like a little bird in a warm nest and I have to see that I will never know why.

I know now that I was foolish to blame myself. I have committed no crime, no sin so bad that God, the merciful God of my childhood prayers, would punish me with such an awful grief as this. There could be no good God who would take away such a sweet baby, such a perfect baby with such blue eyes, as an exercise of His divine will. I know in my heart that such a thing cannot be, such a God cannot be. Even though in the first worst outpourings of my grief I blamed myself and I blamed God, I know now that it was not a punishment for sin. I know that I kept my promise, Arthur's promise, for the best reasons; and God has me in His keeping.

The awful, icy, dark fact of my baby's loss seems to recede with the awful cold darkness of that English winter. One morning the fool came and told me some little jest and I laughed aloud. It was as if a door had opened that had long been locked tight. I realise that I can laugh, that it is possible to be happy, that laughter and hope can come back to me and perhaps I might even make another child and feel that overwhelming tenderness again.

I start to feel that I am alive again, that I am a woman with hope and prospects again, that I am the woman that the girl from Spain became. I can sense myself alive: poised halfway between my future and my past.

It is as if I am checking myself over as a rider does after a bad fall from a horse, patting my arms and legs, my vulnerable body, as if looking for permanent damage. My faith in God returns utterly unshaken, as firm as it has ever been. There seems to be only one great change: my belief in my mother and my father is damaged. For the first time in my life I truly think it possible that they can have been wrong.

I remember the Moorish physician's kindness to me and I have to amend my view of his people. No-one who could see his enemy brought as low as he saw me, and yet could look at her with such deep compassion, can be called a barbarian, a savage. He might be a heretic – steeped in error – but surely he must be allowed his own conclusions with his own reasons. And from what I know of the man, I am certain that he will have fine reasons.

I would like to send a good priest to wrestle for his soul, but I cannot say, as my mother would have said, that he is spiritually dead, fit for nothing but death. He held my hands to tell me hard news and I saw the tenderness of Our Lady in his eyes. I cannot dismiss the Moors as heretics and enemies any more. I have to see that they are men and women, fallible as us, hopeful as us, faithful to their creed as we are to ours.

And this in turn leads me to doubt my mother's wisdom. Once I would have sworn that she knew everything, that her writ must run everywhere. But now I have grown old enough to view her more thoughtfully. I was left in poverty in my widowhood because her *contract was carelessly written. I was abandoned, all alone in a foreign country, because – though she summoned me with apparent urgency – in truth it was just for show; she would not take me back to Spain at any price. She hardened her heart against me and cleaved to her plan for me, and let me, her own daughter, go.*

And finally, I was forced to find a doctor in secret and consult with him in hiding because she had done her part in driving from Christendom the best physicians, the best scientists, and the cleverest minds in the world. She had named their wisdom as sin and the rest of Europe had followed her lead. She rid Spain of the Jews and their skills and courage, she rid Spain of the Moors and their scholarship and gifts. She, a woman who admired learning, banished those that they call the People of the Book. She who fought for justice had been unjust.

I cannot yet think what this estrangement might mean for me. My mother is dead, I cannot reproach her or argue with her now, except in my imagination. But I know these months have wrought a deep and lasting change in me. I have come to an understanding of my world that is not her understanding of hers. I do not support a crusade against the Moors, nor against anyone. I do not support persecution, nor cruelty to them for the colour of their skin or the belief in their hearts. I know that my mother is not infallible, I no longer believe she and God think as one. Though I still love my mother, I don't worship her any more. I suppose, at last, I am growing up.

Slowly, the queen emerged from her grief and started to take an interest in the running of the court and country once more. London was buzzing with the news that Scottish privateers had attacked an English merchant ship. Everyone knew the name of the privateer: he was Andrew Barton, who sailed with letters of authority from King James of Scotland. Barton was merciless to English ships, and the general belief in the London docks was that James had deliberately licensed the pirate to prey on English shipping as if the two countries were already at war.

'He has to be stopped,' Katherine said to Henry.

'He does not dare to challenge me!' Henry exclaimed. 'James sends border raiders and pirates against me because he does not dare to face me himself. James is a coward and an oath-breaker.'

'Yes,' Katherine agreed. 'But the main thing about this pirate Barton is that he is not only a danger to our trade, he is a forerunner of worse to come. If we let the Scots rule the seas then we let them command us. This is an island; the seas must belong to us as much as the land or we have no safety.'

'My ships are ready and we sail at midday. I shall capture him alive,' Edward Howard, the Admiral of the Fleet, promised Katherine, as he came to bid her farewell. She thought he looked very young, as boyish as Henry; but his flair and courage were unquestioned. He had inherited all his father's tactical skill but brought it to the newly formed navy. The Howards traditionally held the post of Lord Admiral, but Edward was proving exceptional. 'If I cannot capture him alive, I shall sink his ship and bring him back dead.'

'For shame on you! A Christian enemy!' she said teasingly, holding out her hand for his kiss.

He looked up, serious for once. 'I promise you, Your Grace, that the Scots are a greater danger to the peace and wealth of this country than the Moors could ever be.'

He saw her wistful smile. 'You are not the first Englishman to tell me that,' she said. 'And I have seen it myself in these last years.'

'It has to be right,' he said. 'In Spain your father and mother never rested until they could dislodge the Moors from the mountains. For us in England, our closest enemy is the Scots. It is they who are in our mountains, it is they who have to be suppressed and quelled if we are ever to be at peace. My father has spent his life defending the northern borders, and now I am fighting the same enemy but at sea.'

'Come home safely,' she urged.

'I have to take risks,' he said carelessly. 'I am no stay-at-home.'

'No-one doubts your bravery, and my fleet needs an admiral,' she told him. 'I want the same admiral for many years. I need my champion at the next joust. I need my partner to dance with me. You come home safely, Edward Howard!'

The king was uneasy at his friend Edward Howard setting sail against the Scots, even against a Scots privateer. He had hoped that his father's alliance with Scotland, enforced by the marriage of the English princess, would have guaranteed peace.

'James is such a hypocrite to promise peace and marry Margaret on one hand and license these raids on the other! I shall write to Margaret and tell her to warn her husband that we cannot accept raids on our shipping. They should keep to their borders too.'

'Perhaps he will not listen to her,' Katherine pointed out.

'She can't be blamed for that,' he said quickly. 'She should never have been married to him. She was too young, and he was too set in his ways, and he is a man for war. But she will bring peace if she can, she knows it was my father's wish, she knows that we have to live in peace. We are kin now, we are neighbours.'

But the border lords, the Percys and the Nevilles, reported that the Scots had recently become more daring in their raids on the northern lands. Unquestionably, James was spoiling for war, undoubtedly he meant to take land in Northumberland as his own. Any day now he could march south, take Berwick, and continue on to Newcastle.

'How dare he?' Henry demanded. 'How dare he just march in and take our goods and disturb our people? Does he not know that I could raise an army and take them against him tomorrow?'

'It would be a hard campaign,' Katherine remarked, thinking of the wild land of the border and the long march to get to it. The Scotsmen would have everything to fight for, with the rich southern lands spread before them, and English soldiers never wanted to fight when they were far from their villages.

'It would be easy,' Henry contradicted her. 'Everyone knows that the Scots can't keep an army in the field. They are nothing more than a raiding party. If I took out a great English army, properly armed and supplied and ordered, I would make an end of them in a day!'

'Of course you would,' Katherine smiled. 'But don't forget, we have to muster our army to fight against the French. You would far rather win your spurs against the French on a field of chivalry which will go down in history than in some dirty border quarrel.'

Katherine spoke to Thomas Howard, Earl of Surrey, Edward Howard's father, at the end of the Privy Council meeting as the men came out of the king's rooms.

'My lord? Have you heard from Edward? I miss my young Chevalier.'

The old man beamed at her. 'We had a report this day. The king will tell you himself. He knew you would be pleased that your favourite has had a victory.'

'He has?'

'He has captured the pirate Andrew Barton with two of his ships.' His pride shone through his pretence of modesty. 'He has only done his duty,' he said. 'He has only done as any Howard boy should do.'

'He is a hero!' Katherine said enthusiastically. 'England needs great sailors as much as we need soldiers. The future for Christendom is in dominating the seas. We need to rule the seas as the Saracens rule the deserts. We have to drive pirates from the seas and make English ships a constant presence. And what else? Is he on his way home?'

'He will bring his ships into London and the pirate in chains with him. We'll try him, and hang him on the quayside. But King James won't like it.'

'Do you think the Scots king means war?' Katherine asked him bluntly. 'Would he go to war over such a cause as this? Is the country in danger?'

'This is the worst danger to the peace of the kingdom of any in my lifetime,' the older man said honestly. 'We have subdued the Welsh and brought peace to our borders in the west, now we will have to put down the Scots. After them we will have to settle the Irish.'

'They are a separate country, with their own kings and laws,' Katherine demurred.

'So were the Welsh till we defeated them,' he pointed out. 'This is too small a land for three kingdoms. The Scots will have to be yoked into our service.'

'Perhaps we could offer them a prince,' Katherine thought aloud. 'As you did to the Welsh. The second son could be the Prince of Scotland as the first-born is the Prince of Wales, for a kingdom united under the English king.'

He was struck with her idea. 'That's right,' he said. 'That would be the way to do it. Hit them hard and then offer them a peace with honour. Otherwise we will have them snapping at our heels forever.'

'The king thinks that their army would be small and easily defeated,' Katherine remarked.

Howard choked back a laugh. 'His Grace has never been to Scotland,' he said. 'He has never even been to war yet. The Scots are a formidable enemy, whether in pitched battle or a passing raid. They are a worse enemy than any of his fancy French cavalry. They have no laws of chivalry, they fight to win and they fight to the death. We will need to send a powerful force under a skilled commander.'

'Could you do it?' Katherine asked.

'I could try,' he replied honestly. 'I am the best weapon to your hand at the moment, Your Grace.'

'Could the king do it?' she asked quietly.

He smiled at her. 'He's a young man,' he said. 'He lacks nothing for courage, no-one who has seen him in a joust could doubt his courage. And he is skilled on his horse. But a war is not a joust, and he does not know that yet. He needs to ride out at the head of a bold army, and be seasoned in a few battles before he fights the greatest war of his life – the war for his very kingdom. You don't put a colt into a cavalry charge on his first outing. He has to learn. The king, even though a king, will have to learn.'

'He was taught nothing of warfare,' she said. 'He has not had to study other battles. He knows nothing about observing the lie of the land and positioning a force. He knows nothing about supplies and keeping an army on the move. His father taught him nothing.'

'His father knew next to nothing,' the earl said quietly, for her ears only. 'His first battle was Bosworth and he won that partly by luck and partly by the allies his mother put in the field for him. He was courageous enough, but no general.'

'But why did he not ensure that Henry was taught the art of warfare?' asked Ferdinand's daughter, who had been raised in a camp and seen a campaign plan before she had learned how to sew.

'Who would have thought he would need to know?' the old earl asked her. 'We all thought it would be Arthur.'

She made sure that her face did not betray the sudden pang of grief at the unexpected mention of his name. 'Of course,' she said. 'Of course you did. I forgot. Of course you did.'

'Now, he would have been a great commander. He was interested in the waging of war. He read. He studied. He talked to his father, he pestered me. He was well aware of the danger of the Scots, he had a great sense of how to command men. He used to ask me about the land on the border, where the castles were placed, how the land fell. He could have led an army against the Scots with some hopes of success. Young Henry will be a great king when he has learned tactics, but Arthur knew it all. It was in his blood.'

Katherine did not even allow herself the pleasure of speaking of him. 'Perhaps,' was all she said. 'But in the meantime, what can we do to limit the raids of the Scots? Should the border lords be reinforced?'

'Yes, but it is a long border, and hard to keep. King James does not fear an English army led by the king. He does not fear the border lords.'

'Why does he not fear us?'

He shrugged, too much of a courtier to say any betraying word. 'Well, James is an old warrior, he has been spoiling for a fight for two generations now.'

'Who could make James fear us and keep him in Scotland while we reinforce the border and get ready for war? What would make James delay and buy us time?'

'Nothing,' he declared, shaking his head. 'There is no-one who could hold back James if he is set on war. Except perhaps only the Pope, if he would rule? But who could persuade His Holiness to intervene between two Christian monarchs quarrelling over a pirate's raid and a patch of land? And the Pope has his own worries with the French advancing. And besides, a complaint from us would only bring a rebuttal from Scotland. Why would His Holiness intervene for us?'

'I don't know,' said Katherine. 'I don't know what would make the Pope take our side. If only he knew of our need! If only he would use his power to defend us!'

Richard Bainbridge, Cardinal Archbishop of York, happens to be at Rome and is a good friend of mine. I write to him that very night, a friendly letter as between one acquaintance to another far from home,

telling him of the news from London, the weather, the prospects for the harvest and the price of wool. Then I tell him of the enmity of the Scottish king, of his sinful pride, of his wicked licensing of attacks on our shipping and – worst of all – his constant invasions of our northern lands. I tell him that I am so afraid that the king will be forced to defend his lands in the north that he will not be able to come to the aid of the Holy Father in his quarrel with the French king. It would be such a tragedy, I write, if the Pope was left exposed to attack and we could not come to his aid because of the wickedness of the Scots. We plan to join my father's alliance and defend the Pope; but we can hardly muster for the Pope if there is no safety at home. If I have my way, nothing should distract my husband from his alliance with my father, with the emperor and with the Pope, but what can I, a poor woman, do? A poor woman whose own defenceless border is under constant threat?

What could be more natural than that Richard, my brother in Christ, should go with my letter in his hand to His Holiness the Pope and say how disturbed I am by the threat to my peace from King James of Scotland, and how the whole alliance to save the Eternal City is threatened by this bad neighbourliness?

The Pope, reading my letter to Richard, reads it aright, and writes at once to King James and threatens to excommunicate him if he does not respect the peace and the justly agreed borders of another Christian king. He is shocked that James should trouble the peace of Christendom. He takes his behaviour very seriously and grave penalties could result. King James, forced to accede to the Pope's wishes, forced to apologise for his incursions, writes a bitter letter to Henry saying that Henry had no right to approach the Pope alone, that it had been a quarrel between the two of them and there is no need to go running behind his back to the Holy Father.

'I don't know what he is talking about,' Henry complained to Katherine, finding her in the garden playing at catch with her ladies-in-waiting. He was too disturbed to run into the game as he usually did and snatch the ball from the air, bowl it hard at the nearest girl and shout with joy. He was too worried even to play with them. 'What is he saying? I have never appealed to the Pope. I did not report him. I am no tale-bearer!'

'No, you are not, and so you can tell him,' Katherine said serenely, slipping her hand in his arm and walking away from the women.

'I shall tell him. I said nothing to the Pope, and I can prove it.'

'I may have mentioned my concerns to the archbishop and he may have passed them on,' Katherine said casually. 'But you can hardly be blamed if your wife tells her spiritual advisor that she is anxious.'

'Exactly,' Henry said. 'I shall tell him so. And you should not be worried for a moment.'

'Yes. And the main thing is that James knows he cannot attack us with impunity, His Holiness has made a ruling.'

Henry hesitated. 'You did not mean Bainbridge to tell the Pope, did you?'

She peeped a little smile at him. 'Of course,' she said. 'But it still is not you who has complained of James to the Pope.'

His grip tightened around her waist. 'You are a redoubtable enemy. I hope we are never on opposing sides. I should be sure to lose.'

'We never will be,' she said sweetly. 'For I will never be anything but your loyal and faithful wife and queen.'

'I can raise an army in a moment, you know,' Henry reminded her. 'There is no need for you to fear James. There is no need for you even to pretend to fear. I could be the hammer of the Scots. I could do it as well as anyone, you know.'

'Yes, of course you can. And, thank God, now you don't need to do so.'

Autumn 1511

Edward Howard brought the Scots privateers back to London in chains and was greeted as an English hero. His popularity made Henry – always alert to the acclaim of the people – quite envious. He spoke more and more often of a war against the Scots, and the Privy Council, though fearful of the cost of war and privately doubtful of Henry's military abilities, could not deny that Scotland was an ever-present threat to the peace and security of England.

It was the queen who diverted Henry from his envy of Edward Howard, and the queen who continually reminded him that his first taste of warfare should surely be in the grand fields of Europe and not in some half-hidden hills in the borders. When Henry of England rode out it should be against the French king, in alliance with the two other greatest kings of Christendom. Henry, inspired from child-hood with tales of Crécy and Agincourt, was easy to seduce with thoughts of glory against France.

Spring 1512

It was hard for Henry not to embark in person when the fleet sailed to join King Ferdinand's campaign against the French. It was a glorious start: the ships went out flying the banners of most of the great houses of England, they were the best equipped, finest arrayed force that had left England in years. Katherine had been busy, supervising the endless work of provisioning the ships, stocking the armouries, equipping the soldiers. She remembered her mother's constant work when her father was at war, and she had learned the great lesson of her childhood – that a battle could only be won if it was thoroughly and reliably supplied.

She sent out an expeditionary fleet that was better organised than any that had gone from England before, and she was confident that under her father's command they would defend the Pope, beat the French, win lands in France, and establish the English as major land-owners in France once more. The peace party on the Privy Council worried, as they always did, that England would be dragged into another endless war; but Henry and Katherine were convinced by Ferdinand's confident predictions that a victory would come quickly and there would be rich gains for England.

I have seen my father command one campaign after another for all of my childhood. I have never seen him lose. Going to war is to relive my childhood again, the colour and the sounds and the excitement of a country at war are a deep joy for me. This time, to be in alliance with my father, as an equal partner, to be able to deliver to him the power of the English army, feels like my coming of age. This is what he has wanted from me, this is the fulfilment of my life as his daughter. It is for this that I endured the long years of waiting for the English throne. This is my destiny, at last, I am a commander as my father is, as my mother was. I am a Queen Militant, and there is no doubt in my mind on this sunny morning as I watch the fleet set sail that I will be a Queen Triumphant.

The plan was that the English army would meet the Spanish army and invade south-western France: Guienne and the Duchy of Aquitaine. There was no doubt in Katherine's mind that her father would take his share of the spoils of war, but she expected that he would honour his promise to march with the English into Aquitaine, and win it back for England. She thought that his secret plan would be the carving up of France, which would return that over-mighty country to the collection of small kingdoms and duchies it once had been, their ambitions crushed for a generation. Indeed, Katherine knew her father believed that it was safer for Christendom if France was reduced. It was not a country that could be trusted with the power and wealth that unity brings.

It was as good as any brilliant court entertainment to see the ships cross the bar and sail out, a strong wind behind them, on a sunny day; and Henry and Katherine rode back to Windsor filled with confidence that their armies would be the strongest in Christendom, that they could not fail.

Katherine took advantage of the moment and Henry's enthusiasm for the ships to ask him if he did not think that they should build galleys, fighting ships powered with oars. Arthur had known at once what she had meant by galleys; he had seen drawings and had read how they could be deployed. Henry had never seen a battle at sea, nor had he seen a galley turn without wind in a moment and come against a becalmed fighting ship. Katherine tried to explain to him, but Henry, inspired by the sight of the fleet in full sail, swore that he wanted only sailing ships, great ships manned with free crews, named for glory.

The whole court agreed with him, and Katherine knew she could make no headway against a court that was always blown about by the latest fashion. Since the fleet had looked so very fine when it set sail, all the young men wanted to be admirals like Edward Howard, just as the summer before they had all wanted to be crusaders. There was no discussing the weakness of big sailing ships in close combat – they all wanted to set out with full sail. They all wanted their own ship. Henry spent days with shipwrights and ship-builders, and Edward Howard argued for a greater and greater navy.

Katherine agreed that the fleet was very fine, and the sailors of England were the finest in the world, but remarked that she thought she might write to the arsenal at Venice to ask them the cost of a galley and if they would build it as a commission, or if they would agree to send the parts and plans to England, for English shipwrights to assemble in English dockyards.

'We don't need galleys,' Henry said dismissively. 'Galleys are for raids on shore. We are not pirates. We want great ships that can carry our soldiers. We want great ships that can tackle the French ships at sea. The ship is a platform from which you launch your attack. The greater the platform, the more soldiers can muster. It has to be a big ship for a battle at sea.'

'I am sure you are right,' she said. 'But we must not forget our other enemies. The seas are one border and we must dominate them with ships both great and small. But our other border must be made safe too.'

'D'you mean the Scots? They have taken their warning from the Pope. I don't expect to be troubled with them.'

She smiled. She would never openly disagree with him. 'Certainly,' she said. 'The archbishop has secured us a breathing space. But next year, or the year after, we will have to go against the Scots.'

Summer 1512

Then there was nothing for Katherine to do but to wait. It seemed as if everyone was waiting. The English army were in Fuenterrabia, waiting for the Spanish to join with them for their invasion of southern France. The heat of the summer came on as they kicked their heels, ate badly and drank like thirsty madmen. Katherine alone of Henry's council knew that the heat of midsummer Spain could kill an army as they did nothing but wait for orders. She concealed her fears from Henry and from the council but privately she wrote to her father asking what his plans were, she tackled his ambassador, asking him what her father intended the English army to do, and when should they march?

Her father, riding with his own army, on the move, did not reply; and the ambassador did not know.

The summer wore on, Katherine did not write again. In a bitter moment, which she did not even acknowledge to herself, she saw that she was not her father's ally on the chessboard of Europe – she realised that she was nothing more than a pawn in his plan. She did not need to ask her father's strategy; once he had the English army in place and did not use them, she guessed it.

It grew colder in England, but it was still hot in Spain. At last Ferdinand had a use for his allies, but when he sent for them, and ordered that they should spend the winter season on campaign, they refused to answer his call. They mutinied against their own commanders and demanded to go home.

Winter 1512

It came as no surprise to Katherine, nor to the cynics on the council, when the English army came home in dishonoured tatters in December. Lord Dorset, despairing of ever receiving orders and reinforcements from King Ferdinand, confronted by mutinying troops, hungry, weary, and with two thousand men lost to illness, straggled home in disgrace, as he had taken them out in glory.

'What can have gone wrong?' Henry rushed into Katherine's rooms and waved away her ladies-in-waiting. He was almost in tears of rage at the shame of the defeat. He could not believe that his force that had gone out so bravely should come home in such disarray. He had letters from his father-in-law complaining of the behaviour of the English allies, he had lost face in Spain, he had lost face with his enemy France. He fled to Katherine as the only person in the world who would share his shock and dismay. He was almost stammering with distress, it was the first time in his reign that anything had gone wrong and he had thought – like a boy – that nothing would ever go wrong for him.

I take his hands. I have been waiting for this since the first moment in the summer when there was no battle plan for the English troops. As soon as they arrived and were not deployed I knew that we had been misled. Worse, I knew that we had been misled by my father.

I am no fool. I know my father as a commander, and I know him as a man. When he did not fling the English into battle on the day that they arrived, I knew that he had another plan for them, and that plan was hidden from us. My father would never leave good men in camp to gossip and drink and get sick. I was on campaign with my father for most of my childhood, I never saw him let the men sit idle. He always keeps his men moving, he always keeps them in work and out of mischief. There is not a horse in my father's stables with a pound of extra fat on it; he treats his soldiers just the same.

If the English were left to rot in camp it was because he had need of them just where they were – in camp. He did not care that they were getting sick and lazy. That made me look again at the map and I saw what he was doing. He was using them as a counterweight, as an inactive diversion. I read the reports from our commanders as they arrived, their complaints at their pointless inaction, their exercises on the border, sighting the French army and being seen by them, but not being ordered to engage; and I knew I was right. My father kept the English troops dancing on the spot in Fuenterrabia so that the French, alarmed by such a force on their flank, would place their army in defence. Guarding against the English they could not attack my father who, joyously alone and unencumbered, at the head of his troops, marched into the unprotected kingdom of Navarre and so picked up that which he had desired for so long at no expense or danger to himself.

'My dear, your soldiers were not tried and found wanting,' I say to my distressed young husband. 'There is no question as to the courage of the English. There can be no doubting you.'

'He says . . .' He waves the letter at me.

'It doesn't matter what he says,' I say patiently. 'You have to look at what he does.'

The face he turns to me is so hurt that I cannot bring myself to tell him that my father has used him, played him for a fool, used his army, used even me, to win himself Navarre.

'My father has taken his fee before his work, that is all,' I say robustly. 'Now we have to make him do the work.'

'What do you mean?' Henry is still puzzled.

'God forgive me for saying it, but my father is a masterly double-dealer. If we are going to make treaties with him we will have to learn to be as clever as him. He made a treaty with us and said he would be our partner in war against France, but all we have done is win him Navarre, by sending our army out and home again.'

'They have been shamed. I have been shamed.'

He cannot understand what I am trying to tell him. 'Your army has done exactly what my father wanted them to do. In that sense, it has been a most successful campaign.'

'They did nothing! He complains to me that they are good for nothing!'

'They pinned down the French with that nothing. Think of that! The French have lost Navarre.'

'I want to court-martial Dorset!'

'Yes, we can do so, if you wish. But the main thing is that we still have our army, we have lost only two thousand men, and my father is our ally. He owes us for this year. Next year you can go back to France and this time Father will fight for us; not us for him.'

'He says he will conquer Guienne for me, he says it as if I cannot do it myself! He speaks to me as a weakling with a useless force!'

'Good,' I say, surprising him. 'Let him conquer Guienne for us.'

'He wants us to pay him.'

'Let us pay for it. What does it matter as long as my father is on our side when we go to war with the French? If he wins Guienne for us then that is to our good; if he does not, but just distracts the French when we invade in the north from Calais, then that is all to the good as well.'

For a moment he gapes at me, his head spinning. Then he sees what I mean. 'He pins down the French for us, as we advance, just as we did for him?'

'Exactly.'

'We use him, as he used us?'

'Yes.'

He is amazed. 'Did your father teach you how to do this – to plan ahead as if a campaign were a chess board, and you have to move the pieces around?'

I shake my head. 'Not on purpose. But you cannot live with a man like my father without learning the arts of diplomacy. You know Machiavelli himself called him the perfect prince? You could not be at my father's court, as I was, or on campaign with him, as I was, without seeing that he spends his life seeking advantage. He taught me every day, I could not help but learn, just from watching him. I know how his mind works. I know how a general thinks.'

'But what made you think of invading from Calais?'

'Oh, my dear, where else would England invade France? My father can fight in the south for us, and we will see if he can win us Guienne. You can be sure that he will do so if it is in his interest. And, at any rate, while he is doing that, the French will not be able to defend Normandy.'

Henry's confidence comes rushing back to him. 'I shall go myself,' he declares. 'I shall take to the field of battle myself. Your father will not be able to criticise the command of the English army if I do it myself.'

For a moment I hesitate. Even playing at war is a dangerous game, and while we do not have an heir, Henry is precious beyond belief. Without him, the safety of England will be torn between a hundred pretenders. But I will never keep my hold on him if I coop him up as his grandmother did. Henry will have to learn the nature of war, and I know that he will be safest in a campaign commanded by my father, who wants to keep me on my throne as much as I want it; and safer by far facing the chivalrous French than the murderous Scots. Besides, I have a plan that is a secret. And it requires him to be out of the country.

'Yes, you shall,' I say. 'And you shall have the best armour and strongest horse and handsomest guard of any king who takes the field.'

'Thomas Howard says that we should abandon our battle against France until we have suppressed the Scots.'

I shake my head. 'You shall fight in France in the alliance of the three kings,' I assure him. 'It will be a mighty war, one that everyone will remember. The Scots are a minor danger, they can wait, at the worst they are a petty border raid. And if they invade the north when you go to war, they are so unimportant that even I could command an expedition against them while you go to the real war in France.'

'You?' he asks.

'Why not? Are we not a king and queen come young to our thrones in our power? Who should deny us?'

'No-one! I shall not be diverted,' Henry declares. 'I shall conquer in France and you shall guard us against the Scots.'

'I will,' I promise him. This is just what I want.

Spring 1513

Henry talked of nothing but war all winter, and in the spring Katherine started a great muster of men and materials for the invasion of northern France. The treaty with Ferdinand agreed that he would invade Guienne for England at the same time as the English troops took Normandy. The Holy Roman Emperor Maximilian would join with the English army in the battle in the north. It was an infallible plan if the three parties attacked simultaneously, if they kept meticulous faith with each other.

It comes as no surprise to me to find that my father has been talking peace with France in the very same days that I have had Thomas Wolsey, my right-hand man, the royal almoner, writing to every town in England and asking them how many men they can muster for the king's service when we go to war in France. I knew my father would think only of the survival of Spain: Spain before everything. I do not blame him for it. Now that I am a queen I understand a little better what it means to love a country with such a passion that one will

betray anything – even one's own child, as he does – to keep it safe. My father, with the prospect on one hand of a troublesome war and little gain, and on the other hand peace, with everything to play for, chooses peace and chooses France as his friend. He has betrayed us in absolute secrecy and he fooled even me.

When the news of his grand perfidy comes out he blames it all on his ambassador, and on letters going astray. It is a slight excuse; but I do not complain. My father will join us as soon as it looks as if we will win. The main thing for me now is that Henry should have his campaign in France and leave me alone to settle with the Scots.

'He has to learn how to lead men into battle,' Thomas Howard says to me. 'Not boys into a bawdy house – excuse me, Your Grace.'

'I know,' I reply. 'He has to win his spurs. But there is such a risk.'

The old soldier puts his hand over mine. 'Very few kings die in battle,' he says. 'Don't think of King Richard, for he all but ran on the swords. He knew he was betrayed. Mostly, kings get ransomed. It's not one half of the risk that you will be facing if you equip an army and send it across the narrow seas to France, and then try and fight the Scots with what is left.'

I am silent for a moment. I did not know that he had seen what I plan. 'Who thinks that this is what I am doing?'

'Only me.'

'Have you told anyone?'

'No,' he says stoically. 'My first duty is to England, and I think you are right. We have to finish with the Scots once and for all, and it had better be done when the king is safely overseas.'

'I see you don't fear overmuch for my safety?' I observe.

He shrugs and smiles. 'You are a queen,' he says. 'Dearly beloved, perhaps. But we can always get another queen. We have no other Tudor king.'

'I know,' I say. It is a truth as clear as water. I can be replaced but Henry cannot. Not until I have a Tudor son.

Thomas Howard has guessed my plan. I have no doubt in my mind *where my truest duty lies. It is as Arthur taught me – the greatest danger to the safety of England comes from the north, from the Scots, and so it is to the north that I should march. Henry should be encouraged to put on his most handsome armour to go with his most agreeable friends in a sort of grand joust against the French. But there will be bloody work on the northern border; a victory there will keep us safe for generations. If I want to make England safe for me and for my unborn son, and for the kings who come after me, I must defeat the Scots.*

Even if I never have a son, even if I never have cause to go to Walsingham to thank Our Lady for the son she has given me, I shall still have done my first and greatest duty by this, my beloved country of England, if I beat the Scots. Even if I die in doing it.

I maintain Henry's resolve, I do not allow him to lose his temper or his will. I fight the Privy Council who choose to see my father's unreliability as another sign that we should not go to war. Partly, I agree with them. I think we have no real cause against France, and no great gains to make. But I know that Henry is wild to go to war and he thinks that France is his enemy and King Louis his rival. I want Henry out of the way this summer, when it is my intention to destroy the Scots. I know that the only thing that can divert him will be a glorious war. I want war, not because I am angry with the French, or want to show our strength to my father; I want war because we have the French to the south and the Scots to the north and we will have to engage with one and play with the other to keep England safe.

I spend hours on my knees in the royal chapel; but it is Arthur that I am talking to, in long, silent reveries. 'I am sure I am right, my love,' I whisper into my clasped hands. 'I am sure that you were right when you warned me of the danger of the Scots. We have to subdue the Scots or we will never have a kingdom that can sleep in peace. If I can have my way, this will be the year when the fate of England is decided. If I have my way, I will send Henry against the French and I will go against the Scots and our fate can be decided. I know the Scots are the greater danger. Everyone thinks of the French – your brother thinks of nothing but the French – but these are men who know nothing of the reality of war. The enemy who is across the sea, however much you hate him, is a lesser enemy than the one who can march over your borders in a night.'

I can almost see him in the shadowy darkness behind my closed eyes. 'Oh, yes,' I say with a smile to him. 'You can think that a woman cannot lead an army. You can think that a woman cannot wear armour. But I know more about warfare than most men at this peaceable court. This is a court devoted to jousting, all the young men think war is a game. But I know what war is. I have seen it. This is the year when you will see me ride out as my mother did, when you see me face our enemy – the only enemy that really matters. This is my country now, you yourself made it my country. And I will defend it for you, for me, and for our heirs.'

The English preparations for the war against France went on briskly with Katherine and Thomas Wolsey, her faithful assistant, working daily on the muster rolls for the towns, the gathering of provisions for the army, the forging of armour and the training of volunteers to march, prepare to attack, and retreat, on command. Wolsey observed that the queen had two muster rolls, almost as if she was preparing for two armies. 'Are you thinking we will have to fight the Scots as well as the French?' he asked her.

'I am sure of it.'

'The Scots will snap at us, as soon as our troops leave for France,' he said. 'We shall have to reinforce the borders.'

'I hope to do more than that,' was all she said.

'His Grace the king will not be distracted from his war with France,' he pointed out.

She did not confide in him, as he wanted her to do. 'I know. We must make sure he has a great force to take to Calais. He must not be distracted by anything.'

'We will have to keep some men back to defend against the Scots, they are certain to attack,' he warned her.

'Border guards,' she said dismissively.

Handsome young Edward Howard, in a new cloak of dark sea-blue, came to take leave of Katherine as the fleet prepared to set sail with orders to blockade the French in port, or engage them if possible on the high seas.

'God bless you,' said the queen, and heard her voice a little shaken with emotion. 'God bless you, Edward Howard, and may your luck go with you as it always does.'

He bowed low. 'I have the luck of a man favoured by a great queen who serves a great country,' he said. 'It is an honour to serve my country, the king . . . and,' he lowered his voice to an intimate whisper, 'and you, my queen.'

Katherine smiled. All of Henry's friends shared a tendency to think themselves into the pages of a romance. Camelot was never very far away from their minds. Katherine had served as the lady of the courtly myth ever since she had been queen. She liked Edward Howard more than any of the other young men. His genuine gaiety and his open affection endeared him to everyone, and he had a passion for the navy and the ships under his command that commended him to Katherine, who saw the safety of England could only be assured by holding the seas.

'You are my knight, and I trust you to bring glory to your name and to mine,' she said to him, and saw the gleam of pleasure in his eyes as he dropped his dark head to kiss her hand.

'I shall bring you home some French ships,' he promised her. 'I have brought you Scots pirates, now you shall have French galleons.'

'I have need of them,' she said earnestly.

'You shall have them if I die in the attempt.'

She held up a finger. 'No dying,' she warned him. 'I have need of you, too.' She gave him her other hand. 'I shall think of you every day and in my prayers,' she promised him.

He rose up and with a swirl of his new cloak he went out.

It is the feast of St George and we are still waiting for news from the English fleet, when a messenger comes in, his face grave. Henry is at my side as the young man tells us, at last, of the sea battle that Edward was so certain he should win, that we were so certain would prove the power of our ships over the French. With his father at my side I learn the fate of Edward, my knight Edward, who had been so sure that he would bring home a French galleon to the Pool of London.

He pinned down the French fleet in Brest and they did not dare to come out. He was too impatient to wait for them to make the next move, too young to play a long game. He was a fool, a sweet fool, like half the court, certain that they are invincible. He went into battle like a boy who has no fear of death, who has no knowledge of death, who has not even the sense to fear his own death. Like the Spanish grandees of my childhood, he thought that fear was an illness he could never catch. He thought that God favoured him above all others and nothing could touch him.

With the English fleet unable to go forwards and the French sitting snug in harbour, he took a handful of rowing boats and threw them in, under the French guns. It was a waste, a wicked waste of his men and of himself – and only because he was too impatient to wait, and too young to think. I am sorry that we sent him, dearest Edward, dearest young fool, to his own death. But then I remember that my husband is no older and certainly no wiser, and has even less knowledge of the world of war, and that even I, a woman of twenty-seven years old, married to a boy who has just reached his majority, can make the mistake of thinking that I cannot fail.

Edward himself led the boarding party on to the flagship of the

French admiral – an act of extraordinary daring – and almost at once his men failed him, God forgive them, and called him away when the battle was too hot for them. They jumped down from the deck of the French ship into their own rowing boats, some of them leaping into the sea in their terror to be away, shot ringing around them like hailstones. They cast off, leaving him fighting like a madman, his back to the mast, hacking around him with his sword, hopelessly outnumbered. He made a dash to the side and if a boat had been there, he might have dropped down to it. But they had gone. He tore the gold whistle of his office from his neck and flung it far out into the sea, so that the French would not have it, and then he turned and fought them again. He went down, still fighting, a dozen swords stabbed him, he was still fighting as he slipped and fell, supporting himself with one arm, his sword still parrying. Then, a hungry blade slashed at his sword arm, and he was fighting no more. They could have stepped back and honoured his courage; but they did not. They pressed him further and fell on him like hungry dogs on a skin in Smithfield market. He died with a hundred stab wounds.

They threw his body into the sea, they cared so little for him, these French soldiers, these so-called Christians. They could have been savages, they could have been Moors for all the Christian charity they showed. They did not think of the supreme unction, of a prayer for the dead, they did not think of his Christian burial, though a priest watched him die. They flung him into the sea as if he were nothing more than some spoiled food to be nibbled by fishes.

Then they realised that it was Edward Howard, my Edward Howard, the admiral of the English navy, and the son of one of the greatest men in England, and they were sorry that they had thrown him overboard like a dead dog. Not for honour – oh, not them – but because they could have ransomed him to his family and God knows we would have paid well to have sweet Edward restored to us. They sent the sailors out in boats with hooks to drag his body up again. They sent them to fish for his poor dead body as if he were salvage from a wreck. They gutted his corpse like a carp, they cut out his heart, salted it down like cod, they stole his clothes for souvenirs and sent them to the French court. The butchered scraps that were left of him they sent home to his father and to me.

This savage story reminds me of Hernando Perez del Pulgar who led such a desperately daring raid into the Alhambra. If they had caught him they would have killed him, but I don't think even the Moors would have cut out his heart for their amusement. They would have acknowledged him as a great enemy, a man to be honoured. They would have returned his body to us with one of their grand chivalric gestures. God knows, they would have composed a song about him within a week, we would have been singing it the length and breadth of Spain within a fortnight, and they would have made a fountain to commemorate his beauty within a month. They were Moors; but they had a grace that these Christians utterly lack. When I think of these Frenchmen it makes me ashamed to call the Moors 'barbarians'.

Henry is shaken by this story and by our defeat, and Edward's father ages ten years in the ten minutes that it takes the messenger to tell him that his son's body is downstairs, in a cart, but his clothes have been sent as spoil to Madame Claude, the daughter of the King of France, his heart is a keepsake for the French admiral. I can comfort neither of them, my own shock is too great. I go to my chapel and I take my sorrow to Our Lady, who knows herself what it is to love a young man and to see Him go out to His death. And when I am on my knees I swear that the French will regret the day that they cut my champion down. There will be a reckoning for this filthy act. They will never be forgiven by me.

Summer 1513

The death of Edward Howard made Katherine work even harder for the preparations of the English army to leave for Calais. Henry might be going to play-act a war, but he would use real shot and cannon, swords and arrows, and she wanted them to be well made and their aim to be true. She had known the realities of war all her life, but with the death of Edward Howard, Henry now saw, for the first time, that it was not like in a story book, it was not like a joust. A well-favoured, brilliant young man like Edward could go out in the sunshine and come home, butchered into pieces, in a cart. To his credit, Henry did not waver in his courage as this truth came home to him, as he saw young Thomas Howard step up to his brother's place, as he saw Edward's father summoning his tenants and calling in his debts to provide troops to avenge his son.

They sent the first part of the army to Calais in May, and Henry prepared to follow them with the second batch of troops in June. He was more sombre than he had ever been before.

Katherine and Henry rode slowly through England from Greenwich to Dover for Henry's embarkation. The towns turned out to feast them and muster their men as they went through. Henry and Katherine had matching great white horses and Katherine rode astride, her long blue gown spread out all around. Henry, riding at her side, looked magnificent, taller than any other man in the ranks, stronger than most, golden-haired and smiling all around.

In the mornings when they rode out of a town they would both wear armour: matching suits of silver and gilt. Katherine wore only a breastplate and a helmet, made from finely beaten metal and chased with gold patterns. Henry wore full armour from toes to fingertips every day, whatever the heat. He rode with his visor up and his blue eyes dancing, and a gold circlet around his helmet. The standard bearers carrying Katherine's badge on one side, and Henry's on the other, rode either side of them and when people saw the queen's pomegranate and Henry's rose they shouted 'God Bless the King!' and 'God Bless the Queen!' When they left a town, with the troops marching behind them, and the bowmen before them, the townspeople would crowd the sides of the road for a good mile to see them ride by, and they threw rose petals and rose-buds on the road in front of the horses. All the men marched with a rose in their lapels or in their hats, and they sang as they marched: bawdy songs of old England, but also sometimes ballads of Henry's composing.

They took nearly two weeks to get to Dover and the time was not wasted, for they gathered supplies and recruited troops in every village. Every man in the land wanted to be in the army to defend England against France. Every girl wanted to say that her lad had gone to be a soldier. The whole country was united in wanting revenge against the French. And the whole country was confident that with the young king at the head of a young army, it could be done.

I am happier, knowingly happier, than I have been since the death of our son. I am happier than I had thought possible. Henry comes to my bed every night during the feasting, dancing, marching tour to the coast, he is mine in thought and word and deed. He is going on a campaign of my organising, he is safely diverted from the real war that I will have to fight, and he never has a thought, or says a word, but he shares it with me. I pray that in one of these nights on the road, riding south to the coast together, in the heightened tension that comes with war, we will make another child, another boy, another rose for England as Arthur was.

Thanks to Katherine and Thomas Wolsey the arrangements for the embarkation were timed to perfection. Not for this English army the usual delay while last-minute orders were given, and forgotten essentials desperately ordered. Henry's ships – four hundred of them – brightly painted, with pennants flying, sails ready-rigged – were waiting to take the troops to France. Henry's own ship, blazing in gold leaf with the red dragon flying at its stern, bobbed at the dock. His royal guard, superbly trained, their new livery of Tudor green and white, spangled with sequins, were paraded on the quay, his two suits of gold-inlaid armour were packed on board, his specially trained white horses were in their stalls. The preparations were as meticulous as those of the most elaborate of court masques and Katherine knew that for many of the young men, they were looking forward to war as they did to a court entertainment.

Everything was ready for Henry to embark and sail for France when in a simple ceremony, on the strand at Dover, he took the great seal of state and before them all invested Katherine as regent in his place, Governor of the Realm and Captain General of the English forces for home defence.

I make sure that my face is grave and solemn when he names me Regent of England, and I kiss his hand and then I kiss him full on the mouth to wish him God speed. But as his ship is taken in tow by the barges, crosses the bar of the harbour, and then unfurls her sails to catch the wind and sets out for France, I could sing aloud for joy. I have no tears for the husband who is going away because he has left me with everything that I have ever wanted. I am more than Princess of Wales, I am more than Queen of England, I am Governor of the Realm, I am Captain General of the army, this is my country indeed, and I am sole ruler.

And the first thing I will do – indeed, perhaps the only thing I will do with the power vested in me, the only thing that I must do with this God-given chance – is defeat the Scots.

As soon as Katherine arrived at Richmond Palace she gave Thomas Howard, Edward's younger brother, his orders to take the cannon from the armouries in the Tower, and set sail with the whole English fleet, north to Newcastle to defend the borders against the Scots. He was not the admiral that his brother had been but he was a steady young man and she thought she could rely on him to do his part to deliver the vital weapons to the north.

Every day brought Katherine news from France by messengers that she had already posted along the way. Wolsey had strict instructions to report back to the queen the progress of the war. From him she wanted an accurate analysis. She knew that Henry would give her an optimistic account. It was not all good news. The English army had arrived in France, there was much excitement in Calais and feasting and celebrations. There were parades and musters and Henry had been much congratulated on his handsome armour and his smart troops. But the Emperor Maximilian failed to muster his own army to support the English. Instead, pleading poverty but swearing his enthusiasm to the cause, he came to the young prince to offer his sword and his service.

It was clearly a heady moment for Henry, who had not yet even heard a shot fired in anger, to have the Holy Roman Emperor offering his services, overwhelmed by the glamorous young prince.

Katherine frowned when she read that part of Wolsey's account, calculating that Henry would hire the emperor at an inflated amount, and would thus have to pay an ally who had promised to come at his own expense for a mercenary army. She recognised at once the double-dealing that had characterised this campaign from the start. But at least it would mean that the emperor was with Henry in his first battle, and Katherine knew that she could rely on the experienced older man to keep the impulsive young king safe.

On the advice of Maximilian, the English army laid siege to Therouanne – a town which the Holy Roman Emperor had long desired, but of no tactical value to England – and Henry, safely distanced from the short-range guns on the walls of the little town, walked alone through his camp at midnight, spoke comforting words to the soldiers on watch, and was allowed to fire his first cannon.

The Scots, who had been waiting only until England was defenceless with king and army in France, declared war against the English and started their own march south. Wolsey wrote with alarm to Katherine, asking her if she needed the return of some of Henry's troops to face this new threat. Katherine replied that she thought she could defend against a border skirmish, and started a fresh muster of troops from every town in the country, using the lists she had already prepared.

She commanded the assembly of the London militia and went out in her armour, on her white horse, to inspect them before they started their march north.

I look at myself in the mirror as my ladies-in-waiting tie on my breastplate, and my maid-in-waiting holds my helmet. I see the unhappiness in their faces, the way the silly maid holds the helmet as if it is too heavy for her, as if none of this should be happening, as if I were not born for this moment: now. The moment of my destiny.

I draw a silent breath. I look so like my mother in my armour that it could be her reflection in the mirror, standing so still and proud, with her hair caught back from her face, and her eyes shining as bright as the burnished gilt on her breastplate; alive at the prospect of battle, gleaming with joy at her confidence in victory.

'Are you not afraid?' Maria de Salinas asks me quietly.

'No.' I speak the truth. 'I have spent all my life waiting for this moment. I am a queen, and the daughter of a queen who had to fight for her country. I have come to this, my own country, at the very moment that it needs me. This is not a time for a queen who wants to sit on her throne and award prizes for jousting. This is a time for a queen who has the heart and stomach of a man. I am that queen. I shall ride out with my army.'

There is a little flurry of dismay. 'Ride out?' 'But not north?' 'Parade them, but surely not ride with them?' 'But isn't it dangerous?'

I reach for my helmet. 'I shall ride with them north to meet the Scots. And if the Scots break through I shall fight them. And when I take the field against them I shall be there until I defeat them.'

'But what about us?'

I smile at the women. 'Three of you will come with me to bear me company and the rest of you will stay here,' I say firmly. 'Those behind will continue to make banners and prepare bandages and send them on to me. You will keep good order,' I say firmly. 'Those who come with me will behave as soldiers in the field. I will have no complaints.'

There is an outburst of dismay, which I avoid by heading for the door. 'Maria and Margaret, you shall come with me now,' I say.

The troops are drawn up before the palace. I ride slowly down the lines, letting my eyes rest on one face and then another. I have seen my father do this, and my mother. My father told me that every soldier should know that he is valued, should know that he has been seen as an individual man on parade, should feel himself to be an essential part of the body of the army. I want them to be sure that I have seen them, seen every man; that I know them. I want them to know me. When I have ridden past every single one of the five hundred, I go to the front of the army and I take off my helmet so that they can see my face. I am not like a Spanish princess now, with my hair hidden and my face veiled. I am a bare-headed, bare-faced English queen. I raise my voice so that every one of them can hear me.

'Men of England,' I say. 'You and I will go together to fight the Scots, and neither of us will falter nor fail. We will not turn back until they have turned back. We will not rest until they are dead. Together we will defeat them, for we do the work of heaven. This is not a quarrel of our making, this is a wicked invasion by James of Scotland; breaking his own treaty, insulting his own English wife. An ungodly invasion condemned by the Pope himself, an invasion against the order of God. He has planned this for years. He has waited, like a coward, thinking to find us weak. But he is mistaken for we are powerful now. We will defeat him, this heretic king. We will win. I can assure you of this because I know God's will in this matter. He is with us. And you can be sure that God's hand is always over men who fight for their homes.'

There is a great roar of approval and I turn and smile to one side

and then the other, so that they can all see my pleasure in their courage.
So that they can all see that I am not afraid.

'Good. Forward march,' I say simply to the commander at my side
and the army turns and marches out of the parade ground.

As Katherine's first army of defence marched north under the Earl
of Surrey, gathering men as they went, the messengers rode desperately south to London to bring her the news she had been expecting.
James's army had crossed the Scottish border and was advancing
through the rolling hills of the border country, recruiting soldiers
and stealing food as they went.

'A border raid?' Katherine asked, knowing it would not be.

The man shook his head. 'My lord told me to tell you that the
French king has promised the Scots king that he will recognise him
if he wins this battle against us.'

'Recognise him? As what?'

'As King of England.'

He expected her to cry out in indignation or in fear, but she
merely nodded, as if it were something else to consider.

'How many men?' Katherine demanded of the messenger.

He shook his head. 'I can't say for certain.'

'How many do you think?'

He looked at the queen, saw the sharp anxiety in her eyes, and
hesitated.

'Tell me the truth!'

'I am afraid sixty thousand, Your Grace, perhaps more.'

'How many more? Perhaps?'

Again he paused. She rose from her chair and went to the window.
'Please, tell me what you think,' she said. 'You do me no service if,
thanks to you, trying to spare me distress, I go out with an army
and find before me an enemy in greater force than I expected.'

'One hundred thousand, I would think,' he said quietly.

He expected her to gasp in horror but when he looked at her she was smiling. 'Oh, I'm not afraid of that.'

'Not afraid of one hundred thousand Scots?' he demanded.

'I've seen worse,' she said.

I know now that I am ready. The Scots are pouring over the border, in their full power. They have captured the northern castles with derisive ease, the flower of the English command and the best men are overseas in France. The French king thinks to defeat us with the Scots, in our own lands, while our masquing army rides around northern France and makes pretty gestures. My moment is now. It is up to me, and the men who are left. I order the royal standards and banners from the great wardrobe. Flown at the head of the army the royal standards show that the King of England is on the battlefield. That will be me.

'You will never ride under the royal standard?' one of my ladies queries.

'Who else?'

'It should be the king.'

'The king is fighting the French. I shall fight the Scots.'

'Your Grace, a queen cannot take the king's standard and ride out.'

I smile at her, I am not pretending to confidence, I truly know that this is the moment for which I have waited all my life. I promised Arthur I could be a queen in armour; and now I am. 'A queen can ride under a king's standard, if she thinks she can win.'

I summon the remaining troops; these will be my force. I plan to parade them in battle order, but there are more comments.

'You will never ride at their head?'

'Where would you want me to ride?'

'Your Grace, perhaps you should not be there at all?'

'I am their Commander in Chief,' I say simply. 'You must not think of me as a queen who stays at home, influences policy by stealth, and bullies her children. I am a queen who rules as my mother did. When my country is in danger, I am in danger. When my country is triumphant, as we will be, it is my triumph.'

'But what if . . . ?' The lady-in-waiting is silenced by one hard look from me.

'I am not a fool, I have planned for defeat,' I tell her. 'A good commander always speaks of victory and yet has a plan for defeat. I know exactly where I shall fall back, and I know exactly where I shall regroup, and I know exactly where I shall join battle again, and if I fail there, I know where I shall regroup again. I did not wait long years for this throne to see the King of Scotland and that fool Margaret take it from me.'

Katherine's men, all forty thousand of them, straggled along the road behind the royal guard, weighed down by their weapons and sacks of food in the late summer sunshine. Katherine, at the head of the train, rode her white horse where everyone could see her, with the royal standard over her head, so that the men should know her now, on the march, and recognise her later, in battle. Twice a day she rode down the length of the line with a word of encouragement for everyone who was scuffing along in the rear, choking with the dust from the forward wagons. She kept monastic hours, rising at dawn to hear Mass, taking communion at noon, and going to bed at dusk, waking at midnight to say her prayers for the safety of the realm, for the safety of the king, and for herself.

Messengers passed constantly between Katherine's army and the force commanded by Thomas Howard, Earl of Surrey. Their plan was that Surrey should engage with the Scots at the first chance, anything to stop their rapid and destructive advance southwards. If

Surrey were defeated then the Scots would come on and Katherine would meet them with her force, and fling them into defence of the southern counties of England. If the Scots cut through them then Katherine and Surrey had a final plan for the defence of London. They would regroup, summon a citizens' army, throw up earthworks around the City and if all else failed, retreat to the Tower, which could be held for long enough for Henry to reinforce them from France.

Surrey is anxious that I have ordered him to lead the first attack against the Scots, he would rather wait for my force to join him; but I insist the attack shall go as I have planned. It would be safer to join our two armies, but I am fighting a defensive campaign. I have to keep an army in reserve to stop the Scots sweeping south, if they win the first battle. This is not a single battle I am fighting here. This is a war that will destroy the threat of the Scots for a generation, perhaps forever.

I too am tempted to order him to wait for me, I so want to join the battle; I feel no fear at all, just a sort of wild gladness as if I am a hawk mewed-up for too long and now suddenly set free. But I will not throw my precious men into a battle that would leave the road to London open if we lost. Surrey thinks that if we unite the forces we will be certain to win, but I know that there is no certainty in warfare, anything can go wrong. A good commander is ready for the worst, and I am not going to risk the Scots beating us in one battle and then marching down the Great North Road and into my capital city, and a coronation with French acclaim. I did not win this throne so hard, to lose it in one reckless fight. I have a battle plan for Surrey, and one for me, and then a position to retreat to, and a series of positions after that. They may win one battle, they may win more than one, but they will never take my throne from me.

We are sixty miles out of London, at Buckingham. This is good speed for an army on the march, they tell me it is tremendous speed for an English army; they are notorious for dawdling on the road. I am tired, but not exhausted. The excitement and – to be honest – the fear in each day is keeping me like a hound on a leash, always eager, straining to get ahead and start the hunt.

And now I have a secret. Each afternoon, when I dismount from my horse, I get down from the saddle and first thing, before anything else, I go into the necessary house, or tent, or wherever I can be alone, and I pull up my skirts and look at my linen. I am waiting for my monthly course, and it is the second month that it has failed to come. My hope, a strong, sweet hope, is that when Henry sailed to France he left me with child.

I will tell no-one, not even my women. I can imagine the outcry if they knew I was riding every day, and preparing for battle when I am with child, or even in hopes of a child. I dare not tell them, for in all truth, I do not dare do anything which might tilt the balance in this campaign against us. Of course, nothing could be more important than a son for England – except this one thing: holding England for that son to inherit. I have to grit my teeth on the risk I am taking, and take it anyway.

The men know that I am riding at their head and I have promised them victory. They march well, they will fight well because they have put their faith in me. Surrey's men, closer to the enemy than us, know that behind them, in reliable support, is my army. They know that I am leading their reinforcements in person. It has caused much talk in the country, they are proud to have a queen who will muster herself for them. If I were to turn my face to London and tell them to go on without me, for I have a woman's work to do, they would head for home too – it is as simple as that. They would think that I had lost confidence, that I had lost faith in them, that I anticipate defeat. There are enough whispers about an unstoppable army of Scotsmen – one hundred thousand angry Highlanders – without me adding to their fears.

Besides, if I cannot save my kingdom for my child, then there is little point in having a child. I have to defeat the Scots, I have to be a great general. When that duty is done, I can be a woman again.

At night, I have news from Surrey that the Scots are encamped on a strong ridge, drawn up in battle order at a place called Flodden. He sends me a plan of the site, showing the Scots camped on high ground, commanding the view to the south. One glance at the map tells me that the English should not attack uphill against the heavily armed Scots. The Scots archers will be shooting downhill and then the Highlanders will charge down on our men. No army could face an attack like that.

'Tell your master he is to send out spies and find a way around the back of the Scots to come upon them from the north,' I say to the messenger, staring at the map. 'Tell him my advice is that he makes a feint, leaves enough men before the Scots to pin them down, but marches the rest away, as if he is heading north. If he is lucky, they will give chase and you will have them on open ground. If he is unlucky he will have to reach them from the north. Is it good ground? He has drawn a stream on this sketch.'

'It is boggy ground,' the man confirms. 'We may not be able to cross it.'

I bite my lip. 'It's the only way that I can see,' I say. 'Tell him this is my advice but not my command. He is commander in the field, he must make his own judgement. But tell him I am certain that he has to get the Scots off that hill. Tell him I know for sure that he cannot attack uphill. He has to either go round and surprise them from the rear; or lure them down off that hill.'

The man bows and leaves. Please God he can get my message through to Surrey. If he thinks he can fight an army of Scots uphill he is finished. One of my ladies comes to me the minute the messenger has left my tent, she is trembling with fatigue and fear. 'What do we do now?'

'We advance north,' I say.

'But they may be fighting any day now!'

'Yes, and if they win we can go home. But if they lose we shall stand between the Scots and London.'

'And do what?' she whispers.

'Beat them,' I say simply.

10th September 1513

'Your Grace!' A page boy came dashing into Katherine's tent, bobbed a most inadequate, hurried bow. 'A messenger, with news of the battle! A messenger from Lord Surrey.'

Katherine whirled around, her shoulder strap from her halberk still undone. 'Send him in!'

The man was already in the room, the dirt of the battle still on him, but with the beam of a man bringing good news, great news.

'Yes?' Katherine demanded, breathless with hope.

'Your Grace has conquered,' he said. 'The King of Scotland lies dead, twenty Scottish lords lie with him, bishops, earls, and abbots too. It is a defeat they will never rise up from. Half of their great men have died in a single day.'

He saw the colour drain from her face and then she suddenly grew rosy. 'We have won?'

'You have won,' he confirmed. 'The earl said to tell you that your men, raised and trained and armed by you, have done what you ordered they should do. It is your victory, and you have made England safe.'

Her hand went at once to her belly, under the metal curve of the breastplate. 'We are safe,' she said.

He nodded. 'He sent you this . . .'

He held out for her a surcoat, terribly torn and slashed and stained with blood.

'This is?'

'The coat of the King of Scotland. We took it from his dead body as proof. We have his body, it is being embalmed. He is dead, the Scots are defeated. You have done what no English king since Edward the First could do. You have made England safe from Scottish invasion.'

'Write out a report for me,' she said decisively. 'Dictate it to the clerk. Everything you know, and everything that my lord Surrey said. I must write to the king.'

'Lord Surrey asked . . .'

'Yes?'

'Should he advance into Scotland and lay it waste? He says there will be little or no resistance. This is our chance. We could destroy them, they are utterly at our mercy.'

'Of course,' she said at once, then she paused. It was the answer that any monarch in Europe would have given. A troublesome neighbour, an inveterate enemy lay weakened. Every king in Christendom would have advanced and taken revenge.

'No. No, wait a moment.'

She turned away from him and went to the doorway of her tent. Outside, the men were preparing for another night on the road, far from their homes. There were little cook-fires all around the camp, torches burning, the smell of cooking and dung and sweat in the air. It was the very scent of Katherine's childhood, a childhood spent for the first seven years in a state of constant warfare against an enemy who was driven backwards and backwards and finally into slavery, exile and death.

Think, I say to myself fiercely. Don't feel with a tender heart, think with a hard brain, a soldier's brain. Don't consider this as a woman with child who knows there are many widows in Scotland tonight, think as a queen. My enemy is defeated, the country lies open before

me, their king is dead, their queen is a young fool of a girl and my sister-in-law. I can cut this country into pieces, I can quilt it. Any commander of any experience would destroy them now and leave them destroyed for a whole generation. My father would not hesitate; my mother would have given the order already.

I check myself. They were wrong, my mother and father. Finally, I say the unsayable, unthinkable thing. They were wrong, my mother and father. Soldiers of genius they may have been, convinced they certainly were, Christian kings they were called – but they were wrong. It has taken me all my life to learn this.

A state of constant warfare is a two-edged sword, it cuts both the victor and the defeated. If we pursue the Scots now, we will triumph, we can lay the country waste, we can destroy them for generations to come. But all that grows on waste are rats and pestilence. They would recover in time, they would come against us. Their children would come against my children and the savage battle would have to be fought all over again. Hatred breeds hatred. My mother and father drove the Moors overseas, but everyone knows that by doing so they won only one battle in a war that will never cease until Christians and Muslims are prepared to live side by side in peace and harmony. Isabella and Ferdinand hammered the Moors, but their children and their children's children will face the jihad in reply to the crusade. War does not answer war, war does not finish war. The only ending is peace.

'Get me a fresh messenger,' Katherine said over her shoulder, and waited till the man came. 'You are to go to my lord Surrey and tell him I give him thanks for this great news of a wonderful victory. You are to tell him that he is to let the Scots soldiers surrender their arms and they are to go in peace. I myself will write to the Scots queen and promise her peace if she will be our good sister and good neighbour. We are victorious, we shall be gracious. We shall make this victory a lasting peace, not a passing battle and an excuse for savagery.'

The man bowed and left. Katherine turned to the soldier. 'Go and get yourself some food,' she said. 'You can tell everyone that we have won a great battle and that we shall go back to our homes knowing that we can live at peace.'

She went to her little table and drew her writing box towards her. The ink was corked in a tiny glass bottle, the quill especially cut down to fit the small case. The paper and sealing wax were to hand. Katherine drew a sheet of paper towards her, and paused. She wrote a greeting to her husband, she told him she was sending him the coat of the dead Scots king.

In this, Your Grace shall see how I can keep my promise, sending you for your banners a king's coat. I thought to send himself to you, but our Englishmen's hearts would not suffer it.

I pause. With this great victory I can go back to London, rest and prepare for the birth of the child that I am sure I am carrying. I want to tell Henry that I am once again with child; but I want to write to him alone. This letter – like every letter between us – will be half-public. He never opens his own letters, he always gets a clerk to open them and read them for him, he rarely writes his own replies. Then I remember that I told him that if Our Lady ever blessed me with a child again I would go at once to her shrine at Walsingham to give thanks. If he remembers this, it can serve as our code. Anyone can read it to him but he will know what I mean, I shall have told him the secret, that we will have a child, that we may have a son. I smile and start to write, knowing that he will understand what I mean, knowing what joy this letter will bring him.

I make an end, praying God to send you home shortly, for without no joy can here be accomplished, and for the same I pray, and now go to Our Lady at Walsingham, that I promised so long ago to see.

Your humble wife and true servant,

Katherine.

Walsingham, Autumn 1513

Katherine was on her knees at the shrine of Our Lady of Walsingham, her eyes fixed on the smiling statue of the Mother of Christ, but seeing nothing.

Beloved, beloved, I have done it. I sent the coat of the Scots king to Henry and I made sure to emphasise that it is his victory, not mine. But it is yours. It is yours because when I came to you and to your country, my mind filled with fears about the Moors, it was you who taught me that the danger here was the Scots. Then life taught me a harder lesson, beloved: it is better to forgive an enemy than destroy him. If we had Moorish physicians, astronomers, mathematicians in this country we would be the better for it. The time may come when we also need the courage and the skills of the Scots. Perhaps my offer of peace will mean that they will forgive us for the battle of Flodden.

I have everything I ever wanted – except you. I have won a victory for this kingdom that will keep it safe for a generation. I have conceived a child and I feel certain that this baby will live. If he is a boy I shall call him Arthur for you. If she is a girl, I shall call her Mary. I am Queen of England, I have the love of the people and Henry will make a good husband and a good man.

I sit back on my heels and close my eyes so the tears should not run down my cheeks. 'The only thing I lack is you, beloved. Always you. Always you.'

'Your Grace, are you unwell?' The quiet voice of the nun recalls me and I open my eyes. My legs are stiff from kneeling so long. 'We did not want to disturb you, but it has been some hours.'

'Oh, yes,' I say. I try to smile at her. 'I shall come in a moment. Leave me now.'

I turn back to my dream of Arthur but he is gone. 'Wait for me in the garden,' I whisper. 'I will come to you. I will come one day soon. In the garden, when my work here is done.'

Words have weight, something once said cannot be unsaid, meaning is like a stone dropped into a pool; the ripples will spread and you cannot know what bank they wash against.

I once said, 'I love you, I will love you forever,' to a young man in the night. I once said, 'I promise.' That promise, made twenty-seven years ago to satisfy a dying boy, to fulfil the will of God, to satisfy my mother and – to tell truth – my own ambition, that word comes back to me like ripples washing to the rim of a marble basin and then eddying back again to the centre.

I knew I would have to answer for my lies before God. I never thought that I would have to answer to the world. I never thought that the world could interrogate me for something that I had promised for love, something whispered in secret. And so, in my pride, I never have answered for it. Instead, I held to it.

And so, I believe, would any woman in my position.

Henry's new lover, Elizabeth Boleyn's girl, my maid-in-waiting, turns out to be the one that I knew I had to fear: the one who has an ambition that is even greater than mine. Indeed, she is even more greedy than the king. She has an ambition greater than any I have *ever seen before in a man or a woman. She does not desire Henry as a man – I have seen his lovers come and go and I have learned to read them like an easy story book. This one desires not my husband, but my throne. She has had much work to find her way to it, but she is persistent and determined. I think I knew, from the moment that she had his ear, his secrets, and his confidence, that in time she would find her way – like a weasel smelling blood through a coney warren – to my lie. And when she found it, she would feast on it.*

The usher calls out, 'Katherine of Aragon, Queen of England, come into court'; and there is a token silence, for they expect no answer. There are no lawyers waiting to help me there, I have prepared no defence. I have made it clear that I do not recognise the court. They expect to go on without me. Indeed, the usher is just about to call the next witness . . .

But I answer.

My men throw open the double doors of the hall that I know so well and I walk in, my head up, as fearless as I have been all my life. The regal canopy is in gold, over at the far end of the hall with my husband, my false, lying, betraying, unfaithful husband in his ill-fitting crown on his throne sitting beneath it.

On a stage below him are the two cardinals, also canopied with cloth of gold, seated in golden chairs with golden cushions. That betraying slave Wolsey, red-faced in his red cardinal's robe, failing to meet my eye, as well he might; and that false friend Campeggio. Their three faces, the king and his two procurers, are mirrors of utter dismay.

They thought they had so distressed and confused me, separated me from my friends and destroyed me, that I would not come. They thought I would sink into despair like my mother, or into madness like my sister. They are gambling on the fact that they have frightened me and threatened me and taken my child from me and done everything they can do to break my heart. They never dreamed that I have the courage to stalk in before them, and stand before them, shaking with right-eousness, to face them all.

Fools, they forget who I am. They are advised by that Boleyn girl who has never seen me in armour, driven on by her who never knew my mother, did not know my father. She knows me as Katherine, the old Queen of England, devout, plump, dull. She has no idea that inside, I am still Catalina, the young Infanta of Spain. I am a princess born and trained to fight. I am a woman who has fought for every single thing I hold, and I will fight, and I will hold, and I will win.

They did not foresee what I would do to protect myself, and my daughter's inheritance. She is Mary, my Mary, named by Arthur: my beloved daughter, Mary. Would I let her be put aside for some bastard got on a Boleyn?

That is their first mistake.

I ignore the cardinals completely. I ignore the clerks on the benches before them, the scribes with their long rolls of parchment making the official record of this travesty. I ignore the court, the city, even the people who whisper my name with loving voices. Instead, I look at no-one but Henry.

I know Henry, I know him better than anyone else in the world does. I know him better than his current favourite ever will, for I have seen him, man and boy. I studied him when he was a boy, when he was a child of ten who came to meet me and tried to persuade me to give him a Barbary stallion. I knew him then as a boy who could be won with fair words and gifts. I knew him through the eyes of his brother, who said – and rightly – that he was a child who had been spoiled by too much indulgence and would be a spoilt man, and a danger to us all. I knew him as a youth, and I won my throne by pandering to his vanity. I was the greatest prize he could desire and I let him win me. I knew him as a man as vain and greedy as a peacock when I gave to him the credit for my war: the greatest victory ever won by England.

At Arthur's request I told the greatest lie a woman has ever told, and I will tell it to the very grave. I am an Infanta of Spain, I do not give a promise and fail to keep it. Arthur, my beloved, asked me for an oath on his deathbed and I gave it to him. He asked me to say that we had never been lovers and he commanded me to marry his brother and be queen. I did everything I promised him, I was constant to my promise. Nothing in these years has shaken my faith that it is God's will that I should be Queen of England, and that I shall be Queen of England until I die. No-one could have saved England from the Scots but me – Henry was too young and too inexperienced to take an army into the field. He would have offered a duel, he would have chanced some forlorn hope, he would have lost the battle and died at Flodden and his sister Margaret would have been Queen of England in my place.

It did not happen because I did not allow it to happen. It was my mother's wish and God's will that I should be Queen of England, and I will be Queen of England until I die.

I do not regret the lie. I held to it, and I made everyone else hold to it, whatever doubts they may have had. As Henry learned more of women, as Henry learned more of me, he knew, as surely he had known on our wedding night, that it was a lie, I was no virgin for him. But in all our twenty years of marriage together, he found the courage to challenge me only once, at the very beginning; and I walk into the court on the great gamble that he will never have the courage to challenge me again, not even now.

I walk into court with my entire case staked on his weakness. I believe that when I stand before him, and he is forced to meet my eyes, he will not dare to say that I was no virgin when I came to him, that I was Arthur's wife and Arthur's lover before I was ever his. His vanity will not allow him to say that I loved Arthur with a true passion and he loved me. That in truth, I will live and die as Arthur's wife and Arthur's lover, and thus Henry's marriage to me can be rightfully dissolved.

I don't think he has the courage that I have. I think if I stand straight and tell the great lie again, he will not dare to stand straight and tell the truth.

'Katherine of Aragon, Queen of England, come into court,' the usher repeats stupidly, as the echo of the doors banging behind me reverberates in the shocked courtroom, and everyone can see that I am already in court, standing like a stocky fighter before the throne.

It is me they call for, by this title. It was my dying husband's hope, my mother's wish and God's will that I should be Queen of England; and for them and for the country, I will be Queen of England until I die.

'Katherine of Aragon, Queen of England, come into court!'
This is me. This is my moment. This is my battle cry.
I step forwards.

Author's Note

This has been one of the most fascinating and most moving novels to write, from the discovery of the life of the young Katherine, to the great question of the lie that she told and maintained all her life.

That it was a lie is, I think, the most likely explanation. I believe that her marriage to Arthur was consummated. Certainly, everyone thought so at the time; it was only Dona Elvira's insistence after Katherine had been widowed, and Katherine's own insistence at the time of her separation from Henry that put the consummation into doubt. Later historians, admiring Katherine and accepting her word against Henry's, put the lie into the historical record where it stays today.

The lie was the starting place of the novel but the surprise in the research was the background of Catalina of Spain. I enjoyed a wonderful research trip to Granada to discover more about the Spain of Isabella and Ferdinand, and came home with an abiding respect both for their courage and for the culture they swore to overthrow: the rich tolerant and beautiful land of the Moslems of Spain, el Andalus. I have tried to give these almost forgotten Europeans a voice in this book, and to give us today, as we struggle with some of the same questions, an idea of the *conviviencia* – a land where Jews, Moslems and Christians managed to live side by side in respect and peace as 'People of the Book'.

A note on the double hearts

The double hearts at the chapter headings are the artist's impression of a carving said to have been found in Ludlow Castle in Arthur's chamber. The carving was sketched in 1684 but the original carving has been lost. They are a good example of the layers of reality that I often encounter: the carving is legend, the sketch is history, and the thought that they were carved by Arthur to show his love for Catalina, his young wife, is fiction.

A note on the songs

'Alas, Alhama!', 'Riders gallop through the Elvira gate . . .' and 'There was crying in Granada . . .' are traditional songs, quoted by Francesca Claremount in *Catherine of Aragon* (see book list below).

'A palm tree stands in the middle of Rusafa', is by Abd al Rahman, translated by D. F. Ruggles and quoted in Menocal, *The Ornament of the World* (see book list below).

The following books have been most helpful in my research into the history of this story:

Bindoff, S. T., *Pelican History of England: Tudor England*, Penguin, 1993
Bruce, Marie Louise, *Anne Boleyn*, Collins, 1972
Chejne, Anwar G., *Islam and the West: The Moriscos – A Cultural and Social History*, State University of New York Press, 1983

Claremont, Francesca, *Catherine of Aragon*, Robert Hale, 1939

Cressy, David, *Birth, Marriage and Death: Ritual Religion and the Life-cycle in Tudor and Stuart England*, OUP, 1977

Darby, H. C., *A New Historical Geography of England before 1600*, CUP, 1976

Dixon, William Hepworth, *History of Two Queens*, vol. 2, London, 1873

Elton, G. R., *England under the Tudors*, Methuen, 1955

Fernandez-Arnesto, Felipe, *Ferdinand and Isabella*, Weidenfeld & Nicolson, London, 1975

Fletcher, Anthony, *Tudor Rebellions*, Longman, 1968

Goodwin, Jason, *Lords of the Horizon: A History of the Ottoman Empire*, Vintage, 1989

Guy, John, *Tudor England*, OUP, 1988

Haynes, Alan, *Sex in Elizabethan England*, Sutton, 1997

Loades, David, *The Tudor Court*, Batsford, 1986

Loades, David, *Henry VIII and His Queens*, Sutton, 2000

Lloyd, David, *Arthur Prince of Wales*, Fabric Trust for St Laurence, Ludlow, 2002

Mackie, J. D., *Oxford History of England: The Earlier Tudors*, OUP, 1952

Mattingley, Garrett, *Catherine of Aragon*, Jonathan Cape, 1942

Menocal, *The Ornament of the World*, Little, Brown, 2002

Mumby, Frank Arthur, *The Youth of Henry VIII*, Constable, 1913

Núñez, J. Agustín, (ed.), *Muslim and Christian Granada*, Edilux SL, 2004

Paul, E. John, *Catherine of Aragon and Her Friends*, Burns & Drates, 1966

Plowden, Alison, *The House of Tudor*, Weidenfeld and Nicolson, 1976

Plowden, Alison, *Tudor Women: Queens and Commoners*, Sutton, 1998

Randall, Keith, *Henry VIII and the Reformation in England*, Hodder, 1993

Robinson, John Martin, *The Dukes of Norfolk*, OUP, 1982

Scarisbrick, J. J., *Yale English Monarchs: Henry VIII*, YUP, 1997

Scott, S. P., *The History of the Moorish Empire in Europe*, vol. 1, Ams Pr, 1974

Starkey, David, *Henry VIII: A European Court in England*, Collins & Brown, 1991

Starkey, David, *The Reign of Henry VIII: Personalities and Politics*, G. Philip, 1985

Starkey, David, *Six Wives: The Queens of Henry VIII*, Vintage, 2003

Tillyard, E. M. W., *The Elizabethan World Picture*, Pimlico, 1943

Turner, Robert, *Elizabethan Magic*, Element, 1989

Walsh, William Thomas, *Isabella of Spain*, Sheed & Ward, 1935

Warnicke, Retha M., *The Rise and Fall of Anne Boleyn*, CUP, 1991

Weir, Alison, *Henry VIII: King and Court*, Pimlico, 2002

Weir, Alison, *The Six Wives of Henry VIII*, Pimlico, 1997

Youings, Joyce, *Sixteenth-Century England*, Penguin, 1991

Meridon

Philippa Gregory

Meridon, the desolate Romany girl, is determined to escape the hard poverty of her childhood. Riding bareback in a travelling show, while her sister Dandy risks her life on the trapeze, Meridon dedicates herself to freeing them both from danger and want.

But Dandy – beautiful, impatient, thieving Dandy – grabs too much, too quickly. And Meridon finds herself alone, riding in bitter grief through the rich Sussex farmlands towards a house called Wideacre – which awaits the return of the last of the Laceys.

Sweeping, passionate, unique: *Meridon* completes Philippa Gregory's bestselling trilogy which began with *Wideacre* and continued in *The Favoured Child*.

'In other hands this would be a conventional historical romance. But Ms Gregory uses her historical knowledge of the haves and the have-nots of those times to weave a much more subtle and exciting story.'   *Daily Express*

ISBN 0 00 651463 4

Bread and Chocolate

Philippa Gregory

A rich selection of short stories from bestselling novelist Philippa Gregory.

A TV chef who specialises in outrageous cakes tempts a monk who bakes bread for his brothers; a surprise visitor invites mayhem into the perfect minimalist flat in the season of good will; a woman explains her unique view of straying husbands; straying husbands encounter a variety of inventive responses. These are just some of the treats on offer in this sumptuous box of delights.

'This stunning collection is about modern relationships – and modern women. Every twist and turn, nuance and delicacy of the mating game is portrayed. It is a significant accomplishment.'
Daily Mail

'Tastily enjoyable.' *The Times*

ISBN 0 00 714589 6

The Favoured Child

Philippa Gregory

The Wideacre estate is bankrupt. The villagers are living in poverty and Wideacre Hall is a smoke-blackened ruin.

But in the Dower House two children are being raised in protected innocence. Equal claimants to the inheritance of Wideacre, rivals for the love of the village, they are tied by a secret childhood betrothal but forbidden to marry.

Only one can be the favoured child. Only one can inherit the magical understanding between the land and the Lacey family that can make the Sussex village grow green again. Only one can be Beatrice Lacey's true heir.

Sensual, gripping, sometimes mystical, *The Favoured Child* sweeps the reader irresistibly into the 1790s and a revolutionary period in English history. This rich and dramatic novel continues the saga of the Lacey family started in Philippa Gregory's bestselling and enduringly popular first novel, *Wideacre*.

Acclaim for the *Wideacre* trilogy:

'Subtle and exciting'   *Daily Express*

ISBN 0 00 651462 6

The Wise Woman

Philippa Gregory

Passion and betrayal fuse in this powerful novel of Tudor England.

Alys joins the nunnery to escape poverty but finds herself thrown back into the outside world when Henry VIII's wreckers destroy her sanctuary. With nothing but her looks, her magic and her own instinctive cunning, Alys has to tread a perilous path between the faith of her childhood and her own female power.

When she falls in love with Hugo, the feudal lord and another woman's husband, she dips into witchcraft to defeat her rival and to win her lover, only to find that magic makes a poor servant but a dominant master. Since heresy against the new church means the stake, and witchcraft the rope, Alys's danger is mortal. A woman's powers are no longer safe to use...

'Compulsively readable'   ANDREA NEWMAN, *Sunday Express*

'Gregory's principal feat in this elaborate novel is the irrefutable artistry with which she lends her prose a constant sense of history'   *Sunday Times*

ISBN 0 00 651464 2

Wideacre

Philippa Gregory

Wideacre Hall, set in the heart of the English countryside, is the ancestral home that Beatrice Lacey loves. But as a woman of the eighteenth century, she has no right of inheritance. Corrupted by a world that mistreats women, she sets out to corrupt others. Sexual and wilful, she believes that the only way to achieve control over Wideacre is through a series of horrible crimes, and no-one escapes the consequences of her need to possess the land.

'The eighteenth-century woman is a neglected creature but, in the figure of her heroine, Philippa Gregory has defined a certain kind of witness...This is a novel written from instinct, not out of calculation, and it shows.' PETER ACKROYD, *The Times*

'For single mindedness, tempestuousness, passion, amorality, sensuality and plain old-fashioned evil, [Beatrice Lacey] knocks Scarlett O'Hara into short cotton socks.' *Evening Standard*

ISBN 0 00 651461 8

The Virgin's Lover

Philippa Gregory

In the autumn of 1558, church bells across England ring out the news – Elizabeth is queen. One woman hears them with dread: Amy Dudley, wife of Sir Robert, knows that with Elizabeth on the throne he will return to the glamorous Tudor court. Amy's hopes that the ambitions of the Dudley family had died when Robert's father was beheaded are ended. The triumphant peal of bells summons her husband once more to power – and to a passionate young queen.

Elizabeth has inherited a bankrupt and rebellious country. Her advisor William Cecil warns that she will only survive if she marries a strong prince, but the only man Elizabeth desires is her childhood friend.

Robert is sure that he can reclaim his destiny at Elizabeth's side. And as queen and courtier fall in love, Dudley begins to contemplate the impossible – setting aside his loving wife to marry the young Elizabeth…

'A simmering mixture of intrigue, lust and betrayal' *Daily Mail*

'[A] gripping novel that brings Tudor England to life… Historical fiction at its best' *Choice* magazine

ISBN 0 00 714 731 7

9/5/20

KT-450-581

20p

This book should be returned/renewed by the latest date shown above. Overdue items incur charges which prevent self-service renewals. Please contact the library.

Wandsworth Libraries
24 hour Renewal Hotline
01159 293388
www.wandsworth.gov.uk

Wandsworth

9030 00004 9442 8

Olivia's Luck

CATHERINE ALLIOTT

PENGUIN BOOKS

PENGUIN BOOKS

Published by the Penguin Group
Penguin Books Ltd, 80 Strand, London WC2R ORL, England
Penguin Group (USA) Inc., 375 Hudson Street, New York, New York 10014, USA
Penguin Group (Canada), 90 Eglinton Avenue East, Suite 700, Toronto, Ontario, Canada M4P 2Y3
(a division of Pearson Penguin Canada Inc.)
Penguin Ireland, 25 St Stephen's Green, Dublin 2, Ireland (a division of Penguin Books Ltd)
Penguin Group (Australia), 250 Camberwell Road,
Camberwell, Victoria 3124, Australia (a division of Pearson Australia Group Pty Ltd)
Penguin Books India Pvt Ltd, 11 Community Centre,
Panchsheel Park, New Delhi – 110 017, India
Penguin Group (NZ), 67 Apollo Drive, Rosedale, Auckland 0632, New Zealand
(a division of Pearson New Zealand Ltd)
Penguin Books (South Africa) (Pty) Ltd, Block D, Rosebank Office Park,
181 Jan Smuts Avenue, Parktown North, Gauteng 2193, South Africa

Penguin Books Ltd, Registered Offices: 80 Strand, London WC2R ORL, England

www.penguin.com

First published by Headline Book Publishing 2000
Published in Penguin Books 2012
001

Copyright © Catherine Alliott, 2000
All rights reserved

The moral right of the author has been asserted

All characters in this publication are fictitious,
and any resemblance to real persons, living or dead,
is purely coincidental

Set in 12.5/14.75 pt Garamond MT
Typeset by Jouve (UK), Milton Keynes
Printed in England by Clays Ltd, St Ives plc

Except in the United States of America, this book is sold subject
to the condition that it shall not, by way of trade or otherwise, be lent,
re-sold, hired out, or otherwise circulated without the publisher's
prior consent in any form of binding or cover other than that in
which it is published and without a similar condition including this
condition being imposed on the subsequent purchaser

ISBN: 978-0-241-95831-5

Export edition ISBN: 978-0-241-96131-5

www.greenpenguin.co.uk

Penguin Books is committed to a sustainable
future for our business, our readers and our planet.
This book is made from Forest Stewardship
Council™ certified paper.

ALWAYS LEARNING   **PEARSON**

For my brother, Stephen

LONDON BOROUGH OF WANDSWORTH	
9030 00004 9442 8	
Askews & Holts	17-Mar-2016
AF	£7.99
	WW15023289

Chapter One

Alf regarded me with his one good eye. It was brown and troubled and beginning to look as glassy as the other one. He frowned as he tried to make sense of it all.

'What – you mean he's left you, like?'

'That's it, Alf.'

'For good? Scarpered?'

'So it appears.'

He struggled with this conundrum. 'And – and so what, ain't he never coming back then?'

I caught my breath at the brutality of my husband's plan laid bare, swallowed hard. 'No, Alf, apparently not. Total desertion does indeed seem to be his overall game plan.' I raised my chin and somehow cranked up a smile.

Alf continued to look mystified. He scratched his grizzled old head, and then the penny – slow to drop at the best of times – began its gradual descent. It finally fell with a deafening clunk.

'Well, bugger me,' he gaped, stunned.

I licked my lips. 'Quite.'

Leaving him to his open-mouthed astonishment, I turned briskly to my other two builders, who, thus far, had been silent throughout this gnomic exchange, though more, I suspected, from pity and embarrassment than lack of comprehension.

Alf's brother, Mac, the foreman, the boss-man, and the

brains of the team, was watching me closely, his blue eyes assessing this dramatic shift in situation, whilst Spiro, the emotional young Greek in my incongruous masonry trio, was having trouble keeping his jaw from wobbling. His black, mournful moustache drooped low and his dark eyes were filling ominously, but then, if you told Spiro it looked like rain he tended to reach for his hanky.

'He *leave* you?' he spluttered incredulously. 'Your husband *leave* you? Alone, here, with a young child and a dreadful falling-down house and bad drains and rats and peeling walls and –' his eyes grew wide as he regarded me with horror – 'looking so *terrible*?'

'The house, I hope, not me, Spiro,' I quipped nervously. He frowned. '*Ti?*'

'Um, no, never mind. Yes, well, of course, you're right, the house *is* in a terrible state but then we're bang in the middle of rewiring and replumbing, aren't we?' I said brightly. 'We're stripping it all back, Spiro, laying it bare, getting back to the bones. It's bound to look worse before it looks better, but once it's gutted –'

'*You're* gutted!' he roared. '*I'm* gutted! I cannot believe what sort of a man *do* this to you! What sort of – of an *animal*!' With that he snatched his tea-cosy hat from his head and, with a great wail, buried his face in it. I had a sudden urge to snatch it from him and do exactly the same. Instead I patted his shoulder.

'Come on now, Spiro,' I muttered. 'You're sweet but, well, it's not as bad as all that. It's going to be fine, honestly.' I waited while he composed himself, blowing his nose violently into his hat and then plonking it back on his head at an unusual angle. His dark eyes blazed.

'All men are bastards,' he informed me unequivocally, shaking his finger furiously. '*All* men.'

Well, I wasn't going to argue with that. In fact I rather approved of his fixed-bayonet relish. Perhaps we could both pull on our snotty hats and go and kill the bastards together. Spiro's blood was certainly fiery, and when it was up, it was hot.

Mac, meanwhile, was clearing his throat ostentatiously. He spat dexterously on to the concrete beside him.

'So you'll be giving all this up then, will you, luv?'

I straightened up to my working foreman, ever the pragmatist, ever the one to get straight to the point, and met his bright blue eyes defiantly. He wasn't much bigger than me, fiftyish, tiny, spry and, unlike his bear-like brother, Alf, very switched on, very sharp.

'How d'you mean, Mac?'

'Well, now that it's all gone pear-shaped you're not gonna want to carry on, are you? You're not gonna want to cope wiv all this malarkey just for yourself and Claudes, are you?'

He jerked his head dismissively at the building site around us: the excuse for the kitchen where we were standing, with its open rafters covered by a flapping blue tarpaulin; the soggy concrete at our feet; the rotten sash windows with their broken cords; the sixties-style Formica units – half of which had been ripped from the walls, the rest still clinging on tenaciously – and finally, the huge gaping hole in the back wall, to which Spiro, on hearing that Greece had been knocked out of the World Cup, had accidentally taken a sledgehammer, and then been so mortified none of us had had the heart to berate him. Yes, this 'malarkey' that was my home.

I cleared my throat. 'Actually, Mac, that's exactly why I've asked you all to take a break and down tools for a minute. You see, the thing is, I fully intend to go on.' I drew myself up to my full five foot three and tucked my short dark hair meticulously behind my ears, struggling to look braver than I felt. 'Fully intend. The mere fact that my husband has seen fit to abscond is neither here nor there, because as far as I'm concerned, we're going on as planned. We're going to finish the kitchen, get all these units out, replaster the walls, put the new cupboards in, get the wooden floor laid, replace all the rotten windows and then, when we've finished that, we're going to start on the upstairs, OK?'

'She so brave,' whispered Spiro in a choked voice, woolly hat back to mouth. I couldn't look at him. I raised my chin, suddenly feeling a bit Churchillian.

'Give up?' I warbled. 'Good heavens, no. I took on this tip of a house with the sole intention of restoring it to its former glory, and that's still very much the plan, very much my dream.' Crikey, I was Martin Luther King now, but there was no stopping me. 'And I'm not going to skimp either,' I warned, swelling my oratory to a preacherly roundness. 'I don't want you to rush things and cut corners just to get it finished any old how so I can flog it, because I'm not going to flog it! I'm going to live in it, and I'm going to live in it for a very long time, and – and if I feel like having Rococo in the bathroom or . . . or – I don't know . . .' I cast about wildly, 'gilding in the guest room, or gazebos in the garden, I'll jolly well have it. As far as I'm concerned this is still a forever house and I want it done properly. I want to match up the old panelling, do the

4

picture rails, the dados, and doodahs, and whatnots, the whole blinking shooting match. The master bedroom needs a complete makeover, a total rethink –' I broke off as, to my horror, my voice wobbled at the mention of this.

Around me, there was a bit of embarrassed scuffing of toes in the dirt and faces turned to the floor. A moment later I'd regained my composure. I swallowed hard.

'Listen, boys, I'll level with you,' I said quietly. 'I wanted to put you in the picture because I know there's been talk – ' I eyed Mac beadily here – 'and I know you've all been wondering where the hell "the guv'nor" is. Well, frankly, I'm fresh out of ideas. I'm right out of management buyout courses he might be on, or corporate finance lectures he might be attending, or – or weekend golf tournaments that seem to go on all week, and squash matches and – oh God, I'm just sick to the back teeth of having to lie. Constantly. To you, to my friends, to everyone at Claudia's school. In fact if you must know, I feel like renting a ruddy great billboard and pitching it outside the front gate with – "MY HUSBAND'S LEFT ME, OK?" plastered all over it.'

There was a short and sympathetic silence. Then Mac spat in his dirty hand and, ever the gentleman, wiped it on his trousers. I had a nasty feeling that hand was coming my way for a warm, supportive shake so I braced myself, had mine at the ready. He stuffed it in his pocket.

'What about the moolah then, luv?'

I blinked. 'Sorry?'

'The dough, the money.'

'I'm not with you, Mac.'

'Well, I hate to seem heartless, but this place is costing

you an arm and a leg, and if he's done a runner and we're gonna go on wiv the work as planned, we need to be clear that at the end of the day, we're gonna get paid. That everyfing's sorted.' He raised his eyebrows and gave me a wry, quizzical smile. 'Know what I mean?'

'I know exactly what you mean, Mac,' I said smoothly, 'and I understand your concerns, but believe me, you've got no worries on that score. My husband might have seen fit to remove himself physically, but financially, I'm OK. Huge and guilty contributions are still being paid regularly into the Privy Purse – which no doubt assuages his conscience – so money is not a problem. You will be paid.'

'At the end of ev—'

'At the end of every working week.'

'In the usual –'

'In the usual, mutually acceptable manner of folding readies in a big brown envelope – yes, Mac, business as usual.'

Mac pursed his lips thoughtfully. Then he smiled. It was a slow illumination. He turned to his workforce.

'I suppose we'll have to say that that's all right then, won't we, boys?' He raised his eyes to his towering older brother, who, whilst higher up in the vertical scale, was lower down the evolutionary one, where thought processes were slow.

'You mean,' he said at last, glass eye flashing in bewilderment, 'you mean we're *not* gonna get paid, like?'

'No, you dozy prat, we *are* gonna get paid, that's what she's just bin saying!'

'Has she? Oh. Oh well, yeah. Yeah, that's all right then.' He scratched his head, still mystified.

Mac nodded. 'Zorba?'

'I would work for you for nothing,' hissed the young Greek passionately. 'I consider it an insult to be asked. On my honour I would feenish the job with my dying breath. I curse the Meester McFarllen who has done this to you. I speet on his mother's grave and his grandmother's grave and then I speet –' he demonstrated with a flash of saliva to concrete – 'on his crotch. May it be sore and blistered, may his piles hang like grapes, may his backside gush like a donkey's, may –'

'Oh, thank you, Spiro,' I broke in breathlessly. 'That's so – so supportive of you! So spirited!' Heavens, if I didn't cut him off in mid curse he'd be impaling himself on his plumbing rods next, kamikaze style.

He seized my arm and brought his face very close to mine. 'I want you to know that I will toil sweat and blood for you, Meesis McFarllen. But him –' he curled his lip scornfully and I tried not to flinch as I felt his whiskers – 'pericolor testatosis!' he finished emphatically.

'Well, quite,' I murmured, backing away. 'Um, thank you, Spiro.'

As I surreptitiously wiped some spittle from my face I wondered what the devil that was all about. I was pretty sure the 'testatosis' bit wasn't particularly polite, though. Young Spiro had his fair share of earthy directness and only the other day he offered to show me his little stiffy. I hadn't liked the sound of it at all but, being too polite to say no, was just preparing to faint nonchalantly, when I realised he was reaching into his jeans pocket for a crumpled photograph. Stiffy, it transpired, short for Stiff-ano, was his baby son; six months old, almond-eyed and

7

adorable – or at least I thought so, so relieved was I to see him. I sighed. Actually, I couldn't help thinking a bit more honour and crotch speeting wouldn't go amiss amongst the jobsworthy Englishmen.

'We'll get on wiv it then, shall we, luv?' said Mac kindly, as if reading my mind. 'Get back to work, like?'

'Please, Mac.' I smiled gratefully, but I also knew that this was my cue to leave. Now that the delicate little matter of the money had been 'sorted', the interview was over as far as Mac was concerned. No worries, just so long as they all got paid.

As I left them to it and moved on through to the hall, I couldn't resist turning back for a moment, watching them unobserved. 'Getting on wiv it' in Mac's book merely meant that the morning's work was over and that the lunch ritual was about to begin. At five past twelve it wasn't worth picking up tools again, and anyway, the table had to be laid. To this end, Alf was lumbering across the concrete floor in search of a milk crate for them to gather round, and various boxes to sit on. He carried this furniture back heavily, seeming always to veer slightly to the left pursued by the rest of his body, then set it all decoratively in the middle of the room, his mouth taut with concentration.

Mac, meanwhile, pale, sinewy, and dressed for this sweltering weather in a vest and navy-blue shorts, his marble-white legs hairless, and looking nothing like the powerhouse he really was, was attending to the more domestic side of things. Bending down to gather filthy mugs from the floor, he reached also for the broken Pils can that served as the sugar bowl and plonked in a couple of sugar-encrusted spoons. Then he swilled the milk around in its cheesy carton, before plugging in the kettle and preparing to be 'Mum'.

Only Spiro, I observed gratefully – who was only in this country in order to earn himself enough money to return to his remote Ionian island, build himself a house, install his young family and set himself up as the local master builder – was still bristling with righteous indignation. Standing alone and ramrod straight, he flicked out a Rothmans, lit up, and puffed away furiously, too distracted to eat or drink.

Alf and Mac, of course, had no such qualms. They lowered their backsides slowly to their wooden boxes, Alf gave a great ceremonial belch in lieu of grace, and then they were off, tucking into their usual fishpaste sandwiches and PG Tips with relish. To be fair, in between mouthfuls, there was a degree of deliberation on the downfall of my marriage, and even some pondering on man's inhumanity to woman.

'Bastard.'

'Yeah.'

''S not on.'

''S right.'

'Not wiv a kiddie.'

'Nah.'

'Pot Noodle?'

'Yeah, go on then.'

Oh no, they weren't completely heartless.

I took one last look at the happy domestic scene unfolding under the flapping blue tarpaulin, which, crackling in the sunshine, cast a light like some subterranean swimming pool, then turned and went on through to the hall.

'Mind you,' Alf's muffled tones stopped me again, ''s not gonna be easy for her, is it? I mean – how old d'you reckon she is?'

I didn't hear the entirety of Mac's response, but enough to suggest that had I been a chicken, it certainly wouldn't be springtime. Clenching my fists and swallowing hard I passed by the front door, stopped at the loo, opened the door, and pausing only to take the briefest of glances at my bloodless reflection in the mirror, turned to the lavatory pan and threw up.

Chapter Two

I'd been testing some Crown Matchpots in the front hall when Johnny had announced his intentions.

There I was, behind the front door, painting away merrily above the skirting boards, when I heard the garden gate go, heard his familiar footsteps up the gravel path. Knowing instinctively that hot foot from his evening commute, from the human lasagne of the City trains, he'd be tired, bad-tempered and in need of a drink, I knew better than to smile brightly and enquire, 'Good day, darling?' to which he'd probably snap irritably, 'Tedious, thank you,' and instead, sat back on my heels and arranged my expression into one of amused contemplation. As his head came round the door, I looked up with a wry smile.

'You know, anyone would think they aim these paints at the dirty-mac brigade,' I said, holding up my two little pots. 'You have a choice here, my darling,' I waggled them at him, 'Beaver or Muff!'

I grinned, enjoying my little joke and waiting for him to laugh, but as he stared back I noticed his face was very pale, his lips tight.

'I don't care what colour you paint the sodding hall,' he muttered. 'I'm leaving.'

And so saying, he pushed past me and on up the stairs, at which point I do recall that I at least managed to say –

in a voice fully intended to travel – 'Beaver it is then!' Knowing full well he'd prefer Muff.

Yes, that was how my husband left me. Those were the very special words with which he chose to end our marriage. I remember sitting there with my paintbrush in my hand thinking – in a shocked and stunned sort of way – that you had to hand it to Johnny. Not for him the usual garbage departing husbands give about needing to find themselves and having room to breathe, blah, blah, blah. No, his was very much in the Rhett Butler school of departure, because frankly, my dear – I paused. Except that, no, that wasn't true either. Up until recently he *had* given a damn. Up until five months ago to be precise, and for the last five months I'd certainly seen this coming but, in the same way as one sees the articulated lorry hurtling round the corner, it's still quite a shock when it hits you.

Functioning on automatic I dipped my brush conscientiously into the turps to stop it drying out, then rested my head back against the wall and shut my eyes tight. Squeezed the life out of them, in fact. For a while there I couldn't move, but I knew I had to, because, after all, he was only upstairs packing a suitcase, and in a few minutes' time he'd be pounding downstairs again before exiting through the front door, and I surely didn't want to be the stepped-over wife, as well as the passed-over one, did I?

Somehow I eased myself up and stumbled blindly towards our tiny makeshift kitchen. Originally I think it had been the old scullery, but now it just housed an ancient Baby Belling stove, a small sink I'd found in a junk yard and a mini fridge, a temporary arrangement all cobbled together any old how because, after all, we were only using it until our splendid new kitchen was finished. In the middle was a small pine table. I sat down shakily, resting my elbows and clasping my hands together, almost in an attitude of prayer. I listened. Upstairs, drawers were shooting in and out with a vengeance, coat hangers were clanking and the wardrobe slammed shut – wham bang – all sounds of a speedy exit. As I reached for a cigarette I noticed my hand was shaking. I shut my eyes again, and his pale, tight-lipped face swam to mind. Chin jutting out, that hard, impenetrable look in his eye – now where had I seen that look recently . . . ?

Well, it was just a few Sundays ago, actually, at a tense, silent, lunch in this very room, the majority of which Johnny had spent behind a propped-up newspaper, the only evidence of his continued existence on the planet being the disappearance of French bread and Stilton behind the broadsheet. Claudia and I had sat in silence too, gazing bleakly at the back of *The Times*, until Claudia could bear it no longer and, pausing only to shoot me a swift what-the-hell's-up-with-Daddy look, had slipped from the room and gone upstairs to play on her computer. I'd done quite a bit of ostentatious sighing, and then in my usual, martyred fashion, got up to clear the plates. There I'd been, elbow-deep in suds at the sink, when I'd turned for a moment to scrape some rubbish in the bin, and as I'd done so, I'd seen his face. He'd left the table and was standing at the window, staring out at the rain-soaked lawn, in the middle of which sat a huge pile of rubble from our gutted house. As I'd watched, he'd raised his eyes to heaven and mouthed 'Jesus Christ'.

I'd turned back quickly so he didn't know I'd seen, but

I went very cold. You see, I'd known what he was thinking: Jesus Christ, is this all there is? After a few moments I dropped the greasy plate back in the water and turned, smiling, wet hands on hips.

'Oh, by the way,' I said brightly, 'I saw something in the back of *The Times* last week, in the classified ads section. There was this thing about a hot-air ballooning weekend in Normandy and I thought – well, why not? You've always wanted to do it and it sounds quite fun, so why don't we go for your birthday? What d'you think?'

Johnny had turned slowly from the splattered window-pane, raised one partially interested eyebrow and said, 'Where?'

'Here.'

Quickly wiping my hands on a tea towel I'd scurried to get the paper from a drawer, spreading it out hastily, knowing exactly which page it was on and which column to find, because I'd saved it for just such an occasion. I'd pointed, then stood back to let him read the ad, hardly daring to breathe as I'd watched his face get gradually brighter. It was a slow transformation, but by the time he'd got to the end, he'd been almost excited.

'D'you know, this isn't such a bad idea, Livvy. We could get the ferry across and maybe ask Marcus and Jane if they want to join us.'

'Exactly. That's what I thought.' I'd stepped forward tentatively.

'And we could all go in one car – pointless taking two – and take the Michelin too, do a sort of gastronomic tour of the local hostelries. It's all cream and Calvados country round there – we'd be spoilt for choice!'

'Precisely. All those cheeky cheeses –'

'Plenty of *vin rouge* –'

'Hoovering up the *escargots* –'

'And we could leave Claudia behind with your mother.'

I paused. 'Yup.' We could. We always left Claudia behind with my mother.

'In fact the weekend after next is a bank holiday so, hang on . . .' he'd gone to the calendar on the door, 'if I took the Friday off . . .'

I'd joined him as he'd flipped the pages over. 'And we came back on the Monday night . . .'

'We'd still be back in time for the Palmers' drinks party on the Tuesday! Good idea, Livvy.' He always called me Livvy rather than Olivia. 'I'll go and ring Marcus, see if he's up for it. Bound to be, mad bastard!'

Oh, bound to be. And off he'd scurried to the phone, full of beans, full of plans, equilibrium restored. And I'd shut the paper slowly, put it back in the drawer, pushed it in softly. Right. So. Suddenly, we were off to France for four days. We couldn't afford it; I'd miss Claudia; Mac and the builders needed constant supervision in this wreck of a house; and I wouldn't get the runner beans in either, but no matter – the crisis had been averted. I remember turning to watch him through the kitchen door as he'd spoken on the phone to Marcus, his face a picture now, all animation and smiles, like a small boy cajoled out of a sulk by a trip to the zoo.

In case you think I'm the kind of girl who'd rather get the runner beans in than embark on a gastronomic tour of Normandy, I'd like to make it clear that I'm not. It was simply that Normandy was the latest in a long line of exotic treats designed to take Johnny's mind off life. Oh, I conjured them up almost weekly. I'd only have to turn from the television to make a remark and find that he was watching me, staring at me intently – and not in a way that suggested he was mesmerised by my beauty – and I was nervously reaching for the phone. Somehow, in a matter of minutes, I'd have the last few Eric Clapton tickets to be had at the Albert Hall, some front row seats at Brands Hatch, a few impossible-to-come-by Twickenham tickets – heavens, at this rate we'd be holidaying at Sandringham soon. I felt like a door-to-door salesman unpacking my sample bag – here, how about this, or this? – but whilst Johnny smiled and nodded and accepted my wares, I knew that one day I'd empty it all out on the doorstep and he wouldn't want anything. No, I don't want that, or that, or that – not today, thank you.

Well, I thought wryly, dragging my cigarette down to my Docksides as I sat at the tiny kitchen table, that day had come.

I stubbed the butt out in an old saucer and cocked an ear above. It was quieter upstairs now, but I could tell he'd moved to the bathroom and was rummaging around in the cabinet, getting his shaving things together, his tooth-brush. I fumbled for my cigarette packet and immediately lit another, blowing the smoke out in a long straight line to the fridge. I stared. On it was an ancient photograph of me and Johnny. It was one Claudia had found at the bottom of a drawer, pounced on in delight, and screaming with laugh-ter at our impossible eighties clothes and hairstyles, had stuck up with a magnet. I narrowed my eyes at it now. I was about, ooh, seventeen, I suppose, and in someone's garden,

Johnny's perhaps. There I was, small, skinny, awkward-looking, with wide-apart grey eyes and a slightly too large nose – gamine, my mother would say, or even Audrey Hepburn, at which I'd guffaw. And there was Johnny beside me, who to my mind hadn't changed. Tall, broad-shouldered, laughing merrily, those bright blue eyes staring frankly and challengingly at the camera, and a flop of blond hair falling permanently in his eyes, as it still did. In the background I could see Imogen and Molly, and maybe even Peter too so – yes . . . it must have been about seventeen years ago. Half my life, when I'd first met Johnny.

I'd been with the witches at the time, of course. Everything I did in those days was with the witches and, to a large extent, still is. 'The witches' was Johnny's name for the three of us, Molly, Imogen and me. 'Full of bubble, but an *awful* lot of toil and trouble!' he'd hiss, stirring an imaginary cauldron, and we'd giggle like mad over that, secretly delighted that three such hard-working, sheltered, inseparable convent girls, who'd never been in a scrape in their lives, could be regarded as 'trouble'. Mad, bad and dangerous we certainly weren't, but it was a nice idea.

It was Molly who saw him first, at the fair on the village green that Saturday night, believe it or not, the first Saturday night I was ever allowed out on my own.

'You get nasty rough types at a fair,' my mother had sniffed, scrubbing away at our tiny Formica kitchen. 'Gippoes and all sorts, but then again, that's probably why you want to go.'

'No,' I said patiently, 'I just want to have some fun with the girls.'

'Well, you wouldn't catch Lady Diana going to a fair at your age,' she snapped. 'She'd still be locked up at school!'

'Yes, and look where that's got her; nineteen years old and about to become a virgin bride. Talk about a recipe for disaster. And for the last time, Mum, I am not Lady Diana!'

'No, you're not, and you're a long way from coming anywhere close to her, my girl.' She whipped a dishcloth around an immaculate stainless-steel sink. 'Go on then, off you go. Go and flaunt yourself.'

I stared at her in amazement for a moment, but then I was out of that back door like a shot. When you got a green light from Mum, you didn't hang around for it to turn.

And so there I was that night at the fair, trying to keep the huge excitement of being out at night to myself, trying to pretend it was nothing new. Of course, for Imogen and Molly it wasn't. Going to discos and cinemas had been part and parcel of their lives for a couple of years now, but not mine, and I hugged the experience excitedly, loving it all: the flashing lights against the dark sky, the bustle and noise, the smell of candyfloss and toffee apples, the thumping disco music, the lithe boys jumping on and off speeding carts, that heady sense of danger and excitement which stirred my teenage soul. Shrieking with laughter we made our way round every single ride, and were all piling out of a Dodgem car, ready to go round again – when Molly spotted him. She stopped dead; seized my arm.

'Holy *Moley*!' (As I said, we were quite sheltered.)

He was standing with a couple of friends in the queue

for the big wheel; tall, tousled, blond, with wicked blue eyes, his hands in his pockets, head thrown back and roaring with laughter at something one of them had said. He oozed glamour but also, at a glance, that automatic social ease that comes from an expensive education, a mother who'd never had to do her own ironing and a father who was quite possibly in the Shadow Cabinet. Our plan had been to head back to the ghost train, but without a word of discussion, the three of us turned as one, and made our way to the big wheel. Molly, vivacious, curly-haired, with dark, dancing eyes, pranced up, and deliberately queue-barged her way in front of him, with Imogen and me giggling in her wake.

'Hey, what's your game?' he rounded on her.

'Sorry, we didn't realise you were queuing,' she smiled sweetly.

'Oh right, so what did you think we were doing then – standing in a line behind total strangers just for the hell of it?'

Molly's dark eyes widened. 'Well, it's a possibility. You look sad enough to try and make friends that way, but to tell you the truth, I really hadn't considered you at all.'

Nudging and giggling we then piled into the next empty cart as it conveniently came to a standstill in front of us, and Johnny and his friends had to make do indignantly with the one behind. As we soared up into the night sky they hooted and catcalled after us, pelting us with peanuts, and we dutifully squeaked and ducked, pretending to be outraged, but loving every minute of it. I remember swinging round right at the top and catching Johnny's eye, shrieking as he took aim, wondering – as his peanut hit the mark, like a perfect Cupid's arrow, right between the eyes – if he knew the effect he had on people. I believe he did.

Of course, we lurked around after the boys for the rest of the evening then, trailing them mercilessly and popping up giggling behind every shooting range and coconut shy they went on, as they, in turn, went through the adolescent ritual of groaning and trying to lose us. Inevitably, though, all six of us ended up together outside the only pub on the green, equipped with far too many goldfish, candyfloss in our hair, cigarettes glowing competitively, and all eyes bright with possibility. Johnny, aged eighteen, went in for the drinks and we sat on the grass outside. We gleaned from the other two boys that they were all at Harrow, but that such was the enlightened attitude of boarding schools these days, they'd been allowed out for the evening. 'So long as we're back by – ooh –' one of them coolly flashed his Rolex – 'about midnight, I suppose.' Suitably impressed by their bravado but just about managing not to show it, we'd sipped our lager-and-limes; Molly, flirting like billyo, Imogen, blonde and beautiful and not needing to, and me, certainly needing to but not having the confidence. As ever, I wished I wasn't so tongue-tied, but Molly made sure every silence was filled, which gave me a chance to observe.

'Posh-gob Scot' was how Johnny described himself, with generations of Scottish ancestors behind him, but brought up in England and sent to Harrow like the rest of his family.

'Only child, I'll bet,' said Molly, her dark eyes flashing with amusement, 'of totally indulgent parents. Ponies for

Christmas, a convertible for your birthday, the apple of Mummy and Daddy's eye. They probably peel you grapes for breakfast.'

He grinned. 'Wrong, actually. Three sisters.'

'Ah, only boy. Yes well, that explains it.'

'Explains what?'

'Your godlike demeanour. Clearly the world revolves around you at home and you're waited on hand and foot. Loo seats are probably warmed for you and you've been mistakenly led to believe in the superiority of the male species. They obviously think the sun shines out of your wotsit.'

He laughed. 'God, I wish! Those wretched sirens torment me, gang up on me, they probably stick pins in little effigies of me.'

'Ah, shame. So you're put upon?'

'You bet.'

'Misunderstood?'

'Totally.'

'In need of a little analysis?'

'No fear. Those shrinks would have a field day with me!'

'Even so, worth a try. Here – lie down on my couch.' She patted her lap and Johnny, grinning, obligingly put his head in it. Oh, to have Molly's nerve. She frowned with mock concentration. 'So . . . a tortured soul, eh, teased mercilessly by your sisters, and I imagine Mummy's no help because – let me see now – Mummy's always in the beauty parlour having her nails done?'

'Christ – in her dreams!' he chortled.

'And Daddy, well, Daddy's no help either because he's –

let's think, what would Daddy be? Certainly something in the City; something fairly enormous. Pr-o-bably the Governor of the Bank of England, and pr-ob-ably called – Peregrine?'

'Wrong again. His name's Oliver and he's a trainer.'

'What, fitness?' I said without thinking.

Johnny sat up, startled. Then he and the other boys hooted with laughter.

'No, racehorses!' he cried. 'God, fitness. I'd like to see Dad in a leotard!'

We all laughed, but I felt foolish and could feel myself reddening as I joined in. It didn't escape Johnny and he shot me a kind look. I don't believe he meant to embarrass me.

'So back to your mother then,' persisted Molly, yanking his shoulders down into her lap again. 'Shut your eyes, please. I must have total concentration in my counselling rooms. If she's not in the beauty parlour, she's . . . ?'

'Oh Mum, well, she's a bit dizzy. "Creative" is how I'm sure she'd like to be described.'

'Ah, a bit off-the-wall.'

He opened one eye. 'Well, only in the sense that loo paper is.'

We giggled, and then for some reason we couldn't stop laughing, and we all fell about on the grass in a heap.

We roared at Johnny's jokes for most of that summer. After that first meeting, it somehow seemed only natural for the six of us to hang around together. The schools were breaking up for the holidays, we all lived relatively close to each other in the stretch of green belt that wrapped itself around the foothills of the Chilterns – it was fun, it was convenient, it was easy. Secretly I think the boys felt they were too old to be hanging about at home and should have been spending their final holiday from school backpacking in Istanbul, or smoking ganja on some remote Caribbean beach, but since they weren't, they deigned to swagger along beside us, to the events on offer locally. Keen to be equally cool, we girls sneeringly dismissed the discos and parties as 'so-o-o incredibly tame' – quick flick of the hair, quick drag on the cigarette – as they no doubt were, but there was no convincing my mother. She saw drug pushers and rapists at every Pony Club dance and tennis club party, and I had practically to shin down the drainpipe to join my friends.

On one occasion when she forbade me to go to a concert in London, I rather daringly ignored her and went anyway. Halfway through some throbbing Supertramp keyboard number, a man came on stage, interrupted the music, and asked if an Olivia Faber could please leave now because her mother was waiting for her in the car park. I remember going literally rigid with shock in my seat, then blushing to my roots. I didn't move. Molly and Imogen on either side of me both reached out and squeezed my hands. A few minutes later the music resumed, but then ten minutes after that, the man was back. Could Olivia Faber *please* leave now, because otherwise the police would be called and the concert could not continue. I got to my feet, puce with shame, and passed down along the rows. I remember going past Johnny, who caught my eye sympathetically, and then, to titters of 'home to Mummy', left the stadium.

Sure enough, Mum was waiting. I got in the car without a word and maintained a tight-lipped silence all the way home, as did my mother. To this day we've never spoken of it. I think we both knew that she'd overstepped the mark, but then again, so had I, and there was a delicious symmetry to it which resulted in a stalemate. Looking back, I wonder we didn't hurl more insults and recriminations at each other, but we never did, we were more careful. Once those things are said, they're out there for ever, hanging in the air and, at the end of the day, we loved each other. She was all I had, and vice versa. Thereafter, though, I did detect a perceptible loosening of the reins, and certainly towards the end of the summer, there wasn't a party I didn't go to or a dance I didn't make.

It's incredible to me now that I can only just remember the names of the other two boys. Peter, I think, and Ben. All eyes were firmly on Johnny, you see, and there was no question of second best. As the summer wore on, though, it became clear that one of our number was forging ahead in the popularity stakes, and two of us would have to resign ourselves to back seats. It was Molly, after all, who'd spotted him first, Molly, who'd wooed him, Molly who'd put in all the hard, flirtatious work, and now Molly who was firmly staking her claim. Every slow dance was hers, every joke addressed to her, every look came winging her way, whilst Imogen and I sat dumbly by, enviously awaiting the first kiss.

During this time we more or less lived at Johnny's parents' house, which, like son and heir, was something of an eye-opener. I'd never seen anything quite like the McFarllens' estate, and probably never will. It was huge, it was

Jacobean, it was turreted – it was even *moated*, for God's sake – in short, it was the sort of place where you suppressed a 'bloody hell' as you went up the drive. Here they talked of land rather than garden, watered the orangery rather than the conservatory, and had a clock tower instead of a weather vane. The lifeblood of the place was, of course, the stables, or 'the yard', as I came to call it, which was adjacent to the house, and run like a slick, well-oiled machine – just like the thoroughbred racing machines it housed, who nodded their elegant, arched necks over every green stable door.

Inside, the house was full of colour and drama. There was a blood-red dining room, a pale blue morning room, vibrant chintz in the sitting room, murals in the bathrooms and, at every window, curtains as thick as duvets hung from fabulous, coroneted pelmets. Every bedroom was painted a deep jewel colour – sapphire, ruby or emerald – and as I crept around upstairs one day on a rather spurious search for a loo, I was also startled to note that each bed had a huge crucifix hanging over it. This, it transpired, was down to Oliver, Johnny's father, who, born a Protestant, had apparently seen the light in later life and made a sweeping and dramatic conversion to Catholicism. Like most born-agains he was messianic in his belief and, insisting that the rest of his family should join him on his road to Damascus, had filled the place with the trappings of his new-found religion. Huge church candles and prayer books loitered in the most unlikely places – next to a pile of *Horse and Hound* in the loo, or in the case of the candles, chewed to bits by the latest puppy in its basket, because for all Oliver's religious fervour, one didn't have to look far to find signs of a hedonistic lifestyle. A velvet curtain, ripped accidentally during a raucous party a few years ago, still hung forlornly by threads from its pelmet, there were shot gun cartridges in the bath, empty whisky bottles behind the loo, and betting slips in every overflowing ashtray, all of which, I thought, gave the place a thrilling air of debauchery.

Oliver McFarllen, tall, handsome and urbane as he strutted about the place in his breeches in an impossibly Mr Darcy-like manner, was altogether a glamorous, if formidable figure. We were all rather in awe of him and kept out of his way, but he wasn't unfriendly and always shot us a cheery 'Hello there!' and a flashing smile if he strode by us in the yard. His moods were mercurial, though, and having once been shocked to a standstill as we heard him bawl out an unfortunate stable girl for not mucking out a filthy stable, we knew better than to hang about in the yard for too long, particularly if clients were viewing their horses. Johnny also told us that the barns at the back of the house, which held Oliver's prized collection of classic vintage cars, were quite simply out of bounds.

The sisters, all younger than us, were terrifyingly good-looking in a pale, consumptive sort of way, and I distinctly remember being introduced to them in the icy splendour of the morning room as they lolled around reading *Tatler* and *Harpers*, glossy blonde hair spilling on to the equally glossy pages. The three of us, Molly, Imogen and I, had stood in the doorway awkwardly, fully prepared to be coolly appraised, then whispered about as we left the room, but to our surprise the McFarllen girls jumped up, pounced on us and dragged us off to the stables, insisting we see their ponies. Once in the privacy of the stables they'd grilled us rigid, bitterly disappointed that none of us had had our tummy buttons pierced, tattooed our bottoms, or at the very least, had sex with their brother. They pretty much ran wild about the place, and rode bareback like demons, and I remember once watching them race their ponies around the gallops for a laugh, waving and shrieking to their father, who was standing up in his ancient, convertible Bristol, binoculars to eyes, playing 'the trainer' for them. As he laughed and roared them on, I remember thinking how alien their world was to mine.

And of course I drank it all in thirstily, parched as I was of this sybaritic lifestyle. It spoke to me, released something pent up and suburban in my soul, as indeed did Angie, Johnny's mother. Bright-eyed, copper-haired and beautiful, with Johnny's brilliant, languid smile, it was she who held the whole chaotic shooting match together, she who was the pivot around whom the household revolved. The kitchen was her domain – although I don't believe she ever cooked in it – but she treated it as her salon and welcomed everyone to it. I can see her now, sweeping saddles from the vast oak table and calling for everyone to sit down together around a steaming pot of soup, placing a trainer next to an old soak, next to a schoolgirl, next to an elderly widow. Once her table was full she'd sit at the head, satisfied that everyone was about her, and then entrance us all, telling stories – but listening too, leaving no one out – and inviting our confidences, until I think I'd told her more about myself than I'd told any adult. I believe Peter and Ben were secretly in love with her, and her husband certainly was, liking nothing more than to show her off.

After a typically liquid lunch with fourteen or so of us around the kitchen table, Oliver, plastered, his pale blue eyes swimming rheumily, would stagger round to her end and try to persuade her to sing.

'She's got a bloody good voice, you know; trained as an opera singer before she met me. God, she should be captivating the front row of Covent Garden instead of a crowd of reprobates like you! Come on, Ange, the girls would love it, wouldn't you, girls? Ask her to sing, Molly; she'll do it for you.'

'Bugger off, Olly,' Angie would laugh, swatting him good-naturedly with her napkin and not moving from her chair. 'Why is it that when you're in your cups you have to have everyone on their feet hollering "Flower of Scotland"?'

'Don't tempt me!' he'd shout, 'Oh God, it's too late – help me Johnny – "Oh fl-o-wer of Sco-tland . . ." and off he'd go, standing up on his chair, belting it out, head back, roaring at the ceiling, with the rest of the table – son, daughters, family, friends – joining in the bits they knew.

My mother had raised delicately plucked eyebrows when I'd foolishly let this slip back home.

'Singsongs,' she'd murmured. 'How delightfully rustic. Do they light a campfire too, I wonder?'

But she could sneer all she liked, I'd fallen in love with the entire family, the whole, compulsive package. Never in my life had I come across such warmth, such unbridled fun for the sheer hell of it, such a house that rocked, almost literally, with laughter, and in the middle of it all, of course, the golden boy, Johnny.

But the summer didn't last for ever, and that October,

after a final, wild goodbye party at the McFarllens', Johnny and the boys went off to university. Molly and I still had another year together at school, but Imogen, being bright as well as beautiful, went up to Oxford a year early to read Fine Art. Coincidentally, Johnny also went up to Oxford, to read Classics, and funnily enough, within a week or two of term beginning, he'd asked Imogen out.

Looking back, I wonder why on earth it hadn't occurred to us before, why it came as such a huge shock. He'd waited for her, you see, waited all summer to make a move, to claim his prize, but being too much of a gent to pluck her right from under Molly's nose in full view of everyone, had hung on until the right moment. And that moment had to be away from the rest of us, out of the spotlight, far from the madding crowd, where Johnny could swing into full, wooing mode, and let the romantic, thirteenth-century hallowed cloisters of Balliol do their damnedest.

Naturally it came as a severe blow to me, losing, as I suddenly had, my partner in rejection, but it was a colossal blow for Molly. She was distraught, understandably, and spitting blood for a while too. She wouldn't speak to Imogen or Johnny when they first came back at Christmas, wouldn't even acknowledge Imogen's letters. Gradually, though, after a couple of months, it all calmed down. It had to. Molly, Imogen and I had known each other since we were seven. We'd played in each other's bedrooms, been in the same netball teams, copied each other's homework, listened to each other's records, borrowed each other's clothes, and Molly was neither stupid nor vindictive. It was easy to forgive Imogen because she loved her, and she wrestled with her pride to forgive Johnny too, which was harder, because she loved him more.

Imogen and Johnny went out for three years, all their time together at Oxford, whilst Molly and I kept watch from less traditional, more redbrick, seats of learning. And they were surely the golden couple: Imogen, tall, slim, with her sheet of blonde hair slipping silkily down her back, slanting blue eyes and high forehead – cruising for a First with an icy cool nerve – whilst Johnny held up the more extrovert, exuberant side of the partnership. A raucous rugby blue, a man's man, partying and drinking till all hours, playing sport until he dropped, scraping a Two-two – 'A gentleman's degree,' he told us with a broad grin, 'means I've had a good time' – and always with the serene, unflappable Imogen on his arm. Deliriously happy, yes, but when they came out of university together, still very young. Still only twenty-one. And, of course, no one had even given a thought to marriage.

As I sat in my tiny, makeshift scullery kitchen, I blew a stream of smoke at the faded old photo on the fridge. Yes, it was funny really, I reflected. Molly had claimed him, Imogen had loved him, but at the end of the day, it had been me who'd married him.

Chapter Three

There wasn't a great deal of joy in the house I grew up in. My father had left home when I was four, but before he'd flown off to Canberra with Mum's best friend, Yvonne, he'd thoughtfully provided for my education by leaving the wherewithal for me to stay at The Sacred Heart Convent School until I was eighteen. I wasn't too sure if he was even a Catholic – in fact I wasn't too sure of any of the details about my father, aside from a blurred old photo I'd found in Mum's dressing-table drawer of a man in RAF uniform – but the convent was no doubt a last-minute, guilty sop to Mum, who was as devout as they come.

Whether her religious fervour was as strong before Dad's departure as it was after, I'm not sure, but I do know that once deserted, alone and grief-stricken, she'd transferred any passion she had left in her soul to God, the Royal Family and Jean Muir, and not necessarily in that order.

The bizarre Jean Muir fixation had come about because in her previous, normal working life – before she took up tormenting teenagers – she'd worked as a fitter in the fashion world. During this period she'd spent some time in Miss Muir's couture house, and such was the impression it had made, that from that day on, she dressed solely in navy-blue shift dresses, with only a single string of pearls and earrings as adornment, her hair styled neatly in a dark, black bob, all very chic, all very à la Jean.

She was also half French, as she never failed to remind me, picking me up from school and greeting me with a cool '*Ça va?*' – to which I was supposed to respond accordingly. Mostly I did – every day in fact – but one day it got on my nerves and I snapped, 'Oui, ça va bloody bien, OK?' She never said it again and that memory fills me with remorse.

Mum's standards were high, and, frankly, I found it hard to live up to the Almighty, the Royals and Jean, and privately staged my own mini rebellion, deliberately skipping my Hail Marys, wearing a 'Sod the Royal Wedding' T-shirt under my jumper, and dressing as sloppily, and as unlike her mentor as possible. All very adolescent and futile, but I think because I looked very like Mum – small-boned, dark and petite – I was rather afraid of ending up like her, and made a supreme effort to be different. Genes will out, though – Parisian ones particularly – and however baggy my clothes I still had an unhappy knack of whipping a scarf around my neck and tying it just so, adding a good, chunky leather belt, some unusual earrings, some witty little shoes, so that according to Imogen and Molly I always looked 'together'.

Looks were everything to Mum, and she hoodwinked the world quite successfully, so that it always came as a surprise to people to realise we were poor. After all, I went to an expensive private school and Mum looked like she'd fallen out of *Vogue*, so it was only when people came to the house – a tiny, Victorian terraced villa with threadbare carpets and cheap furniture – that the dawn came up. On the flip side, though, Mum equally loathed ostentation. I remember one occasion, just after I'd left university, when, as usual, I was off to a party at the McFarllens' and hastily bolting a cheese sandwich at the kitchen table, waiting for Johnny and Imogen to pick me up. She'd stood over me, fingering her pearls more nervously than usual.

'You're off to those McFarllens again then, are you?' she sniffed.

I didn't bother to look up. 'You know I am, Mum,' I muttered, stuffing in the sandwich, knowing she was rotating the earrings now, radiating disapproval.

'Well, you know my views.'

I chewed on in the silence, and at length she tried again, walking around the table so she was facing me on the other side. She rested her palms on the Formica.

'You haven't met many nouveau riche people, have you, Olivia?'

I cleared my throat. 'Quite a lot of the girls at school had money, if that's what you mean,' I said smoothly.

'Yes, but they didn't flash it about, did they?' she retorted quickly. 'Imogen's parents, for instance – they're wealthy, but you'd never know. They've got far too much breeding.' She shuddered. 'Unlike these dreadful people.' I munched on in silence. New money was quite a theme of Mum's, as if we had any old. She sat down opposite me, flicking an imaginary speck of dust off her immaculate skirt.

'I saw him in the paper the other day,' she said tartly, 'splattered all over the back page. Tie askew, hair standing on end, holding a bottle of champagne and grinning from ear to ear like an idiot. Now if *Dick* had won the handicap stakes –'

'Hang on.' I looked up. '*Who* did you see in the paper the other day?'

'Whom, actually. Oliver McFarllen, of course.'

'Oh, right, and *whom*, exactly, is Dick?'

'Major Dick Hern,' she said patiently. 'The Queen's trainer.'

Ah yes, of course. Just plain Dick to Mum.

'Now when *Dick* wins,' she went on, 'he just smiles politely, tips his hat everso decorously, and bows out of the ring to let the owner take all the glory. None of this posing around to get his face in all the papers lark.'

I nodded. 'Quite right. Thanks, Mum. Remind me to give Oliver that little tip.' He'll be *everso* grateful, I thought privately, then hated myself for it.

Johnny hooted his horn from outside. I jumped up. 'They're here,' I said quickly, grabbing my bag and giving her a guilty peck on the cheek. 'See you later, Mum,' and I flew off down the passage and out of the front door, leaving her to shut it behind me.

As I ran down the path to his bright red Morgan, Johnny looked past me in amazement to the vision standing in the doorway.

'Blimey,' he said as I squeezed in behind Imogen to the tiny space in the back, 'is that your mother? She looks like one of those Dior fashion plates.'

'Oh, she'd love that,' I said, hugging my knees up in the obligatory garden gnome position. 'I'll tell her when I get home. She might change her opinion of you.' As soon as I'd said it, I wished I hadn't. He turned round, startled.

'Really? Why, what does she think of me then?'

'Oh well, she hasn't really met you, of course,' I said

quickly, 'but she's — well, she's always had a bit of a thing about . . .' I hesitated.

'She thinks you're a flash git,' put in Imogen helpfully.

He roared with laughter. 'Does she? Christ!' He blinked. 'Well, she's probably right!'

'Probably?' murmured Imogen, raising her eyebrows as he overrevved the car.

He laughed. 'All right, Miss Ice Maiden, I haven't heard you complaining much.'

She lit a cigarette and gave him a secret smile, and he reached across and squeezed her knee in return, territorial gestures that Molly and I were still getting used to.

'Still,' he mused, glancing admiringly at me in the rear-view mirror, 'I can see where you get "the look" from, Liv.'

'Oh, Livvy was born chic,' commented Imogen. 'I wouldn't be surprised if she was doused in Saint-Laurent talc as a baby and snapped into Chanel nappies.'

I'd laughed, but I couldn't help feeling pleased, too. I'd spent my entire youth wishing Mum wouldn't stand at the school gates in navy-blue couture, complete with gloves, hat, and pigskin handbag, and be like the other mums in a tracksuit, trainers, a Sainsbury's carrier in one hand and a buggy with a toddler in the other, but for the first time in my life, I felt a rush of pride for her. And of course, I liked Johnny all the more for admiring her.

The venue that particular night was the McFarllens' barn, and the occasion, the youngest sister, Tara's, seventeenth birthday. Johnny had rigged the place up in a parody of a seventies disco, with flashing strobe lights and a juke box belting out Abba in the corner, and Tara and her friends were giggling in flares and headbands. Entering into the spirit of the thing, Molly, Imogen and I pranced about around our handbags, whilst the boys played imaginary guitars, shutting their eyes and banging their heads together in mock ecstasy. While we danced, I remember looking out through the open barn doors to the house beyond, which as usual was lit up like a vast beacon in the night sky. Through the dining-room window a dinner party was in full swing, with twelve or so people around a table awash with silver and crystal, and Angie and Oliver at either end. As I watched, I saw Oliver get up, take the decanter around the table, and pause to kiss his wife on the back of her neck before refilling her glass, laughing in the candlelight.

Later, after we'd all piled out of the barn and into the swimming pool, hot and exhausted from dancing, they'd joined us; Angie, ostensibly leading her guests out through the French windows for a drink by the pool, but secretly anxious lest one of Tara's friends had had too much to drink and sank to the bottom, and Oliver, puffing on a cigar, following soon after. I recognised a few racehorse owners from the yard: complacent, florid, mostly overweight men, pleased with themselves and laughing too loudly, with younger, trophy wives on their arms. They were all pretty tanked up too, and as they watched us swim relay races, one particularly loud, portly individual peeled off his dinner jacket and prepared to join us, making a fool of himself in his Union Jack boxer shorts. As he jumped in, suddenly a shout went up from Johnny, and he and his sisters rushed to ambush him, intent on debagging. Amid the inevitable splashing and shrieking, I crawled out of the other end, laughing and enjoying it all but, as ever, not wanting to get too involved. Oliver was beside me. He handed me a towel, and as I wrapped it around me, shivering – giggling as fat man got his comeuppance – I wondered where on earth my own clothes were. I knew it was pretty late and I had to get a move on. I turned to go.

'Perfect, aren't they?' he murmured.

I glanced back and followed Oliver's gaze to where Johnny and his three sisters were still streaking through the pool, their tanned, lithe bodies glistening in the moon-light.

I smiled. 'Perfect.'

Then I turned and scurried off, picking up a skirt here, a shoe there, a bra – where was my bra? – oh God, *there*, on the rose bush, then climbing back into them all before dashing back and badgering Molly for a lift home, living in fear of the navy-blue avenging angel arriving to collect her daughter, breathing fire over the hedonists in the pool, a rolling pin in one hand, pigskin bag swinging wildly in the other.

I mention this partly because I remember it well. It was the last one, you see. Because a couple of weeks later, something happened that was to change all our lives. On an equally balmy, hot August evening, Oliver McFarllen left his stifling bedroom, wandered downstairs, and pausing only to get a drink of water, went out of the back door into the night. He walked quite a long way, apparently, right across his paddocks to the edge of his land, where, on reaching a far corner of a distant field, he put a gun to his head and shot himself.

The party line was that it had been an accident. That

he'd been climbing over a fence and had fallen on top of his gun which he'd propped up carefully on the other side, and that it had simply gone off. But Oliver McFarllen had been handling a shotgun since he was twelve; he shot regularly on the Scottish and Irish grousemoors, he hosted a corporate shoot on his own land, and apart from anything else, he'd been found alone, in the middle of the night, in his dressing gown. Accidental death didn't hold much water, so suppositions abounded. Some suggested that Angie had taken a lover; others, that it was Oliver who had, and some scandalmongers even claimed that he was gay. Another rumour went that he'd lost all his money, that he was bankrupt, a broken man, living on credit, but like most tall stories, they all turned out to be unsubstantiated and baseless, because the fact of the matter was that no one knew why on earth he'd done it, least of all, Angie.

The grief almost swallowed her whole. She clung to her family, but their world had gone black too, and they fumbled around in the dark together, reaching for each other, not believing, not understanding. The house, which I eventually timidly visited – knocking on the front door, getting no answer, finding it open and tentatively tiptoeing down the familiar long corridor to the kitchen – was silent. Where once it had throbbed with vitality, it now seemed full of Oliver's shimmering absence. Grief had washed over it and I found the McFarllens clinging to the wreckage. Tara had locked herself in her bedroom whilst the other two girls were down at the stables, weeping into their horses' necks.

Angie, meanwhile, was in the kitchen, sitting at her huge oak table, her beautiful face pale but composed, as she said goodbye to a neighbouring farmer who'd called to offer his sympathies. As he left, pink-faced, his hat twisting nervously in his hands, she reached out and caught my hand.

'Livvy, so sweet of you to come,' she whispered, '*so sweet.*'

I mumbled how sorry I was, not knowing whether to hug her or run away, not wanting to intrude on her grief, but as she motioned with a trembling hand for me to sit down, I sat beside her, dumbly. At that moment Johnny appeared silently in the doorway. As he stood there, his face white and drawn, jeans and T-shirt creased where he'd clearly slept in them, I realised with a jolt that actually it was Johnny for whom the world had really stopped turning. His beloved father, whom he believed himself to be so like, only not so magnificent – to have ended it all in this terrible way. As he stumbled towards us, his blue eyes helpless and staring, wide with misery, I held out my hand and he clutched on to it. For a while there he stood motionless, gazing straight ahead, and then he sank down into a chair, put his head in his hands, and wept. Angie stroked his blond head absently, staring abstractedly out of the window to the paddocks beyond, her face full of longing, full of other days.

Imogen came back immediately, of course. She'd just started a post-grad fine arts course in Florence – had beaten countless hopefuls to get the place – but she put down her paintbrush and was by Johnny's side for the funeral. Elegant in a long black suit, weeping quietly into her hanky, she was right beside Johnny in his grief, and for a couple of days after, too. But then, of course, she had to go back. Life goes on, and all the other usual clichés, and she couldn't just abandon her course.

Johnny understood. Weeks went by, and he too had to struggle on as normal, making his daily trudge to the City where he'd started in the corporate finance department of a large investment bank. But more than six weeks later, with plenty of weekends in between, still Imogen didn't return. Johnny, too proud to ask, sent a cryptic postcard, which read: 'They paved paradise and put up a parking lot', to which Imogen – perhaps not knowing that the previous line of the Joni Mitchell song went: 'Don't it always seem to go, that you don't know what you've got till it's gone?' – had written back: 'Well, they've got to park somewhere.'

Johnny, baffled, flew out to Florence, and took a taxi straight round to her flat. Hot and dishevelled from his journey, and having climbed a million steps to get to her tiny, top-floor apartment, he was greeted at the door by a swarthy young Latin called Paolo, who, wearing nothing but a towel and a cynical smile, had informed him that Imogen was busy. Johnny, furious, didn't stop to find out more and flew straight home, whereupon Imogen, distraught, phoned every hour, begging him to believe that Paolo was just a friend – a neighbour, actually – whose hot-water tank had broken down, and who was just using her shower until it was fixed. But Johnny was like prosecuting council, questioning and cross-examining, pushing her to admit that the Italian wasn't a neighbour at all, or even a friend, that he was a lover, and that she was having an affair. Finally, she broke down and admitted she was.

Johnny was not a man to take infidelity lying down, as

it were, and against a backdrop of his father's death, there was no mitigation, no room for forgiveness. A wall of silence went up between them, made worse by the fact that Imogen continued to see Paolo. Molly and I were appalled, but she was adamant that she was the victim.

'He cast me aside, don't you see? If he'd loved me he'd have forgiven me one small indiscretion.'

'Yes, but you're still seeing Paolo! You're making it a huge indiscretion now – what's he supposed to think?'

'Well, what am I supposed to do, live out here like a nun while he's on the other side of Europe? He can think what he bloody well likes!'

And Johnny did, indeed, think a great deal. When I met him for our customary lunchtime drink in the City, where I was doing a poxy secretarial course and he was shinning up the greasy banking pole, he was erudite on the subject.

'She's a tart,' he said simply. 'She's not getting it from me and she can't go without it. She's always been highly sexed.'

'Oh, Johnny, that's unfair,' I murmured loyally, uncomfortably aware of her nun reference.

'It's true, Livvy. She doesn't love him, does she? Has she told you she loves him?'

'Well, no but –'

'So what's she doing with him then?'

I sighed. This was typical of Johnny. If you weren't wholehearted, what was the point? Wholeheartedness had been part of his father's make-up, and therefore part of Johnny's. Oliver had raced horses to win, not to come second; he lived in the most spectacular house, was married to the most beautiful woman, and had the most sought-after, glamorous children – what was the point of being a runner-up in life? But then, I thought, picking at some candlewax on the checked tablecloth in front of me, if one's standards were so high, surely one was destined to be disappointed?

'How's Angie?' I asked, changing the subject.

Johnny reached for the bottle of Chardonnay and refilled our glasses.

'Sad,' he said simply. 'Sad and quiet. Come and dig with her this weekend, Livvy. You know how she loves that. Come and stay.'

I smiled. It had been a long-standing joke from way back, this eccentric – at my age apparently – love of gardening. Like his mother, I liked nothing more than to be down amongst the slugs and the earthworms, sowing and separating and potting on, and this secretarial course was really only to mark time until I got up the nerve to tell Mum that that was what I really wanted to do – to take a course in garden design that I'd applied for at Cirencester. She'd be horrified, of course.

'I don't know where you get this strange, earthy streak,' she used to say, wrapping her cardigan tightly around her as she watched me trowelling away in our two square foot of back garden. 'Must be your father's side. There's nothing remotely agricultural about the Du Brays.'

Yes, well, there was nothing remotely human about the frigging Du Brays either. My maternal grandmother had fallen out with my mother years ago, and although she lived only a matter of miles from us, in the centre of St Albans, as a child I was forbidden to see her. I did try to make contact once, when I was about sixteen, but had been told very sternly by the elderly woman on the other end of the phone in a heavy French accent that 'your grandmother ees not at home', although it was quite clear it was she I was talking to. As I'd put the phone down I'd had a sneaking sense of regret for Mum. With a mother like that, was it any surprise she'd ended up as she had?

Yes, so Mum was sniffy about my gardening, but Angie McFarllen, on the other hand, had treated it as a wonderful surprise. She'd found me, early on in my days at her house, crouched down in her herbaceous border, pulling a few weeds from around the tender young shoots of her aspidistras, and had recognised that same, avid light in my eyes. She'd pounced.

'Good God, Livvy, are you one of us? Are you a secret horticulturist?'

'Well, not exactly,' I'd blushed, sitting back on my heels. 'Mum and I haven't exactly got much of a garden. I'm just an enthusiast really.'

'Then for heaven's sake come and enthuse with me! No one else in this wretched family does. They're all too busy playing tennis or fiddling with their stupid vintage cars. I've got acres here, and no one to attack the weeds but poor old Ron, who's on his last legs, and I certainly haven't the heart to tell him, poor devil. Come on, let's get cracking. Help me separate these flaming day lilies before they take over the garden like triffids!'

And so had begun our horticultural relationship. In the days before Oliver's death, we'd dug away furiously together, breaking forks in her hard, uncompromising chalky soil and roaring with laughter at yet another broken prong, but more recently, as Angie went quiet and withdrawn, just on our knees, weeding around the scented pelargoniums and the lavender, silently and companionably.

On one of these latter, quieter days, I'd looked up from the greenhouse where we were pricking out and potting on more peonies, to see Johnny, charging around the paddock in an open-topped Land Rover with two squealing sisters in the back. I'd straightened up from the bench where we were working, and shaded my eyes to watch. He'd always loved speed, whether it was careering round on a quad bike or performing wheelies on a clapped-out old motorbike he'd found in the back of the barn. In the old days, we'd all ridden in turn on the bike behind him, tearing down the drive, eyes shut, numb with terror, and I remember flushing with pride one day as he'd careered to a stop in front of the others and said: 'You know, Livvy's the only one who's got the guts to lean into the curves. The rest of you are dead weights, like carrying a sack of potatoes. Just watch and learn!'

Well, this was the first time I'd seen him back in the driving seat, as it were. Just for fun, for a laugh. I'd caught Angie's eye as she set aside a seed tray.

'Almost like old times,' I'd murmured.

'Almost.' She'd paused. 'Except his heart's not in it. He's still very vulnerable, Livvy.'

Perhaps she hadn't meant it as such, but I'd taken this as a warning shot across my predatory bows. I buried my face in the baby peonies and took up my trowel again.

Later on, though, as I looked at him across that half-drunk bottle of Chardonnay in that dark City wine bar, I realised that actually she was right. Death had changed him. I hadn't thought that I could be any more attracted to Johnny than I already was, but vulnerability could be awfully attractive, especially in such a confident man.

'OK,' I said, putting down my glass, 'I'll come this weekend. I need to sort out your herb garden, anyway. The ground elder's practically taken over there. It's a disgrace.'

He laughed. 'Sometimes I think we ought to pay you for this.'

'Of course you should.'

He looked startled. 'Oh! Oh well, Livvy, why didn't you say? I mean, I'm sure Mum –'

'Oh, don't be ridiculous. Belt up, Johnny and pour me another drink. If anyone owes anyone anything, it's me.'

'What d'you mean?'

'Oh, I don't know.' I slid away from his blue gaze. 'For offering me a glimpse of another life, I suppose. A different sort of life.'

He didn't say anything, but as he dropped his eyes to the table, I spotted recognition in them. He'd seen my mother, of course. And he'd seen Hastoe Villas.

To tell you the truth, I'm not entirely sure how it happened – how one weekend's gardening turned into another, and then another, which in turn led to pub suppers alone with Johnny, then trips home on his motorbike under the stars, with me really leaning into those curves, and finally, of course, trips to bed. To me it seemed entirely natural – after all, I'd been dreaming about it for years, so it didn't exactly take me by surprise – and it was utter, utter bliss, but I suppose if it took anyone by surprise, it was Johnny. He sat up in bed one summer afternoon as I lay back on the pillows in his bedroom

45

overlooking the fields, and raked a bewildered hand through his hair. He blinked out of the window.

'D'you know, Livvy, you're an absolute tonic. I swear to God I feel like a new man, I reckon I could jump out of that window, clear that apple tree and race right around those gallops! And I mean – Christ, who would have thought?'

'Who would have thought what?'

'Well, you and me!'

He turned, and I narrowed my eyes at him from my nest on the pillows. 'What, you mean Johnny the *grand fromage* from the big house and little old Livvy?'

He threw a pillow at me. 'Bugger off, I didn't mean that at all. But you must admit, you've crept up on me, Liv. You're a dark old horse.'

'Ah yes, that's me,' I smiled. 'The rank outsider. Long odds, not much to look at in the paddock, pretty dodgy pedigree, but coming up hard on the rails at fifty to one.'

He frowned. 'Why d'you always do that?'

'Do what?'

'Put yourself down?'

I shrugged. 'I suppose I like to get in there before anyone else does.'

He grinned and lay down on top of me. 'Oh, so do I.'

I giggled and wriggled away. 'Hang on, I thought you were about to hurdle some apple trees, race around the gallops like Champion the Wonder Horse!'

'Still might,' he muttered, grabbing me back, 'but I forgot something.'

'Please don't say it's your oats.'

'You've talked me into it, you smooth-talking seductress you!'

After an inevitable scuffle, the rest of the afternoon passed predictably enough, but later on, I thought about what he'd said. Actually, I knew I'd crept up on him. I knew because it had happened before. It wasn't a deliberate ploy on my part, but I'd noticed, over the years, that guys I'd been quite friendly with at university and who I'd knocked around with in a matey sort of way, had suddenly had a habit of going into frenzied stares over their cooling fish and chips in the canteen, or popping up beside me in the library, shooting me hot looks over their Jean-Paul Sartres. I was never the obvious choice, I didn't have the stop-the-traffic looks of Imogen, or the fizz and crackle of Molly, but mine, apparently, was more of a slow burn.

Imogen had to be told, of course, and Johnny certainly wasn't going to do it, so I wrote a long and guilty letter about how it had just sort of happened and how – since she was still with Paolo – I hoped she didn't mind.

'Go for it!' came back her instant missive on the back of Michelangelo's *David*.

I couldn't be more pleased for you, Livvy. You're far more suited to him than I am and, apart from anything else, you won't be bringing an enormous ego into the equation to compete with his!

I allowed this veiled slur on Johnny, tucked the card discreetly into a drawer, and heaved a huge sigh of relief.

Meanwhile, the motorbike rides, the pub suppers, the swimming, the larks, and the bedroom romps continued apace, until, that is, one Saturday, when I received a letter. I didn't say anything, but later on that day, as Johnny was helping me scythe down some nettles in Angie's wild flower meadow behind the barn, he stopped suddenly, put down his scythe.

'What's up?'

I rested on my scythe for a moment, panting. 'What?' I squinted towards him, into the sun.

'I said, what's up?'

'Nothing's up, why?'

'Well, you've been totally silent all morning. In fact you've hardly said a word since you got here. What's occurring?'

'Oh. Have I? Oh, well, nothing really.' I shrugged and gave a half-hearted attempt at the nettles again. Then I stopped. 'It's just . . . well, it's just, I got a letter this morning. I've got into Cirencester. I'll start there in September.'

He gazed at me for a long moment. 'But that's great,' he said slowly.

I swallowed. 'Yes. Isn't it?'

We picked up our scythes again and worked away in silence for a bit. Then he put his down.

'Marry me, Livvy.'

I straightened up, gawped. 'Oh, don't be ridiculous!'

'What's ridiculous?'

'You don't mean that!'

'Yes I do. Don't go to Cirencester, marry me. Let's stay together.'

'Johnny,' I said gently, 'you don't have to marry me for us to stay together.'

'Oh, but I do. I don't want to lose you, Livvy, and I know that if you go up to Cirencester, the chances are some beefy farmer will snap you up and take you off to his ghastly piggery in Shropshire or – or even worse, some stately pile in Scotland, and I just couldn't bear that. You and I were made for each other, you must see that. We want the same things!'

'We do? Like what?'

'Like – all this!' He swung his arm around and I knew instantly what he meant. Not the house exactly, but more the metaphorical hearth: the family, the unit, something I'd never had, and something he'd lost and desperately wanted to recapture. It was true, already we knew each other too well. Knew each other's dreams.

'And?' I challenged, meeting his eye.

'And I love you.'

'You've never said.'

'I'm saying it now.' He walked forward and took my filthy hands in his. 'I love you, Olivia Faber, with all my heart. Don't give up on me, Livvy, don't go away, please. Stay, stay with me, and do me the honour of becoming my wife.'

Well, what could I say? It was an undeniable truth that I loved him completely and uncritically and always had done, so I was on a hiding to nothing. I didn't even pause for breath, didn't let my heart skip a beat, didn't waver for one moment. I just looked into his bright blue gaze and said – yes. Yes, Johnny, yes, of course. Marriage was not something I'd envisaged being even remotely on the cards, but now you came to mention it . . . Mrs Olivia McFarllen? Oh sure. Oh yes, I wanted that more than anything in the world.

Johnny told Angie privately, in the kitchen, with me shaking with nerves in the greenhouse. Eventually she came out to find me and declared herself delighted.

'Really?' I gasped, looked anxiously into her hazel eyes.

'Really,' she assured me, smiling. 'I know you'll make him very happy.'

My face split in two with relief. 'Oh, I will, I will,' I beamed back, not pausing for a moment to wonder if he'd make me happy, or even, whether that mattered.

My own mother, of course, was another matter. Her back was to me as she scrubbed the life out of a pan at the kitchen sink, her dark bob shaking with the effort, not even deigning to look at me.

'So you got him,' she sniffed. 'You "bagged" him, as they say. It all paid off in the end, all that hard work. Jolly well done, Olivia.'

'Mum, listen –'

'No,' she swung round, 'no, *you* listen. You make your bed in the McFarllens' household, young lady, and you'll live to regret it. No one takes a shotgun to a field, puts it into his mouth, stares down the barrel and pulls hard without very good reason, my girl!'

'What's that got to do with my marrying Johnny!' I screamed.

'It's got *everything* to do with your marrying Johnny!'

'But you hated them *before* any of this happened! You've *always* hated them!'

'And with damn good reason, so it turned out!'

'What's that supposed to mean?'

But she wouldn't say. In fact, tight-lipped and pale, she said very little, right up to the day of my wedding.

In my heart I think I knew Angie wasn't entirely happy, and I certainly knew Mum wasn't. As she helped me get ready on the morning of my wedding, I turned in delight at the reflection of my ivory gown in her bedroom mirror, and suddenly thought how small and fragile she looked beside me, standing watching me in her dark blue coat. I swooped to hug her but, to my dismay, tears poured down her cheeks.

Johnny and I were ecstatic, though, and not even Mum's distress could dampen our spirits. Nothing could detract from our delight. We couldn't take our eyes off each other, and as I swept out of that little Catholic church on the village green with Molly, Imogen and Johnny's three sisters in shocking pink behind me, I thought I must be the happiest girl alive. We'll prove them all wrong, I thought as I smiled confidently into the camera, tossing the confetti from my hair. They'll see, we'll show them!

And so we did. We moved into a tiny basement flat in Hammersmith, which was all we could afford, and were blissfully, ridiculously happy. Johnny continued to trudge to the City, but he began to enjoy it more. He was in Futures now, and he enjoyed watching the millions roll back and forth, riding on the waves of adrenalin, hardly bobbing when it rolled the wrong way, unlike some of the nervier, less sharp boys. As for me, Cirencester forgotten, I got a job at a very smart nursery in Chelsea, which amused my mother no end.

'A garden centre! You've got an English degree and you end up as a shop girl!'

'Not for long,' I assured her sweetly, and it wasn't. Within a year or so I was managing the place, which to my fury, amused her even more.

'Ah, so now you're the manageress!' she hissed happily.

I gritted my teeth and swore to God I'd own the bloody

place before long, set up a flipping chain of them just to show her, but before I could embark on my grand, horticultural Empire, a spanner was chucked smartly in my works. All of a sudden I was throwing up in the staff loo, feeling faint at the smell of egg sandwiches, and having trouble with the zip of my jeans. Johnny was delighted.

'But this is what we wanted!' he declared, leaping up on to our terrible old sofa and bouncing about like a child. 'This is marvellous!'

'You don't think it's a bit soon?' I said doubtfully, peering at the wholly conclusive Predictor blue line.

'Of course not!' He jumped off and hugged me delightedly. 'The sooner the better! A family, Livvy!'

Imogen and Molly were not so enthusiastic.

'A baby!' shrieked Molly. 'Bloody hell, what's the matter with you two? You're only twenty-three! God, if you carry on taking life at such an alarming rate you'll be taking P&O cruises when you're thirty!'

Perhaps she had a point, but there was no going back now, and Claudia was born that Christmas. Six weeks premature; tiny, delicate, sickly, unable to sleep, unable to feed from me, and perhaps, not quite what Johnny had in mind.

'Why won't she sleep?' he said as we lay in bed together, exhausted, listening to her scream.

'Because she can't, I suppose.'

'Is she always going to scream like that? I mean, all night?'

'Of course not,' I said, hauling myself out of bed, numb with tiredness. 'She'll settle down. It's just these first few weeks.'

But it wasn't the first few weeks, it was eighteen months before Claudia settled into anything like a routine, and even then, she was always fragile; an asthmatic, sickly child, susceptible to any bug going, allergic to milk, totally distraught if left with anyone other than me – an exhausting child. We adored her unreservedly, of course, but longed for a bright, bouncy boy to pep her up a little, spark her off, put a bit of colour in her pale cheeks with his boisterous games, save her from being quite so precious, and more like Johnny's little sisters had been, exuberant tomboys, full of life.

Nine years later we were still longing. Strangely, while Claudia had been an accident, suddenly, there was not a sausage, not even a glimmer of a Predictor blue line upon the horizon. I suppose it's fair to say we were disappointed, but we weren't obsessive about it, perhaps because Claudia had been such hard work. And equally, whilst I wouldn't say our marriage floundered during this time, it's also true to say it went into remission.

We'd moved to a little house in Fulham and I no longer worked at the nursery but looked after Claudia full time, too nervous of her disposition to leave her with a nanny. Johnny was working harder and harder in the City and now earned a deal of money, but I felt his heart was no longer in it. It was as if he was going through the motions, and if, at times, he became more distant at home, I learnt to cast around to provide some distraction to take his mind off the present, and possibly even the past.

Strangely enough, it was my mother who provided the necessary diversion. She rang one Sunday afternoon as the three of us were slumped in front of an old black and white movie, steadily working our way through a tin of Quality Street.

'Good news, darling! Your grandmother's dead!'

'Mum!' I was deeply shocked.

'Oh, you won't be so pi when I tell you the really good news. She left you the house.'

'What – her house? To me? But why?'

'Well, she wasn't going to leave it to me; she hated me.'

'But she didn't even know me.'

'Which is precisely why she didn't hate you too!'

'Thanks, Mum.'

There was something disarming about her lack of hypocrisy, though, and I have to say, Johnny and I were secretly thrilled. We'd sell it, of course – some ghastly terraced house just north of Watford with a bypass whizzing by its nose, no doubt, and then we'd sell our own poky house, and with the proceeds, move to somewhere central and spacious and light and, oh golly – Holland Park maybe, or even Notting Hill! It was just the boost we needed; it would be a turning point in our lives.

Full of plans we leapt into Johnny's old Bristol – and in fact Oliver's old Bristol – and went off to see it. Amazed that it took us only half an hour to get to this old Roman City of St Albans, we then spent another half-hour trying to find the wretched house. Finally, when we'd walked every cobbled backstreet, grudgingly admired the pretty period buildings, peered in antique shops, climbed the steep hills and marvelled at the ancient, towering Abbey, we found a lane, tucked away behind some cloisters, which led to a crescent of beautiful Georgian town houses. Just as the crescent ended, almost tacked on as an afterthought, was a high old brick wall, with green, double barn doors, slap bang in the middle.

'This must be it,' I said doubtfully, consulting my instructions and map. 'Orchard House, The Crescent.'

'Aptly named for a house in the middle of a city,' said Johnny sardonically.

'Oh, I don't know,' I said, lifting the latch on one of the doors and pushing on through. 'It might be – Oh crikey, look at this!'

We both stopped still and caught our breaths.

'Bloody hell,' muttered Johnny.

There, before us, was the most exquisite little Queen Anne house; white, perfectly proportioned, pretty and low, and surrounded by about an acre of tangled, unkempt garden. On one side was the remains of what had most certainly once been an orchard, and to the other, an over-grown rose garden, which fought with ancient clematis, honeysuckle and the inevitable elder. Even from here, one could see that down at the back, the lawn – which was dominated by a huge old cedar tree – swept down to a stream fringed with bulrushes, which in turn flowed across and along the back of The Crescent. All was walled, all was totally private, and all was a million miles from what either of us had been expecting.

'Oh, Johnny, it's heaven!' I breathed.

'Hardly. It's completely dilapidated and that's just the outside. Don't get excited, Livvy.'

'I won't,' I promised, but I already was. That garden – oh that garden!

Obediently I followed him inside. It was, of course, just as an old lady had left it, with a general air of death and decay, lots of heavy oak furniture, antimacassars on every chair, a frayed rug in front of a gas fire, and chipped Formica and sliding glass doors on the cupboards in the kitchen. But I saw none of that. I saw, like a dolls' house, four, perfectly square and symmetrical rooms downstairs and four above, all with working fireplaces, floor-to-ceiling sash windows, cornices and picture rails, and all, what's more, with views of the garden.

'There's no central heating,' warned Johnny, gazing around upstairs, but I could tell he was impressed. He was jangling his change in his pocket, which was always a good sign.

'OK, so we'll put some in.'

'Oh, it'll need more than that. It'll need gutting, rewiring, replumbing, a new bathroom and a totally new kitchen. We're talking big-time building works here, Liv.'

'So we'll sell the house in London and use the money to renovate it.'

'Lots of money. Lots of time too.' But the jangling continued.

'Fine!' I laughed. 'We've got plenty of both now! Oh gosh, you can see the cathedral from here! Look, Johnny, there, across the rooftops and – oh! Look!'

I had my head well out of the window now, marvelling at the view, but suddenly I popped it back in. I grabbed his hand and ran downstairs, pulling him out through the French windows, across the terrace to the lawn. As we slid down the bank on the other side together, we came to a halt at the bottom, panting. Johnny stared. There, tucked away behind a tall holly hedge and beneath a riot of ivy, was a small, brick-and-timbered barn. It was ancient, its roof was clearly rotten, but it was still standing, albeit by the skin of its teeth.

'I could keep the Bristol in here, maybe get Dad's old Lagonda in too!' he said excitedly. He walked in and peered up at the beams.

'Quite!' I squeaked. 'And you'd never get a double garage in London, no matter where we lived!'

He bit his lip thoughtfully, patted the thick old walls. Then he turned to me. 'We'll see, Livvy. Let's go home and think about it; do our sums, and see, OK?'

'OK!'

We did, but I knew then he was as smitten as I was. The idea of being half an hour from Central London – which let's face it, one could still be in Camberwell or Clapham – and living in a pretty period house with an acre of garden for me, and plenty of garaging for classic cars for him, was not to be sniffed at. We dutifully did our sums, consulted a few intelligent people who told us we were barking mad – and jumped in with both feet.

That autumn, Orchard House became our home and we were blissfully, ridiculously happy. So what if the eccentric East End builders we'd employed, together with their Greek sidekick, had practically moved in with us? So what if they watched our television, monopolised and stank out our lavatory, smoked my cigarettes and fundamentally ruled our lives? So what if the fires smoked and we were freezing to death, huddled in front of smelly blow heaters? So what if there were rats in the cellar and bats in the attic – all these problems were minor, could be sorted by Mac and the boys, and jolly well would be. Johnny surprised me by being very enthusiastic in the

DIY department, I was ecstatic in the garden, squealing with pleasure as I uncovered more and more neglected plants, and Claudia was positively flourishing, happy at her new school, not needing her inhaler nearly as much, loving the garden, delighted to have trees to climb, a stream to fish, and plenty of friends to bicycle with in The Crescent. So all was fine. All was peachy. For a while, anyway.

Until ... something happened, something ... that I couldn't quite put my finger on, but as I say, I reckon it happened about five months ago. Something went wrong. And despite my frantic attempts at Twickenham tickets and ballooning weekends in France, my husband continued to stare out of rain-soaked windows. I'd lost him. And now as I sat here, at our kitchen table, in my paint-spattered checked shirt, staring at a photograph on the fridge that was taken seventeen years ago, I realised I was about to find out why.

I glanced up at the clock: seven forty-five. It seemed to me he'd been upstairs for ever, but it must only have been a few minutes. He'd come back on his usual train, after all. Suddenly I jumped. Yes, now I could hear movement on the landing. He was coming down. I quickly lit another cigarette and was just exhaling the smoke as he came past the kitchen door, jacket on, a case in each hand. He saw me sitting there, stopped, and then stepped backwards so he was framed in the doorway. As he gazed at me, his blue eyes were full of remorse. Blue eyes I loved.

'Sorry, Livvy.'

I nodded. Swallowed hard. 'Johnn–' I tried again; my voice wouldn't work. 'Johnny,' I managed, 'is there someone else?'

He held my eyes for a moment, then slid them down to his shoes. 'If you mean am I having an affair, then yes, I am.'

I squeezed my legs together hard. 'And do you —' Couldn't say it. Couldn't say the love word. 'Is it serious?'

He took a deep breath. 'It wasn't . . . was never meant to be . . . but now . . . yes. Yes, it's serious.' His eyes came back to me. 'I'm so sorry, Livvy.'

I nodded. Raised my chin high. And then against my better judgement, out came, 'So where does that leave me?'

He stared. I looked away quickly from the silence.

He hesitated a moment longer, picked up his cases, opened the front door, closed it softly behind him, and set off down the path.

Chapter Four

'I don't believe you.'

'Please try to.'

'Livvy, you are *kidding*?'

'I'm not bloody kidding. Would I kid about something like that? Molly, do me a favour, don't quiz me on the phone. I'm really not up to it. Just get over here, OK?'

There was a stunned silence. 'But I'm shocked. Honest to God, I am so unbelievably shocked! *Johnny!* Of all people!'

'*Molly!*'

'Yes! Right. Right, I'm coming. And Imogen?'

I swallowed. 'Please. But, listen, could you tell her?'

She paused then: 'Course I will, darling. I'll see you soon.'

Half an hour later Molly was ringing my bell. I opened the door to find her clinging to the doorframe, hugely pregnant, panting hard, one arm holding her bump and the other, just about holding Henry, who at eleven months was puce in the face with fury, screaming and kicking to be set free. Molly's dark curls were damp with sweat, her eyes wild.

'Jesus Christ,' she gasped, 'don't let anyone talk you into unprotected sex in October. I tell you, lugging three extra stone around in a heat wave as well as this little bugger is no joke.'

'I think sex, protected or otherwise, is rather off the agenda for me at the moment.'

'Oh, Livvy!' She dropped Henry, put her arm round my neck and hugged hard. 'Livvy, my love!' I gulped gratefully into her damp curls, feeling her bump against me.

'Fine, I'm fine,' I muttered finally. 'Come on in.'

She followed me into the chaos of my tiny kitchen, neatly sidestepping a clothes horse laden with wet washing, noting, I'm sure, the tottering pagodas of washing-up in the sink, the newspapers on the floor soaking up the rush matting which had got drenched when the washing machine overflowed, but happily releasing Henry into it all, like a ferret down a burrow.

'So when did he go?' she gasped, collapsing into an old Lloyd Loom chair and lighting a cigarette.

'About two weeks ago.'

'Two weeks ago!' She sat up. 'My God, why didn't you tell me?'

'Couldn't.' I plucked a cigarette from her pack. 'Couldn't speak to anyone for about a week, Molly; couldn't even get out of bed. I finally broke it to Claudia, who I'd been fobbing off with a Daddy's-got-a-conference-in-New-York-again line, and then when she'd gone off to school, collapsed in a heap again.'

'How did she take it?'

'She said she knew. Suspected, anyway – had done for a while. She's not stupid, Mol.' I bit the skin round my thumb.

'And is she OK?'

I sighed. 'Seems to be, but you know how Claudes is. Never lets much show and takes everything in her stride, but you can never really tell with children, can you? All the books say the emotional scars and all that sort of scary baggage come later.' I gulped and dragged on my cigarette.

'Books?' scoffed Molly. 'What do they know, a bunch of half-baked psychologists spouting out their university theses? Listen, she'll be fine. God, it's *you* I'm worried about. Has he spoken to you?'

'Oh yes. He rang last week to speak to Claudia, and when I picked up the phone he very sweetly gave me his telephone number in case I should care to call him. Or Her? I asked. Sorry? he said. Well, I explained, surely it was Her telephone too? Oh, he said hurriedly, he'd just meant in case of an emergency. I felt like saying the only bloody emergency would be getting the gore off my hands when I'd finished disembowelling the cow.'

'Ah. So there is a cow?'

'Oh yes, didn't I mention that? Most definitely there is. That's why he's gone.'

'But you don't know who she is?'

'No idea.' I gazed beyond Molly, out of the window. 'No idea at all.'

She dragged hard on her cigarette. 'Jesus,' she muttered, flicking ash on to the newspaper on the floor beside her and shaking her head in disbelief. '*Je*sus. And you didn't see any of this coming, Liv? I mean – is this a complete and utter bolt from the blue?'

'Total. Well, the girl and the moving out bit is. He certainly didn't leave any clues – no lipstick on shirts, no condoms in pockets or anything – but . . .' I hesitated, 'if I'm honest, Mol, I knew something was up. *Have* known something was up for ages really. I just stupidly never thought it would be this.' I gave a hollow laugh. 'An affair! Never thought it would be an affair, for heaven's sake, the most obvious thing in the world!' I reached up to a shelf for a wine glass, but as I tried to find a space amongst the debris to set it down and pour a drink, I realised my hand was shaking violently.

She got up, took the glass and reached into the fridge for the bottle.

'He'll be back,' she said firmly, pouring out a large one and handing it to me.

'Of course he will,' I said quickly, grateful for that, wanting her to say that, wanting more.

'After all, this is what men do, isn't it?' she said warming to her theme, knowing she'd hit the right note. 'I mean, this is the seven-year itch, isn't it?'

'Twelve.'

'The flighty forties –'

'Thirties.'

'The classic mid-life crisis, the "oh my God, where did my youth go, am I going bald and does my willy still work?"'

'Precisely.'

'And then before you know where you are, he'll be crawling back here with his tail between his legs, and you'll be force-feeding him humble pie for weeks! Actually, it'll probably be the making of your marriage, especially if you sort of worry him for a bit.'

'What – you mean dither about having him back?'

'Exactly, do a bit of, "Ooh, Johnny, I'm not so sure. You see, I'm making my own way now. I don't know whether you'll fit into my amateur dramatics group, my gym classes, my –"'

'"Tennis lessons with the wolfish young pro"?'

'Much better! And then all of a sudden he'll see his whole life slipping away into a grotty little flat with yet another Fray Bentos meal put in front of him by a floozie who can't iron shirts, and in that split second – which is all it takes – he suddenly won't be able to remember what on earth he saw in her, and he'll be positively *begging* you to have him back!'

'Well, quite.' I took a huge gulp of wine. I'd been doing quite well there, but the mention of the floozie who might not wield an iron spectacularly but who might have other, more exotic talents, made me feel slightly less gung-ho. 'Bastard,' I muttered.

'Oh yes, that goes without saying,' Molly agreed, 'but – *Henry, no!'*

She lunged as Henry, left to his own devices, was quietly helping himself to the delights of a tool box left open by the builders and about to insert a six-inch nail down his oesophagus. Molly grabbed it, but then a frantic struggle ensued with Henry intent on keeping that nail, and prepared to sink his brand-new teeth into his mother's hand to secure it.

'Ouch! You little –' She bared her teeth viciously at him and snarled back. Miraculously, he dropped the nail.

'Well, that certainly worked.'

'Oh yes,' she panted, pinning him to the ground in a half-nelson. 'He bit me the other day, you see, and I bit him back – in Tesco's, actually. Caused quite a stir in the checkout queue. Someone even ventured to ask if I was fit to have another baby, to which I replied no, I'm not, so

64

give me your address and I'll let you have it. And there'll be plenty more where that one came from, I assured the rest of the queue. At the rate I'm breeding, no one need go empty-handed.'

I smiled. Within weeks of giving birth, Molly had fallen for that fatal old wives' tale which tells you you can't get pregnant while you're breast-feeding. Now, on the point of having two children under thirteen months, she was living proof that you can. Married to a lovely, penniless actor called Hugh, who was always *just* on the brink of making that big Hollywood break but meanwhile doing Bonio adverts to tide them over, she lived from hand to mouth in a tiny rented cottage not far from here that was possibly even more squalid than mine. But Molly didn't see the damp marching up the walls, or the confetti of final demands on the breakfast-room table; she had Hugh, she had Henry, she had her bump, and she was bright enough to know that was more than most. Molly had always been effortlessly, unashamedly herself. She wore anything that came to hand – jodhpurs, felt hats, crochet waistcoats – making fashion decisions faster than a speeding bullet, and I'd often felt that if I were more like Molly, it might give me more confidence, more vigour, make being myself less of a labour. She'd never felt she had a thing to prove, you see – which reminded me.

'Did you get hold of Imogen?'

'Yes. She said she was working late, just locking up the gallery, but she said she'd come straight down, be here about nine. Actually, the way she throws that Mercedes about I'm surprised she didn't get here before me.'

'How did she sound?'

'About what?'

'Well – when you told her about me.'

'Oh. Oh well, to be honest, I could hardly hear her – her mobile was cracking up – but, well, shocked, I suppose.' She frowned, trying to remember.

I reached across and grabbed another one of her cigarettes, then paced the little room nervously. I gazed out of the window. The light from the caravan just across the stream at the bottom of the garden shone out like a beacon in the fading evening light. Mac and the boys, sick of trawling in from Billericay every day and getting stuck on the M25, had asked if they could stay during the week, and since it was in my interests to have them start at eight o'clock rather than ten, I'd said yes, fine, as long as you accommodate yourselves and don't expect me to put you up. Bed and breakfast, I'd presumed, down the road somewhere, but the next thing I knew their truck had arrived dragging a socking great caravan. Later that afternoon, after they'd put in a hard day's work, Claudia and I had stood and watched, fascinated, as they'd bustled around it like three little housewives; pulling down beds from the walls, making hospital corners with the sheets, getting crockery out of dinky little cupboards and even plumping up cushions on the banquette seating, before settling down in front of the telly, a six-pack between them, a vindaloo apiece, with no nagging wives, no bloomin' kids – feet up and all ready to watch the footy. Magic.

Claudia was fascinated by this little menage, and one afternoon, when she'd been feeling rather brave, had knocked on their door. I'd found her there later watching the racing – Pils and vindaloo happily substituted by 7-Up and crisps – looking very important and clearly feeling very grown up. My mother had been horrified when I'd mentioned it, but frankly I could see nothing wrong with her watching the 5.40 from Kempton with my workforce before I called her back to do her homework. Right now, of course, she was tucked up in bed, and they were no doubt in there watching something far more risqué.

I turned back to Molly. 'I haven't seen her for ages.'

Molly was on her knees, changing a nappy.

'Who?'

'Imogen.'

'Oh, right. No, neither have I, really. Not since she split up with Dominic anyway.'

I swung around. 'She split up with Dominic?'

'Yes, didn't you know?'

'No! When?'

'Oh God, I don't know, four or five months ago?'

'Four or fi– but she didn't tell me!'

'Oh, well, Heavens,' she looked up, awkward suddenly, privy to information I wasn't, 'you've been so busy with this house, Livvy, and she's been frantic at the gallery – she's had a rush of private views on recently – it's hardly surprising. Anyway, she was never really serious about him.'

'She's never been really serious about anyone except –' I shook my head. 'And I've spoken to her loads of times, Molly. She never even mentioned it!'

'Oh well,' she shrugged and snapped the new nappy on, 'perhaps she wanted to see you to tell you. You know what Imo's like. Listen, are you going to open those Pringles I've just spotted lurking in that cupboard down there,

67

or are me and my appendage here going to have to starve to death?'

I ignored her, knowing full well she was changing the subject, and seized her hand as it went for the crisps.

'Four or five months, Molly. Don't you see? That's exactly when it started, four or five months ago!'

'Stop it!' Molly shook me off, horrified. 'Livvy, how could you? Of *course* it's not Imo!'

'Why not?'

'Because she's your best friend!'

'Doesn't count, Mol.' I shook my head violently. 'Love cancels out everything like that. Friendship, loyalty – it all goes out of the window and, God, they were *so* in love all those years ago and –'

'Livvy, you have got to stop being so insecure about that! Just because he went out with her, for God's sake!'

'It was more than that and you know it. She broke his heart with Paolo, and then through her own stupid pride broke her own heart too. Imo's never found anyone else, Mol, and look at her now, chucking in the towel with one guy after another!'

I was ranting now, pacing the floor, all the pent-up, horrid, suspicious thoughts I'd had over the last few weeks spilling out like serpents from my mouth.

'Don't you see, Molly, it would *have* to be someone as serious as Imo! Johnny would never leave me just for a fling with a floozie. It's not his style. He despises philanderers! He'd rather slit his wrists than join that sordid little band of –'

I froze as I heard tyres on the gravel drive.

'Don't you dare,' breathed Molly, staring at me.

I held her gaze for a moment, then went to the door. I stood for a moment, regarding the paintwork. The doorbell went, I waited a moment longer, then finally opened it.

She was standing on the doorstep, looking as beautiful as ever in a grey, sleeveless Ghost dress, her blonde hair slipping silkily over her shoulders, her pale blue eyes wide, like a baby's. They filled up with tears when they saw me.

'Oh, Livvy! You poor darling!'

I was so glad she hugged me. So glad I could hide my shame in her hair. I was wrong. So wrong. I knew that instantly. But this was what he'd done to me, you see. This was what the love of my life, the ache in my gut, had done. Made me see treachery in childhood friends.

'How are you?' She held me at arm's length and scanned my face anxiously.

'Terrible,' I grinned. 'Despicable too, and nasty with it, but all the better for seeing you. Come on, come in before Molly and I finish all the wine.'

'Molly's drinking?' she enquired doubtfully.

'Er, well, just a thimble or two.'

'And smoking!' she said, catching Molly hurriedly stubbing out a cigarette.

'My doctor says it's fine,' she said defiantly. 'He says the shock to my heavily addicted, twenty-a-day system would be far greater if I stopped and that one or two is not going to hurt, *plus* a little glass of wine and *plus*, Imo, if *you* were seven months pregnant, flatulent, exhausted, incontinent, and with a one-year-old with a charming habit of projectile vomiting, *you'd* have the odd ciggy too!' Molly got up to kiss her friend. 'How are you anyway, you old bag?' She plonked Henry's bottle in the microwave.

'Well, sorry I spoke, since you ask. But – blimey, it can't be all that bad, surely? I mean, let's face it, millions of women do it every day, don't they? Have babies?' She gave a bright smile, perfectly designed to wind Molly up.

Molly ground her teeth. She and I longed for Imogen to get pregnant. We longed for that perfect size ten figure to swell up to monolithic proportions; for her to scratch and sweat, for her feet to swell, for her tummy button to pop out, and more importantly, for her to suffer the indignities of childbirth. Sadly though, we secretly knew that if Imogen were to get pregnant, she'd just look as though she'd swallowed a doughnut, and that when the time came for the doughnut/baby to be delivered, she'd effortlessly slip the perfect specimen into a gorgeous gynaey's hands, who'd gaze at her with lust and admiration as, pausing only to deposit the babe into the arms of a waiting, uniformed nanny, she shimmied out of his private delivery suite in her size ten jeans, and headed back to the art gallery she ran in Walton Street for a refreshing spritzer with a client.

She sat down now on the only available seat – which, to her credit, was an upturned milk crate – and somehow managed to make it look like a Conran original. After crossing her elegant legs and flicking back her long, blonde hair, she cleared her throat.

'Livvy darling, I'm afraid I've got something to tell you.'

My heart stopped. I lunged for my glass; spun round to face her like a machine gun. Ah, so this was it, then; my hunch had been right. The serpents slithered back up my throat and I met her eyes challengingly. But Imo's slid away. Imo's eyes never slid like that.

'What?' I whispered.

'He's seeing someone else.'

I nodded. 'I know.'

'You know?' She glanced back at me.

'Yes, he told me.'

'Ah.' She paused for what felt like an eternity. 'And did he tell you who?'

I shook my head. Couldn't speak.

She gave a brief confirmatory nod. 'Her name's Nina Harrison.'

My jaw dropped. 'Nina . . . what? Who? Who the hell's Nina Harrison?'

She shrugged. 'Search me, but I saw them in a restaurant about a month ago. It was round here actually. I came home for Mum's birthday and we took her to that new Italian place on Hollywell Hill. They were in there having supper together.'

'No!' I gaped. 'Why didn't you tell me?'

'Oh sure, come on, Livvy. What – tell your best friend that you've just seen her husband with another woman? And how was I to know it wasn't a colleague from work or something, or even just a brief fling that would be much better you didn't know about?'

'Better I didn't . . .' I was speechless for a moment. 'Well, God,' I blustered finally, 'I think I might have told *you*!'

'Oh, me, maybe, but I'm single with no kids. But think about it, Livvy. Would you have told Molly? Pregnant? With a small baby?'

'Oh, I'd have been highly delighted,' said Molly as she took the bottle from the microwave and handed it to a grabbing Henry. 'I dream of Hugh having a concubine. I'd be very happy with light scullery duties, just so long as she took over in the bedroom and breeding department. Really.' She gave a bright smile and I knew she was trying to lighten the atmosphere.

'So how come you know her name?' I persisted, stunned.

'Looked at her credit card. She paid the bill – which was why I thought it could have been a client or something – and then when the waiter took the saucer away to the counter, I crept to the loo with my pashmina over my face. Saw it as I went past.'

'Did you see her?'

'Not clearly.'

'But?'

She shrugged. 'Small, fairish – not blonde – and pretty, I suppose, but in a very mousy, nondescript sort of way. Nothing special at all, Livvy, and certainly no competition for you.'

She was being kind. Being protective. Dear, sweet Imo, who twice in the space of five minutes I'd cast as a she-devil in my husband's bed, a temptress, a Jezebel. But lovers on the skids have no redress. No dignity either.

'And did Johnny . . . ?'

'Oh God, no, he didn't see me. I made sure of that. And anyway, they left more or less as soon as we arrived, thank goodness. I was terrified Mum would spot him.'

'Off for a night of spine-shattering sex, no doubt,' I said bitterly.

'She didn't look the spine-shattering type, Liv.'

'They never do,' I said sadly.

I got up and cleared away some glasses. I knew my eyes were filling up, so I ran the taps at the sink and dithered ineffectually with a dishcloth to hide my face.

'Very odd,' murmured Molly to Imogen behind me as she sat Henry on her lap, rubbing his back to wind him. 'I mean, Livvy's right, a tacky affair with a mousy blonde, it's not exactly his style, is it?'

'Hardly,' said Imogen drily, 'and he's always been erudite on the subject of extramarital sex; always been very happy up there on the high moral ground. Well, how the mighty have fallen.'

Down in the sink a plate almost came to pieces in my hands as I wished, not for the first time, that they didn't know quite so much about my husband, about my marriage. I wouldn't dream of making disparaging remarks about their partners, but Johnny, it seemed, was fair game. He was public property, you see, belonged to all of us, always had done, and whilst –

'*Christ!*' Imo shrieked suddenly. I spun round to see her clutching her head, as a stream of yellow liquid splattered on the wall behind her.

'What was that!' she yelled, frozen to her milk crate.

'Projectile vomiting,' muttered Molly, grabbing a dishcloth and hastening past her to mop it up. 'I believe I mentioned it earlier. So sorry, Livvy, your wall. I'll – Oh, Imo, did it get in your hair? Here, I'll –'

'*Not with that!*' screeched Imo, leaping to her feet as Molly brandished a vomit-soaked rag. 'No, really, Mol, he missed,' she breathed. 'I'm fine, truly.' She sat down again shakily, smoothing her hair. 'Jesus, does he always do that?'

'Periodically,' admitted Molly, scrubbing away, 'although he's supposed to have grown out of it. Most babies do at about three months, but not my Henry. He doesn't know when the joke's over. I wouldn't mind betting that in years to come he'll be offering you a gin and tonic and still be taking aim at your highlights.'

Imo shuddered. 'That'll charm the pants off the girls. Let's hope his incontinence clears up by then. Although I have to say,' she smiled smugly, 'whilst I don't know much about children, I don't think you can claim the monopoly on that, Mol. I'm pretty sure all babies are incontinent.'

'Oh, Imo, I'm afraid you misheard,' smiled Molly. 'That's my affliction, not his.'

Imogen looked appalled. 'Molly! God, how *awful*, poor *you*!'

'Yes, poor me. Still lactating with number one, sick as a parrot with number two, and now, thrillingly unpredictable in the waterworks department too, but don't worry, Imo, it only happens when I laugh, and believe me, there's precious little to laugh about in my life at the moment.'

'Evidently,' said Imogen weakly. 'God, remind me to avoid this child-bearing lark. I'll have one in a test tube, or adopt. Yes, that's it, I'll send out for one, like a pizza – except, hang on, now here's one I *would* take home with me. Hello, darling, how's tricks?'

Claudia appeared in the doorway in her nightie.

'Claudes!' I jumped up. 'It's ten o'clock! What's the matter?'

'Couldn't sleep,' she said, fumbling across to the dresser

for her glasses. She put them on. 'But tricks is fine thanks Imo. I like your dress.'

She kissed her godmother, fingering the grey silky material covetously – very much a Du Bray in the clothes department was our Claudia – before going to kiss her other godmother and pick up the baby.

'How come Henry isn't in bed and I am?' she said, crouching down.

'Henry doesn't sleep, darling,' said Molly, ruffling her hair fondly. 'He's a changeling. He doesn't behave like other, normal babies. He's only been put on this earth to vex his mother. He's from the planet Thwart.'

Claudia giggled, then suddenly looked serious. She straightened up, folded her arms. 'She's told you then, has she? About Daddy?'

There was a silence. I hastened across to her anxiously. 'I did actually, darling. Do you mind?'

'Course not,' she said, pushing her dark fringe back impatiently. 'I said you should share it more, not bottle it up.'

'Well, quite,' I agreed nervously. My daughter was ten, going on twenty-four.

'And how do *you* feel about it, my love?' asked Molly gently.

'Oh, I'm OK. Daddy says he'll see me on Sundays and I know from books that he'll feel really guilty about making me a product of a broken home, so I'll probably get loads of treats and things, and trips to Thorpe Park, which'll be cool. I won't get spoilt, though. Susan, in *The Chalet School* adventures, hasn't got a father, but she's not spoilt 'cos her mother's strict but fair, so I expect I'll be the same.' She nodded firmly.

'Good, good,' said Molly faintly.

'And, anyway, it'll all come right in the end. Something good will come out of it, I'll be bound.'

'I'll be —' Molly turned wide eyes on me.

'Angela Brazil,' I muttered. 'She found all my old books.'

'Ah.'

'And Mummy should get out more,' Claudia said firmly. 'Don't you think?' She rounded on her godmothers.

'Oh yes, absolutely,' they chorused quickly.

'Mrs Parker, Clarissa's mother in *The Faraway Island*, was devastated when Mr Parker went off to America, but she busied herself, and lo and behold, he came back!'

'So — how do you suggest I busy myself, my darling? Bustling round the kitchen baking scones? A bit of embroidery, perhaps? Then lo and behold —'

'Oh no,' she interrupted scathingly, 'those are just meaningless chores invented for the enslavement of women. No, I thought you could go to the pub with the builders.'

I gulped at this child of mine.

'Why not?' she insisted. 'They go out every single night to the Fox and Ferret before picking up their curries. Well, you could go with them, Mum, get a curry too. You like curries.'

'And some tinnies too, perhaps?' murmured Imo.

'Good idea. And then when Dad comes over to pick me up, you could be down in the caravan, watching telly with them. It's tactics, Mum. I saw it on *EastEnders*. Bianca did it to Ricky. You've got to get Dad to wake up a bit, make him jealous!'

'Right, darling.' I nodded. Tactics. From a ten-year-old

girl, drawing on an eclectic mixture of fifties boarding school books and contemporary soaps.

'And you've got to find yourself, too,' she declared importantly.

I sighed. 'Even if I did, my love, I'm not sure I'd recognise her.'

'Oh, don't be so wet,' she retorted. 'It's just a case of getting out and about. I mean, Nanette's *always* asking you over.'

'Oh God, not Nanette, Claudes.'

'Who's Nanette?' pounced Molly.

'She lives in The Crescent,' said Claudia, turning to her. 'She's always having things called fork suppers with men in blazers called Clive, and Mum never goes.'

'I think you get the picture,' I muttered drily, clearing the glasses.

'Sounds rather fun,' grinned Molly maliciously. 'Where exactly does this Nanette hail from?' She got up and peered out of the window, knowing that, such was the nature of The Crescent, most houses could be clearly seen.

'There, over there on the end.' Claudia joined her, pointing eagerly at a lighted window with frilly Austrian blinds. As I joined them, to my horror we saw a hand wave back.

'Oh God, she's *seen* you, Claudes. She thinks you're *waving*!'

'Well, that's OK.'

'And now she's disappeared! She's probably coming over!'

'Well, fine, that's fine. She can have a drink. I like her, Mum.'

'And I do too, darling. She's very kind, but –' I spotted her garden gate opening. 'Oh no, she *is* coming over – hide!' I dived down under the table. 'Tell her I'm out,' I muttered, face pressed down into the rush matting.

'Mummy, that's silly. She'll *know* you're here; your friends are here, for heaven's sake. Of *course* you can't hide.'

'I think Claudia has a point, Livvy,' said Imogen. 'And anyway,' she paused, lifting the curtain again and peering out of the window, 'if Nanette looks anything like Cruella de Vil I'm afraid it's too late.'

There was a familiar crunch of gravel, then 'Coo-ee!' – and a rap of jewelled knuckles at the door. Claudia flew to open it, and two seconds later in came Nanette, just as I was crawling out.

'Olivia! Goodness, you're always crawling around under that table! Every time I pop by you seem to be down there looking for something!'

'Dropped my lipstick this time,' I muttered, since make-up was the first thing that came to mind as I looked at her face. Blimey, she always wore the works, but tonight it looked as if she'd applied it with an industrial high-pressure hose. Mid-fortyish and resplendent in a tight cerise sweater which had a sequinned bird of prey lurking ominously over one shoulder, skin-tight white pedal push-ers and high pink mules, she also had lipstick all over her teeth when she grinned.

'Nanette, it's lovely to see you,' I lied as I scrambled up. 'Um, come in and sit down. We were just having a drink. This is Molly Piper, by the way, and Imogen Mitchell, my best friends.'

'Oh, *really*?' Nanette looked enchanted, especially by

Imogen, and extended a bony, suntanned hand. 'Gosh, and what a shame, I'd *love* a little drinky but I can't stop, I'm afraid. I'm just on my way out to my evening class. It's my sexual awareness and crochet group tonight, you see, but I've heard *so* much about you both,' she lied, 'and I'm thrilled to meet you at last!'

'You too,' murmured Molly and Imogen, looking totally fascinated and agog at this vision.

'But what I *have* brought,' Nanette went on, brandishing a leather-bound book, 'is my diary, and I intend to pin you down once and for all, Olivia! *So* sad about all this ghastly business,' she murmured *sotto voce*, turning to Imogen and Molly, for all the world as if I wasn't there. 'Of course she's told you . . . ? Well, of course she has and, actually, I'm afraid everyone knows. Half the county's talking about it – but don't you think she should get out more? Show that randy old so-and-so – Oops,' her hand went to her mouth, ''scuse my French, Claudia. You know how I adore Daddy really – show him just who's boss around here?'

'I'll get Mummy's diary!' chirruped Claudia happily, as my friends nodded mutely at her. 'Here!' She grabbed it off the dresser and handed it to Nanette.

Two heads then bent low together, as my daughter and my neighbour compared, conspired and pencilled in, with Molly and Imogen – less wide-eyed now, and more highly amused – exchanging mouth-twitching, eyebrow-raised glances.

As I scrubbed a plate savagely in the sink, I found myself turning, and looking with new-found hatred at Nanette's jet-black hair. So. She adored 'randy Daddy', eh? So perhaps it was her? Yes, why not? She was local, they'd been seen together in a local restaurant, she was probably a sex maniac, so yes, perhaps it was Nanette that Imogen had seen, in a blonde wig? Nanette – Nina – of course. My eyes flew to the breadknife on the side. I could plunge it into her back right now, just as she bent over the diary, watch the blood spurt out, see the horror on my friends' and my daughter's faces. I frowned. Would they instantly call the police? Where exactly would their loyalties lie? As I gazed at her, wondering what the devil I'd do with the corpse – freezer perhaps? Compost heap? – I suddenly came to. I shuddered and turned back to the sink. God, I was a low form of life, wasn't I? Capable of anything at the moment. And, of course, this was a form of madness, I thought miserably. I suspected anyone and everyone, including my kind neighbour, who wasn't my type – or Johnny's either come to that – but who was only trying to help, and had simply come over to invite me to supper. Nanette snapped her diary shut, satisfied.

'Friday next week then. Nothing too formal, more of a smart but casual affair, six or maybe eight of us in all, and I'll make sure you're suitably paired off, Olivia.' She tapped her pencil on her diary and narrowed her eyes thought-fully. 'Ye-s, I'll probably do something fairly simple, a salmon en croute perhaps, with a choice of desserts – tiramisu, banoffee pie, that sort of thing – oh, and I'll probably be wearing my beige suede suit, Olivia – you know, my Gucci.' She shot Imogen a quick look to tell her she knew her labels. 'So maybe something like your silk palazzo pants? With a new sweater? I gather Romano's in Radlett have got a sale on at the moment, maybe we could –'

'Thank you, Nanette,' I interrupted weakly, 'that would

be lovely, and don't worry, I'll sort myself out, sartorially speaking.'

'Super,' she beamed, 'and I'll make sure the guest list is suitably yummy, particularly *à l'autre côté à toi*!' Nanette had somehow discovered our French ancestry and had a disconcerting habit of breaking into Franglais at a moment's notice. Imogen and Molly were looking more and more enchanted.

'So! *A bientôt, mes chéries,* and don't forget, Olivia, Friday the ninth, eight for eight fifteen, canapés on the patio, Kir Royales in the conservatory, be there or be square! Toodle-oo!' And with that she bustled out backwards with a dinky little wave.

'Toodle-*oo!*' chorused my friends and daughter joyfully.

The moment the front door closed behind Nanette I chucked a plate in the water, strode to the counter, seized the breadknife, raised it high above my head, and with a blood curdling screech of 'HYAA-AACK!' plunged it straight into the heart of a granary loaf.

'Traitors!' I bellowed. 'The lot of you!'

'Oh, Mum, it'll be fun!' insisted Claudia, giggling.

'Of course it will,' gasped Imogen, wiping her eyes. 'It'll be brimming over with gorgeous Clives, and possibly a few Nigels too. You'll love it!'

I thought back to when we were at school, scanned the rows of desks, searching for the girl I wanted: frizzy-haired, cunning-eyed, mean-spirited, never sharing her sweets, let alone her homework, very smelly feet. 'I would rather,' I said carefully, 'spend an entire weekend in Brenda Archdale's company, massaging her toes with my teeth, than endure the evening that is about to befall me.'

'Oh God, really?' Molly looked suitably shocked for a moment. Then she caught Imogen's eye and they both dissolved into giggles. They clutched each other for a moment, until abruptly Molly froze. Her eyes bulged.

'Oh *God*!' She squeaked, snapping her legs together. 'Help!'

'Serves you bloody well right,' I said callously as I reached into Henry's changing bag and chucked her a nappy. 'Here, try this on for size.'

Chapter Five

A few days later I was lying in bed mulling it over. Nina. *Nina*, for God's sake. Who on earth was called Nina these days? It sounded so pre-war, like she wore a cardy and slippers, or sold smellies in Boots, or even – yes, that's it – maybe she was foreign? Nina Mouskouri – no, no that was Nana – or, OK, Nina Simone? Oh God, I couldn't compete with that, I thought hastily, some dark, exotic, dusky maiden. No, far better she was the cardy type. Or could it be an aristocratic name perhaps? I wondered, with a jolt. Wasn't one of the Mitford sisters called something like – No. No, that was Nancy. I sighed and turned over, bunching up the pillow – then stared. Claudia was beside me, feigning sleep, eyelids flickering. I groaned.

'Oh darling, you said you'd try not to *do* this any more.'

'I know, but I couldn't sleep. And anyway, Daddy's not here, so there's plenty of room.'

Well, there was no arguing with that. The sun was also streaming persistently through the curtains now, so I turned back and seized the clock, peering myopically at it. Twenty to eight.

'Claudia! It's twenty to eight!' I shot up like a rocket.

'I know.'

'Well, don't say I know, flaming well get a move on! You'll be late for school – again!'

She rolled out of bed, pulling the duvet with her, and

dragged herself to her bedroom. 'That, Mother dear, was precisely the idea,' she muttered sardonically.

I flew around the room looking for clothes, desperate for a shower but knowing there wasn't time, listening to Claudia slowly opening drawers and dragging her feet. Hardly the sounds of frenzied activity.

'Claudia, come *on*!'

'I *am*!'

I sat down abruptly on the bed feeling a bit of head rush. I held my fingers to my temples. Oh God, I shouldn't have yelled like that so early in the morning. It always made me feel nauseous. And anyway, so what if we were late, just for once? Sometimes Claudia had a point. I flopped back on the bed. She was so like me in so many ways, and so unlike me in others. Aesthetically speaking, it was plain to see we were a mother-and-daughter act: skinny-framed, beaky-nosed and wide-eyed – which, together with pebble glasses and an unusual dental arrangement, was not a combination Claudia enjoyed at ten years old – but, as I kept assuring her, she'd grow into her looks, as I had done.

'What, and end up looking like you?'

'Is that so terrible?'

'No, but it's just a bit boring to already know what I'm going to look like in twenty years' time.'

This was classic Claudia. Not exactly bored with life, but resigned to it, slightly world-weary. She excelled at school academically, but didn't find it particularly stimulating, so almost as if to compensate, in a minor way, she'd recently become something of a troublemaker. She avoided all games and sports citing her asthma – although these days that was rare — she cheeked the younger teachers — taking care not to tangle with the battle-axes — and wore her skirt hiked up at a ridiculous angle, socks well down, tie in her pocket along with her chewing gum. On one ghastly occasion recently, she'd even been caught stealing a comic from Smiths, whilst ostensibly on a school trip.

'I can't believe she did that!' I'd shrieked down the phone to Molly.

'Why not? We've all done it.'

'We have?' I'd gasped.

'Of course. Remember the make-up counter in Boots? Max Factor lipsticks? Those quiet afternoons of jiggery-pokery on the way home from school?'

'No! Not me. That was always you and Imo.'

'Ah, perhaps.'

'And you were at least fourteen!'

'So she's precocious. Relax, Livvy, it's nothing outrageous. She's just showing a healthy lack of respect for authority. Just ground her for a few days.'

'How can I ground her when she's not allowed out yet!' I'd shrieked.

Nothing outrageous, I'd thought, putting down the phone, but all the same, all acts of rebellion that I, at ten, would have been horrified by. Mine had always been a timorous spirit, eager to please, careful not to offend, yet Claudia seemed unable to pledge allegiance to any values that conflicted with her own. I grudgingly admired her for this, knowing full well from whence it came. She got her looks from me and her balls from Johnny.

The one time Johnny and I had really seen her shine,

and revelled in the reflected glory, was when she took the lead as Alice in Wonderland in the school play. She'd left the rest of the cast standing, and when we'd congratulated her afterwards – full of pride as so many parents patted her on the back, then whisking her away to the hamburger joint of her choice by way of celebration – she'd confided that the reason she'd loved it so much was because she could pretend to be someone else. This had filled me with dread.

'But what's so wrong with being Claudia McFarllen?'

'Oh, nothing,' she'd said coolly, sipping her milk shake. 'But it's just nice to get away from her once in a while.'

Being a normal, angst-ridden, middle-class mother, of course I'd been sent into a flat spin by this, and for one mad moment I'd almost felt compelled to whisk her off to a child psychologist, such was the contemporary vogue for these people, but Johnny had been appalled.

'Christ Almighty, the one time she gets a buzz out of something and you want her psychoanalysed! Relax, Livvy.'

Relax, Livvy, relax, I thought, heaving myself off the bed and dragging myself, like some rough beast, over to my dressing table. I sat down heavily. That was a word I'd come to hear a lot of over the years. I peered blearily at my reflection in the mirror and sighed. The hair badly needed a cut so I tucked some of it behind my ears, then peered again, hoping perhaps for a miraculous transformation, blinking out through the fringe. On a good day, adjectives like 'elfin' or 'principal boy' came to mind, and on a bad day, 'Oxfam' or 'hermaphrodite'. Today was a bad one. I reached for my nail scissors and had a go at the fringe. Lop-sided, of course. I switched hands and attacked from the other side, ending up looking like Julius Caesar. God, just give me a laurel wreath. I sighed and went to the window.

At the far end of the garden I could see movement in the caravan. The door opened and Alf came out. I watched his listing movement across the grass, large and lumbering in his blue overalls, bound, no doubt, for the Portaloo and a few quiet moments with the *Sun*. The Portaloo had arrived with the caravan, and was sent from heaven, as far as I was concerned. So outrageous had been the pong in mine on one occasion that I'd been forced to race, clenched buttocked, round to Nanette's, banging on the door to use hers.

Alf was soon followed by Mac, coming down the caravan steps and looking critically up at the sky. Far too blue for his liking – what they needed was some rain to curdle the cement, to make bricklaying out of the question, to ensure that they could huddle under the blue tarpaulin and smoke and drink tea for a bit. Finally, came Spiro, woolly-hatted even in a heat wave, dark eyes peering into the sun, and naturally, clutching his Wotsits. Despite a monumental fry up in the caravan every morning, Wotsits were essential to get these boys through the next half-hour, together, of course, with their mobile phones. These wonders of modern technology were never out of their hands, and they could quite easily plaster a chimney breast with one hand and talk to her indoors with the other: Spiro to her in Greece, Mac to his third wife, and Alf to his first, with whom he'd notched up twenty years' hard labour. Her name was Vi and she was a legend in her own front room, according to Mac; a shrew of the first order, who nagged Alf 'something rotten' and bent his ear at the slightest opportunity.

As Alf came out of the loo now, his phone went. Vi, of course. My bedroom window was open and I could hear him as he approached the kitchen.

'Orright, luv, the lean-to, yeah, I'll sort it . . . Yeah, I know, it's a mess . . . OK, it's a buggerin' mess . . . Yeah, I will, I'll do it on Sunday . . . Orright, Saturday, yeah . . . As soon as I get home, yeah. Love you. Bye.'

Harangued but devoted, you see. Perhaps that's where I'd gone wrong? I'd noticed recently, as I analysed marriages, that women who harangued and nagged on a permanent basis generally had very well-behaved husbands. I looked at mine as he grinned out at me now from our wedding photo on my dressing table. Bloody photos were everywhere, I thought, glaring at it. Every flaming room I went into, there he was, leering at me again. I should have smashed the lot of them, of course, especially after yesterday. I leant my elbows on the table, put my head in my hands and groaned.

Oh God, yesterday had been awful. The first Sunday Johnny had been over to pick Claudia up, and the first of many, no doubt. I, of course, in a frenzy of anticipation, had spent the two hours before his estimated time of arrival prowling the house, disastrously picking a spot on my chin, checking my hair repeatedly in the mirror, and wondering how the hell I was going to play this. What exactly was the estranged wife form? Should I ask him in? Should I give him a cup of tea, or should I simply open the front door and punch his lights out? And I'm ashamed to say I considered my wardrobe very carefully, too. Casual, of course, so shorts, since it was ninety degrees in the shade and my legs were brown, but teamed with a skinny white T-shirt and a rather snazzy little denim jacket I'd found in River Island, which was probably a bit young for me but looked terrific. My freshly washed hair was blown casually just so, I added a hint of lipstick, a slick of mascara – how the hell was he going to resist me? Unfortunately, though, when the big moment came and as I heard his car arrive in the front drive, I was having a nervous evacuation in the downstairs loo, and as I charged out, zipping up my shorts, I realised I'd left the crucial denim jacket in the garden. Claudia began to clump downstairs.

'Don't go without saying goodbye!' I shrieked. 'I'm just getting my jacket!'

Out into the garden I raced, down to the deckchair under the spreading cedar, seized the jacket, wriggled into it when – damn.

'Hulloa, Mrs McFarllen!' Mr Jones, my next-door neighbour, very Welsh, a highly competitive gardener – very into his leeks and radishes – and always with a roguish twinkle in his eye, stuck his head over the garden wall.

'Oh – morning, Mr Jones. I'm sorry I can't stop now, I'm –'

'Ooa, I woan't take up much of yewer time, like, but I just wanted to say how sorry I am, reely reely sorry. Only Gwyneth told me, see, told me last night about yewer terrible predicament!' He twiddled his moustache nervously, gazed abstractedly at my bosom.

'Ah.' I hovered. 'Right. Thank you, Mr Jones.'

'Wha' a thing to happen, eh? Wha' a shock! Terrible. Terrible! You must be devastated, like!'

'Well, yes, quite upset, but bearing up, thank you, under the circumstances.' I glanced nervously through the French windows to see that Claudia was already opening the front door. I tried to inch away.

'Ooa, yes, I dare say yewer are, like, an' I was sayin' to Gwyneth oanly last night, yewer a bewetiful young girl, feisty too, and yew'll bounce right back like nobody's business, but even soa, 's not easy, is it? Soa I was wondering, like,' he reached down behind the wall and picked something up, twinkling at me the while, 'could yew use one of these?' With a sudden flourish he produced a cucumber.

I gaped at it. Blinked. Finally found my voice. '*Sorry*, Mr Jones?'

'Only I've got soa many, I don't know what to do with them, see!'

'Well, I'm not sure *I'd* know what to do with it!' I spluttered.

'And when Gwyneth told me about that rat getting into yewer greenhouse and destroying all of yewers, and all those luverly tomato plants with it, I thought oo *noa* – and I went straight out into the garden to pick yew the biggest one I could find!'

'Oh!' I breathed. 'Oh, yes!'

'And here it is!' He beamed. 'Must be about two foot long, see, and thick with it! Feel that, girl!'

'Yes, yes, I do see. Gosh, how marvellous!'

Out of the corner of my eye I noticed that Claudia was grabbing a jacket from the banisters, picking up her duffel bag. She turned and spotted me in the garden. 'Bye, Mum!' She waved.

'So I said to Gwyneth, I said I'll give her this one, Gwyn, and –'

Suddenly I lunged across the wall and seized it from his arms. Short of decapitating him, it was the only way to shut him up. 'Yes, thank you, Mr Jones,' I gasped, 'thank you so much!' And with that I beetled back to the house, running as fast as my legs would carry me.

'Are you off?' I managed to gasp, racing through the French doors and into the hall – just as the front door was closing. To my relief it opened again.

'Yes, well, Dad's here so I –' She stopped. They both stared at me in astonishment, Johnny looking blond and tanned and lovely in old shorts, deck shoes, and a blue sailing shirt that matched his eyes.

'What's that?' Claudia gaped.

I glanced down, panting. 'This? Oh, this! A cucumber, of course.'

'Yes, but it's huge. And so fat!'

'Yes, isn't it?' I grinned maniacally.

Bloody thing, what could I do with it? I cast around desperately. The last thing I'd envisaged when greeting my estranged husband at the door was to be found panting hard and clutching an outsized cucumber. Finally I flung it on the floor behind me. They both looked startled as it rolled about.

'And whose jacket is that?' persisted Claudia.

'Hmm? Oh, it's mine.'

'I've never seen you in that before. Is it new?'

'What – this old thing?' I laughed. 'No, darling, I've had it for ages!'

'Blimey, you must have done. Either that or you had a

complete rush of blood to the head in the high street! That's real teen gear, Mum. Looks like something out of River Island!'

Sometimes I just wanted to kill my daughter. I ignored her and turned to Johnny. 'So. Where are you off to then?' Smoothly, I hoped, with a hint of a cynical smile.

'Oh, London.'

'Ah.' Narrows it down. Was it rude to ask where, exactly? I hesitated. 'Well. Have a good time then!'

'Will do.'

'Bye, my darling – Claudia!' I added quickly, just in case Johnny thought I meant him.

'Bye, Mum.'

I went to shut the door behind them, my head spinning. God – two hours of bathing and hairwashing and make-up and wondering what to say – just for that? For that two-second interview with my husband at the front door? I hesitated. Should I walk them to the car, perhaps? Or maybe, yes, maybe just down to the gate? Hell, I'd see any other visitor off the premises, wouldn't I. Why not?

I tossed back my head, smiled broadly, and strolled out after them into the sunshine. Whistling. Which I never do. They turned round in surprise.

'Have fun!'

'We will,' said Claudia, cautiously.

On I strolled, shoving my hands into my tiny, waist-high denim pockets, which was a mistake, because when I tripped over a protruding paving stone, I couldn't get my hands out in time.

'Ooomph!'

They turned to see me sprawled on the ground, nose in the gravel.

'Mum! Are you all right?' Claudia started back.

'Fine!' I gasped. 'Fine, darling. On you go!' Bugger. Also shitsville.

As I got up, gasping, winded, picking gravel out of my nostrils, I was in time to see them get in the car and to hear Johnny mutter *sotto voce*, 'Is your mother all right?' I'm quite sure he wasn't referring to my fall.

Claudia shrugged noncommittally, and off they went. I, meanwhile, gave a bright, cheery wave, a demonic little smile, and went sailing back into the house. Once inside I slammed the front door, seized the cucumber and slammed it viciously against the wall, smashing the living daylights out of it until I'd reduced it to a green pulp. Finally I dropped the shattered remains.

'I'm your wife, damn you!' I screamed at it.

As I raised my head from my hands at the dressing table now, my eyes went back to the photo. I could swear he was laughing at me. Then they caught the clock.

'*Claudia!*'

I jumped up and raced across the landing to her bedroom. 'Claudia, will you hurry up and get downstairs! We're going to be – Oh, for God's sake!'

Claudia was tucked up in bed again, open-mouthed, thumb just adrift, and sleeping like a baby.

We finally swung into the school gates three-quarters of an hour late, with Claudia insisting she was going to claim a doctor's appointment and that I should write a note to that effect.

'But that's a bare-faced lie, Claudia. I'm not doing that!'

'Oh Mummy, you're such a goody-goody. Everyone else does.'

'I don't care what everyone else does, we are not "everyone else".' My God, did I sound like my mother or what? 'And I will not have you being mendacious. No, we will simply say that we got held up by the builders.'

'But that's a lie.'

I screeched to a halt in the car park.

'Claudia,' I snarled, 'would you kindly stop splitting hairs and remember that I am the mother and you are the ten-year-old girl!'

I got out and slammed the door behind me, then raced round the back to the boot where, puffing and blowing, I lugged out her games bag, her lacrosse stick, her flute, her gym kit, her swimming bag, and all the other energetic paraphernalia that she regarded with such cynical detachment and refused to use. As Claudia yawned and leant against the car, I threw it all on to my back and, like a trusty old packhorse, made off, puffing away across the playing field, with my daughter, shuffling along behind me, hands deep in her pockets. Through a chink in the hall curtains I could see that assembly was still in full swing and, yes, 'Lord of the Dance' was wafting towards us on the air waves. With any luck she could sneak in at the back.

'Go on,' I whispered, giving her a little push. 'I'll put your stuff in your locker and you creep in. If anyone asks, say you've been here for ages, went to the loo or something.'

Claudia opened her eyes wide. 'Mum — *another* bare-faced lie!'

I ground my teeth. 'Claudia McFarllen, one of these days –'

'OK, OK, I'm going!' She reached up, gave me a quick, disarming peck on the cheek then, grinning widely, saun-tered off, no doubt pushing her socks down and hiking her skirt up en route to the hall, if indeed she was even *going* to the hall. I sighed and watched her go. Smart kid that.

As I trudged off to the locker room to dump her stuff, I went past the nursery school. Outside the window I saw a mother I knew, Sarah, struggling with a screaming baby. She had him hoisted up on her hip and was trying to quieten him as she peered through the nursery window at her four-year-old. She had a daughter in Claudia's class too, and I'd often watched her with her brood and thought – by rights, that should be me. Ten, four, and nine months, three children and a busy home to run. I'd watched with envy, as I'd watched other mothers too, unloading young children out of Discoveries and into buggies, tucking a little one under an arm. And I always counted.

'Is he OK?' I asked, coming up beside her and peering through the window.

'Oh, hi, Olivia. No he's not – look.' She jabbed her fin-ger at a screaming four-year-old, his fists clenched, red in the face from sobbing, on the other side of the glass.

'They've got a new teacher this term. Miss Pinter's retired, and the new one's really sweet, but it takes Ned ages to settle with anyone new.'

'Plus he knows you're out here,' I pointed out.

'Yes, but if I just leave him I'll feel terrible.'

Ned was opening his lungs and giving the performance of his life now.

'I'll tell you what. I've still got to dump Claudia's stuff. Why don't you sit in the car and when I come back past, I'll tell you if he's OK? I bet you anything he's calmed down.'

'Oh, would you? Only this one's dying for a feed so I could give him a bottle in the car.'

'I'll see you there in a minute.'

She scurried off gratefully to her car and I wandered off to find Claudia's locker in the changing rooms. A smelly cacophony of gym shoes, sweaty socks and verrucas met my nostrils, and memories of Imo, Molly and me came flooding back. Imogen, of course, had been captain of everything, I'd tried hard but had been terminally useless, and Molly had just skived as much as possible. We'd learnt to smoke in changing rooms like these too, and I wondered how many years it would be until Claudia was hugging a radiator and executing perfect smoke rings with her Ten Number Six or – excuse me – Silk Cut Extra. Probably only about six months, the rate she was going.

As I came back out, I went down the internal corridor to get a better look at young Ned Parker through the double glass doors. Sure enough, there he was, dry-eyed, not a care in the world, busy revving up a tractor and going 'Vrrooooom!' as he ran it up and down a small girl's leg. I smiled, remembering Claudia's nursery days in London. My God, she'd had to be dragged screaming and kicking, had clung like a sobbing barnacle, had had to be prised off with no anaesthetic, but the moment my back was turned, had apparently cut the crap and slipped off to single-handedly commandeer the pedal car from the big boys. I gave Ned one last glance and was about to move on, when the sign on the classroom door caught my eye. I stared. Miss Harrison. I stared some more. I went hot, and then very cold.

My eyes came up from the sign. I gazed through the glass. An elderly woman looked up from the pasting table where she was helping a child do something seasonal with dandelion clocks and a Pritt Stick. She smiled at me. I knew her; she was one of the assistants, Mrs Hooper – she'd been there for ever.

'Can I help?' she mouthed.

My eyes flashed around the room like a Colditz search-light. The new teacher wasn't visible. She could be in the plastic house, of course, or maybe helping a child go to the loo. Mrs Hooper came bustling towards me, but just before she reached me, I turned and shot off before she could open the door. I ran, panting, gasping, all the way down to the car park. Sarah, sitting in her car, saw me through her windscreen. She saw my face and clutching her baby, shot out of the front seat, hand to mouth.

'Oh my God – what's happened! Is he all right?'

'He's fine, Ned's fine,' I gasped, clutching the top of her open door. 'Sarah – the new teacher in there, Miss Harrison, is it?'

'Yes, why?'

'Have you met her?'

'Yes, of course.'

'Have you any idea what her first name is?'

'Her first name?' She screwed up her face and thought for a moment. 'Oh God, yes I do know, because one of the other mothers told me . . . something funny. Something very old-fashioned and . . . let me see now . . . Nina! That's it, Nina Harrison.'

Chapter Six

'She's a bloody teacher at her bloody *school*!'

'Terrible, terrible. Here, have an aspirin.'

'I mean, what am I supposed to do, walk past her class-room every morning and say, good morning, Miss Harrison, and how was my husband's performance last night? It's *outrageous*!' I bellowed.

'Course it is. Here, a nice cup of tea.'

Mac handed me the cup while Alf stirred some sugar in. Spiro was bustling around my feet with a stool. 'Up, up,' he muttered, lifting my legs, 'then the blood go straight to the brain.'

'Spiro, there's enough blood storming round my brain at the moment to float an Armada,' I hissed. 'If I have any more I'll bloody haemorrhage!'

Nevertheless, I succumbed to having a stool positioned just so under my feet, then leant my head back and gazed around in a dazed fashion. I appeared to have collapsed in the sitting room and I stared bleakly at it now with its half-stripped walls, ripped-up floorboards, broken windows and, in the foreground, a slightly blurred vision of my workforce, my three burly men, standing over me clutching aspirins and mugs of tea, faces full of concern. I groaned.

'She look pale,' murmured Spiro, peering in.

I stared blankly at him. 'She'll have to be sacked!' I snapped.

He jumped back.

'Of course she will,' soothed Mac.

'The head won't stand for that. What, having an affair with one of the pupil's fathers? *Hah!* No, no, she'll have to go!'

'Hang her!' spat Spiro. 'Or dip her,' he added brightly, 'like they used to do to witches on the island where I come from.'

'You're right, Spiro,' I sat up. 'She *is* a witch. A conniving, insidious, poisonous –' I clutched my mouth. 'Oh, my poor Claudia! My little girl! Imagine the shame, the humiliation – ooooh . . . my poor baby!'

'I go,' said Spiro, turning. 'I go now and keel the beetch!' He shook his fist.

'No, no, Spiro.' I put a restraining hand on his arm. 'You're sweet but, actually, we can't kill her. We can just render her unemployed.'

Mac sucked his teeth dubiously. 'Yeah, well, if you *can*, like, luv. Only it ain't so easy to shift workforce these days, and I should know. They've got written conditions, see, employment rights.'

'*Rights!*' I screeched. 'How can she talk about rights? What right does she have to be shagging my husband? And then, goddamit, to go and teach innocent children! God in heaven – one minute she's pirouetting naked around a bedroom, licking honey off my husband's buttocks, and the next thing we know she's singing "Incy Wincy Spider" to four-year-olds! It's scandalous! No one in their right *mind* would allow it!'

'Of course not, of course not. Head back,' soothed Mac. I obediently crashed my head back on to the chair in fury and Mac began to massage my shoulders in a very businesslike manner. 'You're very tense, you see, very tense indeed. This is what you need, now relax.'

'He very good,' confided Spiro in my ear. 'I had one. I went bye-byes.'

'I wouldn't mind going bye-byes for bleeding ever,' I muttered grimly as Mac attacked my shoulders.

'Give her the tea now, Spiro,' Mac ordered, pummelling away like billyo.

Spiro obediently put it to my lips like a baby, not letting me hold the handle. 'I do it,' he muttered fiercely. 'I do it for you. Now, more aspirin.' He took one from Alf's hand and popped it in my mouth like a Smartie.

This is surreal, I thought as I crunched away maniacally. Here I am, in this chaos of a building site, collapsing in a pathetic heap, whilst one of my builders pats my feet, another massages my shoulders and another administers the drugs. Jesus! I've lost it, I've totally lost it. I shut my eyes tight. But a teacher. A bloody *teacher*! My eyes snapped open suddenly, like searchlights. So how the hell had he met her then? At a parents' evening or something? Sidled up to her after the school concert and given her the eye? But Sarah had said she was new . . . yes, of course, and I'd never seen her before either. My brain went scurrying into overdrive. Right – so he must have met her just after we moved here – about six months ago – that way the timing made sense. But, good grief, a nursery school teacher? That didn't make sense at all! Because despite the terrible name, I'd secretly had her down as a glamorous investment banker, shooting him hot looks across the dealing-room floor, flicking her ash-blonde hair back over her Armani suit, brushing behind him as he sat at his screen, wafting Chanel up his nostrils. In my worst nightmares I'd even seen her driving him back to her Chelsea pad in her Porsche, peeling off her silk underwear to reveal a seamless tan, slipping seductively between her designer sheets, an aristocratic filly who probably wore her tiara in bed and whinnied at the moment critique, and all the time – all the time she really *was* just a bit of a Nina! I shut my eyes and groaned.

Simultaneously, in my left ear I heard, 'What d'you fink then?' in an anxious undertone. 'Only I got money on it.'

I opened one eye. 'Money on what, Alf?'

Mac, still at my shoulders, cleared his throat. 'Well, Alf was just wondering, like, since we're here an' that, if we could just turn the telly on for a minute an' have a butchers at the 11.40 from Newmarket. Only we've had a little flutter.'

'What?' I peered around as three expectant faces gazed down at me. I sighed. 'Oh, fine, fine, yes, go on,' I said weakly. 'God, I may as well lose total control here.'

Mac gave Alf an economic nod and Alf instantly flicked the switch. Alf then settled at my feet, Spiro crouched down close beside me – clearly not wanting to leave my side – and then kindly slipped me a bag of Wotsits. I gazed at them blankly in my lap. He sighed, opened the packet, took one out and popped it in my mouth. I munched listlessly, watching blankly as the horses raced out of their starter gates.

'Come on, my darling,' Mac breathed ecstatically in my ear, still massaging furiously, which was a bit disconcerting. I shifted uncomfortably in my seat. 'Come on, my gorgeous . . . my gorgeous . . . little . . . beauty!'

'Who are we on?' I muttered.

'Creamy Carmel,' he said, 'and she goes like a tiger.'

'Bully for her.'

At length there was a collective groan. 'Well, she did last week, anyway,' said Mac, matter-of-factly. 'Put the kettle on, Alf.'

I was vaguely aware that not a lot of work was being done around here, but Mac's fingers had gone into overdrive and I appeared to be glued to my seat, paralysed, eyes shutting and head nodding, totally unable to take command. After a bit Mac spoke.

'I bin meaning to talk to you about that kitchen.'

'Oh yes,' I mumbled. Kitchen. Good. We could call this a site meeting.

'Yeah, it's about them cupboards.'

'Mmm, yes,' I muttered. 'There does seem to be a curious lack of cupboards, Mac, and you did say —'

'I know, I said I'd make them for you, nice and farmhousey, like, stressed pine.'

'Distressed, I believe, but give them ten minutes in this house and they'll be stressed too.'

'Whatever. Anyway, the fing is there's a lot of them buggers to make, more than I originally fought, and I reckon I'm gonna need more labour.'

'Oh?'

'Yeah,' he sighed. 'I mean what wiv Spiro on bricklayin' and Alf on concrete, I can't do all the joinery meself, so I was thinking of bringing in my Lance.'

'Your lance?' I frowned. Jousting came to mind. Wimples and knights. 'Would that help?' I muttered helplessly as visions of Mac, galloping round the kitchen spearing cupboards into place, sprang to mind.

'Yeah, my boy Lance – he's my eldest, like. He's a chippy by trade, like me.'

'Ah.' Yes, well that cleared something up. I'd been wondering what Mac was.

'He'll be down here by the end of the week and then we'll get cracking on them cabinets straight away, orright?'

I gulped nervously. 'Yes but, heavens Mac – four labourers!'

'Now don't you go worrying your head about the money, luv,' he soothed, kneading away furiously now. 'I'm doin' you a nice little package deal here, bein' as how you're in straitened circumstances an' that. Never let it be said that Mac Turner would squeeze money out of an abandoned woman!'

'Ah, so Lance is free?' I asked hopefully.

'Nooo,' he said cautiously, 'not exactly, but he'll be doin' it for half whack, orright? An' he'll be staying in the caravan too, so there's no need to worry 'bout accommodation.'

'Well, I hardly thought he was staying with me!'

'And that way we'll have that kitchen of yours sorted in no time. There.' He gave my shoulders a final slap. 'You're done, luv. Ready for anything now, and if you don't mind my sayin', what I suggest you do – now that you're nice and relaxed – is get down to that school double quick and give them merry hell. If you look sharp and get your skates on you could bend that headmaster's ear in his lunch hour.'

I sat up and glanced at the clock. Gosh. Yes. He was right. If I went now I might just catch old Michael Harty before lessons started. And, how peculiar – I shook my head – I really did feel better – I got unsteadily to my feet – if a bit woozy. I wondered if that really was aspirin Spiro had been slipping me, or valium perhaps. I staggered a bit and then lunged for my handbag. Blimey, anyone would think I was drunk. My audience watched my performance politely and I noticed that nobody seemed to be getting up to do any work, but then again, they had been very sweet, hadn't they? Very considerate. It seemed churlish to mention it.

'See you later then, boys.' I tottered unsteadily to the door.

'Ta-ta, luv.' Alf settled back comfortably and surreptitiously turned up the volume a bit with the remote control. Spiro's eyes seemed to be slowly shutting.

'Bye, luv,' smiled Mac, who, as the foreman, at least had the grace to get up and see me to the door. 'Now don't forget, give them hell,' he said as he followed me out to the hall. 'Oh, and by the way . . .' He plucked at my sleeve, glancing round to make sure no one was listening.

'What?' I whispered, hand on the doorknob.

He found my ear. 'You'll like my Lance.'

I flushed. Pulled away. 'Well, I'm sure I will, Mac.'

'No, but, you know,' he nudged me. Winked. 'They all like Lance.'

'Excellent,' I muttered faintly, deliberately misunderstanding him. 'Lovely to have popular children. Can't wait to meet him,' and with that I bustled out to the car.

God, that was all I needed, I thought as I slammed the door and crunched the gears into first, roaring out of the drive. Some gum-chewing, heavily biceped beefcake, plastered with tattoos and making goo-goo eyes at me over the cement mixer. Terrific. I shuddered and put my foot down, roaring off down the high street and simultaneously reaching for my mobile phone as I went, careering through an amber light and breaking the speed limit. Molly was out, but I managed to track Imogen down, similarly on her mobile, but in the dealing room of Sotheby's pursuing some fine art. I'm not sure it was entirely convenient, but she loyally listened to my tirade and was suitably outraged, albeit in hushed tones.

'They'll have to sack her,' she hissed firmly. 'She's completely compromised you – be with you in a minute, Damien – put you in a totally invidious position. We'll get a lawyer on to this, Liv. I know the most marvellous chap in the City who'll stitch her up in no time, but the school will have to let her go, anyway. Quite frankly, they've got no other option.'

Sadly, Mr Harty seemed to think they had quite a few. After much corridor marching I finally ran him to ground in the upper school dining room as he sat at a table that was brimming over with upper fourth and testosterone, his eyes glazing over and looking defeated as he toyed listlessly with his treacle sponge.

'A word please, Mr Harty,' I muttered sweetly in his ear.

He looked up, startled, then recognising a wild-eyed mother, and knowing the breed of old, paused only to wipe the treacle from his moustache before getting up and following me wearily from the dining hall. Hundreds of fascinated pre-teen eyes followed his exit, and somewhere amongst those eyes, I spotted my daughter's. I have an idea they were horrified.

Safely ensconced in his office, Mr Harty scuttled hastily behind his large desk and sat down relieved, presumably hoping that two square metres of reproduction oak gave him the edge. He was a moon-faced man with a totally bald head, who apparently had grown the bushy moustache to compensate. His shiny pate reputedly shone more when he was anxious and, I have to say, by the time I'd finished with him, it was glowing like a beacon.

'Well, this is, of course, a very delicate situation, Mrs McFarllen,' he faltered, fiddling nervously with a pencil on his desk. 'We must tread very carefully here, as I'm sure you'll agree.'

'There's nothing delicate about it at all, Mr Harty. She's having a totally *in*delicate affair with my husband, Claudia's father!'

'Well, quite, and I can see how difficult that must be for you, but the problem is, she's an awfully good teacher and that's so important in the nursery, you see – so crucial in the formative years. The parents will be up in arms if I let her go.'

'And I'll be up in arms if you let her stay!' I hissed, getting to my feet and resting my palms on his desk. 'What am I supposed to do, say, "Good morning, Miss Harrison, and how was pillow talk with my husband this morning?" Compare notes or something?'

He laughed nervously. 'Ha ha, no, no, but then in all honesty, that situation is not likely to arise, is it? I mean you don't exactly come across her on a daily basis. Claudia's not in the infant school and –'

'That's not the point!' My voice was shrill. 'It's the indignity of the whole thing the – the – God – it's everyone *knowing*! And apart from *my* pain, apart from my abject humiliation, what about the message it sends to the children? Hmm? Answer me that one, Mr –' I nearly said Farty, the children's nickname for him – 'Harty. What sort of moral guidance are you giving these children in your care – what sort of direction? Because, believe me, they'll all know about it, you can bank on that. You can't keep it from them. Oh, mark my words, within minutes it'll be all round the school – Claudia's dad's having an affair with Miss Harrison – and how d'you think Claudia will feel about that? Oh no, Mr Harty, Miss Harrison's position here is totally untenable. You must see that. She has to go!'

I was shaking with rage now, glaring at him over his oak desk. I wanted her head on a plate and I wanted it now. Mr Harty looked like he'd just run in from an icefield, he was glowing so much. He squirmed some more in his swivel chair, fiddled with his wedding ring, his *second* wedding ring, if I remembered rightly, because . . . oh God, it was all coming back to me now. He'd left his first wife, hadn't he? For the biology teacher. Dumped the first Mrs Harty for a certain Miss Quigly, she of the wiggling hips and the burgeoning bosom, all of which had seen quite a bit of action in the photocopying room. There'd been a hell of a furore about it at the time, but Mr Harty, being *such* a good headmaster, and being *so* well thought of, had stayed on and married Miss Quigly in double-quick time, who in turn had produced twins precisely nine months later. I groaned; held my head. If Miss Harrison produced twins in nine months' time I'd bloody top myself. And her. I picked up my bag from the floor.

'Well, Mr Harty, I can quite see how this is a tricky one for you, bearing in mind your own personal domestic history. Miss Harrison is hardly a trail blazer, is she?' I eyed him beadily. 'It's a well-worn path, isn't it, and of course, one wouldn't want to appear hypocritical, would one? Wouldn't want to reek of humbug?' I ground my teeth as he failed to answer. 'OK,' I spat, 'fine. Do nothing. But, believe me, you haven't heard the last of this. I shall fight my corner despite your inertia. I shall be writing to the governors, voicing my concerns. I shall be lobbying other parents for their support. I shall even chain myself to the school railings, if needs be, and rest assured, Mr Harty, I shall have Miss Harrison out of this school within the week. Good day.'

With that I swept out of his office, head high, cheeks burning. I strode to the car park, roared home at top speed – narrowly missing a group of cyclists on a blind bend, who careered nervously into the back of each other in confusion – before screeching dramatically to a halt outside my house. I sat for a moment, feeling the anger thickening inside my head – clotting actually. Finally I got out and slammed the door. Hard. I set my teeth. And if they're not working in my bloody kitchen, I seethed to myself as I strode up the path, if they're still in *my* sitting room, watching *my* television, swigging *my* PG Tips . . . I flounced in, all guns blazing, ready for action, and slammed the front door behind me so it rattled on its hinges.

'MAC!' I yelled at the top of my voice as I stood on the doormat, fists clenched. Nothing. I strode off down the hall. 'MAC! Oh!' I stopped; stepped back as I went bellowing and stomping past the kitchen. 'Hello, Mum.'

My mother raised herself delicately from the dusty Lloyd Loom chair she'd perched herself on in the little scullery and daintily brushed the back of her skirt.

'Mr Turner is working at the other side of the house in your new kitchen,' she informed me. 'I presume that's what you employ these people to do?'

'Oh, yes. Yes, it is. Um,' I held my head for a minute. It was throbbing madly. 'Right. How are you, Mum?'

'I'm well, which is more than I hear can be said of you.'

I took my hands from my head and met her eyes. Cold and grey. I sighed and brushed past her. Damn. All I needed right now. Really, all I needed.

'Yes, well, things aren't too great around here at the moment,' I admitted, dumping my bag and reaching for the kettle.

'And I have to be the last to know?'

I spun round. 'I'm sorry, Mum. I would have rung only —'

'Mrs Hinton, the greengrocer, told me when I went in for some Granny Smiths. Said she was so sorry to hear about my little Olivia, being left on her own with a kiddie like that. Said it had happened to "her Kylie" too, who'd been left on her own without any "social" either.' She shuddered. 'Yes, that's how I heard that my daughter had separated.'

'Yes, well I'm sorry, Mum, but I was a bit distraught, OK?' I slammed the kettle down angrily on the counter. 'And I didn't want to break down in front of you because I knew I wouldn't get any sympathy either, just a lot of I-told-you-sos. I thought I'd wait until I was a bit stronger before I tackled you, all right? Look, I'm the one that's been left, Mum; I'm the injured party here, not you. Don't make me apologise, OK?'

She regarded me for a moment, then sniffed and sat

down again, folding her hands in her lap and crossing her ankles.

'There's a cup of tea in the pot. It'll still be hot.'

'Oh. Right.' I turned and found the pot with its tea cosy on, which she'd given me and I never used. I filled up the cup she passed me and one for me too. Cups and saucers. Never mugs. I turned and leant against the counter, sipping it, watching her.

'This place is a disgrace,' she said, looking round. I followed her gaze around the room, taking in the cracked sink, the piles of washing-up, newspapers everywhere . . . God, she had to see it like this, didn't she? Today of all days.

'I know,' I said flatly.

There was a silence.

'When did he go?'

'Three weeks ago.'

'Is there someone else?'

'Oh yes,' I laughed hollowly. 'And I don't know what's worse. To be left for someone else, or to be left because he simply couldn't stand me any longer.'

'The former, I think,' she said quietly.

I looked up quickly. God, how stupid of me to miss the parallel. Of course. This had happened before.

'It was . . . the comparison that I couldn't bear,' she said softly.

I nodded, and a chill went down my spine. Never, never, had I thought I'd be in the same boat as my mother. Sitting here comparing notes. I cast around desperately. I couldn't talk about this to her, couldn't do this. I wasn't her, never would be.

'Do you know who she is?'

'Yes, she's a teacher at Claudia's school.' I didn't recognise my own voice. Flat, toneless. 'I'm going to get her sacked.'

'I see.' There was a silence. 'Do you think that's wise?'

I paused, my cup midway to my lips. My eyes darted to hers. 'What?'

'I said, d'you think that's wise?'

'Yes, I heard you, I just couldn't quite believe it. She's at Claudia's *school*, Mum.'

'Do you want him back?'

'Yes, of course I want him back.'

'You do? Really?'

'*Yes*, dammit, really!'

'And so d'you think that getting his popsy sacked is going to further your cause? Do you think that he's going to look favourably on you, think: dear little Livvy, how well she's behaving, how controlled, how dignified? Or d'you think he'll think: poor, sad, vindictive little bitch?'

I opened my mouth dumbly. She put down her cup, leant across and, for the first time in years, held my hand.

'I've been here, Olivia,' she said softly. 'And I did it so wrong. I did all the things you're about to do. I ranted, I raved, I went berserk, I threw plates, I slashed clothes, poured paint on cars, wrote terrible letters. I did all the things you can't possibly imagine me doing. And do you know what? I found out later, from another friend, that it had only been a whim, him and Yvonne. A drunken nonsense after a party, a quick roll in the sack, as you might put it. He would have come back, apparently, and she would have gone back to Derek, but I drove them relentlessly together, Olivia. And I not only drove them together, I drove them away. Drove them from the country. They emigrated to Australia, I made their lives such a misery. I did it all so terribly, terribly wrong. Don't follow my example.'

I gazed at her. 'I never knew that.'

'I never told you. Too much pride. Have some now, Olivia. Walk tall and hold your head high as you go to that school. Do nothing, say nothing. If you see her, smile, say good morning, be polite, but most of all, have pride. He'll be back. Men are intrinsically stupid and vain, but give him six months and he'll wonder what he ever saw in her. But you get her sacked and you'll never see him again.'

I stared, my teacup cold in my hand. So rarely did I ever hear anything from her lips that rang true. But this had bells pealing all over it. I gulped.

'Thanks, Mum. I think you might be right.'

'I know I'm right,' she said, getting to her feet. She reached for her handbag. 'I've got to get back now. I've got a man coming to service the boiler. And if you're going back to get Claudia soon, I'll have a lift. I had to get the bus over.'

'I'll take you home.'

'I can walk from Claudia's school.'

'I'd *like* to take you home.'

We didn't talk as I drove, but when we got to her house, my old home, I stopped the car and just sat, staring at the place. Up there was my bedroom window, the glass I'd pressed my nose against countless times, dreaming of being somewhere else. I couldn't wait to get away from that dismal pile of bricks, with its tiny front room, back kitchen, downstairs bathroom, two bedrooms upstairs and its patch of dry lawn at the back. No fun, no laughter – how I'd longed for that – just a mother who'd set her nose to the grindstone and concentrated on the grim task of bringing up her only child, suffering in silence. And she thought she'd never burdened me with her pain. Oh, but she had. If only she'd told me, confided in me, talked it over with me in a chatty, mother-to-daughter sort of way, but her silence had just deepened the suffering. It had dragged her down, and made me desperate not to sink into the quicksand with her. How different it might all have been.

As she got out, I leant across and kissed her cheek. 'Thanks, Mum.'

She gave her usual tight little smile. 'Give my love to Claudia. Oh, and I collected these for her.' She handed me some coffee jar labels. I'd forgotten that Claudia was collecting the tokens for something, but Mum always remembered, sent them in the post. I smiled.

'Thanks.'

As I drove back to the school, glancing at the little bundle of labels on the seat beside me, I felt ashamed. I knew in my heart I'd always mentally dismissed my mother, wanting to stand alone, not beside her, not wanting to be associated with her, but one never could. And rightly so. Flesh and blood was what made one tick, ultimately.

Before I swung into St Luke's gates for the third time that day, I popped home quickly, collected something from the hall table, then crawled back into the half-empty car park. I was early, and Claudia wouldn't be out for another ten minutes, but some of the really tiny children were already straggling on to the blistered playground, hats falling over their eyes, drowning in outsized blazers. I loitered by the nursery, watching, as each toddler with its bundle of wet paintings and egg-box alligators fell into the arms of an adoring parent. When I was sure every one of them had been collected, I sailed into the empty classroom.

Mrs Hooper I'd already seen, trussed up in her headscarf even in this sweltering weather, and heading for home, and the other assistant had gone too. Nina was bending over the story mat, picking up bricks, cars and other toys that had been fiddled with during the tale of 'The Enormous Caterpillar', but discarded the moment their mothers had arrived. Her back was to me, and she was bent at the waist, straight-legged as she picked up things from the floor, which showed an element of elasticity. She was wearing a calf-length, Laura Ashley-style spriggy cotton skirt, a white T-shirt through which I could see her bra strap, and her hair was short and fair. The back of her neck looked curiously vulnerable. Suddenly she heard me, turned with a smile.

'Can I hel– Oh!' She started, hand to mouth.

Ah. So she recognised me. I smiled warmly, taking it all in quickly, noting that she was quite pretty in a pink-cheeked, healthy sort of way, and also quite pneumatic, but heavens, Imo was right, nothing special. She had that sort of skin that blushed easily, and the colour rose up.

'Hello,' I smiled. 'Look, I just thought I'd pop in because I realise this situation could potentially be very embarrassing for both of us, so I wanted to break the ice and say hi. We're obviously going to be seeing each other around a bit and I thought – well, far better to be grown up about it and not let everyone think we're at each other's throats, don't you think?'

'Oh! Yes, well –' she faltered, flushing to her roots.

'I also wondered,' I went on, 'if you'd be kind enough to deliver these to Johnny.' I handed over a package of his letters. 'Only I've been sending them to his office every day, which costs a fortune, and it seems crazy when I could quite easily give them to you.'

Her mouth went slack with shock. 'Oh! Well – yes, I –'

'Is that OK then? If I just pop them in periodically? Thanks so much.'

Without waiting for an answer I bestowed yet another warm smile on her, turned, and pushed out through the glass swing doors. I made off down the long corridor. Off to collect my daughter. On the way I passed plenty of waiting mothers hovering outside classrooms, some of whom I knew, and some of whom, quite possibly, already knew of my predicament. My head was high, though, and my chin well up. Thanks Mum, I thought, my heart pounding as I strode along. Thanks for the tip, but actually, I can go one better.

Chapter Seven

Days passed and Nanette's dinner party loomed. On the day of the actual event, I tried to get out of it a few hours beforehand by coughing wretchedly into a bloodstained hanky, but Claudia wasn't impressed.

'Alf saw you do that in the kitchen with the tomato ketchup bottle,' she informed me sternly as I sat on my bed clutching hanky to mouth. She had her back to me at my open wardrobe and was riffling through my hangers. 'We all thought it was pretty sad of you, actually. Alf was on the phone to Vi at the time, and when he told her about it she said that you should definitely get out more and had you thought of taking Prozac? What's Prozac?'

'Jesus!' I flopped back on the pillows. 'Now my labourer's wife is pitching in with her two pennyworth, is she?'

'Don't say Jesus, Mummy – Oh! Hang on. What about this?' She pulled out a hanger and threw a short red dress at me.

'Oh, don't be ridiculous, Claudia. I haven't worn that in years! Not since puberty. Ooooh . . . God.' I shut my eyes and clutched my forehead. 'I do feel rotten.'

'Mum, I told you, the game's up. We all know you're faking it. Oh look, what about this one then?' Some equally ancient miniskirt came winging my way. I snatched it up, then threw it on the floor, swinging my legs round to get up.

'Claudia, if I'm going out at all I'm wearing my black, and that's final – *if* I'm going out.'

'Oh, Mummy, not your black *again*,' she wailed. 'You always wear that; you look like Batman.'

'Rubbish. I look thin and mysterious,' I said, wiggling into black trousers and a velvet shirt.

'And old and tired.'

'Thank you *so* much, my angel.'

'Well, you could at least wear chunky jewellery or some-thing, like Nanette does.' She leapt up on my bed and bounced up and down in her nightie, a packet of crisps in her hand, 'or that pashy thing.'

'My pashmina –' I reached for it.

'No, not the grey one, the red one, and look, you tie it like this . . .'

'Yes, I know how to tie it.' I snatched it from her salty hands and sat at the dressing table to arrange it. Then I dropped it. Groaned. 'Oh God, what am I *doing* here? Dressing up to go to some godawful party of Nanette's to talk to some ghastly greasy Herbert she's lined up for me?'

'How d'you know he's going to be greasy? How d'you know he won't be absolutely gorgeous? And if he is, for heaven's sake *smile*, Mummy, flash your rings, tell him you're a rich divorcee or something.'

I gazed at her a moment in the dressing-table mirror; turned. 'Claudia, what's the *matter* with you? Don't you want Daddy to come back? You can't want some slimy accountant sneaking about the place, surely?'

'Of course I don't. I've told you, Mum, this is tactics. Apparently you can bring a man to his knees by pretend-ing to be in love with someone else, and Dad's got to see you're having a good time,' she insisted. She knelt up on the bed urgently. 'And even if you're not, you've got to pretend, Mum. I know you think I'm the only one in my class from a broken home – I've heard you wailing about it on the phone to Molly – but I'm not. Chloe Chandler's dad went off with a floozie, and d'you know what Mrs Chandler did?'

'No idea.'

'She went straight down to B&Q where lots of men hang about, followed a few around with power drills and things in their baskets, and when she found one she liked, she brought him back home and – guess what – Mr Chandler came back the very next day!'

'Claudia –'

'And it doesn't have to be a Homebase-type thing. Chloe says you can do it anywhere. For instance, you could go to a bookshop, Mum – you like books – or – or yes, a garden centre! Mum, go to a garden centre! There's bound to be some there. They're everywhere!' She opened her eyes wide. 'Men are everywhere!' she repeated with awe. She flopped back dramatically on the bed, arms wide like a starfish.

I shut my eyes. 'Claudia, I am not popping down to B&Q for a DIY enthusiast, nor am I creeping round garden centres looking for a like-minded soil tiller, and neither, my love, is your father going out with a floozie.'

'Teacher then.'

I swung round aghast. 'How did you know that?'

'He told me last Sunday. Said in case I found out from someone else.'

'And how do you feel about it, my darling?' I got up and

hastened anxiously to the bed. Hurt? Bitter? Murderous? Do you want to squash her peachy little face right into her blackboard? Poke chalk in her eyes? I know I do.

She shrugged. 'OK, I suppose. I'm glad she doesn't teach me, though.' I clutched my mouth at this horrific thought. She screwed up her nose. 'She's pretty average too, don't you think? I had a look at her in the playground. Not vampy and black-knickerish like I expected.'

I shut my eyes again. I didn't want to think about the colour of her knickers. Although I was sure they were white and came in a pack of three. I sighed. It never ceased to amaze me how much straight-talking children could take, and come back with too. Or was it just my child? My one and only, mature beyond her years.

'Daddy said you went to see her.'

'Oh yes?' My eyes snapped open.

'Said you were quite . . .' She puckered her brow.

'What?' I pounced.

'That word. What the missionaries do to the savages.'

My mind boggled. Missionaries? Savages? Had I tied her up, popped her in a cooking pot and boiled her to death, and let it slip my mind?

'Civilised.'

'Oh!'

I waited. 'Anything else?'

'Nope.'

I turned back and picked up my mascara. Well, whoo-pee. One tiny little brownie point from my estranged husband because I'd behaved well. I couldn't help think-ing it was a better 'tactic' than shagging DIY shoppers, like Mrs Chandler, though.

'It was Granny's idea, wasn't it?' she went on, munching her crisps.

'What?'

'Granny told me she'd told you to be nice to her.' She leant forward eagerly. 'Granny also said there was a curse on all the women in this family, because Great-grandpa left French Granny, and Grandpa left her, and now Daddy's left you. D'you think that's true? D'you think it'll happen to me or d'you think I'll break it? Break the curse, fair maiden!' She raised both hands and plunged an imaginary sabre into the duvet.

I slammed down my hairbrush and spun round. 'Your grandmother talks far too much to a girl of your age! Curse, my eye. You're to stop going there so much, Claudia!'

Her eyes widened. 'What, you mean I'm banned? Like Granny said you were banned from seeing French Granny?' She grinned. 'History repeating itself, Mum!'

I stared at her for a moment. Then I stood up, snatched up my pashmina and swept it around my shoulders. 'Don't be silly, I just said not so much, that's all.'

It hadn't escaped my notice that Claudia spent more and more time in my mother's company. Mum lived only a few roads away from the school and often picked Claudia up, taking her home for a cup of tea and a jam sandwich. When I went to collect her, I'd find Claudia lying on her tummy in front of the gas fire, engrossed in old letters and photograph albums, all of which had been locked away when I was a child. In those days I'd be told that it was none of my business, to go to my room, to be quiet. She was always irritable, like a bad-tempered terrier, always snapping at the heels of childhood. Sit still! Don't slouch! Get out of my kitchen! Not so with Claudia. How old were you when you got married, Granny? When did you first fall in love? Can I see the pictures? Oh, she'd grumble, sure, but she'd get them out, and talk Claudia through them, too. Was it just a mellowing of age? I wondered. Or was it simply Claudia's style – chirpy, probing, authoritative – taking life by the scruff of its neck, so unlike my own cowering self at that age? Well, I thought, striding to the door, they could dissect *her* broken marriage to their hearts' content, but I didn't want them delving into mine, and I'd tell Mum that, too; tell her to cut the chat.

'Claudia, I want you in bed by nine o'clock tonight.' I swept out to the landing.

She gasped. 'That is way, way too early!'

'I disagree.'

'Who's baby-sitting?' She snatched up her crisps and followed.

'Mac. He's downstairs in the kitchen, I think.'

'Not Spiro?'

I turned halfway down the stairs; eyed her beadily. 'No, Claudia. Not Spiro. Spiro is in the Fox and Ferret having a pie and a pint. He's twenty-four-years old, married with a child, and you, my darling, are ten.'

'I know!' She coloured dramatically. 'Just asking, OK?'

'OK. Just telling.'

'Oh!'

Her exclamation came as we both came barging through the kitchen door together, sniping at each other, arguing loudly, before the extraordinary vision before us stopped us in our tracks. A devastatingly attractive man, tanned, blond, with eyes nearly as blue as Johnny's and wearing black jeans and a white T-shirt, was sitting at the little scullery table eating a bowl of Frosties.

'Blimey!' Claudia added, just for good measure. 'Adonis!'

He got to his feet in confusion. 'God, I'm so sorry. My father said you were out and that he was going to baby-sit or something. I had no idea – you must think I'm appalling, sitting here eating your food.' He smiled an apologetic but faintly winning smile.

'Good gracious, you must be Lance then,' I said, recovering, and coolly extending my hand. Would I extend a hand to Alf? I wondered.

He shook it warmly, grin still in place.

'That's it. I'm really sorry if I surprised you, but I've been travelling for about six hours and my father said you wouldn't mind.' He gestured to the bowl.

'No! No, not at all.' Heavens. My father? Not Dad? Pop? The old man? And when had any of my other workers ever got up when I'd come into a room? Most of them promptly sat down.

'We've got Coco Pops too,' piped up Claudia, 'if you prefer?' She dashed to the cupboard and flung it open, brandishing the packet, grinning rather too widely.

'That'll do, Claudia,' I said briskly. 'Go and brush your teeth, please.'

But Claudia didn't move. And after a moment I realised we were both just sort of staring at Lance. He really was very, very good-looking. Suddenly I came to.

'Right! Well, I must be off. I take it you're joining your

da– father while he baby-sits for Claudia, so if you could just tell him I'll be back at about –'

'Right here, luv,' said Mac, coming in through the kitchen door behind me, wiping his hands on a rag. 'Just bin checking the generator down in the cellar, went a bit haywire the ovver day. You've met my boy then?' He nodded at Lance.

'Yes! Yes, indeed.' I smiled brightly. 'And I hope he's recovered from his journey.' I frowned. 'Was it really six hours, Lance? From Billericay?'

'Oh no,' he laughed. 'Florence. I had a couple of days off, you see, and I've got a bit of a thing about Botticelli so I went to have a look at those fabulous paintings in the Uffizi gallery again. My God, that guy could wield a brush. Have you seen them?'

'Oh! Um, yes.'

'When, Mum?'

'Oh, years ago, darling, when you were a baby.'

'But I thought you said you'd never bee–'

'Now run along, Claudes, there's a good girl. Half an hour of television and then bed, OK?' I turned to Mac. 'You know where I am, don't you?'

'Number 32, down the other end. The sequinned busybody.' He looked at me approvingly. 'You look smashing, by the way, luv, don't she, Lance?'

'I think that's something of an understatement,' grinned Lance. 'Have a good time.'

'Will do,' I managed as I scuttled to the door.

I shut it gratefully behind me. Phew. Feeling a bit hot in there, for some reason. Bit sort of sweaty-palmed. I tripped thankfully down the steps. Suddenly I stopped, wrapped my shawl dramatically around my shoulders, lifted one eyebrow and growled, 'I think that's something of an understatement.' I giggled, then tried it again as I turned left down the street, poshing up the accent until I resembled the Duke of Devonshire. Really, I mused, if it weren't for his obvious parentage I would never have guessed his provenance. One tiny clue, though, I thought with a grin, as I skipped along the cobbled street towards the Abbey, my heart feeling lighter and my step quickening by the second: Florence, the lifting of the bottom from the chair and the educated accent were all very fine, but if I wasn't very much mistaken I was sure I'd caught a glimpse of a gold chain nestling beneath that T-shirt. I'd also spotted a tin of Old Virginia and a packet of Rizlas on the table, too. Still, I reflected as I reached Nanette's steps, the vast old Abbey towering right above me now, pale and golden in a beautiful evening sky, he might be more interesting than most labourers to have around. He was certainly more decorative.

Moments later Nanette opened the front door and my high spirits took a dive.

'Darling!' She stepped back for me to admire. She was dressed in an extraordinary sort of embroidered silk pyjama ensemble; her neck weighed down with heavy silver beads; her feet skippy in floppy gold sandals; her toenails bright red and dazzling. Rude not to comment.

'Nanette, you look . . . amazing.'

'Isn't it divine? Roger had the whole lot sent across from Hong Kong and I simply *had* to wear it. It's desperately see-through, of course, so I'm wearing a thong – Roger's idea – although he's devastated he's not here to see it. Poor bunny, he's still stuck out there in the Far East, I'm afraid. I can't *wait* to get him back and kiss him to bits!'

'Ah, so he's not here?' That was something of a bonus, anyway. Roger was her current amour, a computer sales-man: smooth, dark, and very, very softly spoken – a deliberate ploy, as I'd discovered to my cost one day, when I'd leant in close to catch his drift and a hand slipped up my skirt.

'No, still trying to screw money out of the slit-eyed nips, as Prince Philip would say, but I have got some *super* people for you to meet, Olivia. Come on, come on through!'

I followed her jangling beads and floppy sandals down her shiny parquet hall and into her ornate, swagged, dragged, beribboned and bowed drawing room. Four people stood in a silent, awkward circle around a glass coffee table, each clutching a glass of pinkish wine and gazing through the table to the carpet. Nanette clapped her hands prettily, as if to break up the bustling chatter.

'Everyone! Oo-oo! This is Olivia, my very good friend from just along The Crescent, and Olivia, these dear people are Cliff and Yolanda Blair, who are desperately old friends of mine –'

'No relation!' piped up Yolanda. 'But I'm a big fan of Cherie's!' She pronounced it like the drink, but it was clearly her habitual opening gambit so I smiled politely.

'– and Sebastian, who, actually, you *might* know because he lives in The Crescent.' Nanette always referred to The Crescent by its name, never 'the road'. 'And Malcolm here, who if I was a single girl I'd want to keep *all* to myself

126

because he's a complete and utter cutie-pie and makes an absolute *fortune* at the BMW concession in Luton!'

I wanted to turn and run right now, but we all smiled and I shook hands; first with Yolanda, a broad-beamed lady, who managed to prise her hand from Cliff's arm for literally two seconds before firmly replacing it, then with Cliff who was tiny and frail and failed to meet my eye, then Malcolm who was very golf-club tie and belted grey slacks, and finally with Sebastian, tall, pale, with watchful slanting eyes and rather too long dark hair, and who, now you come to mention it, I did recognise.

When I'd first moved in here, Nanette had made it her business to bustle straight over with a kettle and a fruit cake. She'd introduced herself as 'a very merry widow' and swept around my scullery in a full-length fur coat. I later discovered that Nanette nearly always wore her fur coat, even in a heat wave, and even after the nasty incident in the high street when a militant youth had approached her shouting, 'And what poor creature had to die just so you could put that on your back!' To which she'd replied, 'Er, my mother-in-law' – yes, even after that little débâcle she kept it firmly round her bony shoulders, and on that, our very first meeting, had sunk down into it in my Lloyd Loom chair and proceeded to give me the lowdown on the entire neighbourhood. This one, Sebastian, was apparently, 'decidedly odd'. Not only, she'd hissed to me over the Nescafé and the fruit cake, did he pace up and down at his window all day long, waving his arms about, mouthing obscenities at anyone who passed and shaking his head like a mad dog, but he'd also been seen squeezing the grapefruit in Waitrose, wearing his pyjamas. Apparently he refused to answer if anyone spoke to him in the street, and at thirty-six, still lived at home with his mother. I'd already spotted his mother actually: a thin, pinched little woman who hurried everywhere, her head well in advance of her bent waist and her scuttling legs, always hastening back to her house with her shopping, slamming the door behind her and giving very black looks to anyone who caught her eye. They were Irish, apparently, had only been in The Crescent about six months, and according to Nanette, the *on dit* was that since they were only renting, most people were keen they didn't stay. In some small way, the son apparently taught at the boys' school in town, but Nanette reckoned it was just a way of integrating him back into the community. And now here he was, at my left elbow, staring distractedly at a spot somewhere above the top of my head.

'Now, you'll have a little drinky, Olivia?' Nanette fluttered her hand bossily in Malcolm's direction. 'Do the honours, Malc, there's a love. It's Kir, Olivia – I don't know if you've had that before? And then if you'll excuse me for just two secs, I'm going to put the finishing touches to the canapés in the kitchen. Don't fight over her now, will you, boys!'

Well, that surely put the kiss of death on any intelligent conversation. We stood about a bit more in the awkward circle, and somehow, Malcolm and I managed to exchange a few, polite words about the traffic congestion in the city, Sebastian continued to stare above my head, and Yolanda persisted to whisper urgently – and in my view, rudely – in Cliff's ear. After several minutes of torture I made my excuses and escaped, on the pretext of helping in the kitchen.

'Nanette!' I hissed as she squirted some squiggles of pâté out of a tube and on to some tired-looking Ritz biscuits. 'What the bloody hell's going on here!'

She paused mid-squiggle, raised heavily made-up eyes. 'Sorry?'

'Well, isn't that the arm-waver in there? Are you trying to set me up with a nutter?'

'Ah!' She put the tube down. 'Yes, Olivia, listen – I was going to warn you about him –'

'It *is* him, isn't it!'

'Yes it is, but listen, he's fine, honestly. I had a chat to him in the street the other day and he was wearing perfectly ordinary clothes and I really think he's absolutely normal!'

'Oh, come on, you've changed your tune! You told me he was certifiable!'

'Well I know, but I really think that was just a phase or something. After all, we all get depressed, don't we? And when I saw him in the street I did just feel a tiny bit sorry for him, and anyway,' she went on hurriedly, 'Gerald cancelled at the last moment so I just sort of asked him, otherwise you'd have been the odd girl. He's terribly shy and lonely, Olivia. He just needs bringing out.'

'Well, not by me!' I hissed. 'I might bring out a lunatic!'

'Ssh, he'll hear you. Well, OK, Malcolm then? Christ, I gave you a choice! Malcolm's lovely, known him for years, he used to be in oil with my brother – hair oil, actually – but now he's with BMW. He's a complete catch, you know.'

'Nanette, I do not want to "catch" anyone! I wouldn't have come if I'd known you were matchmaking!'

'Oh, don't be ridiculous, Olivia. You can't hunker down like a hermit for ever. You've got to live a little. Johnny has to be shown that you're a very desirable woman!' And with that she picked up her plate of pâté and marched past me with her canapés into the drawing room.

If drinks were torturous, supper was worse. I made a mental note to tell Imogen and Molly that my foresight had been extraordinary: it was far worse than an evening with Brenda Archdale. Malcolm, beside me, of hair oil and now BMW fame, told me in confidential I-wouldn't-share-this-with-just-anyone tones, exactly why the sixteen-valve fuel-injected 318IS was a superior machine to the 1SE, and how he could never go back to an eight-valve even though it was more competitively priced. He even hinted that if I played my cards right, he might take me for a test drive.

'You get sleeker body styling,' he murmured confidentially, ticking off the points on his fingers, 'you get alloy wheels, you get sports suspension, and you get all that for less spondulos than any other car in its class. What more could you want?'

'Very little,' I agreed. He had the most enormous open pores on his nose.

'And it does nought to sixty in 9.7 seconds, too.' He sat back in his chair and raised his eyebrows in awe. 'Incredible, isn't it?' He leant forward urgently again. 'And you see, the mistake you little ladies make is that you think you don't *need* something with that much poke, am I right?'

'Quite possibly,' I murmured, maniacally smearing cucumber mousse around my plate, longing for oblivion, longing for going-home time.

'Take you, for instance, tootling off to the shops, taking the kiddies to school – what car do you drive?'

'Hmm?' I raised my eyes from the psychedelic pattern I'd created on my plate, and suddenly remembered Johnny's garage. My tired eyes flashed in their brave old sockets.

'I've got a Bristol and a Lagonda 3-litre Drophead Coupé.'

As he spat his cucumber mousse across the table, I turned coolly to Sebastian.

'I gather you're a teacher,' I said gently. After Malcolm I could be kind. I could bring him out, just an inch or two.

'Well, yes, occasionally. Just a couple of days a month really.'

Ah, so it was like day release.

'That's good. You must enjoy that?'

'Yes, I do.'

'It's nice to get out, isn't it?'

He frowned at this. Didn't answer. Too difficult perhaps. I persevered.

'And what is it you teach, exactly?' Even more softly.

He paused, perhaps trying to remember. 'Music,' he intoned eventually.

I clasped my hands and contrived to look enchanted. 'Music! Lovely! Songs, and things?'

'Um, some . . . songs, yes.'

'Super!'

A silence ensued.

'And do you play?'

'Sorry?'

'An instrument, you know, the violin or –' oh God, no – 'the recorder? I used to play the recorder!'

'Really.' Rather drily perhaps.

'Yes, at school. Not any more. If people ask "What do you play?" I just say, "Oh, the fool!"'

Suddenly I cringed. Oh God, you idiot, Olivia – the fool! He'll think you're taking the mickey! I cast around desperately.

'I – um, and – how is your mother?'

He turned almost 180 degrees to look at me. Really rather closely. 'She's well, thank you. How's yours?'

'Oh! Oh, fine. No, no the reason I ask is because I see her around quite a lot.'

'Who?'

'Your mother.'

He stared at me with his slanting, dark eyes, as if I had two heads, but happily Yolanda was causing a diversion on the other side of the table and the silence was averted. Nanette was bustling around her, changing plates.

'I'm *so* sorry, Nanette, it's such a bore, but they do say no liver, no blue cheese, no unpasteurised products and absolutely nothing that's been in the microwave. I take it the mousse had raw egg in? Ah yes, well, that's why I left it, and I'm afraid this hollandaise sauce is out, but if you scrape if off I can eat the salmon, and then what is it to follow . . . chocolate pots? More raw egg! Gosh, anyone would think you were doing this on purpose, you naughty girl! No, no, don't worry about me. Bumpy and me will be fine with an apple or something for pudding, won't we, bumpy?'

She patted what I now realised was a burgeoning stomach and smiled smugly at Cliff, the father, it transpired, of her five children. For these weren't newly weds who couldn't keep their hands off each other as I'd originally imagined, but a fabulously fecund couple who were about to inflict their sixth child on the world.

'I'll take the sauce off,' muttered Nanette, removing the plate.

'Oh dear, what a shame, and it looks so lovely, but one really can't be too careful and I'd never forgive myself if anything happened. Five perfectly healthy ones and then God forbid disaster should strike. Has anyone else got little ones here? Nanette, yours are all grown up now, aren't they?'

'Er, well. Not so grown up.'

'But teenagers, surely? At university?'

'Just.' Nanette ground her teeth and, as she replaced the salmon, I could have sworn she wiped a smear of hollandaise back on top.

Malcolm held up his hands and was quick to claim absolutely no offspring whatsoever, so no paternity suits, please, ho, ho, ho. Sebastian failed to answer and looked at her blankly, and I was forced into admitting I had one.

'Just one? A baby then, is it? The first?'

'No, she's ten.'

'Ah, I see!' Yolanda laid down her knife and fork for dramatic emphasis. 'Oh, I *am* sorry.'

All eyes were on me. 'Well, no, please don't be,' I stammered nervously.

'Oh, but I know what it's like.' She leant forward, all concern. 'Friends of ours have been to hell and back with it, haven't they, Cliff? All those blood tests, laparoscopies, Clomid injections, in and out of the infertility clinic – not to mention poor Bernard doing unmentionable things into a test tube with a porno mag – and all for absolutely no reason! You see, quite often, *just* like you, a child has already been conceived – as Bernard and Gill's child was – *totally* naturally, and there's no rhyme or reason why another one hasn't popped along after it! The one thing that everyone *does* say, though,' she confided, lowering her voice, 'is to relax about it. The more het up you get, the more it's just not going to happen, and d'you know, that's absolutely true. The number of couples I know who've adopted as a last resort and then – hey presto – the wife gets pregnant! They've stopped *thinking* about it, you see, stopped fretting, and another little tip – even more extraordinary – get a puppy. Sounds odd, I know, but it's the stroking apparently, the caring, the release of all your pent-up maternal instincts. You see, you're looking after something tiny and vulnerable and – what? Nanette, did you kick me? Am I opening my big mouth again? *Oh!*' Her hand flew to her big mouth. 'Oh gosh, I *am* sorry. Nanette did say, but I forgot.' She puckered her brow in consternation. 'You've had a sadness, haven't you?'

Naturally, I'd been busy blushing away throughout her weighty monologue, but this last remark really shot an extra bathful of blood up the back of my legs. A sadness. Christ!

'Well, no one's died,' I muttered.

'No, but didn't your husband –'

'Shall we all sit soft?' warbled Nanette gaily, getting to her feet and coming firmly to my rescue. 'Through into the lounge for coffee?'

Cliff was the first up from the table, but Yolanda sprinted to his side, then marched just ahead of him into the room. As I followed Cliff through, I noticed him grit his teeth and flick a quick V sign at her ample behind. It was a futile, childish gesture, and one that he'd meant to go unobserved, but one that I – after I'd got over my initial astonishment – applauded wholeheartedly. I hadn't categorised, or even noticed Cliff during the evening, except as a small, cowed appendage to his large, domineering spouse, but I began to realise that all was not quite as it seemed in that camp. Was Cliff unhappy? Was Cliff considering heading for the wide open spaces? And if so, how much better, I mused as I collected a cup of coffee from the tray, to be abandoned with one child than to be abandoned with six.

Cliff was settling himself down on a sofa in the corner, and I determined to have a word in his ear about the merits of the single life, about how Johnny was absolutely loving it, and how I was sure he'd thoroughly recommend it to him. God, I could even give him his telephone number. Yolanda, though, with bristling antennae, seemed to be alive to this possibility and as I sat down, scuttled to squeeze her large backside between us on the two-seater sofa. As we all sat squashed together, elbows in, she confided to me in a loud, pseudo-jolly voice that she never let Cliff go off on any sort of golfing weekend or boys' nights out because that, in her view, was where all the trouble started. It became clear that poor Cliff was a prisoner in his own home, purely there to procreate and pay the mortgage, and that any thoughts he might have of escaping had been crushed long ago.

'I don't let him out of my sight!' she warbled, nudging him gaily and spilling his coffee. 'Do I, darling? Heaven knows what he might get up to!'

Cliff forced a tight little smile, then resumed his

contemplation of his coffee. Black and hot, he stirred it in measured silence, his eyes a trifle wild. Suddenly he got to his feet. I shrank back, half-expecting him to tip it all over his beloved's head, but he simply gathered some coats from a chair and spoke.

'The baby-sitter will be waiting, my love. We must be off.' Calm, measured, but gritted. The voice of a man on the edge.

At the mention of babies she was instantly galvanised, fussing about midnight feeds and bed-wetting and getting up at six to make breakfast, as Cliff helped her into her coat. His hands were shaking, though. Ah no, I reflected sadly, desertion was not on the cards for poor old Cliff. He'd never even make it to the wire, let alone send a postcard back from Blighty. No, no, this was a desperate man with only desperate measures left to him. And either way, he was facing a life sentence.

They left, and the evening limped on without them. Sebastian stood at the window, staring fixedly at a tassel on the curtains, Nanette snuggled up to Malcolm and explained in hushed tones exactly why a thong was so incredibly comfortable, and I threw the hottest coffee imaginable down my throat.

'Finished,' I gasped. 'Must be off, Nanette. Mac will be waiting.'

She followed me to the door, where I promised her that I'd had the most fantastic evening, that of course I'd come again, and agreed that Malcolm was indeed a complete honey.

'He really liked you,' she hissed, glancing back over her shoulder. 'In fact I think he might ring you!'

'Excellent,' I said, too tired to argue. 'Couldn't be more pleased.'

As I turned and walked back up the dark cobbled street, it occurred to me to wonder whether it was my knickers he was trying to get into, or my Lagonda.

Alone in bed that night I lay staring at the ancient brown William Morris wallpaper that still had to be stripped from the bedroom walls. Blue, Johnny had said, and I'd agreed, even though a pale yellow would have been more my choice. I swallowed hard. Nights were always the worst. Still, I reflected, blinking hard, if I couldn't be with Johnny, at least I was alone. That was something of a solace. How much better to be here by myself than with a ghastly Malcolm, or a sad Sebastian, or anyone else you care to mention, desperate to start a relationship, desperate to get to the point at which Johnny and I had already been. That point of absolute familiarity, intimate honesty, that point that took years to get to and which marriages are made of. How could I contemplate embarking on that with someone else? Why would I want to? And even if I did, what was I supposed to do with the deep, abiding love I had for Johnny? Freeze it? Deny it? Stuff it under the pillow and suffocate it? I'd found my soulmate, found him years ago, grown up with him, married him, had a child with him. I'd never thought for a moment of looking for another.

I pictured him now, in bed with Nina, something I'd never yet allowed myself to do. The tears rolled down my face in torrents. I imagined that openness, that intimacy that was mine by rights, not hers. The pain was so great I had to sit up, gasping, pinch my arm hard to stop myself going further down that road. Then I lay back on the pillows feeling weak, staring at the ceiling. So how can you ever have him back? After that? a small voice asked. Oh, but I could. I knew I could. Scarred, damaged, as our lives would surely be, but I'd have him. The alternative, that which I'd glimpsed over the horizon tonight, was too horrific to contemplate.

Chapter Eight

The following Wednesday, Claudia and I bumped into Molly in the school car park.

'What are you doing here? You've got at least two years before Henry's eligible!'

'God, two years is nothing,' she said as she levered herself heavily out of her car. 'You have to put embryos down for some schools these days. No, I've left it late, and much as I'd like to just shove his name on a list, apparently I have to be shown around the wretched place first.'

I grinned. Molly was nothing if not relaxed. Some mothers liked to inspect the plumbing and shake hands with all the dinner ladies.

'Mrs Travis, apparently, I have to see,' she said, consulting a piece of paper. She held her side and puffed across the playing field beside me, the breeze flattening her denim dress against her huge stomach. 'God, it's hot. Where will I find her then, in the office or something?'

'She's the deputy head,' Claudia informed her. 'And she's totally sad.'

'She's sweet,' I assured Molly. 'I'll take you there. Bye, my darling.'

Claudia peeled off to her classroom and I escorted Molly to the office. Passing the main hall, we discovered there'd been a catastrophe. One of the pipes had burst and both the head and the deputy head had been tasked off to deal with the water board, a distraught caretaker was trying to mop up a flood with a roll of kitchen paper – like sticking a finger in the Aswan Dam – and two dozen seven-year-olds were lined up outside in tutus, poised, whispering and giggling, to have ballet and tap in there.

'Oh, Mrs Piper, I'm *so* sorry,' twittered Audrey, the school secretary, wringing her hands melodramatically, when we got to the office. 'What *must* you think of us? *Such* a muddle, I do apologise, but there's simply no one here to show you around! I'd do it myself only I've been tasked off to take Mr Harty's French class and all I can say in French is *je t'aime*! They're always getting me to do this and I'm not qualified to teach a flea!' She flung her hands apart in silly-me appeal. A great advertisement to a prospective parent, I thought. 'You couldn't come back again tomorrow, could you? When we're a teensy bit more organised?'

Molly groaned. 'I could, it's just that it took me ages to arrange a child-minder for Henry, and I dread the thought of bringing him with me – not that he's not an angelic little boy, of course,' she added quickly. 'I couldn't just have a wander round on my own, could I? Peer in some classroom windows, put his name down and come back for a better look nearer the time?'

'Of course, of course!' Audrey fluttered, rummaging in a drawer for a list. 'Here, put his name down here.'

Molly grabbed the pen eagerly. 'How early do you take them?' she muttered, scribbling.

'How old is he now?'

'Nearly one, but he's very mature,' she said firmly.

Audrey looked taken aback. 'Oh, er, well, not for another eighteen months or so –'

'As much as that?'

'Oh, it'll fly by! I tell you what, why don't you just go to the nursery today? That's the first class he'll be going in to. Perhaps Mrs McFarllen would show you where – Oh!' Her hand shot to her mouth. Her cheeks flushed. 'I'm so sorry, Mrs McFarllen, I –'

'Don't be silly,' I said smoothly. 'Of course I'll take Molly to see Miss Harrison.'

'Oh, but I didn't mean to put you to any – I – I didn't think, I –'

'It's quite all right. Come on, Molly.'

I took her arm and we swept out.

'She knows,' muttered Molly as we marched along.

'Of course she bloody knows. Everyone knows, the whole bloody school knows.'

'But that's outrageous!' she gasped. 'It's so embarrassing for you. I don't know how you can bear it!'

'I don't know how I can bear it either,' I mused. 'But I do.'

As we approached the nursery, Molly suddenly stopped short. 'Livvy, I'm not sure I can do this.'

'What?'

'Well, be introduced to her by you when she's living with your husband! What – say howdy-doody when I know my goddaughter's father is having a ding-dong with her? No, thanks, I'll come back another day. In fact – come to think of it – I don't think I want Henry to be taught by her at *all*! How can I form a relationship with someone who's doing this to you? No,' she shook her head vigorously, 'he can go to the nursery in the village. Come straight into the reception class here after that, bypass Miss Whiplash altogether. In fact, why don't you take me to see the reception teacher? I'm sure –'

'Don't be ridiculous, Molly. You know as well as I do this is the best nursery for miles around. Christ, they all sniff the Copydex at the one in your village. Come on.' I seized her arm. 'To tell you the truth, I don't mind this at all. I rather enjoy encountering her.'

She gave me a strange, sideways look, but it was true. I'd noticed recently that instead of going round the back of Claudia's classroom and out to the car park, which was my usual, quicker route, I made a point of coming through the main entrance and going right past the nursery doors. There she'd be, on her hands and knees with the teeny-tinies, doing jigsaws, playing with sand, her backside often presented to me as she leant forward on her elbows. It was wider than mine, but not huge. Small cervix too, I bet. She'd get up, drift across to help another child, the rhythm of her rolling buttocks in her long skirts languid, hyp-notic, like a black girl's. If I had a small silver pistol I could draw it from my bag, aim, and shatter her coccyx, I was sure. I only got a quick glimpse each morning, of course, didn't stand and stare, but it was enough. Like a fix, it set me up for the day. Why? I wondered. Was I stalking her, for God's sake? Sometimes I horrified myself. And why did I want to hurt myself every morning? Because there was no doubt about it, that's what it did: gave me a short, sharp stab of pain. It was almost as if I didn't want that pain to go away, like daily opening up a sore. I've often heard that when someone dies, the grief-stricken, the left behind, want to mourn constantly. They don't want to feel better, don't want to stop crying or stop poring over photographs, because by feeling better, they'd be distancing themselves from the deceased. That was how I felt. I wanted to keep that distance short between me and Johnny, and Nina was my link.

She was sitting on one of those miniature chairs, showing a little blonde girl how to draw around a stencil as we approached. Molly hesitated but I pushed straight on through those glass doors, like barging into a saloon. When she saw me, she stood up hurriedly, knocking over a jar of crayons. She flushed scarlet. Molly glanced awkwardly out of the window.

'Oh, Miss Harrison, Mrs Travis is having a terrible time with a burst pipe in the hall and Audrey asked me if I'd bring Mrs Piper in here to see you. She's thinking of bringing Henry here in – what would it be, two years, Moll?'

'Um, yes, about that,' admitted Molly, scuffing her toe. 'He's two in August next year.'

'Oh, er, yes, well, I'd be glad to show you around.' She shot me a quick, nervous look. 'Um, I don't know if you want to wait here, Mrs McFarllen, or –'

'Hmm?' I raised my eyebrows, deliberately misunderstanding. And I wanted her to have to say that again. The Mrs McFarllen bit. I ran my eye over her quickly and noticed her T-shirt was pink today, but slightly see-through again. Did Johnny like to see her bra straps or did she just buy cheap tops, I wondered?

'Well, I just thought you could either have a chair here, or –'

'Oh no, no, don't worry about me, I'll wait outside. I'll see you in the car park, Molly. Oh – incidentally, more

143

letters!' I produced a bundle from my bag with a flourish. 'Just like Christmas, isn't it! Would you be an angel and pass them on? How is he, by the way?'

A feather could have dropped audibly in the silence. Molly and Nina cringed to their toes.

'Fine,' she gasped eventually.

'Good, good. He hasn't got his hayfever, then?'

'Um, a bit,' she admitted, staring at the floor.

'Oh God, what a bore. Those antihistamine pills I gave you the other day should help, though, and what I meant to tell you was that he never used to have a down pillow at home. The feathers tended to set it off, so I bought him one of those squashy ones – you know, with a bit of foam inside. I could bring it in, if you like. Still,' I mused, peering out of the window, 'they do say it's going to rain soon and that usually sorts him out, gets rid of the pollen. I must say, my garden could really do with a good downpour. It's as dry as a bone! Is yours?'

Now I couldn't have been nicer, could I? I wasn't patronising her, I wasn't picking on her, I was just making chatty conversation, and still the pair of them cringed and blushed.

As I left them to it and walked to the car park, though, I had to delve into my handbag for a tissue. The palm of my hand was bleeding. There were deep nail marks in it.

Later, when Molly reappeared from her interview, she stalked straight past me in the car park.

'I don't know how you could have done that, Livvy,' she muttered, making for her car and putting her key in the lock.

'Done what?' I followed her.

'Prattled away like that about Johnny. It's so – so demeaning! God, I thought you were going to offer to make their bed! Dig their garden for them, pop out for some more hayfever pills – or condoms!'

'I want her to think I don't care,' I said slowly.

'But she knows that's not true!' She rounded on me fiercely. 'She knows it's an act – don't you see? You're making a fool of yourself! I mean, fine, I agree with your mother, you don't have to spit in her eye or get her sacked, but you don't have to pretend she's your new best friend either!'

'Oh, so what do you suggest I do, avoid her? Go out of my way not to go near her, so everyone thinks – poor Olivia, she can't bear it?'

'No, but you don't have to go the other way! You don't have to offer to bring bouncy bedding in for them! What about a bit of silent dignity?'

I stared at her. Started to blink. 'It helps,' I said shortly. 'It helps me to know how he is.' A lump came to my throat. 'The thing is . . . I sort of pretend . . . that she's just a friend of his. Our mutual friend.'

She stared. 'Oh, Livvy!' She flung her arms around me and hugged me hard. I stood like a stone. Gulped.

'I'm in trouble here, aren't I, Moll?'

She drew back and put her hands on my shoulders. 'Maybe you should see someone,' she said gently. 'A counsellor or something, I don't know. And maybe you could go together? Would he come?'

I shook my head. 'Don't want to. Too real somehow, too painful. What – raking through our lovely marriage with a perfect stranger? He'll come back, Molly, you'll see. It's just a phase.'

She narrowed her eyes at me. 'I'm worried about you, Liv.'

I nodded. 'I know.'

She took my hand. 'So's Imo. She wants to know if he's mentioned divorce.'

'Divorce!' I gave a cracked laugh. 'Don't be silly, we're not that far gone! No, no, we're – well, we're not even officially separated. Just estranged. We don't want a divorce.'

'Have you asked him?'

'Of course not!' I said, stricken. 'Why would I want to force the issue?'

'So that you'd know. So that you'd be in the driving seat for once. I kind of feel that you've gone backwards these last few weeks. Your first reaction was downright bloody fury, and rightly so – how dare he? Let's get the bitch sacked immediately – and now you're much more . . .' she hesitated.

'Pathetic?'

'Accepting of the situation.'

'Deluding myself it'll be all right? Some day?'

'Well, yes, and you could be helping yourself, Livvy!'

'How!' I wailed.

'By grasping the nettle a bit more, turning the tables, confronting him. When did you last talk to him?'

I shrugged. 'When he last picked Claudia up. Two seconds at the front door. When he rings I pass her straight over to him.'

'But what do you do about practical matters – finances, the house, school fees, paying the builders? How d'you sort all that out?'

I shrugged again. 'I just do. We've always had a joint

account. I just pay the necessary out of that as usual. It hasn't come up.'

She sighed. 'It's as if none of this is happening, isn't it? As if you're in denial, no decisions to be made, and meanwhile you carry on renovating that bloody house. I mean, have you talked about that? About whether you should stop? Sell it?'

'Of *course* not, Molly!' I said aghast. 'God, it's – it's our dream, our project! We wouldn't sell it. We love it!'

Molly sighed, rubbed her forehead. She shook her head sadly as she started to get in her car.

'But don't you see, Moll,' I urged, leaning into her open door, '*he's* not doing anything either! I'm just following his lead! If *he* doesn't want any major decisions to be made, why should I force his hand? He doesn't want to rock the boat, does he? Otherwise he'd be saying, "Come on, let's sell" or, "Sign this decree nisi, Livvy" – but he's not, so that must mean he's coming back!'

'Or it could mean,' she said darkly, 'that he's a complete and utter coward and can't face telling you, can't face the truth. It's as if you're both putting your lives on hold, warding off reality.'

'There's only so much reality a person can take,' I said sadly as I shut her car door. 'Maybe he's had his fill of it too.'

As I drove home I was ambushed by tears. They fled down my face in torrents, and whilst one hand whipped them away like a hysterical windscreen wiper, the other gripped the steering wheel hard. 'Oh God, you complete and utter bastard,' I muttered to the dashboard, 'look what you've done to me.'

When I'd recovered some equilibrium I stopped off at

Waitrose. I wanted to feel normal again, like a normal housewife cruising those aisles, shopping for her family. Cheese, I thought decisively, striding in, proper smelly cheese – I haven't had that for weeks. But when I got to the cheese counter I realised I didn't know what to buy. Parmesan, Johnny always had to have, in a huge chunk, and Roquefort too, but now – I didn't know. Didn't know what I liked. I suddenly felt panicky as I stood there clutching my numbered ticket, the girl behind the counter in her white hat and apron raising her eyebrows patiently. I dropped my basket and fled from the shop. Out in the car park, as I tried to open the car door, I realised my hands were shaking like crazy. I touched my forehead. God, perhaps I did need something. Perhaps Vi was right, Prozac maybe. I took great gulps of fresh air instead and, after a minute, got back in the car and drove home.

As I drew up to the house I realised there was a car in my usual parking place. I knew this car, this blue BMW. I drew up behind it and sat for a moment. Well, it had to happen, but right now, on what could not, in all honesty, be classed as a good day, it was all I needed.

After a moment I got out and walked past it, noticing a huge dent in the front wing. That looked nasty. I trailed round to the back door to give myself a moment to compose myself before I went to the sitting room where I was sure she'd be but, as I turned the corner, I realised my mistake. It was a beautiful day and, of course, the party was taking place in the garden. Down by the stream, under the spreading cedar tree, draped in various positions about my white, wrought-iron garden furniture, my builders were At Home.

Alf was standing pouring tea from a china pot, Spiro sat cross-legged on the grass, Mac relaxed in a deck chair and Lance was mixing what appeared to be a large gin and tonic. Sitting centre stage, looking radiant in a crisp white shirt and brown linen trousers, her copper-coloured hair shining in the sun, was Angie. I smiled in spite of myself. Wherever Angie went, people flocked around. Not that my builders needed much excuse to flock.

'Livvy!' she called to me, raising her hand in a wave, just as if nothing had happened. As if her son hadn't left me. As if she'd seen me since. I bit my lip and walked towards her, down the gravel path edged with lavender bushes, under the rose arbour, stooping, as I reached her, to kiss her cheek.

'Angie, it's lovely to see you.' I suddenly meant it; felt almost choked at the sight of her.

'Darling, forgive me for not getting up but look what I've done to my stupid foot! Too maddening.'

I glanced down and noticed her shoe was off and that her foot was badly swollen. Spiro – whom I seemed to remember attending to my own feet very recently – was lifting it gently and wrapping a wet towel around it.

'Should be in hospital,' he muttered grimly. 'I say so, but no one listen.'

'Some lunatic pranged into me just as I was coming round your corner – didn't even stop!'

'Oh Angie, how awful. I saw your car but didn't realise you'd just done it!' I dropped down on the grass beside her. 'Are you OK?'

'No, she not,' growled Spiro.

'I'm absolutely fine, and this dear boy is doing wonders.

I just banged my foot on the pedals, that's all. In fact *all* these boys have been absolute sweethearts. Thank you, Lance.' She looked up and took her gin with a smile.

'I just thought something stronger than tea might do the trick,' he explained. 'Angie directed me to your drinks cupboard. Hope you don't mind.'

'This is my second one,' she admitted with a wink. 'But the boys are on tea.'

'Of course I don't mind.' Heavens, it had certainly all been very matey here, hadn't it? First-name terms and buckets of gin.

Angie swirled the ice around in her glass and giggled. 'I was just telling Lance here about that time when you and I flew to Paris for a shopping weekend, remember? And that woman beside us on the plane said to the steward in a very imperious tone, "I'd like a G&T, please. That's a gin and tonic to you." And he retorted, "Ice an' a slice, madam? That's a bit of frozen water and piece of citrus fruit to you." Her face! D'you you remember, Livvy? God, how we laughed!'

'I do,' I smiled, remembering.

'Oh – and Lance has been showing me all his marvellous bits and pieces!'

I boggled. 'Has he?'

'Yes, didn't you know? He makes coffee tables, chess boards – all kinds of things, and all with the most marvellous inlay and marquetry – terribly talented. Has he not shown you his portfolio?'

'I only arrived the other day,' explained Lance quickly, looking slightly embarrassed, as well he might. Yes, he'd only arrived the other day and so far I'd seen him do little more than eat my cornflakes, drink my tea and mix my gin.

'There hasn't really been time, has there, Lance?' I said smoothly, but Angie caught my tone. She looked around.

'Well, boys, now that Mrs McFarllen's back, I'm sure I'm going to be absolutely fine,' she said, beaming. 'Thank you all, *so* much.' Despite her charm, there was no disputing the fact that this was a directive for them to leave. Even Mac, who'd been falling asleep in his chair, got to his feet, yawning widely, and as was his wont, scratched his balls. 'Come on, lads, back to work,' he muttered. 'Let's leave these ladies to their tinctures.'

'Oh, Livvy darling, you haven't got one,' said Angie. 'Lance, would you –'

'Sure.' He turned to go but I stopped him.

'Thank you, Lance, but I'll stick to tea. I'd be grateful if you'd take a look at the waste pipe under the scullery sink, though.' I eyed him beadily. 'I think it's sprung a leak.'

Let's get things straight around here, I thought as he wandered off, hopefully put in his place.

'Nice boy,' murmured Angie, to his departing backside. 'Reminds me of David Gower. And, as I say, very talented. More of a cabinet-maker than a chippy. Strange to think he's the fruit of his father's loins.'

'Strange to think anyone would consider utilising Mac's loins in the first place,' I muttered irritably, getting up from the grass and sinking into his vacated chair. Why the hell were we talking about Mac? Intuitively, Angie stretched out and squeezed my hand.

'How are you, my dear?'

I delved into my bag for my sunglasses and put them

on quickly. 'Pretty good, normally, but for some reason I'm having a bit of a bad day today.'

Spiro put his head around the French windows. 'Lance found a very big leak!' he announced importantly. 'It's all gone slippy-sloppy up your back passage.'

Angie snorted with laughter. 'Heavens – what a ghastly thought!'

'Shall I mop it up?' he went on.

I sighed. 'I'll come, Spiro.'

'No, let him.' Angie put a restraining hand on my arm. 'Yes, please, Spiro!' she called. 'And tell Lance we've changed our minds, we'll have that other gin and tonic after all!' She dropped her voice. 'You look like you need it, Livvy, and we might as well make use of the extra hands about the place.'

'Yes, except that I seem to be paying fifteen quid an hour for the privilege.' I blinked behind the shades. 'Feel I'm losing control a bit here actually, Angie. Feel I'll come home one day to find they've done the washing up, cooked my supper, and that one of them's tucked up in my bed or something.'

'Well, just so long as it's not that one,' she muttered as Alf, bending to pick up some bricks, gave us the classic builder's behind. We giggled, but then a silence ensued. I waited for her to speak, not trusting my voice.

'The garden looks lovely,' she said conversationally, sipping her gin, but not looking at me. 'You've made a super job of those borders, which, let's face it, were rather dull and conventional. I love the way you've contrasted those mauve campanulas with the Boule de Neige. It works beautifully with the *Alchemilla mollis* at the front and the dark foliage behind.'

'It's my refuge,' I said quietly. 'I've lost interest in the house, but this is where I get rid of all my angst. Blow out my passion.'

She nodded. 'I remember when Oliver died, I had this strange compulsion to have my hands in the soil at all times – remember? Sometimes I'd find myself out there in the middle of the night, pulling away at the weeds. It made me feel closer to him, somehow. At first I thought it was because we'd buried him, so there I was in the dirt with him, earth to earth, as it were, but now I think it had something to do with control. Which you mentioned earlier. Controlling nature when I hadn't been able to control someone else's. Hadn't controlled Oliver.'

Another silence broke over us. Suddenly I could bear it no longer.

'Have you seen him?' I blurted out.

'I have.'

'So – he's told you?'

'He has. A couple of weeks ago.'

A couple of weeks ago. But she hadn't come to see me.

'I didn't want to intrude, Livvy,' she said gently. 'Hoped you'd come to me.'

'Well, I – just wanted to be on my own for a bit. You know.'

'I understand.' She patted my hand.

'Did you . . . meet her?' I managed.

'Yes.'

God. Already. 'Where?'

'Johnny and I met for lunch. She just came for a drink first.'

'And so . . . what did you think?' Vocalising it was awful.

She turned to face me fully for the first time. 'Well, if I was being kind I'd say she was a sweet little thing, but as you and I both know – since it appears that by some horrific coincidence she teaches at Claudia's school – that's generous. She's *très ordinaire*. What the devil's he up to, Livvy? I expected Claudia Schiffer at the very least but, good heavens, that bosomy little nobody – and to leave you for her!'

I sighed. 'I know. Defies belief, doesn't it? And there was I thinking you might be able to shed some light on it, tell me he'd always had a penchant for plain, buxom women.'

'The only light I can shed is the little I gleaned when she left the restaurant – which she tactfully did when she'd had a drink.'

'And?'

'Well, it seems . . .' she hesitated, 'it seems he'd been rather unhappy.'

I jumped. 'Here? Did he say *I'd* made him unhappy?'

She shifted in her chair, looked uncomfortable. 'Not in so many words, my darling, but –'

'Yes?'

'Well, he said . . . said he was tired of you always trying to please him.'

I stared at her. 'What?'

'Said it bothered him that you had no life of your own. That everything you did revolved around him, that he wished you'd do something for yourself.'

'He said *what*?'

'Apparently you were always running around after him, fixing up treats, weekends away, with his friends, not yours. Accommodating him.'

'But – but I thought he liked that! Jesus, he'd go into a steep decline if I didn't do all that, and that made *my* life unbearable! I *had* to think of things to do! Christ, and I bust a gut doing it!'

She sighed. 'I know. There's just no pleasing some people. I'm not judging, Livvy, just reporting back.'

'Jesus!' I slumped back in my chair in disbelief, eyes wide, staring. 'Hang on, let me get this straight. I made *him* unhappy by being too nice to him? Is that it?'

She leant forward. 'Think about it, Livvy,' she urged. 'What sort of people are we attracted to? Not ones who hover around us solicitously, but ones who impress us, ones who make things happen!'

'And what does *she* do that's so bloody impressive!'

'Oh, apparently she does all sorts. Ran the marathon a couple of years ago – God knows how, with that bust – wants to swim the Channel one day apparently, does a lot of deep-sea diving. Oh – and they go off on mountain bikes together. She bungee jumps too, if you're interested.'

I stared at her incredulously. 'Bike rides and bungee . . . Angie, are you telling me he gave up on our marriage because I wouldn't fix a bit of elastic to my back and jump off the Tamar Bridge?'

'No, I'm not saying that,' she said patiently, 'but what I am saying is that maybe, subconsciously, you've put your life on hold because of him. Because of that huge personality of his – and, believe me, I know what I'm talking about. I had it with Oliver too, and how. In that grand racing world I could quite easily have slipped under the quicksand of money and glamour and beautiful women, but I made a conscious decision early on that I wouldn't just be Oliver McFarllen's wife, that I'd go my own way. And I always did. He ran around me.'

I thought back. It was true. She'd always been elusive, never at his beck and call, and he was always anxious about *her*. Striding in from the stables – 'Is Angie OK? Has she got enough help in the kitchen? Are you girls lending a hand? How about someone laying the table. I don't want her tired, we're going out tonight.' No, Johnny had never been like that. But then I'd never been like Angie. God, only a few months ago I'd turned down a job at the Chelsea Physic Garden, thinking it would clash with the building works, with family life.

'You're too flipping considerate, Livvy, that's your problem,' she went on. 'You're even being considerate about Her, too, which, incidentally, Johnny cites as being totally typical of you.'

'Oh, *does* he,' I seethed. I was dimly aware that Angie was deliberately trying to rouse me to anger, and that she was doing a damn good job of it.

'Yes, he said, "You see, Mum? She's even making a friend of Nina. It's unreal!"'

I jumped up. 'Oh, *is* it bloody unreal, well, we'll soon see about that!'

'I think he needs a bit of a shock, Livvy.'

'He'll get one!' I hissed, pacing around my chair.

'I think he needs to see that you're not just sitting about waiting for him to come back.'

'Too bloody *right* I'm not!' Lance approached down the garden with my drink.

'That you're your own person –'

'Of course I am!'

'Still a very attractive woman —'

'You *bet* I'm attractive! God, I'm — I'm fucking gorgeous!'

'Still highly desirable —'

'Yes!' I shrieked, banging the back of the chair with my fist, 'yes, yes, *yes*!'

'And I think he needs to see —'

'A man!' I interrupted, eyes wide. 'That's it: he needs to see a man!' I swung round wildly, looking for one, just as — 'Lance!' I seized his arm. 'Lance — you'd be perfect! Absolutely perfect! Just like David Gower!'

'Sorry?' he blinked.

'Lance,' I breathed, 'listen. I — I need to borrow you, not for long but I —'

'Er, thank you, Lance,' Angie said hastily, prising my fingers from his arm and taking the drink. 'Mrs McFarllen's just a little overwrought. It's the heat. Thanks so much for the drink.'

Lance looked startled, but turned and went on his way.

'Perhaps you could be a little subtler than just grabbing the nearest builder that comes to hand!' she hissed.

But I was well away. 'And a job,' I breathed. 'I need a job. I'll ring the Chelsea Physic, see if that's still up for grabs, tell them I'll take it on any sort of salary.' I paced up and down, gripping my gin. 'Yes, it has to be in London. And clothes — I must buy clothes, expensive ones. Clothes, a job, a man — that'll do the trick, that'll show him!'

'Now slow down, darling, slow down,' said Angie anxiously. 'Don't forget you're doing this for *you*. It sounds to me as if you're plotting all this for him again, to paint a picture for him!'

I stopped in my tracks; stared at her. Then I sat down slowly, the wrought-iron seat cold beneath me. 'Well, yes I am. Of course I am.' She was right.

'Make sure it's what *you* want,' she insisted, sitting down beside me. I stared at her even harder. Blinked.

'But I don't know what I want. I've been pleasing him for so long, Angie, I don't know what I want any more. You're right. He's right. I'm just a frigging please machine. Press my buttons and I'll please you. I don't want a job or new clothes, I just want my husband back. Is that totally sad, as Claudia would say?'

'No, it's totally understandable,' she said slowly. 'All I'm saying is . . . enjoy the process. Enjoy the means to the end. Because, believe it or not, if you approach it that way, you may enjoy the means, even more than the end.'

I thought about this. 'Unlikely, but I take your point. I also agree that it's got to be more fun than sitting around waiting for him.'

'Of course it has!' she squeaked. 'That's the spirit!'

I blinked at her. 'It is?'

'Of course! Fun!' She raised her glass. 'You, Olivia McFarllen, are about to have some fun!'

I looked at her excited face. A slow smile spread across mine. 'OK,' I said raising my glass too. 'Here's to fun then.'

She crashed her gin enthusiastically into mine, spilling both. 'Attagirl!'

Chapter Nine

The following morning, I rang Imogen. 'D'you know any nice men?' I demanded.

She paused, taken aback. 'What sort of men?'

'Attractive, sexy, single men, of course. Come on, Imo, you must know loads!'

I felt her switch the phone to her other ear, give a little cough and shuffle her chair around. Perhaps the gallery was busy. 'What d'you want one for?' she muttered.

'I want to make Johnny as jealous as hell, of course. What d'you think!'

'Ah, right. That old chestnut. I wondered when you'd come round to that way of thinking. Hang on, I'll get my address book.' She broke off for a second. 'Right, now, let's see . . .' I heard her flipping through the pages. 'Well, there's Giles, of course, who would have been perfect . . .'

'Yes?'

'But sadly he's come out. Such a waste.'

'Oh.'

'So then there's James, who's gorgeous, but then he's rather gone the way of the Brompton Oratory brigade, bit pious now, so . . .' more page flipping . . . 'Ah – hang on, Rollo! Yes, now Rollo's lovely. He'd be very suitable. Works for the foreign office, frightfully rich, terribly intelligent, just split up with his girlfriend – he ditched her – fabulous flat in South Kensington –'

'Sold,' I purred. 'Perfect, Imo. He sounds totally perfect. Invite me to dinner tomorrow. Then I'll invite him back here this weekend.'

'Tomorrow! God, you must be kidding. For a start he's in Russia at the moment, and for another thing I couldn't possibly suggest anything for his diary without a couple of weeks' notice.'

'A couple of weeks!' I shrieked. 'God, that's no good. I need him on Sunday!'

'Sunday. Gosh no, I'm sorry, I don't think I'd be able to deliver the goods by then, Livvy,' she said doubtfully. 'There's Simon Franklin, I suppose – he likes to do things fairly impulsively – but even he gets pretty booked up, although he might have a space for dinner in July –'

'Never mind, never mind,' I said quickly. 'Forget it, Imo. Thanks anyway.'

'Sorry, but, listen, I'll tell you what. I was going to take the parents to that big concert they're doing in the Abbey next week on the fifteenth. Dad really wants to go and Rollo's a real music buff. Why don't I fix that up anyway? You could come with us? It's something to have in reserve if nothing else.'

'What big concert?' I said dully.

'You *know*. God, it's on your doorstep, for heaven's sake. Faulkner's new orchestral piece. It's going to be absolutely packed.'

'Is it? Oh, OK, fix it up as a stopgap, but meanwhile I need some more immediate crumpet. Speak to you soon, Imo.'

I put the phone down. Clearly Imogen's friends were so rarefied and sought after there'd be no getting into their

Filofaxes, or indeed anything else, this millennium, and that was no good; I needed results and I needed them now. By Sunday actually, three days' time. I gritted my teeth. Malcolm. It would have to be Malcolm. Oh God, could I really bring myself to? Yes. Yes, I could. This was an emergency, and needs must. Before I could change my mind I hurried to the back door, slipped on my old gardening boots, which were all I could find, and hastened round to Nanette's for his number.

Was he really so unattractive? I tried to remember as I scurried across the cobbles. No, quite good-looking actually, average height and with rather a lot of dark hair, I seemed to recall – hopefully it wasn't a toupee – no sign of a paunch, reasonable teeth – yes, he'd do fine. I'd have to light him properly, I reflected as I hurried along – subtly, you know, in a dark corner of the sitting room. Thank God for dimmer switches, candles even – and if his clothes were too appalling I'd lend him something of Johnny's. Yes, brilliant. Johnny's old dressing gown or something – that would really set the cat amongst the pigeons, and he could be naked underneath. Suddenly I felt sick. The thought of Malcolm naked apart from a toupee made me stop, clutch a lamppost. I hung on to it for a moment and breathed deeply, tried not to think about it. When I'd recovered, I went on up Nanette's steps, and rang her bell.

Nanette answered the door with Roger, beaming away behind her, clasping her from behind, as it were, both in matching kimonos and both looking very post-coital. Ah, so he was back. She was nearly sick with excitement when I told her my mission.

'Oooh, I just *knew* you two would hit it off! Didn't I say so, Rog? I'm *so* glad you liked him, Olivia! He's such a poppet, dear old Malc, and a great mucker of yours too, isn't he, darling? Hey, perhaps we could all go out as a foursome sometime!'

The very vocabulary set my teeth on edge, but I nodded gamely. 'Great!'

'The old dog!' hooted Roger. 'Getting his feet under your table in double-quick time, eh? Blimey, Malcolm and his trouser snake pop up in the most unlikely places, although I wouldn't have thought he'd have the class for you, Olivia!'

'Oh, heavens, I thought he was totally charming.'

'And now you can't wait to get your hands on him, eh? Ha! Terrific! Well, I must say, I thought it was more the form for the boy to ring the girl, but then I don't know many emancipated women, do I, Pumpkin?' He nuzzled Nanette's ear. 'Lucky dog!'

'To be honest, Roger, I'm not that emancipated myself, but this is a bit of an emergency,' I said grimly. 'Thanks, Nanette.' I took the piece of paper she'd scribbled the number on, hurried down the steps, and back home to my telephone, fingers itching to dial. Time was of the essence.

Malcolm seemed delighted, if astonished, to hear from me. I could almost hear him loosen his tie, lean back in his chair and work up a bit of a sweat from the plate-glass office of his Luton car showroom.

'Sunday? Er, yes, sure. Shall I book a table somewhere? What sort of time – eight thirty-ish?'

'Eleven o'clock in the morning,' I said firmly. Johnny would be arriving at eleven thirty to take Claudia out.

'Oh! Right. At your place?'

'That's it.'

'And then lunch?'

'Er, no. No, I've got to go out to lunch, I'm afraid.' God, I couldn't cope with him for any longer than was absolutely necessary.

'Ah. Right. So – what time are you going out?'

'Oh, about twelve. Thirty,' I added charitably. Didn't want to seem mean.

'So . . . you want me to pop round for about an hour and a half. On Sunday morning. Is that it?'

'That's it,' I agreed brightly.

'OK . . . fine. And then we'll take it from there, shall we?'

'Yes, why not?' I agreed blithely. 'Oh, and, Malcolm, um – what will you be wearing?'

'Sorry?'

'Well, just so I have an idea myself. Casual? Smart?'

'Oh. Well, smart-casual, I suppose. The blazer perhaps –'

'No, no, not the blazer,' I said quickly. 'What about a T-shirt and some chinos?' I suggested, catching sight of Lance through the window, looking good in something similar, sawing boards on a workbench in the garden. But what would Malcolm look like in a T-shirt? No, ghastly, like Tony Blackburn probably, I dithered.

'A suit,' I said firmly. 'Have you got a nice suit?'

'On a Sunday?' He sounded bewildered. 'Just for coffee?'

'Yes, you're right, you're right, too over the top. Just a shirt and trousers will be fine.'

'Right,' he said faintly. 'See you then, then.'

'Excellent, Malcolm, see you then.' I replaced the receiver. I hoped to God he wouldn't overdo the after-shave – he looked the type who might – but I was sure I could kill it with something stronger, outblast him with Chanel, perhaps. But otherwise – perfect. I nibbled my thumbnail nervously. So. Three days' time. And mean-while all I had to do at the appointed hour was look totally alluring, very much in love, and as if I was having the time of my life.

The following day I raced into London and took Knightsbridge by storm. I flew around Harvey Nichols as if my life depended on it, charging in and out of changing rooms, sending curtains swishing back and forth on their rails, wriggling into far tighter and sexier outfits than I would normally entertain, finally rejecting them all, and instinctively settling on a very elegant cream linen dress with capped sleeves and a pair of kitten-heeled, navy mules. If I say so myself, with my short dark hair and my eyes – which as my face got thinner, were getting huger and hungrier by the minute – the whole effect was very fey. Very *Roman Holiday*.

That was Friday, but the complicated bit of the plan revolved around Saturday. It dawned and, as I sat at the scullery table in my old jeans, cradling my tea, ignoring my breakfast, and drumming my fingers on the old Formica, I grew thoughtful. The thing was, I didn't particularly want Claudia around, a) to see Malcolm and double up with mirth, b) to witness any potential shit hitting the fan depending on whether Johnny, i) hit the roof, ii) hit the road, or iii) hit Malcolm. So. I drummed some more. She was due to go to her best friend Lucy's house for the day, and had originally been asked for the night, too, but I'd refused on the grounds that Johnny would be coming to collect her on Sunday morning. However, a quick call to Lucy's mother could change all that . . .

I was just replacing the receiver, when Claudia sat down for her cereal. She was showered and dressed and ready to go, and hurriedly shook out a bowl of Frosties, sloshing milk on top. I hovered next to her.

'Still going to Lucy's?'

'Mm-hm.' She nodded, mouth full. 'Can you drop me there in about ten minutes? I want to get there really early. We're going to make a ouija board.'

'Sure. Is anyone else going?'

'Lottie and Saskia. *They're* both staying the night.' She glared at me as she munched away.

'Are they? Well, darling, I've been thinking – seeing as it's become a bit of a party, why don't you stay too? You could see Daddy next Sunday. I'm sure he wouldn't mind.'

She nearly dropped her spoon. 'Really? Oh, cool, Mum! Oh, that is totally cool! They're going to see a film on Sunday morning, and have lunch in Café Rouge. Can I do that too?'

'Of course.'

'Of *course*? Good grief, what's happened to you? This is brilliant! I'll just go and pack a bag.' She jumped up.

'I've done it, darling. There.' I pointed to her rucksack at the bottom of the stairs. She stared.

'Oh! Great. Did you put my inhaler in?'

'I did.'

'But – hadn't we better ring Lucy's mum?'

'I've done that too,' I smiled.

'Oh, Mum, you are awesome this morning!' She ran to pick up her bag, then stopped. Turned. 'Oh – but what about Daddy? Will he mind?' She looked anxious suddenly.

'Of course not, my darling, and I'll explain that it was a very special sleepover, planned ages ago. He'll be fine!'

'OK,' she said doubtfully. 'And give him lots of love. Oh – I know, why don't I ring him and tell him? Would he like that?'

'No, no,' I said quickly, 'I'll do that. I've got to ring him anyway about something else. You just get your jacket and we'll be on our way.'

'Thanks, Mum. Hey,' she turned and looked at me suspiciously as we got to the front door, 'you're not by any chance seeing anyone tonight, are you?'

I flushed. 'Of course not. Why?'

She grinned. 'Just wondered. You seem awfully keen to get me out of the house, that's all.'

'Don't be ridiculous!' I spluttered as I ushered her through the door. 'The very idea! Now get in that car, young lady, before I change my mind!'

Sunday dawned even brighter and sunnier than the previous few days. Ninety-four degrees was predicted in old money; thirty-four in new. Either way, the heat was on. As I came in from the garden and went up to the bathroom to have a shower, I paused at my bedroom to gaze out at my handiwork. I smiled. Under the cedar tree, down by the stream, I'd put a small round table, covered it with a red gingham cloth, and placed two French café chairs either side. A posy of white roses was set just so already, but in an hour or two, when Malcolm got here, I'd add a basket of warm croissants, a jug of orange juice, fresh coffee, and a pot of raspberry jam. There Malcolm and I would be, talking intimately and laughing softly, so that when Johnny arrived for Claudia, rang the bell, got no answer because, of course, I could pretend I hadn't heard it from the garden, and walked round the back, he'd be presented with an arresting tableau: his wife and a strange man, sharing not just a tender moment, but what could only be construed as a very late breakfast. A breakfast after the night before. A lovers' breakfast. (At this point I'd reach out and clutch Malcolm's hand, or something equally appropriate.)

Yes, OK, I couldn't do the subtle lighting job on Malcolm that I'd previously envisaged, but I could at least put him in deep shade with an old Panama hat of Johnny's – quite familiar, I thought, to lend him that – pulled down over his eyes. Right down.

I was just about to move away from the window and hop into the shower, fizzing with nerves and excitement now, when something stopped me. I stared. To my horror, I saw the caravan door open. Good grief, hadn't they all gone home for the weekend? It was Sunday, after all. Did they have to live with me permanently? The door stayed open, but no one appeared. Oh terrific, I seethed furiously. All my sylvan scene needed was Mac, belching and scratching his balls, Alf, bending down for bricks and showing us half his backside, and Spiro, sobbing away in a corner somewhere – Jesus! I watched in fury as finally Lance came down the steps, dressed in shorts and a T-shirt, his tool bag under his arm. Suddenly I remembered he'd said he was going to work this weekend because Mac wanted to get the Aga in next week and the cabinets had to go in first. Damn. I didn't particularly want him ligging around, sniggering behind his hand at me and Malcolm, but at least, I reasoned, he was less obtrusive than the rest. And if he was ensconced in the new kitchen with his lathes and drills going, and Capital Radio blaring, he probably wouldn't be any trouble. I followed his journey up the path, under the rose arbour, across to the terrace and – ah, that's exactly where he was headed for. Good. He shut the kitchen door behind him, and, relieved, I hopped in the shower.

As I lifted my face up to the warm water I felt nervous, but strangely excited too. Gosh, perhaps Angie was right. This taking control lark was rather stimulating, and if Johnny took the bait, heavens knows what sort of passions and jealousies could be aroused. I wondered briefly if the posy of flowers was a bit too much . . . No. Why not? Flowers were always delightful, and what about a straw hat for me? Very Vita Sackville-West in her garden. Or was she a lezzie? She was certainly very Bloomsbury and blue-stockinged, but I couldn't quite remember which way she'd leant . . . forget the hat. The garden was stunning enough anyway, just at its most magical at the moment, with the Albéric Barbier in full flower, the lavender borders brimming over and – Damn. I paused mid-scrub as the telephone rang from my bedroom. Swearing and dripping I grabbed a towel and ran to get it.

'Hello?'

'Hello, Olivia? It's Malcolm.'

'Malcolm! Hi!' Gosh, I was almost delighted to hear

from him, almost as if he really were my lover. I could quite get into this role-playing.

'Olivia, I'm awfully sorry, but something's come up.'

I blinked. 'What?'

'Well, I'm so sorry, but I've just realised I'm supposed to be somewhere else this morning. I do apologise, but I'm afraid I'm not going to be able to make it.'

I stared, horrified and dumbstruck, into the mouthpiece. What did he mean, he had to be somewhere else? Where else could a man possibly be on a Sunday morning, apart from church, the pub or a car-boot sale, for God's sake? I sat down heavily on my bed, aghast.

'Malcolm, I don't believe it. Where have you got to be?'

Silence.

'Malcolm?'

There was another pause, then I heard him clear his throat. 'Olivia, am I right in thinking you're separated?'

'Yes.'

'And you have a young daughter?'

'Yes.'

'Who, presumably, your husband has visiting rights to on a Sunday?'

I licked my lips. Couldn't speak. My tongue seemed to be entwined with my tonsils.

He sighed. 'Olivia, when you've been single as long as I have, you get to know the ropes. A lot of the girls I know are gay divorcees, but some are not so happy about it, and the Sunday morning routine is an old one. I don't particularly want my lights punched out by your estranged husband, if it's all right by you.'

I was speechless. All my plans, my schemes, dripped off

me, evaporated into the duvet. But a small part of me felt awful too. There'd been a sadness in his voice. A jaded resignation.

'Malcolm, I'm so sorry. I feel dreadful now, and I really did like you.' I crossed my fingers hard here. 'I didn't ask you over just to – well to –'

'Use me?'

I gulped. Licked my lips. 'Um, look. Maybe – maybe we could get together some other time?' I said generously.

'I don't think so, do you?'

'Er, right. No, no, maybe not.'

'Goodbye, Olivia.'

'Goodbye.'

I replaced the receiver. Stared at it. Bugger. Bugger, bugger, bugger! Now what the hell was I supposed to do? God, Johnny would be here in – I glanced at the clock – an hour. I'd got the linen dress laid out on the bed, the croissants poised ready to be warmed in the oven, Claudia was away for the night – gosh, that had been difficult enough to arrange – I couldn't waste all that effort! Couldn't do it all over again next Sunday, could I?

I paced about the room wrapped in a towel, racking my brains madly. For an awful heady moment I wondered if I could borrow Roger. He was in insurance or something, wasn't he? Could I possibly ring and ask Nanette if he'd come over and take a look at my policy? No – no, he'd probably rape me in the undergrowth hooting 'Lucky dog!' before hoovering up all my warm croissants and, anyway, I had a feeling Johnny had met him once so he'd know he belonged to Nanette. He'd also know he was a complete prat. No, that was no good. So what on earth was I going to do!

I wrung my hands wretchedly, gazing out of the window at my perfect table, my flowers, when suddenly, right underneath my window, from out of the kitchen door came Lance. I stared down at him. He was wearing old khaki shorts, a faded pink T-shirt, and was carrying a couple of skirting boards, destined, no doubt, for the workbench, which he'd set up outside the back door. I blinked. Of course! Why didn't I think of it before? Lance! Hell, in anyone's book he was completely bloody gorgeous, far more gorgeous than Malcolm – and certainly Roger. Yes, yes, Lance was perfect! But the only problem was, I thought, chewing my lip maniacally now, how to organise it? How on earth could I set it up without him suspecting anything, and without him – heaven forbid – thinking I fancied the pants off him? I chewed my lip even more furiously, paced about the room a bit more. I glanced nervously at the clock. Ten o'clock. I didn't have much time. Suddenly I remembered something. Quick as a flash I got dressed in the cream dress, the navy shoes, the pearl earrings, brushed my hair, tucked it neatly behind my ears, added lipstick and mascara, and went downstairs.

Out in the garden Lance was planing away, his broad back bent low over the bench as he worked, his shoulders rippling under his T-shirt, the blond curls curling at the nape of his brown neck, just slightly damp with sweat as he – Blimey, I'd be sweating myself soon; I was rather warming to this idea.

'Hi!'

He turned. I gave a breezy smile. A dinky little wave.

'Oh, hi there.' He looked me up and down. 'You going out?'

'Um, no, just sort of, felt like a change from jeans, really.'

'Oh, right. Very smart. Not much good for your usual grovelling about in the flowerbeds, though.' He turned and went back to his planing.

'No, I suppose not.' I walked round the bench so that I was facing him. 'Um, Lance?'

'Yes?' He paused, looked up.

'I was having a look at that brochure of yours just now. You know, the one you showed Angie the other day, with all your tables and chairs and things in it?' I produced his portfolio from behind my back.

'Oh right,' he brightened.

'Yes, and I was just wondering, would you have time to make Claudia a bedside table? Nothing fancy –' keep it cheap – 'it's just that – well, she's got nowhere to put her books and things and I'm sure she'd love it.'

'Sure, I can do that. Which one caught your eye?' He moved across to take the book from my hand. I held it back.

'Well, I was wondering if we could discuss it later. You know, have a sort of meeting. At about eleven thirty?'

He shrugged. 'OK, but I can talk you through it now if you want. I'm not that busy.'

'Er, no, that's all right. I've got to – do the washing-up. But I thought, if we could catch up later, ooh, let's see, say under the cedar tree? Over there where the table is?'

He turned and followed my gaze. Slowly he took in the

two chairs, the checked tablecloth, the flowers, the jam, the coffee cups. He looked startled for a moment, then his face cleared. As he turned back, his eyes glinted, as though he'd just had a brush with possibility.

'Sure,' he grinned. 'Under the cedar tree it is. Shall I have a rose in my teeth?'

'Don't be ridiculous,' I spluttered. 'But – you might put some trousers on.'

He blanched. 'Sorry?'

'N-no – nothing,' I hastened. 'Forget it.' God, so *stupid*, Olivia. Why on earth should he change his shorts, for heaven's sake?

He gazed down at his shorts. His mouth twitched.

'You don't like my legs?'

'Don't be ridiculous. I've never even looked at them!' I could feel myself blushing.

His brow wrinkled. 'But you think . . . Ah yes, that's it, you think that if you *do* look at them, *and* my brochure, you'll be so overcome, you'll start panting and have to loosen your clothes?'

'Idiot!' I spluttered. 'Forget I said it. I'll see you by the tree at eleven thirty, wear what you bloody well like. Now if you'll excuse me I've got jobs to do.'

I turned and stalked off, hopefully with dignity, towards the back of the house. But after a moment, just as I was crossing the terrace, his voice stopped me in my tracks.

'What time's Johnny coming?'

I turned. Flushed.

'What?'

'I said,' he strolled towards me, hands in his pockets, 'what time is your husband coming?'

'I – don't know what you mean!'

'Oh, I think you do, Olivia.' His voice was gentle now. Less flippant.

He gazed at me, blue eyes very intense. I took a deep breath. Raised my chin. After a long moment, I spoke.

'Eleven thirty. And yes, Lance, how clever of you, how sharp. You've seen right through my little plan. I did want to make him jealous, wanted a reaction from him, but unfortunately, the candidate I originally picked for the job also smelt a rat and cried off, so I panicked and asked you instead, satisfied? You see, naïve and new to this game as I am, I thought I'd hit on an original formula. Thought – I know, I'll pack Claudia off to a friend, be caught by my husband having a cosy *à deux* with my lover under the tree and then, terribly flustered, say, "Oh, Johnny, I'm so sorry! I was so caught up with lover-boy here, I forgot to ring and tell you Claudia wasn't here!" ' I smiled ruefully. 'Little did I know I'd picked a well-worn, sad divorcee's path, one that all you predatory, prowling, single men can sniff out at twenty paces. Forget it, Lance. I'll still have the bedside table, if you don't mind, but I'll just mark the brochure and give it back to you later.'

I turned and started to go towards the house, tears already pricking my eyelids. Just short of the French windows, he caught up with me.

'Hey, hang on. Don't go off in a huff!'

I walked on.

'I just think you could do it better than that, that's all.'

I stopped. Turned to face him. 'What?'

'You want to make him jealous, right?'

'Well, yes I –'

'And is sipping tea with some stuffed shirt under the cedar tree really going to make him see red?'

'Well I thought it might just –'

'What time did you say he was coming?' he interrupted. 'Half eleven.'

He glanced at his watch, interrupting. 'He'll be here in ten minutes. Right. We have to get a wiggle on. Now, what we need are a couple of these,' he walked across to the washing line, reached up and grabbed a couple of towels, 'and a rug, possibly – have you got a rug? Oh yes, I know. I've seen one in the cloakroom.' He marched inside and, as my heart began to beat faster, reappeared a moment later with it under his arm. He laid it on the grass with the towels.

'Now,' he frowned, 'let's see . . . I'll take off this –' he whipped his T-shirt over his head – 'and these –'

'No!' I squeaked as his hand went for his flies.

He grinned. 'Only teasing. No, I'll just lie down like this, I think.' He settled back on the rug, arms locked behind his head, legs stretched out, brown chest, with its smattering of golden hair, bared. His merry blue eyes squinted up at me, into the sun. He shaded them with his hand.

'You look ridiculous, if you don't mind me saying so. If you'd just had a romp with your lover you'd hardly be prissed up like that. You look like you're going to the Tory Party Conference – all you need is a frigging hat – and apart from anything else, it's eighty-five degrees. Go on, go and get your kit off and put your cossy on. Oh, and grab some suntan lotion while you're at it. Come on, chop chop, we haven't got much time!'

I gazed down at him incredulously. Get my kit off? Suntan lotion?

'But –'

'What?'

'Well, he'll hit the roof, won't he? Seeing us laid out out here, all sort of –'

He raised himself on one elbow. I have to say, he looked completely gorgeous. 'All sort of . . . naked? And isn't hitting the roof the general idea?'

I gulped, hovered tremulously for a moment, but didn't make the mistake of hesitating again. He might change his mind. As a wave of hysteria threatened to engulf me, I ran inside, up the stairs, across the landing and into my bedroom, pulling out drawer after drawer, riffling around for my costume. My costume – oh God, could I do this? My hand stayed abruptly. I shut my eyes tight. Thought of Johnny. How I wanted him. Yes, I bloody could.

What I actually came down in – rather sheepishly – was something of a compromise: a bikini top and shorts, not quite having the nerve to go the whole hog which would involve exposing my thighs, which, since I lived in shorts, were horribly white and, as Claudia put it, 'rather porridgey'.

I crept nervously to the rug. He was still prone, hands locked behind his head and eyes – thankfully – shut. I was grateful for that small amount of tact, for not looking me up and down as I slunk down beside him.

'Got the Ambre Solaire?'

'Yes,' I whispered, my heart going like a bongo drum.

'Good. To be applied later. With vigour. Now, what would you like me to be, a solicitor? Architect? Famous artist? And shall I change my name to Jeremy?'

I giggled. 'Oh, well, now let me see . . .' I paused. 'How about Lance, the cabinet-maker?'

He grinned across at me, seeing me for the first time with not a lot on.

'That's very loyal of you, Olivia, but actually, I think it would be better if I wasn't a chippy or anything too manual and close to home. It would look a little slutty of you to have bonked one of your workforce already, don't you think?'

His eyes danced at me. I shaded mine to see him more clearly. I could never quite tell if he was laughing at me or not. Slutty? Would it? Well yes, of course it would! I inched away from him hurriedly on the towel, suddenly having severe second thoughts about this charade, when at that moment, the doorbell rang.

'Shit!' I squeaked, flipping over, face down on to the towel. 'He's here!' I shoved my fist in my mouth. 'Oh God, Lance, I'm not sure I can do this. I think I'm losing my bottle!'

'Don't be ridiculous, of course you're not. Here –' he passed me the Ambre Solaire – 'have this one. Now, sit up and rub it into my shoulders. Firmly, please, I don't want any namby-pamby business.' I hesitated. 'And don't forget, Olivia,' he murmured into the towel, 'I'll bet he's just given that Nina of his a right good seeing to.'

That did it. I knelt up, emptied half a bottle on to Lance's back, and got stuck in. His skin was soft and velvety, already warmed by the sun, and I could feel my heart pounding for various reasons as I kneaded the lotion in. A silence prevailed. Just my heavy breathing and a couple of swallows, warbling away in the treetops. Then the bell rang again. I was almost shaking with nerves now – in fact, I had a feeling I might have to run for the loo in a minute. Thank God I had my back to the side passage and wouldn't see his face immediately. All went quiet. For ages.

'Oh God, he's not coming round!' I hissed, panicking. 'He's going to go away!'

Lance raised himself up on his elbows. 'Quite normal,' he whispered. 'He feels he doesn't live here any more, you see, so he wouldn't presume to come round the back. I'll go and see him.' He jumped nimbly to his feet.

'Lance! No, you can't! What are you going to say?' I gasped.

'Oh, I'll say you're in the bath, soaking, and that in all the excitement you forgot to ring and tell him Claudia was away. I might yawn a bit too, scratch my sleepy head, and then as he goes, I'll turn and walk back upstairs to the bedroom.'

'Lance!' I shrieked, but it was no good. He'd gone.

I flung myself down on the towel and stuffed the corner in my mouth. *Omigod omigod!* He'd freak! He'd go insane, he'd – he'd hit him! Would he hit him? I took the towel out of my mouth. I had a feeling Lance was just a little bit bigger, and Johnny wasn't a fisticuffs sort of man but, oh Lord, the fur would most certainly fly. I shut my eyes tight and counted – one elephant, two elephant – like Claudia did to will the seconds by.

'Enjoy that, did yew girl?' A voice came sailing over the fence. I shot up on my elbows. Mr Jones was grinning at me from his garden.

'Sorry?' I whispered, clutching the towel to my bare-ish bosom.

'I said, did yew enjoy that, like!' He winked salaciously.

'Enjoy . . . what?' I flushed.

'The cucumber!'

'Oh!' Oh, the relief. 'Delicious,' I assured him. 'Really, really yummy.' God, go *away*, Mr Jones! I craned my head and peeked nervously round the side passage. Still no sign. Couldn't hear anything either, no voices.

'Good, good,' he purred. He gazed thoughtfully at the spot Lance had just vacated. 'Like 'em young and firm, do yew, girl?'

'What?' I gasped.

'I said, yew like 'em young and firm! Best way. Leave 'em in the greenhouse too long and they're past it, see? Start to droop at the end; can go a bit soggy too, like!'

I gulped. Heavens. What a thought.

'And I'll have some bewtiful ripe tomatoes for yew soon!'

'Oh! Oh . . . good!'

Happily he seemed to have had his say, and his head disappeared as he went on his way, back to his greenhouse to urge on his bewties, no doubt. I flopped back on the towel, and just as I was thinking I might actually faint from a combination of frayed nerves and heat, Lance reappeared. He strolled back through the house, out through the French windows, hands in his shorts pockets, whistling merrily. He sat down beside me with a grin.

'Well?' I breathed, sitting up.

'He's gone,' he smiled.

'And?'

'And, he seemed most put out. Astonished. Stunned even, and,' he frowned, 'yes, very taken aback.'

'What did he say?' I squeaked, kneeling up.

'Oh, well he spluttered fairly incoherently for a bit – particularly when I explained how exhausted you were – but then he finally said something about ringing you later.' He grinned. 'I said that m-i-ght be all right, but to give it a while because you really were shag – shattered and would probably still be asleep.'

'Oh!' I squealed, clutching my mouth. 'You didn't!'

'Yes, and as he turned to go I said that if he hung on for a minute I'd walk with him because I had to pop out for more baby oil. He scarpered like a scalded cat.'

'Oh, Lance, that's a bit over the top!'

'Not at all. I always put baby oil in my bath.'

I lay back nervously on the towel. Blimey, what would Johnny think? Well, he'd think naked massaging, that's what. I felt a bit queasy now, but then abruptly my blood boiled. After all, that was probably what *he* got up to, wasn't it? If not worse! Why should I feel guilty? Serves him bloody well right, I thought fiercely.

Lance lay down beside me. I shut my eyes, feeling the sun beating down. At length, he murmured something.

I turned and shaded my eyes. 'What?'

'I said, so you definitely want him back, do you?'

'Of course I do,' I muttered. 'He may be a bastard, but he's my husband, Lance.'

So we'd given him a nasty shock, had we? Good. Excellent news. Yes, see how that feels, Johnny, a nice sharp jab in the heart. I'd been having those coronary pains for months now, although, I realised with relief, I felt stronger now than I had for ages. Of course. Control. That was it.

'But he's poking another woman.'

I turned my head. Squinted. 'What?'

'I said he's been unfaithful. Doesn't that bother you?'

'Of course it does. Of course.' I frowned. 'But he's not a serial philanderer, Lance, that's the difference. It's a one-off. He's never done it before, and once he's back, he'll never do it again. You're looking at it from the idealistic, hearts-and-flowers, single person's point of view,' I reasoned sensibly. 'And I probably thought exactly like you before I got married, but real life, grown-up life, isn't like that, Lance. Some marriages do go through a blip like this. You can't just ditch twelve years for one indiscretion.'

'But it's not an indiscretion, he's still doing it,' he persisted. 'It's not like he's been caught with his trousers down and – oops, up go the hands, fair cop, big disgrace, been a naughty boy but home he goes with his tail between his legs. It's still going on. I think most affairs, or blips, as you call them, end in the guilty party slinking home, but he seems to have chosen to stay away. He's chosen her, Olivia.'

I wasn't quite ready for this amount of straight-talking, and whether or not Lance knew this and was deliberately shooting from the hip to shake me, I don't know, but I found I couldn't answer him. Had neither wind nor words to draw on. He's chosen her. Yes, that was enough to knock the stuffing out of me. A few well-chosen words designed to bring a lump to my throat, tears to my eyes, and a ruddy great boulder to sit on my heart. Thanks, Lance.

When I'd gulped down all the detritus, I turned my head back to him, trying to think of ways to explain to a fine young chappie like this what twelve years of marriage, three homes, numerous holidays, friends, commitments, responsibilities and a child of our own felt like. How I couldn't give it up. But his eyes were shut now, and his breathing, slow and measured. Eighty-five degrees in the blazing sun and no worries. Morpheus had swept him away.

As he slept, I gazed, uninhibited now, on those fine features; that straight nose, full lips, the dark lashes brushing his bronzed face. Of course, I reasoned, if one was going to have an affair, this was exactly the sort of man to do it with. Single, uncomplicated, just a spot of undiluted fun to get the blood coursing through the veins, make me feel vibrant and sexy again. But that wasn't what I wanted.

I turned my face back to the sky and shut my eyes against the scorching rays. No, it wasn't what I wanted, not right now. I felt the sun on my eyelids, my skin soaking up this heat. Unlike Lance, worries I most certainly had, but the temperature was getting to me now, making me drowsy. I mustn't drop off, though, I thought sleepily, my skin would absolutely scorch out here. Just two minutes, then I'd get up.

Some time later, I was woken by the doorbell. It was ringing and ringing. I opened my eyes and sat up, startled. Lance was still kipping deadly beside me, snoring away. It rang again, then again, sharp, and insistent.

'OK, OK!' I muttered, staggering to my feet. I weaved sleepily up the garden, through the French windows – hanging on briefly to the doorframe for support – then propelled myself towards the front door. When I reached the hall, I caught sight of myself in the mirror. My face and chest were a livid red, and my hair, wet and sweaty, plastered to my head. I groaned. Oh no, how could I have fallen asleep like that? With my skin? The bell went again.

'I'm bloody *coming*!' I shrieked, as I reached for the doorknob. I swung it back with irritable emphasis.

There, on my doorstep, stood Johnny.

'Johnny!' I gasped, taking a step back. I wrapped my arms protectively around my bare midriff.

'Hi, Livvy.'

'Wh-what are you doing here?'

He frowned. 'What d'you mean?'

'Well – did you – forget something? Come back for something?'

'Come back? No, I've just arrived. Sorry, I suppose I am a bit late, but the traffic was appalling.'

'Late for what?'

'Well, I've come to collect Claudia, of course.'

Chapter Ten

I stared at him, aghast. 'But – you came earlier!'

'What?'

'Didn't you come earlier?'

'What d'you mean?'

'Well – someone came!'

'To collect her?'

'I don't know, I didn't speak to him!'

'So who did?'

'Lance! He's my – my cabinet-maker.'

'Your cabinet-maker?' He blinked. 'Blimey, exactly how rarefied are these builders getting, Livvy? You'll be telling me you're employing gilders next. OK, so where's Claudia?' He peered behind me.

'Oh! Oh no, she's not here!'

Johnny paled. Stared at me. 'You mean . . . you let her go? With this person? This person who came to the door, spoke to your cabinet-maker and – and handed over my *child*?'

'No! God, no.' I pushed my hands desperately through my sweaty hair. 'She's at Lucy's, you see. She stayed the night there, and I meant to ring you and tell you, Johnny, but – well, I forgot.'

His eyes widened with comprehension. 'Ah.' He nodded. 'Right. So . . . I've just sat on the sodding Ml for two hours, in greenhouse conditions, when you could have made a quick phone call, is that it?'

'Well I *meant* to ring, of course, but I've been so busy, you see!' God, this was desperate. All I'd done was make him angry.

'Clearly,' he said drily. 'Well, don't let me hold you up any longer.' He glanced behind me, through the French windows to the garden beyond, where Lance was spread-eagled on a towel, mouth open, snoring loudly.

'I take it that's the master craftsman?'

'Yes . . .' I hesitated, 'that's – Lancelot.'

He snorted. 'Lancelot! Blimey, that's a good one. So – let me guess – you're Guinevere? Lots of "Aye, my lord, and wither my wimple? Chase me round the Round Table"?'

I regarded him for a moment. He looked totally irresistible, of course, this love of my life, this ache in my tubes, this short fuse to my heart. Tall, tanned, his blond hair sun-bleached, standing on my doorstep in his ancient shirt and shorts that I knew so well, had washed, hung out, and ironed so many times. After a moment, I folded my arms and raised my chin at him.

'Johnny, do I poke fun at your relationship? Do I make derogatory remarks about your fluffy, winsome, bosomy little teacher? Or do I make an effort to be as pleasant and as civilised as possible about this horrific situation I find myself in?'

He looked suitably chastened. Nodded. 'No, no, you're right. Sorry, that was cheap.' He scratched his head sheepishly. 'Sorry, Livvy. You're behaving very well. Much better than I am.'

Oh, this was worse, far worse. A lump came to my throat, and as his blue eyes apologised, I wanted to throw myself on him, hug him to bits, smell that shirt, his hair, his skin, say, 'But I don't want bloody Lancelot! I don't want to be standing here going through the motions of this ridiculous charade. I just want you!' But I didn't. Because isn't that the truth? There's always something to behave about.

'So –' he scuffed his Docksiders on the doorstep – 'it is a relationship, then?'

Ah, so he'd picked up on that. Gone after that little word I'd tossed him like a dog would a bone. Even sounded a mite territorial about it. Good. I gave a dismissive little shrug.

'I'm not sure yet. It's still early days.' Play it cool, Livvy, dead cool.

He nodded. 'Right. Well, anyway, it's none of my business,' he said hurriedly. 'I'll be away.'

'You don't want to –' I stood aside to let him in – 'get a drink or anything? I mean, if you've been in the car for ages –'

'No, no,' he said quickly, glancing at Lance. 'No thanks.' He gave a wry smile. 'I don't think I'd be quite as civilised as you, Livvy.'

I smiled back, tears filling my eyes. 'It doesn't come naturally, I can assure you.'

He nodded. 'I know.' As he turned to go, he glanced back. 'Incidentally, I should put something on that chest. You're going to be as raw as hell in the morning. And give Claudes my love. Tell her I'll see her next week.'

I nodded. Couldn't speak now. He walked to his car and raised his hand in a final salute as he got in. I waved back, watched as he drove off, then sat down on the bottom step of the stairs and burst into tears. Damn him. Damn him for being all I'd ever wanted.

After a while I wiped my eyes and blew my nose violently. Get a grip, Olivia. I peered in the mirror again. God, I couldn't have looked more awful, though, could I? I thought with awe. Bright red skin, sweaty hair – I hardly presented a seductive spectacle, and actually, I felt a bit cold and shivery now. I grabbed a cardigan from the banisters, threw it on and went out into the garden. Lance wasn't exactly looking his best either, I thought ruefully, snoring away like that, mouth open, catching flies. Shame Johnny had had to see him like that, but then again, if he'd met him at the door, it appears he might have resorted to some uncivilised behaviour, which was something, anyway, I conceded grudgingly. But then – oh God! Who *had* met Lance at the door? My hand flew to my mouth. I hastened across the lawn to wake him.

'Lance! Lance!'

I crouched down and shook him hard. *'Lance!'*

He came round sleepily. 'Hmm? What?' He raised himself up on one elbow and peered blearily at me. 'Christ,' he muttered, 'what time is it?'

'Almost twelve. We fell asleep. Listen, Lance, you know the guy who came to the door?'

He sat up and yawned widely, scratching his head. 'Johnny?'

'No! No it wasn't Johnny! Johnny's just been. He got stuck on the M1!'

'Oh. Really?' He frowned, looked bewildered.

'Yes, really, so what the hell did he look like?'

'Who?'

187

'The other guy!'

'Oh.' He peered into the middle distance, trying to remember. 'Well – quite tall, I suppose, longish dark hair, and sort of . . . yes, slanty eyes.'

I stared. Sat back on my heels. Tall . . . long dark hair . . . slanty – 'Oh God!' I clutched my mouth.

'What?'

'Oh no, I think I know who that is! Did he look slightly . . . not quite there?'

'He looked completely not quite there, especially when I gave him the baby oil bit.'

I groaned. 'Oh no! Oh God, Lance, I think that was Sebastian, from down the road! And there you were, socking it to him in graphic detail, telling him I was recovering from a monumental seeing-to and douching away upstairs! Didn't he try and stop you?'

Lance shrugged. 'I suppose I didn't give him much of a chance. I was giving it plenty of verbal, see, and all the time, hopping from foot to foot, getting ready to dodge in case a fist came flying my way, although,' he paused, 'I must say, he didn't seem inclined to do that. He just gazed at me sort of –'

'Vacantly?'

'Well, speechlessly, anyway. Blinked a bit, too.'

I stuffed my feet into my deckshoes and groaned. 'Oh God! Now I'll have to go and bloody *see* him, won't I! Have to explain, apologise, do *something* otherwise it'll be all round the flaming neighbourhood – how the abandoned wife at Orchard House spends her Sunday mornings. Nanette will have a field day!' I stood up and chewed my lip thoughtfully. 'I know, I'll say you're my brother or something, and — and you're staying here, and that your wife's just had a baby – hence the oil – and that the reason I was soaking in the bath in the middle of the day was because – oh, because I'd been doing some heavy gardening. Digging. Something like that.'

He shrugged, locked his hands behind his head and lay back. 'Could do, but I don't know why you have to bother. What does it matter if he thinks you're a goer? It's no bad thing.'

'Isn't it?' I gasped.

'Of course not. Contrary to what you might think, us men like girls with a bit of oomph, with a bit of weh-hey about them. Listen,' he sat up, 'up to now he's just thought of you as yet another up-tight housewife from down the road. He'll probably look at you in a completely different light now!'

'Lance,' I hissed, lowering my face to his, 'I do not wish him to see me in any other light than that of a neighbour, OK? He's the local oddball, for heaven's sake! In all probability he's as mad as a meat-axe. The last thing I want is some nutter turning up on my doorstep looking for a bit of "weh-hey"!'

'Is he?' he frowned. 'A nutter? Blimey, he looked all right to me.'

'Oh, what would you know?' I snapped as I buttoned up my cardigan. 'You think all single women should behave like prostitutes, have a bit of oomph about them – except your wife and your mother, I presume, who you'd no doubt like strapped into their pinnies and welded to the stove. It's the classic madonna-whore syndrome. You're probably as barking as he is!'

'Right. Sorry I spoke,' he muttered, settling back and shutting his eyes again.

I ignored him and marched off round the side of the house, out on to the road. I strode off along the cobbles, needing to go while I still felt brave, while I was still fired up, and practising my apology as I went. Happily it didn't matter that my face was the colour of a tomato since I was about to blush heavily anyway. How about if I started with something like, 'Sebastian, good gracious, what must you think? Do let me explain. You see, my brother and his wife are staying and –' Oh, I don't know. Something like that, anyway.

I climbed the steps to his tall, elegant town house, peering first into the basement below, which in Nanette's house was the kitchen. No lights on, no sign of life. I rang the bell and gazed for an inordinately long time at the red front door. I was just about to go away when his mother opened it. Just a fraction. She peered at me around the two-inch crack she'd conceded, almost as if she'd come up from the bowels of the earth and hadn't seen daylight before. I'd never seen her close up before, and I nearly gasped. She was sensationally ugly: her upper teeth protruded and were slightly pointed, making her look like a small, anxious rodent, and her steely grey hair was tied back in a bun so tight, it pulled her eyebrows up, giving her a startled ferret expression.

'Yes?' she whispered.

'Oh! Um, hello!' I smiled brightly. 'I'm Olivia McFarllen, from down the road. I've, um, seen you around, but we've never actually been properly introduced!' I held out my hand matily. She glanced at it, shot out a white hand and almost touched my fingers. Almost.

Oh God, had he told her already? Was I a Scarlet Woman in her eyes? Not to be touched? I flushed.

'Well, I really came to see Sebastian. Is he in?'

'No, he's not.'

'Ah, right. Will he be long? D'you think?'

'I've no idea. I'm going out myself now, though, so if you'll excuse me . . .' She made to shut the door.

'Oh, well, it's just that he knocked on my door. About an hour ago. And I just wondered – what he wanted.'

She frowned. Opened the door a bit wider. 'You didn't answer it?'

'Um, someone else answered.'

'But didn't come and get you?'

Not so stupid, this old bag. Superior thought processes were apparent. 'Er, no. You see, I was very busy. Very involved.' Oh, no, not *involved*, Olivia!

'Well, I wouldn't worry. I don't suppose he specifically wanted to see you. He was out delivering leaflets.'

'Oh, leaflets! Lovely!' I enthused. 'Getting out and about then?'

She narrowed her eyes at me suspiciously, declined to answer. No, quite right. Probably fiercely protective.

'Well,' I hastened on, 'when he comes back, perhaps you could just say – that I'd love to have a chat? When he's around?'

'I'll give him the message.'

She shut the door and left me staring at the paintwork again. God, what an old harridan, I thought as I turned and went slowly down the steps. Poor old Sebastian. Heavens, it was no wonder he was like he was with a mother like that. She probably smothered him as a child, hadn't let him play with any rough boys, probably hadn't even let him go to school. I'd hazard a guess she still ironed his pants for him, tucked his pyjama top into his bottoms at night. It was years since I'd seen it, but she reminded me of that nutty mother in *Psycho*, the one at the top of the house in the rocking chair, which I suppose made Sebastian the creepy son . . . although now I came to think of it, hadn't the son dressed up as the mother? Yes, that's right, there hadn't been a mother at all. I glanced back nervously. Could that have been – Oh, don't be ridiculous, Olivia. She's half his size! None the less, I thought with a shiver, no showers for me until I'd safely explained away Lance's sexual marathon story. I didn't want him thinking we were poking fun at his own sexual inadequacies; didn't want him meat-cleaving his way round to my place.

I slowed my pace as I approached my gates and stopped. Hesitated. It was funny, but now that I was out, and it was such a beautiful day, I didn't much feel like going back. I also didn't feel like facing Lance. However accommodating he'd been this morning, now that it was all over I felt slightly foolish. I wanted to distance myself from him. Wanted to get back to that more formal employer-employee relationship we'd had yesterday, forget the cosy, reclining-about-on-rugs-half-naked relationship of this morning. I always kept a ten-pound note in the car in case of petrol emergencies, so not wanting to pop into the house, I stopped by to pick it up. I shoved it in my shorts pocket and strolled on. Yes, that's it: I'd go into town, buy a bar of chocolate, get the papers, wander around for a bit – why not? And with any luck, by the time I got back, Lance might just have eased himself up from his supine position on the lawn and gone back to making cupboards for my bloody kitchen – which, let's face it, was what he was contracted to do in the first place, I thought (a little uncharitably, perhaps, under the circumstances). I joined the footpath, walked on through the park and out on to the steep hill that led to the high street.

Being Sunday, the town was fairly empty – just a few tourists, sitting around in cafés and wine bars, studying guidebooks, heading no doubt for the Roman ruins. I bought the Sunday papers, and suddenly realised I was starving. I hadn't eaten since breakfast, which I'd hardly touched, so I stopped off in one of the sunnier watering holes and sat down outside, under a shady umbrella. As I shook out the review section of the newspaper, for one startling moment I felt a delicious sense of freedom. No Sunday lunch to cook, no Johnny to worry about, no volatile moods to pander to; no joint to wrestle out of a steaming oven, no apple sauce to make, no pudding – which I never ate but which Johnny and Claudia liked – to spend half the morning preparing. Just me, a glass of chilled white wine – I studied the menu, and – yes, a Caesar salad. I snapped it shut and smiled up at the rather attractive Italian waiter who was hovering, and gave him my order. Well, I thought, lighting a cigarette, which Claudia would have objected to, with dire threats of 'death, Mummy, really slow and lingering, and me an orphan, with no one to look after me.' Well. I smiled into the sunshine. This really wasn't so terrible, was it? A beautiful day, with no one to please but myself. Yes, in theory, I would have had it differently, but actually, in reality, it was not so unpleasant. Was I even warming to it? This single life?

When I'd finished my lunch and read most of the papers, I paid the bill and strolled back, taking a short cut through the West Gate of the Abbey and down a cobbled side street. I passed the Abbey nearly every day of my life but never failed to be moved by it. I stopped now and stared up at the square, red tower, which had been built in something unbelievable, like 1080, from Roman tiles that had already been hanging around for – ooh, about eight hundred years. In anyone's history book, that made it pretty ancient. I strolled on round to the more recent, Gothic façade, but stopped short at the door.

When we'd first moved here, I'd gone in quite a lot, marvelling at the vast painted ceilings, exploring the nave, the crypts, the chapel of the first martyr, enjoying the history, the architecture. Claudia loved it too, and I occasionally accompanied her to evensong, which she liked, but never with Johnny. Having been quite a strict Catholic, he'd suddenly taken against it all, declaring it a load of papist mumbo jumbo – which was odd, because in London he'd chivvy us all into going at least a couple of times a month. Now he no longer went at all. Too much to confess, I thought bitterly. And to be honest, with no one to bully me into it, I didn't choose to worship much either. It didn't bother me that this church wasn't my denomination – and, anyway, they did hold Catholic services here. It was just that I'd always felt attendance a duty, an onerous one, to be done under duress. But as I stood there on the main steps, worn down by centuries of pilgrims' feet, I realised I missed it. It was imbued in me, this religious ritual, whether I liked it or not. A combination of my mother, the nuns at school and, to a lesser extent, Johnny and his family, had seen to that. I missed the contemplation, the peace of prayer. In truth, I missed that still, small voice of calm that I'd kicked against all my life.

On an impulse, I stuffed the rather gaudy Sunday papers in a bin and walked in, abruptly conscious of my shorts. I pulled the turn-ups down a bit. The morning service had finished and the tourists had taken over, swarming about the place. On the South side, orchestra stands and chairs were also being noisily assembled, possibly for a rehearsal of the concert Imogen had mentioned. I stopped, disappointed. Something pompous about not causing a commotion in my father's house came to mind, but in truth, I think the bustle annoyed my romantic sensibilities more than my religious ones. It was at odds with my vision of myself as a young Sophia Loren-like figure, alone in a huge cathedral, black headscarf tied under chin, kneeling to ask my maker for guidance, for forgiveness, whereupon a rather sexy young curate would approach, see my bent head – and, of course, my sylphlike figure and finely chiselled profile – sit beside me and place a hand on mine.

'You look troubled, my child.'

'Yes, well,' I'd sigh. 'You'd be troubled if you'd been left for a complete bimbo, and were having to contend with the builders, not to mention –'

At this point my fantasy lost any religious fervour it might have possessed and plunged into mediocrity. I grinned. Just as well the place was packed, I decided, as I came out through the Chapel door, and I couldn't attempt my prayer/fantasy. Who knows where it might have ended, and anyway, declothing vicars was a rather serious offence, I believed.

I smiled as I rounded the bend into my road, admiring the roses that cascaded over my garden wall. Madame Alfred Carrière was such a good doer. It didn't last all summer, of course, like the modern hybrids, but, my goodness, that flash of splendour made up for its brevity. I was also pleased to see the back of Lucy's mother's car parked outside: the Range Rover lookalike, with its spare wheel giving free advertising to the garage of purchase, that badge of the upwardly mobile, school-running mother. Ah good, Claudes was back then. I realised with a guilty pang that I hadn't really missed her at all, as I usually did. Too preoccupied, no doubt. As a treat, I thought, I'd make her pancakes for supper. Let her eat them in front of the telly, in front of *Ballykissangel* – or *Ballykissarsehole*, as Johnny used to call it – with a packet of Jaffa Cakes between us for pudding, as was our wont.

Lucy's mother, Amanda, was sitting in the front seat. When she saw me in her rear-view mirror, she shot out of the car. I saw her face and stopped short, as if I'd hit a barrier.

'Is she with you?' she called. I'll never forget the sound of her voice. 'Have you got her?'

Her face was pale, strained. I made myself go on, broke into a run.

'What?' I called stupidly, knowing.

'Claudia, is she with you?'

'Of course not! She's with you, isn't she?'

Amanda's face crumpled as I reached her, her hand clutched her mouth.

'Oh God, Olivia, this is all so awful and it's all my fault! I'm so sorry.' Her voice cracked as she reached out and gripped my arm. 'Claudia's gone missing!'

Chapter Eleven

'What d'you mean, gone missing?' I felt my stomach heave, my heart leap into my throat.

'Well, she wanted to come back, you see, this morning,' Amanda fell over her words in her distress, 'and so I brought her back because she seemed so anxious, and then, of course, you weren't here and – and stupidly I left her because she said she'd be fine, and then I panicked and rang and you still weren't back and *she* wasn't here either and – oh God, Olivia, I'm so sorry!' She hid her face in her hands and burst into tears.

Feeling sick to my stomach but knowing I had to stay calm, I sat her on the garden wall.

'From the beginning, Amanda,' I said trembling. 'Slowly. Tell me exactly what happened.'

She wiped mascara from under her eyes with the tips of shaky fingers. Nodded. 'Sorry.' She seemed to pull herself together for a moment. Took a deep breath. 'Well, she was fine last night. I let them have pizza in front of a video and then they all slept on mattresses on the floor in Lucy's room and giggled for ages. Claudia was as cheerful as the others, had a great time – midnight feasts, dancing to pop music, that sort of thing – but then this morning at breakfast, well, she seemed rather quiet. The others were still shrieking away, very overexcited and hyped up, but she wasn't, and she didn't eat anything either. I asked her if she was OK and she said she was fine, and then a bit later on, I dropped them off at a ten o'clock matinée of *Titanic*. When I picked them up outside, the other three were larking about as usual, but Claudia was still withdrawn, so I took her aside and asked her what was wrong. Her eyes filled with tears. She said she normally saw her daddy on a Sunday, but she'd chosen to come here instead, and now she felt awful because she thought he might be upset, think she'd chosen her friends instead, that she didn't want to see him.'

'Oh, Claudes!' My hand flew to my mouth.

'So I said, well, OK, what time did Daddy normally come round? And she said, oh, about lunchtime, I think, so I said – well, look, Mummy's probably put him off, but d'you want to go home and check, and maybe ring him to see if there's still time to see him? Well, her face lit up at that, and she said she did.' Amanda paused for breath, took a huge gulp of air. 'Anyway, I said, OK, that's fine, I'll drop you off, so we all piled in the car and drove straight over, but you weren't here. There was a note on the door from someone called Lance who said he was in the Fighting Cocks if you wanted to join him, but otherwise the place was deserted.' She gave a tremulous sob. 'Except that the back door was open, and Claudia said that if you'd left it open like that you wouldn't be long and you'd probably only popped to the shops, and that, in any case, the builder would be back soon.' Amanda raised her chin to hold back tears. 'Anyway, the other three were going on and on about how I'd promised them Café Rouge and how they were starving, and Claudia was insisting that she didn't want to come, and then the baby started screaming and – oh God, Olivia, in the end I just left her here!' She turned guilty eyes on me.

I nodded. 'It's OK, Amanda. I might well have done the same.'

'So off we all went for lunch and, of course, sitting there in the restaurant, I worried, so I rang to make sure you were back but there was no answer. Then I really panicked. I hurried the girls through their pudding but it took ages to get the bill and then I dropped them all off with my neighbour before dashing back over here. The back door was still open and I looked all over the house and the garden and she just wasn't here. Then I looked down the road and then I thought – well, maybe you'd come back and you'd both gone out together and I'd missed you or something, but then you came back and – Oh God, Olivia, I feel sick!' She held her hand over her mouth, eyes full of fear. 'What are we going to do!'

She felt sick. I swallowed. Right. So she'd searched everywhere and Claudia wasn't here. My head told me that she was very sensible for her age and that she wouldn't be far, maybe across the stream in the thicket at the back, or maybe even next door with the Joneses, but my heart told me that she was ten years old and she was on her own somewhere, had been for two hours, and I didn't know where.

'Should we ring the police?' trembled Amanda.

'Not yet. You go and ask next door. I'm going to check out a few places near the river.'

I flew round the back of the house and down the garden. Most people assumed the stream was our boundary, but our land – such as it was – carried on over the other side. Amanda wouldn't have been down here. I ran over the bridge and into the little thicket where Claudia had her tree house. Oh, please let her be sulking up here, I begged as I climbed the rope ladder, please let her be reading a comic, cross that I wasn't around to get hold of Daddy for her, please! I reached the top and peered in. Empty. I clattered back down again and ran to the back fence. My hands clutched the black railings. There was a park beyond with wide pathways where we sometimes went roller-skating up to the lake. I shaded my eyes. No sign. Just a few teenage girls immobile on the grass with skirts pulled up, and an old couple asleep in deck chairs. I ran back, across the bridge, then veered off left to the caravan. I flung open the door. Nothing. I felt panic rising, but made myself stop and rack my brains. As I shut the door I had a thought: the note on the door from Lance. If she'd read it, and thought – oh, Mum's gone to join him in the pub – then she'd surely come and find me there! Of course! And there was a garden there too, so she was probably on the swings, or having an orange juice and a bag of crisps with Lance, happy as Larry!

I ran breathlessly back to Amanda in the drive.

'She wasn't next door!' she shouted.

'No, it's OK, stay here in case she appears, but I think I know where she is.'

'Oh, thank God!' She clasped her hands. 'Where d'you –'

But I didn't wait to explain, I was gone. The Fighting Cocks was only a couple of hundred yards from our house, at the end of The Crescent, and in the summer it teemed, mostly with teenagers having their first illicit pint, loafing around on the grass, laughing loudly as it reached the relevant parts, or even just hanging out on the wall with an orange juice. The garden was heaving when I arrived. I glanced at the swings, but they were being ridden by much older children, showing off, standing two to a swing, facing each other, making them soar in the air. I spun around, squinting against the sun to spot her. There were children everywhere, running amongst the tables, eating chicken nuggets with their parents – but no Claudia. Then suddenly I spotted Lance. He was sitting at the end of a long table he was having to share with a multitude of others, one hand holding his mobile phone to his ear, the other, shading his eyes as he gazed, rather grimly, at the table. My hand shot up.

'Lance!'

I dashed across. 'Lance – is Claudia with you?'

He glanced up quickly from his phone. 'Speak to you later,' he informed someone abruptly. He snapped it shut. 'Ah! You made it at last.' He smiled. 'D'you want a drink?'

'No!' I shrieked, gripping the table with two hands. 'Is Claudia with you!'

The rest of the table caught the hysteria in my voice and paused, drinks and sandwiches halfway to mouths.

Lance got up. 'No, she's not, why?'

'Oh, Lance, she's missing!' I gasped, rapidly losing control. Vocalising it was so awful. My baby. Missing. He came round the table, took my arm and led me away.

'When was she last seen?' he muttered gently.

'Lucy's mother brought her home – I think about an hour and a half ago. We must have both just left the house!'

'You mean, she left her there?'

'Yes, because she thought I'd be back in a minute!'

'Well, an hour and a half's not long. She must be around here somewhere.'

'Yes, I suppose, but where?' I wailed, spinning around, as if vainly hoping to see her sitting at another table, with another family perhaps, tucking into a ploughman's, grinning and waving a fork at me. We pushed our way through the throng to the gate. 'Where?' I repeated hysterically.

'Now don't panic. She's a sensible girl, and it's not as if she's a baby, for heaven's sake. She's probably just popped round to see a friend or something.'

'No.' I shook my head, knowing he was talking about a different world. A friendlier, latch-key world, an every-mum-in-the-street-is-an-auntie world, not the closeted, privately educated, socially divisive world Claudia belonged to. 'It's not like that, Lance. She doesn't go to the local school, none of her friends live round here, she gets ferried everywhere by car. Oh God, where is she?'

I started to run up the road, my eyes darting about, heart pounding. I didn't know where I was running, I just knew I couldn't walk. I belted down a side street, stopped, spun around and dashed back again. Lance was waiting.

'Why did she come home?' he said, walking fast to keep up with me as I started running back up our road. 'I thought she was staying for lunch?'

'She was, but she wanted to see Johnny. She felt bad about going to Lucy's when she usually saw him on a Sunday.'

'OK, so then wouldn't she have rung him? Possibly gone to find him?'

'What – in London?' I shrieked, stopping dead in my

tracks. Suddenly I saw her. At Piccadilly Circus, on the steps up to Eros, lying with the homeless in a cardboard box, hair matted, eyes dark and hollow, syringe hanging out of her arm, predatory pimp hovering.

'OH CHRIST!' I roared. I had to hold on to Lance's arm for support.

'Steady – *steady*,' he insisted nervously. 'No, I doubt if she'd actually *go* to London – she's not silly – but she might try to contact him, surely?'

'Yes! Yes, you're right, she might!' Hope flooded back for a second. 'I'll ring him.' I hurried on. 'And the police?' I threw over my shoulder. 'Should we ring them too?'

'No, not yet,' he said firmly, jogging to keep up. 'I know you're worried but I think it's a bit premature. Let's explore all the possibilities first because, let's face it, that's all the police will do.'

Amanda came running down the road to meet us. 'Well?' she shouted.

I shook my head.

'Oh God, this is awful!' She clutched her mouth. 'And it's almost *more* awful for me because it's someone else's child!'

She was getting hysterical, and actually, I didn't want to hear about how awful it was for her. I felt like giving her a good slap. She was sobbing now, and Lance was trying to calm her, leading her to her car, knowing she was doing me no good at all, talking to her in the voice one reserves for – who was it now? – yes, that's it, the bereaved. Send her home, send her home, I prayed. She was nodding as he cajoled her into the front seat, and I saw her reach, sniffing, for the ignition key. As I watched her drive off, I wondered if I was actually here at all. Wondered whether this was real, or if I was actually in a hospital bed – I felt sick enough – coming round from some ghastly anaesthetic dream which would disappear just as soon as the gas wore off. Lance came back to me.

'I gave her a job. She's going to ring all the girls in Lucy and Claudia's class, just to make sure she hasn't tried to get hold of one of them. That sent her packing.'

I was in the hallway now, front door open, looking desperately for Johnny's number on the hall table. I felt incredibly dizzy.

'So they'll all know,' I trembled. 'All her friends will know she's missing.'

'We can't keep it a secret, Olivia. We have to find her, that's all that matters.'

I touched my forehead. Of course that was all that mattered. What was I thinking of? Losing face amongst the class mothers?

'Now, Johnny?' He picked up the receiver, raising his eyebrows expectantly.

'Yes, I know but I can't find the bloody number!' I sifted through papers, lifting them up and letting them drop with hopeless hands.

'Well, what's it written on?'

'The back of a milk bill, I think – ah! Here!' My trembling fingers pounced on the scrap I'd jotted it down on, not wanting the number in my address book. Too permanent somehow. I dialled. Nina answered.

'Is Johnny there?' I barked. No niceties now. And she knew it was me. Didn't bother to ask. Yet I'd never rung there before, he always rang here. He came on.

'Livvy?'

'Johnny, is Claudia with you?'

'Of course not. I've just this minute got back from you. Why?'

I explained in a quavering voice. He was silent. I waited for the storm to break, the how-could-you-have-let-her-out-of-your-sights, the recriminations.

'Oh Christ, this is all my fault,' he said quietly. 'I've put her in this mess. This is my doing. She came back to see me.'

I was stunned, but I rallied. 'Of course it's not your fault, Johnny, but we must find her. Ask Nina, has she tried to ring while you were out?'

He turned and I heard him talk to her. I had to close my eyes, clench my teeth, so painful did I find the sound of their murmuring voices. He came back.

'No, she hasn't. Livvy, I'll come down. Ring the police and I'll come down.'

'No, Johnny, she may be coming to see you! She's got your address, remember, and you won't be there!'

'Nina will be here in case she arrives. I have to be with you on this one, Livvy.'

I shut my eyes again. He had to be with me. But he'd qualified it. *On this one, Livvy.*

'OK.' I put down the phone, swung round to Lance. 'She's not there. Now I'll ring the police.' As I went for the receiver, his hand closed on mine.

'In a minute. Just check first – has she taken any money?'

'Oh!' I dropped the receiver. 'I don't know . . . Wait!'

I raced upstairs two at a time, dashed into her room and seized her china pig. I pulled out the plug. I knew she had about thirty pounds, enough to get her to London and back. It was still there.

'No!' I screamed as I crashed back down the stairs. 'It's still there – that's good, isn't it?' I panted, hanging over the banisters, pleading for confirmation. Surely it meant she wasn't in London, and what on earth could happen to her round here?

'I think it is,' he said slowly. 'I think it means she isn't far away. Nanette?'

'Oh God, of course! Nanette!'

I jumped the last few steps and lunged again for the phone. Roger was in, Nanette was at her mother's, and no, he hadn't seen Claudia. I could feel my courage draining.

'Who else?' demanded Lance. 'Your mother?'

'Yes – brilliant, my mother! But she'd need money to –'

'Ring her anyway.'

I did. She was out. Her answer machine was on. Lance paced up and down the hall, biting his lower lip, eyes narrowed. I watched helplessly.

'What would she do,' he muttered, 'on a normal day, on a normal Sunday morning? What would she do?' He swung round, his eyes interrogating me. I fought to think.

'Read maybe, or – or go upstairs and play on the playstation, write an E-mail to a friend.'

'OK, but if she was outside?' he urged. 'If she was out in the garden?'

'Well, her bike, I suppose, or – Her bike!'

I ran out of the front door and round the side passage to the shed. Lance followed.

'It's gone!' I yelled. 'Her bike's gone!'

'Right,' he breathed. 'Now we're getting somewhere.'

'Oh, Lance, she's just gone for a bike ride! That's all, isn't it?'

'Hopefully. And Lucy's mother's ringing all her classmates because there's a good chance she'd ride to one of them, isn't there?'

'Well, not normally. She's not allowed out of The Crescent, but –'

'OK, so where else did she ride it? With you, maybe, but today she tries it on her own. Think!'

'In the park,' I said quickly. 'We'd both ride together up to the lake, and also along the tow path by the stream; it runs along the back of The Crescent.'

'Right. I'll take the park and the lake, you take the tow path. If we meet back here with no joy in ten minutes, we'll call the police.'

'Shouldn't we do that now? They could take a description of her and –'

'Time,' he interrupted. 'All of that takes time, all those questions, forms to fill in – and the chances are, if we're quick, we'll catch up with her.'

'OK,' I agreed, 'but back here at –' we glanced at our watches – 'quarter to.'

Off I raced, back down the garden, but this time, with a slightly lighter heart. She wasn't on a train, she wasn't in London, she wasn't doing drugs in a squat. She was just pootling about on her bike, waiting for Mummy to come home. Oh, thank God. I crossed the bridge and turned right along the tow path. I liked to go the other way, where the trees dipped into the water and the moorhens gathered underneath with their broods, but I knew Claudia preferred this way. This was her beat, with lots of rises and dips to pedal up fast, and shoot down again. As I hurried round a bend, I nearly mowed down an old lady walking her pug.

'Oh – sorry!' I steadied myself, holding her shoulders. 'Have you seen a girl?' I panted. 'Of about ten, riding her bike?'

'I haven't dear,' she said, startled. She adjusted her cardigan where I'd held her. She made to move on, but as I broke into a run again, she called me back.

'Oh – I say!'

I swung about.

'There is a bike, though. Further along, in the hedgerow. I noticed it as I came round.'

I stared at her. Couldn't speak. She raised her walking stick in salute, and went on her way. A bike. In the hedgerow. Full of fear and foreboding I raced around the corner – and there it was. Claudia's bike. Pink, too young for her she'd insisted recently, too Barbie doll, with a basket on the front, and in her basket, an apple and a book. No Claudia.

My eyes shot about. 'CLAUDIA!' I screamed, my heart pounding. Silence.

'CLAUDIAAA!' I felt bile rush to my mouth. My eyes darted back to the bike, abandoned on its side, front wheel at an acute angle, like a silent distress signal. Oh God, she must have been dragged off the path, into the bushes! A strangled sob reared up my throat. Through the bracken I crashed, sobbing now.

'CLAUDIA! CLAUDI-AA!'

Low branches tore at my clothes and face as I plunged off in all directions, going round in circles, always coming back to the same spot, glancing helplessly at the bike before tearing off again.

'Oh God, oh God,' I sobbed, stumbling further down along the tow path. A couple of amorous teenagers, arms and tongues entwined as they walked blindly towards me, eyes shut, were suddenly confronted by a mad woman, face scratched and bleeding, sobbing wildly.

'Have you seen a girl!' I cried.

'What?' The spotty youth unstuck his lips and blinked, startled.

'A girl! Look, there's her bike back there – about ten, in red shorts probably – have you seen her?'

'Nah, sorry, luv.' He made to move on.

'Oh yeah, hang abou'.' His girlfriend held his arm. 'Yeah, we did, remember? What about the one wiv that man, Gary? You know, the one back there?'

'What man!' I roared, voice hoarse but nearly fainting with fear.

Gary shrugged. 'Dunno.'

'Yeah, he was, he was wiv one,' she insisted. She turned to me. 'A little girl. She was wearin' red shorts an' all, and he 'ad her by the arm.'

Oh God. Oh dear Jesus and God. 'Which way?' I choked.

'Over there.' She pointed behind me. I swung about. She was pointing across the other side of the stream, back to The Crescent, to the row of back gardens.

'She was cryin' an' that, too, weren't she, Gary?'

'Dunno.'

'Yeah, she was, an' I watched them go, 'cos I fought it was funny, wasn't sure if he was her dad, an' he took 'er up that parf, into that house there.'

'Which one?' I breathed.

'There, that one wiv the green back door, over there.'

She jabbed her finger. I followed it. Stared – then froze with horror. My heart nearly stopped completely. Oh God. Oh dear God Almighty. Sebastian. It was Sebastian's house.

Chapter Twelve

I flew across the footbridge and down the path that led along the back of The Crescent gardens. Sebastian's house was in the middle, tall, and red brick at the back, in contrast to its white stucco façade, and with a strip of immaculate lawn stretching down to wrought-iron railings and a gate at the bottom. With a pounding heart I ran along the path to the gate. He'd forced her through here, sobbing, the bastard. Had her arm in a vicelike grip. The gate was still open. I ran through, then, realising the French windows at the back of the house were also wide open, veered left and shot behind a shed. I flattened myself against it for a moment, panting hard. I had to get her out of there, but I had to be careful. If I charged in, all guns blazing, he might put a kitchen knife to her throat, hold her hostage or something. Oh yes, I thought, my mind racing, it was all becoming very clear now. He was obviously taking some sort of warped revenge for having my sexual exploits thrust in his face by Lance. Perhaps he was impotent, or – or maybe he had designs on me himself, was plucking up the courage to ask me out and had come to the door on the pretext of delivering leaflets, but then had had to listen to Lance's account of me, wallowing in Radox, bug-eyed with sexual exhaustion. Well, that was enough to send anyone remotely remedial into a complete lather, enough to make him bide his time, wait, watch, and then take revenge. Enough to make him take my baby. A sob tore up my throat. I gulped it back down, clenching my teeth.

Peering cautiously round the shed, I narrowed my eyes. I could just about see into the drawing room, but the bright sunlight made it too dark for me to determine if anyone was in there. I had to make an angled dash across the lawn, aim for the outside wall of the house, flush with the French windows, and hope for the best. Head down and bent forward, I went for it, leaping an immaculate flowerbed and making it to the relative safety of the wall. I flattened myself against it, heart going like a bongo drum. Slowly I inched my way along the doorframe and peeped round. I could hear noises, voices, and for a moment I thought there were a few people in the room, until I realised the television was on. I couldn't see any-one, except – yes. Suddenly I realised that that was Claudia, sitting hunched in an armchair at the back of the room. Except I hardly recognised her. Her hair looked lank and too dark, and she was wearing a dressing gown. A man's dressing gown. *His* dressing gown. A little yelp escaped my lips and I could bear it no longer. A garden rake was propped up against the wall beside me. I seized it and charged in.

'CLAUDIA, GET BEHIND ME!' I shrieked, spreading out my arms and brandishing the rake at the rest of the room. Claudia looked up from the television in aston-ishment.

'Mum!'

'Get behind me!' I yelled.

'But –'

'JUST DO IT!'

Claudia, never having seen me in totally-lost-it mode, waving a rake, leapt up and scuttled behind me.

'Why?' she whispered.

'Where is he?' I barked.

'Who?'

'Sebastian!'

'Oh well, around, I think.'

Around. I swung about, pushing her behind me, still shielding her with my body, glancing furtively in corners, waiting for him to pounce out from behind one of those dark pieces of furniture at any moment.

'Now, back,' I hissed.

'What?'

'Back! Go backwards, out of the French windows!'

Catching the madness and urgency in my voice, Claudia obeyed. Clutching her dressing gown to her, she started reversing out, wide-eyed. I backed with her, eyes darting everywhere.

'Did he touch you, my love?' I whispered brokenly.

'What d'you mean?'

'Well, did he –' I choked back a strangled sob – 'hurt you in any way?'

'Of course not!'

I swung round to see her staring in astonishment at me.

'But he took your clothes?'

'Yes, but –'

'The bastard!' I spat. 'The rotten, dirty, filthy bastard. How *dare* he – *aha*!'

A figure materialised from the shadows. A figure coming through the far door, bearing a tray of tea and biscuits. Sebastian, in a white shirt and faded brown cords, blinked in surprise as he confronted a scratched and bleeding woman in his sitting room, legs planted wide apart and bent at the knee like a sumo wrestler, hands gripping either end of a horizontal garden rake, kung fu style.

'*Aha!*' I cried again, bracing myself, head stuck forward and moving slowly from side to side, like a bull facing a matador. 'So! You've finally slunk out, have you, you little piece of filth! Come one step closer and I swear to God I'll – *Stay where you are!*'

Sebastian stopped, astonished. 'Good Lord, what on earth –'

'Don't you Good Lord me,' I hissed, 'you dirty, scummy degenerate – *Keep backing away, Claudia!*'

Claudia, who for a moment had popped her startled head out, hastily obeyed and began making her way out to the garden.

'Now run!' I yelled over my shoulder. 'Run home and I'll cover you. I'll follow later. Now! GO!'

Claudia didn't wait to argue with a mother in this mood. She took to her heels and scampered off, scared witless, no doubt.

'Mrs McFarllen, are you taking drugs?' enquired Sebastian calmly.

'How *dare* you?' I breathed as I slowly followed my daughter, backing out, but keeping my rake rigid at chest level. 'How dare you abduct a poor defenceless child? You're not just a harmless halfwit like everyone says, you're a bloody pervert! The lowest of the low! D'you know what happens to people like you in prison? Hmm? Do you? Do you know what your fellow inmates will do to you?'

'Good god,' he muttered. 'You need help.'

'Help!' I barked derisively. 'Ha! You're the one who needs help, you little creep, and I'll see that you get it – in spades! You were seen,' I hissed, curling my lip, 'by a decent, upright young couple out walking, seen dragging an innocent child, screaming, *sobbing*, on her knees practically, into *your house*!'

'This is outrageous!' His face clouded and he came towards me.

'NO CLOSER!' I bellowed, swinging the rake so it pointed straight at him. I brandished it at his chest. 'No closer or I'll –'

THWACKK! As he took another step I jerked the rake up, slamming it under the tray and sending it flying. It performed a neat somersault, and steaming Lapsang Souchong and garibaldis leapt high in the air – then splashed straight down in his face.

'Christ!' he clutched his eyes.

Temporarily blinded, he staggered about a bit, and I took advantage. I flung down the rake, shot one last look at the stumbling, gasping figure with his face in his hands – then fled. Up the immaculate lawn I tore, leaping the flowerbed, through the gate, down the tow path, through our own wrought-iron gate, then back down the garden, through the French windows – and home. I slammed the glass doors shut behind me, shooting bolts across at top and bottom with quivering hands. I spun round.

'Claudia!'

No answer.

'CLAUDIAAA!'

'In here,' came a flat, dead-pan voice.

I flew off in its general direction and found her, sitting with Lance, at the kitchen table. She was still huddled in the dressing gown and drinking orange juice straight from a carton. I dropped to my knees beside her.

'Darling, oh, my poor darling,' I sobbed, hugging her knees. 'Are you all right? Shall I call the police?'

'Don't be ridiculous, Mum. You've made a complete and utter pill of yourself,' snapped Claudia, shaking me off. 'I'm so embarrassed. He didn't hurt me at all, he just hauled me out of the river.'

My mouth fell open. I sat back on my heels, then stood up. 'Wh-what?'

'My bike hit a rut and I went in headfirst, bumped my head on a rock. He was at an upstairs window and saw what happened. He came out to help me. I was absolutely soaking so he lent me a dressing gown and put my clothes in the tumble dryer.'

'But – they said you were crying,' I gasped. 'And being held by him!'

'I *was* crying. I cut my knee, look.' She lifted the dressing gown to show a newly bandaged knee with blood still seeping through. 'It hurt like anything, and he wasn't holding me, he was just helping me 'cos I was limping so much. I could hardly walk. I've never been so embarrassed in all my life, Mum. He was so kind and put a bandage on, and made tea and everything, and then you appear like bloody Boadicea, looking totally insane, screaming and hollering, with blood all over your face and twigs and things coming out of your head, and a *rake*, for God's sake. You looked like such a spasmo.'

'Oh God.' I sank down on to a chair. 'You mean he didn't –'

'No, of course he didn't, and I'm really disgusted by your mind sometimes, Mum. You thought he was showing me his privates, didn't you?'

'Well I –'

'I'm going up to change.' She got up and stalked out.

I sat, staring after her for a minute. Then slowly, I leant my elbows on the table, pushed my hands into my hair, clutched my head and groaned.

'Oh Lord!' I whispered. 'Oh Lord, Lance, I went berserk. She's right. I went totally, indescribably, doo-bleeding-lally berserk! I was like a mad woman in there! Called him names, all kinds of terrible – oh Christ – *ghastly* names and – oh God –' my head shot up and my eyes bulged with horror as I remembered – 'I threw hot tea all over him! Scalded him, gave him third-degree burns! He'll probably have me up for assault!'

'Probably,' Lance agreed calmly, pouring me a cup from the pot he'd just made. 'But I'm sure we can get you off with a decent brief and some cock-and-bull story about it being the wrong time of the month and you being emotionally unstable or something. Tends to work. Anyway, the main thing is, Claudia's back.'

'Yes,' I breathed, leaning back in my chair with relief. 'Yes, you're right, thank God. Helped out of a river by Sebastian.' I raked my hands desperately through my hair again, punishing it. 'Oh Lance, I must go back,' I groaned. 'I must go straight back – yet again – and apologise, sort

things out. Poor, simple, decent, innocent man! I've probably scarred him for life!'

'What, with the tea or the insults?'

'Both! Oh, how appalling of me, Lance. Imagine what
that could do to a man like that? I must make it up to him
somehow. Maybe I could take him and his friends on an
outing? To the zoo, or something? Hire a minibus?'

'Olivia, I'm not convinced he's as – Oh-oh.' He broke
off suddenly, glancing out of the window. 'Forget the
Whipsnade trip, I think you'll have to go and make your
neighbourly peace some other time. Right now you have a
visitor.'

I glanced out of the window.

'Johnny!' I breathed, as the old yellow E-type screeched
to an emergency halt outside. 'Oh God, I'd forgotten
about him. I should have rung him on his mobile, told
him she was OK! Blimey, he got here in double-quick
time; must have driven at a million miles an hour!'

'I'll make myself scarce,' muttered Lance, getting up
and making for the back door.

Johnny's face when he got out of the car was very pale,
his mouth set in a taut line. I jumped up and raced out to
meet him. I knew that every moment of thinking she was
missing was torture, and that if I ran, I could spare him
one or two.

'It's OK!' I cried as I flung open the front door. 'She's
back! She went for a bike ride and fell in the stream, but
she's fine!'

He stopped still at the gate. His face cleared. 'Thank
God. Oh, Livvy, thank God.' He broke into a run, and as
I raced out to meet him, he swept me up in his arms and

caught me to him. As he held me tight, my face pressed into his chest, my arms round his warm shoulders, I could feel his heart pounding. I shut my eyes. I wanted to sob. It was like a drop of water to a parched soul.

'Where is she?' he said, releasing me, holding me at arm's length.

'Upstairs, changing. I'll tell her you're here. Oh, Johnny, I'm sorry, I should have rung you on your mobile. You've had to come all this way again on a wild-goose chase!'

'Wild-goose chase?' He stared. 'Don't be silly, I'd have wanted to be here anyway. She's my daughter, Livvy.'

'Yes. Yes, of course,' I nodded meekly, humbled. 'Sorry.' I hung my head.

I seemed to be getting it all wrong today, didn't I? I was all over the place, apparently. We turned to go in, just as, clattering downstairs, in leggings and a pink T-shirt, and framed in the open front doorway, came Claudia. She yelped with delight when she saw Johnny. He ran, and she leapt the last few steps into his arms.

'Hello, pixie,' he muttered into her hair. 'I hear you've been having huge adventures. Lone bike rides and falling into rapids, very Enid Blyton. You'll have to let me come with you next time.'

'Daddy,' she pulled back from him, 'I'm – I'm sorry about this morning, about not seeing you.' Her voice cracked and it broke my heart. I don't imagine it did much for Johnny's, either. He held her gently by her shoulders, gazing at her.

'Don't be silly, Claudes. That wasn't your fault, it was mine. Why should you have to choose between me or your friends? You should be able to have both – see me when you get up in the morning and then go out to play with your friends. I've done this to you, it's my fault. I made you choose.'

I found myself nodding boisterously behind him and had to arrest my neck muscles. Steady. Don't want your head to drop off into the flowerbed, Livvy. All the same, it sounded encouraging, didn't it? Sounded like he'd seen a degree of light. Perhaps this misadventure of Claudia's was going to have a little morality tale at the end of it? Be a bit of a catalyst for a happy ending? Encouraged, I followed them inside, but as they made to go into the kitchen, Johnny turned.

'Livvy, d'you mind if I have a quick word with Claudes? I just want to get one or two things straight in her mind.'

I blinked. 'Sure! No, gosh, good heavens, you go ahead. You, um, go in there and I'll – well, I'll wait in the sitting room.'

They disappeared within and the door closed.

I stared at the white, panelled door. Frowned. What? I wondered. What was it he wanted to get straight in her mind? And what did he want to say that he couldn't say in front of me? That he'd fallen out of love with Mummy? That he was sorry if it inconvenienced her, but that was what happened to grown-ups sometimes? Their sudden closeness surprised me too. I felt very . . . well, excluded. More so, I suppose, because it hadn't always been thus. Claudia had always been very much a mummy's girl. I vividly remembered a time when she was about three, in London, and Paddy, our beloved tabby cat, died. I'd dreaded telling Claudia, but finally had sat her down and broke the news. Oh dear, what a shame, she'd said, before skipping out to play. I'd been surprised but relieved, but the following morning, had found her sobbing inconsolably in our cleaning lady's lap, because Vera had said how sad it was about Paddy. 'But, darling,' I'd said, dropping to my knees beside her, 'I told you yesterday. I told you Paddy was dead!' She'd raised an anguished, tear-stained face. 'I thought you said Daddy!' Johnny had roared with laughter when I'd told him, but I'd noticed, thereafter, a tendency to come home from work slightly earlier, to make it through the door at bathtime, to read her a story at bedtime, and I suppose it had worked. At some stage, they'd bonded closely, only for Johnny to test that bond now, some seven years later.

I inched a few steps closer to the door, inclining my head towards it. I could hear muffled voices within, but nothing clearly. Then I went the whole hog and put my ear to it. Johnny said something about loving her just as much as ever, and Claudia said something I couldn't make out, and then Johnny said in a loud voice, 'Livvy, d'you want to come in?'

I gasped and leapt away.

'We can see your feet, Mummy,' explained Claudia. 'Under the door.'

'Oh! Oh no..I – I was just wondering if you wanted a cup of tea?'

'Well, we can make it ourselves, can't we?' came back Claudia, witheringly. 'We're the ones in the kitchen.'

'Of course, darling, sorry,' I trilled back. Crikey, she sounded so – chilly. Still cross, I suppose, for humiliating her in front of Sebastian.

I crept shamefully off to the garden to wait; picked up

my trug from a bench. Well, they could only be talking about me, couldn't they? I reasoned bitterly. What else was there to talk about? I went to the end of the garden and buried myself in the herbaceous border, savaging a piece of ground elder that had seeded itself around the delphiniums, taking advantage of my abstraction these past few weeks. As I straightened up to chuck it on the lawn, I saw movement through the caravan window. I squinted. Ah, so Lance had made himself scarce in there, had he? Well, that showed a degree of tact, anyway. In the dim, distant past of all of three hours ago, I seemed to recall that he was supposed to be my lover, my boisterous young lothario, but in the light of a missing child, I didn't think having a spare lothario about the place was necessarily a good thing. I heard the back door open and crouched down again, busying myself amongst the earthworms where I belonged, waiting for them to come to me.

'I'll be off then, Livvy,' said Johnny from a short distance.

I gave a little jump, just to show I'd been totally absorbed. As I turned, though, his blue eyes held me. Squeezed my heart. He shaded them with his hand against the sun. I wiped my perspiring face with my hand and realised it was covered in mud. Yes, yet again, I thought bitterly, I'd dressed up for Johnny. Scratched and battered by brambles, and now covered in earth, I'd made myself utterly desirable. I thought longingly of the cream linen dress and my kitten-heeled shoes upstairs.

'Bye, then,' I said with a cheery grin. 'See you in a couple of weeks.' I went to go back to my border.

'Look,' he took a step closer, 'I'm just going to pop in and thank that chap down the road. It seems he did Claudia a really good turn.'

I swung back. 'Oh! Hang on, no, don't do that, Johnny!'

'Why not?'

Claudia strolled up beside him. I shot her a nervous glance. Had she . . . ? No, bless her, she clearly hadn't told him about the bellowing harridan episode.

'Oh, well,' I faltered, 'because –'

'Because Mum wants to. Don't you, Mum?' She eyed me beadily. 'We thought we'd go together.'

'Yes, that's it,' I breathed. 'Take some flowers, do it properly, you know.'

He shrugged. 'OK. But be sure you do, won't you?'

'Of course I will,' I bristled. God, anyone would think I was a child.

'Bye then.'

'Bye.'

He hesitated, and for an awful moment I thought he was going to kiss my cheek. Like social acquaintances. I quickly bent down to collect my trug, concentrating on separating weeds from stones. By the time I'd straightened up, he was on his way – back up the lavender walk, through the rose arbour and round the side of the house. I watched him go. Claudia had gone with him, and I could hear her now, clattering about in the kitchen. I picked up my trug and walked slowly back to the house. Whatever happened, I thought, I mustn't ask her what Johnny had said in the kitchen. That would be an intrusion on her privacy and on her relationship with her father. I put the trug by the back door, breezed in, humming a little tune, and put the kettle on. She was reading an old *Beano* annual at the kitchen table.

'All right now, darling?'

'Yes, thanks.'

My hand went for the tea caddy. I paused. Turned. 'Um, Claudes?'

'Hmm?'

'What did Daddy say?'

She glanced up from her book. 'What?'

'You know, your, um – little chat.'

'Oh. Oh, just stuff about wishing it didn't have to be this way. Hoping I'd understand when I was a bit older. The usual bollocks.'

'Claudia!'

'Sorry. Just a bit fed up with it all at the moment.'

She got up and left the kitchen. I dithered for a moment, then hastened after her into the sitting room.

'Claudes, how about helping me make some pancakes? And then when we've eaten them, we could trough our way through a packet of biscuits in front of the telly!'

'No thanks, I'm going upstairs. I've got some home-work to do.' She reached for her book bag behind the sofa and brushed back past me again. I bit my lip.

'Claudia, I'm sorry. I've said I'm sorry. I was worried about you, that's all.'

She turned. 'Well, I'm worried about you, Mum. You really lost it today. You've got no brakes.'

'Of course I've got brakes!'

'You haven't, you're out of control. I was talking to Lucy's mum about it.'

'Claudia!'

'No, she was really helpful.'

'Was she indeed!'

'Yes, she said that she got a bit unhinged after her last baby. Said maybe you should take up yoga.'

'Yoga!'

'Yes, Lucy's mum does yoga and she's really calm. Really tuned in.'

Is she, by jingo? Well, she wasn't so flipping tuned in today. I nodded thoughtfully, though, pretending to take it on board. At least it wasn't the men in white coats. 'Right, yoga. Yes, that's sounds fun. I might look into that.'

'You should. Lucy's mum can put her ankles behind her ears.'

Diverted that this should calm me down and not have me screaming for the fire brigade to come and unhook me, I nodded again. 'Right. And . . . you think that might help me, Claudes? Feet behind the ears?'

She shrugged. 'It might, you never know. Might stop you overemoting.'

My mouth hung open as she turned and mounted the stairs. Overemoting? Christ! She was ten! Bloody ten! Where was she *getting* all this? I gazed incredulously after her.

Later that evening I rang Molly.

'Where's it all coming from?' I whispered, aware that Claudia was still working upstairs. 'Do the teachers feed them this rubbish, d'you suppose?'

'I blame the media. You only have to open one of those innocent-looking *My Little Twinkle* comics to find it's full of psychobabble. "Dear Tina, I feel a bit depressed at the thought of having to do my homework . . . Dear Jessica, have you thought of getting some counselling?" Honestly, they'll all have disappeared right up their backsides by the time they're teenagers. Why's she so concerned about you, anyway?'

I confided the details of my hideous day, graphically depicting the ghastly Sebastian episode.

'Well, I'm not so sure you weren't right,' she said slowly. 'In fact, I'm not convinced you didn't do exactly the right thing. I mean, why did he take her back to his house? Why not your house? It's just as close. And I don't like the idea of her handing over her clothes to him, either.'

'Don't you?' I yelped, reaching for a cigarette.

'No, but having said that, I'm quite prepared to accept that I'm totally paranoid and I've only got like this since I've had children. If you'd told me that story three years ago I'd have said, "Gosh, what a perfectly sweet, helpful man," but now I've got Henry I see paedophiles at every corner. I can't read him *Fireman Sam* without wondering if Sam's waving his hose about in a rather provocative manner. It's biological, I'm afraid. Once you've had children all that a-stranger-is-a-friend-I've-yet-to-meet crap goes right out the window. A stranger is a potential child molester. It's symptomatic of our overprotective natures.'

I sighed. 'Perhaps, but you should have seen me, Molly. I was like a mad woman in there. I reckoned if I'd had a knife in my hand instead of a rake, I'd have stabbed him with it.'

'So he was lucky then. Just the tea and biscuits. I really don't know what you're worrying about, Livvy, and I'd certainly forget about the flowers. That might put all sorts of ideas into his head. In fact, I wouldn't even bother to apologise in person. Just pop a little note round saying you're sorry if you got the wrong end of the stick. But make sure you keep that "if" in there. Because if ever I heard an iffy story, it's this one.'

Chapter Thirteen

The builders were back the following morning, and with them, an uncharacteristic air of doom and gloom. As they unloaded their spluttering, terminal lorry and dragged in the usual hundredweight of cable, copper piping, planks, bags of plaster, bolts and brackets with which to decorate my kitchen, their faces were long, their voices muted.

'What's up?' I whispered to Mac as I staggered in with a steaming tray of tea, the first of many morning cuppas.

Mac glanced round to make sure we were alone. 'Alf's wife's left him,' he confided soberly. 'He got back on Friday night to find a note on the kitchen table. Said she'd had enough of him, and don't try to find her 'cos she ain't never coming back.'

'No!' I set the tray down, aghast. 'Vi? But they're on the phone night and day. I thought they adored each other!'

'Oh, he adored her orright – couldn't please her enough – but she bossed him around somefing chronic. She always had the upper hand, like, and he's done as he's told all his bleedin' life, and now she's up and left him, ungrateful bitch. Gone to Spain.'

'Spain!'

Mac took his cap off and scratched his head. 'Yeah, well, she's always bin on about wanting to live on the Costa Brava, run a bar an' that, sit in the sun wiv all those fat gits wiv gold chains, knockin' back jugs of Sangria, but

229

Alf's never bin for it. He won't go furver than Margate, Alf won't – needs his family about him, and who can blame him? She don't give a monkey's about anyone's family, though. She's a right cold fish, that Vi, and I've always said so. She don't need nobody, never even wanted kids, and that's not natural, is it?'

'Oh, so there are no children?'

'Nah. Alf would have loved 'em, dotes on his nieces and nephews, he does, but she wouldn't have it. She likes her own company and she's welcome to it. Got it in spades now, hasn't she? Fancy buggerin' off just like that! Took the video an' all.'

'Gosh, poor Alf.'

I glanced across at his huge sorrowful bulk as he passed by the window, head bent, water sloshing from his buckets.

'So, is he very –'

'Gutted,' said Mac, averting his head politely and spitting dexterously to the concrete floor. 'Totally gutted. He's given his life to that cow and then she ditches him wivout so much as a by-your-leave. Silly tart.'

Spiro sidled up beside us with a piece of skirting board on his shoulder. 'I theenk she go with another man,' he confided. 'I smell rats. I don't theenk she go alone, I theenk she go off to do Olé olé and Viva España with a toy of a boy.'

'You may well be right, Spiro, my son,' agreed Mac soberly. 'She's certainly stupid enough, but then I can't see any man in his right mind wantin' to give her one. She's built like a bleedin' matchstick, not an ounce of flesh on her, tits like teabags. Reckon she'd snap in two as soon as look at you, but then my Karen says she had enough black undies in her bottom drawer to sink a battleship, and that Bernie Mundy down the offy said she was always in there buyin' her Baileys and giving him the eye, so who's to say, eh?' He blew his nose, took a peek at the contents of the handkerchief, and replaced it in his overall pocket.

'He so sad,' muttered Spiro, shaking his head. 'He cry in the lorry today.'

'No! Oh, Spiro, how awful!'

Spiro got out his hanky. 'He say his life is over.' He blew his nose noisily. 'He say – he say that now it all gone pear-shaped he has nothing left to live for, and I theenk to myself – oh, bleeding heck, eet is just like poor Mrs McFarl-len. All alone and lonely weeth nothing to live for either!'

Crikey. I blinked.

'And he say he want to die. He say – he say – oooooh!' Emotion overwhelmed him, the woolly hat came off and he dabbed at his streaming eyes. 'And you all so nice!' he sobbed.

I patted his shoulder. 'Come on now, Spiro, you're diluting the tea. Be a good chap and –'

'Get a grip boy,' growled Mac. 'We've got a lot to do today. I don't want any fairies sobbin' down their tutus. I want that concrete plinth put in for that Aga toot sweet and I want it six by four, an' I want that stove plumbed in by tomorrow, no messin'. Now get mixing, Zorba my son. We've got work to do!'

Spiro hastily replaced his hat and shuffled over to the mixer. Through the window I could still see Alf, bent over his plaster palette outside. I went to see him, approaching tentatively. His face was hidden as he concentrated on stirring the soggy pink mess with a trowel.

'Alf, I'm so sorry,' I said gently. 'Mac told me.'

He nodded, but I could tell speech was going to be difficult. Even more so than usual. He didn't raise his head and kept on mixing. I was about to tiptoe away, when finally he managed, gruffly: 'You're orright,' which I'd come to learn was East London for anything from, 'No, thank you, I don't take sugar in my tea,' to, 'Yes, please, I'd adore to be King of the Pygmies.'

I left them to it. Mac seemed to be marshalling his troops with a power and a vigour hitherto unseen, barking out orders and strutting about like a mini masonic tyrant. Lance appeared from the caravan and fell in seamlessly, greeting me with a low 'Have you heard?' – to which I nodded back my sympathies, and then the three of them scurried around under Mac's direction, hammering, mitring and plastering like whirling dervishes. Presumably Mac thought that if he got them working flat out it would take their minds off their troubles, and who was I, the mere recipient of their labours, to disagree?

Work had been occupying my mind lately, too. I was dimly aware that I'd promised both myself and Angie I'd write to the Physic Garden, offering my services. The trouble was, though, that every time I sat down to draft a letter, I'd wonder why on earth they should even consider me, rather than the hordes of fresher, cheaper, younger graduates who flooded out of Cirencester's gates each year, or even the older, far more experienced gardeners whose seamless careers were uninterrupted by childbirth, house restoration, or even marriage restoration. And what about all those smart young London gardeners, fingers on the horticultural pulse, who exhibited at Chelsea and charged a grand for a morning's consultation? Why me? At this point I'd gulp insecurely, doodle a bit, sigh even more, gaze out of the window, screw up the paper and finally wander out to my own little patch, where, I told myself, at least I was improving my practical skills, even if I was only deadheading the lilies or restraining the Rambling Rector from strangling Madame Hardy.

On this particular morning, I dutifully sat down for the obligatory doodle, sigh, gaze and screw, but as I got up guiltily from the writing desk, pushed open the French windows and ambled out into the blazing sunshine to till my soil, it occurred to me to wonder why on earth I would even *want* to slog to London on an overcrowded commuter train, and spend a back-breaking morning in a stifling greenhouse tilling someone else's soil, before slogging back home again? It wasn't as if I needed the money – although of course it would come in handy. No, it was the independence, I told myself sternly. I knelt down amongst the frilly and abundant *Alchemilla mollis* and tugged at a dandelion root. Who was it said that work was the only dignity? Scott Fitzgerald, or someone equally dissolute, but he had a point and, let's face it, I was pretty short on personal dignity at the moment. I shuddered as I remembered yesterday's débâcle. And of course the ability to write my own cheques without drawing on the joint account would certainly show Johnny. Show him I was making my own way. And then, of course, there was the stimulation, I thought wearily, reaching for my trowel. I sat back on my heels for a moment. Yes, let's not forget the sodding stimulation, eh? What did that really mean, I wondered? When people bandied that word around? Did it mean talking to people? Because I could talk to my friends, who were far more intelligent than a lot of the gardeners I knew. Using my brain, then? Well, surely a good book would do more for the grey matter than pricking out dahlias? No, what it really meant, I decided, was no longer feeling guilty about doing nothing. It gave one a badge to wear, a tick to put by one's name. Olivia McFarllen has a job. She occupies her time with more than her house, her garden and her child. She stood up and she was counted. And, of course, at the moment, it was more important than ever that I was seen to have a life, because I couldn't even include 'getting my husband's supper and ironing his shirts' in the domestic equation, as Claudia had so succinctly pointed out to me on the way to school this morning.

'Mrs Chandler's got a job now,' she'd informed me sternly, 'and Mr Chandler was really impressed by that. Said it was more than his increasingly expensive strumpet had.'

I cast my mind back, at the same time trying not to go up a lorry's backside. 'Mrs Chandler? Chloe's mother?'

'That's it.'

'Whose husband left her?'

'Yep.'

'But . . . wasn't she the one that went off with some loose-limbed youth from B&Q, whereupon Mr Chandler came back with his tail between his legs?'

'Ah yes, he did,' she twisted excitedly in her seat to face me, 'but you see it's all changed now. Mr Chandler *did* come back, but then his strumpet —'

'Must you say that word, Claudia?'

'Yes, I like it – his Strrrr-umpet,' she trilled, 'mounted a

234

huge campaign, cycled past his factory gates with her shirt undone and no pants on, that sort of thing – and he went back to her.'

'Right,' I'd said weakly, negotiating a roundabout. 'So, then Mrs Chandler got herself a job, in – don't tell me –'

'B&Q.'

'Naturally.'

'And now she's selling rotary saws and that type of thing, and all on commission, Mum. Chloe said she made an extra eighty-four pounds last week.'

'Excellent,' I said faintly. 'And, um, her young man?'

'Oh, well, Mrs Chandler claims she got bored with him and gave him the boot, but Chloe says she was sitting in the back garden with him only last week and Mrs Chandler came out in a bikini to sunbathe looking *really* hideous – you know, flabby white tummy, saggy underarms and those spongy bits on the tops of the legs, like you've got, Mum, only much worse – and Chloe said that Len – that's his name – took one look, made a face like he was going to be sick, and legged it. They've never seen him since.'

'But . . .' I struggled with this information as I swung into the school gates, 'but surely he'd seen Mrs Chandler before?' I was dimly aware I shouldn't be having this conversation with my ten-year-old daughter, but couldn't quite stop myself.

'What, you mean nudey?'

'Well, yes.'

'No, because Chloe says they always did it with the lights off.'

'How would Chloe know?'

'Because she peeped through the keyhole, der-brain.

Crikey, Mum, get real. We've got to get *some* sort of sex education before we go up to the upper school. If it wasn't for Alice Cassidy's parents, who are practically naturists and wander round the house naked and do it in the conservatory, we wouldn't know *what* was going on.'

I pulled to a halt in the car park. 'Well, three cheers for Mr and Mrs Cassidy. Sorry Daddy and I were never so obliging. I hope you don't feel too deprived.'

She shrugged as she got out. 'I'll survive. Oh – it's OK, Mum,' she said quickly as I went to get out my side, 'I'm a bit late so I'll just run in. Oh, by the way, that letter's for Sebastian. Can you put it through his door? Plus the one from you, too,' she added meaningfully.

I glanced down at the note she'd left on her seat as she scampered off. So. My daughter no longer wanted me to accompany her to the classroom door. Didn't want me to make a fool of myself, no doubt. A bit of a loose cannon, these days, Claudia's mum, and, of course, what with her husband's mistress up there, who knows *what* she might do. I sighed and picked up the letter. It was sealed, of course; show me a child who doesn't lick an envelope. I turned it over and wondered what she'd written. Sorry about my barking mother? She really should get out more, sell a few rotary saws and cycle round St Albans with no pants on? I sighed again, put it down. No, she was right. I must pop it through his door, and add sincere apologies of my own, too. I riffled around in the glove compartment for a bit of paper. No point going home and agonising over the Basildon Bond, I'd write one in the car right now, on any old scrap of paper, pop it in, and then that would be the end of it.

I finally found an old shopping list on the floor under my seat, scribbled out 'Domestos, butter, Immac', and wrote on the back –

Dear Sebastian,

I'm so sorry. What must you think of me? I got totally the wrong end of the stick yesterday, made a complete fool of myself and couldn't be more ashamed.

Best wishes,
Olivia McFarllen

There. Short, gushing, and to the point. Perfect.

On the way home, I stopped outside his house and ran up the steps. I slipped Claudia's note through the letter-box, and was about to add mine to the doormat when I suddenly realised I was being watched. I glanced down and saw the mother, her toothy, ferrety face pale and watchful, staring up at me from the basement window below. I hesitated. My note wasn't actually in an envelope, and she'd most certainly read it, and then what on earth would she think? Why was I so ashamed? So foolish? What stick, exactly, had I grasped the wrong end of? And on a scrappy old shopping list, too. No no, I thought hastily, I'd go home, write it out again, do it properly and then drop it by later.

I tucked it in my pocket and glanced down nervously. I couldn't actually see her now, but I was sure she was still there, hovering about in the shadows. I hurried back down the steps, feeling those sharp grey eyes in my back all the way to my car. I shivered as I got in. Perhaps Molly was right. Perhaps there was something 'iffy' about that whole setup there; perhaps she was his accomplice or something. She certainly looked like she could have been an embalmer in a previous life. I shot off down the road, scurried up the drive to my house, ran in, and shut the door fast behind me. Home.

The day limped on, and by mid-afternoon, the temperature had hit the nineties. Claudia was dropped home by a friend, and lay in a cool bath for half an hour before taking to her bedroom. I, meanwhile, wilted restlessly on the terrace, listening to the sounds of banging and crashing as the boys ploughed on. At one point Lance and Spiro beetled off for more supplies, but other than that, relentlessly, unceasingly, through the heat, with no radio blaring, no chatting, no whistling, no breaks for tea, no stops to execute the perfect roll-up on an upturned milk crate – on they toiled. I was astonished, but deeply impressed. Later, when they'd finally drooped back to the caravan to collapse, I crept in to inspect their handiwork. I was even more impressed. Golly, I thought as I gazed around in wonder, all this in one day. Just shows what they can do when they really pull their fingers out.

The flapping blue tarpaulin had gone, and in its place, the ceiling and walls were pink and plastered. The soggy concrete floor had also been replaced, by a gleaming, reclaimed wooden one. At the far end of the room, the huge, concrete plinth was in situ, ready for the Aga to be enthroned, and around the perimeter of the room, some of Lance's carefully sculpted oak cupboards were already in place. I scurried across the shiny floor and pulled out a drawer. Smooth as silk. I spun around, a delighted smile slowly spreading across my face. My goodness, yes, it was really taking shape, and it was perfect! Just perfect. And just as I'd imagined, too. Finally, after all these months, it was beginning to come together.

The old sash windows had been restrung, deep skirting boards were nailed in and ready to be painted, granite work surfaces were propped up waiting to be fixed, but what really surprised and pleased me was that I could get pleasure from it. Yes, even without Johnny here beside me, admiring it too, it made me smile, and I'd thought that would be impossible, you see. Thought it was all tied up with him, this dream house, and I was astonished to realise it might not be. Was I actually getting stronger then, I mused as I wandered around, or was it just time healing, as people so often – and thoughtlessly – told one it would? Perhaps a bit of both.

By way of celebration, I went back to the old scullery, poured myself a glass of chilled Sancerre from the fridge, and strolled out to the garden, making for the cedar tree where I always sat on a summer's evening. Claudia was tired and had gone to bed early, and all was quiet. The garden seemed to breathe at me, to open its arms, and I sank contentedly into its embrace, the air heavy with the musky whiff of tobacco plants and trailing jasmine. Soft cascades of broom brushed my skirt as I sauntered down to the seat beneath the tree, but as I got close, I realised – damn. On the opposite side of the stream, directly in front of me, the lads had spilled out too. Out of their caravan and on to the grass, lying stretched out or propped up on their elbows. I hesitated. I could hardly sit here drinking just a few feet away, could I? Perhaps I should sit on the terrace?

But on the other hand, I wanted to sit here. I always did. And this was my garden, damn it. I sat, firmly. Mac turned and caught my eye. I raised my glass.

'Kitchen looks great!' I trilled merrily.

'Yep. It's coming along.'

Silence. I smiled inanely into my lap.

'You like yer war?' he ventured.

'Sorry?'

'I said, d'you like yer floor?'

'Oh yes, very nice!'

Lance glanced across, smiled. I smiled back. Looked down into my lap again. I shifted uncomfortably. Heavens, this was ridiculous. They were only a few feet away, and the whole point of sitting here was to gaze into the sylvan scenery, not at them.

I cleared my throat. 'Um, listen,' I called. 'This seems rather silly. D'you want to come across and have a celebration drink? There's some wine and beer in the fridge?'

It was as if I'd cast a magic spell. As if I'd snapped my fingers and – abracadabra – they were across. The stream was leapt – or in Spiro's case, waded – and in an instant they were beside me; sitting on the grass around my chair, grinning up at me like delighted pixies. Lance instantly became barman.

'Right, lads,' he said, rubbing his hands together, 'beer or wine, or shall I bring both?' He looked at me for confirmation.

'Please do,' I purred.

Christ, I felt like Lady Bountiful now, sitting here under my cedar tree with my faithful swains about me. I slid my bottom off the chair and shifted down to the grass. That's better, I thought, hugging my knees, chummily. Much less us and them.

Lance disappeared, only to reappear moments later with a tray of glasses, a bottle of wine wrapped in a fabric cooler that he'd found God knows where, a six-pack of cold Stella, and a huge bowl of Hula Hoops. Crikey, he really was Mr Fixit, wasn't he? I thought admiringly as he set it all down on the grass, and looking particularly attractive this evening in khaki shorts and a baggy white T-shirt. Clean, too, I noticed, as actually, I realised, glancing around, they all were. Did they have a power shower in that TARDIS of a caravan, as well as satellite TV and beds that came whizzing out of the wall? I must ask Claudia.

A moment later the air was filled with snapping and fizzing as ring-pulls were zapped back and a cork was popped, then the happy sound of contented glugging as Stella went down dry red necks, and a cumulative 'Aaaahh . . .' as the business of thirst was attended to. Even Alf looked slightly less wretched as he downed his can without troubling a glass, and lay down to shut his eyes.

'How is he?' I whispered to Lance.

He shrugged. 'He's OK. It's the shock more than anything, and I think that's starting to wear off. And he's not so bad here, you see, working with the boys. It's just at home. Empty kitchen, bedroom, you know.'

I took a slug of my wine. Oh yes, I knew. And how.

'Ees so very, very like you, ees it not, Meesis McFarllen?' said Spiro, on my other side, muscling in on the conversation and warming to his theme again.

I groaned inwardly.

'And always it happen to the good people,' he mused. 'Nice people, smiley people, like you and Alf. He just like you, always if I ask – can I have a ciggy, Alf? – he say yes, or – can I borrow radio, Alf – he say yes, yes!'

'Well, maybe that's the problem, Spiro. We're too free with our yesses.'

'And you know,' he hissed in my ear, 'he only forty-eight! Ees incredible, no? And he still very fit and able to do things.' He smiled at me, flashing perfect white teeth, and suddenly, I saw the way Spiro's mind was going. Alf, my fit and able labourer, my eighteen-stone, glass-eyed, flatulent of bottom and gushing of armpit bricklayer, was being offered in my general direction. Alf, good Alf, *smiley* Alf, Alf, the man who liked to say yes, was being proffered for my delectation by his friend, the woolly-hatted, perpetually sobbing Greek.

I leant towards him. 'No, thank you, Spiro,' I said firmly.

Lance stifled a giggle beside me.

Spiro looked puzzled. 'You no like him?'

'Oh, no, I like him very much, but just not in that way, savvy?'

He sighed, nodded. 'Savvy.' Then he paused. 'So ... perhaps you like the younger man, yes?' His eyes drifted past me to Lance. They sparkled excitedly. 'Perhaps you like –'

'Spiro,' I interrupted urgently, 'what I'd *really* like is another bottle of wine. Would you mind getting one, only this one seems to have mysteriously evaporated.' I waved the empty bottle in his face.

He sighed, took it resignedly, and got to his feet. 'OK. I go.'

'Attaboy,' grinned Lance, as Spiro retreated up the garden path. 'What you have to realise,' Lance went on in my ear, 'is that Spiro comes from an island called Mexatonia.'

'Where's that?'

'Exactly. No one's ever heard of it. It's a tiny disputed territory just off Albania. It's so minute that when the goat-herder dies, his widow automatically marries the fisherman instead. So instead of sex, cooking and mucking out the goats, it's sex, cooking and mending nets, that's all.'

'Right.' I nodded thoughtfully. 'So instead of sex, cooking and Eurobonds, I'd get sex, cooking and my plumbing sorted, is that it?'

'Exactly.'

We giggled companionably, and for a moment I felt ridiculously, absurdly happy; lolling about here with my boys, sharpening our wits, cracking a few jokes, the mayflies buzzing about us, dancing in the low beam of the evening sun. I glanced contentedly about me. Alf was beginning to exhibit signs of sleep. Another can of Stella had done its worst, and he was snoring softly now.

'What happened to his eye?' I asked Mac, who had stealthily usurped the Greek beside me.

'Our stepfather stabbed him wiv some scissors when he was a nipper.'

'Good God!' I sat bolt upright. Felt sick. 'How *terrible*!'

'Yeah, dreadful. I was six at the time, and he was about four. We bofe went off to boarding school after that.'

'Boarding school. Heavens, I wouldn't have thought . . .' I tailed off, about to say – you'd be able to afford it.

'Barnardo's,' he offered helpfully.

'Oh! Right.' I took a slug of wine. Fell silent for a moment. 'Gosh, Mac, you and Alf, you've – well, you've had a pretty traumatic time then.'

He shrugged. 'Could be worse. We've always had each ovver, and we've always looked out for each ovver.'

'You mean, you've always looked out for him,' Lance put in softly.

'Yeah, well, you do, don't you? If you're brovers. Anyway, it weren't that bad. We could have been brung up in Kosovo, couldn't we? Could have had bombs dropping on our beds, could have had –'

'Coo-ee!'

Any extension of this incisive, sociopolitical discussion was brought to an abrupt halt by a loud trill. We all turned in its general direction and saw Nanette, up on my terrace, on the steps of the French windows, wobbling about on pink high heels, wearing the skimpiest of miniskirts, and waving a bottle of champagne.

'Is it a party? Can I come down? I've brought my own bubbly!'

Well, she was coming anyway. Before the 'Of course!' was out of my mouth, she was teetering across the lawn towards us.

'I spotted you all out of the bathroom window,' she called, 'having a little drinky, and I thought – well, I'm damned if I'm going to celebrate up here on my own. Why not go and join them?'

'Why not indeed,' I said, getting up to greet her and give her a kiss. 'But what are you celebrating, Nanette?'

'Oh!' she gushed, clasping her hands together, eyes shining. '*Too* exciting. Roger's asked me to marry him!'

'Oh Nanette, that's wonderful!' I hugged her.

'Isn't it just? And it was such a surprise! There I was, on my hands and knees polishing the parquet floor because Brenda makes such a frightful mess of it, and he just walked in the front door and popped the question! Then he said, "Nanette, I can never resist a woman who goes down on her knees for a man, so while you're down there . . ." Isn't he awful! Oh Lord,' she clasped a jewelled hand to mouth, 'and here I am pouring out all my personal effects, and we haven't even been properly introduced!'

'Sorry, Nanette.' I turned hastily. 'Um, well, you've probably seen these boys around because they're my builders.'

'I have indeed,' she purred, 'but I haven't seen this one.' She plucked admiringly at Lance's sleeve.

'Ah, well, this is Lance, he's quite new, and this is Mac, his father, who's the foreman, and Spiro from Greece, and Alf, who's sleeping it off on the grass.'

'Nanette,' she purred, 'as in Newman, but I don't have to do the washing-up!' She gave a tinkly laugh as the boys regarded her blankly. 'I say, this is all so thoroughly modern of Olivia, isn't it?' she beamed at them. 'All socialising together? So egalitarian, hmm? I do think you're lucky to have an employer like this!'

'And I think you're lucky to have any teeth!' beamed back Mac, quick as a flash, but as she blinked, uncomprehendingly, Lance stepped in quickly.

'Er, can I open that bottle for you, Nanette?'

'Oh, thank you, young man, and bring me a glass too, if you would.'

'Of course,' said Lance, his mouth twitching as he turned.

'Now he's *nice*, Olivia,' she whispered to his not quite retreating backside. 'For a bit of rough, I mean. Obviously he's not in the same league as Roger, but he's quite nicely spoken. You could do worse, you know.'

'Jesus.' I raked my hand despairingly through my hair.

She frowned. 'Sorry, have I said something?'

'No, it's just – well, everyone seems intent on . . . Never mind. Sorry, Nanette. Tell me about Roger. When are you getting married?'

'Christmas,' she said happily, 'just a quiet little ceremony, we thought, except that of course he is Jewish, so we might have to stamp our feet a bit and pin money on our clothes or whatever they do.'

I laughed. 'Sounds fun.'

'Did you know?' she pounced. 'I mean, could you tell?'

'What?'

'That he was Jewish?'

'Er, no, but then I've never really thought about it.'

'Oh yes, he is, frightfully.' She nodded. 'You can tell by the way he parks in The Crescent, just leaves it slap bang in the middle of the road. And of course his mother's an absolute nightmare, but then they always are, aren't they? And *her* mother, who's barely alive, is even worse and still speaks with a ridiculous Polish accent, although I swear she puts it on. But I do love their warmth and culture, don't you? I mean, I think they're pretty much accepted over here now, don't you?'

I frowned. 'Who, the Poles?'

'No, the Jews!'

I looked at her in astonishment. 'Well, of course they are, Nanette!' I spluttered.

'No, no, just checking,' she said quickly, 'only I *am* prepared for people to be a tiny bit – you know – funny. After all, it is a mixed marriage, and you'd be amazed how narrow-minded some people can be, still thinking they're a load of tight-fisted, big-nosed –'

'Um, where is Roger?' I interrupted, looking round nervously. Heaven forbid he should overhear his bride's views on his chosen people. 'Is he coming over?'

'Oh no, he's had to go to some sales conference or other with a load of men in brown suits, too dull for words. You know, it always amazes me how interesting Roger is when he works with such dreary people – Thank you, young man.' She beamed this last up at Lance as he handed her a drink. She patted the grass beside her. 'Now, come and sit beside me and tell me how you know Olivia.'

'I work for her. I'm a carpenter.'

'Of course you are, I keep forgetting! You simply don't look like one, that's all! He's very like Malcolm, don't you think, Olivia?'

She leant back to survey him with narrowed eyes as he dutifully sat beside her.

'He's nothing like Malcolm!' I spluttered, and was about to expand on their striking physical differences, when I realised Nanette had introduced Malcolm simply to inform Lance – softly, so he had to lean in close to hear – exactly where I'd gone wrong with Malcolm. I sighed and sipped my drink, pretending not to care, and actually, I discovered I didn't. Occasionally I'd catch snippets like: '. . . *rang* him, for God's sake, came on much too strong,' or, '. . . doesn't exactly *look* desperate, but you know, it starts to *show*.'

I smiled. Night was stealing up on us now. I leant back against the ancient cedar and gazed into the midnight-blue vault of the heavens. Stars were beginning to twinkle down, and I thought, with a wry smile, what an eclectic gathering we were in this warm, airless summer night: Alf, fast asleep, curled up in the foetal position, thumb practically in his mouth, his face sad, even in slumber; Mac, beside him, quietly sipping his beer, watching over his brother, half his size but with twice his brain power – who knows what horrors they'd been through together? Spiro, far from home, and far from his wife, who perhaps even now was standing at her open doorway in her village, her baby in her arms, gazing up at the same stars but in a different sky; Nanette, from Dagenham, who'd pulled herself up from her roots by her bra straps, who thought that keeping a man and her figure was a sufficient lifetime accomplishment, but who'd fallen in love with a man who every nerve and sinew of her narrow-minded, prejudiced body resisted; and beside her, Lance, blond, beautiful, and generous of spirit, who was letting her flirt and prattle on, instinctively knowing that Nanette was one of those people for whom a response is not important, just an inert body, and then, of course, there was me . . .

After a while, Lance stood up, stretched.

'Night, all.' He raised his hand and wandered off towards the bridge, back to the caravan. I watched him go with regret. Breaking up the party, eh, just as I was beginning to enjoy myself. Nanette seemed peeved too, and gave a little wriggle of her buttocks, a regrouping gesture.

'I'm going to take you shopping,' she hissed, still watching Lance, but leaning against me now, mouth drooping dramatically at one corner. Her eyes were glazed and I realised she'd drunk most of her bottle herself. 'I came through your kitchen just now and saw your bra in the laundry basket. Nobody's going to be driven crazy by that, Olivia. What you need is one of these.' She pulled down her top and shoved her well-upholstered bosom under my nose. 'Plunge and lift, see? Not squash and separate. Get a grip, Olivia. I'll take you to Pollyanna's in Harpenden next week.'

She prattled on about silks and pads and gussets, but she was right, I mused, as I watched Lance disappear through the caravan door, I must get a grip. Not on my underwear, but on my life. The door closed behind him and I looked beyond, into the dark horizon. The great weight that had been gathering for weeks in my chest was still there, but tonight, for the first time, I felt as if it wasn't sitting so tight, and that, were a strong gust to shift it westwards, clearer skies might follow. So was it in my making, I wondered, to shift it? Or would it take something more magnificent to send it scuttling away? The stars twinkled knowingly above, but I couldn't tell.

Nanette was still talking beside me. 'Roger says I should floss more,' she confided. 'Says it's terribly important.' I gazed out at the lilies on the riverbank. Tall, strong and optimistic. 'He has lovely gums,' she said dreamily.

Mac offered me a cigarette and I took it. I hardly smoked at all these days, yet I'd smoked like fury when Johnny left. Fury. That's what had gone. Or was going, anyway. I dragged the smoke down deep. It was strong, and made me feel slightly ill, but I liked the strange, groggy feeling, mixing with the scent of the tobacco plants and the warm night air. So, I wondered dreamily, was this just a transitory blurring of the senses I was experiencing? Or could it really be that, at last, my continued existence on this planet was not causing me quite so much dismay?

Chapter Fourteen

Imogen rang the following morning.

'Right, I take it you're still on for tonight?' she said briskly.

'What's happening tonight?'

'The concert, remember? In the Abbey?'

I put down the glass of Alka-Seltzer that had been half-way to my dehydrated lips and pulled my dressing gown around me.

'Oh. Right.' Well, yes. OK, somewhere, dimly, at the back of my fuddled mind, it rang a bell; something about rustling up a bit of crumpet for me. In fact I believed I might have even instigated it, but right at this moment I didn't feel quite so instigatory, if that was even the word. I leant against the scullery wall and rubbed my throbbing forehead.

'Um, listen, Imo, if it's all the same to you I had a bit of a heavy night last night,' I mumbled. 'Bit of a session. I wouldn't mind just curling up on the sofa with Joanna Trollope and a Horlicks.'

'Oh no you don't, and it's not all the same to me! It's taken me ages to organise this and get seats and every-thing, and Rollo's coming especially for you!'

'Rollo?' I blinked. I wasn't sure I could take anyone with a name like that entirely seriously. 'What, as in Rollo-me-over-lay-me-down-and-do-it-again?' I giggled. A mistake.

'That's the spirit!' she enthused brightly. 'Honestly, you won't be disappointed, Liv. He's totally gorgeous, and so excited about meeting you.'

'If he's so gorgeous,' I said suspiciously, 'why aren't you going out with him?'

'Oh, I know him far too well,' she said airily. 'Shared a house with him at Oxford. He's like a brother to me really. Come on, Livvy. You've got to come. Mum and Dad are dying to see you too.'

'Oh all right,' I caved in pathetically, although why anyone should be excited about meeting a recently separated, neurotic, single mother unless she'd lied through her teeth about me, I had no idea.

'Great. Parents' place for drinks at seven o'clock and we'll go on from there, OK?'

'OK, OK,' I agreed wearily. I could tell Imo was in no mood for shrinking violets.

Imogen's parents lived some distance from the city. Twenty minutes to the west, in fact, in a glorious, unspoilt part of the Hertfordshire countryside, where, on a summer's evening, with the swallows swooping and calling to each other across the valley, and with the wind in the right direction deflecting the low hum of the M25, you could almost believe you were in Devon. Tonight was just such a night, a sultry, misty evening, and as I drove up the bumpy track to their house, a low, rambling, Elizabethan farmhouse complete with beams and gables and tiny leaded lights glinting in the evening sun like shining eyes under the brows of the eaves, I couldn't help feeling a surge of pleasure. I'd spent a lot of time in this house as a child, had some happy times, and I was quietly confident it wouldn't have changed one jot.

Inside it had always been shabbily chaotic; very dark so one fumbled around a bit, and I remember following Imo around in our school uniforms, feeling along walls and stumbling over books, papers, and stacked-up files, all piled up on the stairs, to get to her bedroom. Imogen's father was the headmaster at the local boys' school and her mother an elegant, but slightly eccentric don at Oxford. The written word was a priority in this house, but food wasn't, and mealtimes here had always been something of an eye-opener for me and Molly. In the first place nothing was prepared, nothing cooked. One was simply invited into the rather grubby kitchen to view the freezer and choose an individual M&S meal, which Mrs Mitchell then shoved in the oven. So, for example, I might be having a chicken Kiev, beside Mr Mitchell who was tucking into salmon en croute, opposite a brother demolishing a lamb biriani, and another brother with turbot in a white wine sauce. Sometimes Mrs Mitchell decanted them from their foil containers, and sometimes she didn't, depending on how the mood took her. Reading was pretty much mandatory, though, and Imo, her brothers and her parents would all drift to the table with whatever happened to be clasped in their hands – anything from Kierkegaard to *The Hobbit* – prop it up against a handy pepperpot, and munch away distractedly. I'm fairly sure this rule didn't apply if proper guests were present, but as a school chum of Imo's, I clearly didn't count. My mother, of course, had been horrified when I'd told her.

'You see what comes of overeducating children? They think they're all so flaming clever, but let's face it, it's no better than a telly supper!'

She had a point, but then my mother always had a point, and generally, a disparaging one. It sprang from insecurity, of course. I very much doubt if Jeffrey Archer had ever been propped up at the Mitchells' table.

As I walked up the path to the front door tonight, Ursula Mitchell, a tall, elegant, faded blonde with a rather hawklike nose, and wearing a bright red shot silk ensemble, was outside greeting her guests and directing them round to the terrace, where I realised drinks were being served by caterers to twenty or so people. Quite a party.

'Olivia!' She took both my hands in hers and swooped for a kiss from her great height. 'I'm *so* glad you came!'

'I'm glad too,' I smiled up at her, and I was. It was years since I'd seen these lovely people.

'Come and meet everyone,' she insisted, linking my arm in hers. 'I'm bored with standing sentry at the door so I'm going to show you off. You look simply marvellous, my dear, and I must say, your Rollo seems rather divine too. I hadn't met him properly before tonight, but I assure you, he's quite a dish!' She winked. 'So isn't that perfect?'

As she beamed conspiratorially at me I nervously smoothed down the cream linen dress which had finally got an outing but had creased disastrously in the car. My Rollo, eh?

'And Imo?' I asked, as I followed her through a wrought-iron gate, noticing her hair was quite grey at the back now, but that her ankles were still worth watching. 'Does she have a dish of the day?'

'Oh, my dear, haven't you heard?' She stopped, turned, and for extra emphasis, touched my arm confidentially with cold fingertips. 'The conductor, Hugo Simmonds! He's on the podium tonight and he's absolutely mad about her! He's been here for dinner a couple of times because Gerald got quite involved with the organisation of this concert, and d'you know, Olivia, I have to say he couldn't take his *eyes* off her!'

'I think quite a lot of men have that problem,' I remarked with a smile.

'Well, quite, but does she give them half a chance? No! They're all nuts about her and then they're lucky if they last two weeks! To be fair, the vast majority are no-hopers anyway, but I worry about her, Olivia. What's wrong with the child?' She frowned petulantly. 'And, you know, she's not getting any younger; time is marching on.'

'Mrs Mitchell! And you an ardent feminist – I'm shocked!' I laughed.

'Feminism be damned,' she grinned, taking my arm again, 'I'm a mother first and a feminist when it suits me, and it's Ursula, Olivia, although I know childhood habits die hard.' She sighed as we walked down the stone steps to the crowded terrace together. 'I *do* worry about her, though. She never seems to give anyone a chance, and Hugo *is* rather special. She'd be mad to pass him up. Darling, have a word if you can, would you? Tell her how scrummy he is?'

I laughed. 'I'll try,' I promised. 'Is he here?' I looked around.

'No no, he's limbering up with his baton at the Abbey. You'll see him later, and it's to be hoped that when she sees him strutting his stuff her heart will melt and – ah, now here we are – Imo! Imogen darling!'

She called to her daughter, who was talking to a tall, slim man on the other side of the terrace. Imo turned. Her pale, golden hair was piled up on her head with tendrils escaping and curling at the base of her neck, Grecian style. She wore a simple, black shift dress, pearls, was lightly tanned, and looked amazing.

'Livvy!' She came over, simultaneously catching the tall man's sleeve and dragging him with her. 'God, *fin*ally! I had a nasty feeling you were going to do a bunk. You look terrific, by the way.'

'Thanks,' I grinned, 'so do you.'

'Oh Livvy, this is Rollo. Rollo, Olivia McFarllen, who together with Molly Piper, who *should* be here but is predictably even later, is my dearest friend.'

I shook hands with him. 'Molly's coming?' I said delightedly. 'I didn't think this would be her sort of thing?'

'Of course it isn't, I bullied her into it. Told her a bit of culture would do her good instead of gormlessly watching *Friends* and *Frasier*, who she's beginning to believe *are* her friends, she's so welded to that sofa of hers. Anyway, I've got to go off and relieve Mum at the door, so I'm going to stop wittering on, dear hearts, and leave you both in peace. Toodle-oo!' And with that she gave a dinky little wave and off she skipped. Just like that.

I gazed after her. Blimey, don't make it too obvious, will you, Imo? And couldn't you at least have given us a starting point? This is Rollo, he's in conglomerates, or – even better – this is Rollo, he's an incredibly wealthy polo player?

'Imogen's tact is legendary, of course,' said the tall man, smiling down. 'She once had the hots for a friend of mine in the diplomatic service, but I told her she'd make a disastrous diplomat's wife. You can't just plonk John Prescott next to the King of Tonga, tell them they've got a weight problem in common and then swan off hoping for the best.'

I laughed. But first, I had to wipe my face. Because good-looking though Rollo undoubtedly was, with his toffee-coloured hair, which rather cunningly matched his toffee-coloured eyes, set wide apart in an endearingly boyish face – he had a problem. He spat. I took a discreet step backwards, lobbed up a social 'And what do you do?' and studied him closer.

Yes, it was the front teeth, I decided as he prattled away happily about the foreign office. Too big, and too far apart. Way too far, as Claudia would say. I reached for a canapé and made a mental note, as I munched and smiled politely, occasionally managing, 'Oh really?' out of the side of my mouth, and, 'Gosh, the South African desk, that must be interesting,' that Claudia must have as much orthodontic treatment as she needed, as soon as she needed it, whatever the cost. I didn't want her growing up with an impediment like this and, let's face it, it *was* an impediment. I reached for another canapé, a tray of which had been handily placed on a table beside me. God, I was starving. I really must make an effort to eat properly now I was on my own. Trouble was I couldn't be bothered, especially in the evening when – Bugger. He was gazing expectantly at me.

'Um, sorry?'

'I said, what do you do?'

'Oh! Oh nothing much.'

He raised startled eyebrows.

'I mean, nothing much now,' I hurried on. Crikey, I'd forgotten he was Imogen's friend and that 'nothing much' was tantamount to admitting you sucked worm's blood. 'I mean, I used to garden, you know, pre-children. Professionally, I mean. I used to do garden design.'

'Terrific!' he brayed. 'Gosh, I'd love to do something creative like that. You should keep your hand in. Did you ever do Chelsea?'

'Er, not as such.' I reached nervously for more food.

'Shame. Great mate of mine exhibited there every year, as well as at Hampton Court. You might know her actually – Saskia Soames?'

A giant prawn, centimetres to my lips, froze. Saskia Soames had had an unfortunate effect upon it. On top of the prawn, perched and glistening, sat a huge, shiny globule of saliva. I lowered it carefully.

'Er, no, I don't know her.'

'Oh, you must meet her, she's such a gas. I'm surprised actually, because Imo knows her. We must get you both together!'

'Yes, we must.' I looked round desperately for a handy dog, or a bin. Could I chuck it in the flowerbed? No, of course I couldn't.

'I'm sorry – you're eating,' he said, following my gaze, 'and I'm bombarding you with questions. Pop it in and I'll shut up for a minute.'

I gazed. Pop it in? Are you kidding? I stared at it hard. 'Is this fish?'

He peered at it, then up at me, incredulously. 'Yes, it's a prawn.'

'Is it? Heavens! I can't eat fish!'

'But – you've just eaten about six!'

'Have I? Good God, I'll come out in the most almighty rash tomorrow. All over!'

At this unattractive concept Rollo palpably flinched. 'Golly, poor you,' he muttered. 'Oh well,' he brayed, recovering, 'it's clearly my fault. I must have been distracting you! Disarming you, even! Ha, ha!'

'Yes, clearly!' Prat.

'Tell you what, I'll have it,' he offered, opening his mouth gallantly.

I didn't hesitate. In fact I more or less chucked it in, and then we both beamed delightedly as he munched away. There was something pleasingly apposite about it I felt, back to its maker, as it were. Suddenly my hand shot up.

'Molly!' Oh, the relief. 'You made it!'

'Finally,' she hissed, coming over and kissing me rather damply as she reached into her shirt to hitch up her bra strap. 'Bloody baby-sitter was late and then Henry sodding well threw up over me as I kissed him good night – do I stink?' she asked anxiously.

'No,' I promised, then realised she did. 'Here,' I handed her my bag. 'There's some Chanel No. 19 at the bottom, and do your other eye – you've only got one made up.'

'Have I? Damn. Thanks,' she muttered, grabbing the bag, and was about to scuttle off when she spotted Rollo, hovering territorially. She raised her eyebrows and shot me a quizzical glance.

'Oh! Sorry, Molly Piper, Rollo . . . ?'

'Somerset,' he offered toothily, complete with ocean spray. Molly flinched but, quick as a flash, I'd turned to kiss Hugh, her husband. All yours, Moll.

Hugh, small, clever, and very theatrical, was gazing about him at the crowd, blinking with mock wonder. 'People,' he muttered dreamily. 'People talking . . . socialising . . . yes, yes, I remember now, it's all coming back.' He sniffed his drink. 'Alcohol too.'

I giggled. 'You're not about to tell me you don't have a life any more, are you, Hugh?'

'Oh, but I don't, my love, I don't,' he said, putting an arm round my shoulders and leading me away. 'Just a pukey little toddler and a soon-to-be-podding wife, and wait till that one pops out: you won't see us for years. We'll come up for air, ooh, in about ten years' time I should think, when hopefully the world will still be turning and those who we chose to call our friends will still be out there, smiling and offering us a glass.' He gazed blankly into his champagne. 'You know, I really can't imagine why we all embark on this procreation lark in the first place, Livvy. Vanity, I suppose. An insatiable desire to recreate in our own image, and look where it gets us? Sunk in the mire of shitty despair.' He knocked back his glass in one go and smiled abruptly. 'You, on the other hand, dear heart,' he said, waggling his glass at me, eyes twinkling, 'seem to have it all worked out. You manage to make this whole childcare business look graceful and effortless, and all on your tod now, too, I gather. Tell me,' he added more gently, 'is it a mid-life crisis, or has he just gone blind? You've never looked lovelier.'

I smiled. 'He's a bit young for a crisis, isn't he, Hugh?'

'Lord no, everyone's doing things so much earlier these days. Life's become so accelerated, you see. Girls of eleven are having babies and sexually speaking one's finished at forty. Johnny's obviously doing a spot of panic-buying while he can still get it up, and making a total dick of himself in the process.' He grinned. 'His loss, not yours. Oh, excuse me, young man.' He grabbed a passing waiter. 'That was so delicious, I believe I'll have another.' He put his empty champagne glass on the tray, plucked another full one, and emptied it in one, smacking his lips. 'Yum yum.'

I giggled. 'Hugh, I'm not convinced this is quite the place to get plastered.' I glanced around at Ursula's cronies.

'Oh, but it is, my love, it is. Not only have we got all these stiffs to talk to here, but we've got the wretched concert to get through yet. If I drink myself to a standstill, with any luck I'll sleep through it. Oh, by the way, I'm armed.' He slipped a hand in his pocket and brought out a hip flask. 'Stick by me, kiddo, and you'll be OK.'

I giggled as Molly came charging up, still half made up. 'He spits!' she reported in horror.

'Doesn't he just?' I agreed.

'Bloody hell, don't I get enough bodily fluids at home without being subjected to more at a party?' She wiped her cheek. 'Outrageous! Is he supposed to be yours? What is Imo thinking of? Send him back!'

'Shh, he'll hear. Oh Christ – look out, we're being hounded.'

We smiled sociably as Ursula Mitchell bore down on us. She swooped, encircled our shoulders with bony arms, then confided in hushed tones, 'The seats *are* numbered, my dears, but it's better to get there early, otherwise it's such a crush. If you youngsters wouldn't mind making a move to the cars then I think the others will take the hint and follow. I just thought that if we got there in good time, Imogen might manage a few moments with Hugo, you see.'

Out of the corner of my eye I saw Imo, in no rush, still happily chatting away, and I wanted to say, 'Look, Ursula. Knowing Imo as we all do, don't you think that nothing is going to make her run a mile more than this sort of pressure?' But I didn't. She was happy and excited, and dreaming of a society wedding in New College Chapel, orange blossom tumbling from the pews. So instead I dutifully followed Molly and Hugh to the loo, to the coats, to the door, to the cars, and thence, to the Abbey.

Any qualms I had about venerable old cathedrals being used as venues rather than places of worship were quashed as I joined the glittering throng that waited outside to enter the Abbey. It looked fabulous, lit up and glowing in the clear night sky, and the chattering, excited crowd that jostled politely to get through the huge oak doors couldn't have been more appreciative, ooh-ing and ah-ing as they strained their necks to get a glimpse of the vast, vaulted ceiling. I suppose if The Man Himself were to burst through the double doors and demand to know what the devil we were doing, tanked up, bejewelled – armed, even, in Hugh's case – and awaiting entertainment, we might have had our work cut out convincing Him, but tonight I was happy enough to join the ranks of the great and the good – who were no doubt pious to a man, and who were out in force. I spotted the High Sheriff, the local MP, a brace of High Court judges with their wives, but also quite a few students, eager to hear the London Symphony Orchestra doing their stuff.

'Blimey, I had no idea,' muttered Molly, reading a poster as we went in.

'Me neither,' I admitted. 'No wonder it's so packed.'

As I went up the steps, dutifully escorting Rollo, I couldn't help noticing the young couple ahead of us. They were no more than seventeen probably, in duffel coats and college scarves, close, but shy, as they studied a programme together. He bent his head to hear what she was saying, as she, blushing into her straight fair hair, enthused falteringly about the pieces we were about to hear. He nodded, smiling, turned shining eyes on her, encouraging her. I felt a stab of pain. They were only just embarking, but already they'd found each other. And how lucky they were. For finding is everything.

In the area just within the doors, people milled about talking loudly, waving programmes above their heads to friends they'd spotted in the crowd, and despite frantic attempts of officials to try to guide them to their seats, there was a general unwillingness to move on. This was too much of a social event to hurry, too much of an occasion. With elbows tucked in, and taking tiny pigeon steps, our party gradually made its way through the chattering throng, with Ursula, beckoning us on madly from the front like a wild-eyed scout leader, keen to get front-row seats. As I nudged through – 'Excuse me, so sorry, oops, can I just squeeze through' – I stopped suddenly. The back of a woman's head, a few feet away to my right, looked terribly familiar somehow, but I just couldn't place her. I peeled off from Rollo for a minute, took a quick peek around the side – and gasped. Stopped dead in my tracks. It was my mother. Except that I hardly recognised her. Her face was lightly made up and shining as she smiled and chatted. She was wearing a peach linen coat dress with peach lipstick to match, and her hair, which had been lightened and subtly streaked, was swept off her face in waves, tucked behind her ears, before curling softly at the edges. At her throat was a turquoise necklace which matched the bracelet on her wrist, and, I noticed, the sparkling gems in her ears. There was no dark helmet of hair, no pale, dramatic make-up, no navy-blue shift dress, and not a pearl in sight.

'Mum!' My mouth, literally, hung open.

She turned. Saw me. 'Oh, hello, darling. I wondered if you'd be here.' She kissed my cheek. I stared. For a moment I simply couldn't utter. Then I untwisted my tongue.

'M-Mum – what are you doing here?'

'Hmm?' She looked surprised. 'Oh well, I was invited, of course!'

'Really?' I looked around. The women's group? Or the church perhaps. 'But, Mum, this isn't our church, so –'

'Oh no,' she laughed, 'no, not the church, darling. Howard asked me.'

'Howard?'

It was then that I realised there was someone standing right beside her, right by her arm. I just hadn't connected them. He was mid-fiftyish, tall, with a hint of a paunch, silver-grey hair and a moustache to match, and he was smiling proprietorially down at my mother.

'Howard, this is my daughter, Olivia.'

'Oh!' I gazed, shook his extended hand, but couldn't speak.

'At last,' he grinned. 'I've heard so much about you but, I must say, I was keen to meet the real thing. You get a great press from your mum. Talk about proud mother and all that!'

'Oh!' I said it again, gormlessly too, aware that my mouth was still open.

'Howard's a doctor,' offered Mum, helpfully. 'We met when I took my usual stack of old magazines into the hospital.'

He grinned. 'The nurses kept telling me about this glamorous lady who was keeping them, not only in English *Vogues*, but in French and Italian ones too. I'm ashamed to say they plotted our meeting in an orthopaedic waiting room and I was an entirely willing participant!'

I gazed. Don't say 'Oh' again, you moron, just don't. 'S-so you're a doctor then?' I stammered.

'Well actually, I'm a urologist.'

I racked my brains. 'Ears?'

He laughed. 'Not even close. If I said that renal canals were a speciality, would that help?'

'Oh! Yes, it would!'

We laughed. *Mum* laughed. Mum, who couldn't even mention a front bottom without pinched lips, was laughing at renal canals? I gaped at her. And the *peach* number! I just couldn't help it.

'Mum – the clothes!' I blurted out. 'I mean – I've never seen you in anything remotely like that, ever!'

She laughed. 'I know, isn't it strange? But Howard said

he couldn't be doing with all that navy blue. He bullied me out of it, said it reminded him of one of the sisters on his ward.'

'A particularly repressed one,' put in Howard, with a sly grin. 'Rumour has it she keeps a cane in the dispensary cupboard, to whip the other nurses into shape.'

I giggled. I loved him. Oh God, I loved him already.

'So what d'you think?' Mum glanced at me shyly and for a moment I thought she was asking about Howard. She smoothed down her coat.

'Gorgeous!' I enthused. 'I love it, Mum. You look fab! I just can't wait to tell Claudia. She won't believe it!'

She laughed, blushed a little too. 'Go on, darling, catch up with your party. I saw Imogen go past ages ago.'

I turned, realising that the rest had gone on, but that Rollo was still hovering, not exactly beside me, but quite close, studying a programme. I hesitated. No, I couldn't introduce him, not after Howard. It would be such an anticlimax.

'See you later, Mum.' I kissed her warmly and beamed at Howard. 'Goodbye, *so* good to meet you.'

'You too,' he smiled, and I'd swear he winked too.

'Sorry, Rollo,' I muttered, as I fell in beside him, 'got — caught up.'

'That's OK,' he smiled, tucking the programme away.

We walked on in silence. Maybe I should have explained. Explained that that was my mother, only I hadn't recognised her because she'd changed beyond all recognition and I'd been too astonished to introduce him. I realised, with a pang, that I hadn't seen her for ages. Oh, I'd spoken to her, sure, but hadn't seen her for — what, golly, weeks now, probably. I'd been so preoccupied lately, I hadn't even stopped to think how she was. But then, she was always . . . the same. I turned back and caught a glimpse of them finding their seats, Howard ushering her along a row, his hand gently guiding her peach linen elbow, handing her a programme as she straightened her skirt beneath her to sit down, both chattering away the while, smiling. I turned back, shook my head in wonder. My God. For years now my mother had been pained, irritable and bitter. Could it be that one man was changing all that? Could it be that one, single, beating heart had caused her to transform herself, to come alive again? What power! Just as one had snuffed her out, all those years ago, another, years later, was lighting the blue touchpaper again. I didn't know if that depressed or elated me, because whilst it was wonderful to see her like this, all those wasted years hurt. So many years! And wherein lay the moral for me? Was it that I'd better move fast? Turn those years into months, at the very least? Seize the disastrous dental arrangement beside me, or maybe the blond Adonis back in the caravan, or even the slick salesman lurking in the BMW showroom – pick one of them up and run with it? Make the best of it? God Almighty! I shuddered. And what about a career, a child, both of which my mother had had – shouldn't all *that* have been enough? Shouldn't that have filled the need? Or was it simply that, in the words of The Beatles, love is all you need?

I wandered on, lost in thought, and almost walked past her, I was so distracted, until I realised she was actually plucking my sleeve.

'Olivia!'

It was Angie.

'Oh – hi!' I peeled off from Rollo once again.

She was looking stunning in a pale, silver-grey suit, and as I went to greet her I realised two of her daughters, plus husbands, were with her as well. I glanced around fearfully. Surely not Johnny too? I couldn't help it being the first thing I said as I kissed them all.

'Johnny isn't here, is he?' I murmured anxiously to Angie.

'I'm afraid he is, my dear.'

'But not with us,' put in Serena quickly. She squeezed my arm. 'We couldn't stomach him being in our party, told him to sod off on his own. I'm sure you won't see him. They're way down at the front.'

'They?' My mouth dried.

She nodded, tight-lipped. Hugged me hard. 'Bastard,' she muttered in my ear.

Lovely Serena, quite the prettiest of all, with her husband, Angus, who laid a sympathetic hand on my arm. Gosh, it was almost as if he'd died, wasn't it? And for a moment, I wished he had. It would be so much easier to bear, somehow, so much more clear cut, and I could have had some dignity as a widow. Instead of which, half the county was crammed into this church – many of whom I'd grown up with, many of whom were bound to know us – and he'd seen fit to bring her along, to what – to torture me? To humiliate me? I lived two seconds away, for Christ's sake; there was an odds on chance I'd be here, surely? In an instant Imogen was beside me. I held her arm, felt genuinely giddy.

'He's here,' I whispered.

'I know, I've just seen him. Came to find you.'

'Imo, I'm not sure I can do this. I'm going to slip out.'

'Don't be ridiculous,' she hissed. 'He might have already seen you and you can't just disappear, it looks wet. Stick that head up high and walk with me. I've seen her, and she looks like a dog's dinner and you, my darling, have never looked better. Come on.'

I took a deep breath and walked down the aisle with her. When we got to about four rows from the front, she bundled me in, sandwiching me between her and Rollo, who'd already taken his seat.

'Where is he?' I gasped, as I sat down.

'Other side of aisle, about two rows ahead of us to the left. I'll tell you when to look.' She paused. 'Now.'

I shot my eyes across and saw Johnny, in a dark suit, blue shirt, spotty tie, tanned and very handsome, of course, his blond head bent with hers over a programme. She, Nina, had her hair pushed back in a velvet hairband, very average blue shirt, grey skirt too short for her legs, twenty denier tights. All of this I took in in a nanosecond, then looked away. Their heads. Touching like that. I had to breathe very deeply. Felt sick, physically sick.

'OK?' Imo squeezed my hand.

I shook my head. 'No.'

'You're fine. You're doing fine.'

I watched in a daze as the orchestra, high up on a specially constructed platform in the nave, tuned up. Tears threatened. I raised my eyes to the heavens and concentrated hard on the intricate painted panels of the choir ceiling. I'd read in a guidebook somewhere that years ago, they'd been restoring this particular area of ceiling, and whilst they were up there on ladders and scaffolding, carefully cleaning away, they'd discovered this, an older, much more beautiful ceiling with a medieval painting on it, underneath. I tried to imagine the excitement that must have caused, the shouts of joy from way up there as the restorers unearthed the vision I gazed at today, and gradually I felt the bile go down. I swallowed hard, slowly lowered my head. Happily, Rollo was engrossed in his programme.

'But this is very exciting,' he was muttering as he read avidly. 'It says here that this is the first time this piece of Faulkner's has ever been performed.'

I nodded politely, couldn't speak. He leant across to Imo.

'Imogen, is that right? That this is the first time this symphony's been performed in this country?'

I spread my programme across my lap to catch the drips. Imo leant in eagerly for a meeting of minds.

'Yes, apparently he wrote it some time ago but recently changed it, and has only now allowed it to be performed.'

'But that's amazing, because he hasn't written anything of any note since that marvellous overture, has he?'

Despite my turmoil I was dimly fascinated to observe that Imo wiped her wet face without even appearing to notice. They were on a higher intellectual plain, of course, where things like personal hygiene were too trivial to worry about.

'No, nothing at all,' she said excitedly, 'and of course that was premiered at the Festival Hall with Simon Rattle conducting, remember? We all went in our final year. Gosh, this is such a treat!'

A treat? Really? They sat back, on tenterhooks, and I reached resignedly in my handbag for a tissue. I wiped my programme with deliberate ostentation, but he didn't appear to notice. Oh yes, I thought bitterly, tucking the hanky away, such a treat. Particularly for me, of course, to be closeted here with my husband and his floozie, for all the world to see – maybe even my mother, I thought with a sudden pang – and with my consolation prize of Spitty Dicky beside me. I caught Molly's eye further down the row and she grimaced sympathetically in Johnny's direction. I nodded and raised my eyebrows indicating that yes, I too had clocked them.

Suddenly there was a hush, and then a roar, as Hugo Simmonds took the podium to tremendous applause. He greeted his orchestra, then turned to the audience and smiled. Out of the corner of my eye I saw Ursula Mitchell straighten her back as she clapped madly. Actually I could see her point. He had quite a presence, if you liked narrow, pale faces with high foreheads, swept-back fair hair, and slightly hollow cheeks. There was something very English, very clever, and extremely intense about him. His sharp grey eyes darted about the audience, quickly searching the rows until he'd found what he was looking for. His gaze fell on Imo, beside me. I could almost feel the residual heat. Cool as a cat, Imo acknowledged him with a slight inclination of her blonde head and a Grace Kelly smile. She didn't blush or squirm as I would have done; she wasn't embarrassed to be singled out before hundreds of people; she was gracious, she was relaxed. I marvelled, briefly, but then again, I reasoned, she was used to it. If every time you batted an eyelid it started a stampede, you would get used to it. If every time you stood up, a queue formed, you'd get to take it in your stride.

Satisfied, if not satiated, Hugo turned his back on us, and faced his orchestra. His raised arms paused briefly in mid-air, then came down with a flourish, and the music began. I sank back in my chair and let it wash over me. Modern, explosive occasionally, but at the same time strangely melodic, whatever it was, it was a relief, and I was thankful for it. Thankful for its blanketing effect, for being able to shut my eyes and hide behind it.

So many thoughts churned through my head. I thought of my mother and Howard, meeting in that hospital waiting room, and of Howard, with his twinkly, northern charm, somehow asking her out. How on earth had he managed it without getting the cold shoulder? I thought of Angie too, alone, yet never lonely, surrounded as she was by her huge, loving, extended family. But most of all, I thought of Johnny. I remembered his head touching Nina's, and then, all of a sudden, I had one of those awful, monstrous flashes that I'm subject to occasionally, of the two of them entwined in bed together. An obscene vision, it lurked like some dreadful, leering Caliban at the back of my mind, awaiting its chance, always keen to spot a gap and roar in. I held my breath and stared furiously at the stained-glass windows on my right until it passed, until I was breathing normally again. The urge to look to my left, though, across the aisle, was becoming more overpowering, and as the music went on I found I did – continually, compulsively, couldn't help it – until eventually the inevitable happened. She looked too. I caught her eye, looked away, and realised she'd tell Johnny I was here. In that split second, knowing he'd glance across, I dived my head play-fully into Rollo's shoulder, gazing up at his face. He glanced down, surprised but pleased, and as I turned back, I was just in time to see Johnny turn away, a slight flush on his cheek. Good, I thought viciously. I hope that hurt.

Rollo, on the other hand, was far from hurt. Hugely encouraged, he nestled in close, and every so often he'd peer round at me with a questioning little smile and an alarming look in his eye. I groaned inwardly. Oh hell, I didn't want him getting the wrong idea. I hesitated, then armpit dived him again, only this time made damn sure my face was upturned to the glorious ceiling.

'It's lovely,' I breathed by way of explanation – unfortu-nately, just as the trumpets sounded.

He looked surprised, then smiled. 'Thank you,' he whispered.

I froze. Thank you? Christ, did he think I'd said '*You're* lovely'?

I cleared my throat. 'The Abbey,' I muttered quite loudly. 'The lovely ceiling, the way they've lit –'

'Shhh . . .' He silenced me gently, as one or two people turned and frowned. He smiled, put his finger to his lips. 'Later,' he whispered excitedly, squeezing my arm.

I sank back in horror. Later? God, did he think I was rampant or something? Couldn't wait? Was sitting here twitching away in an agony of erotic anticipation? I shook my head in disbelief and listened on in silence.

On and on. Interminably. No interval, of course, I discovered gloomily from my programme, so held in thrall were we all supposed to be by this sodding symphony. Oh no, an interval would no doubt be deemed to break the mood, spoil the atmosphere. Just the two hours of purgatory then, looking rapt and cultured with an aching heart and an aching bottom, waiting for the agony to end.

Finally, of course, it did, and to my astonishment, the applause was deafening. There was a sudden roar of approval, tremendous clapping, and then the audience got to its feet as one. Dropping my handbag and programme I hastily followed suit, catching Molly's eye as she nudged Hugh awake and he too got up, rolling his eyes at me in mock horror at the ordeal. All around, people were calling out in rapture, and some, like Imo and Rollo beside me, even stamped their feet which I thought was a bit childish, but by all accounts, judging by the flushed, enthusiastic faces of those in the know, it had been a towering success.

Hugo Simmonds, flushed, elated and dripping with sweat, raised his hands and gave us his orchestra. They stood and bowed, as Hugo, with elaborate gestures, singled out the stars: his leader, his flautist, his brass section, his percussion, before finally, turning himself to bow to thunderous applause. He soaked it up for a moment, stood, waved, then turned and disappeared off stage, only to reappear a moment later and receive the same treatment. But still the applause went on. Louder now, and more insistent, as if something was missing, some need waiting to be gratified. Hugo Simmonds smiled, nodded knowingly, and flicked back his damp fair hair. Then he simply gestured to someone near the front of the audience to come up. For an awful moment I thought he might be looking at Imo, but then a few rows ahead of us, a tall, dark man in a dinner jacket stood up with his back to us. As people craned their necks to see, murmuring,

'There he is!' I realised it must be Faulkner himself. He brushed back his hair, and slid along the row to the end, where he went to the front to mount the stage. As he got to the top step and turned to the audience, there was a deafening roar of approval, and for the first time I saw his face. My hand shot to my mouth.

'Bloody hell!'

I gaped in horror, unable to take in what I was seeing. Unable to quite believe my eyes. For up there on the podium, smiling shyly but delightedly, bowing, and waving occasionally to acknowledge the tremendous applause, was Sebastian.

Chapter Fifteen

I gaped, wide-eyed and frozen with horror. The vaulted ceiling, the medieval panels, and all the ancient Roman tiles above it, seemed to fall in on my head. Sebastian. Sebastian was . . . Faulkner? How on earth could that be? Despite the pressure of several tons of masonry on my shattered skull, what was left of my brain strung the names together. Sebastian . . . Faulkner. God, yes, of course, even I, with my modicum of classical music knowledge, had just about heard of him. I flushed to my roots, jaw hanging, boggling at him up there on the podium, bowing and smiling.

'Christ,' I murmured.

'What's up?' yelled Imo into my ear, above the applause.

'I know him,' I muttered.

'What?'

'I said I know him!'

'No!' she squeaked, swinging excitedly around to face me. 'How come?'

I opened my mouth to speak, but happily, didn't have time to elucidate, as in a matter of moments, Ursula was upon us, bustling importantly along the row, knocking into people's knees, sending programmes flying, eyes shining.

'My dears, *such* a thrill,' she breathed ecstatically. 'Hugo Simmonds has conveyed to us by means of a sweet note, that he'd be delighted to have us all join him backstage for a small celebration. Imagine, Imo, we'll meet Faulkner too!'

'Oh, but Olivia already knows him,' said Imo excitedly, 'don't you, Livvy?'

'Er, well,' I gulped, 'sort of . . . ish.'

'No!' Ursula gasped. 'My dear, why didn't you say?' Her eyes shone alarmingly. 'Is he *totally* enchanting?'

I swallowed, and it was on the tip of my tongue to explain that I wasn't the best person to ask since the last time I'd seen him I'd brandished a rake and cast aspersions on his moral character, so the chances of him being overly enchanting to me backstage were minimal, but instead I edged away, smiling nervously.

'D'you know I'm – not sure, Ursula, because to be honest I don't know him terribly well, and – and actually, what with the baby-sitter waiting I really must be getting –'

'Nonsense,' she insisted, seizing my wrist urgently, the possibility of a personal introduction gleaming in her eyes. 'Imogen was telling me how wonderful your builders are, always stepping in to help you out. They won't mind another hour. Come!' She called me to heel, dragging me firmly by the arm. 'How absolutely splendid to make an entrance with someone who's actually acquainted with him,' she squeaked. 'I can't wait to tell Hugo! How exactly do you know him, my dear?' She swooped, hawklike, her sharp nose level with mine as she propelled me from the nave, through the crowds, bumping into people's backs with no regard at all as she made for the back of the Abbey in a frenzy of excitement.

'Um, he lives in my road,' I muttered, glancing around desperately for a convenient side exit.

She stopped, clapped her hand to her forehead. 'Of course he does! In The Crescent! Which is precisely why he wanted the first rendition of this work to be performed here, giving something back to his city, rather than it going straight to the Festival Hall!' She marched on again. 'The powers that be were dead against it of course – wanted it in London – but he was absolutely adamant – and what a success! Tell me,' she breathed, 'right there at the end, throughout that final recapitulation, did you or did you not have goosebumps literally all over?'

'Um, yes.' Not a lie, but from fright rather than ecstasy, and actually they were beginning to reform.

'Come along, my party!' Ursula threw back imperiously over her shoulder as we marched on, glancing round to check that Imo, Rollo, Molly and Hugh were all trailing dutifully behind. Suddenly Ursula stopped.

'Damn. Wait here,' she hissed, parking me by a pillar, but never for a moment loosening the grip on my arm.

She turned and beamed delightedly. 'Charles! Sonia! So good of you to come! Did you enjoy it?' This she addressed to a rather mousy, elderly couple who'd followed, a trifle bemused, in our wake. 'I'm *so* pleased,' she enthused without waiting for an answer. '*Lovely* to see you again,' and with this she kissed them with a definite air of finality.

But Charles and Sonia, camel-coated and seventy-odd, were slow to catch her drift. They were inclined to linger, chat a little, become expansive, come with us even, and Ursula was going to have her work cut out explaining that they were the last people on earth she wanted cluttering up her backstage salon; just the young, the vibrant, the chic and, of course, me, the sick at heart. I glanced about wildly for a handy escape route or even just a pew to hide behind, but I was comprehensively hemmed in on all sides now: Ursula to my right, her hand on my arm, a pillar behind me, and Rollo, quivering with excitement and hopping stupidly from foot to foot, to my left.

'What fun, a party!' he squealed as he pranced skittishly.

Berk. I regarded him with complete disdain. Total, utter, berk. I'd really gone off him in a major way. He was the sort of intellectual giant who clutched his sides when the fool pranced on in a Shakespeare play, the sort who pooped a stupid horn at the last night of the Proms, wearing an oh-so-funny Union Jack hat. Hugh sidled up to me, elbowing Rollo out of the way, and found my ear.

'What's going on?'

'Party, backstage,' I muttered. 'Ursula's idea, but I'm out of here.'

Hugh brightened. 'You mean we get another drink? Splendid, I'm game.'

'Why don't you want to go?' asked Molly as I slipped behind Hugh, past Rollo, and then behind another pillar.

'Because,' I hissed flattening myself against it, 'that chap I told you about, the one who lives down my road and I thought had abducted Claudia – turns out to be bloody Faulkner! It's bloody Sebastian Faulkner!' I inched sideways, spotting, with relief, the Chapter door to my left.

Hugh's eyes widened. 'Faulkner abducted Claudia? I didn't hear about this.' A *Daily Mail* exclusive lurked alarmingly in his eyes.

'No! Of course not, but I thought he had! I made a mistake, but I can't possibly go in there now, it'll be excruciatingly embarrassing! Now for heaven's sake go away and stop talking to me – I'm trying to be discreet, for God's sake. Cover me or something useful.'

I scurried off to the side door, with Molly and Hugh dutifully turning back and shielding me, helped by Molly's huge bulk. Seizing with relief the high iron handle on the old oak door, I turned it. Rattled it dementedly, in fact. Damn, locked. As I swung around frantically, about to leg it to the main entrance, I saw Ursula bearing down on me, with Molly shrugging helplessly behind her. My deodorant was beginning to let me down.

'Wrong way, Olivia!' she called. 'They're using the refectory for the party!'

She linked my arm and made to pull me away, but I dug my heels in hard.

'Ursula, listen,' I said desperately. 'I'm – I'm awfully sorry but I can't come. I feel terribly ill. In fact, I think I'm going to be sick.'

'Oh, I know, it is frightfully stuffy in here, isn't it? Terribly close. But once we're out of this madding crowd you'll feel heaps better, I promise!' She yanked my arm.

'But I –'

'Listen, Olivia, I'll be honest with you.' She dropped her voice dramatically and lowered her head. 'I didn't get a note from Hugo, although I rather hoped I would, but then again he is terribly shy. All the same, I know he'll just be dying to see Imogen, but it would help enormously if you came too. Just to sort of ease our path through the stage door, seeing as how you're a personal friend of Mr Faulkner's and all that.'

I gaped. 'N-no, but listen, Ursula, I'm not, I –'

'Mum, what *is* going on?' Imogen came up looking totally bewildered. 'Are we supposed to be going backstage or not? Everyone's waiting!'

'Yes, of course we are, darling. We're just coming, aren't we, Olivia?' She turned pleading eyes on me. I stared. Looked at Imo. Back to Ursula. Nodded dumbly. 'Excellent!' she breathed. 'Come along now!'

Her iron grip once more took up position under my elbow, and as she marched me, lamblike to the slaughter, along the ancient stone passages, beaten almost hollow with age, I realised where Imogen got it from – this desire to be first; to be top; to be the best. As long as I'd known her she'd striven for perfection, which of course was laudable, but it also meant she couldn't settle for anything less. And Imo had yet to settle.

'Here we are!' Her mother stopped suddenly, raised her knuckles, and gave a sharp tap at the refectory door. It was instantly opened by a lackey.

To my relief, the room was packed. Teeming, actually, full to the brim with the orchestra, presumably their friends and relatives, and various sundry hangers-on. Ursula looked momentarily disappointed since we clearly weren't the chosen few – let alone the chosen multitude – but, happily, Hugo Simmonds was close to the door. He spotted her instantly and, raising his glass above the crush, came squeezing across to greet her.

'Ursula!'

'Hugo! My dear I hope you don't mind us barging in, but Olivia here knows Sebastian *terribly* well and we just wanted to pop by and congratulate you both! Imo – say hello to Hugo!'

'M-mind? Heavens, I'm d-delighted!' he said, flicking

his hair back nervously. He almost came out in a muck sweat as Imogen diligently obeyed orders and kissed him on the cheek. His glasses all but steamed up.

'It's l-lovely to see you, Imogen. D-did you enjoy it?' he stammered. I was stunned. Was this the same commanding man of moments ago?

'It was wonderful,' Imo enthused warmly, 'really wonderful, Hugo.'

'Thank you,' he gasped. 'I'm s-so glad you came. I w-wanted to ask you but w-wasn't sure if you'd . . . I-I must say, Imogen,' he gulped, 'you look absolutely marvellous.' His grey eyes roved admiringly over the Grecian curls, the tanned, smooth shoulders, the slim brown legs and for a moment, he forgot to stutter. 'An absolute vision,' he declared roundly.

'He wants to give her one right now,' muttered Hugh in my ear. 'Behind the choir stalls. Can't wait. And I'll tell you something else, old Ursula Mitchell wouldn't mind if he did.'

I giggled, but I was simultaneously scanning the room nervously for Sebastian. Ah, there he was, right over the other side, thank God, with his back to me. His dark head protruded a couple of inches higher than the swarm of people he was talking to. If I stayed right here by the door, had a quick drink and slipped away in two minutes flat, I'd be fine. I'd done my duty, got old Ursula in; yes, I could be away. I kept my eyes firmly on that head lest it should suddenly turn, took a glass of champagne from a tray as it passed by, and sipped and stared. As I did, I grew more and more incredulous. I simply couldn't believe it. Could *not* believe who he was. Christ, I mean, he'd never said, had he? Never mentioned it, and he'd had ample opportunity, surely? Had he, though? I racked my brains, trying to remember where I'd first met him. Of course, at Nanette's. God, bloody Nanette, who knowing no better had billed him, first as a lunatic, and then as a *teacher*, for heaven's sake. What planet was she on?

'I think he's rather cute,' murmured Molly in my ear, crunching a pistachio nut. 'Can't think why you thought he was certifiable.'

'Molly, you thought so too!' I hissed. 'When I told you about Claudia turning up in his house, you said I shouldn't apologise in person because it all sounded very iffy! I distinctly remember!'

'Yes, but that was before I knew who he was, before I'd seen him in the flesh. Anyone can see the man's totally normal. In fact,' she squinted, 'he's really rather handsome.' She inched round to get a better view of the side of his face, pulling me with her. 'You told me he was a long-haired loner who ran about in jim-jams.'

'Yes, well, he's wearing a dinner jacket now, isn't he, and he's had his hair cut.'

I had to agree, though, that with a good couple of inches off his hair so that one could see those dark, slightly slanting eyes which ran parallel with high cheekbones, he looked a different person. Quite a presence.

'He's got such a sensitive face,' she murmured.

'Oh rubbish,' I scoffed. 'If anything he's got an arrogant face. You're only saying that because you know he's a composer. If he was a doctor you'd say he had a caring face, and if he was an artist you'd say he had an artistic face, and for heaven's sake stop staring, Mol. He'll see us!'

I realised in panic that we'd drifted away from the door, and that our exit was now blocked by a few more newcomers. I desperately tried to fight my way back, simultaneously scrabbling in my bag for my car keys. Time to go. Definitely time to go.

'He can't see us, Livvy,' Molly said as I rooted about in my bag. 'He's far too swamped by all those luvvies. Just look at them fawning. They're practically kissing the hem of his jacket.'

Having at least found my programme in my bag, I used it to shield my face and peep over. She was right: people were literally queuing up to talk to him.

'Was he nice when you went over?' she whispered, eyes glued.

'What?'

'When you went round to apologise, what did he say?'

'Oh, I didn't go round in the end. I did as you said, I sent a –' Christ. A note. Had I sent a note? My mind fled back. I'd written one, certainly, and failed to drop it in because of his mother, so then I'd gone home to write another, but . . . I went cold. 'Oh God!'

'What?'

'I forgot to write a letter!' I clasped my mouth. 'Oh, Molly, I forgot to do it! Forgot to apologise!'

She looked at me in horror. 'You mean . . . he still thinks – that you still think –'

'I've got to get out of here, Mol,' I said urgently. 'Got to, before he sees me. Come on,' I turned and lunged for the door.

'Too late,' she muttered in my ear.

I swung my head to see – Sebastian Faulkner, pale-faced, stony-eyed, who had not only seen me, but was making determined strides in my direction, pushing fixedly through the madding throng, his dark eyes as hard as a couple of flints.

'Help!' I squealed, as I pushed for freedom, but we were three deep from the door now, and Molly's heavily pregnant state made it nigh on impossible to shove through. I felt like a fox being hunted, the hounds right on my tail, but as I glanced back, panic-stricken, I suddenly saw Ursula Mitchell step out right in front of him, blocking his path.

'Mr Faulkner, *might* I say how absolutely marvellous I thought that was!' she gushed. 'I honestly don't think I've enjoyed a piece of music so much since I heard Pascalle conduct Beethoven's Fifth with the Berlin Philharmonic in Rome, which I was privileged enough to go to last year with a great friend of mine Lady Farqurson, and I have to say, that even *that* occasion, momentous though it was, didn't *quite* send shivers up my spine the way that *your* symphony did tonight! Truly magnificent, maestro!'

He gave a small bow. 'Thank you,' he muttered, and made to sidestep her, his eyes still fixed and predatory, but dear old Ursula hadn't finished. She blocked his way – bless her – and gave him another earful, just as I, managing to barge past Molly and make a desperate lunge for the door, arrived to find that the only obstacle between me and freedom was Rollo, leaning laconically against it, and holding forth about Faulkner to a couple of credulous college students.

'. . . such powerful stanzas, yet such insight into the common lot. One feels almost humbled by his power, his presence, his – Ow!' he yelped weedily as I barged up. 'That was my foot!'

'Move,' I hissed shamelessly, elbowing him roughly.

'Sorry?'

'Move out of the way!'

'Sorry?'

'Oh, for Christ's sake get out of my way and stop bloody spitting at me!' I shrieked, wiping my face.

He frowned. 'Olivia, are you all right? You look a bit –'

'Tra-la-la-la-la-diddly-dah!' trilled a loud soprano behind us. I jerked my head back to see Ursula, who, much to Imo's embarrassment, was now giving the composer her own cringe-making rendition of her favourite bits, still blocking his path. 'That's the phrase I just adored,' she beamed, 'at the beginning of the second movement. *So* bewitching with that lovely lilting melody, and such a contrast to the first movement. In fact, I was saying to someone . . .' She tried desperately to catch Sebastian's eyes, which were not on her at all. 'Mr Faulkner, I was saying to –' she gave up and followed his gaze. 'Olivia! I was saying to Olivia, who, of course, you know!'

In one bony swoop of her arm, like python snatching its prey, she lunged out, plucked my arm, and pulled hard, sweeping me into her inner circle. I felt like a child being hauled before the head. My knees began to knock, and my eyes, when I finally dared to raise them, found his: cold, dark and forbidding. He gave me a look that froze my spine.

'You *do* know each other, don't you, Olivia?' insisted Ursula, in case I'd made it up.

'Yes, we, um, do.' I faltered.

'Unhappily,' he barked sharply, and I could see his hands clenching by his sides.

Ursula's social smile quivered. 'I-I'm sorry, did you say –'

'Oh, thank God!' shrieked a shrill voice behind us. Suddenly Molly burst through, pushing people out of the way, clutching her huge stomach, eyes wild. 'I've got the most frightful pains, Livvy, terrible stomach cramps, and Hugh's too drunk to drive! I've been looking everywhere for you. Would you be an angel and take me home?'

'Oh, my dear!' Ursula was all consternation. 'Are they labour pains, d'you think? Are you about to have it? Do you need an ambulance?'

Molly staggered about a bit, enjoying herself hugely. 'Noo, noo,' she gasped bravely, 'I think I'll be – AAARGHHH!' She clutched my arm suddenly and sank to her knees. Ursula jumped back in horror. 'No, I'll be fine, really,' she gasped, straightening up, face racked with simulated pain. 'I'm sure it's too soon, not due for days yet, it's just that I must lie down, you see, put my feet up and – Hugh!' She gasped with relief as her husband pushed his way through. 'Oh, Hugh darling, so sorry, ghastly pains. Livvy's going to drive us home! Bye, all, thank you *so* much Mrs Mitchell, lovely party, lovely concert!'

She'd played her part perfectly, and we'd undoubtedly have made a seamless exit were it not for Hugh, who, loving a drama, and having not worked in one for a while, was delighted to stumble across this one. He threw himself into it shamelessly.

'Darling!' he cried. 'Oh God, darling, are you all right? Shall I ring Mr Kenny?'

'Mr Kenny?' Ursula blinked. 'Isn't he the Queen's gynaecologist?'

Hugh straightened up. 'He's my wife's gynaecologist,' he informed her soberly. 'What he does in his spare time is his own affair, we all have to make a living. Come, my dear.' He supported Molly's bulk as she collapsed, groaning, on to his shoulder. 'Come, I'll help you to the – Christ!' Hugh leapt back theatrically as there was a sudden splash on the floor between Molly's legs. Everyone gasped.

'Oh God, it's your waters!' cried Hugh, a mysteriously empty glass in his hand, insanity in his eyes.

Molly looked genuinely horror-struck. 'Good God.' She stared down at the puddle. Blinked. 'I didn't even feel it!'

'Ah well, that's mother nature for you,' muttered Hugh, manoeuvring his wife expertly through the gaping throng, which was parting like the Red Sea now, and towards a hurriedly opened door. 'It eases you into it gently, lulls you into a false sense of security but, mark my words, it'll be the stirrups and the forceps for you before the night is out. You'll be biting through my hand, kicking innocent bits of furniture and being sensationally abusive to the medical team. It'll be just like Henry all over again! Come, Livvy, to the hospital, please, and don't spare the horses! Mind your backs, good people, mind your backs. Bye all, wish us well!'

'Bye!' I managed to squeak as Hugh ushered us out.

As the door shut behind us, we fled down the corridor. Back through the nave we raced, down the side aisle of the empty Abbey, our feet echoing wildly on the flagstones. Hugh and I were on either side of Molly, who, the size of a barrage balloon, was running for England. Down the steps we clattered, through the huge oak doors and out into the garden, where, under a leafy tree and the safety of darkness, we threw ourselves on to a bench, collapsing in an hysterical, giggling heap.

'Oh God,' I gasped, as we fought for control. 'Oh Molly, you were marvellous. I didn't know you had it in you! You should be the one out there treading the boards. I thought you were going to have it right there and then!'

'Bloody hell, so did I!' she gasped. 'It took me a moment to realise my waters hadn't gone!'

'Ah me,' sighed Hugh, wiping his eyes happily, 'I haven't enjoyed myself so much since I was a spear carrier in *Hamlet* and Ophelia sat on my spike. Did you see Ursula's face? Horrified that Molly might be about to commit the ultimate social sin of *dilating in public*! I was about to offer to have a quick peek at your cervix, Mol, but I thought that might be going too far.'

'Far too far,' I agreed sternly, mopping my eyes, 'the Frascati on the floor was bad enough.'

'Ah, but we saved your bacon, eh, Livvy old girl?' Hugh slung an arm round my shoulders as we struggled to our feet. 'Christ, he was going to have you for breakfast! I've never seen such murder in a man's eyes. It damn nearly wiped the smile off my face, I can tell you, and it takes a lot to do that. He was hopping mad.'

'But justifiably, surely,' I said more soberly, as we made for the car park. 'Don't you think? I mean, after what I'd accused him of?'

'God, I should say,' agreed Molly warmly. 'I'm surprised he didn't just biff you on the nose and have done with it.'

I stopped. 'And then he had to witness our ridiculous charade. And I'm sure he knew it was a charade. I saw his face at one point. He knew I was trying to slip through the net again, so once again I've done him a disservice, haven't I?' I bit my lip. 'I didn't go and apologise when I should have done, and I couldn't even stand my ground in there and do it then.' I swallowed.

Molly looked at me in horror. 'Livvy, you're surely not thinking –'

'Liv darling, he'll have your guts for garters,' interrupted Hugh gently, taking my arm. 'And not just for garters. He'll make suspenders out of them, believe me. The man's world famous, he has a name to protect and, God, even if he hadn't, even if he was as small a fish as I am, he'd be so bloody furious about being accused of – Well, Christ, if anyone said that about me I'd – I'd – bloody . . .' For once he was lost for words.

'Precisely,' I said quietly. 'So don't you see? I have to go back. It's so awful, what I've done, and now I've made it worse. I have to go back.' I turned.

Molly caught my arm. 'Wait a bit,' she urged. 'Hang around out here and wait until everyone's gone. Catch him on the way out. At least then he won't be surrounded by all those bloody sycophants.'

I shook her off. 'No, I'm going. If I don't go now I'll never pluck up the courage, and then I'll never do it.'

They watched in silence as I walked away from them. I retraced my steps, up into the Abbey, down the side aisle that we'd just this minute raced through, bubbling over with laughter, down towards the altar. I tracked right through the nave, past the tombs, the monuments, round the vast painted column at the far end, and then, full of fear and dread, went down through the great gothic arch and the wooden steps to the refectory. I stopped for a second, my hand on the handle, heart pounding. There was still plenty of noise coming from inside, chattering and laughing – and for a moment I almost lost my nerve. Molly was right: I didn't have to do this. Not here. Not now. Some other time perhaps. Then – damn it. Get on with it, Livvy. I turned the handle and walked in.

The room was still crowded, but not nearly so tightly packed. It had thinned out a little and it was possible to walk around. I slid along the sides, my eyes darting, searching, until quite quickly I found who I was looking for. He saw me at exactly the same moment. Broke off abruptly from talking to the cluster of ten or so people around him who were listening intently. I wouldn't say you could hear a pin drop, exactly, because the rest of the room was still buzzing, but certainly as the group around Sebastian fell silent, it provoked something of a ripple effect. I noticed Imogen and Ursula to the right of me, staring.

'Excuse me,' muttered Sebastian to his neighbour. He came towards me, a muscle going in his cheek.

'Mrs McFarllen,' he said in a low voice, 'you've made your way back to my party. Is that wise? Are you so deprived of social engagements that you seek out even those where you are clearly unwelcome?' His voice was soft, but bitter and scathing, and it seemed to me that at this point, the rest of the room caught his tone and went quiet.

In an instant Ursula and Imogen were beside me.

'Olivia, what is it?' hissed Ursula. 'What's going on?'

I cleared my throat. 'I've come to apologise,' I said, looking up into his stony face. 'I made a very foolish mistake the other day, and accused you,' I made myself meet his cold brown eyes, 'of a dreadful thing.'

'What? What dreadful thing?' urged Ursula, just a little too agog.

'She accused me of being a child molester,' said Sebastian in a level voice. 'A paedophile.'

A horrified gasp went round the room.

'No!' someone breathed, Then, 'Good God!' and, 'Slanderous!'

'Olivia, how could you!' gaped Ursula.

I felt incredibly giddy and a bit light-headed, but I managed to meet his eyes.

'How could I?' I said. 'Because I was frightened. Terrified, actually. I don't know if you have children, Mr Faulkner, but let me tell you, the most frightening thing in the world is losing them. I lost my child,' I said, forcing myself to look round the room, to catch anyone's eye who was interested, 'last Sunday. My ten-year-old. She slipped off on her own on her bike, and when I followed the route I imagined she'd taken, through the woods, down by the river, I found something that confirmed my worst fears. Her bike, dragged into the bushes, and abandoned. When I asked a passer-by – no, screamed at a passer-by – if she'd seen a little girl in red shorts, she said yes, going into a nearby house, sobbing, and being taken by a tall man. This tall man.'

Even Ursula looked slightly askance at this. She shot a look at Sebastian, who was still staring at me.

'So without stopping to think, and imagining only horror, I stormed into that house, all guns blazing, to find my little girl, sitting in this same man's house, and wearing nothing at all, but his dressing gown.' I paused. 'Now what would you have thought?' I asked, trembling now. 'Ursula, what would you have thought?' I turned demanding eyes on her.

'Well I – I . . .' she floundered, turning bewildered eyes on Sebastian.

'Exactly. You'd have thought the same as me. But you'd be wrong, as it happens, and that's why I'm here. To apologise. I apologise, Mr Faulkner.'

There was a stunned silence.

'S-so what happened?' stammered Ursula. 'I'm confused, I mean, if he didn't –'

'Claudia fell in the river,' I said. 'She hit a rut on her bike and went headfirst into the stream, banged her head on a rock. Mr Faulkner saw from an upstairs window and rushed out to help her. He dried her clothes, gave her a dressing gown, and made her some tea. I have a lot to be thankful for. She had a pretty bad bump and had he not seen her, had she been floundering about in the river for longer, it could have been a different story. I might even have lost her. As it was,' I turned back to Sebastian, 'I called you every foul and vile name under the sun. In my defence I might say that I had no idea who you were, although I doubt that would have made any difference. To an enraged mother a famous composer is just as culpable as a man in a dirty mac. But I was wrong.' I was aware my voice was beginning to wobble so I speeded it up. 'Very wrong. I slandered and insulted you and I'm deeply sorry and ashamed. I'd like to thank you for being so quick-witted and helping Claudia, and – and I deeply regret,' I rushed on, 'any pain I've caused you. I'm sorry.'

With that I turned, and without waiting to hear his, or Ursula's views on the subject, walked out of the room. I went back down the Abbey, and out into the night, whereupon I promptly burst into tears.

Chapter Sixteen

That night I slept fitfully. I dreamt I was up on the Abbey stage, a key member of Sebastian's orchestra, performing his masterpiece with a vast, outsized cello clamped between my legs. As I screeched and scraped away hopelessly, making a terrible din and ruining the symphony, the front row of the audience became mutinous.

'Off! Get her off!' they yelled.

I glanced up from my bow, sweat pouring off me, to see Angie, Howard, my mother, Imogen, Ursula, Johnny and Nina, their faces all contorted with rage, shaking their fists, baying for my blood.

'She never could play!' yelled Johnny, on his feet now. 'She's a fraud!'

In the row behind, Alf, Mac and Spiro, still in their work overalls, feet up, and swigging Stella from cans, were booing and making obscene gestures involving strenuous wrist action. A can came flying my way. 'Off, get 'er off!' they jeered.

Finally Sebastian stalked on from the wings, enraged. 'Mrs McFarllen,' he spat, 'in the words of the great Sir Thomas Beecham, you have between your legs something that can bring pleasure to millions, and all you can do is *scratch* it!'

'I can't play!' I wept. 'I never said I could, I –'

'Mummy, Mummy!' I was being bounced up and down

now, my head nearly coming off my shoulders as it rocked back and forth.

'Aaggh! Don't! I'll learn, I swear to God I'll learn, I'll – Claudes!'

I opened my eyes to see Claudia, astride me, dressed in her stripy summer school uniform, bouncing me up and down on the bed. The sun was streaming in through the windows.

'Learn what?' She frowned down at me.

'Oh my God,' I breathed, blinking sweaty eyelids and pushing back my hair. 'What a nightmare. What a godaw-ful, terrible, horrific, nightmare. I feel sick. What time is it?'

'Twenty to eight, and I've got my ballet exam today.' She yanked the duvet off me. 'Oh yuk! You're all sweaty!' She dropped it back in disgust.

I sat up and clutched my head. She was right, my hair was plastered to my scalp, my T-shirt sticking to me. I shot my eyes to the bedside clock.

'Christ! Your ballet exam! You're supposed to be there in twenty minutes!'

'I know.'

'All tutu'd up with a hairnet on!'

'I know.'

I stared. 'And you deliberately didn't wake me earlier because you don't want to do it! Claudia, you are such a devious, mendacious little –'

'Don't say the F word.'

'I wasn't about to say the F word!'

'It shows lack of character. And, anyway, what's the problem? I'm waking you now, aren't I?'

'Claudia, I'll give you lack of character!' I seethed, leaping out of bed and grabbing my jeans. I plunged my legs into them. 'Just get your tail downstairs *now*, grab your tutu and get in that car and I'll join you there in two minutes! *And don't forget the bloody hairnet!*'

Three minutes later, unwashed, dying for a cup of tea, mouth like the bottom of a budgie's cage and armpits decidedly pongy, I was nevertheless reversing at high speed out of that drive. I can move when I feel like it and, amazingly, I thought, glancing smugly at the clock, we'd make it. She'd be in that exam room in precisely ten minutes, strapped into her pointes and doing the dying swan if I killed us both on the A41 in the process.

'You'll make it,' I snarled as she sulked beside me.

'Yeah, I know,' she sighed, resignedly. She'd had a go, but I'd had a better one.

I caught sight of myself in the rear-view mirror and pushed desperate hands through greasy hair. 'Oh, Claudes, *look* at me! Pass me my –'

'Here.' She'd already reached into the glove compartment and found my dark glasses.

I shoved them on. 'Thanks.'

'And this?' She picked up an old baseball cap from the floor.

'Please.' I rammed it on.

She was still rummaging around. 'Mint?'

'Definitely.' I opened my mouth and she popped in a Polo. I sucked for a bit, then shot her a sideways glance. Winked.

'Heavy night?' she offered sympathetically.

'Terrible,' I groaned, sucking hard. I rubbed my forehead with my fingertips, remembering. 'Oh gosh, *really* terrible, actually.' What an evening. What an absolutely, awful evening!

'I had a great time last night, Mum.'

'Good, good,' I murmured distractedly, shooting straight across the top of a mini roundabout, four wheels off the ground. God, what a disaster! First Johnny and Nina all snuggled up together in hand-holding cosiness, and then bloody Sebastian! Up there on the *stage*, for heaven's sake! I shook my head in disbelief.

'It started off really badly 'cos Alf was so sad and grumpy and still upset about Vi, but then Spiro came over from the caravan and said that their telly wasn't working so did I think you'd mind if they all came over and baby-sat with Alf. I said you wouldn't. You wouldn't, would you, Mum?'

'Hmm?' Oh God, and *Molly*, practically giving *birth* like that!

'Mum?'

'What, darling?'

'Watching the telly?'

'Yes, no, fine. Lovely.'

'Oh good. So anyway, they all came over and we got loads of pizza and stuff out of the freezer and they drank lots of beer – *lots* of beer, actually – and Spiro got really happy and larky. Oh Mum, it was so funny. He was doing Greek dancing on the table and throwing plates and catching them – we used those big Spanish bowls you've got – and I was doing it too, all in my nightie!'

'Excellent, excellent, my love,' I murmured distractedly, as I remembered yet another shaker. What about my mother? Turning up with a *man*, for goodness' sake!

'And then in the middle of being really happy, Spiro suddenly got really sad because he missed his wife and son so much – you know how he cries – so I had a brilliant idea and said, why didn't he ring her up! You don't mind, do you, Mum?'

'Hmm?' Unbelievable really. My mum. God, after all those years. All those arid years.

'Mum?'

'What, darling?'

'Using the phone?'

'Of course you can use the phone.' Heavens, and talking of mothers, what about Ursula! In fine ambitious form, throwing Imo to that conductor like a Christian to the lions.

'So anyway he rang and talked for ages, all in Greek, of course, and then because he was so cheered up and happy, we decided to have a disco, and we turned the music up really loud and Mac was the DJ and he did all the rapping stuff, you know, and Alf – oh gosh, Mum, Alf was *so funny*! He was like, really, really drunk – could hardly stand up by now – and he was burping and everything, and then he started doing this striptease dance – you know, like in *The Full Monty* – de da de da de da!'

But it was Sebastian who was really making my toes curl in their trainers this morning. I cringed down low behind the wheel, hiding under my baseball cap. I'd never forget his face, gimlet-eyed as he pushed through that room towards me. I glanced across at Claudia, who for some reason was slipping her blazer off one shoulder and rolling her eyes like Shirley Bassey. 'Put it on, darling. You know Mr Harty likes you to at least turn up in it.' I hoiked it back up. Yes, crikey, those *eyes* of his – wouldn't like to come across them in a dark alley. I shivered.

'And then he got up on the sofa and was mucking about and sticking out his bare tummy, which was really fat and hairy like a dog's, and he was rubbing it and everything, and we were laughing and laughing, and suddenly – he was sick! But *luckily* Spiro held out a bowl, so most of it – "Puyaka!" – went in the bowl! Wasn't that lucky, Mum?'

'Hmm? Christ!' I just managed to screech to a halt as a lollipop lady stepped out in front of me. 'What?'

'I said wasn't it lucky it went in your Spanish bowl?'

'Oh. Yes. I expect it looked nice.'

Claudia frowned. 'No, it didn't look nice. But, anyway, we chucked it down the loo and Alf had another beer and said he felt better, and then we did this brilliant kanga – you know, de-da-da-da-da-da – DA! De-da-da-da-da-da – DA! – all holding on to each other in a line all over the house. We even went upstairs and tramped all over the beds – it was brilliant!'

'Good . . . good.' And then to try and escape like that with Molly and Hugh, like – like flipping adolescents! What must he have *thought* of us? But at least I'd gone back, I thought, with a degree of relief as I swung in through the school gates. That was something, anyway. Imagine how I'd feel this morning if I hadn't!

'And while we were up there, in your bedroom, some undies of yours were lying on a chair, and Alf put your bra on, and it was *so funny*, Mum. He had this great big hairy tummy and teeny tiny bosomy things and he was doing a really silly dance and singing, ". . . with-a-little-bit-

of-this, and-a-little-bit-of-that, and-shake-your-bum, just-
like-your-mum."'

'Bottom,' I said vaguely, recalling Sebastian's face visibly pale as I'd gone back into that room.

'What?'

'Bottom, not bum.'

'Oh right. Well, anyway, then Lance came back from
the pub –'

'Lance?' I swung around.

'Yes, he'd been at the pub all night, hadn't been with us,
you see, and he got really cross!'

I stopped the car in the car park and frowned. 'Why?'

'Exactly!' She shrugged incredulously. 'I have *no* idea! I
mean, you're not cross, are you?'

I shook myself. 'Cross? Should I be?'

'Well, anyway, *he* was.' She rolled her eyes dramatically.
'Livid. He went absolutely doolally, kicked the others out
of the house and back to the caravan –'

'But . . . what were they all doing there? Wasn't Alf
baby-sitting?'

She groaned and reached on to the back seat for her
reading bag. 'I *told* you, Mum, their telly broke so they
came over. *And* he told me to go to bed –'

'Who?'

'Lance, when it wasn't even him that was baby-sitting, it
was Alf.'

'Well, darling –'

'*And* he turned my light out without even letting me
read!'

'It was probably well past nine o'clock.'

'Huh!' She slammed her door and came round the front to my open window.

'Bye, my love, have a good day. I'm shooting off now.'

'Because you haven't got your make-up on and you don't want to bump into Nina.' She grinned.

I pulled her straw boater down over her eyes. 'You're too sharp for your own good, young lady.'

'I know, just call me Razors.'

I smiled. 'Well, here's something I'll bet you don't know, Razors.'

'What?'

'Granny's got a boyfriend.'

'No!' Her eyes widened with disbelief. '*Granny!* Brilliant! Since when? How d'you know?'

'Since I don't know, but I met him last night, at the concert.'

'Cool! A boyfriend! What's he like?'

I suddenly had a vision of Claudia's idea of a boyfriend, something young and blond, something out of Steps, maybe.

'Well, he's about her age,' I said quickly.

'Oh!'

'But *very* nice and smiley.'

'Handsome?'

'Mmm, Claudes, he's *her* age. Tubbyish and grey, but kind-looking. Stares at her a lot, you know, into her eyes.'

'Oh yum!' She was excited by that. 'Can I meet him?'

'Of course. I thought we'd ask them for tea on Sunday, and listen,' I added quickly, 'whatever we think, Claudes, it's lovely for her, don't you think?' I asked anxiously.

'Oh *yes*. And I think if Dad doesn't come back it would

be lovely for you too, Mum, even someone tubby and grey. Think how you've worried about Granny all these years, wished she hadn't been so lonely. Well, that's going to be *me* worrying, if you're not careful!'

I ground my teeth. 'Claudia, shall we discuss this when you're twenty-five and have been worrying for fifteen years, and not, perchance, when you're ten and have been worrying for all of two months? Anyway, you're a child, for goodness' sake, you don't need to worry about me!'

'Children feel things very keenly,' she informed me soberly. 'Don't you know that? Esther Rantzen knows that. She says it a lot on Childline. Don't keep me talking, Mum, I've got a ballet exam to get to.'

'Oh Christ, your exam!' I yelped, clutching my head in horror. 'I'd forgotten again – go – GO!' I pushed her. 'Why aren't you running!'

'I'm going, I'm going,' she said as she turned and trudged wearily across the car park, the weight of the world on her shoulders, dragging her bag and her feet. I watched her go, aghast. Heavens – her exam! That's why we'd been rushing! Oh God, I was losing it. I shook my head hopelessly as I shoved the gears roughly into reverse. There was no doubt about it, I was really, really, losing it.

And I must keep more of an eye on that young lady, I reflected sagely, making for the exit and still watching her in my rear-view mirror. I wasn't sure I was entirely happy about her spending so much time with the builders when I was out. It seemed to be putting all sorts of precocious ideas in her head. And she needn't think she could pull the wool over *my* eyes either, needn't think I didn't know what was going on. Reading after nine o'clock, indeed! I swung out of the gates with a knowing little sniff and headed for home.

When I got back, I made some tea and took it into the new kitchen where, despite their rather splendid surroundings of which they should have been justifiably proud, I found a pretty subdued bunch of boys beavering away. Mac and Alf didn't seem to be able to drag their faces out of the Aga fuse box to look me in the eye, and Spiro had his hat pulled right down over his eyes as he crouched to fix some skirting boards. I frowned as I looked around for somewhere to set the tray.

'You all right, boys? You all look a bit peaky this morning.'

Lance appeared from behind the larder door and took the tray from me. 'Claudia tell you about last night?'

'Last night?' I tried to remember. 'Oh, about coming over to watch the television?' Suddenly I realised they felt they'd overstepped the mark and that a strict line should be taken. I straightened up. 'She did actually, and listen, guys, you know I don't mind if I'm here, but I do draw the line if I'm out, OK?'

'OK,' they mumbled quickly, heads down. I turned to go. Hesitated. It was unnervingly quiet.

'Did she stay up late?' I demanded suddenly.

'A bit,' admitted Mac, quietly.

'And did she watch anything unsuitable?'

There was a long and tremulous pause.

'Not . . . on telly, no,' said Lance, finally.

'Good.' I nodded. 'That's all right then, but another time, please remember she goes to bed at nine o'clock.'

I turned to go, but Mac straightened up to face me for the first time that morning.

'I'd say we'll be out of your hair in a couple of weeks, luv.'

'Really?' I was startled. 'What, finished?'

'Yep, 'bout ten days.'

'Gosh, as little as that.' I realised, with a strange pang, that somehow I'd thought they'd be here for ever.

'Well, now that the Aga's in and the cupboards are nearly there, we've only got the new bathroom suite to plumb in upstairs and you're laughing.'

'Yes. Yes, I suppose I am. Yes, you're right, that'll be it then,' I said, cranking up a smile. I walked across and stroked the top of the shiny, navy-blue Aga which had finally gone in yesterday. Its concrete plinth built, it had been ceremoniously set, then plumbed in upon it, and was heating up nicely now, enthroned and radiating warmth like some plump, benign king of a South Sea island.

'You'll be glad to see the back of us,' said Mac. 'Bet you can't wait to have the place to yourself!'

'Yes!' I laughed, but it had a hollow ring to it. 'I expect everyone's glad to see the back of you, aren't they?'

'Too right they are!'

'Still,' I said softly, 'it'll be quiet without you.'

I drummed my fingers on the hob cover. There didn't seem to be an answer to that. I turned, and as I went, caught Lance's eye. He looked away quickly. Well, of course he would. An embarrassingly sad housewife who was admitting to a flicker of regret at seeing her builders go? Crikey. Most people hung out the flags! Declared it a day of celebration! I wandered through to the front hall, biting my lower lip. And not just regret, I realised in horror, also – yes, I felt a wee bit panicky, too. Alone then, in this house – apart from Claudes – for the first time since . . . well, you know. And you see, because of the boys, I hadn't actually been alone, yet. There'd always been someone to talk to, to share a joke with, to take a cup of tea to.

I stopped and picked up the mail from the mat, marvelling at myself. Good grief, I *was* sad, wasn't I? Genuinely pathetic. Actually admitting that the place wouldn't be the same without a rusty old cream caravan blocking the view of the cherry tree, or a clapped-out lorry monopolising the driveway. Why, only yesterday I'd met Alf, backing out of my downstairs loo – the Portaloo apparently being occupied – and squirting a cheap, lavender spray in a desperate attempt to veil the sensational whiff he'd left behind, the result being a sort of lavender-bush-with-dog-poo-on-it aroma. Well, I could do without that, couldn't I? And what about the constant stench of roll-ups and Pot Noodles, the blaring radio, the empty crisp packets that went forth and multiplied on a daily basis – I wasn't going to miss any of that, surely? I stared out of the window at the bright blue morning-glory that had wound itself around the frame, bursting into transitory flower. Don't answer that, Olivia.

Instead, I turned briskly to the letters I'd picked up, and opened a bill from Barclaycard – before dropping it hurriedly on the mat again. Heavens! Really? As much as that? Were they talking lire? And for what? I peered down, kicking it around so I could see the print. Oh, OK. Wretched linen dress and kitten-heeled shoes. I hated them already.

I leant back against the front door and flicked through the rest of the post. And OK, I conceded, I *would* answer that previous question. What I'd miss, all right, what I'd miss, apart from the jokes and the banter, was the feeling that they were on my side, that they were with me, rather than against me, which frankly, was becoming a rare commodity these days. I mean, take last night for instance. Crikey, if all my enemies had conspired beforehand they couldn't have planned it – Hello, what's this? I stopped flicking through, and turned over a rather smart cream envelope, addressed to Mrs Olivia McFarllen, and penned with something of a flourish. No address or stamp, so hand delivered. I ripped it open quickly. Inside, in the middle of a piece of thick, expensive paper, in italics in black ink was written:

Dear Olivia,

That was a brave thing you did last night. Come for drinks tonight at seven, if you can.

Yours,
Sebastian.

I stared. Read it again. Brave thing. Me. Drinks. Tonight. Me brave. Him Sebastian. Thing. I did. Blimey!

I lowered it for a moment, and stared. How sweet. How very, very sweet, and how – well, forgiving. And, gosh, yes, of course I'd go, but . . . gulped, golly. Talk about going back into the lion's den. But then again, he didn't sound very lionlike, did he? I raised the paper and read it again. No, more dovelike. More dove with olive branch in beak, in fact. I turned and walked slowly upstairs, one hand trailing thoughtfully on the banister rail, one still clutching the note, then sat, my heart hammering slightly, on the edge of my bed.

So . . . off to Sebastian's, eh. Bound to be a terribly smart and sophisticated affair; what on earth should I wear? I jumped up abruptly, and hastened to my wardrobe, flinging the doors wide. I riffled through the hangers with a vengeance, tail up, nose twitching, sniffing my way along. Now . . . let's see . . . which of my lovelies . . . I got to the end of the hangers, blinked in surprise, then went back to the beginning again. Eventually I stood back, folded my arms peevishly. Well, what on earth did one wear for a bevy with a famous composer, for heaven's sake? And was it just me, or would there be others? Because if it *was* just the two of us, anything more than trousers and a shirt would be over the top, but if, say, it were a celebration, a post-concert party perhaps, then something a bit more stylish would be called for. Maybe – maybe this? I pulled out a little black number I hadn't worn in years. Stared at it. What are you thinking of, Olivia? This is drinks with a neighbour, just down the street, not cocktails with a crown prince at St James's Palace. And anyway, why are you so excited?

I hung the black dress up slowly, went back and sat down on the bed. I'm not excited, I reasoned, just – flattered. That's all. And relieved. That he's no longer angry. I raised my chin. Got up and went across to the cheval mirror. But I'm not *excited*. Hell, no. I smiled at my reflection, tucked my hair back behind my ears. Why, only the other day I was calling him Sad Sebastian, for goodness' sake; he was still the same person now, wasn't he? Why should I be any more interested? Quite.

I shut my wardrobe door firmly and turned to my chest of drawers. From the bottom drawer, I shook out a pair of khaki Gap trousers – a bit creased and faded, but perfectly serviceable – and a white shirt. I gazed at them. All the same, that huge talent, that masterful way he clearly had with quavers and semiquavers – you couldn't deny that had a certain glamour, a certain cachet? I mean, Jeremy Paxman wouldn't be the same without his masterful way with dodgy politicians, and what about Alan Titchmarsh's masterful way with turnips, or Imran Khan's – No, OK, Imran Khan would be absolutely delicious whether he was masterful with a cricket bat or not. I sighed and pushed the bottom drawer in with my foot. But there had definitely been something commanding about that man's presence last night, hadn't there? And not just because the luvvies were simpering around him either. No, there was something very . . . watchable about him. Of course, I reasoned, a dinner jacket always helps, and a few inches off those wayward, gypsyish curls . . .

I shook myself and went back to gaze at my reflection in the mirror again. Golly, I looked old. I peered closer. Older still, close up. I put my fingertips on my cheekbones and pulled the skin back. Much better, shame I couldn't hook it behind my ears, took ten years off me. Couldn't smile, of course, but you could see why people fell for it. I dropped the skin and my face fell with a shudder, now resembling a Van Gogh self-portrait. Ah well, perhaps he was an ankles man? I gazed down at them ruefully. It was pretty much all there was left, these days. I glanced back up at my face sharply. Oh, don't be ridiculous, Olivia, the man's an intellectual, he won't be looking at your ankles or your cheekbones, he'll be interested in your mind! I nearly buckled at the knees in terror at this thought, and hurriedly racked my brains to think of any famous pieces of music I could talk about. 'What do you like?' he might well ask. Yes, well, he might well ask. Um . . . Wasn't the theme from one of Claudia's old Disney videos something memorable – *Sleeping Beauty*, was it, or . . . oh yes, the music from the Hovis ad, with the lad trudging up the cold northern hill? I mulled it over for a moment, but fearing that the next thing to spring to mind might be so staggeringly prosaic I'd even horrify myself and be forced to decline the invitation, I abandoned my mind, and instead, with a sigh, went downstairs in search of chocolate to appease my body.

Chapter Seventeen

When I finally ran out of the house at half-past seven that evening, I was hot, flustered, out of control, and not at all in the cultured, sophisticated frame of mind I'd intended. For a start, there had been huge hassles over the baby-sitting. When I'd popped into the kitchen to see the boys and ask Spiro, seeing as it was his turn, I'd been met with such flushed faces and a horrified silence, I was taken aback.

'What? What's the matter?'

Finally Spiro found his tongue. 'Oh, Meesis McFarllen, I feel so badly, I fall on your breast with shame. I theenk you not know, but last night, I seen your shreddies, I seen your jugs jacket, I see –'

'Hang on, seen what? Jugs what? Spiro, what on earth do you mean?'

'I think what Spiro means,' said Mac, stepping in smoothly, 'is that we thought we might go out for a curry tonight. Didn't we, boys?'

They nodded to a man. Beaming with relief until I thought their faces would split in half.

'Yeah, that's right,' agreed Alf happily. 'A curry. Need to get out, see, have a bit of a vindaloo.' He rubbed his stomach and grinned even wider. I feared for my lavatory pans.

'Oh! Oh, well, that's a bit of a blow.' I frowned. God, it

was a blow, actually. Suddenly I saw my sophisticated evening disintegrating. Where the hell was I going to get a baby-sitter at such short notice?'

'Perhaps I could ask Nanette,' I wondered aloud. 'I think she might be on her own this week.'

'And if she can't,' put in Lance quietly, 'I'll do it. I'm not that desperate for a curry.'

'Oh, Lance, that's awfully kind,' I beamed. 'You're an angel. I tell you what, I'll keep you in reserve.'

'You do that,' he muttered with ill-concealed sarcasm. I glanced at him, startled. Now what the hell did he have to be peeved about? His face betrayed nothing, though, so I shrugged. Oh well, I couldn't cope with sulky builders right now. I had bigger fish to fry.

I hastened over to see Nanette, who was indeed Roger-less, and who declared that she'd be delighted. She and Claudia liked nothing more than a girly nail-varnish-and-highlights chat, and they'd already had a couple of cosy evenings together, painting toes, putting face packs on and wading through *Hello!* magazines searching for Posh and Becks, something Claudia complained she didn't get enough of from me.

'Where are you going, anyway?' called Nanette, hanging out of an upstairs window which she'd pushed open when she'd heard the doorbell. She was jangling armfuls of bangles and clutching a duster in her nails.

'Sebastian's,' I muttered, glancing nervously down the street.

'*Sebastian's!*' she shrieked. 'I don't *believe* it!'

'Nanette, you were totally wrong about him,' I hissed, 'he's not a nutter, or a teacher, he's a world-famous musician! A composer for heaven's sake – he's Sebastian Faulkner!'

She frowned. Shook her head. 'Never heard of him. Who?'

'Oh, never mind. Let's not discuss it at the top of our voices in the street. I'll see you later, OK?'

'Be there at seven o'clock.'

'Great.'

Except, of course, that she wasn't. Seven o'clock came and went and I paced about the garden for a bit. Then, when it got to twenty past, I rang her.

'Nanette, are you coming?'

'Of course, darling. Just getting ready.'

'Nanette, you're *baby*-sitting! You don't have to get ready, just come over, please! I'm going to be late!' I wailed.

'Okey-doke.'

Five minutes went by. Then ten, so I rushed off to get Lance.

'She *is* coming,' I yelled through the caravan door, 'but she's going to be late, so I just wondered – Oops – sorry!' The door opened and he appeared with just a towel around his waist, fresh from the shower. I covered my eyes and carried on talking. 'I just wondered, could you possibly come over just till she arrives?'

'Sure, and you can uncover your eyes too. I'm perfectly respectable, you know. You mustn't be so uptight, Livvy.'

'Right, yes. Sorry.'

I dropped my hand and he dropped his towel.

'*Lance!*' My hand shot to my eyes again.

'Sorry, I dropped it,' he laughed.

313

'Oooh, *God!*'

Seething now, I turned and raced back to the house to find Claudia, lying on the sofa reading a teenage magazine.

'Darling, it's half-past seven,' I panted, checking my hair in the mirror, 'and I must go. Lance will be up in two ticks followed by Nanette, OK?'

'Fine. Can I watch *The Simpsons*?'

'No you *can't* watch *The Simpsons*. Do some flipping homework for a change why don't you!'

She looked up from her mag. 'Mum, you're nervous.'

'What?'

'I can tell when you're nervous, you always get stroppy. Take a deep breath and think –' she turned back to her magazine and read – '"I can do this. I can trap this man. I'm gorgeous."'

'Oh, for God's sake!' I snatched the comic from her hands, reached into the bookcase, flung *Anne of Green Gables* at her and stormed out. All of which was not particularly conducive to feeling calm, confident, and collected as I beetled across the cobbles in shoes that, frankly, could have come out of Nanette's wardrobe. I hadn't worn anything like these mules, or the peacock-blue pedal pushers I'd squeezed into, since I was about twenty, but I had a feeling the place might be teeming with trendy arty types and I didn't want to look frumpy. I wondered, as I ran along, tucking back my hair, if I looked too frivolous, though, and tried desperately to look serious and intelligent. Oh, and musical. I hummed a little tune. Abba. Hopeless, Olivia, just shut up. As I ran up the steps to the front door and teetered on the top one to ring the bell, it occurred to me to wonder if mother would be in. I did hope not. I wasn't convinced she'd be conducive to the artistic atmosphere within, unless, of course, it was in some dismal, gothic novel, sort of way.

Two seconds later, well-heeled heels came drumming down the hall, and the door was thrown back to reveal – not mother, but Sebastian. Such was my relief, I beamed.

'Hi!'

His face, which I realised had been on the point of holding back some reserve, relaxed at my smile.

He grinned. 'Hi, come in.'

He stood aside to let me into a huge, smoky-blue hall-way, covered in prints and drawings, with a vast iron and stone staircase which swept up and up, curling finally to an enormous round glass lantern in the roof, storeys high.

'Gosh!' I stared. 'I had no idea these houses were so big!'

'Deceptive, aren't they?' he agreed, following my gaze. 'That's what I liked about it when I saw it. Very under-stated on the outside and full of surprises within.'

He turned back to me, and I suddenly realised that I was exactly the reverse. Very overstated on the outside in these ridiculous peacock-blue trousers, and no surprises at all within. Why hadn't I worn something grey and sub-tle to match the chaste good taste of this house, instead of something more at home in Nanette's all white shag pile? Sebastian himself was wearing ancient cords – the badge of the intelligentsia – and a blue Boden shirt. I did notice, though, that he'd clearly just washed his hair because it was still a bit damp at the edges. We stood there smiling at each other.

'I just wanted –'

'Olivia, I –'

We laughed. 'Go ahead,' he said, scraping back short dark waves, 'you go first.'

I felt my meagre supply of words dwindling but ploughed on regardless. 'Well, I – I just wanted to say how sorry I was. You know, about all that ghastly business with Claudia and then gate-crashing your party last night when I should have known better. I've – well, I've been a total imbecile and I'm sorry.'

He smiled. 'Forget it. God, I meant to say forget it in the note – did I not say that? Come on, let's go through and sit in the garden. It's too stuffy in here.' He guided me through the house. 'Anyway, apart from anything else, you apologised quite enough last night, explained yourself perfectly, and very eloquently too, definitely had the crowd on your side. I got a bit nervous at one point, thought I was going to be lynched, and it made me realise that had I been in your shoes, I might well have thought I was the mad flasher-mac man, too.'

'Really?' I gazed about as I found myself on an elegant terrace, spilling over with urns of ivy and dusty white geraniums. I sat down on the French café chair he held out. Clearly it was just the two of us and I felt hugely relieved.

'Really,' he confirmed, as he sat beside me, a tiny iron table between us. 'I'd forgotten about that tigress instinct mothers have, but looking back I seem to remember mine was just the same. When I was about eight, she once saw me talking to a strange man in our road and came tearing up, demanding to know if he'd offered me sweeties or anything. As the poor man opened his mouth to speak she beat him about the head with her handbag. She wasn't to know he was my housemaster, I suppose.'

'Oh God!' I giggled and took the beautifully chilled glass of Pouilly Fumé he offered me. 'Is she here now?' I glanced nervously around.

'Who?'

'Your mother.'

He put down his glass, sat back and regarded me curiously. 'You know, the first time I met you, Olivia, you showed an inordinate amount of interest in my mother. She lives in Dorset, with my father. Why on earth would she be here?'

'In Dorset! Oh! So – so who's that – that woman then?' I jerked my head back housewards. 'With the hair,' I scraped mine back to demonstrate, 'and the teeth.' I stuck mine out rattily.

'Maureen? She's my girlfriend.'

I dropped my hair. Stared. 'You're kidding!'

He laughed. 'Of course. She's my housekeeper.'

'Oh!'

'Because I live on my own and I'm fairly hopeless on the domestic front, she cleans and puts food in front of me now and again. She's got a flat in the basement. Why on earth did you think she was my mother?'

'Because Nanette said –' I stopped, flushing, as I remembered what Nanette had said. She clearly hadn't a clue, but wanting to appear informed, had creatively filled in the gaps on the strength of very limited information.

He folded his arms, mouth twitching slightly. 'Yes, what exactly *did* Nanette say? I'm keen to learn, if only to discover why, at that godawful dinner party of hers, you addressed me so slowly and distinctly and in words of only one syllable. At first I thought it might be because you were brain-dead, but then when you miraculously recovered your powers of speech to address the rest of the party, it occurred to me that you might imagine I was, am I right?'

I flushed and picked at an imaginary speck of dust on my trousers. 'Oh God, Sebastian, this is all so horribly embarrassing,' I mumbled. 'You see – well, the thing is, Nanette told me you were a bit . . . unhinged.'

'Unhinged.' He mulled the word over, nodding soberly. 'Right. Why so, exactly?'

'Oh, such silly reasons, too stupid to even –'

'No no,' he interrupted, 'I insist on being enlightened. It might happen again you see, and I need to know how to curb my derangement in public. Do I twitch maniacally? Inadvertently sing at table, suck my thumb and twiddle with my hair during pudding?'

I giggled. 'Well, OK she said –' I gazed at my trousers – 'she said you stood in front of your window all day long waving your arms about like a windmill.' I glanced up. 'Oh, and she also said you ran around the streets in your pyjamas.'

'*A la* Wee Willie Winkie?'

I grinned. 'I suppose, but listen, Nanette's hopeless; she gets everything wrong and –'

'No, not, not at all. As a matter of fact, our Nanette is very observant, and I fear I might well have to plead guilty on both of those counts, but would you first like to hear my defence, before you actually send for the men in white coats?'

'Oh, heavens no,' I said hastily, 'please don't bother. I mean we all have our foibles, Sebastian, and to be honest I've got some very odd habits so –'

'The arm waving,' he interrupted, 'is perfectly legit, and stems from me conducting as I compose in my head. Before it gets to the piano, and before it makes it on to paper. Does that make sense?'

'Perfectly,' I beamed.

'But the pyjamas . . .' He scratched his head. 'I can only assume it was that time I ran into her in Waitrose when I was probably wearing some comfortable old stripy trousers I picked up in a market in Afghanistan. I tend to work in them – oh, and a crumpled old T-shirt that probably looked – to our manicured Nanette – like I'd slept in it. And of course I always look appalling when I'm working and haven't had a haircut for months. Mad, probably. Will that do? Or do you need further and better particulars?'

'No no,' I laughed, 'that will do.' His brown eyes were merry and far from steely now as they met mine over the white wine. He had one of those thin, intelligent, Jeremy Irons type faces that leant naturally to the serious, but when animated, was very attractive.

'And the teacher bit?' I blurted quickly, realising I was staring shamelessly. 'Nanette had some crazy idea that you were let loose on small boys on your day release from the institution.' I laughed, then stopped abruptly. 'Oh – hang on, in fact *you* told me that too, I remember, at dinner!'

He nodded. 'Well, it's absolutely true, although teaching's probably overstating it somewhat. But I do go to the High School about once a month to talk to the boys.'

'Oh, right. What about?'

319

'Table tennis.'

I blinked.

'Music, Olivia,' he said patiently. 'Composition and the-ory, that sort of thing.'

'Oh! Of course!' I laughed nervously, but flushed dra-matically. God, you *moron*, Olivia, you must stop sounding so inane. And why are you sitting here like some fearless, probing breakfast TV reporter, getting this world-famous musician to explain why he's yet to be locked up and have the key thrown away? Who d'you think you are, Judy Finnigan? Oprah Winfrey, even? I shut up for a moment, and gazed instead at his immaculate walled garden, the one I'd zigzagged across, Apache style, just a few days ago. It was very well designed, in a tasteful, white-flowers-and-greenery sort of way, and since I so often feel that gardens reflect their owners, I wondered if this was the man. Con-trolled, precise, safe. For some reason, I felt it might not be. One thing was for sure, though, he certainly wasn't a gusher. He chose his words with care, whilst I tended to choose mine with reckless abandon. I tried to think of something intelligent to say.

'I loved your music last night,' I lied.

He smiled. 'Thank you. Was it your sort of thing? I mean, is that what you like to listen to, as a rule?'

I hesitated, sensing a sure-fire way to ingratiate myself, but could I then bluff my way, musically speaking, for an entire evening? I licked my lips.

'Um, listen, Sebastian, could I possibly retract that last remark? Only, the thing is, it was a bit of a fib. I was so preoccupied last night I didn't actually listen to a note.'

His eyes widened. 'Oh. Right.'

'I mean I'm quite sure it would have been my thing,' I hastened on, 'I'm sure I'd have loved it, but the reason I wasn't listening was because my husband turned up with his girlfriend, and I had trouble concentrating on anything other than taking a pot shot at the pair of them.'

'Dear me,' he stammered, scratching his head. 'Yes, that must have been very – difficult.' He reached for the bottle and looked awkward.

Ah, well done, Olivia. You're embarrassing the socks off him now, airing all your dirty linen in public. But something told me to plough on. Something told me that in order to establish any sort of channel here, any sort of rapport, all small talk had to be banned, even if it meant making a monumental fool of myself in the process. The refined good taste of our surroundings somehow made it all the harder.

'He left me a few months ago, you know.'

'Yes, I had heard. Nanette, you know . . .' He hastily refilled his glass, eyes lowered.

'Went off with a teacher at Claudia's school. Of course, that was pretty hard to take, pretty gut-wrenching, but I guess I'm more or less used to it now.' I nodded bravely. 'I guess I'm getting over it.' God, I sounded like I was in therapy now, spilling the beans to some New York analyst – and when had I ever said 'I guess'? Twice!

He smiled, put the bottle down. 'From my experience, Olivia, it takes a lot longer than a few months to get over something like that.'

'Your experience?' I pounced. Ah, now we were getting somewhere.

'Oh, very limited,' he said hastily. 'We weren't married,

like you are, and no children, so . . .' He shrugged dismissively.

'But it was serious?'

He paused. 'Very.' There was another long pause, but I
kept quiet, knowing that was the only way. That he'd go
on only if he wanted to.

'We met about five years ago. Quite late to fall in love,
I suppose – I mean, properly, for the first time. I'd got
to the ripe old age of thirty-two thinking it would never
happen.'

I did some quick mental arithmetic and filled up his
glass shamelessly, even though it was practically brimming
over, keen to hear more. He cradled it and narrowed his
eyes, gazing pensively over his green enclosure. Leaves
dipped and danced against the high brick walls in the long
evening shadows. He turned, looked directly at me.

'It was doomed, right from the start, actually. Madness
when I think about it now. We were both too set in our
ways, too long in the tooth perhaps, and too attached to
our customs, our countries –'

'Our countries?'

'Lara's Russian. She plays in the Russian National
Orchestra and we met when one of my symphonies was
being performed over there. I went across to oversee
rehearsals; she was a first violinist.'

'Oh!'

Gosh, how romantic could you get? My mind flew to a
rehearsal room somewhere, and in the front row of the
orchestra, a beautiful violinist, one arm cradling her
instrument, the other bowing beautifully, revealing slim
arms, a perfect figure, long blonde hair – I was sure – eyes,

full of passion for the music, meeting the dark eyes of the handsome composer over the music stands, as she made his dream, his masterpiece come to life. And Lara! It had to be Lara, didn't it, Zhivago's lost love, calling to her desperately as he crawled through the snow – 'Lara! Lara! Lara!' No doubt she looked just like Julie Christie too. I sighed.

'How romantic. Didn't you try to make it work?'

'Oh, sure. I spent two years in Russia and she spent a couple over here, but I hated the place and couldn't compose there. Musically speaking I dried up completely, and England had pretty much the same effect on Lara. She missed her family, friends, her language – that's what she missed the most, actually, not being able to chatter away, ever, in her own tongue. It's not like being French or German and living over here, because there are plenty of other French and Germans too, but not many Russians, and Lara got very lonely. Felt terribly isolated. She stopped playing, stopped going to the orchestra even.'

'Gosh, how sad! So she went back?'

'Fourteen months ago. Precisely. Which is why I say to you, Olivia, don't expect the scars to fade so quickly. I've been at this lark much longer than you have and mine are still there.'

'I know,' I said in a small voice. 'I was being flippant when I said I was used to it. Of course I'm not. It's like getting used to having your arm chopped off. I don't think I'll ever be whole again.' I took a big shaky breath. 'I miss him so much.' I stared into my lap. Oh God, was I really doing this? I couldn't believe I was. I concentrated hard on a chipped paving stone.

'I know,' he said quietly. 'I know how you feel. And some days are better than others, aren't they? Some days you can kid yourself you're all right, that you're actually staggering from the depths towards dry land, and then just as you reach the beach, a bloody great tidal wave crashes over your head and drags you back in again.'

'That's it,' I wobbled, 'that's exactly how it is. It's like I'll never reach that bloody beach.' To my horror and eternal shame, a great tear ran down my nose and plopped into my lap. I brushed it away furiously, not sure if he saw, but if he did, to his credit, he tactfully pretended not. There was a silence for a while.

'Right,' he said suddenly, standing up, 'enough of all that. Goodbye to all that, in fact. Come on, let's get cracking.' He rubbed his hands together briskly, smiling down at me.

I blinked, nervously. 'Cracking?'

'Oh,' he scratched his head sheepishly, 'sorry, I do that. Think of things without saying them and then go one step further and carry them out.' He grinned. 'Comes from living alone, I think. No, I just thought – well, since you missed out on so much music last night, I'd play you something wonderful tonight. Bach is my big passion at the moment, but I'm open to Schubert on a beautiful evening like this, or perhaps you'd prefer something – I don't know – more joyous? Scarlatti, perhaps?'

'Oh!' I smiled. 'Well, that would be great, but couldn't we listen to something of yours?'

'Of mine?'

'Yes, since that's what I missed last night. Has that Abbey thing been recorded yet?'

He grinned. 'That "Abbey thing" hasn't, as yet. It'll have to be something else, but then again they're all pretty similar.' He turned and went inside through the French windows, crossing the drawing room to the CD player. 'I churn out the same old rubbish, as a rule.'

'What rot,' I said warmly, picking up my glass and following him in. 'Everyone says how marvellous you are!'

'Ah, yes, everyone,' he said scanning his CDs, his back to me. 'Everyone who's desperate to embrace modern music, determined not to seem backward-thinking, keen to be progressive and avant-garde. It's rather like the art world – critics rave about the latest Damien Hirst or whatever, but do they really like it or are they just terrified of not seeming hip?'

'Perhaps they don't understand it,' I said, making what I considered to be my first intelligent contribution that evening.

He turned abruptly. 'D'you know, I really object to that assumption. That's just the sort of obnoxious, smug, pretentious twaddle the darlings of the creative world like to peddle. Art and music are there to be enjoyed, not understood!'

'Oh, er, yes I quite agree. I was just, um, repeating what someone else said.'

'Oh, right.'

'Yes, um. Ursula Mitchell,' I lied disloyally. 'She's terribly sweet,' I added with a surge of guilt, 'it's just that, well, she longs to be part of that arty milieu.' Oh good *word*, Olivia.

He shrugged. 'Well, I don't really know her, but I can imagine. I know the type. Anyway,' he slipped the CD in, 'here goes. Oh, by the way, I'm assuming you'll stay for supper? Maureen put some sort of casserole in the oven. She's a disastrous cook but she's been with me for years now and I haven't the heart to tell her. Would you care to join me in picking the gristle out of her goat's bladder stew?'

I giggled. 'That's the most attractive offer I've had in a long time. I'd love to, but I might just ring home. I told Nanette I'd only be about an hour or so.'

'Sure. It's in the hall.'

When I got back from the phone, Sebastian was sitting up rather straight in a high, wing-back chair on one side of the fireplace, remote control in hand, fingers tapping impatiently. He looked up. 'Ready?'

'Oh, yes, sure!' I hastened to my chair, realising that this wasn't background schmaltz we were about to listen to. We weren't going to chat above it either, or even have it on while we had supper – no, we were going to sit here and listen. I perched rigidly on an identical chair the other side of the marble fireplace and clasped my hands on my knees. What was I supposed to look at, for heaven's sake. Him? Or should I shut my eyes? Or would that be considered smug and obnoxious again? Christ, I hadn't really been educated for this. I hoped I wasn't going to fart in the slow movement or something terrible. His hand went to flick the switch, then abruptly – paused. He frowned.

'I say, this is awfully pretentious of me, isn't it? Asking you round then foisting my music upon you?'

'Don't be ridiculous. You didn't foist anything on me, I asked!'

'Yes, but if I were an acrobat or something, and suddenly on a whim I rolled back the carpet and performed my double backflip, or – or a plumber insisting you inspect my S-bends, or –'

'Oh, for God's sake, Sebastian, just get on with it and put it on!'

'Righto.'

He gave a mock salute and obliged with a grin, but that little exchange had relaxed me. I felt that the somewhat academic atmosphere had been purged. I leant back in my chair and crossed my legs.

'Well, this particular piece is played by the Berlin Philharmonic. It's called *The Rigorous Judgement*.'

Blimey, *The Rigorous Judgement*. I sat bolt upright again. Perhaps I'd been right about that garden, after all. Perhaps he was into order and control. I braced myself and waited.

The Rigorous Judgement, however, began sublimely. Breezy flutes and other pleasant windy things piped softly and wistfully and I imagined we were somewhere – oh goodness, somewhere pastoral and sylvan, with a bird perhaps – a piccolo was it? – lifting the melody. I gazed contentedly into the empty grate, letting myself be lulled along, cajoled by gently rising passages until, abruptly, the mood changed. The bird seemed to cry out in alarm, there was a shriek, and suddenly, it seemed the woods were upon us. Dark, base notes sounded ominously, one after the other, coming like footsteps all the time, and simultaneously terrified piping noises whirled overhead, swooping and crying as the strings gathered momentum. The intensity built, and as drums and cymbals joined the violins, there was a sudden sprawling change of key, as horns and trumpets heralded some sort of procession, some kind of parade. I sat up a bit. Braced myself. More and more triumphant waves unfolded until there was a great orchestral wall of sound, and then suddenly – it stopped. A single flute piped on, to a clearing, perhaps, where the strings started up again, softly. They played quietly for a while until, finally, they too faded away, as the picture faded too, leaving nothing behind, but a tantalising afterglow.

I stared at Sebastian in silence for a moment, realising I was actually on the edge of my seat. For a while there I was speechless. I felt my cheeks flush red.

'Good heavens, that was beautiful!' I finally managed.

'Really?'

'God, *really*!' I gasped. 'I mean, well, I've never sat down and listened properly to that sort of music before so I'm not the best person to ask – a complete philistine, in fact – but I could *see* it, Sebastian, and *feel* it too! I had no idea music could do that to you, had no idea you got pictures with it!'

He laughed. Stood up. 'Good.' He rubbed his hands together briskly. 'Well, come on, let's go down and get some supper, before you start reminding me of some of the more pseudy music critics I know.'

He caught my eye and I laughed, but I could tell he was pleased, and as I got up and followed him down the steps to the basement kitchen, it was with a considerably lighter heart. That music, dark and forbidding though it had been in parts, had somehow changed the mood of the evening. All guards were off and all defences down; it was as if he'd said, 'OK, this is me. Like me or loathe me,' just as I, I thought suddenly, could walk him round to my back yard, swing my arm towards my intricate beds, paths and borders and say, 'OK, well, this is me, too.'

As he struggled to get a huge, red-hot casserole out of the oven, he directed me to a drawer where I found some knives and forks, and I set about laying the table. Uncannily relaxed now – to my amazement he even flicked Capital Radio on – I sat down, as he manoeuvred the heavy Le Creuset across from the stove to the table, and lifted the lid. We stared into it for a moment in silence, then at each other. His mouth twitched. I swear to God, not even a dog, not even a ravenous Labrador, would hoover up that honking, heaving pile of bones.

'Bloody hell,' muttered Sebastian under his breath, and on an impulse, turned and tipped the whole lot in the bin.

He then had a surge of guilt about Maureen's hurt feelings, and giggling wildly, we had to lift out the steaming bin liner, wrap it in three more, and then take it to the dustbins outside. Whilst Sebastian was getting rid of the evidence, I managed to rustle up a mushroom omelette, find some rather good Brie lurking at the back of the fridge, and Sebastian came back and opened another bottle of wine. Finally, we sat down. The wine and the conversation flowed, barriers were lowered – I knew his past, or the important bits anyway, and he knew mine – and it seemed that we could now get on with the business of discussing friends, family – both subjects complicated – work, children, this single life – anything, in fact, of great, little, or no importance that sprung to mind. It was easy, it was relaxed, and later, as I toyed with the cheese, laughing as he recounted some musical anecdote, I even forgot to answer him.

'What?' he demanded.

I looked up. 'Sorry?'

'What were you thinking?'

I grinned. 'I was just thinking how different you are from that night when I first met you at Nanette's. I don't think you said more than two words to anyone, just stared fixedly at the curtains as if you were contemplating eating them or something.'

He wiped his mouth on his napkin. 'Ah yes, the dinner party from hell, with the used-car salesman, the couple who wanted to talk us through all eighteen of their home births, and the strange woman beside me, keen to hear about my macramé classes.' He grinned and I smiled back at him over the table. The kitchen clock ticked on in the silence. Suddenly I glanced up.

'Sebastian, I must go. It's way past twelve, Nanette will be pacing up and down.'

'Is it?' He looked up. 'God, and I've got to do some work tomorrow. Come on, let's get you out of here otherwise I'll be too wide awake to sleep and start tinkering with that wretched piano, composing whatever springs to mind well into the small hours, and then tomorrow I'll feel like death, when I should be wide awake and concentrating hard on doing some proper, paid, commissioned work.'

I laughed. 'Is that what you're like?'

'Oh, totally. It's compulsive, this music lark, I'm afraid, but only when I'm doing what I want. I'm surprised Nanette hasn't observed me tearing my hair out at four in the morning, mouthing obscenities at passers-by, called the police, even.'

We got up and he walked me to the door, opening it on to the warm, dark night, at which point, the first awkward moment of the evening arose. I turned, smiled.

'Good night then, and thanks, Sebastian.'

He scratched his head, which I'd noticed he did occasionally. 'Night, Olivia.'

We hesitated, and then I sort of lunged cheekwards, whilst he, unfortunately, lunged the other way. We laughed as we crashed noses, tried again, and finally accomplished a dignified social peck on the cheek.

'I should walk you back,' he called as I tripped down the steps into the street.

'Don't be ridiculous, you can *see* me back from there.'

He laughed. 'True.'

As I walked across the cobbles in the warm, still air, a crescent moon was rising over the tower of the Abbey, and I was aware and pleased that he was indeed watching me. As I got to my gate, I turned and waved, smiling. He raised his hand back in salute, and then the red front door closed as he went in. My smile faded and I stared at the door for a moment. Swallowed. Yes, that's what I miss, I reflected. Having a laugh. A giggle. Having – well, the companionship of a man. Oh sure, I had masses of girl-friends but I missed – yes, I missed maleness. I sighed, looked up at the stars. It wasn't the same as being with Johnny, of course. Nobody could make me roar like he could, make me literally throw back my head and hoot with laughter, and nobody could make me come alive as he did too, make me want to dive impulsively into bed with him, stay there all day. I absently dead-headed a day lily beside me. In a way, then, I realised sadly, this evening had been something of a poisoned chalice. It had made me realise what I missed: being the female part of a team, moving around the kitchen with a man, getting his perspective on things, laughing at his jokes – but it had also made me realise that nice as Sebastian was, he could never be Johnny. That no one could ever be Johnny. And up to now, that had never been so glaringly apparent, because up to now, I'd only met pretty second-rate men. But this one was first rate, and still he couldn't match up. I stared up at the stars finding the plough, its handle, the pan. Where did that leave me then? Sad and alone for twenty years, as Claudia kept doggedly reminding me, finally tottering into some dentist's waiting room with my gardening mags and seeing the light in a white-coated, middle-aged man's eye as he prepared to repair my molars, as time, finally, did its repair work, too?

I sighed and crunched up the empty drive to the front door. Mac's lorry was missing, so no doubt the curry evening had turned into eight pints and some sampling of the local nightlife, too. There'd be hangovers in the morning.

I put my key in the lock and heard the television quietly humming.

'Nanette? I'm back,' I whispered, shutting the door softly behind me.

I went into the sitting room, but the sofa was empty – no Nanette. She must be in the kitchen then. I turned the television off and went in to look. Apparently not. I tried the loo. 'Nanette?' I called quietly, knocking softly. I pushed open the door. Nothing.

Where was she? Slightly panicky now I dashed upstairs, first into Claudia's bedroom where to my relief, she was fast asleep, breathing peacefully, and still hugging her old blue rabbit. I smiled, pulled up her duvet and tucked her in. Then I frowned. Bloody hell, where on earth was Nanette? Crashed out on my bed? I went next door. No. In the spare room then, having decided it was so late she'd stay the night? I opened that door. Empty. Well, how very peculiar. I stood on the landing, frowning. Had she gone home? I'd told her I'd be late, for crying out loud. Surely she wouldn't do a thing like that? Leave Claudia here on her own? But then again, if Roger had suddenly rung up, announced he was back, been panting to see her . . . there was no knowing with Nanette. I stared out of the landing window. Suddenly it came to me: of course, the garden! It was a warm night – a sultry one, in fact – so she'd be down there, by the river, where we'd all gathered the other evening, sitting under the cedar tree armed with a drink and a magazine and gazing periodically at the stars. I know that's where I'd be.

I ran downstairs and went out, walking confidently down to the river. There I stopped, bewildered. The seats under the tree were deserted, as was – I swung back – the terrace. I turned around, biting my thumbnail. The caravan was in darkness across the stream, but on an impulse, I went across the little bridge towards it anyway. Perhaps Lance hadn't gone for a curry, after all; perhaps he'd know where she was. As I approached, though, I stopped dead in my tracks. Well, how odd . . . I peered. How very extraordinary. That really was the weirdest thing. The caravan was moving. Rocking, and bouncing up and down of its own accord, as if it had a momentum all of its own, as if it was, well, as if it was possessed! I ran up and flung open the door.

'Lance!'

'Shit!' came a voice from the shadows. Lance's voice.

Instinctively I flicked on the light.

At the other end of the caravan, where the beds pulled down from the wall, two naked bodies were caught, mid-writhe, on a lower bunk. Frantic bare arms scrabbled for the duvet on the floor, and as they hiked it up over their heads, naked legs and buttocks were still glaringly apparent below. Two tousled heads shot out from under it, and two pairs of startled eyes blinked at me in the brightness, like rabbits caught in headlamps. Lance's eyes, and Nanette's.

Chapter Eighteen

'Nanette!'

We stared at each other for a second, then I quickly slammed the caravan door.

'Oh, for God's *sake*!' I shrieked furiously at it.

Two seconds later she was out, hair standing on end, and hurriedly tying up a white nylon dressing gown with the legend 'Plasterers Do It Plastered' emblazoned on the front.

'Oh Lord, Olivia, what must you think?' she gasped, raking a hand through dishevelled hair. 'I'm so sorry, can't think *what* came over me!'

'Rampant hormones, I should think. Christ Almighty, Nanette, you're supposed to be baby-sitting my daughter, not shagging my builder!'

'Cabinet-maker,' she corrected quickly.

'And what if Claudia had come downstairs? What if she'd come outside and found you! Talk me through *that* charming little scenario, if you will!'

'Oh no,' she assured me earnestly, clutching my arm, 'I made absolutely sure she was fast asleep. I wouldn't have *dreamt* of doing anything untoward if there'd been the slightest chance she'd come down, really.'

'Don't be ridiculous,' I scoffed, 'you were probably so revved up it wouldn't have mattered if she'd been sitting right beside you on the sofa! Taking notes!'

'Well, at least we made it to the caravan,' she said peevishly, pulling the dressing gown around her. 'That was Lance's idea. He was being frightfully responsible, you know; you really mustn't blame him.'

'Responsible!'

'Well, I don't know why you're so upset, Livvy. It's not as if you wanted him, did you, so why shouldn't I?'

I gaped at her, speechless. 'What the hell has *that* got to do with anything!' I spluttered finally. 'The reason I'm upset, Nanette, is because I'm concerned for my daughter's welfare, and *you* were supposed to be looking after her! I couldn't give two hoots what you do with Lance in the privacy of your own home!'

'Oh no, I couldn't do it there.' She shook her head vehemently. 'It wouldn't be fair on Roger.'

'Roger! You're still planning on being fair to Roger, are you? Jesus! Well, what would he think about all – all this!' I flicked my hand despairingly at the caravan behind us.

'Oh, I think best not to tell him, don't you?' she said, glancing about nervously. 'I think we'll just keep it between ourselves and put it down to premarriage nerves, eh?'

'You didn't look very nervous in there!' I jerked my head back.

'No, no, I wasn't actually,' she agreed guilelessly, eyes wide. She lowered her voice and glanced back at the door. 'If you must know, Olivia,' she whispered, 'I was absolutely *fan-tastic*! Had him positively *squealing* for more, and we did it four times, and the fourth time his teeth nearly went through the duvet like a tatty old sandwich!'

'Nanette, I really don't –'

'And as for him!' She rolled her eyes dramatically. 'Boy,

is he *heaven*. I swear to God, Olivia, you don't know *what* you're missing, and listen –' she clutched my arm as I tried to interrupt – 'I'm really happy to share, honestly. It's frightfully greedy of me, what with Roger as well, and as far as I'm concerned Lance is just a delightful diversion with a cute little backside, but you could really *do* with him, darling. Make you feel *loads* better, I swear, and I'd hate to think I was hogging the lion's share or anything.'

'Ah,' I said folding my arms grimly as Lance appeared, doing up his jeans. 'The lion himself.'

'Oh er, hi, Livvy,' he said rather sheepishly. I must say he looked all in, utterly exhausted as he staggered down the steps.

'Lance, I was just explaining to Nanette here, that with an impressionable ten-year-old about I'd rather you didn't enliven her sex education with practical demonstrations in my back garden, OK?'

Lance shrugged. 'Your back garden, but our caravan, surely?'

'Then move it,' I hissed. 'Tow it to Waitrose car park next time you feel the urge, but *don't do it in my back yard*!'

He regarded me with a quizzical smile. 'I really don't know why you're so upset. Claudia was fast asleep.'

'Yes, and alone! Anyone could have walked in!'

'Oh, come on, being in the back garden doesn't exactly constitute leaving her –'

''Ello 'ello 'ello! I feel like PC Plod breaking up this happy gathering. Wha's going on then?' Mac elbowed his way roughly into our heated little circle and flung a drunken arm round my shoulder. 'What's up, luv? Wha's occurring?'

337

'Ah, good, Mac, you're back,' I said, relieved. 'I was just explaining the house rules, *vis-à-vis* sexual activity, to Lance and Nanette here, hoping to keep it off the premises, as it were. I'm sure you'll back me up.' I folded my arms grimly.

Mac looked from Lance to Nanette. He blinked in astonishment, then a slow, beery grin developed. He took a deep breath, raised a finger, and seemed on the point of making a profound statement, when round the corner Spiro and Alf suddenly lurched into view, arms round each other's shoulders, singing their respective national anthems in their respective tongues, at the top of their voices. As they approached, they stopped singing, slowed down, and came to a halt in front of Nanette. They swayed a bit, and looked her up and down with considerable inter-est. Nervously clutching the neck of the dressing gown, Nanette turned and scuttled back into the caravan. Alf turned to me and raised startled eyebrows.

'Orraaghff?' It was half belch and half interrogative, and roughly translated from troglodyte, I imagine it meant – Good evening, Mrs McFarllen, so what the devil's your neighbour doing in my dressing gown then? I shud-dered. Christ! And to think I'd thought I'd *miss* them!

'You bin a naughty boy, then, Lance?' grinned Mac with road-map eyes, wagging a crooked finger at him. 'You bin a bit of a lad? You dirty devil, you! You see?' he hissed alcoholically in my ear, 'I told you he was a one wiv the birds. Can't keep 'em off him, like flies round a pile of shite they are. Looks like you've missed yer chance there, though, luv. Looks like No No Nanette has turned into Yes Yes Nanette and got in there first!'

I noticed Lance watching me carefully.

'Oh, you conceited idiot!' I hissed. 'You actually think I mind, don't you? You actually think that I'm gnashing my teeth here, cursing my bad luck, because instead of having a delightful supper down the road with an eminent musician, I could have been getting my leg over your "cute little backside" in your SQUALID LITTLE CARAVAN!'

'MUM!'

I froze for a second – then swung round in horror to see Claudia, hanging out of her bedroom window in her nightie.

'Mum, what's going on?' she called sleepily. 'Why are you shouting like that? You woke me up!'

'Sorry, darling, sorry!' I called back in a hoarse whisper. 'Go back to bed, I'm coming!' I made to go towards her, then stopped in my tracks, turned. I took a step towards Lance. 'This is never, *never* to happen again, got it?' I breathed. He gazed at me with strange, heavy eyes, but didn't answer.

'Oh, for God's sake!' I spluttered impatiently, before beetling back up the garden path towards the house, towards my daughter.

I raced in through the back door, through the kitchen, and took the stairs two at a time, arriving to find her kneeling up in bed in her nightie, rubbing her eyes.

'What's happening? What's going on?'

'Nothing, darling, nothing at all. Lie down now and I'll tuck you in.'

'But what was all the fuss about?' murmured Claudia sleepily as I pulled the duvet back over her.

'Oh, nothing really. It was just – well, a fox got into the

garden, that's all. Went down the rubbish bins, made a bit of a racket. Now go back to sleep.'

'Oh.' She turned over to face the wall. 'Mum?'

'Hmm?' I paused, mid-creep to the door.

'What's – getting your leg over?'

I paused. Turned. 'It's . . . a riding expression. It's, you know – how you mount a horse.'

'But why were you talking about it just now?'

'Oh, because . . . because Mac was thinking of chasing the fox. On horseback.'

There was a brief silence. 'But we don't have a horse.'

'Exactly,' I breathed, 'which is why I told him it wasn't such a good idea!'

She turned back, stared at me as I went to shut her door.

'And a horse has a cute little backside?'

I swallowed. 'That's it!' I agreed brightly.

She smiled, turned back to the wall again. 'Nice try, Mum. Really nice try. Very creative.'

I shut the door and groaned. Leant back against it for a moment, eyes shut. Oh God. Sometimes I despaired. Sometimes I really, really despaired.

A moment later I came to, shook my head wearily, and went off down the corridor. To my own room. To bed. And for once, I thought, slamming my bedroom door behind me, I was grateful for the solitude that awaited me there.

The following morning I was decidedly frosty as I delivered the elevenses. As I banged the tray down on the side and made to stalk out, Alf stared in dismay.

'What, no bourbons?'

'Alf, I have to be in an *extremely* good mood to deliver bourbons, and if you must know, I'm feeling distinctly below par today.'

'Ah. Too many late nights,' he offered sagely.

'I don't think so,' I muttered as I turned to go.

''Ere, hang on, luv. Lance has got somefing to say to you, haven't you, Lance?' put in Mac quickly, digging his son in the ribs with a chisel.

'Thanks, Dad,' muttered Lance sheepishly. 'I can speak for myself, and actually I thought I might do this without an audience.'

'Oh come on,' I said, turning to face him, folding my arms. 'I wouldn't have thought that would affect your performance in any way?'

He paused. 'All right.' The eyes that met mine were clear, blue and steady. 'I was out of order last night and I'm sorry. It shouldn't have happened. I've got no excuses besides a couple of beers inside me and the fact that you've got an extremely provocative neighbour, but I shouldn't have risen to it.'

Alf tittered dirtily.

'All right, Lance,' I sighed. 'Let's forget it.'

'I'll say she was provocative,' put in Mac. 'Lance here says she had all the gear – you know, corset, suspenders and stilettoes an' that – had it all on under her jeans, just for comin' round to baby-sit!'

I gaped. 'You're kidding.' So that's what she'd meant by 'getting ready'.

'Nah, straight up, inn't that right, Lance? Said one minute she looked perfectly normal, sitting beside 'im watchin' *Coronation Street*, an' the next, she'd leapt up, whipped all her kit off, an' bugger me if he didn't have Miss Whiplash standing in front of him, legs astride, hands on hips, all in black lace an' rarin' to go!'

I groaned. God, no wonder she'd accepted with such alacrity. She'd probably been waiting for just such an opportunity, planned the whole seduction. She'd certainly had her eye on him ever since that first meeting down by the river.

I licked my lips. 'Yes, well, I'm sure you didn't stand a chance, Lance, and I accept your apology, but at the end of the day it takes two to tango, and before you tell me –' I raised my voice above a cry of protest – 'that you were putty in her hands and what's a poor boy to do –'

'Too right!' cried Mac.

I grinned. 'I'd say we just drop the subject and make sure it doesn't happen again, OK?'

Lance tugged his forelock and grinned. 'It'll never happen again, Miss,' he said soberly.

'Excellent.'

I bent to pick up the empty tray, hiding my smile, glad to be back on bantering terms with the boys, but also, I realised, glad about something else, too. In a funny sort of way, I was grateful to Nanette. I'd like to think I'd never been seriously tempted by Lance, but having said that, he was, let's face it, extremely decorative, and fun to have around, and sometimes, in my lowest moments, I'd found myself looking at him with something approaching wantonness. It would be fun, a little voice in my head had assured me more than once, and fun is exactly what you need right now. A bit of uncomplicated coupling, some warmth, some tenderness, but no strings, no commitments, a place where the body and not the heart is the only participant. But seeing Nanette emerge from that caravan last night, crumpled, dishevelled and deeply undignified, made me realise it was just what I didn't want. Casual sex was not something I'd ever gone in for, and to embark on it now, feeling vulnerable and insecure, would make me feel, I was sure, in the aftermath of the event, even more frayed at the edges, even more alone.

As I went to take the tray out, Mac called me back. 'Oh, by the way, luv, I forgot to mention, you had a visitor last night.'

I turned back. 'Oh really?'

'Yeah, just before we went out for a curry. Alf was monopolising the karzy, right, having a wash and brush-up, so I went for a Jimmy Riddle in the garden.'

'Do I need to know this, Mac?'

'Oh, not in yer 'erbaceous border or anything crass, luv – I'm not a complete heathen – no, I was just takin' a leak in the shrubs round the side. I'm conducting a little experiment, see, 'cos did you know that urine can change the colour of a hydrangea? Straight up, pee on a hydran-gea and it goes from blue to pink. It's the acid see, and –'

'Mac, the visitor!'

'Oh. Oh yeah.' He paused. Scratched his head. 'Yeah, well anyway, there I was, havin' a – Well anyway,' he has-tened on, 'round the side of the house, as I said, out of sight, like, when stone me if someone doesn't cough behind me. Well I swung round, right, which was danger-ous, like, in my predicament – lucky I missed me shoes – and saw this bird sitting on your terrace. The one at the side which you never sit on 'cos it don't get the sun.'

'A bird?' I frowned. 'What, you mean a girl?'

'That's it.'

'Well, who?'

'Well that's just it, I don't know, 'cos I didn't recognise her, see. But I knew it wasn't one of yer Mollys or Imogens 'cos I know them, right, but when I'd tucked me old man away and asked her what she was doing – politely like, 'cos I imagined she was a friend of yours – she said she'd seen Spiro here in the front drive, on his way out to get some fags, and he'd told her you'd only gone for a quick drink down the road and wouldn't be long, so why don't she wait?'

I turned confused eyes on Spiro.

'Ah yes,' he piped up, remembering. 'She look so tired, you see. She walk from the station, no car, so I say – ah, I so sorry, she not here, but you wait inside, she not be long, but she say – oh no, I no do that, but I seet in garden if OK. And I say – sure, ees OK, Mrs McFarllen, she so kind, she no mind!'

'But hang on, who was she? What did she look like, Spiro?'

He shrugged. 'Pretty, I think, but not so much. Blondie hair, a skirty.' He shrugged again. 'I don't know.'

'You know what I think?' said Mac suddenly. 'I think it was his woman. His fancy piece.'

'Whose fancy piece?' My heart lurched.

'Johnny's, your ovver half.'

I stared. 'Why d'you think that, Mac?'

He frowned. 'Dunno.' He shrugged, suddenly all Inspector Morse'd out; reached for his hammer. 'Just a feeling, really.' He put the hammer down. Second thoughts puckered his brow. 'Something . . . about the way she was,

344

though,' he said carefully. 'Really nervous, like she shouldn't be here. Sitting bolt upright on that terrace an' clutching her handbag. Shit scared too, definitely, eyes dartin' about everywhere, and she didn't say who she was neiver, 'cos I asked, and said I'd take a message an' that, but she just said she'd popped by on the off chance, hoping you'd be in.'

'And she didn't say what it was about?'

'Nah,' Mac shook his head. 'And she went soon after, too, just up and left. But if you ask me,' he wagged his hammer sagely, 'it's her guilty conscience rearin' its ugly head!' He nodded triumphantly.

'What d'you mean?'

'Bet you anything you like she'd come round to explain herself. Listen, luv, she knows she's nicked your husband, but it's been a few months now, so the glory's wearin' off a bit and her conscience is beginning to prick her. She don't want to be forever branded as the Scarlet Woman or what have you, 'specially since she teaches at the school an' it all gets about, so she's come to get – what is it the Pope deals out?'

'Er, dispensation?'

'Nah.'

'Redemption?'

'That's it. She's come for a bit of that, come to make it cosy an' above board, get it all off her chest. I know you women,' more hammer wagging, 'you don't like skulkin' about bein' disliked, do you? You want to be over the garden fence again, eh? Like as not she's thought to herself – blimey, she used to be friendly to me, at the school an' that, an' I didn't take her up on it. I could go now, explain myself, then we could be all chummy and everyone wouldn't think what a cow I was. Mark my words if I'm not right.' He grinned, pleased with himself.

'Really,' I said drily. 'Yes, well, thank you for that penetrating insight into the female psyche, Mac. I had no idea you were such an expert.'

'What, wiv five daughters an' her indoors? Do me a favour! There ain't much I don't know about the female mind – or the body, come to that!'

Cue much raucous, dirty laughter, which I took as my own cue to leave. I went, shutting the kitchen door firmly behind me.

Funnily enough, though, I reflected as I abandoned the tray to a sideboard and wandered out gardenwards, I'd be loathe to admit it, but I had a sneaking suspicion Mac might be right. Recently, when I'd taken Claudia to school, I'd sensed that our Miss Harrison had deliberately made it her business to seek me out. I'd spot her lurking near Claudia's classroom, quite out of her normal infant territory, searching furtively for some nonexistent nursery book in the junior bookcase, or on some other equally spurious mission.

I wandered thoughtfully down the lavender path, pulling idly at the fragrant heads and sprinkling the seeds. Likewise, I remembered with a jolt, when I'd gone to watch a ballet display the other day, there she'd been again, making it her business to be bustling around with extra props for the show. She'd obviously been alive to the fact that I'd be turning up, and had tried to catch my eye as I'd walked in. These days I hadn't felt much like catching it, and had swept on in, head high, to take a seat.

I paused for a moment under the apple tree. And now she'd been here, had she? Looking for me. I glanced back to the side terrace and for a moment, my blood boiled. She'd sat here, in *my* garden, on *my* sacred territory. She'd taken in the glorious delphiniums, the stocks, the jasmine round the door, smelt the nicotiana placed carefully in pots around the house for night scent, seen my secret patch on a summer's evening in all its glory. How dare she?

And the reason she'd called unannounced, of course, I realised, pulling savagely at a leaf from a low bough, was because she knew that if she telephoned, I might slam the phone down, tell her to bugger off, inform her I had nothing whatever to say to her. I walked on down to the water's edge and stopped for a moment, gazing across to the other side, to where the dragonflies were darting in and out of the bulrushes, under the heavy boughs of the chestnut tree. I narrowed my eyes into the sun. Nice to know she'd been a bag of nerves, though. I turned and walked back. Yes, good. And she could prepare to get even more nervous, because actually, I was getting stronger by the day. I wasn't the cringing, cowering creature of a few weeks ago, grateful just for a glimpse of her skirt because in some warped way it brought me closer to Johnny. No, she'd had that phase, and she'd blown it. No, no, *these* days, she'd find it much harder to track me down. Harder still to confess her sins and hope for – Golly, what exactly did she want? I stopped still for a moment, dazed. An amicable arrangement or something? A civilised atmosphere, an understanding that Claudia could go to their flat – which I'd point-blank refused to let her do –

and for her, Nina, to maybe join Johnny on trips to the zoo with her? For Claudia to treat her as some sort of stepmother or something? To be a nice, big, happy, dysfunctional family?

I felt my cheeks flush with anger as I walked smartly back to the house, ducking under the rose arbour as I went, brusquely dead-heading it on the way. Oh, dream on, Miss Harrison, dream on. You see the last thing I'm feeling right now – I crushed a perfectly good rose bud viciously between my fingers – is papal.

Chapter Nineteen

Days passed. The weather, if it was possible, grew even warmer and Claudia's school term began to draw to a close. It occurred to me, as I took her in one baking hot Monday morning, that I only had three more days of avoiding Miss Harrison's eye before eight weeks of summer holidays, followed by Claudia passing on into the senior school in September, which, although in the same grounds, was in a totally separate building. It also occurred to me, as it had on many occasions, that being at the same school until the age of eighteen was a hell of a long time, and that although I'd rather lackadaisically assumed she'd stay, it might be time for a change. Maybe the High School in town? It was only round the corner and would certainly make life easier for me – in more ways than one. I resolved to talk to Claudia about it.

On the afternoon that Claudia broke up, by way of celebration, my mother and Howard came for tea. Claudia and I had gone to town; making scones, biscuits, a chocolate fudge cake, piling bowls high with strawberries and cream, and setting it all out on a table under the cedar tree. Deeply giggly about 'Gran and the Man' as Claudia called them, we sat and waited, with Claudia speculating furiously about what he'd be like – a rather twinkly Des Lynam type, she'd decided, with a bristling moustache – and me, fervently hoping Mum wouldn't be too nervous.

Half an hour later they breezed in, arm in arm, and it

349

was Claudia and I who were rendered speechless. Far from nervous they held court, recounting stories of how they'd met, teasing each other and giggling like a couple of children, as Claudia and I sat and stared, our heads going back and forth from one to the other, like the Centre Court crowd at Wimbledon.

'I finally plucked up the courage to ask your mother to a hospital dinner dance, you see. Well, you should have seen the assembled company's faces when "Poor Old Howard" turned up, not only accompanied, but glamorously accompanied!' He squeezed her hand and grinned.

'Poor Old Howard, my eye – you were the life and soul of the party and clearly had been for years! "A guinea a minute" the sister beside me informed me you were!'

'Nonsense, a shy retiring chap like me? No, no, I was brought out of my shell that night.'

'Well, I didn't exactly need a tin opener, did I? I'd hardly finished my coffee when you were on that dance floor, dragging me up!'

'Ah, but I could sense you were itching for a canter, my love. Those dancing feet of yours had been tapping away under the table from the moment the band started up and, my goodness, what a mover! What rhythm! I could hardly keep up; thought I was going to have a coronary!'

'You'd be in the right place for it!'

'Don't you believe it. Some of those colleagues of mine shouldn't be allowed to operate on a rabbit.'

'Oooh, I'll tell them you said that, Howard!'

'Do,' he twinkled. 'That way I'll lose my job and we could *both* take graceful retirement. I could potter about in the garden, digging up plants instead of weeds, tramp mud through the house and get under your feet all day. I'd probably drive you mad!'

'Stark staring, and there's no "probably" about it!'

'Hey – we'd be demons at cribbage, though, wouldn't we, love?' He nudged her. 'We could play all day!'

'Howard,' she laughed, 'we practically do that anyway!'

Well, Claudia's mouth simply wouldn't shut, and as I followed her back into the kitchen with a pile of empty plates I had to tell her to stop staring.

'I don't see why. They don't notice. It's as if we're not even there! Mum, it's so extraordinary, it's like she's a totally different person. It's like – well, like she's possessed or something, like someone's cast a spell! And her hair! All sort of blondie and swept back and – and white jeans, for heaven's sake! Granny doesn't even wear trousers, let alone jeans! And now they're talking about going on a cruise. Granny would have said that was s-oooo . . . what's the French word she says?'

'Bourgeois.'

'Exactly! "Too bourgeois for *words*, darling" – can't you just hear her? Jesus, I just can't *believe* it!'

'Shh, they'll hear you, and don't swear.'

'I'm not swearing, but, Jesus!'

'Claudia!'

She stared at me, eyes still wide. Then she gave herself a little shake. Came to.

'Well, I think it's brilliant,' she said soberly. 'In fact, I think it's more than brilliant, I think it's wicked. But just think, Mum, she could have been like this all along, all sort of fun and larky! Isn't that awful? That it was all lurking inside her and we didn't know?'

I smiled sadly, began wiping up. 'I know. That's exactly what I thought when I saw her the other day.'

'Hey!' She caught my arm. 'D' you think he's got a son?'

'I think he has, actually. I know he's a widower and I'm sure he said he had a boy. Why?'

'For you, of course! Maybe it's in the genes; maybe he could work the same magic for you!'

I put the tea towel down. Turned to face her. 'Claudes, am I a bore? Do I lack fun? Am I a grouch, now that Daddy's gone?'

'Of course not, Mum.' She plucked a strawberry from a bowl and sailed out through the back door. 'You were like that before he went!'

Later, when Claudia took Howard off to see her guinea pigs and Mum and I were alone, side by side in deck chairs and straw hats, mopping our brows periodically – me, hastily averting my incredulous gaze from the pink canvas deck shoes Howard had 'impulse bought her in Harrods' – I shaded my eyes into the distance, to where Claudia and Howard were, down at the hutches.

'Mum, d'you think Claudia's had enough of that school? If she goes on into the seniors she's got seven more years of it.'

'Hmm?' She came back from smiling at Howard's back. 'Oh, she's talked to you then?' She licked some cream from her fingers and set aside her strawberry bowl.

I stared. 'No, why, has she talked to you?'

'Oh yes, she rang the other night. We had a nice long chat. Yes, she's bored there now. She'd be happy to go.'

I sat forward, gaped at her open-mouthed. 'Well, why the hell doesn't she tell *me* that!'

'I don't know, darling.'

'And where does she want to go? To the High School?'

She gave me a sideways glance. 'No. She wants to go to boarding school.'

I stared at her, aghast. '*Boarding* school! No! Why?'

She shrugged. 'Because she thinks it would be great fun, as I'm sure it would.'

I felt very sick suddenly. 'She wants to get away,' I breathed shakily. 'She's had enough of living in a broken home with a distraught, neurotic mother and – oh God – she wants to get out of here!' I clutched my mouth but a small sob escaped. My baby. Wanted to leave home. My only child.

Mum laid a hand firmly on my arm. 'Which is precisely why she didn't tell you. She knew that was how you'd react, so she wanted to sound me out first, and that is absolutely *not* why she wants to go. She's an only child, Olivia; she needs the company. She's read all the books – *Mallory Towers*, Angela Brazil – she thinks it would be a hoot, and so it would!'

I swallowed. 'I never meant her to be an only child. I still think . . . maybe . . .'

'I know you do, I know, and believe me, you'll go on thinking that until your menopause.'

Of course. Like she had, too. Hoping against hope that my father would come back, and me, knowing full well I was destined to be an only child, as Claudia surely did too. And dying to get away. I remembered reading all those books, dreaming of midnight feasts in the dorm, pillow fights, shrieks of laughter, a world away from the sourness that pervaded my childhood. Financially it had been out of the question, of course, but I'd deliberately worked my little socks off at school, dreaming of university when finally, *finally* I could escape. It gave me an actual physical pain in my gut to realise Claudia felt the same way. I breathed deeply, blinking back the tears.

'Think about it,' Mum said, as Claudia and Howard came slowly back up the lawn. 'There's plenty of time. She doesn't have to go this year. She's not eleven for a couple of months, she'd be quite the youngest in her class. She could go next year.'

'But – I'd miss her so much. I'd miss her!'

'Of course you would, but you know, boarding schools are so different now. She'd be back practically every weekend.'

I couldn't speak. But she'd be gone. Effectively, she'd have left home. And she was all I had.

'Promise me you won't talk to her about it until you've calmed down, OK?' muttered Mum urgently.

'OK,' I whispered, for they were back, bearing guinea pigs.

'Howard likes Edward best,' announced Claudia, holding a speckled one aloft. 'But the only thing is, he says he's not Edward at all, he's Edwina, which might explain why, cooped up with Pandora all day, they've never had babies!'

'I knew my medical training would come in handy one day,' laughed Howard. 'If only for sexing guinea pigs!'

Later, when they'd gone, I gave Claudia a big squeeze as she went off for her bath, burying my face in her hair. She stepped back in alarm.

'M-u-um! My shell necklace!'

'Sorry.' I took the broken bits from her. 'I'll mend it.'

She shrugged. 'It's OK, I didn't really want it any more.' She ran up a few stairs, then halted, turned, her hand on the banister. 'I didn't mean what I said about you being a grouch, you know. You're not.'

I managed a grin, but couldn't speak. Nodded instead. My chin wobbled. She was waiting for me to answer.

'I know,' I whispered.

She stared. 'Mum!' She jumped down the last few steps and I dissolved. Hands on face, ambushed by tears. Stupid. Couldn't help it. Didn't want to.

'Mum!' she cried in alarm. I sat on the bottom step and she sat beside me, hugging my neck hard.

'Is it Dad?'

'Yes!' I sobbed, grateful for that. 'Yes, yes, it's Dad.'

She sighed, and hugged me some more, but then abruptly, her arm froze.

She sat back. 'It's not Dad, is it? Gran told you, didn't she!' She wriggled free and moved along the stair so she could see my face properly.

Damn, I rooted in my pocket for a hanky, this was so awful! So like I'd sworn I'd never be, loading guilt on to children, so like my mother – never, never, never! I sat up straight and blew my nose.

'Don't be silly. This has nothing whatever to do with that. I'm just a bit tired and overwrought, that's all.'

'I'm not going,' she said vehemently, shaking her head violently. 'No way, no way. I'm not going. I *knew* this would happen, knew that's what you'd think! You think I want to get away!' she wailed.

My tears dried up the moment hers started. 'Now, Claudia, listen. We must think about it.' I wiped my nose determinedly, stuffed the tissue back in my pocket. 'We certainly mustn't rule it out, and in fact the more I think about it, the more I think it's a very good idea. You're on your own so much here, and now that Daddy's gone –'

'*No!*' She sobbed wretchedly. 'You think I don't love you! You do, you think I don't love you, and it's just not true!'

Well, that set us both off. Tears streamed in torrents down our faces as we hugged, kissed, wailed, reassured each other, said how marvellous we both were, how incredibly special, then wailed some more, until finally, totally spent, we sank back on the stairs, exhausted. Somewhat dazed and startled by our mutual hysteria, we stared into space for a while, sniffing a bit. Then we sat up, blew our respective noses, got to our feet, and arm in arm, went as one to the fridge for the chocolate fudge cake. Setting it between us on the little scullery table we dragged up stools, and armed with a spoon apiece, dug straight into the middle, sniffing loudly. Naturally, in time, our equilibrium recovered, as naturally, in time, our blood sugar levels were raised.

'We'll see,' I said sternly, between dripping chocolatey mouthfuls, back in mother mode again. 'We'll go and have a look at one or two, and then we'll see, OK?'

'But not too far away,' she warned, waving a spoon bossily at me. 'It's got to be close, and back at weekends.'

'Agreed.' I nodded.

We pitched back into the calories again.

'Becky's going,' she said licking her spoon, 'and she's taking her pony. Maybe I could have one too?'

'Becky's going?' I looked up, surprised. Becky was a great mate of Claudia's, and one I thoroughly approved of. A sweet girl with an incredibly close-knit, happy family.

She regarded me wisely over a spoonful of chocolate. 'Mum, you don't *have* to be orphan Annie to go to boarding school, you know.'

I blinked, surprised. 'No. No, I suppose you don't.'

The following day Molly came round. As we basked, beached-whale-like on sun-loungers on the terrace – Molly, considerably more whale-like than me, tossing and turning uncomfortably in the shade, groaning, and swigging intermittently from a strange bottle of chalky white liquid which allegedly assuaged the heartburn and wind – I told her about Claudia. Henry was splashing happily in an ancient paddling pool I'd found, as Claudia dashed inside to find some boats for him to play with. Still such a child, I thought desperately, as she ran back out, armed with the boats. Too young to go, surely?

'It'll be good for her,' pronounced Molly roundly. 'She's incredibly sociable and she'll have a terrific time. God, I never wanted to go, far too cringing and pathetic and tied to Mummy's apron strings, but think how you would have loved it!'

'I know,' I said sadly, knowing precisely why. I gazed at my daughter sailing the flotilla in a circle round Henry, ducking them occasionally and making him giggle.

'Of course, the only one who'll lose out here is you,' said Molly abruptly.

'Precisely.'

'On your own.'

'Thank you, Molly, it had crossed my mind.'

She narrowed her eyes thoughtfully. Was silent for a moment.

I cleared my throat. 'Molly, I do hope you're not about to say, "Perhaps you could get a dog"?'

'No, I wasn't, but – well, how's Sebastian?'

'Oh, thanks!'

'No, but seriously, I thought he was terribly nice.'

'Molly, you met him once, and then you nearly had a baby on his feet.'

'Ah, but I liked him,' she nodded unconvincingly, lips pursed. 'I could tell he might be right for you.' She puckered her brow. 'He had, well, he had, um . . . kind eyes.'

'Nonsense, he was all sort of glowering and wall-punching when you saw him.'

'Yum-yum.'

'And, if anything, he's got a particularly steely gleam to his eye. You couldn't even pick him out of an identity parade. You obviously haven't the faintest idea what he looks like.'

'Even so,' she persisted, sitting up, 'I *feel* I know him.' She cupped her hands around an imaginary crystal ball, shut her eyes and contrived to look mystical, mouth twitching. 'And I feel . . . yes, I feel he could make you . . . very happy . . . my dear.' She reached out and clasped my hand.

'Bog off,' I said, snatching my hand away as she giggled wildly. 'And don't wee on my sunbed, please. It's a new one.'

'I wasn't about to – have to be hysterical for that – and, anyway, it's the wind that seems to ambush me these days.'

She shifted uncomfortably on the bed. 'You know, there's a lot to be said for elective Caesareans. Quite apart from anything else you get them two weeks early – which considering I'm likely to be two weeks late, would mean a month less of this malarkey – and if I'd gone down that route I'd have had the bloody thing by now, straight out of the sun-roof.' She reached into her handbag and lit a cigarette. 'You know in Brazil – first one this week so stop looking so disapproving – in Brazil, no self-respecting Brazilian beauty would *dream* of having a natural birth. What – and get your precious birth canal all shot to bits? Good heavens, what would your average, swaggering, polo-playing husband think about *that*? That's not what it's there for at *all*.'

'Bit late now, isn't it? You told me Henry came out like a human cannonball. Nearly knocked the midwife out.'

'Well, quite, so there's no hope for me,' she said gloomily. She beamed, suddenly. 'So back to you. Back, via birth canals, to Sebastian, in fact.'

'You are so disgusting, Molly Piper.'

'But didn't you say you'd seen him recently?' she persisted, twisting round to face me.

I sighed. I had. More than once, actually. Twice, to be precise. After our supper I'd phoned him to say thank you, and he'd asked if I'd like to see a film with him later on in the week. Naturally that had led to supper in a little bistro afterwards, and then walking home, we'd spotted a poster advertising an open-air concert in the park, which naturally we'd gone to too, a few days later. (On both of these occasions incidentally – and much to Claudia's horror – Maureen had stood in as baby-sitter. I could tell at a glance that nothing would get past those sharp eyes – particularly Lance and Nanette – and after a couple of evenings with Maureen, Claudia had become really quite proficient at needlepoint, which, I thought, on balance was better than oral sex.) But I digress. Yes, Sebastian liked me, that I could tell, and I don't say that with any degree of smugness or insensate conceit, either. It's just that I'm not the sort of girl men instantly fall for, so when it does happen it's all the more apparent. And I liked him too, but not in the same way. I liked his dark, intelligent good looks, he made me laugh, he was droll and dry, and I liked the rather quizzical gleam he got in his eye when he was about to say something amusing. In fact I couldn't fault him but, at the end of both evenings, I was left with that same hollow, empty feeling I'd had when I'd come back from his house that first night. After the concert in the park, I cried when I shut the front door. It was me, of course, I knew that. Not him. I never asked him in for a coffee because I felt it wouldn't be fair, and he never made a move in that direction because he hadn't been given so much as a smidgen of a sign that it would be acceptable. Lately, though, I wondered if I should, just for the hell of it. This wasn't Lance, after all; it wouldn't be *that* casual, would it? This was a man I liked enormously, but whom I just wasn't in love with. Surely then, it couldn't hurt? In fact, it might even help – might help me to fall in love, be better again. I so desperately wanted to be better. To be normal, not to be living in this ghastly limbo land, waiting to see what would happen next.

'Yes, I've seen him,' I sighed.

'And?'

'And . . . well, he's very nice,' I said lamely.

'Thought so,' she retorted smugly. She sat up and pursed her lips. 'Right, tell you what, why not bring him round for supper? Better make it sharpish, though, otherwise I really will have this baby on his feet. How about Friday?'

I turned to look at her properly. She was being suspiciously determined about all this. 'Sure, I could bring him,' I said slowly. 'But what's the rush? Why the indecent haste?'

She was quiet for a moment. Put her sunglasses on, sat back and gazed out at the view, which, with the sun glancing off a riverful of floating water lilies, was carrying on like an Impressionist painting.

'They're going away together, you know that, don't you?' she said quietly.

I swallowed hard. 'I . . . suspected,' I muttered. Johnny had indeed telephoned to say he was going away for a while and couldn't see Claudia for a bit. He hadn't elaborated and I'd foolishly hoped it might be a business trip, but since it fitted in quite seamlessly with the start of the school holidays, it seemed unlikely.

'Where are they going?' I said in a small voice. Molly was friendly with a few of the nursery mothers, so I knew she'd know.

'St-Jean-de-Luz.'

I sat bolt upright. 'St-Jean-de-Luz! That's where we went for our honeymoon!'

'I know.'

I breathed deeply, bit the inside of my cheek hard. 'Tell

361

me the worst, Molly. I know you know, and I deliberately never ask.'

She shrugged miserably. 'I don't really know much, actually, because apparently she's very private, but Tessa Jarvis says – well, she says they're very close at the moment. Nina's told her how incredibly happy she is, how she never thought anything like this would ever happen to her, never thought she'd get someone like Johnny –'

'OF COURSE NOT, BECAUSE SHE'S SUCH AN AVERAGE LITTLE TART!' I bellowed. 'My bloody husband! Never thought she'd – "*get*" – my gorgeous bloody husband! How bloody *dare* she?'

'Breathe,' Molly commanded, reaching out and clutching my wrist. 'Come on, you've gone all purple now, breathe – in . . . out . . . in . . . out . . .'

I sank back and obeyed. God, he had such a weird effect on me, it was like releasing demons. And my language became so exotic too, like that girl in *The Exorcist*. Next thing I knew my head would be rotating.

'Anyway,' I snarled, simultaneously breathing deep, 'Tessa Jarvis doesn't know her arse from her elbow, she's got a huge mouth on her, and *her* bloody husband is the pits! Pinches bottoms at school fêtes, and I should know!'

'Well, quite,' she agreed hastily, 'she's a terrible old gossip, but I'm just telling you what I've heard, that's all. Because I think you should be prepared.'

'For what?' my heart stopped.

'For . . . any serious developments.'

I stared at her. There seemed to be two of her. Two pairs of sunglasses. Two curly heads. I couldn't speak for a while.

Then, at length: 'She came to see me, you know.'

'What, here?' Molly whipped off her glasses, aghast.

I nodded. 'But I wasn't in. She hasn't been back since and I've avoided her at school. Obviously, though, she had something to tell me. Something . . . burning.'

Molly nodded thoughtfully. 'I'd say you might be right,' she said quietly. 'And maybe Johnny didn't want to be the one to say it. Or couldn't say it.'

A long silence prevailed. Eventually, I took a deep breath.

'Molly, we'd love to come.'

She frowned, miles away now. 'Hmm?'

'To dinner, Sebastian and I.'

'Oh good!' She brightened. 'Friday then?'

'Perfect.'

'Spag bol in the kitchen, I'm afraid. It's about all I can manage these days. Oh God, is that all right?' She looked suddenly alarmed. 'He's probably not used to that sort of thing, is he?'

'No, Molly, he only dines at the Connaught. Don't be ridiculous, he's perfectly normal, he even picks his nose like the rest of us, he just happens to be good at music, that's all.' I got to my feet. 'Gin and tonic?'

She consulted her watch and blinked. 'Lord, Livvy, it's only ten thirty for God's sake!'

'I'll take that as a no, then,' I said evenly, as I marched inside, crossed to the sideboard, and with a shaking hand, poured an extremely large one for myself.

Chapter Twenty

Supper on Friday began somewhat inauspiciously. Having assured Molly that Sebastian couldn't be more relaxed, I did actually sneak him a sidelong, nervous glance as we stood for what seemed like an eternity on the doorstep of the Pipers' little flint cottage, getting absolutely no answer at all from their cranky old bell. Finally we tried the door, pushed tentatively through, and happened upon a sitting room that looked for all the world as if it had been burgled. We glanced at each other, startled. There was an astonishing lack of sofas, chairs, tables – or indeed any sort of furniture at all – and all that remained on the rather grubby carpet were piles of books and magazines, a few mouldy coffee mugs, one of Molly's maternity bras, and a brace of apple cores festering quietly on the fender. Neither Molly nor Hugh was anywhere to be seen.

'Looks like they've moved out,' muttered Sebastian, gazing around. 'The thought of me coming for supper was clearly too much for them, they've done a runner, put their possessions on their backs like Kurdish refugees and fled. We'll probably find them halfway down the road, wild-eyed and desperate, dragging an astonished donkey and making a break for the border.'

'Either that or the bailiffs have been,' I said nervously. 'Which, believe me, is entirely possible with Molly and Hugh. They've clearly forgotten we're coming, anyway. Come on, let's go.' We turned hastily back to the door.

'Well, bugger off, then, oh ye of little faith!' cried a voice behind us and we swung round to see Molly, sweeping through the French windows in a billowing maternity smock, like a ship in full sail, a plate of garlic bread poised in her hand.

'We're out here in the garden, and we've got no garden furniture to speak of so we dragged all our stuff outside.' She threw her arms around her barren sitting room. 'Welcome to *Lifestyles of the Poor and Disgruntled!* Makes a refreshing change, don't you think? You don't mind being outside, do you? We thought we'd have a barbecue so Hugh can wear stupid clothes and do macho things with tongs and baked potatoes.' She grinned and kissed me on both cheeks, then beamed up at her guest.

'Ah, Sebastian, what must you think of me? Did I behave *quite* appallingly the other night?' She twinkled merrily at him.

He grinned. 'Quite appallingly, but with remarkable aplomb and presence of mind too. You're obviously a dab hand at rescuing damsels in distress from sticky situations. I only wish I could stash the big-with-child card up my sleeve to deploy in similar circumstances.'

She chuckled. 'Ah yes, privilege of my gender, I'm afraid, and I do like to make the most of my fecundity. It has very little else going for it, believe me. Now,' she linked both our arms with a squeeze and turned us gardenwards, 'come and meet the man responsible for my condition. You can't miss him, he's the one in the vest and the shorts who thinks he looks like Bruce Willis in *Die Hard.*'

We strolled outside with her where, sure enough, scattered about the long, unmown grass and the daisies, was the sitting-room furniture – a sofa, two armchairs and a coffee table – all looking a bit tipsy and off balance, and slightly embarrassed to be outside. And in the middle of this al fresco furniture showroom, was Hugh, in what looked like his underwear, behind a wall of smoke, fighting desperately with a furious, flaming, spitting cauldron that was more reminiscent of Sputnik than a barbecue.

'Remember these, Moll?' he cried, waving a huge pair of barbecue tongs. 'I borrowed them from the maternity ward. They'll be needing them back when you go in!' He clamped them to an imaginary head and pulled hard, rolling his eyes maniacally like Doctor Death. 'Oooh, aahhh!'

'*Au contraire*, my darling,' she sang, 'they'll be needing them back for your vasectomy, for when I have your balls off. Sebastian, this is my husband, Hugh, who you met very briefly last week. He's an out-of-work actor, and as the evening wears on, you'll appreciate why.'

'Not at all,' smiled Sebastian, shaking Hugh's hand, 'I thought your performance in the supporting role of "tense father" the other night was masterful. It was method acting, I take it?'

'But of course,' grinned Hugh, taking a deep bow. 'There's always method in my madness. No offence taken, I hope?'

'None at all,' smiled Sebastian.

'Excellent! Now – a drink! Good God, Molly, call yourself a hostess? These good people haven't even got a bevy!'

A jug of Pimm's was discovered lurking under a table,

the flies were ceremoniously picked out of it, then Hugh poured four huge, lethal tumblers, and the evening slipped happily along. And as we sat, laughing and chatting, slumped in their comfortable old chairs with the springs bursting out of their arms, in their tiny, magical cottage garden, surrounded – more by accident than Molly's design – by hollyhocks, phlox and lupins, our toes in a daisy-strewn lawn, we gazed on to a veritable Constable scene of traditional English haystacks in the fields beyond. As Hugh waved his tongs in a final triumphant flourish we then ate our traditional English barbecue: charred spare ribs, sausages that were black on the outside and raw in the middle, vast baked potatoes that were as hard as bullets but no one seemed to mind, and a salad, that much to everyone's mirth, I insisted on rushing to the flowerbed to decorate with borage and nasturtiums, as meanwhile, the drink and the conversation flowed on.

Molly and I discussed the chaotic state of her garden, as was our wont, with her promising to put into practice all my handy hints, and me knowing full well she wouldn't, whilst Sebastian and Hugh chewed the arts long and hard, alternately eulogising or rubbishing every single play, film, festival or concert they'd ever been to, disagreeing as much as they agreed, and enjoying themselves hugely.

'So what sort of thing do you do yourself then, Hugh?' asked Sebastian finally, picking the charcoal from his teeth.

'When you're not poisoning your guests,' I added, flicking raw sausage off my plate.

'Oh, quite a lot of telly, you know, that type of thing,' Hugh said airily, waving his arm about vaguely.

'He does sanitary towel ads,' said Molly grimly. 'If we're lucky.'

'Sanitary – but surely . . . ?' Sebastian looked perplexed.

'Wrong gender?' Hugh offered brightly. 'No problem. I change sex; after all, I am an actor! No, seriously, dear boy, I am, as my wife so kindly reminded me, in the current ST ads, but I don't wear them myself. No no, I'm the fresh-faced lad playing volleyball with our padded heroine on the beach. Voila!' He jumped up to demonstrate, punching an imaginary ball, a frozen smile on his lips. He held the pose. 'Recognise me?'

'Er, well . . .' Sebastian smiled.

'I'm the gorgeous young buck she bounds confidently up to in her skimpy white shorts – for thanks to Panty Pads, our lass *can* wear skimpy white shorts – and whose shoulders she playfully straddles – for our lass *can* straddle shoulders with no embarrassing repercussions – and whose hair she playfully ruffles. I'm the git who lollops across the sands with the silly cow's arse wrapped round my neck, like so.' He turned to show us his hunched back. 'Recognise me now?'

'It's all coming back to me,' grinned Sebastian as Hugh staggered about under a colossal imaginary weight, like the hunchback of Notre-Dame.

'And, um, when you're not doing important feminine hygiene ads? Dare I ask?'

'He lolls about at home, scratching his bum and getting in my way,' said Molly, preparing to throw the rib bones to her two Border terriers, who were sitting bolt upright, quivering with excitement.

'What my dear wife means,' said Hugh, leaning conspiratorially towards Sebastian, 'is that when I'm not making passionate love to her on a sultry afternoon amongst the buttercups, I am in fact, rehearsing for my play.'

'Ah, and that is?' Sebastian brightened.

'Oh, dear boy, sweet of you to ask, to take an interest and all that, but it's very much a fringe thing. On a considerably lesser stage to the one you inhabit, playing to seriously dwindling audiences, and at a little-known auditorium, a modest venue just off the Hammersmith Broadway.'

'The Lyric? D'you mean the new Simon Gallway play? The Roman one, um – *Death of a Conqueror's Son?*'

Hugh nearly fell off his chair he was so excited. 'Yes!' he rasped, nearly choking on a rib bone. 'Fuck me, yes! Have you seen it?'

'Certainly I have. It was excellent.'

Hugh's chest expanded until it was fit to explode, his face went purple.

'Well then, surely you recognise me!' he squeaked. 'I'm on stage the whole time!'

Sebastian's eyes widened. 'You are? Blimey, I only saw it a few weeks ago, but . . .' he frowned. 'Oh, hang on. You're the centurion, right?'

Hugh shook his head excitedly. 'No!'

'Er, well. The lead?' he said, somewhat doubtfully. 'Peter the Great?'

'Warmer, getting warmer!' Hugh leapt up and down and hopped about excitedly.

'Er, Peter the Great's son? Michaelias?'

'Hot! Really hot – so close!'

369

Sebastian frowned. 'Peter the Great's . . . other son? Alexander?'

'That's it!'

'But – isn't he . . . dead?'

'Precisely! From the word go! I'm the corpse!'

'Oh!'

'Front of stage the whole time,' he said proudly, 'lying doggo and deceased. Remember?' Hugh collapsed flat on his back in the daisies to demonstrate, eyes shut.

'Oh, er, well, yes. I do now. You were . . . unforgettable.'

'Wasn't I just?' beamed Hugh, sitting up. 'If I say so myself I was *bloody* unforgettable. Yep, I really got into that part.' He reached for his glass of Pimm's and took a satisfied swig. 'It's all in the breathing, you know,' he informed us importantly, waving his glass about. 'All in the oesophagus control.'

'He made me see it four times,' muttered Molly, leaning back wearily and shutting her eyes in despair. 'I was eight months pregnant, feeling ghastly, and it was like a sauna in there. And he keeps berating me because I won't go again. And he does nothing! He just lies there, for God's sake!'

'Ah, but I *feel* dead, Molly,' he urged. 'I actually feel it, and I convey my deceased state to the audience. Seb here will back me up, won't you, Seb? Oh – and I'll tell you someone else who will, someone else who was sitting at my feet in the front row, looking starry-eyed at my performance, drinking from the muse. Old Imo and Hugo whatsis-name, the conductor!'

'Imo came?' said Molly. 'You didn't tell me that. Gosh, that was sweet of her.'

'Sweet!' He gasped. '*Sweet!* Why so? I'm not a *charity*, my darling. They came to marvel, to be enlightened! One doesn't rattle one's tin and give generously to poor old Hugh!'

'So they're still together,' I mused. 'That's nice, and it must be a record for Imo. Have you spoken to her recently, Moll? I haven't seen her since the concert.'

'I asked her to come tonight,' said Molly, sucking the orange from her Pimm's, 'but she was frantic in the gallery and couldn't really speak, except to say she had a work thing to go to, so she couldn't come. I did ask how things were going, though, and she said she was besotted.'

'Really! With him?'

'Well, presumably. She didn't say, but I imagine so. I should think Ursula's wetting her pants at the prospect.'

'I saw the pair of them the other night, actually,' said Sebastian. 'The Mitchells asked me to dinner and, having refused two invitations, I thought it only politic to go.'

'Ah,' I grinned. 'So Ursula *is* becoming your benefactress. I knew she would.'

'I must confess I had that same, slightly uncomfortable feeling,' he grimaced.

'And was Hugo there too?' demanded Molly. 'Playing footsie next to Imo and shooting her hot looks over the vichyssoise?'

'He was, although not next to her. I suspect even Ursula's not that obvious. I sat next to Imogen, actually. I thought she was charming. Very easy on the eye and much less intense than her mother.'

'Oh *God*, yes,' I agreed.

'Wouldn't be difficult,' added Molly.

'But scary,' warned Hugh, wagging his finger.

'Imo? No, why?' I said, but I knew what he meant.

'Oh, come on, Livvy, Ursula's overeducated her. Any fool can see that. All those violin lessons at four and cuboid maths at five – you feel you can't open your mouth without her thinking – Christ, what a berk!'

'Entirely valid in your case,' said Molly, getting up. 'More booze, anyone?'

We drank on and on, and I had far more than I should have done, first because I wasn't driving, but also because I felt I might need it. I'd shaved my legs, you see. And my armpits. And as Molly doled out the strawberries and cream, I gazed at Sebastian as he chatted animatedly with her and wondered just how reckless I was being here. Not very, I decided, taking another swig of Pimm's, and eyeing him carefully, and anyway, he'd won the bet. The one I'd made with myself in the bath, earlier on. It went – why string him along if you're not really interested, Olivia? Then – well, I'm not stringing him along, I really like him. Then – OK, so if you really like him, how about it? You said you wanted to get back to the land of the living. Well, live a little, for Christ's sake! At this point, in the bath, I'd seized the Gillette G2 from the soap dish and depilated furiously. But only, I'd told myself, shaving away like a demon, if I'm totally bowled over by him tonight. Only if he makes me laugh; only if I can look at him without thinking of Johnny; and only if he goes down well with Molly and Hugh – although why this should come into the equation I've no idea since Johnny had never got on particularly well with Hugh, thinking him camp and theatrical – 'dodgy' was how he'd once described him – whilst Hugh, who was as straight as a Roman road, had, in turn, found Johnny just a little too hearty and macho for his artistic taste.

I studied Sebastian now, roaring with laughter at something Hugh had said, head thrown back, wiping tears from his eyes, that narrow, intelligent face creased with mirth. He caught my eye as he shook his head in bemused wonder at Hugh, and I grinned back happily, holding his gaze for just a little longer than was strictly necessary. As I finally looked away it struck me, rather gloriously, that some time later this evening, I was indeed going to live again. Some time tonight, after all these arid months of mere existence, I was going to uncurl my dry, dusty old roots and drink again, feel the sap of life. I wondered, with a jolt, if I could remember how to do it. Nah, course I could. Just like falling off a bicycle. I frowned, blearily, into my drink. Hang on, wasn't I mixing my metaphors a bit here? And if I *was* going to do it, where the devil was my cap? Gathering dust in my bedside drawer probably, beside an unmade bed and – Hell, when did I last change the sheets? Suddenly I felt my courage begin to slip through my fingers like fine sand. I hastily took another gulp of Pimm's.

Molly came back, armed with a fresh jug, and crouched down between the boys to gather up some strawberry bowls, demanding to know what they were laughing at. Sebastian told her that Hugh had fallen asleep on stage one night and had snored so loudly he'd had to be surreptitiously kicked awake by Peter the Great.

'Not so surreptitiously,' gasped Hugh. 'Apparently I was out for the count. He nearly broke my ribs!'

'You never told me!' Molly shrieked throwing a napkin

at him. 'You old fraud – getting into the part, my eye – you never told me that!'

I got up to help her clear away, determining at the same time to tell her of my little seduction plan. I needed encouragement and boy, would she encourage me. 'Go for it, Livvy!' I could hear her saying. 'This man is perfect. This is exactly what you need!'

I followed her into the kitchen, and as she wiped her eyes on a tea towel at the sink, still hooting and dissolving with laughter, I stared at her.

'How are you managing this, Molly?'

'What?' she gasped.

'All this hilarity. You haven't laughed like this for weeks!'

'Oh!' She pulled up her dress. 'Plastic pants! Huge ones, absolutely marvellous, men's ones actually. Bought them in Boots this morning, and padded them out with stacks of those wingy ST things Hugh brought back from the shoot. I was so bloody sick of sitting around po-faced as if I had a cucumber up my bottom, I thought – damn it, I'm going to have a laugh tonight. Honestly, I've practic-ally got a nappy on here, Liv, and I can skip –' she demonstrated across the kitchen – 'I can dance – arab-esque – lah-lah-lah!' Her arms flew out and her leg shot up all of two inches behind her. 'Well, almost. And I'm sure I could straddle some gorgeous hunk's shoulders if I really – Shit!' she squeaked, suddenly clutching herself.

'What!' I leapt forward.

She peered down. 'I'm leaking!'

We gazed in frozen horror as torrents of liquid poured down her legs.

'God, that's more than a leak, Moll!'

'My waters! Quick – a bucket!'

'No, no, the loo, hurry – it's closer!' I bundled her towards it.

'No!' she hissed suddenly, digging her heels in. 'I've got to keep some! My midwife told me to, so they can test the amniotic fluid. Get a plastic bag!' She clamped her legs together, bug-eyed with alarm now.

'Where?' I flew wildly round the kitchen.

'Top drawer – there,' she pointed. 'Hurry!'

'They're huge!' I wailed as I pulled a vast John Lewis carrier bag from the dresser.

'Never mind!' she squeaked. 'Just get some of this ruddy stuff!'

I crouched down between her ankles, trying desperately to catch some drops and actually feeling faintly hysterical now. Her legs were no longer dripping, just wet, and the deluge was all over the floor.

'Oh, Moll, I can't!' I gasped hysterically.

'Get a spoon!' she shrieked. 'Look, there's a big puddle. Oh, go away, Digger!' Digger the Border terrier, keen to join the party, looked frightfully excited and all set to clean up. I hurriedly shut him in a cupboard.

'Oh, for God's sake, Molly,' I yelped, bending down again, frantically spooning away, 'you should be at the hospital, not worrying about your amniotic fluid – HUGH!' I flung over my shoulder.

'What?' drifted laconically up from the garden.

'GET IN HERE – NOW!!!'

I reached down deep into my lungs for this, and it did

the trick. Hugh and Sebastian arrived at the double, just as Molly, tottering across the floor towards her husband, collapsed stiffly on his neck like a paperhanger's board.

'It's coming,' she moaned. 'Finally, Hugh! Ten bloody days late, but it's actually, finally coming!'

Sebastian, childless, and probably having only ever seen births on episodes of *Casualty*, where it all tends to happen in ten seconds flat on the floor of a phone box, looked horrified. 'What, here? Now?'

'That's it, mate,' said Hugh, grasping his shoulder. 'This is how she wanted it. On all fours on the kitchen floor, that was her birth plan. Glad you could join us. I'd like you down at the works end, if you will. Wash your hands.'

'No no,' I said hurriedly, seeing Sebastian's aghast face. 'He's joking. She's got a while to go yet, and Molly's not into painful home births either. Come on, Moll, let's get you into the car.'

'We're off, we're off!' chortled Hugh joyfully, hopping about from foot to foot. 'God, I wonder what it is. It's just like Christmas, isn't it!'

'Hardly,' snarled Molly.

'Never mind, my love, we'll have you there in a jiffy and it'll soon be over, you'll see. Come on, my sweet.' He helped his huge wife, who seemed to have gone completely rigid now, out of the kitchen, then abruptly lunged back to grab a pewter hip flask from the dresser.

'Hang on, Moll!' He supported her with one hand and filled the flask expertly with whisky with the other. 'Pain relief,' he grinned, slipping it into his pocket. 'In case her agony is too much for me to bear.'

'Oh, the pain,' she moaned, clutching her tummy.

'What – already?' he asked anxiously.

'No, no, I'm just remembering. I want everything, Hugh,' she warned him, staggering out, 'everything that's going, remember that.'

'I will, my love.'

'I want epidurals, pethidine, gas, injections – whatever's going I want it. Unconscious will be just fine. Tell them, Hugh.'

'I'll tell them, my pet, don't you worry.'

'And don't forget to put a ciggy in my mouth as soon as I come round.'

'It'll be my first priority.'

'And your case?' I asked anxiously, following them out of the front door.

'Boot of the car,' she gasped, 'packed and ready. I knew this would happen, knew it would come in a rush, be a bloody emergency. Oh, bye, everyone!'

She turned, halfway down the path, and waved, grinning from ear to ear, suddenly enjoying the moment. Hugh braced up beside her with a huge cheesy grin, never missing a potential audience opportunity.

'Bye, all,' he cried. 'Back soon!'

'Bye!' Sebastian and I yelled back enthusiastically. It was a bit like waving to a royal couple on the balcony.

'And good luck!' added Sebastian as Hugh helped Molly into the car.

'Thanks, mate!'

Moments later they were away, roaring off in Hugh's ancient MG, roof down, waving frantically, when suddenly – my hand shot up in the air.

'*Stop!*'

Hugh obediently squealed to an emergency halt in the middle of the lane. His head swung back. 'What!'

'You've forgotten Henry!'

Molly and Hugh exchanged horrified looks then – 'Shit!' in unison.

Hugh performed an immaculate three-point turn in the middle of the lane and came roaring back.

'So we have,' he muttered as he raced past me and on up the stairs. 'Well done, Livvy. You're thinking on your feet.'

'But, Hugh, why don't you leave him? Don't wake him up, I'll –'

But he'd gone, and two seconds later was racing back down with a sleeping bundle, wrapped in a duvet, in his arms.

'Hugh, why don't I stay? Or take him back to my house?' I urged. 'He can stay with me.'

'No, no,' he insisted, dashing past me, 'family occasion.' He stopped, turned back. 'In years to come, Livvy, this chap will be able to say that he attended his sibling's birth, and how many boys can say that, eh?' He leant forward confidentially. 'And don't tell Molly,' he whispered, 'but I've got the video camera packed in her case. Thought I'd surprise her, thought we could all be in it, you know, *en famille*, but I'll be down at the sharp end, of course, getting the *moment critique* as she pushes it out, doing a bit of a David Attenborough commentary. Won't she be surprised?' he grinned.

'Oh, Hugh, I'm not so sure she'll –'

'Won't she just love it? And we can play it every year on

his birthday!' He turned and ran. 'Bye, all. Just put the dogs out for five minutes, then slam the front door behind you as you leave!'

We watched as he ran off down the path, bundled Henry in the car – no question of strapping him in, of course, or his wife come to that – and then with a throaty old roar of the engine they were away. I saw two cigarettes burning in the night sky as they sped off, shrieking with laughter. Very close. Very happy. Very Molly and Hugh.

Sebastian and I stood and waved until they were out of sight. All was quiet for a moment. Then Sebastian voiced what I was thinking.

'I envy them,' he sighed.

I nodded. 'Me too.'

There was a pause. I shook myself. 'Come on, let's clear up, see to the dogs and get out of here.'

Much of the drive home was spent in companionable silence. I think we were both exhausted by the events of the last few hours and also, pleasantly mellow, and somewhat lost in our thoughts. At length though, Sebastian chuckled.

'What?' I turned, smiling.

He shook his head. 'Just – that pair. What a riot.'

'I know,' I smiled, pleased to have introduced him to a riot. My riotous assembly. I snuggled down happily in my seat.

After a bit, he pulled up in front of my house. 'Here we are, then.'

I turned. Took a deep breath. This was my moment. 'Um, would you like to come in?'

His dark eyes widened with surprise. I hadn't noticed

before but they were exactly the colour of expensive chocolates. Belgian browns, they should be called, with black nuts in the middle.

'What, with Maureen there?'

'Well, she could go home,' I said, somewhat brazenly. I felt myself flushing. This was wrong, somehow. I should be having this conversation in his arms, hot with passion, lips a-tremble, unable to control ourselves and needing to prostrate ourselves somewhere horizontally, pronto, not two feet apart as if we were at some executive board meeting.

He scraped back his hair nervously. 'A little, um, awkward, don't you think? Bye-bye, Maureen, see you later, nudge-nudge?'

I licked my lips. 'Well, why don't we go to your house then, have a coffee there?' I offered brightly. What was wrong with this man, and what the hell was I doing in the driving seat?

He regarded me for a long moment. Smiled gently. 'Let's leave it, Livvy, eh? Not tonight.'

I stared. It took me a moment to realise I'd been rejected. Not tonight, Olivia. I felt for the door handle, struggled with it, flushing to my toes.

'You're right, it's late,' I said, rustling up a bright smile, 'and coffee only keeps me awake anyway.'

Suddenly he lunged towards me – yes, he couldn't help himself – and I pitched forward too, kissed his ear as he – opened my door for me.

'It does stick a bit,' he confessed as I retrieved my lips from his hair.

'Oh, right!' I gasped. God, did I get away with that? Did

he know I'd tried to snog him? I got out, covered in confusion.

'See you soon then,' I warbled.

He smiled up at me through the open window. 'Definitely. 'Night, Livvy.'

'Good night.' I recovered enough to smile, even challenged him briefly with my eyes. But he didn't seem to notice.

I turned, not waiting to see him drive off the few yards down the road, and walked dazedly up my drive.

When I knew he'd definitely gone, though, I stopped still, turned, and stared back down the empty road. Well. What d'you make of that then? I blinked. Had I got it so wrong? Had I really misread the signs so badly? Had we not, after all, been swimming in a sea of mutual attraction for the best part of the evening? Had he not felt the roaring in his ears, the volts shooting through the old aortas, the throbbing of the pulse points as we'd locked eyes over the buttercups, simultaneously licking strawberry juice sensually from our fingers? I felt – shattered, confused. What was wrong with the man? Was I not right, somehow? Had I said the wrong thing? Offended his artistic sensibilities? I didn't have time to ponder further, however, as Maureen opened the front door.

'Ah, you're back,' she said caustically. 'I thought I heard a car.' Her sharp nose twitched like Hunca Munca's. Probably smelt it too.

'Yes, we're – I'm back.' I sighed. 'Hi, Maureen. All well?' I trudged wearily towards her.

'Fine. Claudia's been asleep for hours. I sent her up at nine, she was so tired, but . . .' she paused.

'Yes?'

'Well, there's a man here.'

'A man? Where?' I peered past her, through the open front door.

'He's sitting out in the garden, on the terrace. Been here for a while, actually.' She swooped forward suddenly and found my ear. 'He says he's your husband!' she hissed.

I stepped back. Stared. 'My . . . Johnny?'

She nodded, wide-eyed, tight-lipped, triumphant. Then she folded her arms importantly and stood aside to let me in. I put my handbag down slowly on the hall table and moved past her in a daze, then realised she was following me down the passage.

I turned. 'Um, thank you, Maureen,' I muttered. 'How much do I owe you?'

'Oh, well, now let me see. I arrived at seven so –'

'Here.' I pressed far too much into her hand, not having time for the mental arithmetic.

She didn't argue and went back towards the door for her coat. 'I'll see myself out,' she called diplomatically, but with a tinge of regret.

I nodded, didn't answer, but all the same waited until the door had shut firmly behind her. Johnny? Here? What on earth for? And why so late? I glanced at my watch. Ten thirty. Not so late, of course, because Molly had abruptly curtailed the evening.

I walked slowly out on to the terrace, tucking my hair carefully behind my ears. My heart was pounding. As I emerged through the French windows, I saw him sitting on the terrace wall, his long, elegant legs dangling. He stood up.

'Hi, Livvy.' His face was strange, taut and pale in the

moonlight, yet I knew he had a tan, and he was smoking, for God's sake. Johnny almost never smoked. Then it came to me. In a blinding flash, I knew. Knew what this was. Why he'd come. This was what Nina had come to tell me the other day, what Molly had hinted at.

'Sorry to crash in on you like this.' He cranked up a smile.

'That's OK,' I said carefully.

He took a nervous drag of his cigarette and stared down between his feet. I moved past him and sat, because I needed to, not too close, but just a bit further along the wall from where he'd been sitting. I held on to the balustrade behind in case I needed to clutch something.

'I thought you were in France,' I said lightly.

'I was, we were, but . . .' He bit his lip. 'Well, I needed to talk to you. It wouldn't keep any longer, so I flew back this afternoon.'

I nodded. Blimey. This afternoon, eh? Guilty conscience keeping him awake at night, no doubt. Spoiling his holiday, putting him off his langoustines, keeping him from concentrating on his Jeffrey Archer on the beach. I noticed he was practically wearing beach clothes too – T-shirt, deck shoes, shorts – as if he'd literally just stood up and brushed the sand off himself. Literally just left her, lying supine and bronzed beside him on her raffia mat in her Topshop bikini, kissed her sun-drenched shoulder a tad regretfully and said, 'It's no good, my love, I must pop back and speak to her indoors. We simply must get this sorted out once and for all. See you back here in the morning for coffee and croissants on the balcony, OK?'

'Right,' I swallowed. 'You couldn't have called?'

'No. I had to see you, Livvy.' His blue eyes were heavy with regret.

I gulped and gripped the balustrade behind me firmly. 'I see. Well, here you are then.' I raised my chin with a brisk, defensive air. 'Fire away.'

He took a quick nervous drag of his cigarette, dropped it and stubbed it out with his toe. His eyes came up to meet mine. Clear as a summer's sky.

'I can't bear it, Liv. I miss you too much. In fact I miss both of you too much. This has been the biggest mistake of my life. I thought I could do it, but I can't, I know that now. I love you so much, Livvy. I want to come back.'

Chapter Twenty-One

I stared at him incredulously. For a moment I couldn't speak. Had neither wind nor words to draw on. My mouth fell open with shock.

'You . . . want to come back?'

He scraped back his hair nervously. 'Look, I know it's a hideous cheek and I should have rung or written – prepared you in some way – but every time I sat down and put pen to paper it sounded so formal, so eighteenth century, I – I just needed to see you.' Suddenly he bounded across to me, took my hands as they lay shocked and lifeless in my lap, and shook them urgently, as if to shake life into me. He gazed desperately into my eyes. 'I needed to plead with you, Livvy, to beg you even, to go down on my knees if necessary, because God knows, I can't do this any more. I'm dying without you. I can't bear it. I just can't bear it any longer!'

I stared into his wide blue eyes, speechless. Then I took my hands away, got up, and walked dazedly round the terrace. I sat down again, my legs feeling very unsteady, and looked down at the moss on the York stone. He wanted to come back? *He* was pleading with *me* to have him back? At length, I unwound my tongue.

'But – you left *me*!'

'I know.'

'For her!'

'I know!'

He shook his head despairingly, scraped frantic hands through his hair again, pulling at the roots as if to punish it. 'And God knows why. Well, no, I *do* know why, exactly why, but that's not important right now. All that matters is that I want to come back, to be a family again, here, with you and Claudia, where I belong.'

'It's important to *me*!' I spluttered. 'Why *did* you leave me, Johnny? And for her! Why her, of all people, and why have her charms suddenly deserted her so dramatically!'

He plunged his hands deep into his pockets and threw back his head. Turned anguished eyes on to the night sky. At length his eyes came down to meet mine.

'Sex,' he blurted out, holding my gaze. 'Pure and simple.'

I nodded. Stared back unflinchingly. Then I took a deep breath. 'Better than with me?'

'No, different.' He shrugged. 'Different person, that's all, so more exciting in the beginning, the thrill of the unknown, that kind of thing. Pathetic.' He gazed down at his shoes, shook his head remorsefully. Then in a low voice: 'I know, Livvy, I know. Sad, clichéd, totally laughable and deeply, deeply, pathetic. A middle-aged man who sees his youth slipping away from him. A man who's always felt young and vital, who can't believe it's all over. Can't believe he's never going to sleep with anyone else, ever in his life again, besides his wife. Puerile, I know. And I'm so, so sorry.' His eyes came up to meet mine, beseechingly.

I nodded, trying to keep calm. 'Well, it's not exactly trail-blazing, is it, Johnny? You're not the first, and you certainly won't be the last, but – God, just for sex! All this – all this pain and heartache, just for sex? Couldn't you have gone off and had an affair? Sneaked off out of hours, seen her in your lunch hour, maybe even had a few old-fashioned dirty weekends, told me you were playing golf with the boys or something, got it all out of your system that way, so no one knew?'

He stared at me, aghast. 'You mean – you'd have *liked* that?'

'Oh, I'd have *loved* it! *No*, Johnny!' I cried. 'I'd have liked it about as much as having a cup of cold sick poured over my head, but I'd have preferred it to – to the cruelty I suffered! Preferred it to the ghastly public humiliation, to the mockery you made of my life, of my marriage, and to the grief and the agony my child went through! *She* wouldn't have known if you'd sneaked off to a grubby motel, half the *county* wouldn't have known, Christ, *I* might not even have known, and since you clearly planned to ditch this woman within a few months anyway, in the long run it would have been tacky but preferable!'

'And deceitful.'

'Oh, Johnny!' I cried, exasperated, banging the palms of my hands on my forehead. 'You and your bloody honour! It's so misplaced, so misguided! You really think you're doing the decent thing by coming clean and walking out on your wife and child and not sneaking around? You really think that's the honourable thing to do, under the circumstances? *Well, I disagree!* The only thing that assuages is your conscience! The only person it helps is you! *You* wanted to feel better, and you couldn't cope with having the guilt hanging round your neck any more! Oh, you could stoop to having the *sex* – that wasn't a problem – but, Johnny, the man of honour, the man with a sense of duty, couldn't stoop to lying, to being deceitful, to not letting me find out. You couldn't stoop to *sparing* me!' My fists were clenched with anger, and for a moment then, I couldn't speak. My voice, when it finally came back, was low, shaky, quivering with rage. 'You destroyed me, Johnny, and you've destroyed our marriage. You've ruined everything! Spoilt it all, and now, months later, as I'm beginning to lick my wounds, beginning to come to terms with the grief, and trying hard to become part of the human race again, you stroll back in here, cool as anything, and declare you'd like to be part of this family again. Lie in your old half of the bed, wash the car, dig the garden, do the washing-up, poke the boring old wife for the rest of your life – well, I'm just not having it, Johnny! I'm just not convinced!' With that I burst into tears. Great racking sobs rent my body and tears poured down my face. I didn't even bother to try to check them, to cover my face in any way. He rushed to put his arms round me.

'*Piss off!*' I shrieked, pushing him away. 'Just piss off!'

He backed off and I sobbed on. Turned my back to him, sat down on the terrace wall and wept. I couldn't stop, actually. It was as if he'd taken a brick out of the dam and it had just burst all over the place, exploded everywhere. He lit a cigarette and perched tentatively a little way along the wall; beside me, but not too close. Eventually my sobs subsided and I got to the catchy breath and shoulder-shaking stage. I threw back my head, wiped my face with the back of my hand and gazed blankly up into the night. I couldn't believe this was happening. Simply couldn't believe it was true. He lit another cigarette and passed it to me. I dragged on it gratefully, right down to my toes, feeling calmer now. Shaky, but calmer.

'You have every right to be furious.'

'Of course I have,' I muttered.

'And every right not to have me back.'

'That goes without saying.'

'And I swear to God this isn't calculated persuasiveness; this isn't me sailing back in here because things aren't working out and I'm wondering if I've been too hasty in abandoning you, abandoning a cosy, settled life. It's much more visceral than that. I'm desperate, Livvy, absolutely desperate without you.'

I couldn't answer.

'Think about it, Liv,' he urged. 'Think about what we had, what we'd be throwing away.'

'I've done nothing *but* think about it!' I replied hotly. Suddenly the rage shot up through my body like a high-speed elevator. I was speechless again, then incensed, incoherent with fury.

'How *dare* you! God, these past few months – what we'd be throwing away – how *dare* you ... what *you've* thrown away, you bastard!' Suddenly I was on my feet, fists raining down on him, pummelling him as he sat on the wall. He stood up to defend himself, went for my flailing fists, caught my wrists, held them tight, and to my horror, as we struggled I was sobbing again. This time he pulled me close. My strength failed me and I collapsed on to him, wept into his cotton T-shirt. It smelt of fresh air, hay. Of Johnny. He stroked my hair, kissed the top of my head, his arms tight but shaky around me. And it was lovely. Normal. Like coming home. I shuddered into his shoulder. No more chasing rainbows, I thought, peering blearily into his T-shirt through wet lashes and soggy mascara; no more awful dates with Malcolms and Rollos; no more rejections from famous musicians; no more making a fool of myself; no more pity from friends; no more sympathy; no more being strong for Claudia and breaking down when I'd put her to bed and shut my bedroom door; no more empty future; no more living in fear of being like my mother – just Johnny, the love of my life, the ache in my gut, the soulmate I'd had beside me since I was a teenager, my only family, back where he belonged. Who wouldn't be tempted?

'It's just a blip,' muttered Johnny fiercely into my hair. 'Our only blip, in twelve years. Three months of madness, that's all, a madness that gripped me. But it's gone now. Gone for ever.'

I drew my head back from his chest. Found his eyes. 'And her? Why not her?'

He sighed. Loosened his grip on me. Looked away. 'It just didn't work, Livvy. She's so – possessive, so jealous. I couldn't move, couldn't breathe, it was suffocating, stifling.'

I thought back to when I'd seen them together, two blond heads bent over the concert programme. 'You didn't look very stifled at the Abbey.'

'God, that was so awful. Seeing you there, with that guy.'

I frowned. Rollo? Yes, it must have been Rollo. And of course Johnny wasn't to know he spat.

'And then tonight, waiting for you, knowing you were

out with someone.' He gazed, hurt clouding his eyes. 'Some guy?'

'It's none of your business, Johnny,' I said quietly.

He nodded, head down. 'No, you're right.'

My God, his penance would be huge, though, wouldn't it? I thought, looking at his blond head, bent low, sorrowful, remorseful. And think of the mileage in that; I could milk it for months, for years. He'd have to toe the line for the rest of his life. I'd have the upper hand entirely, which I wasn't convinced I'd ever had. But would that be healthy? Would that, at the end of the day, help either of us? Surely if this was to work, it had to be with a clean slate. It had to be even-handed, shoulder to shoulder, facing the world together, and with no Sword of Damocles hanging over his head. But how realistic was that? Not very. How often would I be tempted to say as he failed to empty the dishwasher – oh, and I suppose you'd rather be with your bloody whore than tidying up the kitchen! But then again – I gazed up at the night sky and sighed – what was the alternative? To say: no Johnny, sod off, I'm making my own way now, having a great time? Was I? I thought about that one carefully. No, a better time, I decided, but not a great time. And how come I was even weighing it up? I thought, suddenly startled. I pushed an astonished hand through my hair. *Seriously* weighing it up too, genuinely thinking of rejecting him, and not just to play a game, to keep my pride, to make him wait, to have a bit of 'I'll show the bastard' – no, I was seriously thinking of telling him to get lost, and yet this was what I'd longed for, yearned for, all these months!

'Do you still love me, Livvy?' Quietly, it stole out of the night. I took a deep breath. Ah. The trump card.

'Yes.'

Yes I did. Of course I did. How could I not?

'And can you imagine us . . .' he took a deep breath to steady himself, 'not growing old together?'

Sorry, no, *this* was the trump card. The other one was just the knave. Growing old together. Sentimental pictures of white heads and rocking chairs side by side, gnarled hands creeping out from under the knee blankets, and clasping, as we turned wrinkled, faded smiles on each other. I shook my head. My chin wobbled.

'No,' I whispered. 'No, I can't imagine not doing that.'

Don't you dare. Don't you dare play that ace.

'And if not for all that –' he took me in his arms and squeezed me tight. I could feel his heart racing – 'if not for me, for us, then –' his voice cracked – 'for Claudes? And – and, who knows, Liv?' he said, his heart thumping away now. 'Maybe another child?'

A tiny baby in a crib, with Johnny, Claudia and me all standing round, looking lovingly down, sprang instantly to mind, and for the third time that evening I burst into tears. You wouldn't think there'd be any left, would you, but there were. I soaked his shirt, and he'll forgive me for telling you that he soaked mine, too.

We sat on that wall for a long while on that warm, still, July night, talking softly, clenching and unclenching hands, even crying again – Johnny this time, not me – until eventually, it seemed as natural as anything. To take one another by the hand, to walk through the house, and to mount the stairs to bed. Oh yes, by rights, I should have made him fight, every inch of the way, made it much, much harder, but actually, I wanted him very badly. As we stood up from that wall and hugged each other hard, half a bathful of adrenalin shot up the back of my legs and swept force-fully around my body, and as he tightened his arms around me, I could feel his breath coming in spurts, roaring in my ear. I didn't think – oh yuck, he's been with her; and I didn't think – how frigging dare he? I just thought – yesss. He's mine. And he's come home. And I want him.

We were kissing as we went up the stairs, desperate, tor-tured kisses, lips trembling, and then again beside the bed, eating the faces off each other as we struggled out of our clothes, falling together, pulling each other down, our naked bodies fitting like parts of a modular jigsaw puzzle, seamlessly entwined. We made love with a frenzy and a passion that I don't think, in all our years of lovemaking, had ever possessed us before, and a greed too. Like a couple of thirsty camels happening finally upon that water hole. Finally we fell apart, flung back away from each other like deflecting magnets, satiated, replete, relieved. We stared up at the ceiling, panting, the duvet in a heap on the floor, the warm night air stealing in across our naked bodies. All was so still, so silent; just the sound of our breathing.

At length I reached down and pulled the duvet back. We curled up and lay together like spoons, Johnny behind me, his arms wrapped around me, both of us gazing out of the open window beside the bed, at the crescent moon.

'Where is she now?' I asked quietly, as reality came seeping stealthily back. So many questions. So many answers I needed. I wanted to sit up and light a cigarette, but that had never been our style.

'She's back at her flat.'

'Oh. Not in France?'

'No, why?'

I shrugged. 'Somehow I thought you'd left her there.'

'France was a disaster. It was a last-ditch attempt of hers to bring us together. She booked a hotel in St-Jean-de-Luz as a surprise. She wasn't to know we'd spent our honeymoon there, of course, but it couldn't have been more fatal. Couldn't have sounded the death knell of our relationship more conclusively. We spent a ghastly few days in a stifling, hundred-degree heat wave, she, in dark glasses in our room to hide her red eyes and me, walking the streets. I walked everywhere, all around those little back lanes we discovered, with tiny painted houses, balconies and terraces spilling over with geraniums and bougainvillaea – remember? Remember how you made friends with all the madames, took cuttings, filling our room with little jam jars, determined to get them home somehow?'

'I remember.'

'I walked for miles. Came back only for silent meals, picking at food in happy, bustling restaurants, with her, still in dark glasses, sitting opposite me, and surrounded by French children on other tables sharing a late supper with their parents, about Claudia's age, younger too, laughing, chattering into the night. Awful.'

I stayed silent.

'After three days of what should have been a three-week holiday, we booked out.'

'She wanted to go too?'

He hesitated. 'Yes. It was a mutual decision.'

I spotted a lie. The first one. I swam towards it – then let it go.

'And now?'

'Now?'

'Well, either she's accepted the fact that the affair's run its course, or she's distraught and in a heap.'

He swallowed. 'Distraught and in a heap.'

For a brief moment I felt a pang of pity for her. Alone in her flat. But not much of a pang.

'Oh well,' I said, reaching for a glass of water, 'I don't suppose it'll take her long to recover. Don't suppose it'll take her long to find another married man to play with.'

He didn't answer. Ah, I thought, sipping my water. He wasn't prepared to rubbish her, then. I wasn't sure if I liked that or not. Yes, I was. 'Isn't that her game?' I demanded hotly.

'She – got caught up in something,' he said, picking his words carefully. 'By accident. I take the blame. For everything. This has all been my fault.'

Suddenly I was furious. He was defending her. As I struggled to contain my temper, he went on.

'But now, because she's desperate to cling on, she's changed. She's doing everything in her power to keep me. She'd go to any lengths: she tells lies, she's manipulative – downright cunning too.'

This was better. I took a deep breath. 'In what way?'

'In extraordinary ways. Recently she's taken to writing letters to herself. Threatening letters.'

I sat up. 'What d'you mean?'

He propped himself on one elbow and struggled to

explain. 'It all started when Claudes went missing, remember? God, I was upset – so full of remorse, thought it was all my fault, and I'm sure that's when she felt me slipping away, sensed my first seeds of doubt. First she invented aches and pains, limped about the flat clutching her side and moaning, even made me drive her to the hospital, said she thought her appendix had burst. All spurious, of course. The nurses exchanged knowing glances as they examined her and sent her home within minutes, but I remembered thinking then that in some warped kind of way it was a cry for help. I had –' he hesitated – 'been passionate about her, helplessly so, and I think she was trying to rekindle that passion. Trying to say – look, imagine life without me. Imagine if I were to die, remember how close we were. Does that make any sense?'

I blinked. 'Blimey. Bit extreme.'

'She is,' he insisted. 'She's neurotic and extreme.'

'And the letters?'

'That started quite recently. Threatening letters in childish capitals, Agatha Christie stuff, very naïve.'

'But saying what?'

'Oh, death threats, you know – "Dear Nina, you'd better watch out, we're after you" – all designed to make me hugely protective, to make me hole up with her in that flat for ever, barricade the door, put bars on the windows, shut out the world, never let her out of my sight.'

'Good God!' I gazed at him.

'I told you, Livvy, she's nutty. She'd do anything.'

Naturally that frightened me for a second. I thought of Claudes, of *Fatal Attraction*, of boiling bunnies. 'She'd bloody better *not* do anything,' I said hotly.

But I felt stronger, too, because of it. United against her. If she was nuts, it helped enormously. But once again, ridiculously, a pang of sympathy. Because for a while there, I'd been nuts too. I remembered trying to make a friend of her, practically offering to iron her underwear, much to Molly's horror. I shuddered. Lay down beside Johnny.

He turned from his side on to his back and I gazed at his profile. Gazed at this husband of mine, square-jawed and bronzed, lying beside me in the moonlight. His hand, curled in mine, gradually loosened its hold as his eyes shut and Morpheus welcomed him back, down the dark lanes of sleep. And as I stared and stared until my eyes began to hurt, I thought – how weird. How strange. How . . . very curious. Four hours ago I'd been in Molly's garden flirting with another man. Two hours ago, I'd been in aforementioned man's car, as near as damn it propositioning him. And now, here I was, in bed with Johnny. If your probing, investigative, fly-on-the-wall reporter had slunk through my bedroom door right now, crept up to the bed, stuck a microphone under my nose and hissed urgently, 'So how d'you feel, Mrs McFarllen? Our viewers are keen to know?' I'd have had to answer, in the words of the tabloid press – gobsmacked. If he'd persisted, pursued his tack with, 'But happy? Happy, surely, Mrs McFarllen?' I'd have replied – yes. Very. But, I decided, turning over to face the wall, I'd qualify that with 'unsettled'. Happy, but unsettled. Those, I decided as I, too, finally shut my eyes, were definitely my overriding emotions of the moment.

Chapter Twenty-Two

Of course, that's not the way it should have been. As any good counsellor, psychologist or best friend worth their salt would tell you, what I should have done was turf him out. Given him the never-darken-my-door routine, the how-dare-you-come-grovelling-back-after-all-you've-done-to-me malarkey. Sent him away with a flea in his ear. Then, naturally, he'd have wanted me even more. And at some point, weeks – no, maybe even months – later, I might have agreed to meet him for dinner. In an incredibly expensive, swanky London restaurant, looking gorgeous. (Me, not him, hell no, he'd be pale and gaunt, a shadow of his former self.) Oh, I'd *agree* to meet him, but I wouldn't turn up. So there he'd be, at this impossible-to-come-by corner table, chewing his napkin nervously, drinking heavily, trying to avoid the disdainful eyes of the waiters as they scornfully observed his solitary, stood-up status, before emerging hours later, seriously drunk, reeling down Knightsbridge, and stopping every passer-by with the requisite number of ears to inform them just how mush he was in love wish his wife, and how he'd alwaysh been in love with hish lovely wife, before being discovered in the gutter by a passing policeman and taken to the cells for the night.

And meanwhile, of course, I'd be out with my boys. My Malcolms, my Rollos, my Sebastians – the former in a hat and dark glasses and the second under strict instructions not to open his mouth – parading them up and down in front of his nose until it turned green and fell off. Then maybe, *maybe*, I'd agree to meet him again. For, hmm, let me see now – coffee. And on the understanding that he had precisely half an hour to present his case because I was a very busy woman. (By this stage I'd naturally have that aforementioned, much discussed, high-powered job at the Chelsea Physic.) In I'd click in my designer mules – I'd be on the management side, rather than the soil-tilling, gumbooted side – and there he'd be, cowering at a corner table again, sweaty-palmed, getting eagerly to his feet, knocking his chair flying in his haste. Oh yes, it could have gone on and on like that. I could have milked it for months, brought him to his knees, given him to understand that only under very exceptional circumstances would he ever get so much as a toe in my door again. Instead of which, with a belly full of Pimm's inside me as Dutch courage to take another man to bed, I'd taken Johnny instead. Just like that.

More kindly critics might argue that if getting Johnny home was indeed the endgame, the *raison d'être*, why shilly-shally about? Why play the fish, dangle him at length for no apparent reason, when actually, it was the landing of him that was so important? We weren't seventeen, after all; this wasn't an extended flirt, this was serious stuff, this was a marriage.

I suspect there may have been some middle ground, but I didn't find it. I simply saw the green light, put my foot down and went for it. Marriage, it seemed to me, was rather like one of those great big shiny Jeeps, driven by mothers with expensive highlights and crammed full with children at private schools; the whole family perched up high, roaring around bends, confident, loved, cruising into the future, pushing the odd bicycle into the verge, which to me, felt like the single life. Pedalling hard, alone, feeling every bump, every rut in the road, never quite knowing what was around the next corner. I'd been in the Jeep for ten years and then I'd got on the bicycle and I knew which I preferred, which was harder work, and which was more terrifying. Not seeing round corners frightened the life out of me, but now, the future was simply a scene I could cruise back into. What a relief to let go of those handlebars. Weak? Possibly, but on the other hand, who on earth was I supposed to be brave for? Surely this was about me? About what I wanted?

As I lay there the following morning, feeling I really should pinch myself extremely hard, I took in the surreal scene around me. Johnny was still asleep beside me, his clothes in a familiar heap on the floor, his brown arm flung over me in its habitual fashion, one leg sticking out of bed, his eyelids just beginning to flicker. They opened, and as he saw me, a huge smile spread instantly across his face. It was so instinctive, so very much the moment he'd opened his eyes, so free of any ghastly doubt, any 'holy shit, what have I done?' that I beamed back, delighted. And it was at that, highly seminal moment, that the door opened and Claudia appeared in her nightie. She stopped dead in her tracks, her hand frozen on the handle. Her jaw dropped.

'Daddy!'

He turned quickly towards her. She stared in astonishment, her grey eyes huge, first focused on him, then on me.

'It's Daddy!' She gaped incredulously at me, as if perhaps I didn't know. I smiled, waiting.

Johnny sat up and stretched out an arm to draw her close. She came, but slowly, looking to me first for reassurance. I nodded, still smiling.

'Daddy, what are you *doing* here!' she squealed suddenly, leaping forward excitedly, jumping high in the air, and coming crashing down on top of him with her knees bent, catching him neatly in the groin.

'Oooomph . . .!' he groaned, bringing his knees up in pain. 'Aaarrgh! What am I doing? I'm being beaten up by a ten-year-old,' he gasped, 'that's what I'm doing, and on the day of my homecoming too. What sort of a welcome is that?'

'Home . . . ?' Again, wide grey eyes shot across to me.

'Daddy's coming back, darling.'

'Really?' Her mouth dropped.

'Really,' said Johnny firmly.

There was a silence. She didn't whoop, and she didn't shriek, and for a moment there, I was nervous. But then a slow smile spread over her face. She reddened a bit too.

'Well, about time too,' she said hotly, giving him a playful clip round the ear. She folded her arms and pursed her lips, affecting a rolling-pin-wielding, northern harridan style. 'Moother and I 'ave bin worried sick, 'aven't we, moother? All this time without a word, you never call, you never write, we've been that fussed!'

He laughed, catching her wrists as she made to beat

him up with her rolling pin and then they rolled about on the bed, wrestling and fighting amid shrieks of giggles.

I watched them for a moment, tussling away beside me. Just like old times. Extraordinary. Like he'd never been away. How could that be then? Because he had been away. I blinked, shook my head in wonder, then grabbed my dressing gown, rolled neatly out of bed and slipped into it. I smiled down as they rolled about, Johnny pinning Claudes to the bed now, telling her that 'if she gave 'im any more lip e'd come down from mill or oop from pit and give 'er a right good thrashin',' and Claudia shrieking that if he did that she'd 'put on clogs and shawl and get a job oop big house as servin' wench!'

I tied my silk dressing gown around me and gazed out of the window. A hazy mist was hovering over a dewy lawn, full of the promise of sun. The caravan was still in situ on the other side of the river (despite Mac's assertions that they'd be gone soon, predictably, they were still here), and I saw the door open and Lance appear. As I watched him yawn, stretch, gaze up at the blue sky then make his way over the bridge and up the dewy lawn, I realised, in a sudden rush, the enormity of what I'd done. Realised what a huge leap of faith I'd taken. I also realised, with something approaching panic, that having taken that leap, it simply had to work. Shrieks of glee rang out behind me. It had to. If not for me, then for Claudia. We couldn't do this to her only for Johnny to disappear again, could we? But of course that wasn't going to happen, was it? I thought hastily. He was back for good now and we were a family again. As I watched Lance potter off round to his workbench in the garage, I leant forward and rested my forehead on the glass. Was it really that simple? Did we just erase the last few months and start again? Carry on from where we left off without even skipping a beat? I gave myself a little inward shake. Why, yes of course we did, why not? As I turned, I saw Johnny's eyes on me as he tussled with Claudia. They seemed anxious.

I straightened up. 'Right, you lot!' I said with a bright smile. 'Scrambled eggs and bacon in the kitchen in ten minutes, and the last one down washes up the scrambled egg pan!'

I swept out joyfully and clattered downstairs. Well, if they were looking to me for guidance, that was fine. I could do that, I could be the leader. In fact, it would make an extremely pleasant change.

It was a beautiful morning. I threw open the back door and humming happily, gathered some eggs from the fridge. Yes, breakfast in our new kitchen, cooked on my shiny blue Aga, with the sun streaming in on the pale yellow walls, hung now with blue and white plates, casting shadows on the smooth, mellow wooden floor, and all of us here, together, back where we belonged.

As I fried the bacon at the stove, simultaneously laying the table with orange juice, toast, cereal, quickly flicking on the radio as I went past, Johnny and Claudia came bounding in. They flopped happily down at the table, still chattering away, and occasionally, Johnny would catch my eye as in, 'Isn't it great? She's delighted!' And I'd respond with a smile which agreed.

Meanwhile, the laughter and the jokes continued apace. But it seemed to me, as I listened, my hand pausing for a moment as I went to break an egg in the pan, that somehow he was hiding behind Claudia. Something, and I couldn't quite put my finger on it, was wrong. His larking was extravagant, and OK, it always had been, but somehow . . . No. I cracked the egg. No, you're wrong, Olivia. It's just that he's bound to be slightly nervous. Why d'you think you flicked that radio on so quickly if not for some background hum, and aren't you secretly glad that Claudia's here and not round at Lucy's? And after all, I thought, reaching for the milk and sloshing it in, why shouldn't he be in glorious, over-the-top high spirits on this supremely, glorious, heady day?

That day, and the next few, proceeded in much the same pattern. I seemed to vacillate between strange extremes of emotions. I'd notice every nuance, every flicker of Johnny's eye, every intonation in his voice, but as the days progressed, my reactions to these nuances became more pronounced. One moment I'd be almost incandescent with happiness, hugging him to bits, showering him with kisses, and the next, tears of doubt and rage would spring and I'd be stomping round the house in fury, practically spitting in his coffee as I handed it to him. Johnny indulged these moods, knowing, I'm sure, that they were entirely natural and that it was better for me to get it all out rather than bottle it up. He did his best to ride the waves. He also indulged my rather erratic desire for information, as one minute I decided I wanted to know absolutely everything about Nina, and the next, nothing. Sometimes, the minute Claudia had gone out to play, I'd seize his wrist, drag him to the kitchen table, sit him down, and with frenzied, burning eyes demand, 'Where? How? How exactly did it happen – how did you meet her? I want to know precisely – tell me again!'

And he'd light a cigarette and patiently explain, yet again, that the day we'd been to look around Claudia's new school, on the open day, Nina had been there too. As a new teacher, available to meet new parents.

'You picked her up at an open day!' I screeched, fumbling for a cigarette.

'No, I just talked to her, but for quite a while because you were off touring the school. You wanted to see the new science block again, remember? The headmaster took you, and while you were gone, we chatted, that's all.'

My mind scuttled back. Was that right? Had I gone off? Maybe I had.

'And then?' I demanded. 'How the hell did you progress from there? Listen, Miss Harrison, we seem to have a few minutes, fancy a quick one behind the bike sheds while my wife's examining the Bunsen burners?'

'No,' he said levelly, ignoring my sarcasm, 'it happened quite by chance, actually. A couple of months later the gears were playing up on the Lagonda, so I took it into the Classic Car garage in Finchley – you know, the one Dad used to go to, and the one I still use. Well, it was quite extraordinary, because there she was, just coming out of the front door to the flat next door. She recognised me and smiled, and at first I couldn't think who the hell she was, but then I remembered I'd met her at the school. We got chatting and it turned out that her father owns the garage, which is extraordinary really because I've known Bob Harrison for years, and – well, I suppose we laughed about the coincidence, said what a small world it was, talked for a bit.' He shrugged. 'It just went from there.'

'How?' I yelled. 'How did it "just go from there"!'

He sighed, frowned and picked at an eggy stain on the kitchen table. 'I suppose . . . I asked her if she fancied a drink.'

'What – just like that? Oh golly, Nina, what a coincidence, your Dad mends my cars, fancy a lager and lime?'

'Well, it was a hot day, the pub was opposite . . . I don't know. It seemed natural at the time, somehow.'

'Natural?' I sneered. 'But you're married, Johnny. A married man.'

'I know.'

I dragged hard and deep on my cigarette, eyes a trifle wild. 'And then?'

'Well,' he shifted uncomfortably, 'then I suppose we arranged to meet again, only this time it was for dinner, and then –'

'*Stop, Stop!*' I cried, clapping my hands over my ears. 'Stop this minute! I don't want to hear another word!'

And so it went on, with me oscillating wildly between a greed to be informed and a revulsion at the details, between hate and happiness, and in the midst of all this, many bouts of desperate, frenzied lovemaking. Oh yes, there was a definite desperation about it, as if sex was the filling in the sandwich, something which would glue us together, and which we had to have, as much as possible, at any conceivable opportunity, to stop us falling apart. In some ways I was more worried about me than I was about Johnny. He seemed so sure, so strong, so ready to go along with anything I wanted, and I began to wonder if it was me who was the neurotic here, me who was having the mid-life crisis.

I seemed to veer from an insatiable desire to run down the street shouting, 'He's back! My husband's back!' to not wanting to answer the telephone in case it was Someone Who Should Know. My mother, for instance, or Angie, maybe Molly, or Imogen. Of course we did tell these people, we told them all in time, but gradually, letting it leak out over a period of days. Looking back, their reactions fell neatly into two camps: modified rapture from my mother, Molly and Hugh, and unmitigated delight from Angie and Imogen.

My mother's subdued reaction – 'Well, darling, I'm pleased for you, of course I'm pleased, it's what you wanted, isn't it?' – together with a promise, when pressed, to come over soon with Howard, was, in light of her new incarnation as a born-again romantic, a no-longer-passed-over, shat-upon woman, I suppose somewhat predictable. But Molly surprised me.

'And you've taken him back?' she demanded from her hospital bed, newly delivered of a nine-pound baby girl named Flora, after the cottage garden she was very nearly born into, and who, her mother declared, was even more stunning than Helen of Troy, fed beautifully, didn't crack her nipples, and had yet to be sick all over her.

'Well – yes. I have.'

'No questions asked?'

'Of course, Molly, many.'

'Good. Well, I just hope he's got some answers.' A pause. 'Sorry, Livvy, I'm delighted for you, of course I'm delighted. God, ignore me, I'm just hormone soup at the moment. This morning I was in floods of tears because I was convinced Flora was going to grow up to be a lesbian.

407

One of the nurses missed her pink wrist tag and called her a great big bruiser of a boy, and I could suddenly see her in dungarees, with a number-one haircut and a lover called Brenda. I cried for half an hour. Added to which I feel like my undercarriage has been sewn up by some malicious, sharp-eyed seamstress from the WI, while at the back I've got a bag full of jelly beans swinging jauntily out of my bottom. Just ignore me, I'm a mess. Hugh's here and he's thrilled for you, aren't you, Hugh?' She held the phone out to Hugh for confirmation.

'Am I?'

There was some muffled confusion as her hand clamped over the mouthpiece, a fair amount of hissing, then – 'Thrilled!' came back a chipper male voice. 'But tell her I thought she was doing pretty well under her own steam, too.'

Angie cried on the phone, so relieved was she, and promised to come round soon, wondering also if Claudia would like to come and stay a while and give us some space? I turned, the receiver at my ear, to ask Johnny and we both instinctively shook our heads and said – no! Then we stared, anxiously at each other. Why didn't we want space? Why didn't we want to be alone? Because we wanted to be a unit, a family, I decided firmly.

Imogen, though, surprised me most. I left a message on her answer machine at work – she was out at Sotheby's – and that evening she appeared on my doorstep, loaded with flowers, hugging us through her tears and her orchids, hugely overcome and emotional.

'Oh God, guys,' she gasped, 'this is so much what I'd hoped for! It's just the answer to everyone's prayers! I just can't believe it – I'm so, so happy for you!'

'Imo,' I said, touched as she hugged me tight, 'you're so sweet to come.'

She sat in the garden with us a while, shared a bottle of wine with us, but when she left, I closed the front door thoughtfully and went, biting my thumbnail, back to Johnny on the terrace. He was hidden now, behind the *Telegraph*.

'I can't believe she came all that way just to give us some flowers,' I said in astonishment. 'And she's so busy. She's got a private view to organise tonight.'

Johnny didn't answer, immersed as he was in his broadsheet, and suddenly I felt a bit guilty. I adored Imo, always had done, but always from a slightly respectful distance, always from afar, and yet here she was, on my doorstep the moment she'd heard, brimming over with tears for me. I had no idea she'd felt my loss so keenly.

Claudia was skippy and happy most of the time, but cautious too, I noticed. Johnny would pull her on to his lap, maybe after Sunday lunch, and she'd laugh, fool about with him a bit, but be quick to slip away, too. If he noticed, he didn't say.

Once, when she and I were picking strawberries together in the vegetable patch, she suddenly paused, face down in the fragrant, star-shaped leaves. Crouched on her haunches, she said abruptly, 'Is Daddy back for good, then?'

I straightened up. 'Yes, of course, darling. This is for ever. We're a family again!'

She didn't reply.

I frowned. 'Claudes?'

'It's just . . . well, Granny says, "Never say never, and you can't say for ever." '

'Oh, Granny and her little mottoes!' I said, exasperated. 'When did she say that?'

She shrugged. 'The other day.'

'You saw her?'

'No, I rang her.'

'Oh!' Again, panic. She rang her? Why couldn't she talk to me? 'But – but you wanted Daddy to come back, surely?'

'Of course. I'm just asking, that's all. I can ask, can't I?' She straightened up and stared defiantly at me in her blue shorts and ancient Mickey Mouse T-shirt, her cheeks glowing. Yes, of course she could ask, I thought slowly as she threw down her basket, brushed past me and stomped off. Why not? Children have every right to assume their parents will be together for ever, so if one disappears, then comes back to the fold, surely they have every right to question that reappearance, too?

And then of course there was Sebastian. Initially I'd almost gone down on my knees and thanked God that I hadn't seduced Sebastian that night. Thanked God that I hadn't forced him, protesting, back to his towering town house, drugged his wine before dragging him by the hair up all those zillions of stone steps to his bedroom, slammed the door shut, refused to take no for an answer, cracked my whip, thrown him on the bed and given him a damn good seeing to, because look what I'd have been missing in my own back yard? Look who was waiting for me, under the stars, on my very own terrace?

Then again, I thought, running the tap over a lettuce I'd just picked for lunch and gazing out at Johnny through the kitchen window, snoozing in a deck chair with a

Panama hat over his eyes, then again, as every how-to-get-your-man manual would tell you, that probably couldn't have been better. What – to have the errant husband sitting waiting on the matrimonial doorstep until two in the morning, wondering where the hell the abandoned wife was, and then for me to arrive back, panting and dishevelled, knickers in my handbag, very definitely post-coital, very definitely deflowered? Oh perfect, the vengeful would breathe ecstatically, perfect! But I knew better. Johnny, with his code of honour, would have been horrified. He wouldn't have spoken to me, let alone touched me; would have brushed straight past me, stony-faced, got back in his car and roared off, because whilst it was OK for him to be promiscuous, for his *wife* – oh, heavens no. Hadn't he already quizzed me – gently but searchingly – about the possibility of my having seen some action these past few months? Eyes trawling my face for lies? Suddenly I flung down the lettuce and threw open the window in rage.

'Double standards!' I shrieked. 'DOUBLE FUCKING STANDARDS!'

Johnny awoke from his deck chair with a jolt and swung round, astonished, his Panama dropping on to the grass. In the bathroom above, Mac and the boys laid down their tools. It wasn't the first time they'd halted their hammering to listen to the 'domestic' below. By the time Johnny had run in and reached me in the kitchen I was hanging on to the sink, sobbing uncontrollably into the lettuce water. As he rushed up I seized the wet lettuce and slapped it in his face, hitting him again and again with it. He stood there, taking it, soaking wet, eyes shut, bits of green slime all over him, until finally I dropped it and sank down into a chair. Johnny crouched, took me in his arms and held me as I sobbed. You see, this was nothing new. Our days were full of interesting little episodes like this. He never argued his corner – well, let's face it, he didn't exactly have one – just let me get it all out of my system, and then when it was over, went slowly back to his deck chair, his garage, his toolshed, or whatever it was he'd been doing before. Occasionally, though, after one of these outbursts, I'd catch him later in an unguarded moment, and see his eyes, full of sorrow and regret, so profound it shocked me. I hoped it was for me, for what he'd done to me, for the time we'd lost together, but I couldn't be sure. And, feeling my eyes on him, he'd quickly respond with a bright smile and then we'd be back on track again, but often, they were tracks I didn't recognise – polite, dissembling tracks. Where the hell were they going?

And so, as I said, Sebastian had to be dealt with. Had to be visited. Well yes, of course he did, didn't he? I mean, we'd never been lovers, but I was pretty sure we'd been more than friends, and I couldn't exactly have him popping round wondering if I fancied dinner; couldn't just leave it hanging in the air like that, could I? And so I went one afternoon without warning, simply because I saw his car outside and I knew he'd be in. Maureen opened the door.

'He's in the study,' she said with a brisk jerk of her head upstairs. 'Will I tell him you're here?'

'Could I just go up?' I asked tentatively. 'I'll knock, I won't just barge in.'

She gave a hint of a smile. 'Since it's you.'

And so I crept up the millions of stone stairs, knocked gently on the study door, and on hearing a curt 'Come!', entered.

Sebastian was standing at the tall, floor-to-ceiling Georgian window, facing the street, fingertips pressed to temples, eyes shut.

'You old poser,' I muttered brightly as I went in. He opened his eyes and swung round, and for a moment, my heart stopped. I instantly wished I hadn't said it. His eyes were distant and preoccupied, about to be annoyed, but then remarkably, his face cleared, in the way I remembered, but had recently forgotten.

'Olivia!' He was across the room in seconds. 'How extraordinary, sixteen more bars of this wretched piece and I was coming over to see you! Did you get my postcard?'

I nodded and sat down quickly on a button-backed chair, eschewing the sofa on the grounds that I didn't want him too close. 'From Paris, I did. How did it go?'

'Marvellous,' he beamed, dragging up a chair, eyes shining. 'To my utter relief they absolutely loved it, thank goodness, and let me tell you those Parisians are harsh taskmasters. Not so much the audience, who adore anything so long as it lets them get dressed up in their Chanel and pearls and go swanking about town, but the music critics. God, they're sharks. And there they all were, in the front row – where stupidly I'd parked myself too – and I kept glancing along the row, watching their impassive poker faces. My heart was sinking fast, I can tell you, and then at the end there was this horrible hush, and then – thunderous applause! They even got to their feet, for

God's sake, and old Claude Pastiche from the *Figaro* doesn't stand up for his grandmother!'

I laughed. 'Oh, Sebastian, I'm so pleased. You were so nervous about Paris. And Hugo conducted?'

'Quite magnificently. Best yet, actually.'

I smiled. 'Missing Imo, no doubt. Her memory must have stirred him to passion.'

'Oh no, not the memory, no, no, she came out.'

'To Paris? Did she!'

'Oh yes, for four or five days. God, we had some fun, though, the three of us – lots of laughs, lots of gastronomic delights and a huge amount of drinking – too much, actually, bearing in mind that at least two of us were supposed to be working.' He glanced down. 'Oh Christ, Olivia, excuse my clothes. I'm in the old working pyjamas again, my nutter outfit.'

'But how odd,' I mused, gazing past him, ignoring this. 'I mean – I saw Imogen the other day, and she never said. Never even mentioned it.' I glanced back and felt his dark eyes upon me. Abruptly I remembered why I was here. I took a deep breath. 'Look, Sebastian, the reason I've come –'

'If it's about the other night,' he interrupted anxiously, 'after Molly and Hugh's, maybe I should explain –'

'No, no.' I stopped him hurriedly. 'No, it's not about the other night. No, what I came to tell you was –' I went on in a rush – 'well, Johnny's home.'

'Johnny?' He frowned.

'My husband.'

'Oh – oh yes, of course.' There was just a flicker of surprise, as if he'd momentarily forgotten who Johnny was, then his eyes widened in recognition. Slowly, a lovely, warm smile spread across his face.

'But this is wonderful news, Olivia, and just exactly what you'd been hoping for, isn't it?'

'Yes, yes it is.'

'How amazing! And a complete surprise? I mean, did he give you any warning or –'

'Complete,' I breathed, relieved he was taking it like this. 'So unexpected, Sebastian, totally out of the blue. And you know, if I'd known he was coming back, well, I would never have – well, you know, in the car the other night. I hope you don't think . . .' I panicked. What? What was I trying to say? I hope you don't think I was stringing you along? But no, I hadn't been stringing him along. I'd liked him, and, anyway, why was I sitting here explaining myself? Surely he'd rejected me? God, he was probably *genuinely* delighted.

'I'm delighted,' he beamed. ' You're back together again, a family, and it's how it should be. Claudia must be thrilled!'

'She . . . is,' I said, confused. Confused about how I felt, as much as how he felt. I studied his face, lean and elegant with those high cheekbones and dark brown eyes, which gave no clues, but which regarded me kindly now, rather as one would a small child.

'D' you know,' he said thoughtfully, 'I thought I saw her cavorting rather skittishly yesterday.'

'Who?' I said, muddled.

'Claudia. She pogo-sticked down practically the entire length of the road!'

The phone rang and he got up and went to the piano to pick it up. His back was to me. I gazed. I'd forgotten how tall he was. How dark his hair was. He half turned and his face clouded as he listened.

'Yes, yes, I know,' he said, scratching his forehead, 'but, God, Louis, their timing is absolutely lousy. I can't just churn these things out at a drop of a hat. I know they think I can but . . . Yes, yes I know . . . Yes, I said I would so I will, of course I will, but . . . OK, OK, keep your hair on. Yes, they'll get it. Relax . . . You too . . . Bye.'

He replaced the received and grimaced. 'My agent, Louis. Apparently some film director is screaming for this score I'm supposed to be writing, although why I ever agreed to do it in the first place I'll never know.' He rubbed his forehead sheepishly. 'Well, yes, I do know actually, money, together with the promise of popular recognition, but remind me, Olivia,' he wagged a finger, 'never again. There's a joke in the music world that goes – when someone asks you to write a film score you reply, "D'you want it good, or d'you want it on Thursday?" Couldn't be more apposite in this case.'

He glanced surreptitiously at his watch and moved imperceptibly towards the door. Suddenly I realised the interview was over and I was being shown out. I got up hurriedly. God, perhaps I shouldn't have come at all? Perhaps I was overstating my position here. Maybe we hadn't even remotely been 'an item' as Claudes would put it, but surely . . . Oh well. I grabbed my bag and scuttled doorwards.

'There's still your London premiere, isn't there?' I said nervously as he held it open for me.

'At the Wigmore Hall, that's right.'

I wondered for a minute if he was going to offer me a ticket but he seemed miles away.

'Well, good luck,' I faltered.

He smiled. 'Thanks, I'll need it. I'll be a nervous wreck that night. I could really do without this can of worms on my plate, too.' He scratched his cheek anxiously and glanced across to the piano. 'I usually like to be completely free of any work at a premiere, so I can empty my mind.' He continued to gaze past me, then abruptly came to, shrugged. 'Oh well, can't be helped.'

'I should just bung any old thing down and tell them it's a masterpiece,' I joked, in an effort at levity.

He laughed. 'Nice idea, Livvy, but I'm afraid I'm far too analytical and self-obsessed to "bung". No, I won't be happy until these final closing bars lie down and behave.'

'You'll knock them into shape.'

'Let's hope so, otherwise the London music mafia will knock me into shape!'

I went past him and out towards the stairs. 'Oh, you don't have to come down –' I glanced back as he made to follow.

'It's OK,' he said easily, 'I need another pot of coffee and I feel horribly guilty if Maureen has to puff all the way up here. By the time she arrives at the door she has steam coming out of practically every orifice, except the coffee pot, of course, which is stone cold.'

I smiled, but couldn't think of anything to say in reply. I was drained of all wit and words suddenly, and talking to him had always been so easy. Finally we were at the bottom.

'Well, goodbye,' I turned.

'Goodbye, Olivia.'

He smiled, held the front door open for me, lightly

touched my shoulder and kissed me warmly on both cheeks. Out I went.

The red front door shut fast behind me, and the sultry, heavy, mid-afternoon air wrapped itself around me like an electric blanket, hot and oppressive. I walked down the steps and wiped my forehead. God, why the hell did it have to be so hot all the time? This was supposed to be England, for crying out loud, not Madagascar. And talking of crying, I realised with alarm, there seemed to be a bit of a lump in my throat. As I walked up the cobbled street, I appeared to be gulping down a fresh supply of tears. God Almighty, I dragged a hanky from my pocket and blew my nose loudly, where was all this water coming from? Was I compensating for the drought? Doing my bit for the national crisis? I was so flaming overemotional at the moment, so permanently on the point of bursting into floods or punching a wall, and – well, I was supposed to be the happiest girl alive! What the hell was the matter with me?

Chapter Twenty-Three

Various factors combined to convince me to pay Nina Harrison a visit. Outright curiosity, for a start, together with a desire to tie up all the loose ends and to see that all the stories did indeed tally, but I could have resisted both of these impulses, were it not for the fact that Johnny's mood swings were beginning to rival mine. Now, I was allowed to be volatile – I was the wronged wife, for heaven's sake – but over the last few days, Johnny, from a standing start, was whipping up a performance that was positively Wagnerian in style. It certainly knocked my lettuce slapping into a cocked hat. He'd suddenly taken to getting up at dawn, wandering around the garden smoking furiously, and then at about nine o'clock, coming inside to pace the house. From that moment on, the telephone was rarely out of his hand and he'd negotiate urgently all morning, before slamming the receiver back in its cradle, punching the air, and giving an elated cry of, 'Yes!'

'Yes what?'

Yes, it transpired, we simply had to fly to Geneva to stay with some people we hardly knew but who he'd managed to track down, and if he got enough of a party together he'd even hire a private plane to get us there! I'd watch, sweaty-palmed and with a horrible sense of *déjà vu* and memories of Normandy ballooning trips, as more and more of these plans unfurled. I wondered in bewilderment where on earth the rocklike, calming influence of a few days ago had gone. The following morning I'd take him up a cup of tea in bed, only to find that Geneva was off and he didn't even want to get up. At all. Later that morning, though, I'd glance out of the kitchen window to see him still in his pyjamas, but careering around the garden with a squealing Claudia on his shoulders, shrieking with glee and terror as he threatened to throw her in the river. An hour or so later would find us at lunch, Claudia beaming up at her jocular Daddy, who for no apparent reason, would suddenly turn on her, yelling at her with such ferocity about the atrocity of her table manners that the poor child was forced to shrink down in her chair and peer at him from under her fringe, so strong was the stream of his invective.

As this yo-yoing continued I began to wish he'd go back to work, just to give myself time to think, to regroup, to consolidate, but as far as the office was concerned, he was still ostensibly in St-Jean-de-Luz and had time on his hands. Time to dig enthusiastically beside me in the flowerbeds, time to accompany me to Sainsbury's and commandeer my trolley, questioning loudly my need for quilted loo paper and other luxuries, just when I wanted to cruise those aisles in peace and give myself time to think.

But it was Mac and the boys who really took the full force of his boomerang style. Since Johnny had been back he'd been wont, at the end of a very warm day, to take a six-pack from the fridge and wander upstairs to the bathroom, where they'd all be sweltering away amongst the archaic plumbing. There he'd open a can or two with them, take a debrief on the day's work, and perching on the side of the bath, recall his own days as a student, when he too had worked on a building site, joking laddishly with them the while. Now, suddenly, puce in the face with rage, he was telling them their work was shoddy, that they had to redo the entire bathroom, strip the plaster work off, repin the boards underneath and start again.

'You can see great lumps and bumps in the wall, Livvy,' he stormed as he dragged me upstairs one evening to see. 'Look, even *you* can see that's hopeless, surely!'

I ignored the implicit insult. 'But we're going to tile it,' I soothed. 'They'll plaster it over and then the tiles will cover it. You won't even see it.'

'But I'll know it's there,' he hissed. 'And I want it all off!'

My builders were subdued. Johnny's return had been greeted with polite congratulations and a searching look from Lance which I'd ignored, followed by studied concentration, heads down, and a deep desire to finish the job and get the hell out as soon as possible. Any hopes of finishing that imminently, though, were dispelled by Johnny, who made it quite clear – politely or forcibly, depending on which way the wind took him – that much of the work done in his absence had been second rate. Clearly, he seethed, they'd hoped to get away with it, but now that he was back and was once more 'the guv'nor', they wouldn't. Spiro whimpered and twisted his hat in his hands, Alf cowered, Lance looked angry and defiant and Mac was mutinous but tight-lipped, because he'd been a builder long enough to know that keeping shtumm was the only way to get paid.

As Claudia and I sat in the kitchen at breakfast one morning, listening to him berating them upstairs, I felt sad. On the whole I believed their work to be good and professional, but aside from this, I'd been close to these people. They were my friends. They'd helped me when Johnny hadn't been there and seen me through some very dark days. I clenched my hands under the table and felt a sense of betrayal as Johnny's irate voice resounded through the rafters.

'It's just incompetent!' he was saying. 'Just downright incompetent!'

Claudia was wide-eyed over her Coco Pops. 'Why is Daddy so cross?' she breathed.

'I don't know,' I replied. I pushed my chair back and got up. 'But I intend to find out.'

I may have sounded determined as I snatched my car keys from the dresser and grabbed my bag, but as I went into the sitting room to find the A to Z, it was with a thudding heart. I knew Nina Harrison's address off by heart, but as I flipped through the pages to find the route, my hands were shaking. You see, for the first time since Johnny's return, it occurred to me to wonder if the object of his affections had rejected him.

Clarendon Road wasn't hard to find. Plenty of my friends had lived in the Finchley, Highgate area, premarriage, and as I drove around the quaint little back streets, I thought what happy times I'd had here in my single days, tipsy and shrieking with laughter in a girlfriend's basement kitchen, a crowd of us cooking spaghetti bolognese and talking long into the night. In fact, if I remembered rightly, Imogen used to have a flat right – here. I went past her old flat, peering into the familiar windows, then turned down another familiar side street, and left into a mews. I purred along, and drew up slowly, right opposite number 32. I checked my scrap of paper. Yes, 32, next door to a garage Johnny had said. I gazed out of the window. And yes, there it was. Not a tacky, filling-station-type of garage, though, more of a discreet workshop affair, with double barn doors painted bottle green, and opening on to a small forecourt with a couple of classy vintage cars parked outside.

A silver-haired, narrow-faced man with glasses looked up from polishing a hubcap as I got out of my car. He straightened up and wiped his hands on a rag. It was a quiet, dead-end street so I imagined any visitor was some-thing of a diversion. As I locked my door I felt his eyes on me and I wondered if he was just a mechanic or indeed Bob, the father. Either way I ignored him as I walked con-fidently across the street, glancing up at a rather dear little mews house, painted pink with a green door to match the garage beside it, with window boxes and pots spilling over with bright red geraniums. I reached the door and stared nervously at the bell. 32A or 32B. Oh help, which one was she? I couldn't remember. Suddenly I realised the silver-haired man was behind me.

'Can I help?' in a friendly voice.

I turned. I knew at once it was her father. I managed a smile. 'Oh, well, I was looking for Nina actually.'

'Ah, you want the top flat then. We're down below in the servants quarters where we belong.' He chuckled. 'Hang about, I'll see if she's around. Sheila!' He rapped his oily knuckles on a downstairs window.

A net curtain parted and a middle-aged woman appeared between the Fairy Liquid bottle and a spider plant. She was attractive in a faded blonde sort of way, with good bones and pale hair coiled neatly round her scalp, secured with gold hairpins.

'What?'

'Is Nina about?' he yelled.

She shook her head and smiled, indicating by a wave of dithering hands in the air that she couldn't hear a thing. 'Hang on,' she called. 'I'll come out.'

'Deaf as a post,' he grinned. 'Although I always maintain it's selective. She can hear the postman arriving with her new Freemans catalogue halfway down the street!'

I groaned inwardly. Oh God, did we have to get the whole family involved here? Why on earth had I come? In fact, why didn't I just slip away now and forget all about it?

The green door opened and the woman peered around. She was wearing a housecoat and Dr Scholl sandals, and I spotted a wheelchair behind her in the hall.

'This lass has come to see Nina,' explained Bob with a sideways nod at me.

'Oooh, has she now?' she said with evident interest, coming more squarely into the doorway. 'Well, she should be up there, luv. Is she expecting you?'

'Um, well not exactly.' I hesitated. They gazed expectantly at me. 'I'm – I'm a parent, from school. From – her school.'

She beamed. 'Oh well, she'll be pleased to see you, I know she will. She's always keen to get involved with the kiddies, isn't she, Bob? Have you tried the bell?'

'No, I –' haven't had a chance, I wanted to say through

gritted teeth, but stopped short of saying anything at all as I heard a clattering down the stairs behind her. Pink, fluffy slippers appeared, then nylon-encased legs, a floral skirt, and then Nina was beside her mother in the communal hall. She looked tired, dishevelled and unmade up. Her face was very pale. As she stared at me, her right hand slowly reached out and gripped the banister rail tight.

'What d'you want?'

Her parents caught the tone of her voice and turned quickly. They glanced at her, then back at me. As they did, I could see the penny making its slippery way down and, as it dropped, so did their smiles. Her mother's face sagged.

'Well, I – I wanted to talk to you,' I faltered nervously. I flushed, from nerves, sure, but actually, from anger too. Jesus, who was the wronged party around here? Why should I be feeling guilty? Surely the aggressive, defensive tone should be mine, not hers? Who exactly was the floozie here, hmm? Nina's eyes dropped to the lino floor, almost, I thought, in recognition of this. She nodded.

'You'd better come up.'

'Nina, d'you want me to –' her mother shot out an anxious hand. Nina shook it off her arm.

'No, Mum, I'll be fine.'

Her parents watched silently as I followed their daughter upstairs, and as I turned at the top, I saw the man put an arm around his wife's shoulders.

A separate front door opened on to a tiny hallway with a night storage heater and not much else, which in turn issued on to a light, airy sitting room. I followed Nina through and realised it stretched the length of the flat – which wasn't large – with two sash windows on to the street. Coir matting covered the floor and a pair of identical white sofas with rather worn, washable damask covers stood either side of a wooden fireplace. Oatmeal hessian curtains hung at the windows from black, wrought-iron poles and on the white walls or on shelves, driftwood collages, twiggy sculptures and large church candles perched. All was cream, all was neutral, all was very safe and very Habitat. And how unlike my own eclectic, cluttered chintzy home, I thought, glancing around, full of clashing colours and mistakes, but at least they were my mistakes and not Terence Conran's. I tried to imagine Johnny here, full length on one of those creamy sofas, reading the Sunday papers, picking his nose, swigging a beer. Suddenly, I realised I could. Yes, why not? Totally at home, no doubt, his feet on that ethnic wooden coffee table. Fury rose and it strengthened my resolve.

'So this is it,' I sneered. 'The love nest.'

'Would you like a cup of coffee?' she asked, wrong-footing me.

I stared. 'Um, yes, all right,' I muttered. I'd rather expected a defiant stare back.

I followed her into a little white galley kitchen, the paint peeling slightly on the walls, and watched as she fiddled about making real percolated coffee, something we never bothered with at home. I didn't think Johnny liked it. I glanced at the efficient, stainless-steel kitchen. Clearly his tastes had changed. Then I studied her in the silence. Her hair was mussed and flat on one side and there were pillow marks on her cheek. I realised she'd probably been lying on the bed. I used to do a lot of that, too.

'I don't know why I'm surprised,' she said suddenly, snipping the top off a gold foil coffee bag. 'I half expected you to come every day.'

I startled. 'Really? Why?'

She shrugged. 'To fit the jigsaw together, I suppose. Find out about the other side of the story. After all, I came to see you.'

'You did,' I said, remembering how Mac had described her sitting on my terrace. 'And I never found out why.'

She shrugged again. 'An impulse, which I didn't have the nerve to repeat. I wanted to present my case, I think.'

'Which is?'

She turned and handed me a mug. Her eyes were very blue, but pale, like a duck's egg, fringed with blonde lashes. 'Look, why don't you tell me why you've come here, first? Something clearly brought you, and then we can take it from there, eh?'

It was said gently, but I found the 'eh?' patronising. None the less I nodded and followed her back into the sitting room, thinking that even if I looked compliant, I wasn't bloody feeling it. Oh no, I was thinking fast. In the first place I wasn't going to tell her what a mess Johnny was and how worried I was about him, and I wasn't going to enquire as to whether she knew what was driving his erratic behaviour either, and whether it stemmed from her. No no, I could box a bit cleverer than that. I perched on the edge of a sofa as she bustled about getting mats for the mugs. She still had her ghastly fluffy slippers on and I just knew I'd have kicked those off the moment I'd heard the door. Well, actually I wouldn't have bought them in the first place; how could Johnny bear to look at them?

Did she slop around in them all day? They closed neatly together on the coir matting as she perched opposite me. Her face was expectant. I took a deep breath.

'Johnny says – well, he says he left you because he missed me too much. He says he made a mistake and that he should never have gone in the first place, that it was a madness that should never have happened. He's adamant he loves me more than ever now, but I need to know that for sure. I need to know you're out of our lives for good.'

The pain this gave her made her catch her breath, but I didn't care. I'd caught my breath a few times recently too. She gripped her cup, glanced down at the carpet. Presently she nodded.

'Yes, he left me because he missed you.' She raised her eyes. 'And I dare say he loves you above me. There now.' She smiled. 'Is that what you wanted to hear?'

She gazed at me with her steady baby blues, and it seemed to me she was mocking me. I hesitated. Somehow I'd expected her to deny it, say that he'd only returned to me through feelings of guilt, of marital duty.

'Well, obviously I came to get the truth.'

'The truth.' She smiled again, eyes still on mine. She shook her head slowly. 'Well, I'll answer any questions you care to ask truthfully, but what about the ones you don't know how to ask? What about them?'

I stared. 'I . . . don't know what you mean.'

'No. You don't. How could you? And actually, it doesn't matter. You're right, all that matters is that he left me to go back to you.' She picked up a glass ashtray from the table beside her, turned it around in her hands thoughtfully. 'Nothing else matters now.'

I licked my lips, confused. Tried a different tack. 'OK –
so, if that's all that matters, why did you come and see me
that night?'

She sighed and put the ashtray down. 'Because I could
feel him going. I could feel him slipping away. I wanted to
explain to you – to appeal to you, really – try to make you
understand why I needed him so much. It was a last, desperate attempt to hold on, I suppose.'

'To appeal to *me*? But why me, for Christ's sake. God,
I – I probably would have socked you in the teeth!'

Not for the first time her eyes flitted back to the little
table where she'd replaced the ashtray, darting, involun-
tarily almost, to a large black and white portrait photograph
in a silver frame. I realised with a start that it was a picture
of Johnny as a baby, dressed in a sailor suit. It was very
similar to one that Angie had given me. Had Angie given
it to her? Was it some sort of warped, setting-up-home
present? I reached across.

'Where on earth did you . . . ?' I studied it. 'It's Johnny,
isn't it?'

'No, it's not Johnny. Everyone says that, but it's not.'

As I stared I felt the blood drain from my face. Suddenly I dropped it. It clattered down on to the carpet, still
face up. I gazed down. No, it wasn't Johnny. It was too
modern a pose. It was very like him, but – it was his son.
I put my hand to my eyes. Covered them so as not to see.

'Oh God.'

'That's what I came to tell you,' she said quietly, reaching forward and picking it up. 'Johnny wouldn't, couldn't,
but I felt you should know.'

I had a moment of complete light-headed nausea. For

a second, I thought I was going to pass out. They had a son. Johnny had a son.

'I wanted you to know I wasn't just some two-bit tart he'd picked up, that I was the mother of his child too.'

Doesn't stop you being a tart, I thought fiercely. Plenty of mistresses have illegitimate children. But my head was spinning now, full of unanswered questions. The mother of his child. Jesus.

'How – how old is he?' I whispered, staring blankly at the photo again that she'd set back on the table. God, so like Johnny – that nose, those eyes. The smile. The smile destroyed me.

'Nine months.'

'Nine –' My eyes shot back to her. 'But he's only been with you for –'

'Six years.'

My mouth dried. 'Six years!'

She nodded. 'But I've known him a lot longer than that.'

'But how? How can you have?' I blurted out, clenching my fists and realising my voice was shrill and uncontrolled and not at all as I'd intended, but I was shaken to the core.

'Because every Saturday for years, he used to come here with his father, tinkering with cars with Dad. I've known him since I was about twelve, when Oliver gave him his first car, in fact. He must have been – ooh, about seventeen.'

'Seventeen!' I gasped. 'You knew him – shit!' I got up and walked quickly over to the window, gripping the sill hard.

'My parents knew Oliver very well. He brought all his cars here to be serviced, you see, took Dad's advice whenever he bought a new one too. They used to travel all over the country together, to view them.'

'But – but Johnny told me –' I swung round – 'he told me he met you at an open day. At the school, he said –'

'Yes, well, he would, wouldn't he?' she interrupted without a hint of irony. 'Of course he would. He didn't want you to know, did he? Didn't want you to discover he'd been living a secret life for years, had a mistress. What husband would? You might have been a mite upset had you known he came here most Wednesdays, had a chat with Dad and a cup of tea with Mum, before nipping up here and making love to me. I dare say he also didn't mention the fact that last year I gave birth to a son. Of course he didn't!'

My heart was hammering; I couldn't think straight. My God, where did this leave me? And Claudia too, with a brother? I felt sick.

'Where is he?' I whispered, glancing nervously about, half expecting a small blond head to pop up behind a sofa. I didn't want to see him. Ever.

'Peter? He's downstairs with Mum. She has him every morning. Usually I'm teaching, but she still has him for me in the holidays. It gives me a bit of a break.'

'Convenient,' I muttered drily.

'Well, yes, I suppose so, but it's also fairly essential. We all need a break from him now and again. Peter's got cerebral palsy.'

I stared, shocked. 'Oh! God, isn't that – serious?'

'Very. Although some kids are not too badly affected. But Peter's very ill. Very – severe.' She swallowed and her eyes filled.

I gazed. 'I'm . . . sorry.' I was. Confused and angry and shocked as I was, I could still feel sorrow for a handicapped child.

'My God – Johnny!' My hand clutched my mouth. 'How did he –'

She nodded. 'Devastated. Totally devastated. We only found out when Peter was six months old. It wasn't diagnosed until then. That's when he moved in with me.'

I gazed at her incredulously. 'You mean – that's when he decided to leave me? When he heard the child was sick?'

'Yes, he said he couldn't leave me alone with him then. We'd never intended to live together, you see. I'd always known he loved you much more, and I'd always known I was just a harmless diversion, a mistress, and for a while, it suited me. I wasn't unhappy with that. He was great fun and we always had a lark, a good roll in the sack, but I'd always known he was beyond me, totally out of my reach. I thought I was lucky to have him as a lover, but I never thought long term. I'd always assumed that in time I'd marry someone else, someone from my own sort of background. But then Peter came along.'

'But couldn't you have had an abortion?'

'I could, but I didn't want one. Johnny wanted me to, of course. He was horrified when I told him I was pregnant, but I assured him I'd be no bother. I wasn't trying to trap him or anything. I promised I'd have absolutely no contact with him ever again, and I didn't want any money either, said I'd never intrude on his life in any way, that once the baby was born he wouldn't see me for dust. Well, he wasn't happy about it, of course he wasn't, but what could he do? I was absolutely determined to keep it.' She sipped her coffee, two hands cradling the mug. They were trembling.

'Well,' she whispered, gazing at the carpet, 'Peter was born, and Johnny sent some flowers to the hospital, he didn't come to see us, but that was fine, I didn't expect him to. Then a few months later I had this awful shock. Peter had been having all sorts of tests, routine they said, and only because he didn't seem quite as advanced as other babies of that age, but then the paediatrician at the hospital called me in and gave me this terrible diagnosis. Mum was with me, and when we got home, sobbing our eyes out, she persuaded me to tell Johnny, said it was only right; that it was unfair to keep it from him. Well, I didn't want to, but she insisted, and I was in a hell of a state, so I rang him at work.' She gulped. Brought her eyes up from the carpet to meet mine. 'I couldn't believe it. Twenty minutes later a black cab drew up and he was on my door-step, his face as white as a sheet, and when Dad let him in, he cried. I'll never forget it. I came downstairs and he just stood there in the hall, leaning against the wall, the tears streaming down his face. We all cried then. We came up here, Mum, Dad, Johnny and me, and we sobbed. Then after a bit Johnny got all forceful and said he wanted to live with me, said he couldn't possibly leave me with a dis-abled child, that he wanted to share the responsibility. He said it was all his fault and we'd get through this together, bring him up together. We were all astounded, of course, and Mum and I both said don't be ridiculous, what about you and Claudia, and Dad said it was an outstanding offer but one he'd regret later so totally out of the question. We were all astonished. But Johnny kept on, he wouldn't drop it, kept insisting he was moving in. Well, Dad got cross in the end and said, "No – listen, lad, it's just not practical." I can hear him now. "You've already got a family," he said. "You can't just leave one for another, and our Nina here's a grown woman. She knew what she was getting into when she had the baby." Then he held out his hand to Johnny and said that most men would run a mile from an illegitimate baby, let alone a disabled one, and he appreciated the gesture.' She gulped. 'But Johnny wouldn't shake his hand. He said it wasn't a gesture. He was adamant. Said he wanted to be involved, fully involved, and swore he'd devote his life to Peter and me. We were staggered, of course, but all so grief-stricken and confused, especially coming on top of Martin.'

'Hang on,' I said, bewildered. 'Who's Martin?'

'My brother. He's fourteen now, but he's been in a wheelchair all his life, so it seemed like history repeating itself. Anyway, we let Johnny have his say and thought that in the cold light of day he'd probably change his mind, but later that night he arrived, with all his bags, ready to move in, but still as white as a sheet, as if he'd seen a ghost.'

In a flash that night came back to me. The night he'd left me. Is it serious? I'd asked, crouched down amongst my paint pots by the front door in the hall. 'It wasn't,' he'd replied, ashen-faced and sweeping past me with his suitcase, 'was never meant to be . . . but now . . . yes.'

'Anyway,' Nina went on, 'I said, "Oh, don't be a fool, Johnny. Go home, go back to Olivia, I'm going to give up teaching and look after Peter full time. You don't need to worry about me," but he wouldn't have it. He persuaded me to take the job at St Luke's —'

'Yes – How the hell did you end up there? At Claudia's school!'

'That was Johnny. He got me the job. The Montessori I'd been teaching at closed down and reasonably paid private nursery jobs are like gold dust in London. He made a few discreet inquiries and found out that they were looking for someone in the nursery. At first he didn't tell me Claudia was there and I felt really terrible when I found out, but Johnny said it was fine. You know how he does, with that winning smile of his – "It's fine, Nina, don't worry about it! Claudia's going up to the senior school soon, and anyway, no one will make the connection. No one will ever know who you are."' She grimaced. 'Naïve, of course.'

'Just a bit!' I exploded. 'I found out on bloody day one! Along with the rest of the world!'

'I know, and I knew you would, but you know Johnny. Likes to think he's Mr Fixit, Mr Control Freak.'

I knew Johnny. Did I know Johnny? No I didn't recognise this man. This wasn't the man I married.

'Second rate,' I muttered, moving unsteadily back to the sofa and perching shakily on the edge. 'This is second-rate stuff. Sneaking around, betraying his wife – go on, do it, Nina, take the job. Olivia will never find out.' I felt sick.

She leant forward. 'Ah, but Johnny would say he was

being honourable. He'd say he was honouring his commitment to us.'

'But what about his commitment to me!' I shrieked.

'I know, I know.' She gazed down.

The blood rushed to my head. 'And you didn't even bloody want him!'

'Oh yes I did!' she said sharply, jerking her head up. 'I just never thought I'd have him, that's the difference. I'd told myself for years it was unthinkable. Unimaginable. What – Johnny McFarllen? *The* Johnny McFarllen? The one I'd gaped at and admired for years, run to the window to catch a glimpse of since I was a child, breathing on to the glass to see him draw up beside his father in the convertible Lagonda? Blond, gorgeous, languid, laughing Johnny, with his lovely lazy, sexy smile, Johnny from the huge house, from that big, powerful family, with all that wealth, that opulence, that joy? Oh no,' she shook her head vehemently, 'it wouldn't be true to say I didn't *want* him, I just never believed it possible before.'

'Until you trapped him with a disabled child,' I snapped.

'I told you,' she said patiently, 'I didn't want him to stay. I told him to go home, we all did. Then when he wouldn't, when he moved in – well, I told myself not to fall in love with him. Told myself it wouldn't last, that he'd be gone, but how could I help myself?' Her eyes appealed to me. They were very round, the blue exactly in the centre. 'You know how he is, how he lights up even the most dismal, the most mediocre of lives – well, think what he did to mine!' She swung her arm around. 'Look at me, look at this place! I thought I'd died and gone to heaven, thought

436

I was walking on air!' Her pale eyes were bright with emotion now, sparkling. She lowered them to her mug.

'But then, as the weeks went by, and living together in this cramped flat with Peter screaming all hours of the night, needing constant attention and massaging, and my parents running up and down the stairs to help – well.' She grimaced. 'You can imagine. He'd sacrificed himself at the altar of "care" and hadn't realised he wasn't sacrificial material. He thought he'd been "called", thought it was his duty or something equally crappy – God's will if you like – but he couldn't do it. And if anything,' she said sadly, 'he'd made it worse. His fine gesture had worsened the situation.'

'Why?'

'Because I became infatuated with him, and previously I'd never allowed myself to do that. But he was with me every moment of the day now, you see, every night. I couldn't help it. He could see it too – my obsession. I couldn't hide it.' She gulped and picked at some ancient pink nail varnish on her fingernail. 'About a month ago, after Claudia went missing, and after he'd seen you at the concert with someone else, I felt him slipping away. Like sand through my fingers.' She stopped picking and clasped her hands tight. 'I panicked. And the more I tried not to, the worse it became. I've always had a nervous, respiratory thing, a bit like asthma, and when I'm worked up I can hardly breathe. It's all psychosomatic, of course – panic attacks they're sometimes called – but I had to admit myself to hospital to be put on breathing apparatus. Well, what with Peter being so ill, Johnny thought it was outrageous, total histrionics, especially when I strolled out a couple of hours later, right as rain. He thought it was a ruse, thought I was attention-seeking.' She shook her head sadly. 'But I wasn't, that's how it's always been with me. How anxiety takes me. And then there were the notes.'

'Yes, he said . . .'

She reached under the coffee table to a magazine shelf below and took out an old *Cosmopolitan*. She opened it and handed me two pieces of scruffy paper. They'd been torn out of a cheap, ring-bound notebook, and on the top one, in scrawled, capital letters was written: 'KEEP YOUR MOUTH SHUT OR THE KID GETS IT.' The second one read, 'GOOD GIRL. YOU KEEP QUIET.'

I read them again, frowned, then raised my eyebrows at her. She shrugged.

'I have no idea. Dad's convinced it's one of his mechanics. We found out he'd been involved in passing on some cannabis to teenagers and Dad had to sack him. I occasionally work downstairs in the office, and Dad thinks this guy may have thought I overheard him doing a deal one day on his mobile phone.' She gave a wry smile. 'Johnny's convinced I wrote them to myself, though; thinks it was some kind of neurotic attempt to keep him. You know – oh gosh, I've got a disabled son and his life's being threatened. Johnny, you'll *have* to stay now.'

'But you didn't.'

She shook her head sadly. 'No. I didn't.'

'And was this what you came to tell me? That night when you sat on my terrace?'

'No, this hadn't happened then. I came to tell you about Peter, and about how long the affair had been going on. I wanted you to understand where I was coming from. Why I needed Johnny so badly. That I wasn't just some scheming opportunist who'd briefly got her claws into someone else's man, some ghastly husband-snatcher.'

I regarded her for a moment clutching her mug, in her pink slippers, with her pale, unmade-up face and her round blue eyes. I cleared my throat.

'But you are, Nina. That's exactly what you are. Because in the beginning that's precisely how it was. Just a bit of fun, a roll in the sack, with someone else's husband. Oh, you'd never met her, the wife, but sod it, who cares? Some up-tight rich bitch who was probably as frigid as hell and deserved all she got, and anyway, you'd known *him* all your life, hankered after him for years, so somehow, it seemed all right. Somehow, it seemed justifiable. But when the shit began to hit the fan, when the "fun" had some terrible repercussions and you gave birth to a disabled child, you began to think you were entitled to some dignity. Well, I don't think so. You're still the same person, Nina, all that's changed is your situation. You've gone from being a fun-loving mistress to a single mother, only your task as a mother is harder than most. I do pity you, Nina, if pity's what you're after, but funnily enough,' I gave a shaky little smile and reached down for my bag, 'I pity me and my daughter more.' I swung the strap over my shoulder and gripped it hard. I made myself look at her, stared at her coldly, but her eyes couldn't meet mine. They fled to the floor. After a bit, I stood up, turned, and made my way to the door.

'Are you going to tell him we've had this conversation?' she said in a small voice.

I paused, leant against the doorframe for a moment. For support. 'I don't know,' I replied without turning round. 'To be honest, Nina, I don't know what I'm going to do.'

And with that I left the flat.

Chapter Twenty-Four

I drove home in turmoil, my mind racing. The heavy, oppressive weather had finally broken while I'd been in the flat, and a fierce storm had erupted overhead. The windscreen wipers danced at top speed in a manic fashion as my brain cells, at an equally accelerated rate, attempted to clear the chaos in my mind. As I tore perilously around the Finchley back streets, heading blindly for the M1, my insides heaved with revulsion. A love child. A six-year relationship. Not a quick fling with a local girl he'd picked up on a whim since we'd moved house, but a long-running affair with someone he'd known since he was a child. Someone he'd been seeing when we lived in London, sneaking out to sleep with from the office. A mistress – yes, that was the word, that was her job description – who'd been a huge part of his life, had had a role in his life, almost as large as mine, for God's sake, and for a hell of a long time.

Gripping the wheel tightly and totally ambushed by tears, I swerved violently to avoid a lorry as I careered on to the motorway. But how much did this really change things? I thought wildly, wiping the tears desperately with the back of my hand. How much did it actually matter? A lot, my head suggested grimly, but my heart was set on damage limitation. Not necessarily all that much, it declared, defiantly. After all, there was no rule book to consult here, no scale at which one's emotions were deemed to be stretched to the limit and must legitimately snap. This was a purely personal thing. How much could I take? How much could I, Olivia McFarllen, put up with? Or, to put it another way – I squared my shoulders – yes, how strong was I, surely?

Now some women, I was sure, couldn't take adultery in any denomination. One whiff of Chanel on the pinstriped suit and they'd be off, a child under each arm, divorce petition clenched between the teeth, Harvey Nichols account right up to the limit, heading for those wide open spaces. Some, on the other hand, having suspected for years, might quietly have got used to the idea. Got used to all those late meetings and seemingly needless overnight stays in provincial hotels, but having taken a long hard look at their children, at the roof over their heads, at the clothes in the cupboards, the food in the fridge, had decided – Christ, he's only a man, for heaven's sake. What d'you expect? At least he can fix the boiler; at least his armpits don't gush too much; at least he makes good money and, let's face it, if it wasn't him it would be some other bugger, so let's hammer out some sort of *modus vivendi* here, shall we? Let's be a big girl and take it in our stride. I gripped the wheel tight, sniffed hard and let out a long, shaky breath. It all came down to personal choice really: how humiliated and betrayed was one prepared to be to preserve one's world, and how much extracurricular sex was one prepared, metaphorically, to swallow?

Now Nina, no doubt, was hoping I couldn't swallow this at all. She was hoping I'd gag on this latest sensational dollop, spit it out – and Johnny with it – right back on to her plate, where quick as a flash, she'd pick it up and run with it. She was no doubt hoping our conversation had persuaded me he was a cad of the highest order and was, even now, kicking off her fluffy slippers, rolling on her nylons and preparing to glide seamlessly back into his life to pick up the pieces. I gripped the wheel fiercely. Well, we'd see about that.

I realised, though, still gulping down the tears, that on a less emotional level, if I was going to take this on the chin, I needed to deal with the practicalities. Peter, for instance. I caught my breath. Christ, Peter. How much of an impact would he make on mine and Claudia's lives? Well – no more than he had up to now, surely? I thought desperately. I mean, I'd *know* about him, be aware of his existence, but I'd never have to see him, and Nina was clearly determined to be totally self-sufficient. She didn't seem the type to arrive in her clogs on our doorstep, with Peter wrapped in a shawl, demanding ten thousand a year and the right to the McFarllen surname, so in actual fact, what difference did this new revelation make? Oh, it made me hysterical and upset, I knew that from the amount of tissues I was getting through, and the number of stares I was getting from lorry drivers who peered curiously down from their cabs at this pitiful woman dissolving behind her wheel, chucking lighted cigarette butts out of the window every few minutes, but temporary hysteria aside, precisely how torn apart was I going to be on a long-term basis? Just how traumatised was I?

I slowed down a bit and sank back in my seat. The rain was abating and I turned the windscreen wipers down from manic to relatively sober. As I wiped the mascara from under my eyes with a shaky finger I noticed that the tears were drying up slightly too. Yes, now that the storm was over, I could surely assess this in a rational manner. Assess whether or not I'd actually taken so much already that this was just another well-aimed blow that had stunned, but not entirely knocked me for six. A body blow, but nothing critical.

Ten minutes later, with thoughts still jostling furiously for position in my mind, I pulled up in my drive and instantly realised my mistake. God, how stupid! Why on earth had I come straight home? Why on earth had I raced, instinctively, back here when what I really needed was time to think, hours – days in fact – to let this sink in? Now I literally had minutes before I had to confront it all, confront Johnny.

Feeling hot and panicky I fumbled for the ignition, quickly started the car again, and was about to plunge it into reverse and charge out backwards – when I realised it was too late. I'd been seen. Johnny was actually in the drive and was, even now, walking towards my car at the same time as yelling something furiously over his shoulder to Claudia, who was running after him in floods of tears. As I turned off the ignition and slowly opened my door, I spotted my mother and Howard in the porch, looking distinctly shaken, and slinking, heads down, towards their car.

I got out. 'What's going on?'

Howard and my mother stopped, mid-slink, and Mum came scuttling towards me.

'Oh darling, this is all my fault,' she breathed, putting an anxious hand on my arm. 'We just popped round, you see, on an impulse, to see you all together again, and we had a lovely cup of tea in the new kitchen with Johnny and Claudia, but then stupidly, well, I went and put my foot in it, just as we were leaving.'

'What d'you mean?'

'Well, I brought up the business of the schools,' she hissed, wide-eyed. 'You know, the boarding business. I gather Johnny didn't know.'

Her face betrayed nothing, but one never knew with Mum. Never quite knew if she'd been deliberately meddling.

'No, it's out of the question!' Johnny was saying, shaking Claudia's pleading hand off his arm as he strode towards me. 'God, this is ridiculous, Livvy. I don't know why you said you'd even consider it! There's no question of her going away, especially now I'm back!'

'Why, especially now you're back?' I asked calmly.

He stopped in front of me. 'Well, I can see that the two of you here on your own might have seemed a bit quiet, a bit lacking in colour, but now that I'm back, well, we're a family again!'

'Ah. So you make all the difference?'

'I didn't mean it to sound as arrogant as that,' he spluttered, 'but I certainly make *some* difference to home life, surely?'

'It's got nothing to do with that!' sobbed Claudia hysterically. 'I wanted to go away before, I've always wanted to go, even when you were here, before you went! And Mum said I could, didn't you, Mum?'

'I said we'd discuss it,' I said quietly. 'And that's what we will do, but not here, not now, not screaming like banshees in the middle of the drive in front of Granny and Howard.'

I turned to Howard, who was looking distinctly embarrassed. I managed a smile. 'Howard, what must you think of us?'

'I think you have a mighty characterful daughter who knows her own mind,' he said, scratching his chin. 'But I also think it's not our place to get involved. Come now, Sylvia, we'll be on our way.' He held out his arm to Mum, who took it hastily. I walked them to their car.

'Absolutely right,' muttered Johnny in a low voice, coming up behind me. 'Mind your own bloody business.'

Mum and Howard were very definitely in their seats at this point, so didn't hear, but I did. I waved them off, then turned slowly. My hands were clenched by my sides.

'Johnny, he might have heard you.'

He shrugged. 'So what? It isn't any of his bloody business, just as it isn't any of his bloody business how "characterful" my daughter is, either. God – some jumped-up, overweight, ee-by-gum widower from Yorkshire who specialises in bladder problems telling me how I should educate my child? Jesus! And your mother! Honestly, Liv, what a joke!'

'What?'

'Well, I mean those clothes! Mutton dressed as lamb, or what? I hardly recognised her! I mean, turquoise trousers, for heaven's sake, and beads, and her hair!'

'I think she looks lovely!' blurted Claudia, her voice cracking, her pale face stained with tears. 'And we like Howard too, don't we, Mum?'

I turned to her and took her shoulders. 'Darling, go

446

upstairs, wash your face and have a lie-down on your bed. I'll be up in a minute.'

'But –'

'Now, Claudia.' I gazed down at her and she caught my eye and the tone of my voice. With a last defiant glare at her father she brushed past us, marched in, and slammed the front door behind her.

'You must admit, my love,' laughed Johnny, moving to put an arm round my shoulders, 'they don't exactly wear their new arrangement well, do they? I mean, with the best will in the world it's hardly love's young dream, is it? Christ, I found the whole thing positively embarrassing, and I wished to God you'd been here. When they were billing and cooing and holding hands at the kitchen table, I didn't know where to look!' He chuckled and made to lead me back to the house. 'Ah well, you know what they say, there's no fool like an old fool, but I mean – what exactly is the set-up there? I think we should know, shouldn't we, if only for Claudia's sake? Are they living together or something crass?'

I shook his arm off and backed away.

'Johnny, why didn't you tell me you had a son?'

He turned, stared at me. Then he took a step back. I watched him visibly pale. 'You know.'

'Yes, I went to see Nina. She told me.'

His arms came up from his sides, then flopped down limply in a gesture of defeat. His knees apparently wouldn't hold him any longer, because he slumped back on the bonnet of my car. He rubbed his eyes with a shaky hand.

'Livvy, I'd have done anything to have spared you this.'

'So it appears. Like lying through your teeth for years.' I knew I was trembling, but I felt a terrible clenched calmness too.

'Look, it's not that I was never going to tell you,' he said desperately. 'I was, honestly I was, and I've been building up to it. I knew if I came back you had to know, and I was going to tell you – this week, in fact. That's why I've been so upset these past few days. I keep trying to tell you, I've been on the point of it so many times, but it's so hard – *so* hard!'

'Not as hard as it is for me, though, surely, Johnny? Please don't ask me to pity you too. As I told your girlfriend earlier, I'm afraid I'm claiming the monopoly in that department, because nobody, Johnny, not you, not your mistress, not anyone, has taken quite as much shit as I have.'

'Except . . . perhaps my sick son.'

'That's out of my jurisdiction. And Godlike and all-controlling though you most surely think you are, for once, it's out of yours too.'

'Divine retribution,' he muttered, 'for all my mistakes.'

'I doubt it. I doubt if He's that interested in you, particularly since you can't even call them sins. No, Peter's affliction was caused by casual, careless, unprotected sex, together with the law of averages governing the amount of oxygen reaching babies at birth. It was bad luck.'

His face contorted with pain at this. He clenched his fists, rapped his knuckles on his forehead. 'I've tried so hard to make it up to him, to do the honourable thing! I went back, and it was only for the child! I went back! I was prepared to sacrifice everything, I –'

'Oh, don't give me all that honour-and-duty crap, Johnny,' I snapped furiously. 'Was it honourable to poke the garage owner's daughter in the first place? Was it honourable to get her up the duff when you had a wife and child of your own at home? Hmm?'

He gazed at the gravel, couldn't look at me. I stared at that troubled blond head that I'd loved so much, stroked so often, and my heart heaved. Finally he looked up piteously.

'I'll make it up to you, Livvy.'

'Oh really? In what way?'

'I'll never see her again, never see either of them again.'

'That seems a little harsh, particularly in Peter's case. It's all or nothing with you, isn't it, Johnny?'

His blue eyes widened, and the first truth for a long while fell from his lips.

'I don't know how else to be.'

I nodded. 'I know.' I regarded him silently. 'Pack a bag, Johnny.'

'What?' he said, startled.

'You heard me. Pack a bag. I really don't think I can live with you any more. I can't live with your wholeheartedness, your honour, your sense of duty, nor your integrity. I just can't do it.'

With that I turned on my heel, and left him standing, staring after me as I walked into the house.

I went on through the hall, up the stairs and across the landing to Claudia's bedroom. I peeped around the door. She was lying on her side on her bed, fast asleep, as I knew she would be. Sleep had always been her defence mechanism for any sort of upset or trauma. I closed the door softly and went downstairs, turning smartly right at the bottom and going out of the back door so as not to encounter Johnny, then on down to the potting shed.

As I let myself into the cool, dark space, shutting the door behind me, I leant back on it and let out a long shaky, breath. My God. What had I done? I blinked into the woody gloom. Well, I'd sent him packing, that's what I'd done. I'd known instinctively, in those few moments as I stood there facing him, that I simply couldn't take any more. Didn't want to either. Didn't want him in my life. My eyes widened in the darkness, boggling at this revelation. God, had I really admitted that? I was so startled my hand went to my mouth. Surely in the car just now, I'd been so convinced I could overcome it all, could overlook everything . . . I lowered my hand. But I couldn't. I shook my head in bewilderment. Extraordinary. All this time, all that anguish and heartache and now, suddenly, right in the middle of swallowing the crap just as fast as he could shovel it in – I'd gagged.

After a moment I sat down shakily at the potting bench. Peered into my seed trays. Yes, those seedlings were getting a bit leggy. Could do with pricking out. I noticed my hands were trembling as I went about my business, but I also knew that I was quite clear about what I'd done. That I felt lucid and calm. And it was comforting to know that I could quite easily spend the next couple of hours in here and not have to witness his departure.

When I did emerge, a while later, he had indeed gone. To her, I wondered, as I crept around the house? Who cares? At that moment I really didn't; I just wanted to be on my own. Alone with Claudia. As I went upstairs to find her, it occurred to me that I might sell this house. I paused for a moment on the stairs. Stroked the banister, but not regretfully. Oh, I'd loved it in the beginning, we'd both loved it, thought of it as a forever place, but he'd been living a lie in it even then. That soured everything, and I wasn't sure I wanted it any more. On an emotional level too much had gone on under its roof, too many unhappy memories, but on a practical level too, it was too big for us. We'd need something smaller now, the two of us. A cottage maybe, near that school that I knew Claudia was really keen on, but hadn't mentioned because she thought it was too far away. The one on the cliffs in Dorset, with the sea beating against the rocks below, and the ponies in the paddocks above. I'd found the prospectus hidden under her bed, well thumbed and with 'Cool!' scrawled all over it. She'd thrive there, of course, in a place like that, and I could be close by in – yes, I thought wildly – a little whitewashed cottage, with a fabulous cottage garden full of poppies and lupins that she and her friends could come back to at weekends. Oh really, said a wry little voice in my head, and what about you? Would you give up on your own life altogether? Make jam, pickles, grow your own turnips, grow your own underarm hair, become a hermit or something? I sighed and trudged on up the stairs. Maybe, maybe. Because frankly, after all I'd been through, jam, pickles and hairy armpits sounded remarkably alluring.

Claudia was still fast asleep, spreadeagled on her back now, her mouth wide open. I took off her shoes and brushed the hair back from her face. Her forehead was hot and damp and I moved to the window to open it, to let a breeze in. As I flung it open, I hung out for a moment, feeling the wind on my own face, marvelling at what I'd done, at the empty drive below where his car should be. Just to the left of the drive, a stunning white, Himalayan rambling rose was taking over a tiny apple tree, killing it probably. I must chop that out, I thought suddenly. Why hadn't I done so before? Yes, a beautiful, charming killer that, up to now, I'd just watched, transfixed, in a powerless state of fascination. But not any more. Nothing, and no one, was going to get away with that sort of bullying behaviour any more. As I gazed into the hazy sunshine, marvelling at the turn my life was taking, I suddenly spotted Imogen's car. It was coming round the corner. Yes, that was surely her distinctive red Mercedes, indicating right now, and cruising slowly down our road.

I raised my hand in welcome and was about to call out, rush downstairs, throw open the door and drag her in for a much-needed gin and tonic on the lawn, when abruptly, she stopped short. Not outside my house, but Sebastian's. Oh, of course, I realised, she was probably with Hugo. Sebastian's concert was about to be premiered at the Wigmore Hall and he was no doubt having last-minute consultations with his conductor. I watched, disappointed, as she got out, looking stunning in a sleeveless cream dress, her blonde hair swinging and shining like a girl in a shampoo advert, and waited for Hugo to get out the other side. But Imogen was on her own. Oh, so Hugo was clearly inside already. Either that or he was coming along later, under his own steam. As I watched Maureen let her in, I thought what fun they must have all had in Paris. Imo and Hugo, happy and in love; Sebastian, carefree, delighted his piece had been such a hit, high on success. God, if only I'd played my cards right I might have been there with them – made up a jolly foursome, guzzled champagne into the night, trawled the bars and cafés with the best of them, instead of which I'd welcomed my errant husband back with open arms. Fool.

As I crept out of Claudia's room, though, I decided that foolish though I'd most surely been, I was now getting stronger by the minute, and surer than ever that I'd done the right thing. I knew what Claudia would ask in the morning: 'For ever? Has he gone for ever, Mummy?' My insides twisted briefly. My gut feeling was yes, for ever, but I'd say I didn't know. Let it sink in. Say, 'Well, as Granny says, Claudes, never say never and you can't say for ever, but what I do know, darling, is that I'm in the driving seat. For the first time in a long while, your mother, Olivia McFarllen, is calling the shots.' She'd like that. She'd be sad too, of course, and yet . . . and yet . . .

As I made my way slowly downstairs, biting my thumbnail and lost in thought, I suddenly spotted Spiro, hovering on the front step behind the glazed front door. He was twisting his hat in his hands and peering through the glass, clearly looking for me. I stopped, sighed. And so life goes on, I thought wryly. I might, just this minute, have discovered my husband's love child lurking in a North London bedsit, I might, tomorrow morning, have to tell my sensitive ten-year-old that her family unit had once more collapsed, but no matter. Come what may, one still had to deal with the day-to-day. One still had to deal with the builders.

'Spiro, come in,' I said, throwing back the door. 'Do

just walk in and yell if you can't find me. You don't have to loiter outside. Good heavens, you look very smart. Where are you off to?'

His normally unruly black curls were brushed neatly to one side and slicked down with water, his jeans were pressed, he had a clean white T-shirt on, and he was carrying his tea-cosy hat, rather than wearing it.

'Out,' he said, puffing up his chest and beaming proudly. 'But first, Mac, he say to me – can I please bring Meeses McFarllen the latest bill and ask her, very, very kindly, and thank you so much, for an advance on the readies?'

'Oh, he did, did he?' I took the bill he proffered and looked at it. Looked again. Blinked. 'Blimey, as much as that, Spiro? Bit steep, isn't it? How many weeks in advance is this for?'

'Only one, but he say we need so many building supplies, breeks, copper piping, cement and things, and so he order it, but he no pay for it yet. It all here, see?'

He pointed to a shopping list of masonic items in Mac's hand.

I sighed and tucked it in my pocket. 'Yes, I see. Well, I'll go down and talk to him about it. I'll certainly give him some of it, but I'm not sure I can ante up the whole lot right now.'

Spiro looked anxious. 'But he say to be sure to bring it back and –'

'Look, I'll talk to him, Spiro, OK? Now don't you worry, no one's going to shoot the messenger,' I smiled. 'So, where exactly are you off to in your Sunday best, then?'

'Ah yes, well, that also why I want to speak to you.' He twisted his hat nervously. 'You see, I got a leetle job, a very tiny one,' he held his forefinger and thumb apart a fraction, 'and it only take a jiffy, but I don't want to step on your feet, so first, I come here, to ask your permission and see if you don't mind.'

I folded my arms in mock horror. 'Good heavens, another job? Don't tell me one of my staff is moonlighting? Where exactly is it, Spiro?'

'Ees only down the road, at number 42. You know, at your dear friend, Meesis Nanette's.'

I frowned. 'Really? And what exactly are you doing for dear Meesis Nanette?'

'Ah,' he rolled his eyes. 'Poor lady. She have beeg, beeg problems with her bed.'

'Her bed?'

'Yes,' he sighed, 'an antique bed, you see, so very beautiful, but very old, and some of the springs, they go flippy floppy on her. They shoot through,' he demonstrated with a sharp upward thrust of his fist, 'and hurt her something chronic she say. She want me to come with my spanner, you see, adjust them, and she say, "Spiro, you wear clean clothes now, please, because I have a cream carpet, and also, I may need you to lie on my bed to test it."'

'Did she now?' I said grimly.

'Yes, and you know what, *she* may have to lie on *other* side of bed because sometimes,' his eyes widened, 'the springs, they go plippy-ploppy all over! So we do a practical demonstration.' He nodded sagely.

'Ah. And I take it Roger isn't around to help with this

practical? He's not hovering about helpfully with *his* spanner?'

'No, no, so sad. You see Meesis Nanette, she say, "I'm Rogerless, Spiro! And he such a handy man, my Rog, but he not here to do the business!"'

'Is he not? I see.' I nodded. Pursed my lips. 'Spiro, have you ever heard of a nymphomaniac?'

He frowned. 'Nymph? Ah yes, ees Greek, you know, for youth, and beauty.'

'Possibly, and in her dreams, but in England, together with the maniac bit, it means mad about sex.'

He frowned. 'Ti?'

'Sex, Spiro – she loves it. Lots of it, and with dewy young men like yourself and Lance, see? Oh, there's nothing too terrible about it. It's a harmless enough hobby, a frivolous diversion from the ironing and the dusting, something to do between *Neighbours* and *Countdown*, and I dare say it's a marvellous tonic too, but just so long as you know the score. Just so long as you know what you're getting into here. Because tomorrow morning, I really don't want to find you weeping in the back garden, sobbing into your hat about what you've done to your poor Atalanta, when I'd really rather you were rodding my drains.'

'Sex!' he gasped. 'No bad springs?'

'Oh, I should think they're fairly bad, pretty rotten and worn out by now, but I'm sure they're up to just one more hammering.'

'Never!' he spluttered, backing away in horror. 'Never would I cheat on my Atalanta to hammer this woman!'

I patted his outraged shoulder. 'Attaboy, Spiro, that's

the spirit. Now you hold on tight to that righteous indignation and pop down the road and put her straight. Tell her you won't be making an appearance in her boudoir this afternoon. Oh, and while you're there, you might tell her from me that she's a terrible old slapper and to keep her thieving hands off my workforce. Tell her that if she's that desperate for company, she can come and have a gin and tonic on the lawn with me instead. I'll be getting the ice out right now.'

Opening and shutting his mouth he backed away. 'Yes, I go, I go. And I tell her!' Suddenly he stopped, frowned. 'Slapper?'

I grinned. 'That's it.'

He nodded. 'OK.'

He squared his shoulders, turned and marched out of the drive, for all the world like some proud Cretan soldier off to rout a young Turk. Head high and bristling with indignation, he swept the tea-cosy hat out of his pocket and plonked it firmly on his head again.

I watched him go, smiling, imagining Nanette's stunned face. I also felt sure she'd have the nous to see the funny side, though. I could see her, listening incredulously to his indignant, disjointed spiel, then as she shut the door, throwing back her head and roaring with laughter, before charging upstairs, ripping off her black camisole, throwing on her old sequinned jeans and coming over to have a drink with me. I'd tease her mercilessly, of course, and no doubt she'd stay a while, help me see the bottle off, and we'd roar drunkenly into the night. Yes, two single, frustrated women, knocking it back. 'Ha!' I laughed out loud.

Because for the first time for ages, that didn't make me feel either sad or lonely. It simply amused me.

I was still smiling as I went down to the cellar, en route to the safe to get some money out for Mac. As I crouched down and punched in the combination number, I looked at the scrappy piece of paper Spiro had given me. I'd give Mac half, I decided, slowly opening the safe door. Two thousand pounds really was too much all in one go. I counted out the cash, popped it in an envelope, put the rest away, and then shut the safe again. God, no wonder he'd sent Spiro, I thought wryly as I mounted the cellar steps. For a start I generally paid him on a Friday, so this was earlier than usual, and also, I wanted to ask him about all these so-called building supplies. I could have sworn I'd paid for a whole lorryload only last week.

I put the envelope in my skirt pocket and wandered down the garden to the caravan. I could hear voices and a light was on. I glanced at my watch. Four o'clock. Well, they'd knocked off slightly earlier than usual, but I wasn't going to quibble about that. They worked jolly hard during the day. I knocked on the door and Alf answered.

'Oh, Alf, look, Spiro gave me this bill, but I have to say it's rather hefty and I'm minded to give you only half at the moment. I'll speak to Mac about having the rest later. Is he about?'

Alf looked worried. 'It's all kosher, luv, all straight-up stuff.'

'I'm sure it is,' I soothed, 'but if I could just have a word . . .'

'E's in the karzy, luv, d' you wanna wait? He won't be long.'

'Er, well, no I won't, if you don't mind,' I said nervously, eyeing the Portaloo door, not convinced I wanted to encounter Mac before he'd washed his hands. 'Just ask him to pop up and see me, would you?'

Alf took the bill. 'Swear to God it's all stuff we need, on my life. Copper piping an' that for the bathroom, skirting and architrave for round the doors, and –'

'I don't doubt it, Alf,' I interrupted patiently, 'I just want to go through it, that's all, sitting down at the kitchen table. Tell Mac I'll speak to him later.'

'Yeah, orright.' He scratched his head, looked anxious. He glanced at the envelope in my hand. 'I'll take that little lot then, shall I? Just for the minute?'

'Oh – sure.' I handed it over. 'Oh, and could I have a receipt please, Alf?'

'A receipt?'

'Yes, you know, just to say I've given it to you.'

'Oh! Right.' He turned, went inside, and came lumbering back a moment later with a pencil and paper. 'What does Mac do then?'

'Oh, just your name and then write received, from me. You know, Mrs McFarllen,' I said, just in case he didn't.

'Right.' He licked the end of the pencil. It hovered doubtfully over the paper. For an awful moment I thought perhaps he couldn't write, but then slowly he began to etch away and I realised his eye probably gave him trouble. Finally he handed it to me.

'There.'

'Thanks, Alf.' I took it and glanced down.

'FROM MRS O. MCFARLLEN. THE SUM OF £1,000, RECEIVED BY MR A. J. TURNER.'

I was about to stuff it in my pocket, when suddenly I stopped. Pulled it out. I read it again. Stared. I knew this writing. Childish capitals, scrawled on cheap, lined paper, torn out of a spiral-bound notebook. Slowly I looked up and met Alf's eye. I knew in an instant where I'd seen this handwriting before.

Chapter Twenty-Five

I gazed into his eyes, one brown and watery, the other, unfocused and veering off to the right somewhere.

'Orright, luv? That the sort of fing?' Alf nodded down at the receipt, shuffling nervously from foot to foot, clearly keen to shut the door.

'Yes. Yes . . . that's fine, Alf.'

'Right. See you later, then.'

I didn't respond, so with a curt nod of his head, he shut the door anyway.

I stared down at the piece of paper again. After a moment I turned and walked slowly back up the lawn. Then I stopped. Turned back, and looked at the caravan door. For a moment there I was tempted to run back, bang on it, and demand an explanation, but then in another moment I'd changed my mind. I stuffed the bit of paper in my pocket and walked quickly back to the house. I marched through the French windows, made straight for the telephone in the hall, and started riffling furiously around on the chaotic hall table, searching for that scrap of paper with the number scrawled on it that had *still* not made it into the address – Ah! There it was. I pounced on it and punched out the number. Nina answered more or less immediately.

'Oh God, I'm so glad you've rung. I've been really worried about you.'

I was momentarily taken aback. 'Really? Why?'

'Well, telling you all that stuff about Johnny and then letting you get in the car and drive home in that dreadful storm. Mum said it was an awful thing to do, said you must have been in a terrible state. I kept imagining you, blinded by tears, tearing down the motorway and ploughing into the middle of some ghastly pile-up or something!'

I paused. Sat down and crossed my legs. 'No, not at all,' I said slowly. 'In fact, quite the reverse. I'm delighted you gave me the missing pieces to the puzzle. You see it merely confirmed some suspicions I'd had all along, made me realise I'm definitely doing the right thing. But I wasn't ringing about my husband, Nina. I wanted to ask you something else.'

'Oh! Right.' Her turn to be wrong-footed.

'That night you came to see me, the evening you sat on my terrace. Did you see anyone else in the garden?'

'Well, one or two of your builders were about, yes.'

'Which ones – Mac? The small one, quite thin and wiry?'

'Um, yes, I think so. Skinny with bristly hair.'

'That's it. He said he was having a pee in the bushes and turned round and saw you there, is that right?'

'Oh no, he certainly wasn't having a pee. I'd have remembered that. No, he was sitting on that little brick wall round the corner, on the other side of your patio, the main bit. He had his back to me, he was talking to the big one.'

'The big one?'

'You know, huge, funny eye. I couldn't see much because it was dark, but I remember him.'

462

'Alf,' I breathed, and Mac had told me he was alone. Said that Alf had been monopolising the bathroom, getting spruced up for their night out in the curry house.

'What were they talking about? Did you hear?'

'Not really. It was all in whispers. You know, very hushed and urgent. They seemed to be arguing a bit about something, though, and that pushed the volume up occasionally.'

'But you don't know? Not a word?'

She paused. 'No, except . . .'

'Yes?'

'Well, something about – how to get rid of it. But I don't know what. That was all, really. Why, is it important?'

'I don't know,' I said slowly. 'So what happened next? They saw you?'

'Yes, well, I coughed actually, on purpose. I didn't want them thinking I was spying on them or anything, and the small one swung round and saw me. I heard him say "Shit" under his breath, and then the big one scuttled away, back to the caravan, I think.'

'And Mac came over?'

'Oh yeah, he came storming over, wanted to know what the hell I thought I was doing there and I sort of stuttered something about waiting for you. I'd seen the foreign one in the front drive, you see, and he'd said it was OK to wait. This one was pretty mad, though.'

'Was he?' I murmured. Yes, not at all how Mac had related this encounter. A polite conversation, he'd said, about when I might be expected back.

'Um, how is he?' she faltered nervously.

'Who, Mac?'

'No! Johnny.'

'Oh. Oh, fine, I expect. He's not here, though. I rather thought he might be with you. Still, the traffic could be bad on the M1. I'd expect him any time, Nina.'

I heard her catch her breath. 'You mean – he's left?'

'No, no,' I smiled. 'I threw him out.' I found a nail file and picked it up, pushing back a cuticle or two. 'There's only so much crap a person can take, you know, and frankly, I'm grateful to you for showing me just how much was being dumped my way. Goodbye, Nina. Oh, and incidentally, don't throw away any of those little notes you've got tucked away in that magazine. They may turn out to be what I believe is known as admissible evidence.'

I replaced the receiver before she could utter a response. Right. That, I thought with some satisfaction, had surely killed two little birds quite neatly with one stone, hadn't it? In the first place I'd let her know that I wasn't exactly breaking my heart over her liaison with my husband, and in the second place, I'd got her to reveal just a *soupçon* more about what was going on here. I frowned. Twisted round in my chair to face the garden. But only a *soupçon*. Because what exactly *was* going on in my back yard that I didn't know about? What sort of scam was Mac operating here, and was it being conducted from my house? Right under my nose? I took Alf's receipt out of my pocket again. Should I ring the police? Get them involved? I instantly decided against it. God – no, what was I thinking of? What, shop these guys; my friends, who'd helped me through some tricky times, just because my husband's mistress had been threatened by them? No no, I ought to be grateful to them! Pat them on their backs, buy them all a pint, tell them how delighted I was that they'd put the wind up her adulterous knickers, sparked off her neurosis, which, let's face it, had been the catalyst for Johnny leaving her. Only a few weeks ago I'd have been thrilled to bits about that. I smiled. Yes, strange to think, I mused, that in an ironic sort of way, they might have saved my marriage. Only they weren't to know, as I did now, that there was nothing to save.

No, I decided, getting briskly to my feet, no, I wouldn't talk to the police, I'd talk to Mac. He was a shrewd, intelligent man and we'd always got on well, always talked frankly to one another. There was bound to be some terribly simple, innocent explanation to all this. I'd go and see him now, right this minute while I was still feeling bullish and elated about throwing Johnny out, go and have it out with him. Right, absolutely, go for it Olivia. Go call those shots.

I sailed off back through the house, through the French windows and marched back down to the caravan. Smiling and holding my head up high I felt that in my present mood, there was very little I couldn't accomplish right now, very little I couldn't achieve. I rapped smartly on the caravan door. There was a sound of scuffling inside, then Mac stuck his head out.

'Yes?' he barked in my face.

'Oh!' I stepped back in surprise. 'Um, Mac, I'd like a word, if – if I may.' I faltered.

'Oh, sorry, Livvy,' he recovered with a smile. 'I, um, fought it was someone else.'

'Ah.' I blinked. Who? I wondered. In my garden? 'Well – is it convenient?'

He hesitated. 'Yeah. Yeah – hang about.' He pulled the door to for a second and shot back inside. I heard muffled whispers, urgent instructions, but to whom, I didn't know. I crept forward and peered through the crack he'd left. I could just about make out the side of Lance's head, sitting at the table. Ah, so he was in on this too, whatever it was. I stepped back smartly as Mac reappeared. He came right out this time, and shut the door firmly behind him.

'Yes, luv, what can I do for you?' He rubbed his hands together briskly, grinning.

'Mac, I'm a little concerned.'

'Oh yeah?'

'Yes, only I went to see Nina Harrison today. D'you know who I mean by that?'

He scratched the top of his head, looked puzzled. 'Can't say I do, luv.'

'Well, she's my husband's mistress, Mac. She's the one you treated to a grandstand view of an al fresco pee one evening not so long ago, remember?'

He looked startled, but recovered quickly. 'Oh yeah, yeah, it's all coming back to me. I didn't know her name, see.'

'Didn't you? Or her address in Finchley, I suppose?'

He scratched some more. 'Her address?'

'Yes, Mac. You see, today, when I went to see her, she showed me some letters. Two, actually, both anonymous, both threatening, and both written in this hand.'

I got out Alf's receipt and handed it to him. He looked at it. Pursed his lips, but otherwise his face betrayed little.

'She also,' I went on, 'has a very different account of that evening in the garden. You see, you told me that Alf

466

was in the bathroom, but she maintains you were having a whispered discussion with him on the other side of the terrace.'

'What did she say?' he said quickly.

I folded my arms, smiled. 'Ah, Mac, you surely don't expect me to divulge what she overheard, do you? I mean, yes, you're right, she *did* hear quite a lot, but snatches, naturally. Snippets of conversation. She couldn't piece it all together herself, but I dare say if she related it to the police they'd have no problems.'

He looked at me for a long moment. His blue eyes were sharp and hard and I felt a small frisson of fear. It occurred to me that Mac was quite capable of being the affable brickie one minute and the hard-as-nails-East-End-boy the next. As quickly as the look had come into his eye, though, it vanished, and a second later he'd taken me by the elbow and was leading me gently away from the caravan door.

'Orright, luv, I shouldn't tell you,' he glanced about him cautiously, 'but I'm gonna now, 'cos you know too much already. Alf's in trouble.'

'Well, I rather gathered that.'

'Big time, like. It's the gee-gees.'

'Gee-gees?'

'Horses, luv. You know, gambling an' that.' He glanced nervously over his shoulder, then round the side of the house. 'Well, you know how he loves the racing, always sneaking in to watch the two-thirty from Kempton when he should be mixin' cement an' that, and that's 'cos he's always got a bet on, see? He's always gambled – well, we all have, to be fair, all like a flutter – but Alf's got it bad, and he's got himself in a right pickle now. He had a couple of big losers see, big-cheese debts to pay off, so to cover it, the stupid sod went and put all he had in the world on the appropriately named Fool's Gold, which managed to limp home last in the three fifteen Novice's Cup from Newmarket a few weeks back.'

'Oh! Oh dear. So – how much does he owe now?'

Mac rolled his eyes. 'Don't ask. Just don't ask. Thousands, luv. Can't be more pacific. And they're after him for it, an' all.'

'Who, the police?'

'Nah, not the police, the bookies. Gaming debts aren't enforceable by law see, so what the bookies do is they get some heavies on the case. A couple of big leery bastards in jangling jewellery generally turn up in a Ford Capri and ask you ever so nicely if you'd mind coughing up or they'll shorten yer legs for you, that sort of thing.'

'Heavens!'

'That night your friend was 'ere, we was in conference, see, discussing where Alf should go. To hide, right, a safe place, like. Well, when we swung round and saw that tart, Alf got windy. He was petrified she'd overheard and so the stupid git found her number by your phone and rang her to warn her off. Well, he got the muvver instead, didn't he, who says she's taken the baby out.' Mac gave me a sideways glance at this but I didn't even flinch. 'So instead, right, the pillock thinks – ah-hah, a kid! Maybe I'll write her a note instead, put the wind up her a bit, rattle her cage an' that, so he finds her address by the phone and goes for it. Well, I went ape-shit when I found out, but by then it was too late. He'd sent it.' He shook his head sadly, tapped his temple. 'He's never had much up there, our Alf.'

'Evidently. I mean – as if she'd get involved anyway! It wouldn't mean a thing to her.'

'Yeah,' Mac sighed, 'but like I said before, he's not a bright lad, our Alf. He don't fink fings frough, he just panics and gets in a state, don't he?'

'But if Alf's in such danger, why is he still here? I mean, that was a while ago, wasn't it?'

'Yeah, but then again, this is as good a hiding place as any, innit? I mean, who'd fink of looking for Alf here, deep in leafy suburbia? But it won't do for much longer.' He pursed his lips. 'We just got word from some mates down Hackney way that Trinidad and Tobago is on their way, so Alf's out of 'ere first fing tomorrow. We've only got your bathroom to go now, luv, and me an' Lance an' Spiro can handle that.'

'Trinidad and Tobago?'

'The heavies, luv. Big black bastards whose ancestors hail from sunnier climes.'

'Oh! Good grief. Yes, well, I'm delighted in that case that Alf's going. I certainly don't want any broken legs decorating my back yard, thank you very much, and what am I supposed to do if they come to the door?' I asked a trifle nervously.

'Send them straight down to me, luv. I'll sort them out.'

Really? I looked dubiously at Mac's tiny frame. 'Well, I sincerely hope you're right.'

'Oh, they wouldn't touch me. I know too many influential people, see,' he tapped the side of his nose. 'Too many people wiv more subtler, but probably more interesting, mefods of persuasion.'

'Oh! Right.' Bloody hell. Yes, I imagined he did. It occurred to me that Mac had probably led quite an exotic life – this tiny little man who'd protected his big, lumbering, younger brother from a vile stepfather, been through Barnardo's and then out the other side into the turbulent East End. I expect Mac knew quite a few colourful characters.

'So don't you worry, luv,' he said, taking my elbow again, only this time, subtly propelling me housewards. 'We can handle it. Only I'd be ever so grateful if – you know.' He tapped his nose again. 'Mum's the word.'

'Oh – yes, of course. I mean, I don't know anyone to tell, Mac.'

Don't actually know anyone in gangland Hackney who'd be interested in his brother's whereabouts, I thought as I made my way slowly back to the house. It struck me, though, that there were clearly some lawless places out there. Not exactly Al Capone land, but a shady, grey, wheeling-and-dealing area where people still got their legs broken, a place that most ordinary people didn't even know existed. I pulled my cardigan around me with a little shiver. Well, I for one was far happier being blissfully ignorant.

As I wandered back through the French windows I closed them behind me, shooting the bolts up firmly. Now that the weather had broken there was a chill in the air and the wind was getting up. In fact, it occurred to me that the reason it was gushing through here like a raging monsoon was because the front door was wide open.

God, no wonder there was such a gale. As I crossed the room to the hall and went to shut it, someone coughed behind me. I froze. Stood there, paralysed with fear, one hand on the doorknob. Then I swung around. Over the back of the sofa, the top of a man's head was clearly visible. A dark head.

'Who is it!' I yelped, swinging the front door open again. 'Christ! What d'you want!'

'Peace and quiet and a large gin, since you ask.' Hugh's head popped up over the sofa.

'Omigod!' I clutched my thumping chest. 'Oh my *God*, Hugh, don't *do* that! I thought you were Trinidad and Tobago!'

'Who?'

'Trinidad and Tobago, the heavies, well versed in the art of subtle persuasion!'

He frowned. 'What the hell are you talking about, Livvy?'

Still hanging on to the furniture, I told him all about Alf and his debts. He chuckled.

'Blimey, I should think he's scared witless. I'd rather be hounded by the police than those hoods. Can't he raise the money?'

'I think,' I said, collapsing into a convenient armchair, still suffering from shock, 'that if that had been an option he'd have explored it by now, don't you?' Suddenly I sat bolt upright. 'Oh help – I'm not supposed to tell anyone!' I clutched my mouth. 'Oh God, Hugh, I swore I wouldn't breathe a word to a living soul and I've just told you the whole story!'

'Oh, don't worry, my love, I'm not a living soul, just a

grey, shambling wreck inhabiting a living soul's body. Your secret's safe with me. My lips are sealed.'

'Well, they bloody better be or I'm in deep shit,' I said reverting to gangland parlance. 'And anyway, what the hell are you doing here, Hugh, frightening the life out of me? Why aren't you at home changing nappies and rubbing cream into cracked nipples?'

'Because – something terrible's happened.' I realised with a start his face was very grim.

I gasped. 'Oh God, not the baby!' I shot out of my chair.

'No, no, not the baby,' he said hastily. 'Sorry, Livvy, didn't mean to frighten you. No, Flora's fine, that would be tragic, this is merely terrible. No, Millicent's arrived,' he informed me darkly.

'Ah!' I sank back down again. 'God, don't *do* that to me, Hugh. I've had more than enough shocks for one day!'

'Sorry. Still, you must admit it's fairly appalling. She breezed in this morning, totally unannounced, of course. She knows full well we'd go into hiding with Alf if she'd given us prior warning.'

'Oh dear, poor you!' I giggled. Millicent was Molly's huge and formidable mother, truly a woman of substance, about fourteen stone in all, and still firmly entrenched somewhere in the 1950s, when being a housewife really stood for something. She couldn't understand why Molly didn't darn her husband's socks, boil giblets for gravy and knit her children's vests.

'There I was, upstairs,' Hugh went on tragically, 'casting a dreamy, casual eye out of the bedroom window, minding my own business, quietly picking my nose and idly wondering whether Molly would like to be eased gently back into the sexual saddle tonight – albeit a few weeks before she goes up on the ramps for her six-week check-up – when suddenly, a horribly familiar white Fiesta draws up. The door opens, there's a ghastly hiatus . . . and then Millicent's unmistakable bulk is disgorged, a carrier bag in each hand – one, no doubt full of nourishing food (bits of dead sheep to you and me) and the other full of Pingouin knitting patterns – and all I could do was watch, petrified, as she cruised menacingly up the garden path like a battleship under full steam.'

'Oh God! What did you do?'

'Well, first I dropped my bogey –'

'Hugh!'

'Then my fantasy, and then I legged it downstairs and out of the back door, just as her humongous fist was hammering at the front. I tell you, Livvy, it was a close-run thing. I mean, normally I can spot her heaving into view at twenty paces and divert at nineteen, but this time she caught me on the hop.' He shuddered. 'Frankly I'd rather meet your brace of black boys in a dark alley than Millicent in the front hall. Now where's that drink I ordered?'

'Poor Molly,' I sighed, getting up to pour it.

'Ah yes, alas, poor Moll,' he intoned sadly. 'Trapped for hours, nay, days even, being permanently scolded about how she's not looking after the baby properly, and being told how Alison – married to Moll's brother, remember? Mousy little wifey thing? Wears an apron? Probably wears it in bed.'

'Oh yes,' I giggled.

'How Alison – God, quite sexy actually. Naked but for an apron.'

'Get on with it!'

'Oh yes, well how Alison never gave baby Hannah the breast unless it was absolutely bang on four hours since she'd been offered it the last time, whilst my poor Moll sits there, being constantly milked by our demanding daughter and looking like some mad cow, all wild about the eyes, and now about to be driven even madder as Millicent subjects her to reams of photos of young Hannah – who looks like a cross between Boris Yeltsin and a Vietnamese pot-bellied pig incidentally – dressed in cutesy little smocky things, *all* of which the sainted Alison has made *by hand*, whilst the only thing poor Moll has ever made by hand is a mess.'

I giggled and passed him a large gin, sipping my own and sitting down beside him on the sofa, pulling my legs up under me. 'Which is precisely why you should get back,' I said, wagging a finger sternly. 'It's unfair to leave her on her own.'

'I thought we'd do it in shifts,' he said, resting his head back and gazing at the ceiling. 'I thought I'd creep back when it's dark, smuggle her and Flora out, and tell her that your front door is always open – which it was, by the way – and that even better, Johnny's car isn't even in the front drive.' He turned his head, eyed me beadily.

I swirled the ice in my glass. 'Well spotted,' I said levelly. 'I'd noticed that too. But I had no idea,' I went on brightly, 'that you and Molly disliked him so much, Hugh.'

'Oh, I wouldn't say that,' he said lightly, 'nothing so strong as dislike. No, no, we just thought he treated you like dog poo, that's all. And I'm not just talking about the last six months, either.'

'Ah, I see. So, therefore you thought I was pathetic, cringing and downtrodden?'

'You can only be downtrodden, Liv, if someone bigger is doing the treading, but I'll say no more, because I've learnt from past experience that it's a mistake. Only the other day a mate of mine, Tom, confided to me that he'd left his wife and I yelled, "Terrific! I always thought Geraldine was a dog, and you wouldn't *believe* the number of times I've had to wrestle her hand out of the front of my trousers!" Well, bugger me if two weeks later I'm not sitting next to "the dog" at a dinner party, and Tom's shooting me homicidal looks over the salmon mousse. I think Johnny's a wonderful, caring human being, Livvy, and I love him to bits. Now, moving smartly on, the *other* reason I came, aside from not meddling in your domestic set-up and *aside* from escaping Millicent, was to give you these.' He lifted his bottom off the sofa, reached into his jeans pocket and flicked some pieces of paper at me.

'What are they?'

'Tickets for Sebastian's concert tomorrow night. He very kindly sent them, together with some flowers – which was totally uncalled for – as a thank you for supper the other week.' He sighed, wistfully. 'Believe it or not we were actually thinking of going. Moll's got terrible cabin fever – you know, four-walls-and-a-baby-not-to-mention-sodding-Henry – and she thought she could easily feed during the performance and meanwhile we could greedily observe other life forms, be reminded that there *is* a world out there.' He sighed. 'But now that HMS *Splendid*'s arrived our plans lie in tatters. We shall no doubt be sitting down to supper and sampling some of her famous desiccated lamb's heart stew instead.' He shuddered. 'She brings the bits of sheep with her, you know. They're the oldest ewes in Wales. I'm sure she sits on the hillside watching them, waiting for them to die – which they gladly do under her gaze – before smuggling them home and hanging them for six months prior to foisting them on to us.'

I smiled, but I wasn't really listening to his habitual patter, I was gazing at the tickets, turning them over in my hand. 'But – how very kind of him,' I said slowly, as it also occurred to me that – God, he hadn't sent *me* one, had he?

'Wasn't it?' Hugh agreed. 'I popped in to thank him just now, actually, en route here. Didn't stay, though. He was having a bit of a pre-concert drinks do with the musical élite, and they all looked a bit scary and sophisticated to me.'

'Oh yes,' I sat up eagerly, 'I saw Imo's car. She and Hugo are over there, did you see them?'

'I saw Imogen,' he said carefully.

'I wonder if she'll pop over later,' I mused, gazing somewhat wistfully in that direction.

'I doubt it somehow,' he said quietly.

I glanced back. 'Why?'

'Oh – just that it looked like it was going to go on a bit,' he said quickly. 'You know.'

'Oh, right.' I felt a brief pang of jealousy. A roaring pre-concert drinks party, eh, and if I'd played my cards right I could have been there too. Christ, been there – I might even have been the hostess. I chewed my lip ruefully for a moment, then smiled.

'God, I'm *so* pleased about Imo, though, aren't you, Hugh? She's absolutely ecstatic about this guy. Honestly, you should hear her eulogising about him. Molly said she left a message on the answer machine the other day saying she was absolutely besotted, and that's so unlike her, isn't it? She's keeping a hell of a low profile, though,' I said, frowning. 'She popped in briefly when Johnny came back, but I was just thinking, I haven't really had a proper evening or lunch with her since that terrible concert in the Abbey. Does Moll see much of her?'

Hugh took a deep breath. 'Um, Livvy, look. I wasn't going to tell you this, but I think there's something you should – Shit!'

We both jumped and I spilt my drink as a tremendous banging came at the front door.

'Bloody hell!' I squeaked, jumping up. 'I do have a bell!'

The banging came again, only more of a hammering now. Hugh and I gazed at each other, stunned.

'God, who the hell would do that?' whispered Hugh, getting up and moving behind the sofa.

I went to answer it. 'Well, I don't know, but I'm bloody well going to –' I stopped. Swung round. My hand flew to my mouth. 'Trinidad and Tobago!' I breathed.

'Oh, good point,' he muttered with relief. 'For an awful moment I thought it might be Millicent.'

'Quick, in here!' I grabbed his arm and pulled him through into the study, which looked out on to the front drive. We scuttled to the window together and peered out round the red velvet curtain. A small, bald-headed man in a beige, belted raincoat was standing on the step, beside a middle-aged, peroxide-blonde woman in a well-worn, shiny C&A suit.

'Oh. How very disappointing,' observed Hugh flatly.

'They look like insurance salesmen. Either that or Jehovah's Witnesses.'

'Well, thank goodness for that,' I said with relief, going to answer the door. 'They certainly don't look like knuckle breakers, anyway.'

I opened it.

'Mithith McFarllen?' the man enquired softly. He had a lisp.

'Yes?'

'I believe a gentleman named Mithter Alfred Turner ith currently in your employ. May we thpeak with him, pleathe?'

My heart skipped. God, yes, of course, far more sinister. The quietly spoken gunman and his female accomplice, his moll, his *femme fatale*, brought along for cover. Nothing brutal and thuggish, mind, just a single bullet to the head, while the girl wiped the revolver clean with a white silk handkerchief.

'Oh! Well, yes I –'

'Police,' the moll informed me helpfully, flicking out her ID card.

'Oh!' I gasped with relief. 'Good, heavens, I thought you were –'

'Yes?'

'No, no, nothing. Um, yes, well do come in. In fact – no, no, don't come in, there's no point. We'll go round the back. They're down in a caravan, you see, in the garden. Such fun, you'll see!' I breezed nervously. I stepped outside and began to lead the way, when abruptly I stopped. 'Oh – except I have to tell you, I have a feeling Alf won't be there.'

'Really? Why so?' asked Raincoat.

'Well, because they always go to the pub at about this time.' I glanced at my watch. 'Yes, they'll be having a pint.'

'Ah.' He gave a thin smile. 'Well, shall we go and thee, anyway, Mrs McFarllen? Jutht in case? Shall we go and find out?' he gestured with his arm that I should lead on again.

'Oh, yes, OK.' God, he was a bit creepy, wasn't he? A bit – you know – unnecessary? 'Um, coming, Hugh?' I glanced back over my shoulder.

But Hugh was recovering from shock and cowering in the porch, desperately trying to light a cigarette with an empty lighter. 'No, no,' he muttered faintly, 'don't worry about me. I'll be off now. Might even go to the pub myself, have a large Scotch. Toodle-oo, my love, and thanks for the drink.'

'Love to Molly,' I called as he shuffled off down the drive.

Gosh, the police, I thought, my head spinning as I led them away down the garden. Now, that was an interesting development. Hadn't Mac said that gambling debts weren't enforceable by law? But then, perhaps they were here to protect Alf? Yes, that must be it, I decided. They'd probably heard that some unsavoury characters were after him and were here to warn him, offer him some protection, perhaps. Well, thank goodness for that. I wasn't unhappy about a bit of police presence if there were going to be some undesirables knocking about. I banged on the caravan door.

'Mac! Alf!'

Spiro answered. 'Yes, Meesis McFarllen?' with studied politeness.

479

'Oh, Spiro, are the others in?'

'No, Meesis McFarllen, they have gone out. They have gone to the public house.'

It was quite obvious Spiro had been well briefed. He was talking in an even more unnatural and stilted manner than usual, as if he'd rehearsed, and was now regurgitating the words.

'Do you happen to know which public houthe?' whispered the man in the raincoat.

Spiro smiled ruefully. 'I am so very sorry. I am so very afraid that I do not know wheech public house.'

God, he sounded brain dead. Raincoat turned to me. 'What's the nearest local then, Mrs McFarllen, the Fighting Cocks?' He paused. 'Mrs McFarllen?'

'Oh, I'm sorry.' Just behind Raincoat, I'd suddenly caught sight of Mac, hiding in the rhododendron bushes. I'd also spotted Lance, tucked away behind him. Lance put a finger to his lips. I turned wide eyes on Raincoat. 'What . . . did you say?'

'I thaid, is the Fighting Cocks the nearetht?'

'Yes, yes, that's it.'

'But they go on a creep, I theenk,' added Spiro, imaginatively. 'They go creepy crawly.'

The policeman stared.

'A pub crawl, he means,' I put in quickly.

'Ah.' Raincoat nodded, then squinted at Spiro as if he'd never seen anything quite like him before. He pursed his lips. 'Well, how very inconvenient, but I don't believe I shall trouble to "creep" around the local hothtelries after them. Would you thimply inform Mr Turner that I would

480

like a word with him on a matter of great importance, and will be returning forthwith, in other words, tomorrow morning, Mrs McFarllen?'

'Of course!'

'And meanwhile, thank you for your time.' He inclined his head slightly, then with a sharp 'Come!' to his accomplice, they turned to go.

Spiro and I watched as they made their way up the garden, not quite goose-stepping but almost, up the lavender walk, and under the rose arbour. My eyes darted briefly to the rhododendron bushes, but then suddenly, on an impulse, I ran after them.

'Um, excuse me,' I called, 'can I just ask,' I said, breathlessly, catching them up, 'since this is my home, and Alf Turner is staying on my premises – can I just ask what this is all about?'

He turned. 'Yeth of course. It's about his wife.'

'Whose wife – Alf's?'

'Yeth. She appears to be missing.'

'Missing! Oh, oh no, now you see I can help you with that, officer,' I said eagerly. 'If you mean Vi, she's gone to Spain!'

He gazed witheringly at me. 'No, Mrs McFarllen, she hasn't gone to Spain. For one thing she has never in her life possessed a pathport and she certainly hasn't forged one and sneaked her way out of the country. She's missing, believe me. In fact we're very much afraid she may be dead.'

I stared. 'Dead!' My hand shot to my mouth. 'Oh!' I gasped.

'Exactly. Oh,' he repeated quietly. His pale grey eyes bored deep into mine. 'Bear that in mind, Mrs McFarllen, when you answer any more of my questions, hmm?'

And with that he turned and left.

Chapter Twenty-Six

'Dead!' I stared after his retreating back. Spiro came up behind me.

'Spiro, she's dead!' I gasped.

'Who dead?'

'Vi, Alf's wife!'

He gazed at me, open-mouthed. Slowly it dawned. 'Oh! Oh no, so poor Alf! He be so sad, Meesis McFarllen! He have his heart broken in a million tiny pieces, he –'

Mac and Lance materialised from the bushes and came over the bridge, just as Spiro was filling up and reaching for his hat. Mac jerked his head. 'Vamoose, Spiro.'

'*Ti?*'

'You heard, Zorba, beat it,' he snarled. 'Go find a kebab house to loiter in and bring us back a doner while yer at it. Go on, get out of here.'

Spiro's eyes widened. 'Ah yes, yes.' He looked suddenly nervous. 'Good idea, I go for doner.' He backed away.

'Excellent. Now.' Mac's steely-blue eyes met mine. 'We need to talk.'

'We certainly do,' I muttered.

'Over here.'

He led the way back across the bridge, pausing only at the caravan to reach in and grab a six-pack from inside the door. Then the three of us, under his guidance, moved further along the river and sat down on the grassy bank. Lance was silent.

'She's dead, Mac,' I breathed, staring into the water.

'I know.'

'Does Alf know?'

He turned his head, looked at me for a long moment.

'He killed her?' I gasped.

'Didn't think it would take you long. But he didn't kill her, as in murder her, right? It was an accident.'

'Jesus!' I got to my feet, knocking his Pils over. 'He killed her, Alf killed his wife – *Jesus*!'

'Sit down,' hissed Mac, reaching up and taking my arm roughly, dragging me down. 'An' keep yer voice down!'

I glanced around. There was no one about, but I appeared to be trembling. I sat down again.

'Now listen,' he breathed hoarsely in my ear. 'It was an accident, right? A terrible, tragic accident, like a kiddie drowning in a pond while his mum's not watchin', or like knockin' an old lady down 'cos you didn't see her suddenly step off the kerb, and that's not murder, is it? That's manslaughter, innit? See the difference? He's not a bad man, our Alf, orright?' His blue eyes bored into mine.

I gulped and inched back slightly on the grass. 'All – all right.' I nodded. 'What happened?' I whispered.

Mac took a slug of beer, narrowed his eyes across the river.

'That weekend, a while back, when we went home, and Lance stayed here, remember? Real scorcher?'

I thought back desperately. My mind whirled for a moment, then memories of Malcolm standing me up and Lance sitting me down and me slapping the Ambre Solaire

all over him in the garden and Claudia going missing jostled for position so – yes, that weekend, it must have
been . . . 'Yes, yes, I remember,' I muttered.

'Well, previous to that, she'd bin ringin', right?'

'Who had?'

'Vi, on his mobile, ringing and ringing, all week, and
always givin' him earache – remember that? 'Member how
his phone never stopped goin'? An' we all kept groanin'
and sayin', "Bloody hell, it's bleedin' Vi again," an' laughing about it – yeah?'

'Oh yes, yes, I do remember.'

'Well, what it was, right, what she was on about, was
some kitchen cupboard she wanted puttin' up. On an' on
she went, an' she wouldn't let it go. Right bleedin' nag, she
was, always giving it verbal, but old Alf, he don't mind,
see, he never minded, 'cos he loved her, right, and he was
used to it, wasn't he? So anyway, he went home that Friday
night and said – yeah yeah, orright luv, stop givin' me
grief, I'll do it, orright? I'll put it up.

'"Now," she says firmly.

'"Aw, come on," says Alf. "I've had a hard week, I've
just got in, luv. It's bin a long drive, I need me tea. Tomorrow morning, like."

'"No, I want it tonight," she says. "You never do sod all
round this place for me, Alfred Turner, always fixin' up
someone else's place. Well, bleedin' well fix mine up for a
change!"'

Mac sucked his teeth. 'That's what she was like, see,' he
muttered. 'Never mind that he was bringin' home the
dosh "from fixin' someone else's place up", never mind
that he was handin' the whole lot straight over to *her* every

bleedin' Friday night. Oh no, never mind all that.' He took a deep breath. 'So anyways, old Alf, he hauls himself out of his chair, even though he's knackered and he ain't even had his tea or anything, and goes to the shed and gets this cupboard, right? He's made it already, see, made it the weekend previous – and then he gets the step ladder out too, an' he starts fixin' it up, an' all the time she's standing there givin' him earache below about how he's never home and what a useless lump of lard he is. Well, finally, right, he gets this cupboard up on the wall, hammers it home, and he's wobbling about on top of the ladder and he calls down, "About there orright, luv?"

'And she stands back and says – "Bleedin' heck! It's not even bleedin' straight, you useless lump of shit!"

'Well, Alf, he loses it then. He's tired and he's hungry and he's up this ladder, and he slams his hammer down on the floor – chucks it away in disgust. Only what he don't realise is, she's moved forward, hasn't she, and she's standin' right underneath him now. Well, it gets her – WALLOP! – right on the side of the head, right on the temple, and she falls to the floor in a heap, crumples like a pack of cards. Well, the next thing Alf knows, he's tearing down that ladder, and then he's crouched down beside her in a pool of blood, feeling for her pulse, which she ain't got.'

'Oh God,' I breathed.

'So anyways, trembling and sobbin' like, he gets straight on the blower to me. Really cryin' he is, and I can hardly make out a word he's sayin', but I get the gist orright when I hear him say, "I've killed her, I've bloody killed her, Mac!" So I'm shitting myself, right, but I tell him to calm down an' I get round there sharpish and I don't tell no one where I'm going, not even the missus or nofing. Well, when I get there, burst through the door, there he is. Sat there, poor sod, sobbin' his eyes out on the kitchen floor, covered in blood 'cos he's tried to revive her, tried to give her mouf to mouf, the daft sod, and the poor bitch is in his arms, head back, mouth open, bleedin' like a stuck pig, cradled like a baby.'

'Oh Christ.' My hand flew to my mouth. I glanced at Lance. He was hugging his knees tight, staring at the grass. He'd gone very pale.

'Well, I'm in a right state now, aren't I? On the one hand I'm all for ringin' the police an' tellin' it straight, leavin' the steps right where they are, hammer an' everything, all just as it is, but on the other, I've got Alf, see, cryin' his eyes out, huggin' an' kissin' her an' that, and strokin' her hair which is covered in blood and moanin' about how he didn't mean to do nofing, and in that split second I fought – well, who the hell are they goin' to believe? Not my little brother, that's for sure. What, married to some naggin' old witch that everyone knows is a right pain in the arse and would testify to that effect? A right old cow who finally gets her comeuppance in a well-deserved hammer blow to the head? "Just slipped out of my hand, your honour, didn't mean to chuck it, honest?" Do me a favour,' he scoffed. 'And old Alf – he'd be useless in the dock, under fire from some poncy brief – "Er, now tell me, Mr Turner," Mac puffed out his chest and popped his thumbs into an imaginary barrister's gown, "would you concur that you were actually involved in an argument with your wife at the time of the assault?"

'"Well,"' Mac shuffled sheepishly on his bottom, aping Alf, '"Yeah, she was windin' me up a bit, yer honour, yeah."

'"She was . . . Winding You Up. Hmm. I see. And did you therefore lose your temper?"

'"Yeah, well, I was cross an' that but I –"

'"Did you, in fact, slam that hammer down with some considerable force?"

'"Well, I didn't mean to, like, but I suppose –"

'"*Aha!* So you *did* slam the hammer down with –" Nah.' Mac broke off in disgust, spat in the bulrushes. 'He don't stand a cat's chance in hell. He'd be in that slammer before you can say hot porridge, and that's unnecessary.' Mac wagged a finger. 'He's never hurt a fly in his life, old Alf. He's as gentle as anyfing, we all know that, and he don't deserve that.' He reached for his Pils and threw his head back, sucking on his can with a vengeance. As his head came back down, I realised there were tears in his eyes. I remembered the story about Alf's eye – what horrors they'd been through together.

'So . . . what did you do?' I asked tentatively.

Mac swallowed hard and I realised he was in trouble. He shook his head to indicate he couldn't speak. Lance cleared his throat.

'He got her out of his arms – prised her, apparently, Alf was clinging on to her for dear life – stripped off all of Alf's clothes and burnt them, then he took him upstairs and gave him a shower. Dad said it was like washing a baby, said he just stood there, dumb, not resisting or anything. Then of course he had to scrub the kitchen, and the shower, and then . . .' Lance swallowed.

'Then I realised there was no goin' back,' Mac continued gruffly. 'I'd done it, then, see? Burnt the clothes, scrubbed away the blood, got rid of the evidence. All in a matter of minutes. It dawned on me then that there was no way I could go to the police. I had to carry on.'

'And the body?'

Lance shook his head. 'Dad won't tell me.'

'Alf and I dealt wiv that,' said Mac gruffly. 'It's not for the lad to know. He's got enough on his conscience already through no fault of his own, an' it's not for you to know neiver.'

'No! No absolutely not, don't tell me, Mac!' I got up hurriedly, suddenly realising I knew far too much already. I moved along the river bank, hugging myself. I felt so cold, freezing actually. I clutched my upper arms tightly. My mind was spinning. God, I – I was an accomplice now or something, wasn't I? In it up to my neck! Christ, how on earth had I managed to get involved in this? I had to extricate myself forthwith! I had to – well, what did I have to do? I swung around. Mac was watching me closely.

'But – but surely, Mac, now that the police have got a whiff of this, now that they think she might be dead, surely you'll have to come clean? I mean, they definitely suspect Alf. You heard what that guy said, so Alf will have to talk to them now, won't he? Tell them what happened? You could persuade him to, and you could help him, too. I mean I know Alf's likely to get in a muddle and say the wrong thing, but between you, you could both tell them what you've just told me! I mean, I believe you, so why shouldn't they? It looks far more guilty *not* to say anything, *not* to go in and answer their questions!'

'Don't be soft,' he scoffed. 'The only reason you believe

us is 'cos you know us, and trust us. They'd take one look at us, root around in our backgrounds – which are tidy, but not immaculate – see how we've tampered with the evidence, and then they'd be rubbing their hands wiv glee! Oh yes, yet another conviction to pop under the DI's nose, yet another murdering bastard nailed, and a right feaver in their caps, too! Nah, do me a favour. That's right out. There's no question of that, not now, it's too late. Alf's got to get away, that's the only answer. He's gone, anyway, see. Gone to a safe place.' He checked his watch. 'In a couple of hours he'll be out of the country, heading for the Spanish –'

'OH, MAC, DON'T TELL ME!' I shrieked. 'I – I don't want to know!' I swung round, turning my back on him, biting my thumbnail frantically, and staring, horrified, into the gathering gloom of the middle distance. My God, what was I doing even *listening* to this? This was like – well, like getting involved with the great train robbers or something! A nice bunch of cockney lads, kind to animals and old ladies, always sending flowers to their mums, and who'd only meant to rob a train like Butch and Sundance did, who hadn't meant to blow the guard to bits and skip off to Puerto – I swung back. 'And has *he* got a passport?' I demanded. 'Alf?'

'He has now.'

I groaned, clutching my head. Oh God, why did I *ask* that? Now I *knew!* A false passport probably, and – oh crikey, yes, of course, a thousand pounds in folding readies stashed in his pocket. I gulped. Kindly donated by yours truly, not two hours ago. No wonder he'd wanted more.

'And you? You and Lance? They'll be back to question you in the morning, surely?'

Mac lit a cigarette and sucked hard. 'I'm sure they will, and we know nofing. All we know is what Alf told us, that Vi left him. Packed her bags 'cos she'd had enough of 'im and went to Spain to stay with a friend, and as far as we know, that's where she still is. Right, Lance?'

Lance was still staring miserably at his shoes. 'Right,' he muttered bleakly.

'And Alf? Where's Alf, they'll ask.'

Mac shrugged, expressionless, just as he no doubt would in the police station. 'Alf? Dunno. Really, dunno, guv. Christ, I'm not my brother's keeper, am I?' His blue eyes widened innocently at me.

Oh, but he was, he most definitely was, and always had been. And I had no doubt that in the not-too-distant future, Mac would be joining his brother in Puerto wherever-it-was, taking the whole family with him, upping sticks, buying a little villa, running up a few haciendas with the help of his masonic brothers and sons, before going on to buy a bigger villa, with luxury pool and then retiring to run a beach bar. Mac had neatly averted disaster all his life, slipping and sliding, ducking and weaving, just one step ahead of his clumsy, not-so-sure-footed brother, but always there to stretch back a hand to catch Alf, should he need one, should he fall. I crouched down beside him.

'So why tell me?' I breathed. 'Why not just tell me what you'll tell the police? That you're not your brother's keeper and you haven't a clue where he is?'

'Because you know us too well and you know about Alf's stupid letters and you're too bleedin' smart into the bargain. I had you fooled wiv the Trinidad and Tobago stuff, which, incidentally, happens all the time round our neck of the woods, but I knew I'd have to tell you if the old bill came snoopin'. They just came a bit sooner than I'd hoped, that's all. We should have 'ad Alf away days ago, but these fings take time to arrange, if you know wha' I mean.'

'No,' I said firmly. 'I don't.'

And I didn't want to know either. Didn't want to know about false passports, false identities, someone to meet him on the other side, no doubt. Let's face it, there'd have to be. I couldn't see Alf getting to Tooting on his own, let alone Marbella. No wonder it had taken time to arrange – and then a safe house somewhere, with someone to look after him until Mac could get out there. And of course extradition was still lax in some areas on the continent. For all the Spanish protestations that they did their best, if you knew the right people, it was still possible to lie low, and if the heat was turned up, why, you could always get on a boat and hop across to Marrakesh until things cooled down. And meanwhile, yes, meanwhile, poor old Vi lay a-mouldering in a shallow grave somewhere. Mac caught my eye.

'An accident, remember?' he said sharply. 'He loved her, orright? Really loved her. You saw 'ow he was for weeks afterwards, beside 'imself he was, weren't he?'

I nodded. That much was true. I remembered them all coming back that weekend: Alf in tears; Spiro, with presumably not a clue what was going on but joining in on the waterworks front anyway out of sheer solidarity; Mac, pale and tense, hustling them all to work like demons that morning, taking their minds off the horrors of the past couple of days with some hard graft; and Lance – no. No, of course, Lance had been here that weekend. It was the weekend that Claudia had gone missing. I suddenly remembered rushing to the pub to look for her, but finding him on his mobile phone instead, talking to his father, looking deadly serious, grim. And then I remembered his strange reluctance to call the police to find Claudes . . .

I turned. 'You knew? When I found you in the pub?'

'Only that Vi was dead,' he said quietly, 'and that it was an accident. I didn't know what Dad was planning to do, but I knew enough not to get the police round here if I could possibly help it.' He regarded me squarely. 'Although I would have done, Livvy. Had we needed to.'

I nodded. I believed him too. Believed both of them, knew instinctively they were both telling the truth, and knew instinctively that the police wouldn't believe them and would nail Alf, and that life was so unfair. But where did that leave me?

'I'm counting on you to stay shtumm, luv,' said Mac quietly. 'Not to lie or anyfing, not to tell any porkies, right, but just to say nofing. Say you don't know, orright?'

I looked at him, then glanced away. Across the river, the fireflies were dancing in the beams of the low evening sun. It sounded so easy, didn't it? Just don't say anything. Say you don't know. I swallowed.

'You need to know, Mac, that I can't do that,' I said quietly. 'I won't go to the police, won't actually seek them out, tell my story, spill the beans, but if they come here asking me questions, I won't stay "shtumm", either, as you call it. I have to tell them all I know. The letters, everything. You need to know that.'

I held his eye firmly as he looked at me long and hard. Finally he nodded.

'Yeah, well, I rather thought you'd say that. Rather expected it. Two different walks of life, eh, luv? Two codes of practice, somefing to do with morals and duty – rules, too, I expect.'

'Something like that.'

'Yeah, well, when the chips are down, I make me own rules.' He eyed me beadily.

I eyed him nervously back. There was a pause. 'So what are you going to do then, Mac? Boff me on the head to keep me quiet?'

Suddenly he flared up. 'I fought I'd make it clear we ain't like that!'

'Sorry, sorry,' I muttered quickly. 'That was cheap.'

Cheap, but quite a relief to know he *wasn't* going to, actually, I thought nervously.

'No,' he said thoughtfully, scratching his chin, 'but what it does mean, though, is I might have to make tracks sooner than I thought. Might have to –'

'Mac, enough!' I gasped, jumping up. 'Just do what you have to do, but don't tell *me* about it, all right? Don't tell me any more!' I folded my arms and marched off a few paces, then spun round and came back again. I glared down at him. 'Just – keep it to yourself, OK!'

He gazed up at me for a moment, pursed his lips, then sprang athletically to his feet. 'Yeah, yer right,' he agreed. 'The less you know the better.' He jerked his head. 'Come on, Lance, my boy, we've got work to do.'

Lance got miserably to his feet and then they both made to go, but then suddenly Mac turned back, regarded me squarely. 'Lance and Spiro will finish up here, luv. There's precious little to be done in that bathroom, but they'll do it, and you can settle up wiv them later, orright?'

'Orright,' I growled. 'I – mean, right.'

He held out his hand. 'Goodbye then, Olivia. Nice doin' business wiv you. Only do us a favour, eh? Give us a day's grace before you go an' spill the beans?'

I stared at him. 'Well now, how on earth am I supposed to do that,' I said slowly, looking at his outstretched hand. 'They'll be back here tomorrow morning, Mac, first thing. You heard him say so yourself.'

'Ah, but not to speak to you, luv, to us. You could make yourself scarce for the day, couldn't you? Not be there when they bang at the door? Have a pressin' engagement?'

I could feel Lance's eyes on me too now. I licked my lips. Could feel myself wavering for a moment. 'Well, I suppose . . . I could try, but –'

'Good girl,' he beamed. 'You're all right, Olivia. You're straight and you mean what you say. I like that.' He offered his hand again and this time I shook it, albeit gingerly.

'Yes, but listen, Mac,' I said nervously, 'I said I'll try, that's all. I'm not promising anything. I mean – I might not be able to get away, it may not be poss–'

'Oooh, you'll do just fine, luv, believe me. I knew I could count on you. Knew you wouldn't let us down.'

'Well I –'

'*Arrivederci* then,' he said briskly, giving a mock tug of his forelock and turning smartly on his heels. Lance fell in quickly behind him.

I watched, somewhat slack-jawed, as they went quickly back to the caravan, disappeared inside, and then I saw the door slam behind them. I stood for a moment, my mind racing, but with a nasty sickly feeling in my stomach, too. Finally I turned myself, walked slowly over the bridge, and on up the lawn to the house.

Dusk was falling fast now, and the fireflies were doing a last frantic dance in the low, flickering light. My own head was dancing fairly frantically too, and as I ducked under the blossoms of Madame Hardy covering the arbour, I realised, with a sudden start of horror, that Mac had very subtly turned the tables on me there. With his steely blue eyes upon me I'd promised – What exactly had I promised? I stopped still. To disappear for twelve hours so as not to blow their cover while Mac slipped the country? Good God! My hand shot out and clutched the wooden arbour, crushing petals, feeling thorns. Oh Lord, Olivia, that's – that's tantamount to harbouring criminals, isn't it? Or at least aiding and abetting them? Well, it was certainly something dodgy, I wasn't sure what, but on the other hand what else was I to do? I turned, gazed back at the caravan door. I'd more or less given my word, shaken hands even, and I'd feel such a heel shopping them first thing tomorrow, I'd – Well, I'd be a *grass* or something terrible, wouldn't I?

I chewed my lower lip nervously. Should I go back and tell Mac I couldn't do it? Couldn't go through with it? I wasn't altogether sure I could face those piercing blue eyes upon me again, though. Oh God, I thought, raking a hand through my hair, if only I wasn't so thoroughly on my own here! I just longed to *talk* to someone about this, longed not to be so flaming independent, so very solitary, longed to wail, '*Help!* I'm caught up in a murder inquiry here. What the hell should I do? What would *you* do? It struck me, in a flash, that Imo was literally only over the road; dear, smart, sensible Imo. Should I dash over and bend her ear? I blinked. What, in the middle of a smart cocktail party, Olivia? Muscle your way through the rattling jewellery and the clinking champagne glasses to tug at her sleeve, hiss in her ear? And what would she say? Well, you know damn well what she'd say: she'd say go to the police right now, of course she would! And Sebastian? I took a deep breath. No. No, I mustn't even think about Sebastian. That way madness lay, and I certainly mustn't involve him in this. Molly and Hugh I'd love to speak to, but they were both caught up with Millicent and the baby, and although they were both woolly-minded liberals I had a nasty feeling that even *they* might point me in the direction of the police station. In fact, anyone who didn't know these boys, who hadn't heard their story, who hadn't seen Mac's eyes fill up with tears just now, and who hadn't seen Lance's white, scared face, would say just the same. But I had. I had heard them, and I had seen them, and I knew Alf and I knew he wouldn't hurt a fly, and d'you know, I just . . . couldn't do it.

I turned back and walked quickly inside, perching on the first convenient chair that came to hand, just inside the French windows. I bit my thumbnail furiously for a moment, then got up and lit a cigarette. More thumb gnawing as I paced about the room, then – a thought. I stubbed my cigarette and hastened to the calendar in the kitchen. Maybe, just maybe, I *had* got a pressing engagement tomorrow? I mean, you never know, I might be incommoded at the dentist's, be flat on my back at the gynaecologist's or – ah, here, the 22nd, anything doing? . . . I gazed. Blank. Damn. Except – what was this, at the bottom, in pencil? I peered. 'Claudia to Lucy's for night.'

Ah yes, of course, I remembered now. Amanda, Lucy's mother, of the disappearing child episode, was desperate to have Claudes back and prove her worth as a competent mother, so if Claudia was away all day and all night, I reasoned rationally, what would I normally do? What would *any* normal, right-minded mother do on a child-free day in the middle of the school holidays? Well, she'd go to London, of course, that's what! Yes, I thought with a surge of joy, she'd spend the entire morning – nay, the entire *day*, in Harvey Nichols, of course she would! She'd have lunch, maybe take in an art gallery or two, have a leg wax, get her hair done – perfect! Oh golly, yes, *per*fect. My day was really taking shape! And it wasn't even a ruse, I thought happily. I really, honest to God, might well have done just that had I glanced at my calendar in the morning and seen Claudes bolting down her cereal all set with her overnight bag. And if I could set off bright and early, I thought furtively, really bright and early, before Raincoat and C&A Suit had even got a toe on the doorstep, well so much the better.

I quickly lunged for the telephone and rang Amanda, who instantly thought I was cancelling.

'Oh God, Livvy, I'll look after her,' she wailed. 'I swear to God I won't lose her!'

'Don't be silly, Amanda,' I scolded. 'I'm simply ringing to say could you possibly have her slightly earlier than we said? Like – ooh, I don't know, sort of, breakfast time?'

'Of course,' she agreed happily. 'Really, *any* time, Livvy. Drop her off in the middle of the night if you like.'

'Don't tempt me,' I said grimly. 'But rest assured, Amanda, you'll be seeing me pretty bright and early tomorrow morning.'

I put the receiver down and noticed my hand was trembling. I stared. Well, it would, wouldn't it? I thought, regarding it with interest. After all, here I was, an ordinary middle-class housewife, pillar of the local community, erstwhile member of the PTA, coolly, coldly and calculatingly working out the perfect strategy to give the police the slip.

Chapter Twenty-Seven

The following morning the alarm went off at ten to six. I sat bolt upright, felt a bit sick, couldn't think why – then remembered, and felt even sicker. Hand to mouth I leapt out of bed, showered quickly, got dressed, and went to wake Claudia, who was kipping deadly.

'Claudia. Claudes, wake up!' I shook her shoulder.

She moaned and rolled over on to her face. I pulled back the covers mercilessly.

'Claudia, get up! We'll be late!'

'Geddoff!' She tried to wrench the covers back but I had them in an iron grip somewhere down by her feet.

'Up now, darling, with the lark! Be quick!' I trilled brightly.

She turned bleary eyes on her clock. 'But it's only six o'clock!'

'Yes, but you're going to Lucy's, and I have to go to London today, remember? Remember I told you I was going, darling?'

'No,' she muttered, dragging her legs around and stumbling out to the loo. 'I don't.'

I left her to it and dashed downstairs to the kitchen. Seizing the calendar from the larder door I wrote in bold felt pen 'Shopping in London!' Then I smudged it a bit with my finger. There. I stood back and admired my handiwork with narrowed eyes. Looked like it had been there for ever, decades even. Plunging my bare feet into wellies, I then flew out of the back door and raced down the garden, leaping a flowerbed brimming over with dew-soaked *Alchemilla mollis*, dashing down the lavender path, across the lawn, under the cedar tree, and across the bridge to the caravan. I rapped on the door, holding my side and panting. No answer. I rapped again, harder. The door finally opened and Lance stuck out a very tousled, blond head. He yawned and rubbed his eyes.

'Olivia,' he muttered. 'What's happened?'

'Lance, I'm going to London,' I hissed. 'I want you to know that, it's very important.'

'Fine.' He nodded.

'So if the police come,' I urged, 'it's been arranged for ages, OK? I've been excited about this for weeks, OK, Lance?'

'OK, OK.'

'Mac's gone, hasn't he?' I peered past him to the sleeping form of Spiro on a lower bunk. 'I heard his van go last night.'

'Yes, he's –'

'*Don't tell me!*' I shrieked, clapping my hands over my ears and shutting my eyes. When I opened them again, his steady blue eyes were trained anxiously on me.

'Olivia, listen to me. Don't worry about this, all right? Don't panic. This has absolutely nothing to do with you. This is our own personal tragedy and you'll be kept well out of it, OK?'

'OK? OK? Of course it's OK,' I spluttered, 'and of *course* I'm nothing to do with it. Jesus, I – I never imagined for one moment I was!'

I gave him what I hoped was a look of withering magnitude, but probably had more than a hint of frightened rabbit about it, then turned and bolted back up the garden, veering off left in a sudden tangent to glance round the side of the house and just make sure that a flashing blue light wasn't cruising menacingly my way.

Ten minutes later I was hustling a sleepy and protesting Claudia out of the front door, down the drive and into the car. I was just running furtively round to the driver's side, when abruptly – I heard a roar behind me.

'Hang on – I want a word with you, young lady!'

My blood froze. I shut my eyes and stood, sledgehammered to the spot, awaiting the first stone, the first clink of handcuffs. Then I opened my eyes, and forced myself to turn, slowly, to see – Mr Jones, tearing down his path towards me, dressing gown flying, slippers flapping. Oh, thank you, God, thank you! Thou art a real brick!

'Mr Jones!' I cried.

'I'm soa, soa glad I've caught yew, like,' he panted. 'Tried to get hoald of yew yesterday, but yew didn't seem to be abowt. You see – I've heard all about your pickle!'

My heart stopped again. How the hell . . . ? 'But I'm not in a pickle, Mr Jones!' I gasped.

'Oh noa, noa, your chutney! Gwyneth told me, see. Says yew always swear by those Unwin's green tomatoes yew grow, but I'll bet you've never tried making it with one of these boyos, eh?' He held up a whopping great pair of plum tomatoes, hanging pendulously together, side by side.

'Gordon's Bliss!' he hissed dramatically. 'Bet yew've never even seen the like, 'ave you now?'

I blinked. 'N-no, you're right, Mr Jones, never! How splendid, and – how kind. I'll pickle them this evening, shall I?'

I made to reach out for the voluptuous orbs, chuck them in the back of my car and be on my way, but he was too quick for me.

'Oa, steady on now!' he twinkled, holding them aloft, 'thought yew'd be interested, like! John Innes No. 2 and plenty of bone meal is the secret, but not soa fast!' He lowered his pink, excited face to mine. 'Fair dos, eh, girl? I've had my eye on that flat-leafed parsley of yours for some time now; wouldn't mind getting me 'ands on a sprig or two of that before yew pop these boyos in your chutney locker!'

'My . . .' I gazed. 'Oh! Right! Yes, well, be my guest, Mr Jones. Heavens, take the lot, do, only I really must fly. I'm off to London for the day, don't want to be late.' I jumped in the car. 'Really, take the lot!'

He frowned. 'Oooh, noa, noa, I wouldn't do a thing like that. Wouldn't dream of it, girl. I only meant –'

But I didn't hear the rest, I was away, leaving him standing in his dressing gown in a cloud of dust, clutching his vast tomatoes, whilst I roared off at breakneck speed to do business on the other side of town.

Ten minutes later, I was banging on Amanda Harper's mock-Georgian, twin-pillared front door in an immaculate, sleepy little cul-de-sac full of frothy Austrian blinds which were still very firmly down. Claudia was beside me, yawning her head off and looking like a bag lady as she clutched her possessions in a Tesco's carrier she'd had to grab hastily as I'd hustled her out. Finally Amanda appeared in her dressing gown, hair on end, mascara down her cheeks.

'Oh! Livvy. Gosh, I didn't realise you meant sparrow's fart.'

'Amanda, I'm so sorry. I know it's terribly early,' I breathed, 'but I'm off to London today, been looking forward to it for ages. Shopping trip, you know.'

She rubbed her eyes. 'Blimey, at this hour? God, you'll be there in half an hour, there'll be so little traffic. I'm not sure the shops open at seven thirty, do they?'

'Ah, but I'll get a good parking place,' I beamed. 'So exciting. I've been –'

'Looking forward to it for months,' said Claudia wearily, pushing past me with her arms full. 'You've told us that about twenty times. She's lost it,' she informed Amanda as she went on past her and trudged upstairs to find Lucy, whom she'd no doubt crash out next to on her bed. 'She's really lost it this time. We're talking beyond Prozac.'

Oh God, was I overdoing it? I wondered, as I fled back down the path. Making too much of a meal of it? That would look even more peculiar. I must calm down. As Lance had said, this was absolutely nothing to do with me. Don't panic. Nevertheless, as I roared up the M1, every so often an image of Alf, kneeling, and holding a blood-soaked Vi in his arms, like Lear sobbing over a lifeless Cordelia, would spring to mind and make me clutch my mouth with horror, and simultaneously put my foot down in an attempt to distance myself.

As a result, the speedometer hit 90, and I found myself in central London by seven forty-five along with all the early bird commuters. I parked in a Knightsbridge NCP, bought a paper, then had tea and toast in the Brompton Arcade, feeling I really should have a hat and dark glasses on in case someone recognised me and asked me why the devil I wasn't at home, where I belonged. The minutes ticked by. As I sat at the little café table I peered over my paper, gazed around a bit, a little more adventurously now perhaps for a wanted woman, and looked at my watch. Eight fifteen. Good grief, only eight fifteen! What the hell was I supposed to do now?

'Um, what time do the shops open?' I bravely asked my Italian waiter, breaking my cover as he sauntered languidly up with my third cup of tea.

He shrugged, shoulders up around his ears somewhere. 'Ees supposed to be ten, but you know, ees summer time, so . . .'

So – what, the shopkeepers have a lie in? I sighed. Excellent news. Well, the plan was to stay for late-night shopping and go home at about ten o'clock. At this rate I'd have to shop till I was vomiting. More tea was required. I ordered it and read the *Daily Mail* more minutely – from cover to cover, in fact – until I noticed that according to Patrick Walker's replacement, Saturn was dominating my sphere and would undoubtedly be my downfall today. 'Don't expect to come up smelling of roses if you've deliberately deceived someone,' it warned grimly. I put the paper down with quivering hands, wondering if the deceived detective was even now banging on my front door, demanding to see the lady of the house, sniffing around to see which criminals I was harbouring today. Heavens, how brave those Resistance people must have been, with fighter pilots in the attic, whilst here was I, quivering with nerves at the thought of a brace of brickies in a caravan. Calm down, Olivia, just calm down. In an effort to do so, I emptied the entire contents of my hand-bag on to the table and sorted it out methodically. This, in the event, was just as well, because it was during this little operation, that a plan was hatched. You see, as I sorted around amongst the ancient cough lozenges, the parking tickets, the sweetie wrappers and a very tired-looking tampon, there, nestling at the bottom of my handbag, I spotted two tickets. Two tickets to a concert at the Wig-more Hall.

I sat back and stared at them. Of course, Hugh had given them to me, hadn't he, and I must have stuffed them in my bag. I took a sip of tea, turning them over in my hand. Yes, why not? Why not, in fact, spend the entire day preparing for this very event? Why not go to the hair-dresser's, buy a new dress to wear, maybe even have my nails done for the first time in my life, and then, looking drop-dead gorgeous – well, as near as damn it, anyway – swan off to the concert in the evening? Imogen would be there, of course, and we could probably sit together since Hugo would be conducting, and naturally Sebastian would be there too . . .

I took another sip of tea. It was colder than one would wish. I hadn't allowed myself to think about Sebastian yet, you see. Since Johnny had gone, I realised I'd mentally put him up on a high shelf so I couldn't reach him. Not out of my mind, because that was impossible, but out of reach, because that was where I knew him to be. But I missed him – yes, of course I did. I missed the easy friendship we'd had and his downright niceness but, more than that, something deeper, more visceral, something in my heart ached for him too. If I allowed it. Mostly I didn't, but just occasionally I'd let it out of its cage, give myself a glimpse of him, at Hugh and Molly's maybe, his face creasing up with sudden mirth as he chewed gamely on a burnt sausage, or hauling a dripping Claudia out of the river, or just the two of us together, cooking in his base-ment kitchen, giggling as we threw Maureen's putrid casserole in the bin . . .

I traced the gingham pattern on the café tablecloth sadly. I knew I'd blown it, you see. I realised that. I knew I'd always thought of Sebastian as a first reserve, a sort of – well, if Johnny doesn't come back then who knows? Better than Malcolm and Rollo and Lance but not as good as Johnny. And I'd more or less said as much, hadn't I? Said, sorry Seb, old boy, Johnny's back now, I'm afraid, so it's bye-bye and on yer bike, OK? Well, I could hardly turn round now and say – hey, guess what, great news! He's gone, so you're on again! Except that Johnny hadn't gone. I'd thrown him out. Surely that was different? Surely that changed the whole complexion of the situation some-what? And maybe if I explained that to Sebastian, maybe if I didn't ask for too much, no more than our familiar old friendship back, then perhaps – perhaps something deeper could develop? Into what it should have been?

I lit a cigarette and watched a couple go by, arm in arm, the boy turning to drop a kiss on the girl's head. I glanced dreamily down at the tickets and for one giddy moment, saw Sebastian with his arm through mine, turning to drop a – Christ! My eyes suddenly snagged on a headline in the

Daily Mail. 'British girl arrested for her part in cover-up.' I gasped, horrified, and read on. Oh – drugs, oh no, no, I wasn't involved in that, thank heavens, but what was I *thinking* of? Sitting here, mooning about Sebastian, when all the time . . . didn't I have enough on my plate? I mean, I had the murder squad on my doorstep, the boys in blue snooping round my house, what I needed was advice, not frigging romance! I took a deep, deep drag on my cigarette. OK, I reasoned calmly, so forget the romance bit, but – how about if I just talked to him? To Sebastian? About my present pickle? About the almighty Horlicks I seemed to have got myself into? See if he could give me some words of wisdom, some words of advice, because actually, I realised with a jolt, his were the only words I'd care to listen to. If he told me to go straight to the police, do not pass Go, do not collect £200 then I would, unreservedly, and conversely, if he said I was under no compulsion to do anything of the kind, well then, I'd go along with that, too.

Of course, I reasoned, packing up my bag again, it would be nigh on impossible tonight. I could hardly sneak up to him in the interval, tug at his sleeve and hiss, 'Listen, Seb, down at the bottom of the garden where most people have fairies, I've got these self-confessed killers who are frightfully sorry but would like me to cover up for them, what d'you think? Loved the violins in the first half, by the way.' No, no, that would never do. But perhaps afterwards, if I crept backstage and caught his eye, then maybe I could pass him a note? Ask him, if he wasn't too busy, if he could possibly spare a moment tomorrow? At about six in the morning, before the police popped round again?

I gulped and took another terrified drag of my cigarette, but felt relieved at least, to have something of a plan. Something to cling to. Resolving to stick to it, I heaved my by now groaning bladder from the chair, tottered to the counter to pay for four cups of tea, then embarked on my exhausting day.

As I trailed between Harvey Nichols and Harrods, filling in cancelled manicures here, and leg wax appointments there, it occurred to me to wonder how on earth French women managed it? All this beautifying? On a weekly basis? What, face, nails, toes, the lot? How very tiring, and how on earth did they find time to prick out their dahlias? As I emerged from yet another salon, having gamely entrusted myself to a student who'd never plucked an eyebrow in her life but was keen to try, I finally ended up, sans eyebrows, at the hairdresser's, with Marco, a drop-dead gorgeous blond, standing behind me.

I could tell at a glance that Marco was more used to positioning himself behind members of his own sex, and was standing now as though he was slightly uncomfortable, as though there might even have been someone standing behind him last night. Gosh, it could go on for ever, couldn't it, I thought, lines of them, my mind boggling at the possibilities. Marco gave a little sigh.

'So what are we doing today then?' he enquired in a bored little voice, gazing distractedly across the salon to where a fresh-faced young lad was sweeping the floor.

'We're doing sex and glamour,' I informed him firmly.

His peroxide head spun back like a machine gun, and his eyes met mine in the mirror. 'Ambitious,' he murmured doubtfully. Then arching his eyebrows in pained disdain he began plucking sniffily at my split ends. 'But then again,' he murmured, 'I always like a challenge.' Pausing only to shriek imperiously, 'Cindy, a coffee for my lady, please!' he pursed his lips, clenched his tight little buttocks, flexed his scissors, and went to work with alacrity.

Well, I have to say that half an hour later, albeit with a frightening amount of hair on the floor and an exhausted Marco behind me, the end result wasn't half bad. He'd cut it short, shorter than I'd normally have it, but had given me a long and sexy fringe which flopped right down over one eye, and which I had to flick back if I wanted to see daylight.

'What am I supposed to do with this then?' I said, lifting it doubtfully.

He sighed. 'You're supposed to smoulder through it, darling, but if that's a problem I'll cut it off.'

'Oh!' I dropped it. 'No, that's not a problem at all, watch.' I pouted kittenishly at him in the mirror.

He shuddered and reached for the scissors. 'Off, then.'

'No no!' I laughed, stopping his hand, 'I'll practise. Trust me, Marco, in a couple of hours I'll be smouldering so hard I'll have half the men in London spontaneously combusting.'

'Scary,' he muttered drily, tossing his pretty little head and tucking his scissors in his tight back pocket. 'Well, be sure to leave a nice red-hot one for me.'

I assured him that I would and as he minced away I sailed out, feeling really rather sassy and pleased with myself. I kept catching glimpses of myself in the mirrors as I rode the Harvey Nicks escalators, and the effect was so gratifying, it gave me the confidence to sail straight into the hushed portals of the Donna Karan franchise and try on the first little black dress I came across. Yes, OK, it was a bit tight across the bottom and perhaps a bit short – sleeveless and backless too – but, boy, did it look terrific. I bounced out of the changing room delightedly and saw the young, male sales assistant glance admiringly.

'You don't think it's a bit young for me?' I asked with a confident smile.

'You're right,' he nodded, 'it is. How about this?'

Thunderstruck, I watched as he minced to a rail and plucked out a vast black tent. He dangled the hangar from his manicured little pinky and raised his eyebrows quizzically. Bastard. This was clearly Marco's boyfriend and there was obviously some homosexual conspiracy afoot here to put thirty-something women in their place. Well I, for one, wasn't going.

'I'll take it,' I said, smiling sweetly, 'and what's more, I'll be wearing it this evening!'

'Certainly, madam,' he murmured demurely, gliding seamlessly to the cash desk, 'but if you don't mind my saying, madam might want to pop to the beauty salon, first.'

'Bloody cheek!' I seethed. 'Madam has just spent three hours up in the beauty salon, actually!'

'Ah, but not in the depilatory section, I'll warrant,' he purred.

'Oh!' I clenched my arms to my side. 'Yes, right. Well, I'll see.'

Flushing but fuming I paid and stalked away. Actually I was a teeny bit grateful, too. God, imagine hailing Sebastian in the Wigmore Hall, looking like a Romanian shot putter? Flowing freely? I shuddered and dashed to Boots for a packet of Gillette, decorated a lavatory pan in the ladies, and then totally plucked, shaved, coiffured and painted – and somewhat stressed now, too – I hailed a taxi to take me to the other end of the Kings Road, where I was pretty sure the latest Hugh Grant film was showing, and where I was also pretty sure I could hole up for a couple of hours and pick my nails in private.

The first time I watched it I laughed, the second time I slept through it, and then when I awoke, sometime later, it was five thirty. I looked at my watch and blinked. Perfect. I'd had a nice relaxing snooze, felt totally refreshed, and now I had precisely half an hour in which to go back to Harvey Nichols, monopolise the ladies, put on my dress, fiddle with my fringe, apply the make-up, and dump my clothes and shopping bags in the boot of the car.

I arrived at the concert early. For some reason I'd imagined the Wigmore Hall to be somewhere arty, somewhere on the South Bank perhaps, or even in the Barbican, so when I hailed a cab, it was with a good half an hour to spare. I felt slightly foolish when I realised the venue was literally five minutes away in, funnily enough . . . Wigmore Street. Once outside I loitered nervously on the steps for a bit. There was no one else going in and I didn't want to be the first, so I pretended I was studying the programme which was stuck up in a glass case, like a restaurant menu, and which meant absolutely nothing to me, save for the fact that Sebastian's name was writ large at the top.

'*Night of the Spirits* by Sebastian Faulkner; performed by the London Sinfonietta.'

I swallowed. Quite something, really, one way and another, to have one's work performed here by the likes of them, surely? I suddenly wondered if a little black dress and a floppy fringe were quite the thing? I also wished to God I'd thought to ring Imo at work. How stupid of me! We could have gone together, met at the gallery, had a couple of drinks first perhaps. Still, people appeared to be arriving in dribs and drabs now, and even going inside, so I crept in behind a hugely sartorial group, pulling my dress down a bit at the back.

I bought a programme on the basis that I could at least put it across my knees to hide some thigh, and then went into the hall, wondering nervously if Sebastian would already be in the auditorium or perhaps backstage? I realised, with a little leap of pleasure, how excited I was about seeing him. All the ghastly horrors of yesterday and the equally ghastly horrors that would no doubt befall me tomorrow, fell away like a melting drift of snow, as I thought of his kind, sensitive face, relaxing into a smile of welcome as he spotted me. I glanced around. He didn't appear to be about just yet, though, so I found my seat and perched on the edge, peering at the now gathering throng and looking for Imo.

It soon became clear that this was a very sophisticated London audience: there were no waving programmes, no excited shouts of 'Co-ee! Over here!' as there had been at the more provincial Abbey; merely hushed, excited murmurings about the importance – musically speaking, darling – of this supremely momentous occasion. Highbrow to a man – and a woman, too – they were all very much in the Ursula Mitchell mould, until I realised that one of them actually *was* Ursula Mitchell, and that a few paces behind her was her daughter, Imo.

She was coming down the aisle behind a group of her mother's friends looking absolutely stunning in an ankle-length, blue slip of a dress, arms bare and golden, the dress, loose and fluted around her ankles. I instinctively opened my programme on my knees and wished I'd listened to my friend in Donna Karan.

I stood up. 'Imo!' I hissed, waving wildly and blessing my friend for his other tip, but she didn't hear me, and sailed on down the aisle, talking animatedly. I kept my eyes trained on the group, watching closely as they made their way to the very front. Then, seeing them cluster around some seats, murmuring excitedly and fanning themselves with programmes, I left my chair and hastened down.

Ursula was looking very much at home and holding forth in hushed tones to anyone who cared to listen about what a marvellous season the London Sinfonietta were having and what a tremendous violinist Stenbusky was and how lucky we'd been – *we'd been*, mind – to pinch him from the Birmingham Philharmonic, when, mid-stream, she saw me appear.

'Olivia!' She turned in surprise.

Imo swung around. 'Good heavens – Livvy! What on earth are you doing here? How lovely!'

'Molly and Hugh gave me their tickets,' I said with a grin, kissing them both. 'And I was in London anyway, so I thought – why not?'

'Why not indeed?' agreed Ursula, generously. 'And what fun! Tell me, is Johnny with you or is he meeting you from work? You can't *imagine* how delighted I was when Imogen told me you were back together again. That is *such* good news, my dear! Oh, Simon! Lovely to see you!' She turned as someone approached.

'Well no, it's not good news, actually,' I grimaced to Imo. 'You see, we're apart again now.'

'No!' Imo clutched my arm in horror. 'Oh God, I don't believe it! Don't tell me the bastard did it to you again?'

'Noo,' I said slowly, 'actually, Imo, I did it to the bastard this time.' I smiled wryly. 'I just realised how appallingly badly I'd been treated by him, you see. Oh, Imo, you were so right, right back in the very beginning when he'd first left me and you said I'd be mad to have him back!'

'I said that?' Her eyes widened.

'Yes, you did, and that was so incisive of you, but I just couldn't see it at the time! It was almost as if I had to have him back to realise it. It was like – like some sort of warped rite of passage – and I had to be the one finishing it too. In the end I realised – well – I just realised I didn't love him enough to swallow it all, I suppose.'

'Really?' Imo looked startled. Bewildered even. 'Gosh. B-but, Livvy, surely now that it's on your terms, now that you've got the upper hand – well, you can call the shots for a change, can't you? Be in the driving seat for once?'

'No,' I shook my head firmly, 'still wouldn't work, because you see I was in love with a dream. A fantasy Johnny, who just didn't exist. The *real* Johnny McFarllen was a weak, selfish, vain, manipulative man who – Oh, but don't get me on all that now, Imo,' I grinned. 'I'll tell you another time. I promise, there's loads, and when you've got at least six hours and an extremely large gin I'll fill you in on all the details, but what's more important now,' I lowered my voice excitedly, 'and what's *so* thrilling, actually, Imo, is that for the first time in years, I find myself seriously attracted to someone else. Someone who I think is fond of me, but who up to now – well, I've just been so blind to! I was so consumed by Johnny, you see, I couldn't even see this guy, not even when he was right in front of my nose!'

She gazed into my bright, excited eyes. 'Who?' Quietly.

I grinned. 'Sebastian.'

'Sebastian?'

'Yes, Sebastian Faulkner, the composer, silly, our man of the moment tonight! Oh, Imo, I *knew* he liked me and I was so stupid, I simply couldn't do anything about it until I'd got Johnny out of my –'

'Imogen –' Ursula suddenly leant between us and put a hand on her daughter's arm.

'So sorry to interrupt, Livvy, my dear, but I'd just love Imo to meet Simon Allsop, the impresario, and this is absolutely her last chance. Hector!' She called loudly to her husband. 'Hector, darling, introduce Imo to –' She pointed wildly to a man in a flamboyant red coat, then turned her daughter round and gave her a little push in their direction. Hector obediently came to collect her.

'Now.' Ursula turned back to me, smiling broadly. 'Olivia, did you say Sebastian, my dear?'

'Sorry?'

'When you were talking, just now to Imo. About someone you were fond of?'

'Oh! Oh yes, that's right!'

'Well, good heavens, I must warn you, I really must.' Her eyes widened.

'What?'

'Well, Imogen is seeing Sebastian.'

I stared. 'Imogen's . . . what?'

'She's seeing Sebastian. Walking out with him, as we used to rather coyly put it, and they've been together for some time now, quite some time, and terribly in love. They're off to Vienna tomorrow, in fact. Sebastian has a performance out there.' She looked anxious. 'I'm so sorry, Olivia. I'm really surprised you didn't know.'

'But . . . she was seeing Hugo!' I felt panic fly through every vein, strange flutterings besieged me. 'I-I thought it was Hugo she was so infatuated with, so besotted by and –'

'Oh, Hugo,' she interrupted impatiently. 'Heavens, for a bit, maybe, but he was far too puppydog-ish for her. Good Lord, he followed her everywhere, hung on her every word – much too needy for our Imo. No, no, Sebastian is altogether a different kettle of fish, very much his own man, far more cerebral and eminently more suitable for Imo.' She smiled, raised her eyebrows confidentially. 'D'you know, I think I can quite confidently say that This Is It, Olivia? Isn't that marvellous? Because I know that you and Molly – and, good heavens, even Hector and I at times – had almost given up on her, almost despaired of her ever finding the right man and settling down, but I honestly believe that this time, she's finally done it!'

I gazed into the confident, grey eyes beaming down at me. But what about me? I wanted to say. Surely I found him first?

'And you didn't really want him, did you, my dear?' she said softly, putting a hand on my arm as if reading my thoughts. 'You told him so, remember? Although actually, he was terribly embarrassed about that. Came round one afternoon and told us about it.'

'Wh-what d'you mean?'

'Well,' she gave a tinkly little laugh, 'between you and me, he wasn't really aware that there was anything to finish!'

I stared at her. It occurred to me that this was actually an incredibly bitchy remark. I straightened up.

'Well, Ursula, believe me, there was. We'd become very fond of each other. Maybe he was too upset to admit that.'

A spot of colour came into each of her high, pale cheeks. She glared at me.

'Olivia, I've known you for many years, since you were a little girl, in fact. I'd hate to see you make a fool of yourself.'

'I have no intention of doing that.'

'Good, because I feel I must warn you that this time you'd be out of your depth. This time you're in an entirely different league.'

'What d'you mean, *this time*?'

Her sharp grey eyes went cold. 'I mean this time, as opposed to last time. When you crept in and took Johnny right from under her nose.'

I stared at her, aghast. My mouth dropped. 'I did *not*!' I managed to gasp. 'God – how can you *say* that? Imogen finished with Johnny, she –'

'Oh, she cooled it with him, all right,' she said impatiently, 'but she hadn't actually *finished* with him, hadn't actually ended it, and that's the difference. No, no, she was testing him, Olivia. She wanted to marry Johnny, you see, and she was adamant about that – had been right from the very beginning – and we all knew that, the whole family knew, and frankly I'm surprised you didn't, or perhaps you chose not to, hmm?' She sighed. 'But she was so young, you see, still so very young.' She pursed her lips as I gazed, horrified at her. 'For a long time, too, I'd felt that Johnny had had the upper hand in the relationship, was a bit too . . . well, a bit too conceited, too big for his boots, so I concocted a little plan, a way to bring him down a peg or two. To test him out. Imogen was convinced he was the only one for her, but I wanted to see if Johnny was up to it, if he was up to marrying my precious daughter. I wanted to bring him to heel,' she breathed, 'to deserve her, to beg her to have him back!'

I stared at her, astounded. 'What – so you told her to cool it with him?' I gasped. 'To hardly even speak to him after Oliver's funeral, to never come home at weekends and – and to sleep with Paolo in Italy!'

Her face closed. 'Don't be so crude, Olivia. No, I merely suggested she play the fish a little, make him jealous, make him see that there were other men besides him who were attracted to her, desperate to take her out, see what his reaction would be. And he reacted pretty well, I must say. He even trekked all the way out to Italy to get her back, and I was impressed. I thought that with a little more of the same treatment she'd bring him quite conclusively to his knees, have him begging to marry her.' Her eyes hardened. 'But I hadn't reckoned on you, Olivia. Hadn't reckoned on your part in the tale. Because then you appeared on the scene, didn't you? You, with your green fingers and your broken home, wheedling your way into

Angie's garden with your secateurs and that wide-eyed, little-girl-lost routine of yours, winding yourself like bindweed around a broken-hearted Johnny.'

'Mrs Mitchell!' I gasped. 'You're rewriting history! He was devastated about Imo, sure, but he was equally adamant he wouldn't have her back, not after what she'd done!'

She smiled. 'Oh no. *You* persuaded him he was adamant he wouldn't have her back. All those cosy little lunches in the City while you did some two-bit secretarial course and while my talented daughter studied Botticelli in Florence, waiting for him to come to her.' She tilted her chin up at me. 'You played on a vulnerable young man, Olivia, a man whose girlfriend was conveniently studying abroad and whose father had just died. It was insidious, calculated, and very, very shrewd, I'll give you that.'

I gazed at her, aghast. My God. All these years she'd thought this of me, all these years she'd harboured this bitterness, this resentment, considered me the fly in the ointment. And Imo too? I swung round to find her, but couldn't see her. My heart lurched in horror. I also felt shocked into wondering – was this so? Was she right? But I'd asked Imo, I'd cleared it with her when Johnny and I had first –

'I *asked* Imo, Mrs Mitchell. I wrote to her in Florence, got a letter back saying –'

'Oh yes, and that was jolly clever of you too, wasn't it?' she sneered. 'Let's get it in writing. And what did you expect her to reply? Keep your thieving hands off my boyfriend? Over my dead body, you conniving bitch? What – dear, sweet-natured Imo? No, no, you knew darned well she'd give you the all-clear. You're a sharp little thing, Olivia, you always have been. You sneaked in and –'

'I did *not* sneak in,' I trembled. 'I was fully aware of how delicate the situation was and –'

'Not aware enough,' she snapped sharply. 'And actually, for all your sharpness, not smart enough to see what was *really* going on, which was that Johnny took you on the rebound because he couldn't have my daughter!' Her voice trembled. 'Christ, she even came back from Italy to be your bridesmaid. You made her do that, and I'll never forgive you for that because, God help me, I had to pick up the pieces the following day. The poor child nearly had a breakdown.'

I caught my breath in horror. Her face was pale now, taut with pent-up loathing. 'My precious girl,' she breathed, 'you did that to her. And she never found anyone else, never found anyone like Johnny.' She raised her chin high. 'But she has now, you see. She's all right now. She can be whole again – Sebastian's seen to that. And we're all so relieved, so thankful. They're in love, Olivia, very much in love, and I'm not going to ask you not to interfere, not going to ask you not to meddle, because this time, you can't. No one could possibly come between them now. Even if you tried, believe me, you'd be pissing in the wind.'

Something in the vulgarity of this expression, totally out of character, and the flash of steel in her grey eyes made me realise what Molly and I had always suspected. That Mrs Mitchell was a very, very tough cookie. I stared at her jutting jaw and her hawklike nose which seemed to be almost quivering with rage, just as Imogen came rushing up.

'Mummy! Are you all right? What's happened? You . . . you look so upset!'

Ursula raised a brave chin. 'I'm fine,' she whispered. 'I was just explaining something very fundamental to Olivia here. Frankly, I'm surprised she didn't know before. Any of it.'

She held my eyes a moment longer, then turned and walked away.

The orchestra were ready on the stage now, tuning up, violinists brandishing their bows, anticipating the appearance of their conductor. Imo stared after Ursula, then shot me a confused, anxious glance, before hastening to her mother. I watched them go, transfixed, literally welded to the spot by the ferocity of her words. A moment later, I saw Sebastian materialise from a side door. His face wore a defended, public look as he glanced about at the audience. Then, seeing Imo at the front, quickly walked across to join her as she stood, comforting her mother. I watched as he lightly touched Imo's back and kissed her cheek.

Ursula's back was still to me, but I saw her delve into her bag for a hanky and pat her eyes, as Imo reached anxiously across to clutch her hand. What is it, what's wrong? I saw her ask. Ursula began to speak but the strings were growing louder and I couldn't hear what she was saying, could only watch Sebastian's face grow darker, more concerned, more – angry. Imo's eyes widened, her jaw dropped, then as Ursula dabbed with her hanky once more, they both turned and stared in my direction, turning shocked, horrified gazes on me. There was a brief moment when we all locked eyes. Then they turned away, back to Ursula. I saw Sebastian put a hand under her elbow for support, and as she gravely nodded to them both that she was fine, fine now, they helped her into her seat.

The orchestra had gone very quiet and the audience were hushed with anticipation, with only the odd muffled cough punctuating the silence. Imo sat down next to her mother with Sebastian beside her. Realising suddenly that I was the only person in the hall left standing, I turned and made my way shakily back to my place at the rear of the auditorium. A moment later, Hugo Simmonds took the podium to an enormous roar from the crowd. I sat, dazed and bewildered, watching blankly as he acknowledged the audience, then turning his back on them, he raised his arms, brought them down with a flourish, and with a blast of trumpets and horns, the music began. I looked down and realised my programme was shaking on my knees. I must have listened to three, maybe four bars of the piece, before getting up, gathering my bag and my programme, and leaving the hall.

Chapter Twenty-Eight

I don't remember hailing a taxi, sitting shocked and white-faced as I no doubt did in the back, gazing blankly at the thronging London streets as they swept by, or even arriving at the car park, and somehow, dazedly, finding my car, but I suppose I must have done that too. I do remember the drive home, though. I remember how dry my throat felt, how knotted my chest was, and how I had to keep a really firm grip on the wheel to stop my hands from shaking and the car from veering into another lane. But if my body was having problems reacting properly, my mind was compensating by going into overdrive. Imo and Sebastian – of course. God, what a fool I'd been! It was him she'd been angling for all along, not Hugo. Cosy dinner parties at her parents' house, all no doubt arranged by her Svengali, Ursula, and then yesterday – why, I even *saw* Imo, alone, going into his house. Why hadn't I clicked? Even Hugh had hinted at it now I came to think of it, and of course, she'd been so thrilled when Johnny and I got back together, coming round with flowers, hugging us, tears of relief in her eyes: 'Oh God, guys, this is what we've all been hoping for!' Well, of course it was, of course!

I buzzed down the window and gulped in some air. So – how long had it been going on? While he'd been seeing me? If indeed he *had* been seeing me, I thought with a jolt, because actually, in *his* eyes he probably hadn't, which would explain his reluctance to comply when I offered him my body on a plate after Molly and Hugh's barbecue, and his bemused expression when I popped round later to inform him that our tempestuous affair was over. No wonder he'd looked surprised. No wonder he hadn't broken down in floods of tears. As far as he was concerned I was Mrs Friendly Neighbour with whom he had the occasional matey drink when he wasn't canoodling with his main squeeze, Imogen Mitchell! I thought of Imo's beautiful, shining face tilted up to his and a hot flush washed over me. 'Don't make a fool of yourself,' Ursula had said. Well, it was too late for that. I'd done that already. In fact, it occurred to me I'd been doing it for years. About thirteen, to be precise.

Yes, thirteen years ago, I thought with a wave of misery, when Imo had apparently decided she wanted to marry Johnny, but unlike me, had thought through the implications, had known intuitively what she was taking on. She knew full well she had to bring a man like Johnny to his knees, drag him out to Italy, shove Paolo in his face, humiliate him, have him storm off in high dudgeon, but all the while be waiting, waiting for his anger to cool, for his unquestionable passion to surface, for him to beg her, on bended knee, to come back, at which point she'd have tossed her blonde head, slipped on her Gucci mules and returned to have him right where she wanted him. Except that she hadn't reckoned on me, creeping stealthily in, like some fat, spotty teenager who'd never been allowed to join in the games, and who'd spotted a gap and gone for it. Oh yes, in I'd nipped, always on the sidelines, always marginal, but, boy, was I seizing my chance now – but only, mind, only because Johnny had no one else to play with.

I gritted my teeth and breathed hard. And I'd never been enough for him, never – I saw that now. He'd always wanted more, needed more, and so he'd turned to Nina. It wouldn't have happened if he'd married Imo – she was more than enough for any man – and now, because of me, because of my pathetic eagerness to have him at any cost, there was carnage all around. Broken marriages, mistresses, thwarted love affairs and at the heart of it all, a small, fatherless, disabled boy. My heart lurched. My fault. I shot my chin up and swallowed desperately, but it was no good, tears were falling relentlessly, sliding silently down my cheeks as chaos howled inside me. It was all of my making.

And all that time, I thought wretchedly, wiping my face with the back of my hand, all these years Imo must have secretly hated me. Must have swallowed it bravely, but how her guts must have twisted every time she looked at me, every time she saw Johnny and me together, came to our home, sat at our table. Always in her mind – that should have been me! And I never *knew*!

I pulled off the motorway with an astonishing lack of care, horns blaring in my wake, and sped blindly away into more traffic. The sky was darkening overhead and a rainstorm threatened. At length it broke, and I drove the rest of the way in a torrential downpour, concentrating hard on the frantic dance of the windscreen wipers, grateful for their distraction.

When I finally pulled up in my drive I turned off the engine and sat for a moment. The rain had abated to a dismal drizzle and I leant forward and rested my head on the wheel. My insides were twisting themselves into a fierce ball of anguish, but I knew too that monthly abdominal cramps were also to blame. How convenient of my reproductive system to make its presence felt at this particular moment. Thank you, God. I dragged my head wearily from the wheel, massaged my tummy and leant back, reliving for a ghastly moment Sebastian's face as he'd turned to look at me. Shock and disbelief seemed to be the overriding emotion in those dark eyes. So what exactly had Ursula said? That I was intent on the same, destructive course of action that I'd perfected thirteen years ago? That I was determined to muscle my way into his life and crowbar her precious daughter out, at all costs? I rested my head back wearily on the head-rest, and it was at that moment that I realised I wasn't alone.

Just round the corner of the house, in the little car port that no one ever used, was a car I didn't recognise. It was blue, an Escort, I think, and it occurred to me that I didn't know anyone who drove a car as middle-aged as that. Its position in the car port rather than dumped in the middle of the drive gave it an alarming gravitas too, as if it had been carefully positioned, and as if its owner knew they may have to wait some time. Why yes, of course, I realised with a start, it belonged to the protagonists in the *other* disastrous chapter in my life, the chapter which, despite my desperate efforts to keep it under wraps, had clearly been unfolding relentlessly in my absence. The jolly old police. Oh yes, the boys in blue, who no doubt had been told I was out, but armed with a search warrant and an unending ability to sit soft and drink copious cups of tea, had camped out patiently in my sitting room, awaiting my return. Oh good. More music to face, and why not? Might as well get it all over in one day; might as well face a symphony as a string quartet.

I got out and slammed the door hard, rehearsing, slightly defiantly in my head – why yes, officer, I'm well aware that one of my workforce recently knocked off his wife, but seeing as it was a complete and utter accident I decided to give him a day's grace to get away. You see I –

'*Ahhh!*'

I leapt inches in the air as someone stepped out of the shadow of the hedge and caught my arm from behind. Terrified, I swung round.

'Lance!'

'Shhhh!' He put his hand gently over my mouth, glancing quickly about to check I hadn't been heard.

Wide-eyed I stared at him, then nodded to let him know I wasn't going to shriek again. Slowly, he took his hand away.

'What's going on?' I gasped, when I'd regained the use of my vocal cords. 'What's happened?'

'I'm waiting for Spiro,' he whispered. 'The police should be back with him any minute. I don't want them to know I'm still here.'

'Spiro?'

'Yes, poor bastard, he's down at the station. They took him there this morning. He's been there all day, being questioned.'

'Oh God! And you too?'

'Most of the day, but they let me out on bail a couple of hours ago.'

'On bail!' I stared. His face was very pale under his tan.

'But, Lance, you weren't even there when Vi died! You were here with me that weekend. You haven't done anything!'

'Quite, but in the absence of Dad or Alf, Spiro and I are all they've got to go on. You were right to go to London, Livvy.'

'Did they want to speak to me?' I whispered fearfully.

'Yes, but only as a matter of course. Just as a formality, so they said, and certainly not as desperately as they wanted to speak to us,' he added drily.

'But,' I glanced back at the house, confused, 'why is Spiro down there? I mean, if they're up here –'

'Who?'

I jerked my head. 'Isn't that their car?'

He stared, then clicked. 'Oh no, that's your mother-in-law. I let her in. She wanted to wait for you. She's inside.'

'My –'

'Livvy? Is that you, darling?'

The front door opened and Angie stood there framed, peering out into what was now just a light drizzle, shading her eyes in the gathering gloom.

'Good God, does *she* know anything about all this?' I hissed, appalled.

'Of course not,' he hissed back. 'What d'you take me for? No, by all accounts she just came round to discuss the state of your marriage.'

'Oh terrific,' I groaned.

'Livvy, is that you?' she called again.

'Go on.' Lance gave me a little shove. 'Go in and act naturally, for heaven's sake. I'll let you know when Spiro gets back.'

He slunk back to his position behind the hedge, pulling up the collar of his leather jacket and lighting a cigarette, shading the match with his hands and looking for all the world like Orson Welles in *The Third Man*. I raked a despairing hand through my wet hair. God, Angie. She was all I needed right now, but then again I reasoned wearily, she was, admittedly, somewhat preferable to the police. I trudged dismally up the path and kissed her damply on the doorstep.

'Angie, I didn't recognise your car.'

'It's a hire car, darling. Remember I pranged the last one? And the bloody door leaks like a sieve so I have to put it under some shelter when I park. Good gracious, you look all in! Come in and I'll make you a stiff gin and tonic. Are you feeling all right?'

'Period pains,' I said weakly, and not untruthfully. 'But I'll take you up on that gin,' I said following her in and collapsing into the nearest armchair. 'It's the best offer I've had all day.'

She bustled off to the kitchen and I rested my head back and gazed blankly at the ceiling. So, Spiro was, at this very moment, being grilled rotten in some cold grey interview room, was he? Poor boy. Heavens, he'd be terrified, and probably in floods too, wringing torrents out of his hat. I wondered when they'd be back for me. I shut my eyes and rubbed my forehead wearily. I could hear Angie rummaging about in the kitchen, no doubt looking for ice and lemon, which could be a very fruitless search in this house. How long had she been here, I wondered? And what was so important that she had to come over, rather than telephone? And then wait? I twisted uncomfortably in my chair, rubbing my aching tummy, as Angie reappeared with two large gins, predictably, *sans* ice. She handed me one and I took a large gulp as she settled herself opposite. She was looking lovely, as usual, in a pale suede jacket and biscuit skirt which went beautifully with her copper hair, but her face wore an anxious look. She went to take a sip of her drink, then thinking better of it, put it aside and leant forward urgently.

'Livvy, I've got to talk to you.'

'So I gather,' I murmured. I took another gulp. God, it was strong.

She leant back for a second and massaged the corners of her mouth with thumb and forefinger, gazing at a spot somewhere above my head as if for inspiration. Then her eyes came back to me. They were wide and frank.

'Livvy darling, I know what you're up to.'

'Oh?' I blinked. Crikey, I wish I did.

'With Johnny. I know the game you're playing.'

'I'm not playing any game.'

'Yes you are, and you've played it brilliantly, quite brilliantly. But listen, darling – he's desperate. You've brought him comprehensively to heel now, brought him right back into line, so don't make him suffer any more, eh? He so badly needs to come home.'

'Needs?' I muttered.

'Wants,' she corrected quickly.

I frowned. 'So – he's with you?'

'Of course he's with me, where did you think he'd be? He's been with me since you threw him out!'

'Well, funnily enough, Angie,' I said slowly, 'I had a sneaking suspicion he might be with another woman. The woman who, actually, was the initial *cause* of my throwing him out.'

'Oh her,' she said dismissively. 'No, no, that's all finished. He's over her now, and that's all thanks to you, my dear. Golly, you've made him sit up. By showing him the door, just when he thought he'd got his feet under the table again and all was forgiven – oh, that was inspired, Livvy, and I told him so too. Told him he jolly well deserved all he got from you, and that it was up to him to win *you* back now. You've really brought him to his senses, my love, and it was absolutely what he needed – a good kick up the chauvinistic pants. But . . . I'm worried now.' Her well-preserved forehead puckered with anxiety and she clasped her hands tight. 'I'm worried that if you leave him in the wilderness any longer your plan might backfire, that he may get *used* to being out there on his own, find some other form of distraction. Now's the time, Livvy,' she said urgently. 'He's learnt his lesson, bring him in from the cold. He'd crawl back now if you said the word, and with everything out of his system! You've won hands down, darling, but – just be careful. A man like Johnny won't stay on hold for ever.'

I swirled my drink thoughtfully in my glass. Frowned into it. 'But . . . I just told you, Angie. It's not a game. I don't want him back. Ever.'

I looked up and met her hazel eyes. Saw a wave of hurt pass over them. I steeled myself.

'D'you have any idea what he's done?'

She nodded quickly, swept her hair back nervously. 'I – I know how long it went on for.'

'And?'

'And – I know about the child,' she admitted quickly.

'And *you'd* forgive him?'

'Yes,' she nodded, before her eyes darted out of the window. 'Yes, I know I'd find it in my heart.'

'Would you? Really? So – where d'you draw the line then, Angie? What is forgivable and what's unforgivable?'

She didn't answer. Glanced down at her hands. I put my drink aside.

'Come on, Angie,' I urged, 'let's see. What exactly would you forgive? How about – a quick snog on the dance floor with a girl at a party? Well, one would be furious, naturally, but it's hardly grounds for divorce, is it? Well, what about a quick one-night stand then? In a hotel? Or a brief affair? Ghastly, of course, humiliating in the extreme, terribly degrading and the marriage would never be quite the same, et cetera, et cetera, but still, yes, one probably *would* forgive, wouldn't one? Because frankly, what's the alternative? A bleak, single life and a solitary, uphill struggle to bring up one's child?' I shrugged. 'And so one staggers on, bravely, as I staggered on, and I forgave him all that, Angie. But what about a long, long, love affair? A year? Two years? And what if there's a child?'

Angie continued to inspect her nails. 'I still think,' she murmured levelly, 'the home, the breaking up of the family –'

'OK, so what about ten years of infidelity then? Twenty, no – thirty? And what about –' I cast about wildly – 'what about if you knew, for instance, that the moment your betrothed had shaken the confetti from his hair, the moment his honeymoon tan had begun to fade, he was off, dropping his trousers at every conceivable opportunity,

and spreading himself about as thinly as possible? With –
ooh, let's see now – half a dozen bastard children knocking
about the place?' She stayed silent. 'Of course not!' I
exclaimed. 'Of course one wouldn't forgive that, but
don't you see, Angie, it's all subjective. It all comes down
to what one's prepared to stomach, and call me old-
fashioned, but knowing what I know now, I'd advise any
woman to gag after that first snog at a party!' I angrily
knocked back a swig of gin.

'No, not old-fashioned,' she said slowly, her hazel eyes
coming up to meet mine. 'Very modern. You girls want
everything now, don't you?'

'Well, if fidelity's having everything –' I exploded.

'Oh, for God's sake, Livvy, grow up!' she snapped.
'Women have put up with this for centuries! Johnny's not
exactly the first oversexed man who went off to relieve
himself elsewhere!'

There was a pause. I stared into her hazel eyes. Slowly
it dawned. 'You mean . . . ?'

'Oh yes.' She smiled thinly. 'Yes, for years. Scarcely had
Oliver's feet hit the tarmac at Heathrow airport after our
honeymoon in India – you see, I fit very neatly into that
little analogy of yours – than the extracurricular activity
started. Complete with bastard children too. Clearly in
your book I shouldn't have stomached it.'

I stared, incredulous. 'But – you and Oliver. You were
so happy!'

'Exactly.'

'But –'

'Happiness doesn't necessarily conform to the storybooks, Olivia,' she said impatiently. 'We *were* happy, genuinely happy, but we'd ironed out our own *modus vivendi*, not one decreed to us, laid down by society.'

'But didn't you care? About the affairs?'

'Of course! Desperately, at first, of course I did. And he didn't know I knew, but privately I cried myself silly over them, particularly as a young bride. I thought it was the end of us.'

'So why didn't you confront him!'

'Because it would have been counterproductive,' she said patiently. 'I loved him, you see, and I didn't want to leave him. Telling him would have forced my hand, forced me to make an issue of it, make a decision. And in time, I also began to realise that actually, his affairs had no bearing on me, were no reflection on our marriage at all. He loved me, you see, adored me, probably even more so at the height of each adulterous liaison than at any other time. Physically, too, that side of our marriage never died. If anything it just got stronger.'

'So – then why did he need them? Why did he need those women!'

She shrugged. 'Different, I suppose, so therefore exciting. Different women – different sort of sex too, if you know what I mean.' She eyed me beadily.

I blinked. 'No, I –'

'Well, I do,' she interrupted firmly. 'I know. And I tried it once, let me tell you, tried to be novel and imaginative and outrageous, tried to give him the sort of dirty sex he sought elsewhere, and he was appalled. I was his wife, you see, his shining madonna, mother of his children; he didn't expect that from me.' She passed her hand wearily through her hair. 'Oh, I don't know, Olivia. Why have men always gone to brothels?'

'But how could he face you? Wasn't he mortified? Ashamed?'

'Oh, totally, but that was his problem, not mine. I could rise above it all, look after the children, the house, the garden, and all the time he walked around tormented. He was riddled with guilt.'

'Jesus, I'm not surprised! But you're not saying you liked that? That you enjoyed occupying the high moral ground? You surely would have preferred it otherwise?'

'Of course I would, but that wasn't my particular marriage bed. Mine was the one I've just described, and I had to lie in it or go elsewhere. Every marriage is different, Livvy.'

'But it's outrageous that you should have been forced to compromise like that!'

She shook her head. 'I wasn't forced. I loved him, and he loved me. Really, like we'd never loved before. You saw how he was with me, he adored me, worshipped me, and that's why I stayed.'

'But . . . were there always other women?'

'Oh no, not necessarily, but I always knew when one was about, because he prayed incessantly. He was deeply religious, as you know, but the minute he was involved with someone else, there he'd be, kneeling at the foot of the bed, rosary beads winging frantically through his fingers, muttering endless Hail Marys, eyes shut, mouth taut with concentration, and then off he'd rush to confession the next day to absolve himself.' She smiled wryly. 'And maybe you're right. Maybe I did take some perverse kind of pleasure from it as I sat up in bed reading Barbara Pym, with half an eye on my husband kneeling at the foot of the bed trying to save his soul. I certainly felt in a stronger position than he was. He was in torment.'

She gazed up at the spot above my head and I realised her eyes were filling up.

'And . . . is that why . . . ?' I asked softly.

She swallowed. Shook her head. 'No. Well, yes. Yes and no, really. It wasn't *why* he did it, but shooting himself was a direct result of his infidelity. There was a baby, you see.'

'Oh!'

'Only one. Oliver prided himself on being so bloody careful, and that, to him, would be the ultimate sin, to bring an unwanted child, born out of holy wedlock, into the world. When I found out that this particular woman was pregnant, suddenly it all made sense. I realised why Oliver had only been sleeping for two hours a night recently, why he was walking endlessly round his paddocks in the early hours, why I'd find him weeping on the bathroom floor, why, on one occasion, he even tried to tell me, grabbing me round the knees as I found him sobbing, hunched by the bath.' Her face buckled briefly. 'Perhaps I should have let him. Perhaps that was cowardly of me, perhaps I could have saved him, but I didn't want to know. I shook him off. I couldn't, you see. Couldn't let him know I knew his secret. And I knew he wouldn't just tell me about this one woman, I knew the whole lot would come spewing out. And it would change the entire fabric of our marriage. From being a shining innocent, serene and above it all as he believed, I'd suddenly become a downtrodden doormat who knew the whole grimy truth and had to put up with her lot. Put up, or get out.' She took a large swig of gin; stared into space.

'So,' I cleared my throat, 'so when the child was born, is that what pushed him over the edge?'

'No. When the child was born,' she said carefully, 'Oliver was all right. Oh sure, for a day or two he was desperately distracted, but then, he began to calm down. It was as if the inevitable had finally happened and the pressure was off. He didn't know I knew, of course, but I watched him carefully as the days went by, very carefully, and I was relieved. It seemed to me that we could ride this storm, as we'd ridden all the others. But then the terrible news came. The news that all was not well. That the baby was severely disabled. Blind as well as crippled. That evening Oliver went out into the field and blew his brains out. He blamed himself, you see, thought that God's finger was pointing right at him, that his sins had been singled out for retribution, and been manifested in his son. My God, you've gone so pale, Livvy. I've shocked you.'

I was on my feet now. 'No, no . . .' I crossed to the window, my hand clutching the sill, trembling. Disabled. My God. Like Johnny's child. I swallowed.

'Have – have you seen Johnny's baby?' I whispered, staring at the wet lawn.

'Of course not, and neither shall I,' she said staunchly.

'And –' I cleared my throat – 'and, Angie, does Johnny know all this? About his father? About how the baby was?' I turned.

She shook her head. 'No one knows. I prided myself on that, although . . .' she hesitated, 'recently I've wondered if I shouldn't tell Johnny. Let him know that his father wasn't all he was cracked up to be, all that Johnny thought he was. Part of Johnny's problem, I've always believed, was living up to Oliver. He idealised him and thought he himself never quite came up to the mark.'

I remembered how Johnny had stopped going to church when his own affair had been going on, wouldn't accompany me and Claudia, how he hadn't used religion to absolve himself, and how he had at least tried to look after the child when it was ill, and hadn't blown his brains out.

'Knowing what I now know about Oliver,' I said slowly, 'I don't think Johnny's got anything to worry about. He more than surpasses Oliver's mark.' Suddenly Oliver's words came back to me, that night, that last party at the McFarllens', Tara's birthday party, as he and I stood by the pool, watching Johnny and his sisters swim. 'Perfect, aren't they?' he'd said. I shivered. Just before he'd found out, no doubt. Before he'd discovered the condition of his illegitimate son. I cleared my throat. 'And I wouldn't tell Johnny about his father either, Angie, wouldn't disillusion him. To him, Oliver was a god. Let him at least hang on to that memory unscathed.'

If anything could completely destroy Johnny, I thought, this surely would. Like dysfunctional father, like dysfunctional son. And I didn't hate him enough to want him to know himself and his father for what they really were.

We were silent for a while, Angie and I. I thought of little Peter and his struggle through life. Perhaps Johnny would go back to them? How odd that I didn't care; quite wished he would.

'What happened to the child?' I asked suddenly, breaking the silence.

Angie was staring out of the window, blankly. 'Hmm?' She came back to me.

'Oliver's child, what became of him?'

'Oh, he lived, but other than that, I don't know. His mother was one of the few women I ever actually met though, although Oliver didn't know it.'

'She was a friend?'

'No no, not a friend.' She gave a wry smile. 'Oliver was not susceptible to our own class. Only the lower orders brought out the beast in him. No, her husband was a mechanic, he mended Oliver's cars. They had a vintage car place in Finchley, and I had to take one of Oliver's Lagondas in for him once. I saw her there.' She frowned. 'Livvy, what is it?'

I'd crossed to the French windows, shot back the bolts and flung them wide despite the rain. I stood there, letting the cool breeze gust into my face, blowing back my hair. 'Nothing.' I shook my head. 'Nothing, Angie.'

Oh God. Oh *God*. I remembered the faded blonde prettiness of Nina's mother. The kindly, no doubt unsuspecting father who'd believed he'd fathered the crippled, unseeing lad whose chair I'd seen. Nina's brother. Martin. Oliver's child. Tummy churning and feeling quite faint now, I gulped down great gusts of air. Angie was behind me, her hand on my shoulder.

'What is it, darling, what's wrong?'

'Nothing,' I murmured, 'nothing at all. It's all in the past.'

And if it remained Angie's intention to have nothing to

do with Johnny's child, then that's where it would stay, I thought as I shut the doors again and bolted them. She'd never know, and let it remain that way. Let it all stay buried under a mountain of years; years of rich, privileged people playing carelessly with other, less privileged people's lives. Let the little family of the 'lower orders' beside the garage in Finchley, who now had two disabled children to their name, just get on with it, just cope, whilst those who'd created the carnage, those carefree, rich, amorous, glamorous men like Oliver and Johnny, who lay either dead and buried, unable to bear it, or at home with Mummy, unable to bear it, absconded themselves. Whilst Nina and her mother had no choice but to soldier on. Day after exhausting day, bearing the horror and the brunt of living with disability. Of coping with a sick child.

At length, I found my voice. 'Angie, does Johnny know you're here?'

She hesitated. 'Of course not, darling.'

I turned. 'He does. He sent you.'

'N-no, no really, I wanted to come,' she faltered. 'I –'

'It's all right, Angie,' I interrupted wearily. 'I have no intention of shooting the messenger, and actually, it makes more sense to talk through you, because the way I'm feeling at the moment, I'm not sure I could look at him anyway, let alone speak to him.' I folded my arms. 'Please tell him from me, Angie, that I'll be serving him with divorce papers just as soon as I've contacted my solicitor. Tell him that access to Claudia will of course be amicably and cordially arranged, and that I also intend to sell the house and move further away into the country. You can also tell him that –'

'Olivia, you don't mean this!' Angie was on her feet, agitated and pink, her drink spilling over her skirt. 'You're upset, I've upset you with all this talk of Oliver! Think it over, please. You'll regret acting hastily, I swear it! This is *Johnny* we're talking about, not some nobody you can cast aside like yesterday's paper! He's worth more than that, he's – Oh!'

To my everlasting relief – because I truly loved Angie and didn't want to tell her exactly how much her son was worth – at that moment there was a loud bang, as the front door flew open on its hinges. A great gust of wind billowed through the house, and then a moment later, two bodies lurched through, like a couple of desperate souls reaching their journey's end. Staggering down the hallway came Lance, looking wet and bedraggled, and supporting someone I almost didn't recognise. With his black hair mussed all over his face, eyes wild and staring, one arm slung around Lance's shoulder and dragging his feet like a dead man – was Spiro.

Chapter Twenty-Nine

'Spiro!' I ran to them. 'Oh God, Spiro, are you all right? Lance, what did they *do* to him!'

Lance, panting, dragged Spiro to the nearest chair and deposited him heavily, whereupon Spiro, with a great moan of misery, doubled up, put his head in his hands and wept. Angie was on her feet, beside herself with consternation.

'Good heavens, what on earth's happened to the poor boy? Livvy, what's wrong with him!' She wrung her hands.

'Nothing, he's fine,' said Lance shortly. 'He's just upset, that's all.'

'Lance is right,' I said quickly as Lance shot me a meaningful glance and jerked his head towards the door. I picked up Angie's handbag and took her by the arm, trying to propel her doorwards. 'He's absolutely fine, Angie,' I said firmly, 'really he is, but sadly – well, sadly he's had some bad news. From home.'

Angie wasn't going anywhere, though. She stood rooted to the spot at this, appalled. 'Oh Lord,' she clutched my arm. 'Has someone died?' she whispered.

Lance flinched at the mention of death. 'No,' he hissed roughly, 'no one's bloody died. Now listen, why don't you just mind your own bloody –'

'It's the goats,' I breathed quickly, realising as soon as

I'd said it I'd just picked the first Greek thing I could think of. It could have been yoghurt. Or dancing.

'Goats?'

'Yes, they've got some – terrible disease. Scurvy, or something ghastly. Wiped out the whole herd.'

'Oh heavens, how awful,' she breathed, 'and with it his livelihood, I suppose?'

'Exactly,' I agreed soberly as, to my alarm, Spiro looked up in horror.

'My . . . goats?' he croaked, red-eyed.

'Oh, you poor boy,' said Angie, touching his arm. 'But, Livvy, have they really *all* gone?'

'No, no, there's one or two left,' I said wildly, 'now come *on*, Angie.'

'Only . . . one or two?' Spiro gasped, horrified, getting slowly to his feet.

I groaned. Oh God, why hadn't I gone for yoghurt? 'Yes, but the best ones, Spiro,' I soothed, 'the absolute pick of the bunch. Now come on, Angie. You really don't want to get involved in –'

'Because, darling, if there *are* some left, there's the most marvellous vet in Athens,' she insisted. 'Theodore Popolopolus or somebody – Johnny will remember. Oliver flew him over when one of his horses had a rare blood disorder – said he can cure anything. Why don't I –'

'Angie, *please*,' I insisted, shoving her forcefully out of the front door now. 'Heavens, the poor boy's got enough on his plate without forking out for horrendous vet bills. Now come along!'

As I hustled her out and down the drive I had one ear on Lance behind me, listening as he placated a distraught

Spiro, putting him straight on the goat front if nothing else.

Angie shook her head sadly, groping about in her bag for her keys. 'That poor boy,' she sighed, shaking her head and suddenly looking very old, her forehead fretted with fine lines. 'There just seems to be so much sadness about at the moment, doesn't there?' She hesitated. Glanced up hopefully. 'Will I – will I say anything else to Johnny? Give him a few words?'

'Yes,' I said grimly, 'you can give him a few words. Give him –' I stopped, ashamed, as her eyes grew round and fearful. 'Just – give him my best.' I finished lamely.

She nodded, and I saw her eyes fill. 'And if you change your mind?'

'He'll be the first to know. But I won't, Angie, believe me, I won't.'

She swallowed. 'I know. And you know, Livvy, sad as I am about this whole wretched situation, about losing you, I admire you for what you've done. Truly I do. I couldn't have done it.' We regarded each other for a long moment.

'You haven't lost me,' I whispered.

She gave a grateful smile, nodded again, but tears were imminent now, so she didn't speak. Instead she patted my arm, turned, and got in the car. I watched as she reversed out of the car port, turned out of the gateway, and waved as she purred off slowly down the road. Then I stood for a moment, in the empty drive, remembering. Remembering happier times, long ago, when we'd gardened together; roared with laughter as we'd battled against elder and thistles, up to our knees in brambles and –

'LIVVY – GET IN HERE!' Lance's voice came

roaring through my memories, and abruptly I came to. Oh Christ – Spiro!

My hand went to my mouth and I dashed back into the house. Slamming the door behind me, I hurtled to the sitting room where I found Spiro, hunched up in my yellow Colefax armchair, leaning forward now, and being violently sick into a potted plant. Lance looked up grimly and handed it to me.

'Yours, I believe.'

'Oh, help – hang on. I'll get him some water.' I took the pot, hustled it to the loo, couldn't face chucking it in, so just shut the door on it, then, retching violently at the terrible smell, ran back via the kitchen to get a glass of water. As I flew back in, Spiro reached out and took it with a shaky hand. I dropped to my knees beside him and took his hand, appalled.

'Spiro, what on earth *happened* to you in there!' I gasped. 'Was it really as ghastly as all that? God, what did they *do* to you?'

'They didn't *do* anything to him,' said Lance drily, lighting a cigarette and perching on the arm of the chair. 'This isn't Occupied France, you know, Livvy; we're not living with the Gestapo. They didn't pull his fingernails out or anything beastly, they just questioned him, that's all, frightened the life out of him, I expect. I don't know what they said to him actually, he hasn't uttered a word yet.'

I squeezed Spiro's hand. 'Spiro, it's me, Livvy.' He was staring at the carpet between his feet, shaking his woolly head and moaning.

'Come on, Spiro, you can tell me, can't you? You can tell Livvy? What is it? What happened?'

Suddenly he sat bolt upright, his dark eyes wide and strange. His head turned slowly – and his gaze fell on Lance.

'I so sorry!' he blurted out, staring at him.

Lance frowned, shook his head. 'Why, Spiro? Why are you sorry?'

'Because – because they go on and on, questions, questions, and I know nothing of what they speak, but then – then I theenk of something, and –' He broke off, gave a strangled sob, hid his face in his hat.

'What?' Lance insisted. 'What, Spiro?'

Spiro lowered his hat. 'I theenk I let the rabbit out of the bag!'

'Cat.'

'*Ti?*'

'Never mind. What rabbit, Spiro, what did you say?'

He glanced about furtively, as if to check we were alone, then beckoned for us to lean in. Lance and I both bent our heads.

'They want the body!' he hissed.

I jumped back. 'The body!' I yelped.

'I know,' said Lance calmly, 'that's what they kept asking me. Where was she, where was she buried, what have they done with Vi? But we don't know that, do we, Spiro? I don't, so you certainly don't.'

'No, I don't, but they keep saying – theenk, Spiro, where could she be? Where you theenk they could have put her? What were Mac and Alf doing at the time, in those few days of her death?'

'Well, they were working here,' I said staunchly, 'that's what!'

A terrible silence fell.

'Exactly,' said Lance, at length, quietly. 'They were working here.'

Spiro turned to me and nodded, wide eyes full of portent.

I stared at him. 'Shit!' I squeaked suddenly, leaping to my feet.

'And the bald man, he keep saying – where you bury her, Spiro? Where you put her? And I say – I know nothing! And then he say – so if you know nothing, perhaps you were not there to see? And I say – what you mean? And he say – well, did they perhaps get you out of the way, while they got rid of her? And I say – no! No, I work there every day, like a dog, that not possible, I see everything, *everything* that go on, and she not there!'

'Quite right!' I squealed.

'But he so persistent, Meesis McFarllen, he go on and on, and he say *th-e-e-nk*, Spiro, *th-e-e-nk*, and he tap his bald head, like this, like an egg.' Spiro broke off to tap his temple. 'Was there not a day when you go out on an errand? When your services not required at the house? When you sent elsewheres? And I theenk, and slowly, *very* slowly, I say, yes, yes there *was* such a day, because I remember Lance, that day when we have so much to do, so very busy, and we both surprised, because Mac – he send us to builders' merchant for bricks, remember?'

'I remember.'

'Together, both of us, so unusual, both in truck. And when we get there they say – oh no, so sorry, we know nothing of brick order, and we ring Mac and he say – oh, so sorry, I mean *timber* merchant. So we go there, and it take hours in traffic, and when we get there, *they* know nothing either. So we ring Mac again, and he say – oh, no order? Oh deary me, well, get us some bits of four-by-two then – and so we come back with these teeny tiny bits of wood, and it feel *so* much like a wild-boar chase – remember, Lance?'

Lance had gone very pale. 'I remember.'

'And I don't theenk anything about it at the time, I just theenk, oh bleeding heck, with all the work we got to do back there at the house, that *beeg*, heavy job, and Mac – he send us for pieces of wood! Remember, Lance? Remember what Mac and Alf have to do all alone here on that day?'

'I do.' Softly.

'And I hadn't theenk of it before, but the police, they griddle me, griddle me something rotten, and I *say* it – I say it without even theenking and –'

'What!' I gasped. 'What did you say? What job were Alf and Mac doing?'

Spiro went quiet. Glanced down at his hands.

'It's all right, Spiro,' said Lance softly. 'I thought of it too. Not before, but when they were questioning me, down at the station. It suddenly occurred to me, too. I could just as easily have said it.'

'WHAT!' I shrieked. 'What could you just as easily have said? Tell me, you bastards, or I'll – Christ!'

I broke off as a terrible banging came on the door. We all swung around – then stared back at each other. I froze. Only one man knocked on my front door like that. Only one, very small man, with one very bald head, who clearly made up for his lack of height and hair by announcing himself in a big way. My insides curdled as the banging came again.

'They're here,' I breathed. 'It's them.'

Spiro whimpered, got up from his chair and backed away into a corner. Lance had gone very pale.

'Open it, Livvy.'

I nodded and went to the door, holding my side now where the stomach cramps and the shock were searing through me, making me feel light-headed as my hand went up to the latch. I swung it back. Sure enough, the bald-headed man with the big fist and his blonde accomplice, in another shiny suit, were neatly ranged on my doorstep. But this time, they weren't alone. Behind them stood two, much larger men, wearing blue overalls and carrying tool bags, and behind them, stood a couple of uniformed policemen, too. Six, in all.

'Yes?' I breathed.

'Mithith McFarllen, may we come in?' Baldy lisped softly.

'Yes, yes, of course,' I stood aside. 'I see you've brought . . . reinforcements this time,' I managed weakly.

'Indeed we have. How very obthervant of you.' He gave me a thin little smile as he shuffled through with his hands in his mackintosh pockets, closely followed by the rest of the crew.

As I shut the door behind the last one, I went weak for a moment, leaning back on the door and shutting my eyes. It occurred to me that I was heaving around a stomach which under normal circumstances would have had me doubled up on the sofa with a fistful of paracetamol and a hot-water bottle, and I had a nasty feeling I might need

Spiro's pot plant in a minute. As I opened my eyes, though, I realised – no time. No time to exercise that jolly little option. Baldy's pale brown eyes, the colour of a certain doggy detritus, were trained on me like searchlights. I jumped nervously. Me? Why me? I glanced behind, wondering perhaps if there was someone standing behind me, but no, just the empty kitchen. Realising I wouldn't be the one slinking off in there to make the tea, I crept forward nervously. Clearly I was expected to join the party. Still staring, his eyes, it seemed to me, full of hideous portent, he nodded his head almost imperceptibly, but out of the corner of my eye, I noticed one of the overalled men quietly unzip a tool bag in response.

'Mithith McFarllen,' he lisped, 'tho thorry to bother you, but we have here a warrant to thearch your house and garden.' He quickly flashed a piece of plastic at me, eyes pale and watchful.

I held on tight to the back of the sofa. The garden? Christ Almighty, was she out there? Buried under my Bobby Brown rambler perhaps, or – or under the phlox and the delphiniums? Beneath my beautiful clematis-covered pergola?

I felt both hot and faint. 'A-Any . . . particular reason?' I faltered.

'Oh yeth. For the very particular reathon that we believe the body of Mithith Violet Turner to be buried here.' He kept his eyes on me.

'That's Alf Turner's late wife, I take it,' I muttered, edging along the sofa and playing for time, although what I was going to do with it Lord only knows.

'The very thame.'

'I see,' I gulped. 'And did you have any particular place,' I gripped the sofa hard, my legs feeling odd and my head woozy, 'any particular corner of my beloved, much-treasured home or garden in mind for excavation, officer? Or are you just going to dig away indiscriminately at the whole lot?' I managed to raise my chin defiantly.

He took my point, but his eyes slithered away. He wasn't interested in whether or not he was violating my precious home. He wasn't even interested, it seemed, in my garden. His eyes didn't slither that way, you see, to my herbaceous border, for instance, burgeoning over as it was with late lupins and asters, or to my rockery, thick with alpines and heather. Nor did he gaze beyond, down to the cedar tree, to the marshy banks of the river, nor even beyond that, to the caravan on the other side. No, no, Baldy's eyes were trained somewhere much more proximate. On the door-way, in fact, behind me. The doorway which led, via a small passageway, through into the new kitchen, and more specifically, those eyes were trained on something at the far end of that room. I glanced around.

'Yeth,' he said softly, slowly making his way past me in that direction, 'yeth, we do have a particular corner in mind.' He stopped, just beyond me, in the doorway. 'You thee we believe, Mithith McFarllen, that she's embedded in concrete.'

'Concrete!'

'Yes, or to be more precise, in a concrete plinth. A concrete plinth commonly built to support a heavy, free-standing, cast-iron, range.' He turned to face me in the doorway, his nose almost touching mine. 'In fact it's our belief, Mithith McFarllen, that Violet Turner is buried underneath your thtove.'

I gaped. 'My . . . thtove?'

'Your Aga, Mithith McFarllen.'

I jumped – then stared incredulously past him to my new kitchen. To my shiny pride and joy at the far end of the room, surrounded at it was by Portuguese tiles, edged with dados and doo-dahs, with its pine shelf above brimming with pretty plates, antique jugs and Mary Berry cookbooks; where I stood every day, frying the bacon, prodding Claudia's fish fingers, turning occasionally to warm my bottom, contentedly cradling a mug of coffee, chatting on the phone . . . and all the time . . . yes, all the time, stretched out beneath it, face up perhaps, hands clasped across her bosom, or maybe in a black bin liner, curled up in a foetal position, eyes shut, or possibly even wide and staring . . .

As the dawn came up I gasped in horror, as simultaneously a stab of pain seared straight through my abdomen. My hand clutched vainly at my stomach, but I had white lights flashing before my eyes now. My ears roared, my brain sizzled, my fingers slipped from the back of the sofa, as with a little gasp of 'Shit!' I collapsed, insensible, at Baldy's feet.

Chapter Thirty

'Best thing you could have done,' said Hugh, dunking a soldier into his son's boiled egg.

'What?' I raised my head feebly from their breakfast table.

'Faint like that, last night. Makes it so convincing, so much more obvious that you had nothing to do with it.'

'She didn't have anything to do with it,' snapped Molly, opening her dressing gown and clamping Flora firmly on to her left bosom. 'What – you think she might actually have assisted in some way, Hugh? Bundled the body under the Aga in a bin bag and arranged the feet neatly whilst Mac and Alf stood poised, ready to pour on the wet cement mix?'

'Oooh, *don't*,' I groaned, dropping my head like a stone again.

'No, all I'm saying is that when the police rang and asked us to come and get her, it looked pretty good,' said Hugh. 'You were still out for the count, Livvy, flat out on a sofa and completely away with the fairies, whereas poor old Lance and Spiro were shifting about pretty nervously, I can tell you.'

'I still don't quite understand how they came to ring you,' I said bleakly, opening an eye from the stripped pine table.

'Apparently Lance suggested us when the police said

they wanted you out of there,' said Hugh. 'Presumably they couldn't cope with you doing the dying swan all over the place when they had a house to excavate and a body to exhume. I must say I was hugely intrigued. Those guys had bloody nearly shifted that stove when I got there. I reckon she was damn nearly out! I hovered about a bit and tried to play for time by pretending you weighed a ton and that I was having difficulty lugging you off the sofa, then staggering e-ve-rso slo-wly to the door –' Hugh got up to demonstrate – 'then coming back for your handbag which happened to be, oops, in the kitchen, then – ooh yes, better pop upstairs and get your nightie, and then, damn it, just as I was popping back for your toothbrush, that bald chap sussed me and hustled me away. Shame. I reckon two more minutes and they'd have had the old bird out.'

'Hugh!' Molly slammed a milk bottle down.

'Well, it would have been fascinating, Moll. I've never seen a dead body before, and don't forget, I've been there in spirit. Would have been great for research.'

'Macabre,' shuddered Molly. 'And to think you'd been *cooking* there, Livvy, and all that time she was –'

'Oooh, stop it!' I moaned. I raised my head feebly. 'I really don't know how Alf and Mac could have *done* that to me!'

'Well, to be fair, Liv, they never meant for you to find out, and as long as you were none the wiser, so what?' said Hugh, reasonably. 'They had to put her *some*where, and actually I think it was a jolly good idea.' He frowned. 'Can't help feeling she might have got a bit hot, though. Maybe even gone a bit – you know – whiffy.'

'*Hugh!*' Molly was pink. 'God, you are *so* distasteful. Poor Livvy here is *distraught*, and so would I be if I found a dead woman under my cooker! Christ, it's gruesome!'

'All right, all right,' he muttered. 'God, you're so flaming genteel, Moll. I just think it's incredibly exciting, that's all, to be suddenly slap-bang in the middle of a murder like this. Talk about street theatre.'

'I told you,' I growled, 'it wasn't murder.'

'Well, OK, whatever you call a pissed-off husband knocking off his shrewish wife with a swift hammer blow to the head and then squirrelling her away under some kitchen appliances. Rather an apt ending, I feel, for a harridan of a housewife? Back to her roots, as it were?' His eyes gleamed. 'And it gives a whole new dimension to the old Aga saga, eh?'

Molly gave an exasperated little cry and pointedly swivelled round in her chair, turning her back on her husband. 'Liv darling,' she said gently, leaning forward and taking my hand, 'd'you remember much about last night?'

'Not much,' I said miserably. 'Just coming round in the back of Hugh's car, that's all . . . shouting a bit, I think.'

'Shouting a *bit*!' spluttered Hugh, spraying egg everywhere. 'Jesus, you were screaming blue murder! There you were, flat out and comatose on the back seat, quiet as a mouse, when suddenly – "GET ME OUT OF HERE – DON'T LET THEM PUT ME IN THE BIN BAG – OH GOD NO NOT THE BIN BAG SOMEBODY HELP ME!!!" Then the next thing I knew you were crawling over into the front seat with these mad, staring eyes, like something out of a Hammer Horror movie, trying to get me in an arm lock and turn the wheel at the same time. You damn nearly drove us off the road! Christ, I had to stop the car. I was scared witless I can tell you!'

I groaned. 'Sorry,' I muttered, shaking my head. 'God, I'm so sorry, Hugh, I had no idea. I really wasn't with it. When I woke up I just couldn't think where the hell I was!'

'Of course you couldn't,' agreed Molly staunchly, closing her dressing gown and putting Flora over her shoulder to wind her. 'Frankly, I'm surprised you're as *compos mentis* as you are now! If that had been me I'd be on that phone right now, booking myself into the Priory for the next couple of weeks I'd be so unhinged. And what about those two bastards who dropped you in all this? Why aren't they sharing the angst, Mac the knife and Alf the half-wit? Where are they while all this drama unfolds? On the Marrakesh Express or something?'

'I don't know,' I sighed, 'and, Molly, I know it sounds crazy, but they weren't really bastards. Just a couple of hard-working guys who got caught up in a horrific domestic drama and then – well, then did the wrong thing. Ran, instead of facing up to it.'

'All the best murders happen like that,' observed Hugh, sagely, wiping Henry's eggy mouth. 'Ninety per cent are committed within the family, which makes a copper's job something of a doddle really, doesn't it?' He scratched his head and affected a dim PC Plod. 'Er, so what d'you reckon, Sarge, shall I 'ave a word wiv the relatives?'

'So why do they still want to speak to me then?' I said, suddenly fearful. 'If it all hinges on the relatives, why ring me here, at the crack of dawn this morning, and ask me to present myself down at the station!'

'Just routine they said, remember?' soothed Molly.

'Nothing to worry about. What time did they say they wanted to see you?'

'Ten o'clock,' I said, glancing at the clock. My heart was hammering. 'In half an hour. I must go soon.'

'D'you want me to come with you?' She squeezed my hand.

I shook my head. Gulped. 'No, I'll – be fine. You've got Flora to see to and your mother's still asleep and –'

'Well, Hugh's not doing anything today. He could easily take you.'

'No, no really, I'm sure you're right,' I said quickly. 'I'm sure it's nothing to worry about.'

I wasn't entirely sure I could cope with Hugh wise-cracking his way to the police station with yet more corpse jokes, because actually, suddenly, I felt very scared. I wished I could just hole up here in Molly and Hugh's tiny, warm, chaotic kitchen with its airer groaning with bibs and babygrows, and Flora sucking away contentedly at her mother's breast, and Henry eyeing me carefully from his high chair, thumb in mouth, not entirely sure if I was generally present at his breakfast table.

'So what happens next?' said Molly softly, as if reading my thoughts.

I grimaced. 'You mean, what am I going to do?'
She nodded.
'Well, sell the house, of course.'

'Of course,' she agreed quickly, shooting Hugh a look as he opened his mouth to protest.

'And move, I suppose, but God knows where. I'll have to decide soon, though, because Claudia's term starts in September. You know she's been offered a place at St Paul's?'

'No! In London? Blimey!'

'I know. I'd forgotten I'd even put her down for it, must have been ages ago, in an ambitious moment. Haven't had many of those recently.'

'But that's seriously hot stuff, Livvy. Places like that are *fought* over! God, about two hundred girls going for twenty places!'

I sighed. 'I know, can't think how she managed it, although apparently she did rather well at her interview. They asked if she had any hobbies and she said, rather disdainfully, "Certainly not" – you know Claudes. And then they said, "Well, do you collect anything, dear?" And she said, "Yes, money."'

Molly giggled. 'That's my girl. No shrinking violet, eh?'

'Hardly. But do we really want to live in London, Moll? And a day school too – not really what she'd had in mind.'

'A *brilliant* day school, though,' said Hugh through a mouthful of toast. 'Hell of an opportunity. She'd probably end up Prime Minister or something equally bloody frightening.'

'True,' I sighed again. 'Anyway, I'm going to have to think about it.' I hauled myself out of the cosy Windsor chair. 'Right now, though, I have to gird my loins for my chat with Shiny Suit and Baldy. Perhaps it'll be Pentonville for me, with Claudia on visiting rights.'

'Don't be silly. It's quite obvious you were just an innocent bystander,' Molly protested. Nevertheless, I noticed, rather nervously, that they both followed me to the door and that Molly still had her arm round my shoulders when we got there.

'You're welcome to stay here as long as you like, you

know that, don't you?' She gave me a squeeze. 'A year if you want, whatever it takes.'

'Thanks.' I forced a smile. 'But it'll only be a few days. We wouldn't want to cramp your style.'

'We don't have a style,' announced Hugh loftily, sticking his chest out. 'Makes life so much simpler.'

'Speak for yourself,' muttered Molly, 'I wouldn't mind a bit of style.'

'Nonsense, my dear, you're totally à la mode as you are, modelling for us this morning this season's must-have basic, the cheesy dressing gown with baby puke down one shoulder and – Oops! There she goes again!' He caught Flora's sickly projection and grabbed Molly's muslin to mop it up as the baby proceeded to do another mouthful.

'She keeps doing this,' said Molly anxiously. 'I'm getting terrible *déjà vu*. I keep waiting for her to actually take aim and get my mother in the face, like Henry used to.'

'Henry's grown out of that,' I soothed. 'Flora will too.'

'Ah, but you haven't seen Henry's latest trick,' said Hugh proudly. 'Irritated that he can no longer hit Molly's mother in the eye with a stream of puke, he's taken to dropping his trousers, presenting dear Millicent with his bare backside, then letting rip with the most almighty fart.' Hugh sighed, wistfully. 'Something I realise that I, too, have long wished to do myself.'

'Hugh!' Molly scolded.

'Well, I can't see this little angel doing anything as gross as that,' I said fondly, stroking his daughter's cheek.

'She's going to be a stunner,' he agreed.

'And talking of stunners,' Molly rearranged Flora and looked me in the eye, 'I heard about Imo.'

'Ah.' I scuffed my toe on the doormat. 'That.'

'Flaming cheek!' she said hotly. 'You were well in there first!'

Hugh cringed. 'Well In There? Is that how you speak of us gentle menfolk?'

I sighed. 'Yes, but while I was making up my mind, Moll, Imo saw a gap and went for it. And who can blame her?' I added ruefully.

'Saw a gap and . . . ? Good heavens,' gasped Hugh faintly, clutching the doorframe for support. 'We're just a mere line of traffic now, are we? With gaps! Whatever happened to romance?'

'What indeed?' I agreed ruefully.

'And, anyway, I don't know why all this comes as such a big surprise to you girls,' he went on. 'If we're intent on using disgusting analogies, if you ask me, she wormed her way in long ago.'

'When?' demanded Molly.

'Oh, come on, Moll, ages ago, at that backstage party at the Abbey, for starters. And then when I saw her the other day, cosily ensconced at his house . . .'

They debated on, but suddenly I wasn't listening. Suddenly I felt like Flora: I wanted to be sick all over someone's shoulder. Cosily ensconced. Really? For how long? How long had it been going on? I wanted to ask.

'Livvy?' Molly was watching me anxiously. I forced a bright smile.

'Bye then. Wish me luck in the cells.' I made towards

my car, which Molly had driven back last night when I'd been in Hugh's.

'Good luck!' they chorused. 'As if you're going to need it,' added Molly scornfully.

In the event, they were right, I didn't. Down at the city police station Baldy was conspicuous by his absence, and since I'd clocked him as being the more dynamic of the duo, I relaxed when I discovered that Shiny Suit was going to interview me alone. As I followed her into a little grey room, sat down and regurgitated all I knew, I could tell by her demeanour that although she was affecting high dudgeon, she was actually only going through the motions to scare me.

'So why on earth didn't you come straight in and report to us the moment you knew she was dead!' Her eyebrows shot into her overtreated fringe.

'I was scared,' I admitted, with more than an element of truth. 'I knew I should have done, but I'd never been involved in anything like this before. What Mac and Alf told me terrified me. I shot off to London like a bat out of hell, telling myself it was only what I'd normally do on a child-free day.'

'And what did you do in London?'

'Oh, just some shopping, went to a concert, that sort of thing.'

The eyebrows shot up some more. 'Very relaxed.'

'Yes but while I was there I realised I'd done completely the wrong thing,' I added quickly. 'And – and I decided I'd come in and see you the very next day. I really meant to.'

'Did you indeed?' she snorted doubtfully. 'Yes, well, I could mutter on a bit about the road to hell being paved with good intentions and all that,' she shuffled her papers sniffily. Glanced up. 'You know, of course, that I could throw the book at you for sheltering known criminals and withholding crucial evidence?'

I nodded dumbly.

'Staying silent is as much of a crime as actually aiding and abetting. It's calculated corroboration.'

I nodded again. 'Yes, I – I can see that now.'

She sighed wearily. Closed her file. 'But under the circumstances,' she said, pushing it to one side, 'I think it's fair to say you've probably been through the mill enough. It's not every day you find a corpse under your cooker.'

I gulped. Too true. I glanced up and met her eye. 'Thank you,' I whispered gratefully.

'We will, of course, get them, though,' she added, fixing me beadily. 'Your chums, Mac and Alf. There's no question of that.'

'Of course,' I agreed quickly, wishing she hadn't called them 'my chums'.

'Gone are the days of the Spanish being wet about extradition. We'll put a rocket up their backsides and they'll deliver them tout suite. This isn't the Ronnie Biggs era, you know, this isn't the slap-happy, swinging sixties where anything goes on the Costa Brava.'

'Oh no, I know,' I agreed fervently. 'And quite right too,' I added toadishly. Just let me go, please let me go.

'So.' She folded her arms and flashed me a thin, professional smile. 'I imagine you're free to go.'

I sprang to my feet. 'Thank you!'

'Provided,' she warned, 'that you don't wander too far afield. We will need you later on to give evidence and

I don't want to find you've skipped the country or anything dramatic.' She got up and opened the door for me, propping it open so I had to go under her arm. 'Your house has been put back pretty much in apple-pie order, you'll be pleased to hear. Our boys worked fast last night and Forensics have been in and out already. You're not even cordoned off, either, because the press don't know and we didn't want to draw too much attention to the place, so you don't have to wait, you can move straight back in.' She frowned. 'I'm not sure the cooker is fully operational, though. Some people are apparently coming in next week to fix that, but other than that,' she flashed me another wintry smile, 'you wouldn't even know we'd been there!'

I managed a tremulous smile in return and even muttered a thank you before scurrying away. Wouldn't even know they'd been there? I thought, bug-eyed with horror as I sped down that corridor in the direction of the free world. Excuse me, but I think I would. Oh, I'd know all right. I'd know every time I lifted the lid to put the kettle on, every time I bent down to take the roast chicken out of the oven. Know? Bloody hell – I'd *heave*! Christ, I wouldn't stay in that house now if you *paid* me, I thought, barging angrily through some swing doors, and she was right, I *had* suffered enough. So much so that I was having to – Well, I was having to sell up! I stopped still for a moment, shocked by that thought, blinking in horror, and conveniently forgetting, of course, that I'd actually been planning to sell up anyway. Yes, that's right, I thought, slowly walking on, outraged, I was the victim here. I should be offered compensation! God, I could sell my story to the tabloids, spill the beans for millions! I must talk to Hugh about it. He'd enjoy that.

Once in the car park, though, all thoughts of anything other than the fact that I was a free woman paled into insignificance as I threw myself with relief into my familiar old, boiling-hot sauna of a car. Free, I thought, resting my head back gratefully and shutting my eyes. Thank God. I gave myself a little shake and started the engine, then realised, with a start, that I didn't know where the hell I was going. I turned it off again. Frowned. Right. So, Livvy. Here you are on your own again. I bit my lip. And what now? Where to? Long term I had absolutely no idea, but more immediately . . . I narrowed my eyes, frowned into the middle distance, then started the engine again. Yes, yes, I *did* know, actually. Knew exactly where I was going. Before I could change my mind I reversed at speed – slowing dramatically when I remembered I was still in a police station – then once out of sight, roared off. The house. It had to be Orchard House. Let's face it, at some point I had to go back because Claudia and I had no clothes at all at Molly's – as it was I was wearing a skirt of Molly's to avoid climbing into the disastrous Donna Karan number – so I may as well go and get it over with. I was due to pick Claudes up from Lucy's this afternoon and if the poor child had neither a father, nor a home to come back to now, she should at least have a clean pair of knickers.

With a gathering sense of dread I drove slowly down the familiar roads, turning down into George Street, bumping over the cobbles, past the little antique shops, then left into the arched, Abbey gates with the Abbey tower looming over my shoulder. As I turned left into

The Crescent I couldn't help driving very, very slowly and peering up at Sebastian's house. His car wasn't outside so I knew he wasn't in, and for some reason, all the shutters were closed. It looked strangely – well, shut up, as if he'd gone away for some length of time, too. Was he in London? I wondered. Living at Imogen's, maybe? I gritted my teeth and swung into my drive.

I sat for a moment, drumming my fingers on the wheel, steeling myself, and not relishing this little visit one iota. Finally, telling myself not to be stupid – it wasn't as if she was *there* any more, was it? – I got out and marched up to the front door. I propped it open with a plant pot – didn't want it slamming behind me or anything gross – then, studiously avoiding the kitchen from which I reasoned I needed precisely nothing, I nipped upstairs, humming maniacally to calm my nerves. Once there, I dragged a large suitcase out from under a bed and, working quickly, emptied all of Claudia's drawers into it, not forgetting a few books, her jewellery case, her schoolwork, and a much-loved blue rabbit. Then I ran across the landing into my own room, did exactly the same, lugged the almost exploding suitcase heavily back downstairs, dragged it across the gravel, and heaved it up into the boot of the car. I slammed it shut. There. I brushed off my hands and stared back at the house. Now. Anything else? Surely I'd got the bare essentials? And surely I could just get some professionals in to clear the rest? Store the furniture somewhere perhaps? Yes, exactly, except – hang on, the photos in the sitting room; I'd like them with me. Taking another deep breath, I dashed back inside, gathered up all the silver frames full of photos of Claudia, took the albums from the bottom drawer of the chest, and was just about to skedaddle again, when stupidly, I glanced out of the French windows. I paused. And as I did, a lump came to my throat. My garden. My precious, beloved, glorious garden. I could quite happily leave the house, but the garden – oh, that was a huge wrench. I simply had to say goodbye.

I dropped the photos on the sofa and, almost as a reflex action, my hand reached up and shot the bolt across at the top of the French windows. Flinging them wide I wandered sadly outside. Around the terrace, stone urns tumbled with white pelargoniums, hostas and variegated ivy, and in the surrounding beds, day lilies and Michaelmas daisies jostled for position while lamb's tongues crawled towards my feet over the mellow York stones. The lavender path ahead was humming with bees and above it, arches of heavy, tumbling climbers – Albertine, Madame Alfred Carrière and my lovely, lusty Rambling Rector – nodded invitingly to me in the breeze. Dredging up a great sigh from the soles of my feet, I ducked under it for the last time, reaching up to touch a blossom, which, being so overblown, fell to pieces in my hand. Scattering the petals regretfully on the parched grass I went on, on to take a last look at my herbaceous border, stunning now with its great clumps of delphinium, larkspurs and poppies, all finally out together and looking pleased as punch to be so thoroughly synchronised. It brought a lump to my throat to think there'd be no one out here with the hose at seven o'clock as usual tonight, seeing them through this dry spell, giving them just a few more days of precious growth.

Down the yellowing lawn I wandered, my skirt brushing the fragrant brooms and hebes, shading my eyes to the river, to the glorious cedar tree, spreading its branches to give a cool blanket of shade beneath. I gazed across the river to the caravan. Still there, of course, I thought wryly, obscuring the view of the cherry tree as usual, except that – blimey – hang on, no – it was off! The bloody thing was moving! Well, of course it was, because – I squinted hard into the sun's dazzling rays – there was a car attached to it. A car, attached and pulling. I ran down towards the water's edge to watch, but just then the car stopped. Somebody got out, slammed the door, and walked round to peer down at the caravan's wheels, checking to see if they were stuck. I stopped. Lance.

'Lance!' My hand shot up in delight. He turned, shaded his eyes, then waved.

'Livvy!'

I grinned and ran, picking my way across the rickety bridge, brushing against bulrushes, and then along the bank on the other side. By the time I got there, Lance, bare to the waist, bronzed and bleached blond as ever, was busy digging a stone out of the way of one of the caravan's wheels. He straightened up with a smile.

'Well, I didn't expect to see you back here after last night!' His blue eyes found mine, gently. 'Are you all right? I tried to ring you at Molly's but she said you'd gone.'

I nodded. 'I'm fine now, absolutely fine, it was just – well, it was just such a shock, Lance. I don't usually pass out like that, like some nineteenth-century drip having the vapours, but a large gin and tonic on top of a very gippy tummy, plus –' I rolled my eyes – 'well, plus everything else . . .'

'Well, quite. It's not every day you discover a dead body lurking in your kitchen. I tell you, Livvy, I quite felt like passing out myself.' He regarded me earnestly with clear blue eyes. 'And I really didn't know anything about it, Liv, you must believe that. I would never have sanctioned it, however desperate they were.'

I nodded. 'I do know that, of course I do.'

'And I can understand how – well, how you must hate them,' he said with difficulty. 'For what they did.'

'Well, as you said,' I said carefully, 'they were desperate. Desperate men.'

He nodded. Glanced down. Scuffed his toe miserably in the dirt.

I sighed. 'Look – don't feel you have to take responsibility, Lance. It's not your fault. I just wish – well, I just wish they'd driven back via the Thames and gone for the more conventional East End burial ground, that's all.'

He smiled ruefully. 'They shouldn't have done that either; should have gone straight to the police, right from the start.'

'Bit late now,' I said grimly.

Lance scratched his head. 'You'd think so, wouldn't you, but you know, perversely, apparently not. Who knows whether to believe them or not, but the police say there's a good chance they'll get off with manslaughter if they return to face the music. Apart from anything else their story is perfectly true, and since literally everybody will back them up – oh, and apparently there's some marvellous left-wing brief who's prepared to take Alf's case on, and all on legal aid too – he stands a really good chance of getting off. I just have to persuade them to come back, that's all, and that might be tricky.' He grinned. 'Spiro reckons the ouzo will agree with Dad and I can just see Alf –'

'Ouzo?' I interrupted.

'Oh,' he flushed suddenly. 'Oh, no, nothing.' He bent down quickly, attending to the wheel.

Ouzo, I thought, astonished, and Spiro knew about it, so – so not Spain at all. Greece, or to be more precise, I thought rapidly, a little island off the tip of Greece, a Greek-speaking community in the Balkans, a disputed territory just off Albania. Yes, a place where you could disappear, literally for ever, without a hope of anyone finding you. Particularly on a close-knit little island where everyone closed ranks. A little island called Mexatonia. An island where a certain Gullopidus family pretty much ruled the roost, ran the show, owned the boats, the goats, the bars, and where a couple of Englishmen – friends of Mr Gullopidus's son, don't you know, friends of young Spiro, who'd been looked after so magnificently during his stay in England – could quite easily be found shelter, houses, jobs. God, I could just see Alf mending boats on the beach, patching up the fishing nets, whistling away, quiet, contented, happy in his work, and Mac – yes, Mac behind the bar in town, measuring out the Metaxa, turning his quick mind to the lingo – unlike Alf, who'd barely mastered English and certainly wouldn't be mastering Greek – ingratiating himself into local life, becoming part of the community. Yes, Mac, a colourful figure, bringing out his wife, Karen, the grown-up kids coming out for holidays, and running the place; drinking long into the night with all the old men, playing backgammon in the village square, chewing the cud with Spiro and Atalanta up the road . . . I smiled. Well actually, in spite of myself, I grinned, really quite widely. My God, what a life! They'd never come back. And, of course, Mac had very cleverly told me Spain, had let that slip quite deliberately to put me off the scent, and perhaps even hoped I'd tell the police. Which come to think of it . . . I frowned. Had I? Well, I certainly hadn't disagreed when Shiny Suit had mentioned the Costa Brava as the spot she'd be dragging them back from. Well good, I thought suddenly. I probably shouldn't think that, but I did. Good.

'Forget I said that,' muttered Lance, straightening up for a moment.

I smiled. 'Forget you said what?'

He grinned, but I glanced away, point made, but not wanting to prolong that conversation, thank you very much. I gazed back to the house, to the new kitchen, its windows flashing knowingly at me in the sunshine. When I'd turned back, Lance had bent down again and was tightening up a bolt on the wheel. His broad back was smooth and brown. I remembered it well, felt I knew it intimately, in fact, from our suntanning session, together with that blond hair that curled rather seductively on the nape of his neck. I watched him working for a moment. Swallowed.

'Um, Lance, I don't suppose you fancy a drink, do you?'

He straightened up. 'Oh, Livvy, I'd love one, it's just that . . .' He hesitated, glanced down at his oily hands.

'What?'

'Well, it's just that, I sort of said I'd –'

'Lance!'

We both turned as a shrill voice rang out behind us.

'Hey! You said twelve o'clock. It's way past that. Come on!' Nanette was hanging out of her upstairs window, dressed in some sort of scanty, Caribbean sarong affair, complete with a flower in her hair. She waved an armful of jangling bracelets when she saw me. 'Co-ee, Olivia! I say, all sorts of action been going on at your place, eh? Can't wait to grill Lance!'

I turned and raised amused, quizzical eyebrows at Lance. He had the grace to blush.

'Ah, I see,' I murmured. 'Off for a grilling.'

'Well, you know,' he said sheepishly, scuffing his toe in the dirt. 'Seeing as how I'm going today, I thought – well. I thought just for old times' sake I'd pop round and have a drink with Nanette. But you're welcome to join us,' he added quickly. 'I'm sure she won't mind.'

'Oh, I'm quite sure she *will* mind,' I laughed. 'I'm not convinced that's entirely what our Nanette had in mind, are you?'

He looked at me a moment, then grinned. 'Perhaps not. Well, bye then, Livvy. Best of luck.' He leant forward and kissed my cheek.

We regarded each other fondly for a moment, and perhaps even a touch regretfully.

'Bye, Lance,' I said with a smile, then I turned to go, making my way back up the parched lawn. A few steps on, though, his voice halted me.

'Oh, by the way, that musician chappie called round.'

I swung back.

'Oh?'

'Yes, he's gone to Vienna.'

'Oh. Right.' My heart thudded on again. Of course. Ursula had said. With Imo. Hence the shuttered house.

'But he popped in to say goodbye. Left a note, I think.'

'Really? Where?'

He shrugged. 'Kitchen table?'

Kitchen. Bloody kitchen. I hurried on up the garden, heart racing again, through the French windows, then steeled myself to – Yes, yes I could . . . I went in. I avoided looking at the Aga and glanced quickly at the table. Nothing. Totally bare apart from the fruit bowl. In the fruit bowl perhaps? No. Notice board? No. Counters, surfaces, pinned to the larder door? No, no note, nothing. I glanced all about now, even casting a desperate eye at the Aga. All was neat and tidy, and there wasn't a fluttering piece of paper to be seen. He must have changed his mind. Dejected, I turned to go, but just as I was leaving, noticed that the rubbish bin was practically overflowing. Damn, I'd have to empty that or it would stink to high heaven in this weather. Irritated, I pulled out the plastic sack, but as I did, realised there were some balls of screwed-up paper on the top. They were from my telephone pad. I opened one.

Dear Livvy,

I popped round to say goodbye, but I also wanted to say

I opened another.

Dear Livvy,

I'm off to Vienna today, but I just wanted to write to

573

And another.

Dear Livvy,

I dropped them back in. One by one, slowly. Stared at the wall. What? What had he wanted to say? Deep in thought I lugged the bag outside and dumped it in the bin. I locked up the house, then, realising I'd left the photographs on the sitting-room sofa, went back in again, but I was totally distracted now. What? What had he wanted to say, for God's sake? And why start a letter three times? I carried the photos back in my arms towards the front door, just as the telephone rang. I stared at it for a moment on the hall table. For some reason, I felt full of foreboding. Almost didn't answer it. Then slowly, I put my bundle of photos down, and my hand went to the receiver. I picked it up.

'Hello?'

'Livvy, it's Imo.'

I gazed into the hall mirror, saw my eyes widen. 'Imo, hi.'

'Darling, I'm so sorry.'

'What about?'

'My bitch of a mother.' Her voice wobbled.

I lowered myself very slowly on to the hall chair. 'How did you know?' I whispered. 'I mean – did she tell you what she'd –'

'No, no, of course not,' she sniffed. 'When she came across to us in tears at the concert she just said you'd insulted her, called her some terrible names, accused her of being a culture vulture or something, but Daddy overheard the whole thing, he was just too terrified to interfere. We're all too terrified. Have been for years.' Her voice sounded small and sad. Very far away.

'So you know –'

'Not quite everything, but I'm keen to learn because, believe me, it'll all be bollocks,' she rallied defiantly. 'It always is with Mum, and there's no way she's coming between you and me, Livvy, no way on earth. So go on, darling, spill the beans. What's the old cow been up to now?'

I licked my lips. 'Well, she said . . . well, first of all she told me about Johnny. Imo, I had no idea. I never knew you were so besotted back then. If I'd thought for one moment you were still in love with him –'

'You'd never have married him?'

There was a silence. I swallowed hard.

'Don't be silly, Livvy,' she went on quietly, 'you'd have followed your heart, and quite right too.'

'So – you were in love with him then?'

'Oh, back then, yes, I was, but the balls-up on that front was nothing to do with you, it was my own private tragedy, and my own stupid fault, too. You weren't to know what was going on, but yes, there was a plan afoot, instigated by Mum, of course.'

'So that was true? She did intervene?'

'Of course! You know Mum. She knew that I was deadly serious about Johnny and was adamant that if he was going to take me to the altar so young he had to deserve me, or some such crap. Not coming back for weeks on end after Oliver died was her idea. It was all her idea.'

'And Paolo?'

'The son of a gallery owner she knew. He just arrived at my apartment one evening, asking if I'd like to have supper. Oh, I didn't *have* to sleep with him, of course, but in those days I did most things Mum suggested ... "a delightful little dalliance" was her euphemism for it, a brief romance, she said, before settling down as a wife and a mother for good. And I complied. Thought she was right. Thought I needed my last fling. Staggering really; I didn't seem to have a mind of my own. She's a control freak, you see, Liv, totally manipulative, and look where it's got her. One of my brothers is dead from drugs, another one can't stand her and married a hairdresser to thwart her, and the other one lives in New Zealand, so far away she can't get at him. I always wanted to please her – we all did – but I can't do it any longer.' She sucked in her breath. At first I thought she was crying, then I realised –

'Imo – you're smoking!'

'I've smoked for years. Secretly, of course. Mummy would be horrified. And I've never, ever gone against her,' she said vehemently, her words tumbling out in a rush now. 'Oxford, Florence, an art gallery where I'd meet nice, cultured young men – everything was her idea, and I so envied you with your sweet, unpushy mother who never –'

'*My* mother? Jesus, Imo, my mother was a nightmare!'

'Only in your eyes. Molly and I were as jealous as hell. She was so discreet and elegant and unambitious, whilst I had the She-Devil Incarnate to deal with and poor Moll had the ghastly Millicent. But I envied you for defying her, too,' she said softly. 'She was strong, your Mum, no pushover, but you signed up for that Cirencester course against her wishes and married without her blessing. I could never have done that.'

I remembered the rows Mum and I had had when I'd told her I was marrying Johnny.

'Well no,' I said slowly, 'I'd certainly never let her run my life.'

'You see? And I did. And look where it got me. I've gone from man to man to please her. Oh, she thought Hugo was absolutely marvellous in the beginning, but then Sebastian came along and he was even *more* marvellous. It's been the story of my life. I don't even know what I think any more,' she said unhappily.

I licked my lips again. 'She said – Ursula said – that you were in love with him. With Sebastian.'

'Ah. Yes. That much, at least, is true. But then again, it's not the whole story. You see sadly, he's not in love with me. And no point forcing a square peg into a round hole, eh?' She gave a hollow laugh and I heard her drag hard on her cigarette.

'But I thought you were going to Vienna with him! Your mother said –'

'Well, of course she bloody did. That's her oh-so-subtle way of angling for an invitation for me, and warning you off. Christ, I'm surprised she didn't book the bloody ticket, drive me to the airport, shove me on the plane and strap me into the seat next to him, taking absolutely no notice of his horrified face!'

There was a silence.

'It's you he wants, Livvy,' she said softly. 'You must know that.'

'Wh-why should I know that?'

'Because . . .' she struggled. 'Oh, I don't know, don't know for sure, but – listen, darling, I spoke to him this morning, before he left for Vienna. I wanted to set the record straight – *my* record straight, at least. Christ, I've made such a bloody fool of myself one way and another and I wanted to explain things, things that – Oh, but that doesn't matter right now, the important thing is that he was asking about you. I think he might try and get in touch with you, Liv, write to you perhaps, or even –'

'Oh!' I nearly dropped the phone.

'What?'

I couldn't speak for a moment. I went hot, then finally pulled myself together and dragged my eyes away from the window by the door. In the mirror I could see the colour rising rapidly up my neck.

'Imo, it's – it's all right,' I breathed. 'He's here.'

Chapter Thirty-One

'You're kidding!' Imo's voice was still in my ear even though I wasn't with her. I was glued back to Sebastian's eyes again as he looked at me through the hall window. 'Gosh, I thought he'd gone!'

'What?' I whispered.

'I thought he'd gone to Vienna!'

I swallowed. 'Obviously not.'

'Ah. Right.' Her voice went quiet. 'Good luck then, Livvy. You deserve it.'

Her subdued tone made me glance into the receiver. 'Imo?'

'Hmm?' She sounded distant.

'Lots of love.'

She paused. 'You too, darling. You too.'

I slowly put the receiver down and stood up to open the door, my heart hammering around somewhere up by my oesophagus. Sebastian was there on my doorstep, leaning against the doorframe with his hands in his pockets. He was in khaki trousers and a pale blue shirt – quite smart for him, not his usual battered composing kit – but his eyes were the same as ever, dark and glittering, and he was wearing that devastating smile, the one that transformed his face, creasing it up into angles and slanting his eyes. It seemed to me it lit up the whole street.

'Hi.'

'Hi.'

With these modest monosyllables, I found myself to be suddenly wide awake. Alive again. I felt my whole body begin to glow and every nerve tingled.

'Can I come in?'

'Hmm?' I gazed, wantonly.

'Inside?'

I jumped. 'Inside? Oh – no!' Hurriedly I hastened distinctly *out*side, and joined him on the step, slamming the front door firmly behind me. He looked surprised.

'Ah. I see. A doorstep conversation then.'

'Well, it's just that – I'm rather off my house at the moment,' I explained hastily. 'It's – the wallpaper.'

'The wallpaper?'

'So depressing.' Or did that sound neurotic? 'Er – no, OK, it's not the wallpaper, but it's a long story, Sebastian, and a rather tortuous one at that, so I won't go into it right now, but . . .' I glanced about desperately, no, not out the back because Lance might still be there so, 'tell you what, let's go and sit over there.'

I hastened down the drive to the front wall, excitement mounting. It was a bit high and covered in creeper, but somehow, with a superhuman spring, I managed to jump up, and then contrived to look comfortable even though I had ivy up my bottom. He glanced at the filthy wall and in his smart clothes, clearly decided to stand. Suddenly it occurred to me he was spruced up for travelling.

'Oh yes, Imo said you were off to Vienna.'

'Imo?'

I flushed. God, why did I have to mention Imo? Right at this moment? 'Yes, that was her on the phone just now.'

'Oh, right.' He coloured too, then recovered. 'Yes, well, she's right, I am, but the plane's been delayed. I'm leaving any minute actually.' He glanced at his watch. 'The taxi will be here soon. I just came round to say goodbye.'

'Oh! Right.' For some reason the excitement began to drain out of me. Seeped right down into my shoes. This didn't seem to have the makings of an embryonic romantic conversation, more – well, more a matter-of-fact, bon voyage conversation, actually. I wondered if Imo had got the wrong end of the stick. I felt slightly foolish too, sitting up here like a little gnome, with him standing before me, his shoulders level with my knees.

'The symphony's going to be played in the Musik-verein tomorrow evening,' he explained, 'so I'm flying out tonight to listen to the rehearsal. I'm leaving the house, too, hence all the frenetic activity.' He jerked his head down the street. I looked, and realised that his front door was wide open and that two men were busy heaving a heavy desk down the steps to a lorry. 'My desk and my piano are the only things I actually brought with me to the house, so they're going down to the country. The rest stays.' He grinned. 'I thought you might think it a bit odd if I disappeared from the neighbourhood overnight without saying goodbye! I must pop in and see Nanette, too.'

My throat felt curiously dry all of a sudden. 'Oh . . . right. Yes, I'd forgotten you . . . only rent it.'

'Oh yes, I'd never buy it. Renting was ideal. I needed to be here to write the music for the Abbey, because, somehow, being close to the old building got the inspiration going, but now that it's finished, I don't need to be here any more. I'm keen to get away, actually.' He smiled, his eyes creasing up at the corners.

For some reason his words chilled me. 'Of course,' I heard myself saying. 'That part of your life is over. Time to move on.'

'Quite. And my parents have been dying to move out of their house to a cottage in a village nearby. It's far too big for them now, so I'm taking it over. It's an old rectory with a lovely garden, and I'm not really a city person. It'll be good to work in the country again.'

'I see,' I said quietly. I met his gaze. 'You're all set up then, aren't you? I'm moving on too, you know.'

'So I gather.' He grinned.

'Who told you?'

'Your builder, the chap round the back.'

'Ah. Yes, well, I'm sure he didn't tell you exactly why, but believe me, it's out of necessity. I don't have your luxury of choice.' I met his eye, somewhat defiantly perhaps for someone with whom I'd been keen to share a special harmony.

'To Dorset?' He grinned again.

'Sorry?' Why was he grinning at me like that?

'Aren't you going to Dorset?'

'No no, to Chiswick, that's where Claudia's school is.'

'Chiswick!' He looked appalled.

'Yes, she's got into St Paul's Girls' School. It's a hell of an opportunity and it would be crazy of us not to take it up, so I'm pretty sure we're going to be moving up there, although I have to say,' I grimaced, 'I haven't squared it with Claudes yet. Might go down rather badly.'

He stared at me. 'Livvy, is this because . . . is it because of Imogen?'

I frowned. 'What?'

He licked his lips. 'You know, we were never an item.' He ran his hands through his short dark hair. 'I mean I know it *looked* as if we were, and if I'm honest, that's the way I *wanted* it to look. I wanted you to think that I was going out with her, I was so bloody furious.'

I gazed at him, completely lost. What did Imo have to do with me moving to London?

'And I didn't seek her out deliberately, either, didn't make a beeline for her at all, but when she kept asking me to supper at her parents' house, practically zooming into position beside me at the dinner table – with her mother doing most of the shoving incidentally – well, I was so bloody cross, I thought – why not? Why not escort a stunningly beautiful girl for a while? Why not let her arrange a pre-concert party at my house, if that's what turns her on? Why not let her be seen on the composer's arm at the premiere of the concert too, even if I do have to stick her ghastly mother as well!'

'But – why?'

'Why?' he spluttered. 'Because I was feeling very firmly rejected and pissed off, since you ask!'

'Rejected?'

'Yes, Livvy,' he said patiently. 'By you.'

'*Me!*' I gaped. Eventually I found my voice. 'God – how can you say such a thing? Good grief, that – that is so not true!' I slipped into Claudia speak in my outrage. 'I mean, that night after dinner at Hugh and Molly's I practically *threw* myself at you in the car! Asked you in for coffee, fluttered the old eyelashes seductively, the whole damn bit, and you sat there beside me like a frigging ice man, before politely showing me the car door! Oh, no, no,' I said vehemently, 'I think you'll find that if there was any rejecting going on it was instigated by *you*, Sebastian! God – and what about that day I came round to see you, to explain about Johnny coming back, just in *case* there'd been a smidgen of feeling on your part, just in *case* you thought we'd built up something of a relationship those past few weeks – picnics in the park, suppers together, concerts – but you couldn't have cared less! In fact, if I remember rightly, you sat down next to me with a big cheesy grin on your face and said how *pleased* you were for me, yes – gosh, how *nice*, Livvy, your husband's back – and then you couldn't hustle me away quick enough, so desperate were you to see the back of me and get back to your composing! Oh no, I think you'll find the cold-shouldering was all yours!'

He lifted his chin and folded his arms, regarding me, pink and indignant as I was, perched up on the wall.

'Fine, Livvy,' he said quietly. 'OK. Let's take this step by step, shall we? The night you "threw yourself at me," as you put it, after Molly and Hugh's, you were drunk.'

'Oh excuse me,' I blustered, 'I most certainly was *not* dru–'

'Oh yes you were, and you'd intentionally got plastered too. I watched you knocking it back, glug after glug of Pimm's. I watched the way your mind was going too, you were so bloody desperate to forget Johnny and get back into the land of the living, and you kept glancing at me in that garden with "he'll do" written all over your forehead. He'll do, you thought, he's got a pulse, he doesn't smell, he hasn't got dandruff, he's probably got all his own teeth, and, Christ, I've got to do it with *some*one, at *some*time, haven't I, so why not him? Oh, your body might have been with me that night, had I taken you up on your oh-so-generous offer, but your heart most certainly wouldn't have been. It was with that bastard Johnny, as you so neatly proved by opening your arms and your bed to him again that very evening.'

I gazed at him in horror for a moment. Then my mouth shut. 'I had to do that,' I muttered defiantly. 'Couldn't help myself. I had to have him back in order to exorcise him. It was like a rite of passage; I had to get him out of my system.'

'The other occasion you refer to,' he swept on, ignoring me, 'was when you so sweetly popped round a few days later to inform me of Johnny's return. And believe me, that was equally galling. Livvy, I do have eyes in my head. I do live in your street. I do stand at the window every day waving my arms like a lunatic, composing my stupid tunes. I did *see* him, believe it or not, in his *car*, going in and out of the *house*, playing with Claudia in the back garden, helping you pull up your radishes, helping you in with your shopping, and how d'you think that made me feel? Bloody wretched, actually, and very smartly kicked in the teeth, but I damn well wasn't going to show it! Oh, I'm absolutely de*light*ed you found me so cool and distant when you tripped merrily into my study that day, because believe me, I'd had a few days to think about it, and that's precisely how I'd planned it. That's how I fully intended to be!'

'But –'

'And now,' he went on, with a sort of clenched fury, 'you have the gall to sit up there, grinning like a pixie, swinging your little feet around and telling me you're *not* moving to the country after all, you're going up to London! Jesus Christ, what is it with you, Livvy? Can't you make up your bloody mind just once!'

My jaw dropped as I stared uncomprehending at him. Finally I shook my head. 'Sorry,' I said at last. 'Sebastian, I'm really sorry, but you've completely lost me now. I have absolutely no idea what you're talking about. What on earth has us moving to Chiswick got to do with anything?'

'I thought Claudia wanted to board,' he said patiently.

'She does.'

'At a school near Frampton.'

I blinked. 'Well, yes, that was her first choice, why?'

'My parents live near Frampton. Or should I say –' he thumped his chest – '*I* now live near Frampton.'

I gaped. 'You do? Good heavens, what a coincidence!'

'Not really.'

'Why not?'

'Because I suggested the school to Claudia.'

'You . . . ?' I boggled. 'When!'

'Oh, ages ago, when she was chatting about where to go. My niece went there and loved it. It's got an excellent reputation, and I showed her a prospectus. Ponies, swimming, all that sort of thing.'

Suddenly I remembered the much-treasured prospectus under her bed, well thumbed and scrawled over. I also remembered that I couldn't recall where it had come from. He'd given it to her. My head swam. 'But – why?'

'Because I wanted you close by.'

A huge wave crashed over my head. I gazed at him, but actually, didn't seem to see him. My world was starting to spin. Those sweet, precious words: 'I wanted you close

586

by.' He gazed back at me and suddenly the spinning abated, and everything fell into place. Everything went very still. Very quiet. And it seemed to me that, in that silence, his eyes gazed into my very soul.

'Mr Faulkner?' A cab drew up beside us, its familiar purr breaking the exquisite quiet.

'Yes,' muttered Sebastian, not turning.

'I called at the 'ouse, like, but they said you were over 'ere. 'Op in, mate, if you're coming, 'cos we're gonna have to shift if you're gonna catch that plane. The traffic's diabolical.'

'Your taxi,' I muttered, not taking my gaze from those dark, shining eyes.

'I know.'

The sound of running feet didn't distract us either, when towards us, down the street, came Maureen, dragging a case on wheels.

'Well, thank heavens for that,' she gasped, panting. 'I had a feeling you'd be here but you might have said! You'll catch it if you hurry, and they've been ringing from Austria in a right old state asking how long you were going to be delayed. Come on, Sebastian.' She grabbed his arm and hustled him round, out of my garden to the waiting taxi. I watched as Maureen thrust some tickets in his hand. 'Get in or you'll miss it!'

She bundled him in, together with his case, then slammed the door shut behind him and passed his passport through the window. I swung my legs round to the other side of the wall. Jumped down. Despite all that activity, we'd hardly taken our eyes off each other. I'd followed him all the way round. The driver shifted into gear.

'Hang on,' I heard Sebastian say. He leaned out of the window, past Maureen.

'I wanted to give you time, Livvy,' he called, 'that's what you need. I didn't want to rush things. I did that before and it didn't work out, that's why it's good that I'm going away. You *need* that time, Livvy, to recover, to get over Johnny.'

I nodded, greedy with longing. Johnny, bloody Johnny.

'I'll ring you from Vienna and we'll meet when I get back, take it from there.'

I nodded again, tears of joy and relief and all sorts of other scrambled emotions making my eyes swim.

'And while I'm gone, go to Frampton,' he called. 'Go to the school, see if Claudia likes it. She may not!' He grinned.

I opened my mouth to find my voice but the taxi had slowly moved off. All I could do was wave, eyes flooding now, and with a bemused Maureen beside me. I waved until he was out of sight.

'Well then, dear,' said Maureen eventually, when we were left alone in silence. 'What a to-do, eh? Still, must get on.' She gave me a sly, secret smile, squeezed my arm, and then bustled off down the road, leaving me there on that hot, empty pavement.

I stood for a while, then moved on myself. Away from my house, and away from Sebastian's house. I needed to go somewhere quiet and green, like the park. Yes, the park would do, to think, to hug my joy. My feet tripped lightly along the hot pavements. Yes, I'd wait, I thought, dizzy with longing. I mustn't be greedy, mustn't be impulsive. He was right: we both needed time. And then when he got back, we'd see. We'd take it from there, reassess the situation. It might not be right, I might not be right ... And meanwhile – I stopped at the park entrance. Yes, mean-while, I'd be sensible. I bit my lip. And actually, being sensible meant not going to the park and dreaming and longing and hugging myself, because my dreams had a habit of not coming true. Instead – I turned – instead I'd walk to Lucy's and get Claudia. It wasn't that far, and we could walk back together, discuss Dorset, rationally, but I wouldn't mention Sebastian, just in case. Excitement threatened to bubble up again at the thought of him, the thought of those precious words 'I wanted you close by', but I bit it down. No, I mustn't be disappointed again, mustn't be let down, and heavens, I hadn't even kissed him yet. Nothing was certain. But I could ring the school, plan a visit. I could even find a cottage, maybe, go and see some estate agents. There was a lot to do and –

'Livvy!' I stopped. Didn't turn. I must have imagined it. Then: 'LIVVY!' again, only louder. His voice – no doubt about it – and running footsteps too. I swung about. Down the old cobblestones of George Street, worn smooth with the traffic of time, and under the gaze of the ancient towering nave of the Abbey, came Sebastian. At the double. I stood still, could hardly breathe, and waited, until he arrived in front of me, panting hard.

'Come to Vienna,' he gasped. 'Bugger restraint, bugger giving you time – come to Vienna!'

My head swam. 'Wh-what now? I can't, I –'

'Tomorrow, we'll both go tomorrow.' His voice was taut with emotion. 'I can miss the first rehearsal tonight. It always sounds lousy with an unfamiliar orchestra and I wonder how I ever wrote the wretched thing. Come tomorrow!'

I stared. 'Sebastian, I can't, Claudia –'

'Oh, God, kiss me first, and then say you can't.' He took me in his arms and kissed me very thoroughly on the mouth. I could hear his heart pounding against mine, could smell the sweet fresh cotton of his shirt, and when I came up for air, his eyes were glittering intently into mine, searching my face.

'God, you're lovely, Livvy,' he breathed, 'and what really flips my heart over is that you don't know that. No one's ever told you, have they? That bastard Johnny never breathed a word, did he, kept it to himself, and you've lived most of your life thinking that people like Imogen Mitchell are better than you.' He traced my mouth with his fingertip. 'It's criminal, actually. You're special, Livvy. When I saw you I confess I simply lusted after you, but when lust turned to love I was lost. Come with me, Livvy. Come and love me in Vienna.'

I gazed up at him. 'Yes,' I breathed, 'I'll come. I love you too, I know that now. I've known it for ages, actually, and couldn't believe I'd been so stupid. Mum can have Claudia and –'

'Bring her,' he commanded. 'Don't leave her behind. Bring her, we'll all go.'

My head swam. Lovers together in Vienna, holding hands over café tables, walking arm in arm down boule-vards, drowning in each other's eyes . . . with a small, agog, ten-year-old girl in tow. Grey eyes huge behind her specs, fascinated beyond belief. Mum and a *man*! Blimey, she'd be taking notes!

'No,' I said firmly, 'no, she can stay with my mother, she'll be fine there and – *oh*!' Suddenly my hand shot to my mouth. 'Oh God, no, I *can't* go!'

The taxi, with a bemused driver behind the wheel, still full of luggage, had trailed Sebastian back and was trundling up behind us.

'Why not?' demanded Sebastian.

'Because I can't leave the country! I'm sort of on bail!'

'Bail!' He stepped back in horror.

'Yes, well, I was this morning, anyway. You see there was this murder and –'

'Good God!'

'No – no, manslaughter, actually,' I added hastily, 'but the body ended up in my home –'

'Jesus!' He tore at his hair.

'I know, dreadful, under my cooker of all places, and the thing is, I promised the police I'd stay around, but – well, Vienna isn't far away and they won't need me for ages yet. There won't be a trial for some time, I'm sure, so – so maybe if I asked – they're terribly obliging down there at the station – maybe I could come next week!'

He stared at me in astonishment. 'Right,' he said eventually, looking totally bewildered.

'You coming, mate, or what?' from behind us.

'He's coming!' I called. 'Go,' I insisted softly, pushing him gently. 'Go. It's enough for me to know you *wanted* me to come, that you came back for me. I don't *need* to go to Vienna now, but I'll join you when I can, I promise.'

He gazed at me, still with a degree of astonishment, then stepped forward, and gently took my hands.

'Livvy, it seems to me you lead a very unusual and complicated life. You see nutters and weirdos at every corner, you rant and rave and wave rakes in defence of your child, you consort with murderers, you stow dead bodies in your house and you're on intimate terms with the local police. Heaven only knows what I've been doing with my life apart from writing the odd symphony, but I want you to know that I'm keen to be a part of this rich and varied tapestry of yours. If being with you means sitting in damp cellars forging passports, laundering money and stowing spare bodies away, then I'm your man. I'll follow your lead blindly, be Clyde to your Bonnie, if that's what you want.'

I giggled. 'Idiot. I'm not in any sort of real trouble, it's just – well, strange things have happened recently.'

He smiled. 'You're telling me.'

'There's twenty quid on the meter, mate!'

'Go.' I bundled him in, and this time he went. I shut the door, and he held my hand through the window until the taxi started up and trundled away.

I watched Sebastian's face in the back window, and as the cab turned into the main road, I raised my hand in salute, as he did too. I stood on that hot pavement, and knew I had yet more tears in my eyes. But this time, I knew why. I never thought I'd say that to a living soul again, not after Johnny. Those three little words. Not a living soul. Never believed I'd have that sort of luck. But I had. I'd said it, and what's more – I sailed joyfully off along the hot pavements, my shoes feeling as if they'd got wings on – what's more, I meant it.

Catching up with
Catherine

We donned our wellies and trudged
through the mud to meet Catherine
for a catch-up on writing, reading,
and life in the country . . .

Catching up with
Catherine

How and where do you write?

In the garden in the summer, and on a sofa by the fire
in the winter, literally with the nearest pen,
which as a result often runs out.

Any tips for alleviating writer's block?

I'd probably go for a long walk with the dogs but also
never call it writer's block. It's just a day to do
something else; tomorrow will be different.
With luck and everything crossed, the muse
might perch on one's shoulder again.

You live in the countryside in a village not too dissimilar from those you write about. How does country life in your books compare to real life?

There are some remarkable similarities, but obviously
names have been changed to protect the innocent . . .

What do you like to do when you're not writing?

I ride my horses and, recently, wander round poultry
farms. I'm trying to decide which ducks to get for
my new pond: Indian Runners are terribly comical,
Aylesburys would be more geographically
appropriate, yet I'm strangely drawn to good
old Mallards, too. Decisions . . .

If you had to live the life within a classic novel and star as a literary heroine, who would you be and why?

Possibly Jane Austen's Emma Woodhouse,
who lived something of a charmed life,
even if she didn't realize until
it was almost too late.

What's your favourite place to escape to?

Over the hills and far away. The valley behind my
house is actually not very far at all and the Downs
start there so it's very peaceful. Devon is,
of course, heaven, but a little further.

What's the best way to survive a day in the British countryside?

In an ideal world I probably wouldn't take my
own very badly behaved dogs; I would take
someone else's – that way I wouldn't be chasing
them all day shrieking unattractively.

Catherine's top tips
for the perfect countryside break

The same rules apply for children as for dogs (see before), depending on age and reliability of your children – husbands, too.

Never picnic (as in the romantic ideal of rug, hamper, chicken drumsticks à la Delia). Pubs tend to be far more successful, although I am nostalgically drawn to beach picnics. Sand in sandwiches is surely part of any child's education and there's nothing funnier than the man of the family getting to grips with a windbreak in a force-eight gale. Particularly if his own childhood holidays were spent in Tuscany.

Don't be deceived by the English countryside. It looks pretty but can turn on you in an instant.

Leave the horses to the professionals – that doesn't include me. A horse that decides to nap (go home) in the middle of a village which also happens to be something of a tourist magnet is embarrassing for all concerned, particularly the red-faced, middle-aged woman on top.

Again on the subject of horses, 'not a novice ride' means bucks like fury, while 'a fun ride' means carts you into the next county. Male horse-dealers are fond of both expressions, but never forget they are stronger than we are. The men and the horses.

When you answer the door in your coat in winter to a surprised friend who asks if you're just going out, don't be afraid to let them stay an hour or two until they put their coats on too.

If invited to a dinner party in London in January, don't forget there will be women in little dresses who have proper central heating. In the car en route, turn the heater up full blast and try to shed at least three of your layers. Don't forget the Ugg boots. If you stay in the vest and the cashmere roll-neck, you will be in a critical state by pudding, particularly if you're approaching fifty.

If anyone offers you the use of a flat in town in winter, bite their hand off.

Catherine's top ten countryside reads:

The Pursuit of Love
Nancy Mitford

Untold Stories
Alan Bennett

The Irish R. M.
Somerville and Ross

High Fidelity
Nick Hornby

Persuasion
Jane Austen

Pomp and Circumstance
Noël Coward

84 Charing Cross Road
Helene Hanff

The Woman in White
Wilkie Collins

Franny and Zooey
J. D. Salinger

Atonement
Ian McEwan

'Supremely readable, witty and moving.
I adored this' *Daily Mail*

'If I'm being totally honest I had fantasized about Phil dying.'

When Poppy Shilling's bike-besotted, Lycra-clad husband is killed
in a freak accident, she can't help feeling a guilty sense of relief.
For at long last she's released from a controlling and loveless marriage.

Throwing herself wholeheartedly into village life, she's determined
to start over. And sure enough, everyone from Luke the sexy
church-organist to Bob the resident oddball, is taking note.
Yet the one man Poppy can't take her eyes off seems tantalizingly
out of reach – why won't he let go of his glamorous ex-wife?

But just as she's ready to dip her toes in the water, the discovery
of a dark secret about her late husband shatters Poppy's confidence.
Does she really have the courage to risk her heart again?
Because Poppy wants a lot more than just a rural affair . . .

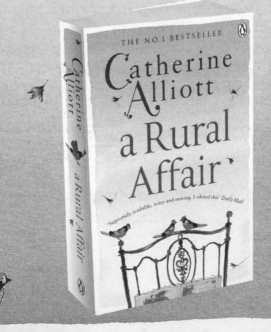

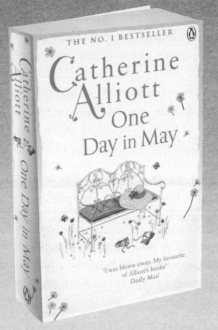

THE NO. 1 BESTSELLER

Catherine
Alliott
One
Day in May

'I was blown away. My favourite
of Alliott's books'
Daily Mail

May is the month for falling in love . . .

Hattie Carrington's first love was as unusual as it was out of reach –
Dominic Forbes was a married MP, and she was his assistant.
She has never told anyone about it. And never really got over it.

But years later with a flourishing antiques business
and enjoying a fling with a sexy, younger man, she thinks her
past is finally well and truly behind her.

Until work takes her to Little Crandon, home of Dominic's widow
and his gorgeous younger brother, Hal. There, Hattie's world is turned
upside down. She learns that if she's to truly fall in love again she
needs to stop hiding from the truth. Can she ever admit what
really happened back then?

And, if so, is she ready
for the consequences?

'A fun, fast-paced page-turner' *OK!*

Evie Hamilton has a secret – one she doesn't even know about. Yet . . .

Evie's an Oxfordshire wife and mum whose biggest worry in life is whether or not she can fit in a manicure on her way to fetch her daughter from clarinet lessons. But she's blissfully unaware that her charmed and happy life is about to be turned upside down.

For one sunny morning a letter lands on Evie's immaculate doormat. It's a bombshell, knocking her carefully arranged world completely askew and threatening to sabotage all she holds dear.

What will be left and what will change for ever?
Is Evie strong enough to fight for what she loves?
Can her entire world really be as fragile as her best china?

'We defy you not to get caught up in Alliott's life-changing tale' *Heat*

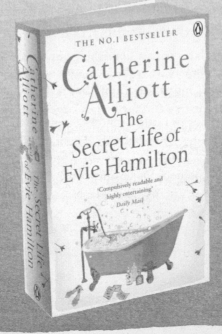

THE NO.1 BESTSELLER

CATHERINE ALLIOTT
The Secret Life of Evie Hamilton

'Compulsively readable and highly entertaining'
Daily Mail

THE NO.1 BESTSELLER

Catherine Alliott
A Crowded Marriage

'Another gem from the
pen of Ms Alliott'
Closer

'Another gem from the pen of Ms Alliott' *Closer*

There isn't room in a marriage for three . . .

Painter Imogen is happily married to Alex, and together they have a son.
But when their finances hit rock bottom, they're forced to accept Eleanor
Latimer's offer of a rent-free cottage on her large country estate. If it was
anyone else, Imogen would be beaming with gratitude. Unfortunately,
Eleanor just happens to be Alex's beautiful, rich and flirtatious ex.

From the moment she steps inside Shepherd's Cottage, Imogen's life
is in chaos. In between coping with rude locals, murderous chickens,
a maddening (if handsome) headmaster, mountains of manure
and visits from the infuriating vet, she has to face Eleanor,
now a fixture at Alex's side.

Is Imogen losing Alex? Will her precious family be torn apart?
And whose fault is it really – Eleanor's, Alex's or Imogen's?

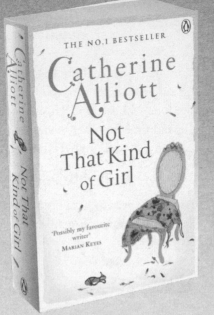

**A girl can get into all kinds of trouble
just by going back to work . . .**

Henrietta Tate gave up everything for her husband Marcus and their kids.
But now that the children are away at school and she's rattling around
their large country house all day she's feeling more than a little lost.

So when a friend puts her in touch with Laurie, a historian in need of a PA,
Henrietta heads for London. Quickly, she throws herself into the job.
Marcus is – of course – jealous of her spending so much time with
her charming new boss. And soon enough her absence causes cracks
in their marriage that just can't be papered over.

Then Rupert, a very old flame, reappears and Henrietta suddenly finds
herself torn between three men. How did this happen?
She's not that kind of girl . . . is she?

'Compulsively readable' *Daily Mail*

Annie O'Harran is getting married . . .
all over again.

A divorced, single mum, Annie is about to tie the knot with David.
But there's a long summer to get through first. A summer where
she's retreating to a lonely house in Cornwall, where she's going to
finish her book, spend time with her teenage daughter Flora and
make any last-minute wedding plans.

She should be so lucky.

For almost as soon as Annie arrives her competitive sister and her wild
brood fetch up. Meanwhile Annie's louche ex-husband and his latest
squeeze are holidaying nearby and insist on dropping in. Plus there's the
surprise American houseguest who can't help sharing his heartbreak.

Suddenly Annie's big day seems a long, long way off –
and if she's not careful it might never happen . . .

'Alliott at her best' *Daily Telegraph*

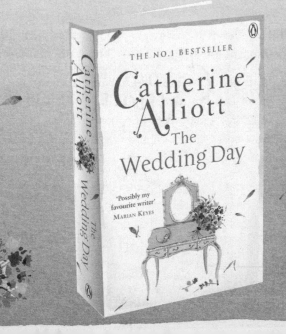

'What could be nicer
than living in the country?'

Lucy Fellowes is in a bind. She's a widow living in a pokey London flat
with two small boys and an erratic income. But, when her mother-in-law
offers her a converted barn on the family's estate, she knows it's a
brilliant opportunity for her and the kids.

But there's a problem.

The estate is a shrine to Lucy's dead husband, Ned. The whole family
has been unable to get over his death. If she's honest, the whole family
is far from normal. And if Lucy is to accept this offer she'll be putting
herself completely in their incapable hands.

Which leads to Lucy's other problem. Charlie – the only man since
Ned who she's had any feelings for – lives nearby. The problem?
He's already married . . .

'Hilarious and full of surprises' *Daily Telegraph*

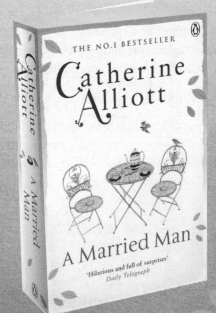

THE NO.1 BESTSELLER

Catherine Alliott

A Married Man

'Hilarious and full of surprises'
Daily Telegraph

THE NO.1 BESTSELLER

Catherine Alliott

Olivia's Luck

'The writing is both intelligent and sparkling'
Marian Keyes

Olivia's Luck

'I don't care what colour you paint
the sodding hall. I'm leaving.'

When her husband Johnny suddenly walks out on ten years of marriage,
their ten-year-old daughter and the crumbling house they're up to their
eyeballs renovating, Olivia is, at first, totally devastated. How could he?
How could she not have noticed his unhappiness?

But she's not one to weep for long.

Not when she's got three builders camped in her back garden,
a neighbour with a never-ending supply of cast-off men she thinks
Olivia would be drawn to and a daughter with her own firm
views on . . . well, just about everything.

Will Johnny ever come back?
And if he doesn't, will Olivia's luck
ever change for the better?

'The writing is both intelligent and sparkling'
Marian Keyes

'Alliott's joie de vivre is irresistible' *Daily Mail*

'Tell me, Alice,
how does a girl go about
getting a divorce these days?'

Three years ago Rosie walked blindly into marriage with Harry.
They have precisely nothing in common except perhaps their little boy, Ivo.
Not that Harry pays him much attention, preferring to spend his time
with his braying upper-class friends.

But the night that Harry drunkenly does something unspeakable,
Rosie decides he's got to go. In between fantasizing how she might
bump him off, she takes the much more practical step of divorcing
this blight on her and Ivo's lives.

However, when reality catches up with her darkest fantasies,
Rosie realizes, at long last, that it is time she took charge of her life.
There'll be no more regrets – and time, perhaps, for a little love.

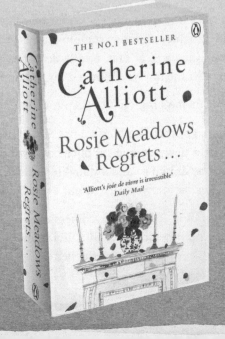

THE NO.1 BESTSELLER

Catherine
Alliott

Rosie Meadows
Regrets...

'Alliott's joie de vivre is irresistible'
Daily Mail

**Every girl's got one – that old boyfriend
they never quite fell out of love with . . .**

Tessa Hamilton's thirty, with a lovely husband and home, two adorable
kids, and not a care in the world. Sure her husband ogles the nanny more
than she should allow. And keeping up with the Joneses is a full-time
occupation. But she's settled and happy. No seven-year itch for Tessa.

Except at the back of her mind is Patrick Cameron. Gorgeous, moody,
rebellious, he's the boy she met when she was seventeen. The boy her
vicar-father told her she couldn't see and who left to go to Italy to paint.
The boy she's not heard from in twelve long years.

And now he's back.

Questioning every choice, every decision she's made since Patrick left,
Tessa is about to risk her family and everything she has become to find
out whether she did the right thing first time round . . .

'You're in for a treat' *Daily Express*

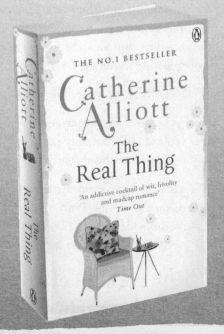

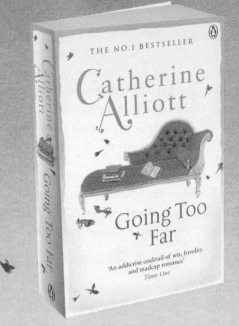

THE NO.1 BESTSELLER

Catherine Alliott

Going Too Far

'An addictive cocktail of wit, frivolity and madcap romance'
Time Out

'You've gone all fat and complacent
because you've got your man, haven't you?'

Polly Penhalligan is outraged at the suggestion that, since getting married
to Nick and settling into their beautiful manor farmhouse in Cornwall,
she has let herself go. But watching a lot of telly, gorging on biscuits, not
getting dressed until lunchtime and waiting for pregnancy to strike are not
the signs of someone living an active and fulfilled life.

So Polly does something rash.

She allows her home to be used as a location for a TV advert. Having a
glamorous film crew around will certainly put a bomb under the idyllic,
rural life. Only perhaps she should have consulted Nick first.

Because before the cameras have even started to roll – and complete
chaos descends on the farm – Polly's marriage has been
turned upside down. This time she
really has gone too far . . .

'An addictive cocktail of wit, frivolity
and madcap romance' *Time Out*

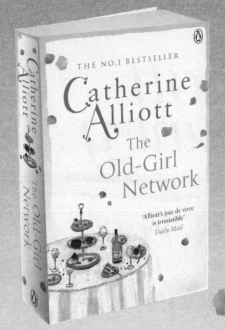

THE NO.1 BESTSELLER

Catherine Alliott
The Old-Girl Network

'Alliott's joie de vivre is irresistible'
Daily Mail

Finding true love's a piece of cake – as long as you're looking for someone else's true love . . .

Polly McLaren is young, scatty and impossibly romantic. She works for an arrogant and demanding boss, and has a gorgeous-if-never-there-when-you-need-him boyfriend. But, the day a handsome stranger recognizes her old school scarf, her life is knocked completely off kilter.

Adam is American, new to the country and begs Polly's help in finding his missing fiancé. Over dinner at the Savoy she agrees – the girls of St Gertrude's look out for one another. However, the old-girl network turns out to be a spider's web of complications and deceit in which everyone and everything Polly cares about is soon hopelessly entangled.

The course of true love never did run smooth.
But no one said anything about ruining your life over it.
And it's not even Polly's true love . . .

'Possibly my favourite writer' Marian Keyes

Step into *Alliott Country*

at www.catherinealliott.com

WIN wonderful WELLIES

by joules

WE'RE GIVING AWAY

10 PAIRS of JOULES WELLIES
MADE TO MAKE A SPLASH WHATEVER THE WEATHER!

To be in with a chance of winning this welly good prize visit www.catherinealliott.com/winwellies

Joules are also giving readers **15% OFF** *plus* **FREE P&P.**

Simply visit www.joules.com and enter offer code **WELLY12** at the checkout.

Competition closing date **31ST AUGUST 2012**

For full terms and conditions and details of how to enter visit www.catherinealliott.com/winwellies